Isaac Todhunter

A History of the Progress of the Calculus of Variations

During the Nineteenth Century

Isaac Todhunter

A History of the Progress of the Calculus of Variations
During the Nineteenth Century

ISBN/EAN: 9783741182532

Manufactured in Europe, USA, Canada, Australia, Japa

Cover: Foto ©Andreas Hilbeck / pixelio.de

Manufactured and distributed by brebook publishing software
(www.brebook.com)

Isaac Todhunter

A History of the Progress of the Calculus of Variations

HISTORY OF THE

CALCULUS OF VARIATIONS.

Cambridge:
PRINTED BY C. J. CLAY, M.A.
AT THE UNIVERSITY PRESS.

A HISTORY OF THE PROGRESS

OF THE

CALCULUS OF VARIATIONS

DURING THE NINETEENTH CENTURY.

By I. TODHUNTER, M.A.

FELLOW AND PRINCIPAL MATHEMATICAL LECTURER OF ST JOHN'S COLLEGE,
CAMBRIDGE.

MACMILLAN AND CO.
Cambridge:
AND 23, HENRIETTA STREET, COVENT GARDEN,
London.
1861.

PREFACE.

In 1810 a work was published in Cambridge under the following title—*A Treatise on Isoperimetrical Problems and the Calculus of Variations. By Robert Woodhouse, A.M., F.R.S., Fellow of Caius College, Cambridge.* This work details the history of the Calculus of Variations from its origin until the close of the eighteenth century, and has obtained a high reputation for accuracy and clearness. During the present century some of the most eminent mathematicians have endeavoured to enlarge the boundaries of the subject, and it seemed probable that a survey of what had been accomplished would not be destitute of interest and value. Accordingly the present work has been undertaken, and a short account will now be given of its plan.

As the early history of the Calculus of Variations had been already so ably written, it was unnecessary to go over it again; but it seemed convenient to commence with a short account of two works of Lagrange and a work of Lacroix, because they

exhibit the state of the subject at the close of the eighteenth
century; the first chapter is therefore devoted to these works of
Lagrange and Lacroix. The notice of the two works of Lagrange
is very brief, for in fact both of them were accessible to Woodhouse, and he has given a good account of all that Lagrange
accomplished. The notice of the work of Lacroix is fuller because
the second edition of that work had not appeared when Woodhouse wrote; it was also necessary to indicate two important mistakes which occur in Lacroix on account of their influence on the
history of the subject; see Arts. 27 and 39.

The second chapter contains an account of the treatises of
Dirksen and Ohm.

The third chapter contains an account of a remarkable memoir
by Gauss, which affords the earliest example of the discussion of
a problem involving the variation of a double integral with variable
limits of integration.

The fourth chapter contains an account of a memoir by Poisson
on the Calculus of Variations. The great object of this memoir is
to exhibit the variation of a double integral when the limits of
integration are variable. The memoir is important in itself, and
also from the fact that it may be considered to have led the way
for those which were written by Ostrogradsky, Delaunay, Cauchy
and Sarrus.

The fifth chapter contains an account of a memoir by Ostrogradsky; this memoir was suggested by Poisson's, and its object is
to exhibit the variation of a multiple integral when the limits of
the integration are variable.

The Academy of Sciences at Paris proposed for their mathematical prize subject for 1842, the Variation of Multiple Integrals.
The prize was awarded to a memoir by Sarrus, and honourable
mention was made of a memoir by Delaunay. The memoir of
Delaunay is analysed in the sixth Chapter, and the memoir of

Sarrus in the eighth Chapter; the seventh chapter analyses a memoir by Cauchy, in which the results obtained by Sarrus are presented under a slightly different form.

Here that part of the present work terminates which treats of the variation of multiple integrals.

The next three chapters treat of another branch of the subject, namely, the criteria which distinguish a maximum from a minimum; these criteria were exhibited in a remarkable memoir published by Jacobi in 1837, which has given rise to a series of commentaries and developments. The method of Jacobi is founded upon one originally given by Legendre; accordingly the ninth chapter first explains what Legendre accomplished, and also what was added to his results by another mathematician, Brunacci, and then finishes with a translation of Jacobi's memoir. The tenth chapter contains an account of the commentaries and developments to which Jacobi's memoir gave rise. The eleventh chapter contains some miscellaneous articles which also bear upon Jacobi's memoir.

The twelfth chapter contains an account of various memoirs which illustrate special points in the Calculus of Variations. The thirteenth chapter contains an account of three comprehensive treatises which discuss the whole subject. The fourteenth chapter gives a brief notice of all the other treatises on the subject which have come to the writer's knowledge.

The fifteenth chapter notices various memoirs which have some slight connection with the subject. The sixteenth chapter notices various memoirs which relate principally to geometry, or differential equations, or mechanics, but the titles of which are suggestive of some relation to the Calculus of Variations.

The seventeenth chapter gives the history of the theory of the conditions of integrability.

The writer has endeavoured to be simple and clear, and he hopes that any student who has mastered the elements of the subject will be able without difficulty to understand the whole of the work.

It may appear at first sight that great disproportion exists between the spaces devoted to the various treatises and memoirs which are analysed. The writer has not considered solely or chiefly the relative importance of these treatises and memoirs, but also the ease or difficulty of obtaining access to them; and thus a work of inferior absolute value may sometimes have obtained as long a notice as another of higher character when the latter could be procured far more readily than the former.

In citing an independent work the title has usually been given in the original language of the work, but in citing a memoir which forms part of a scientific journal it has generally been considered sufficient to give an English translation of the title. Sometimes a mathematician has been named in the history before an account of his contributions to the subject has been given; in such a case by the aid of the index of names at the end of the volume it will be easy to find the place which contains the account. Occasionally in the course of the translation of a passage from a foreign memoir the present writer has inserted a remark of his own; this remark will be known by being enclosed within square brackets.

The writer may perhaps be excused for stating that he has found the labour attendant on the production of this work far longer and heavier than he had anticipated. It would have been easy to have examined merely the introductions to the various treatises and memoirs, and thus to have compiled an account of what their respective authors proposed to effect; but the object of the present writer was more extensive. He wished to ascertain distinctly what had been effected, and to form some estimate of the manner in which it had been effected. Accordingly, unless the contrary is distinctly stated, it may be assumed that any treatise or memoir relating to the Calculus of Variations which is described in the present work has undergone thorough examination and study. This remark does not, however, apply to all the productions which are noticed in the last two chapters of this work.

It will be found that in the course of the history numerous remarks, criticisms, and corrections are suggested relative to the various treatises and memoirs which are analysed. The writer trusts that it will not be supposed that he undervalues the labours of the eminent mathematicians in whose works he ventures occasionally to indicate inaccuracies or imperfections, but that his aim has been to remove difficulties which might perplex a student. In the course of his studies the writer frequently found that remarks which he intended to offer on various points had been already made by some author not usually consulted; for example, the considerations introduced in Art. 366 occurred to him at the commencement of his studies, and it was not until long afterwards that he found he had been anticipated by Legendre; see Art. 202.

The writer will not conceal his own opinion of the value of a history of any department of science when that history is presented with accuracy and completeness. It is of importance that those who wish to improve or extend any subject should be able to ascertain what results have already been obtained, and thus reserve their strength for difficulties which have not yet been overcome; and those who merely desire to ascertain the present state of a subject without any purpose of original investigation will often find that the study of the past history of that subject assists them materially in obtaining a sound and extensive knowledge of the position to which it has attained. How far the present work deserves attention must be left to competent judges to decide; should they consider that the objects proposed have been in some degree secured, the writer will be encouraged hereafter to undertake a similar survey of some other department of science.

The writer will receive most thankfully any suggestion or correction relating to the present work with which he may be favoured, and especially any information respecting those memoirs and treatises which may have escaped his observation, and those of which he has only been able to record the titles; see Arts. 394 and 420.

The writer takes this opportunity of returning his thanks to the Syndics of the University Press for their liberal contribution to the expenses of printing the work.

St John's College,
April 13, 1861.

CONTENTS.

CALCULUS OF VARIATIONS.

CHAPTER I.

LAGRANGE. LACROIX.

1. It is the object of the present work to trace the progress of the Calculus of Variations during the nineteenth century. It will be convenient to begin with an account of three works which exhibit the state of the subject at the close of the eighteenth century. We shall accordingly in this chapter give an analysis of the treatises on the Calculus of Variations contained in Lagrange's *Théorie des Fonctions Analytiques*, in the *Leçons sur le Calcul des Fonctions* of the same author, and in the *Traité du Calcul Différentiel et du Calcul Intégral* of Lacroix.

2. The first edition of Lagrange's *Théorie des Fonctions Analytiques* appeared in 1797, and the second in 1813; the work was also reprinted in 1847. The portion which treats of the Calculus of Variations remains as it was in the original edition, where it extends over pages 198—220; we proceed to give an account of this portion.

3. Having treated of ordinary maxima and minima problems in the preceding pages of his work, Lagrange states that the same principles may be applied to determine curves which possess at every point some assigned maximum or minimum property. For example, required the curve at every point of which

$$\{y + (m - x) y'\} \{y + (n - x) y'\}$$

is a maximum or minimum, where y' denotes $\dfrac{dy}{dx}$.

1

Here it is supposed that at any point of the curve y' is susceptible of variation while x and y are not susceptible of variation; then according to the ordinary principles of maxima and minima problems we differentiate the proposed expression with respect to y' as variable, and equate the differential coefficient to zero. This gives

$$(m-x)\{y+(n-x)y'\} + (n-x)\{y+(m-x)y'\} = 0\ldots(1);$$

therefore

$$y' = \frac{(2x-m-n)y}{2(m-x)(n-x)};$$

divide by y and integrate, thus we obtain

$$y^2 = h(m-x)(n-x)\ldots\ldots\ldots\ldots\ldots\ldots(2),$$

where h is an arbitrary constant.

Differentiate the left-hand member of (1) with respect to y'; this gives $2(m-x)(n-x)$; hence we conclude that at every point of the curve determined by (2) the proposed expression

$$\{y+(m-x)y'\}\{y+(n-x)y'\}$$

is a maximum or minimum according as $(m-x)(n-x)$ is negative or positive. From (2) it appears that the curve is an ellipse if h be negative, and then $(m-x)(n-x)$ must be negative and there is a maximum; also the curve is an hyperbola if h be positive, and then $(m-x)(n-x)$ must be positive and there is a minimum.

This is the first appearance of a problem of this kind. Lagrange intimates that such problems may be proposed involving other differential coefficients besides the first.

4.   Lagrange next considers the more common problem of the Calculus of Variations, namely that in which we require the maximum or minimum value of the integral of a function $f(x, y, y', y'',\ldots)$. He uses ω to denote what is called the *variation* of y, and which is usually denoted by δy. He arrives at the well-known relation which must be satisfied in order that the proposed integral may be a maximum or minimum; this relation he expresses in the following manner;

$$f'(y) - [f'(y')]' + [f'(y'')]'' - [f'(y''')]''' + \ldots = 0.$$

He also obtains the ordinary result for the terms which are free from the integral sign, which must likewise vanish in order that the proposed integral may be a maximum or minimum.

5.   Lagrange now proceeds to the discrimination of a maximum from a minimum value; he takes the case in which the function under the integral sign contains no differential coefficient of y higher than the first.   We will here indicate his method, but we shall use the ordinary notation instead of Lagrange's.   Let p denote $\frac{dy}{dx}$, and suppose $f(x, y, p)$ to represent any function the integral of which taken between certain fixed limits is to have a maximum or minimum value.   Change y into $y + \delta y$ and p into $p + \delta p$; thus $f(x, y, p)$ will become

$$f(x, y, p) + \frac{df}{dy}\,\delta y + \frac{df}{dp}\,\delta p$$

$$+ \frac{1}{2}\frac{d^2f}{dy^2}(\delta y)^2 + \frac{d^2f}{dy\,dp}\,\delta y\,\delta p + \frac{1}{2}\frac{d^2f}{dp^2}(\delta p)^2 + \&c.,$$

where the &c. stands for terms of the third and higher orders in δy and δp.

Now by means of the relation between x and y given by

$$\frac{df}{dy} - \left(\frac{df}{dp}\right)' = 0 \dots\dots\dots\dots\dots\dots (1),$$

and the fact that the integration is taken between fixed limits, the integral denoted by

$$\int \left\{ \frac{df}{dy}\,\delta y + \frac{df}{dp}\,\delta p \right\} dx$$

vanishes.   We must then examine the integral

$$\int \left\{ \frac{1}{2}\frac{d^2f}{dy^2}(\delta y)^2 + \frac{d^2f}{dy\,dp}\,\delta y\,\delta p + \frac{1}{2}\frac{d^2f}{dp^2}(\delta p)^2 \right\} dx;$$

if this taken between the fixed limits is *negative* for all indefinitely small values of δy and δp, the proposed integral is a *maximum* when y has the value which satisfies (1); if it be *positive* for such values of δy and δp the proposed integral is a *minimum*.

The integral which we have to examine may be put under the form

$$\lambda\,(\delta y)^2 + \int\left\{\left(\frac{1}{2}\frac{d^2f}{dy^2} - \frac{d\lambda}{dx}\right)(\delta y)^2 + \left(\frac{d^2f}{dy\,dp} - 2\lambda\right)\delta y\,\delta p + \frac{1}{2}\frac{d^2f}{dp^2}(\delta p)^2\right\}dx,$$

where λ is any function of x; for we can shew immediately by differentiation that the latter expression coincides with the integral which we have to examine. Now assume λ such that

$$\left(\frac{d^2f}{dy\,dp} - 2\lambda\right)^2 = \left(\frac{d^2f}{dy^2} - 2\frac{d\lambda}{dx}\right)\frac{d^2f}{dp^2}\quad\ldots\ldots\ldots\ldots\ldots\ldots(2),$$

then the last expression under the integral sign becomes a perfect square, and the integral may be written

$$\int\frac{1}{2}\frac{d^2f}{dp^2}(\delta p + A\delta y)^2\,dx,$$

where

$$A\frac{d^2f}{dp^2} = \frac{d^2f}{dy\,dp} - 2\lambda.$$

Thus we have to examine the sign of

$$\lambda_1\,(\delta y_1)^2 - \lambda_0\,(\delta y_0)^2 + \frac{1}{2}\int_{x_0}^{x_1}\frac{d^2f}{dp^2}(\delta p + A\delta y)^2\,dx,$$

where x_0 and x_1 denote the limits of the integration, and λ_0 and λ_1 are the values of λ and δy_0 and δy_1 the values of δy at the respective limits. Let us suppose that δy_1 and δy_0 are zero, then we have remaining

$$\frac{1}{2}\int_{x_0}^{x_1}\frac{d^2f}{dp^2}(\delta p + A\delta y)^2\,dx.$$

Hence we may conclude that if $\frac{d^2f}{dp^2}$ be always positive between the limiting values of x the proposed integral has a minimum value; and if $\frac{d^2f}{dp^2}$ be always negative between the limiting values of x the proposed integral has a maximum value.

Lagrange remarks that this result had been published in the *Memoirs of the Academy of Sciences*, in 1786 [by Legendre]; but he adds, that in order to ensure the correctness of the result it ought to be shewn that the value of λ determined by (2) does not become infinite between the limits of integration, and it is generally impossible to do this, because the value of λ cannot actually be found.

6.   Lagrange takes for example the case in which

$$f(x, y, p) = p^2 + 2mpy + ny^2;$$

here $\dfrac{d^2 f}{dp^2}$ is necessarily positive, but Lagrange shews that when n is negative we are not certain of the existence of a minimum.

7.   Lagrange then indicates the method to be pursued in discriminating a maximum from a minimum when the expression which is to be integrated involves differential coefficients of a higher order than the first.

8.   Then leaving the question of the discrimination of maxima and minima values, Lagrange returns to the consideration of the conditions which are common to both maxima and minima values.   He makes some remarks on the case in which the limiting values of the quantities y, y', y'', ... are not given, but only one or more equations connecting them.   He then proceeds to suppose that the function under the integral sign contains, besides y and its differential coefficients with respect to x, another variable z and its differential coefficients with respect to x.   When y and z are independent he arrives at the two well-known relations which must be satisfied in order that the proposed integral may be a maximum or minimum, namely the relation already given in Art. 4, and another which may be obtained from that by changing y into z.   Lagrange also gives the results for the case in which y and z and their differential coefficients with respect to x are connected either by a given equation or by the circumstance that an assigned integral expression involving them is to have a constant value.

9.   As an example of the theory Lagrange considers the problem of the brachistochrone when a particle moves from one given point to another.   Take the axis of x vertically downwards, and let $\sqrt{2g(h + x)}$ be the velocity which the falling particle has when at the depth x below the origin; then the expression which is to be rendered a minimum is

$$\int \frac{\sqrt{(1 + y'^2 + z'^2)}\; dx}{\sqrt{(h + x)}},$$

where $y' = \dfrac{dy}{dx}$, and $z' = \dfrac{dz}{dx}$; here we have not assumed that the required curve is a *plane* curve. Hence in order that the integral may be a maximum or minimum we must have, by the relations referred to in Art. 8,

$$\left\{\frac{y'}{\sqrt{(h + x)}\,\sqrt{(1 + y'^2 + z'^2)}}\right\}' = 0, \quad \text{and} \quad \left\{\frac{z'}{\sqrt{(h + x)}\,\sqrt{(1 + y'^2 + z'^2)}}\right\}' = 0.$$

Integrate these equations; thus

$$\frac{y'}{\sqrt{(h + x)}\,\sqrt{(1 + y'^2 + z'^2)}} \quad \text{and} \quad \frac{z'}{\sqrt{(h + x)}\,\sqrt{(1 + y'^2 + z'^2)}}$$

are both constants; hence by dividing the first of these expressions by the other we have $\dfrac{y'}{z'}$ a constant, and this shews that the curve must be a plane curve. Then by completing the investigation in the usual manner we obtain a cycloid for the required curve. We now proceed to examine whether the proposed integral is thus rendered a maximum or minimum. The terms of the second order are (see Art. 5)

$$\int \frac{(1 + q^2)\,(\delta p)^2 - 2pq\,\delta p\,\delta q + (1 + p^2)\,(\delta q)^2}{2\,\sqrt{(h + x)}\,(1 + p^2 + q^2)^{\frac{3}{2}}}\,dx,$$

where p stands for $\dfrac{dy}{dx}$ and q for $\dfrac{dz}{dx}$. The above expression may be written

$$\int \frac{(\delta p)^2 + (\delta q)^2 + (q\,\delta p - p\,\delta q)^2}{2\,\sqrt{(h + x)}\,(1 + p^2 + q^2)^{\frac{3}{2}}}\,dx,$$

and as this is essentially *positive* the proposed integral is rendered a *minimum;* and thus the cycloid fulfils the conditions of the problem.

10. Lagrange then gives some investigations relating to the *conditions of integrability* of functions; this is a subject to which a separate chapter will be devoted in the present work.

11. The treatise on the Calculus of Variations contained in the *Théorie des Fonctions Analytiques* is very clear, and although the

notation is not so expressive as that which Lagrange originally introduced, it is far preferable to that employed in the *Leçons sur le
Calcul des Fonctions*. We now proceed to give an account of that
part of the latter work which is connected with our subject.

12. In the list of Lagrange's works which is appended to the
Mécanique Analytique it is stated that the first edition of the
Leçons sur le Calcul des Fonctions appeared in 1801 as a portion
of the second edition of the *Séances de l'Ecole Normale*; the *Leçons*
were also included in the 12th part of the *Journal de l'Ecole Polytechnique* in 1804. In 1806 a separate edition of the *Leçons* appeared containing two additional *leçons*, and these were also inserted in the 14th part of the *Journal de l'Ecole Polytechnique* in
1808. The two additional *leçons* are devoted to the Calculus of
Variations.

13. In the edition of the *Leçons sur le Calcul des Fonctions*
which was published in 1806, the part bearing on our subject
extends over pages 401—501 and forms the last two *leçons*. The
first of these two *leçons* extends over pages 401—440; it treats of
the integrability of functions, and also contains a sketch of the
early history of the Calculus of Variations; as we do not consider
the early history of the Calculus of Variations in the present work,
and as we reserve the subject of the integrability of functions for
a future chapter, we shall not here give any account of this part
of Lagrange's work. Lagrange states that the work of Euler,
entitled *Methodus inveniendi lineas curvas...* would have left nothing
to be desired respecting curves which are required to have a maximum or minimum property, if it had been based on an analysis
more conformable to the spirit of the Differential Calculus; Lagrange then adds that the object had been attained by his own
method given in the Memoirs of the Turin Academy. This method
is the well-known use of the symbol δ to express a variation.
Lagrange states that this method has been explained in most works
on the Differential Calculus which have appeared since it was
published, and therefore it will be sufficient for him to give merely
an account of the principles of it; and accordingly a brief sketch
is supplied.

14. Lagrange begins the next *leçon* thus;—"The method of variations based on the use and combination of the symbols d and δ, which denote different differentiations, left nothing to be desired; but this method having, like the Differential Calculus, the method of indefinitely small quantities for its base, it was necessary to present it under another point of view in order to connect it with the Calculus of Functions; I have already done this in the *Théorie des Fonctions*, but I propose to return to the subject now in order to treat it in a manner more direct and more complete."

15. Lagrange proceeds accordingly to expound the subject with the aid of a new notation. Suppose $y = \phi(x)$, and let $\phi(x)$ be changed into $\phi(x, i)$, where i is an arbitrary indefinitely small quantity; then suppose $\phi(x, i)$ expanded in powers of i by Maclaurin's Theorem. The result is expressed thus,

$$y + i\dot{y} + \frac{i^2}{1.2}\ddot{y} + \frac{i^3}{1.2.3}\dddot{y} + \ldots\ldots,$$

so that dots over the symbol y indicate differential coefficients of y with respect to i, it being supposed that i is made zero after the differentiations. The terms of the series after the first constitute in fact the *variation* of y; in this work however Lagrange confines himself to an investigation of the conditions which are common to maximum and minimum values, so that in fact the terms which involve powers of i beyond the first are not used by him. Since the way in which i enters into $\phi(x, i)$ is quite arbitrary it follows that $\dot{y}$ may have any value we please.

16. Lagrange then arrives at the ordinary conditions for the maximum or minimum value of $\int V dx$, where V is supposed to contain x and y, and the differential coefficients of y with respect to x. In his investigation he first supposes that x itself does not receive any variation, and afterwards finds the change in his formulæ occasioned by varying x.

He then proceeds to the case in which V contains besides y another dependent variable z, and its differential coefficients with respect to x; and he gives the relations which must hold in order that $\int V dx$ may be a maximum or minimum both when y and z are unconnected and when they are connected by an equation.

17. Lagrange gives some investigations relative to the maximum or minimum value of a function of two independent variables which involves a double integral. We will indicate how far he proceeds with this problem; but we shall use the ordinary notation instead of Lagrange's. Suppose V a function of x, y, z, p, q, r, s, t, ... where $p = \dfrac{dz}{dx}$, $q = \dfrac{dz}{dy}$, $r = \dfrac{d^2z}{dx^2}$, $s = \dfrac{d^2z}{dx\,dy}$, $t = \dfrac{d^2z}{dy^2}$, ...; and let $U = \iint V\,dy\,dx$; then

$$\delta U = \iint \delta V\,dy\,dx,$$

and

$$\delta V = \frac{dV}{dz}\delta z + \frac{dV}{dp}\delta p + \frac{dV}{dq}\cdot\delta q + \frac{dV}{dr}\delta r + \dots$$

say

$$= L\delta z + M\delta p + N\delta q + P\delta r + Q\delta s + R\delta t + \dots$$

Now by the Differential Calculus

$$M\delta p = \frac{d}{dx}(M\delta z) - \delta z\,\frac{dM}{dx},$$

$$N\delta q = \frac{d}{dy}(N\delta z) - \delta z\,\frac{dN}{dy},$$

and so on; thus we obtain

$$\delta V = \left(L - \frac{dM}{dx} - \frac{dN}{dy} + \frac{d^2P}{dx^2} + \frac{d^2Q}{dx\,dy} + \frac{d^2R}{dy^2}\dots\dots\right)\delta z$$

$$+ \frac{d}{dx}\left(M\delta z + P\frac{d\delta z}{dx} - \frac{dP}{dx}\delta z + Q\frac{d\delta z}{dy}\dots\dots\right)$$

$$+ \frac{d}{dy}\left(N\delta z + R\frac{d\delta z}{dy} - \frac{dR}{dy}\delta z - \frac{dQ}{dx}\delta z\dots\dots\right).$$

In order that δU may vanish it is necessary that the coefficient of δz in the first line of the expression for δV should vanish; that is, we must have

$$L - \frac{dM}{dx} - \frac{dN}{dy} + \frac{d^2P}{dx^2} + \frac{d^2Q}{dx\,dy} + \frac{d^2R}{dy^2}\dots\dots = 0.$$

Then δU consists of terms which involve only one sign of integration, namely, that with respect to x or that with respect to y.

Thus Lagrange is correct as far as he has carried the investigation; but as we shall see hereafter the great difficulty of the question consists in reducing the terms which involve only *one* sign of integration to their simplest form, so as to deduce the equations which must hold for the limiting values of the integrals. The difficulty was first overcome by Poisson. Lagrange adds a remark which is not correct; he says—" The simplest case is that in which the boundary of the surface represented by the equation in x, y, z is supposed completely given and invariable. Then the variations of z and its differential coefficients are zero with respect to the bounding curve and therefore also through the whole extent of the single integrals contained in δU, and the condition $\delta U = 0$ is satisfied of itself." If the bounding curve be given δz vanishes at every point of the bounding curve, but it is not true as Lagrange asserts that δp, δq, ... also vanish.

18. Lagrange illustrates the subject by the discussion of some of the standard problems. He selects the following;—the shortest line in free space or on a given surface, the brachistochrone in a resisting medium, the curve down which a particle must fall in a resisting medium in order to acquire a maximum velocity, and the surface of minimum area. The first three of these problems had been originally discussed by Euler, the last had been originally discussed by Lagrange himself in the Turin Memoirs.

19. The treatise on the Calculus of Variations contained in the *Leçons sur le Calcul des Fonctions* is rather difficult, and the notation is extremely uninviting and perplexing. It may be observed that there is a German translation of the two works of Lagrange which we have considered, by Dr A. L. Crelle; the translation is accompanied by a running commentary which is incorporated with the text. In the translation of the *Leçons* the notation of Lagrange is replaced by the ordinary notation of the Differential Calculus. It seems to have been the design of Dr Crelle to translate all the works of Lagrange, but the only work which appeared besides the two we have considered was the *Treatise on the Solution of Numerical Equations.*

20. We now proceed to give an account of the chapter on the subject contained in the work of Lacroix. The first edition of the

Traité du Calcul Différentiel et du Calcul Intégral appears to have been published in 1797. The second edition of the second volume is dated 1814; it contains a chapter on the Calculus of Variations extending over pages 721—816. There are some additions and corrections extending over pages 716—721 of the third volume, which is dated 1819.

21. In his preface Lacroix states that the Calculus of Variations is treated at much greater length than it had been in the first edition of the work; he considers that he had to effect two things, namely on the one hand to exhibit the Calculus of Variations in all the extent it had reached and with the symmetry which it had gained by means of its peculiar notation, and on the other hand to explain the connexion of the subject with the ordinary principles of the Differential Calculus. He adds that those readers who wish to confine themselves to the Calculus of Variations strictly so called may begin at page 755.

22. The guide whom Lacroix has principally followed is Euler; the third volume of Euler's treatise on the Integral Calculus contains an appendix on the Calculus of Variations, and in the fourth volume of the treatise a memoir on this subject is given which is reprinted from the Transactions of the Academy of St Petersburg (*Novi Comment. Acad. Petrop.* XVI.). Lacroix devotes the first part of his chapter, extending over pages 721—754, to an exposition of the method given by Euler in the memoir just cited; the method is the same as that which was afterwards used by Lagrange in the *Leçons sur le Calcul des Fonctions*. Suppose y any function of x, say $y = \phi(x)$; let there be a new variable t, and let $\phi(x, t)$ be any function of x and t which reduces to $\phi(x)$ when $t = 0$. Then by Maclaurin's Theorem

$$\phi(x, t) = \phi(x) + \frac{d\phi}{dt} t + \frac{d^2\phi}{dt^2} \frac{t^2}{2} + \cdots$$

where t is supposed to be put equal to zero in the differential coefficients with respect to t after differentiation. Then $\phi(x, t) - \phi(x)$ is equivalent to what is usually denoted by δy and called the *variation of y*. If we suppose t small enough we may restrict ourselves to the first term in the series for $\phi(x, t) - \phi(x)$, that is, to $\frac{d\phi}{dt} t$.

Lacroix adopts this restriction and then proceeds to investigate the conditions which must hold in order that an integral $\int V dx$ may have a maximum or minimum value, where V is a function of x and y and the differential coefficients of y with respect to x. The results are of course the same as those which are obtained with the aid of the common notation. We shall make some remarks on various points which occur in this part of the work of Lacroix.

23. On pages 729—731 Lacroix examines some cases of the problem of the *brachistochrone*. At first the starting-point is supposed fixed; the velocity at a point which has y for its vertical ordinate is supposed to be $\sqrt{2g(y-h)}$, where h is a constant. Now let the horizontal abscissa of the final point be supposed given, but not its vertical ordinate; then the usual result is obtained by Lacroix, namely, that the tangent at the final point must be horizontal. Lacroix next supposes that the horizontal abscissæ of both the starting-point and the final point are known, but not their vertical ordinates, and he arrives at the result that the tangents at both points must be horizontal; and he gives a figure which supposes the moving particle to start from the lowest point of a cycloid, and to ascend to the cusp and then to descend down the next arc until it reaches the point which is in the same horizontal line as the starting-point. It must however be observed that Lacroix does not examine the terms of the second order so as to ascertain whether there really is a minimum; and it is obvious that there can be no minimum in the present case, for by taking the starting-point low enough the initial velocity may be made as great as we please, and thus the time of passing from a point with the first given abscissa to a point with the second given abscissa may be made as small as we please without restricting the moving particle to describe a cycloid.

24. On page 732 Lacroix observes that if the expression

$$N - \frac{dP}{dx} + \frac{d^2Q}{dx^2} - \frac{d^3R}{dx^3} + \dots$$

vanishes identically $V dx$ is an exact differential; thus $\int V dx$ taken between limits can be expressed as a function of initial and final values of co-ordinates and differential coefficients, and so the problem

of finding the maximum or minimum value of this integral does
not differ from an ordinary problem of maximum or minimum.
This remark leads him naturally to consider the example given
by Lagrange of finding the maximum or minimum value of an
expression which involves a differential coefficient but no integral
sign. (See Art. 3.)

25. Up to page 734 Lacroix has supposed that the independent variable x is not susceptible of variation; he now introduces
the supposition that x itself receives a variation. This part of the
subject is treated perhaps as well as it could be on the basis.
adopted by Lacroix, but it would probably be obscure to a beginner.
It is perhaps impossible to avoid this obscurity altogether if we
ascribe a variation to the independent variable; and thus it seems
better to adopt the method of some recent writers who vary only
the dependent variable and obtain the requisite generality in their
formulæ by giving small changes to the limits of the integral
instead of varying the dependent variable. (See the works of
Strauch and Jellett.)

26. On pages 742—744 Lacroix expounds a method which he
says in its full extent is due to Poisson. In this method the limiting values of the variables and differential coefficients which occur
in the expression under the integral sign are at first supposed fixed;
then by the ordinary process of the Calculus of Variations a differential equation is obtained, which must be solved, and which will
involve a certain number of arbitrary constants; these constants
Poisson proposes to determine by the principles of the Differential
Calculus. For example, if the problem proposed be that of the
brachistochrone, it would be first inferred from the differential
equation furnished by the ordinary process of the Calculus of
Variations that the curve must be a cycloid; then with the relation
between x and y thus determined, the integral $\int V dx$ may be obtained, and may be expressed in terms of the limiting values of x
and of the arbitrary constants which arise from the solution of the
differential equation; it will now be a problem of the Differential
Calculus to assign such values to the limits of x and to the arbitrary
constants as will ensure a minimum value for the integral. In fact
instead of solving a problem at once and completely by the Calculus

of Variations, Poisson proposes to divide it into two parts and solve one part by the Calculus of Variations and the other part by the Differential Calculus. This method appears to possess no superiority over the common method, and Lacroix seems to intimate the same opinion on page 744.

27. An important mistake in the treatment of the variation of a double integral occurs on page 752, and is repeated on pages 783, 784; this we will now explain, using the ordinary notation. Let V be a function of the independent variables x and y, and of the dependent variable z, and of the differential coefficients of z with respect to x and y; let

$$U = \iint V\,dx\,dy;$$

then it is required to find the variation δU which arises from a variation δz ascribed to z. Let the differential coefficients of z be, as usual, denoted by p, q, r, s, t; and suppose for simplicity that no differential coefficient of z occurs of a higher order than the second. Then

$$\delta U = \iint \left(\frac{dV}{dz}\delta z + \frac{dV}{dp}\delta p + \frac{dV}{dq}\delta q + \frac{dV}{dr}\delta r + \frac{dV}{ds}\delta s + \frac{dV}{dt}\delta t \right) dx\,dy.$$

Lacroix now proceeds to transform these terms by integration by parts, and in doing so he makes a mistake. His process is substantially the following. Let S denote $\dfrac{dV}{ds}$, then

$$\int S\delta s\,dy = \int S \frac{d^2\delta z}{dx\,dy}\,dy = S\frac{d\delta z}{dx} - \int \frac{dS}{dy}\frac{d\delta z}{dx}\,dy \dots\dots\dots(1),$$

thus
$$\iint S\delta s\,dx\,dy = \int S\frac{d\delta z}{dx}\,dx - \iint \frac{dS}{dy}\frac{d\delta z}{dx}\,dx\,dy\,;$$

again
$$\int S\frac{d\delta z}{dx}\,dx = S\delta z - \int \frac{dS}{dx}\delta z\,dx \dots\dots\dots\dots\dots(2),$$

and
$$\int \frac{dS}{dy}\frac{d\delta z}{dx}\,dx = \frac{dS}{dy}\delta z - \int \frac{d^2S}{dx\,dy}\delta z\,dx\,;$$

thus finally $\iint S\delta s\,dx\,dy =$

$$S\delta z - \int \frac{dS}{dx}\delta z\,dx - \int \frac{dS}{dy}\delta z\,dy + \iint \frac{d^2S}{dx\,dy}\delta z\,dx\,dy.$$

The step taken in (2) is generally false. For in a double integral the limiting values of the variable with respect to which we first integrate are in general *functions of the other variable;* thus in (1) after integrating with respect to y, we should have to substitute some function of x for y in the term $S\dfrac{d\delta z}{dx}$. Therefore in the expression $\int S\dfrac{d\delta z}{dx}\,dx$, the symbol δz does not represent a function of the independent variables x and y, but a function of x alone. But $\dfrac{d\delta z}{dx}$ indicates the *partial* differential coefficient of δz taken with respect to x, and is therefore only a part of what we obtain when we differentiate δz with respect to x, supposing y itself a function of x. So that if we denote the complete differential coefficient of δz with respect to x by $\dfrac{D\delta z}{dx}$, we have

$$\frac{D\delta z}{dx} = \frac{d\delta z}{dx} + \frac{d\delta z}{dy}\,\frac{dy}{dx},$$

where $\dfrac{dy}{dx}$ is to be found from the value of y in terms of x which holds at the limit. The process of Lacroix then is wrong because it uses $\dfrac{d\delta z}{dx}$ as if it were $\dfrac{D\delta z}{dx}$.

28. There is no error in the transformation which Lacroix effects of the terms $\iint\dfrac{dV}{dr}\,\delta r\,dx\,dy$ and $\iint\dfrac{dV}{dt}\,\delta t\,dx\,dy$; but the error indicated in the preceding article occurs again in the transformation of terms arising from the differential coefficients of z which are of an order higher than the second. It must be observed that the error disappears when the limits of both the integrals are constants.

29. The error indicated in Art. 27 was alluded to by Poisson and corrected in his memoir on the Calculus of Variations (*Mémoires de l'Institut,* Tome XII. page 296). It seems to have been introduced by Euler; it occurs in Art. 169 of the Treatise on the Calculus of Variations contained in the third volume of Euler's

Integral Calculus. In the memoir however to which we have already referred (see Art. 22), which is reprinted in the fourth volume of the *Integral Calculus*, the error does not occur; there Euler has a result which is equivalent to

$$\iint S\delta z \, dx \, dy = \int S \frac{d\delta z}{dx} \, dx - \int \frac{dS}{dy} \delta z \, dy + \iint \frac{d^2 S}{dx \, dy} \delta z \, dx \, dy;$$

that is, he omits the incorrect equation (2) of Art. 27. He has therefore here not attempted to carry his transformations farther than they are carried in Art. 17, and has left his results in a correct form. It should however be observed that Strauch asserts that Euler's results are not correct, since he has omitted several terms which involve only a single integral (Strauch, *Calculus of Variations,* Vol. II. p. 633). There seems no reason for the assertion made by Strauch beyond the following:—In such a step as

$$\int S\delta z \, dy = S \frac{d\delta z}{dx} - \int \frac{dS}{dy} \frac{d\delta z}{dx} \, dy,$$

we must remember that the integration with respect to y will have to be taken between certain limits, so that the equation just written would more correctly be written thus,

$$\int_{y_0}^{y_1} S\delta z \, dy = \left(S \frac{d\delta z}{dx} \right)_1 - \left(S \frac{d\delta z}{dx} \right)_0 - \int_{y_0}^{y_1} \frac{dS}{dy} \frac{d\delta z}{dx} \, dy,$$

where the first two terms on the right-hand side are respectively the values of $S \frac{d\delta z}{dx}$ when y_1 and y_0 are substituted for y. This is the only point in which Euler's formula is liable to objection, and this can scarcely be called an error, as it is really only an abbreviation which is perpetually used in the *Integral Calculus*. This is probably all that Strauch means by his assertion; in the problem which he has discussed in the pages immediately preceding his assertion he has confined himself to the case in which the limits of the integrations are all *constants*, and his results agree with those of the third volume of Euler's *Integral Calculus*, when we allow for the abbreviated form which Euler adopts, as we have just explained. It may be added that the mistake corrected by Poisson has been preserved in some elementary works which have been published since Poisson's Memoir.

30. In addition to the error already pointed out, it must be observed that on page 752, Lacroix exhibits the result very incorrectly; for he omits all such terms as $\dfrac{d\delta z}{dx}$ and $\dfrac{d\delta z}{dy}$, and δz is the only form in which he introduces the variation of z. In consequence of this, he falls into the same error on page 753, as has been already indicated in Lagrange (see Art. 17). He states that when the lines which bound the area over which the double integration extends are absolutely given, then all the terms in the variation of the double integral vanish except those which remain under the double integral sign; and this of course is not true.

31. Lacroix closes this division of his subject with a remark on the problem of the variation of a double integral when the limits themselves are supposed variable; pages 754, 755. He says that the question is too difficult for him to stop to consider it, but that he will return to it afterwards in order to introduce the reader to some considerations of which *no trace could be found in preceding works*. It is not apparent to which of his subsequent articles Lacroix thus refers; the only place in which he appears to return to the point is page 778, and there he gives scarcely any thing more than had previously been given by Euler.

32. On page 755 Lacroix begins his exposition of the Calculus of Variations properly so called. Here he introduces Lagrange's symbol δ to express a variation. Lacroix devotes his first article to *proofs* of the formulæ $\delta dy = d\delta y$, $\delta dx = d\delta x$, $\delta d^2 y = d^2 \delta y$, ... This article seems to require some observations. After he has considered the case in which y alone receives a variation and not x, he proceeds thus :

" Hitherto we have only varied the ordinate PM or y; but this point of view is too restricted; some questions may require that we should pass from the point M of the curve CE to a point ν of the curve $\gamma\epsilon$ corresponding to an abscissa $A\Pi$ which differs from AP. (See fig. 1.) It is obvious that the variation of PM consists then of two parts, namely of the variation $M\mu$ which is due solely to the change of curve, and of the increment which $P\mu$ receives in the curve $\gamma\epsilon$ when the abscissa AP is changed into $A\Pi$; and we shall have in this case $\delta dy = d\delta y$. For let

$$PM = \phi(x), \quad P\mu = \psi(x), \quad A\Pi = x + \varpi(x) = X,$$
$$AP' = x + dx = x', \quad A\Pi' = x' + \varpi(x') = X';$$

it will follow that

$$\Pi\nu = \psi(X), \quad P'M' = y' = \phi(x'), \quad \Pi'\nu' = \psi(X'),$$
$$\Pi\nu - PM = \delta y = \psi(X) - \phi(x), \quad \Pi'\nu' - P'M' = \delta y' = \psi(X') - \phi(x'),$$
and $\quad \delta y' - \delta y = d\delta y = \psi(X') - \phi(x') - \psi(X) + \phi(x).$

On the other hand, since

$$dy = \phi(x') - \phi(x),$$
$$\delta dy = \delta\phi(x') - \delta\phi(x) = \psi(X') - \phi(x') - \psi(X) + \phi(x);$$

hence $\qquad\qquad\qquad \delta dy = d\delta y.$

It is moreover obvious that by supposing $\delta x = \varpi(x)$ we have separately

$$\delta dx = d\delta x.$$

It follows that $\delta d^2 y = d\delta dy = d^2\delta y$; and proceeding thus we shall obtain the theorem

$$\delta d^n y = d^n \delta y,$$

in virtue of which we may transpose the characteristics δ and d; this may be extended to any function whatever, so that

$$\delta d^n U = d^n \delta U$$

whatever U may be. As the basis of the Calculus of Variations this was enunciated at the origin of the Calculus; but it has always appeared to me that the truth of it had not been proved with sufficient care, and that it was necessary to develop the demonstration by bringing into view the nature of the variations attributed to the abscissa and the ordinate."

33. The proof given in the preceding Article may be exhibited more clearly; it consists essentially of the following process. Let y stand for $\phi(x)$, let d denote the operation of changing x into x' and subtracting the original function from the new function, let δ denote the operation of changing x into X and ϕ into ψ and subtracting the original function from the new function; then

$$d\delta y = d\{\psi(X) - \phi(x)\} = \psi(X') - \phi(x') - \{\psi(X) - \phi(x)\}.$$

and $\delta dy = \delta \{\phi(x') - \phi(x)\} = \psi(X') - \psi(X) - \{\phi(x') - \phi(x)\}$;

therefore $\qquad\qquad d\delta y = \delta dy.$

The proof is certainly sound; it must be noticed however that it is assumed that δ always means a change of x into X and ϕ into ψ and a corresponding subtraction. This however is too restricted a meaning of the operation denoted by δ, for it is necessary to have the power of supposing that the curve $\gamma\epsilon$ in the figure is not throughout determined by the equation $y = \psi(x)$. The curve may be determined by $y = \psi(x)$ for part of its extent, by $y = \chi(x)$ for another part, by $y = f(x)$ for another part, and so on. All the restriction on $\psi, \chi, f, \ldots$ is that there be no discontinuity in the *value* of y or of any of its differential coefficients up to that of the highest order which occurs in the expression we are considering; discontinuity in *form* is admissible, and in fact necessary. Thus the demonstration given by Lacroix in Art. 32 is not perfectly satisfactory, since it involves a limitation of the meaning of the symbol δ.

34. Many elementary writers who have reproduced this demonstration have however omitted that part of it in which the symbols are defined, and thus have rendered it inconclusive. Thus it has been considered sufficient to proceed as follows:—let $AP = x$, $P\Pi = dx$, $PP' = \delta x$, $\Pi\Pi' = \delta(x + dx)$; then P' and Π' are the abscissæ of points on the new curve which are infinitesimally near, and $AP' = x + \delta x$, therefore

$$P'\Pi' = d(x + \delta x);$$

hence $\qquad\qquad P\Pi' = dx + \delta(x + dx),$

and $\qquad\qquad P\Pi' = PP' + P'\Pi' = \delta x + d(x + \delta x);$

therefore $\qquad\qquad \delta dx = d\delta x.$

But in this process the statement $P'\Pi' = d(x + \delta x)$ is quite arbitrary, as there is no definition on which it depends.

35. But in fact there is nothing to be proved, and the subject would be rendered more intelligible by the omission of these and similar propositions which appear in so*many elementary works. Suppose for example that y receives an increment δy, then the first differential coefficient of y with respect to x instead of $\dfrac{dy}{dx}$

becomes $\dfrac{d(y + \delta y)}{dx}$, that is, receives an increment $\dfrac{d\delta y}{dx}$. Hence if we please to denote this increment by δp we have $\delta p = \dfrac{d\delta y}{dx}$; there is here nothing to prove, it is merely a definition of the meaning of δp. Again, let u denote the integral $\int v dx$; if v receives an increment δv then u receives an increment $\int \delta v dx$, which we may denote by δu if we please. Instead then of a formal proposition in which $\delta \int v dx$ is proved equal to $\int \delta v dx$, there is really only a definition of the meaning of δu when $u = \int v dx$.

36. That these supposed propositions are not required in a treatise on the Calculus of Variations may be seen by consulting Airy's Tract on the Calculus of Variations. The subject will be found there treated with great simplicity and clearness, without any introduction of such matter as we have taken from Lacroix in Article 32. It may be added that Euler, who gives the geometrical process of Article 32 in his treatise on this subject contained in his Integral Calculus, gives it rather as an illustration than a proof (*interim tamen juvabit id per Geometriam illustrasse*).

37. Lacroix now proceeds to give the usual formulæ of the subject expressed in the usual notation. He exhibits the variation of an integral which involves both x and y and their differentials, so that in fact x and y may be considered both functions of a third variable. He notices the conditions which must hold in order that a function involving two variables and their differential coefficients may be susceptible of integration, once or more than once, without assigning any relation between the variables. He also investigates the variation of $\int V dx$, where V contains another integral $\int V' dx$ besides x and y and the differential coefficients of y; as this is a point of some difficulty we shall consider it here more fully.

38. An investigation of the variation of an integral formula which itself involves another integral was given by Euler; it occurs in the 4th chapter of the treatise on the Calculus of Variations, which is contained in the third volume of his *Integral Calculus*. Lacroix gives it in his Articles 854 and 871. Lacroix omits a few lines of explanation which are found in Euler, and thus the process which in its original form was not free from obscurity is rendered

still more obscure; in fact, as we shall see, Lacroix does not distinguish between problems which are really different. From Lacroix the process has passed into many elementary works. We will now give the process of Lacroix.

Required the variation of $\int V dx$, where V is a function of x, y, p, q, r, ... and v where $v = \int V' dx$, and V' is also a function of x, y, p, q, r, ...; here p, q, r, ... denote the successive differential coefficients of y with respect to x. Suppose

$$dV = Mdx + Ndy + Pdp + Qdq + Rdr + \ldots + Ldv,$$
$$dV' = M'dx + N'dy + P'dp + Q'dq + R'dr + \ldots$$

Then by the usual formulæ of the Calculus of Variations

$$\delta \int V dx = V \delta x + \int (dx \delta V - dV \delta x);$$

now for shortness let $dV = d\psi + Ldv$, then $\delta V = \delta\psi + L\delta v$;

thus $\quad \delta \int V dx = V \delta x + \int (dx \delta\psi - d\psi \delta x) + \int (Ldx \delta v - Ldv \delta x).$

Also $\quad \delta v = V' \delta x + \int (dx \delta V' - dV' \delta x);$ and $dv = V' dx;$

therefore $\quad \int (Ldx \delta v - Ldv \delta x) = \int Ldx \int (dx \delta V' - dV' \delta x).$

Put $\int L dx = I$; then by integration by parts

$$\int (Ldx \delta v - Idv \delta x) = I \int (dx \delta V' - dV' \delta x) - \int I (dx \delta V' - dV' \delta x).$$

Hence we obtain

$$\delta \int V dx = V \delta x + \int (dx \delta\psi - d\psi \delta x)$$
$$+ I \int (dx \delta V' - dV' \delta x) - \int I (dx \delta V' - dV' \delta x).$$

The three terms which follow $V \delta x$ on the right-hand side of the last equation may be transformed by the ordinary processes of the subject. Thus if $\omega = \delta y - p \delta x$, we shall obtain

$$\int (dx \delta\psi - d\psi \delta x) = \left(P - \frac{dQ}{dx} + \frac{d^2 R}{dx^2} - \ldots \right) \omega$$
$$+ \left(Q - \frac{dR}{dx} + \ldots\ldots\ldots \right) \frac{d\omega}{dx}$$
$$+ \left(R - \ldots\ldots\ldots\ldots \right) \frac{d^2\omega}{dx^2}$$
$$+ \ldots\ldots\ldots\ldots\ldots\ldots$$
$$+ \int \left(N - \frac{dP}{dx} + \frac{d^2 Q}{dx^2} - \frac{d^3 R}{dx^3} + \ldots \right) \omega dx \ldots\ldots (1).$$

$$I \int (d\omega\, \delta V' - d V'' \delta x) = I \left(P' - \frac{dQ'}{dx} + \frac{d^2 R'}{dx^2} - \ldots \right) \omega$$

$$+ I \left(Q' - \frac{dR'}{dx} + \ldots\ldots\ldots\ldots \right) \frac{d\omega}{dx}$$

$$+ I \left(R' - \ldots\ldots\ldots\ldots\ldots\ldots \right) \frac{d^2\omega}{dx^2}$$

$$+ \ldots\ldots\ldots\ldots\ldots\ldots\ldots\ldots\ldots\ldots$$

$$+ I \int \left(N' - \frac{dP'}{dx} + \frac{d^2 Q'}{dx^2} - \frac{d^3 R'}{dx^3} + \ldots \right) \omega\, dx \ldots (2).$$

$$\int I (d\omega\, \delta V' - d V' \delta x) = \left(IP' - \frac{dIQ'}{dx} + \frac{d^2 IR'}{dx^2} - \ldots \right) \omega$$

$$+ \left(IQ' - \frac{dIR'}{dx} + \ldots\ldots\ldots\ldots \right) \frac{d\omega}{dx}$$

$$+ \left(IR' - \ldots\ldots\ldots\ldots\ldots\ldots \right) \frac{d^2\omega}{dx^2}$$

$$+ \ldots\ldots\ldots\ldots\ldots\ldots\ldots\ldots\ldots\ldots$$

$$+ \int \left(IN' - \frac{dIP'}{dx} + \frac{d^2 IQ'}{dx^2} - \frac{d^3 IR'}{dx^3} + \ldots \right) \omega\, dx \ldots (3).$$

Thus far there is no difficulty, but Lacroix adds in Article 871; let A denote the total value of I, that is, of $\int L\, dx$ taken between limits determined by the nature of the question; since this value is a constant it may be introduced under the signs of differentiation and integration, and thus the formula will become

$$\delta \int V' dx = V \delta x + \left\{ (P + AP' - IP') - \frac{d}{dx} (Q + AQ' - IQ') + \ldots \right\} \omega$$

$$+ \left\{ (Q + AQ' - IQ') - \frac{d}{dx} (R + AR' - IR') + \ldots \right\} \frac{d\omega}{dx}$$

$$+ \ldots\ldots\ldots\ldots\ldots\ldots\ldots\ldots\ldots\ldots\ldots\ldots\ldots\ldots\ldots\ldots\ldots$$

$$+ \int \left\{ (N + AN' - IN') - \frac{d}{dx} (P + AP' - IP') \right.$$

$$\left. + \frac{d^2}{dx^2} (Q + AQ' - IQ') - \ldots \right\} \omega\, dx.$$

This last step is not obvious; it will be seen that no change is made in the terms which are denoted by (1) and (3), but that I is changed into A in (2). Now the original integral $\int V dx$ must be supposed taken between some limits, say α and β; thus the first line for example in (2) will really when written at full become

$$\left\{ I\left(P - \frac{dQ}{dx} + \frac{d^2R}{dx^2} - \ldots \right)\omega \right\}_{x=\beta}$$
$$-\left\{ I\left(P' - \frac{dQ}{dx} + \frac{d^2R}{dx^2} - \ldots \right)\omega \right\}_{x=\alpha},$$

and as the value of I when $x=\beta$ will not generally be the same as its value when $x=\alpha$, we cannot as Lacroix does put A for I in the terms included in (2).

Some variety of meaning may occur with respect to I; for by I we may understand simply the indefinite integral $\int L dx$ without any constant added; or by I we may understand $\int_a^x L dx$, so that I vanishes when x has the arbitrary value a, or again, a may be supposed equal to α or to β. None of these suppositions however lead to the result given by Lacroix, although the supposition that I vanishes when $x=\alpha$ or when $x=\beta$ will simplify the correct formulæ. There is another point to be noticed. We have hitherto supposed v to mean the indefinite integral $\int V' dx$ without any constant added; but v may stand for something different, as for example for $\int_a^x V' dx$. In this case in order to find what arises from $I\int(dx\delta V' - dV'\delta x)$, we must take the integral from c to x, then multiply by I and put successively $x=\alpha$ and $x=\beta$ in the result, and subtract the first value of the result from the second. Similar processes must be performed with the terms in (3). For simplicity we will suppose that $I = \int_a^x L dx$, so that I vanishes when $x=a$. Thus, for example, the first term of the first line of (2) is

$$[I\{(P'\omega)_{x=x} - (P'\omega)_{x=c}\}]_{x=\beta}$$
$$-[I\{(P'\omega)_{x=x} - (P'\omega)_{x=c}\}]_{x=\alpha}.$$

The second line vanishes since $I_{x=\alpha}$ is zero, and the first line may be written

$$I_{x=\beta}\{(P'\omega)_{x=\beta} - (P\omega)_{x=c}\}.$$

From considering this result, we see that *if $c = a$*, we may adopt the final form given by Lacroix. Thus the formula of Lacroix must be understood to imply that $v = \int_a^\beta V' dx$, where a is also the lower limit of the integral $\int V dx$.

It is however possible to suppose that v stands for $\int_a^b V' dx$, where a and b are constants. In this case the terms in (2) will give

$$(I_{x=\beta} - I_{x=a}) \int_a^b (dx\, \delta V' - dV'' \delta x).$$

The terms in (3) will give

$$\int_a^b I (dx\, \delta V' - dV'' \delta x),$$

in which we are supposed to make x successively equal to a and β, *and subtract one result from the other;* so that the remainder is zero. Hence in this case

$$\delta \int_a^\beta V dx = (V \delta x)_{x=\beta} - (V \delta x)_{x=a} + \int_a^\beta (dx\, \delta\psi - d\psi\, \delta x)$$
$$+ (I_{x=\beta} - I_{x=a}) \int_a^b (dx\, \delta V' - dV'' \delta x);$$

and nothing remains except to transform $\int_a^\beta (dx\, \delta\psi - d\psi\, \delta x)$ and $\int_a^b (dx\, \delta V'' - dV' \delta x)$ by the ordinary processes of the Calculus of Variations.

Moreover $\qquad\qquad I_{x=\beta} - I_{x=a} = \int_a^\beta L\, dx.$

39. We now arrive with Lacroix at the problem of the Variation of a function of two independent variables. An important mistake occurs on pages 779 and 780, which must be noticed here. We shall use the ordinary notation for partial differential coefficients of a function z, namely p for $\dfrac{dz}{dx}$, q for $\dfrac{dz}{dy}$, r for $\dfrac{d^2z}{dx^2}$, and so on. Lacroix gives the following process.

To find δp and δq. We have

$$\delta p = \delta \frac{dz}{dx};$$

by differentiating the fraction in the ordinary way and changing d into δ, we shall have '

$$\delta p = \frac{dx\,\delta ds - dz\,\delta dx}{dx^2} = \frac{dx\,d\delta z - dz\,d\delta x}{dx^2} = \frac{d\delta z - p\,d\delta x}{dx}.$$

Similarly $\delta q = \dfrac{d\delta z - q\,d\delta y}{dy}$.

The formulæ thus obtained for δp and δq by Lacroix are incorrect; they appear to have been taken by Lacroix from Euler's treatise comprised in his *Integral Calculus*. The true formulæ were given by Poisson; the erroneous steps in the process of Euler and Lacroix were afterwards indicated by Ostrogradsky, and Poisson's results were confirmed. These points we shall have occasion to explain in analysing the memoirs of the two writers last named.

'40. After the error in finding δp and δq Lacroix follows Euler in giving erroneous formulæ for δr, δs, and δt. These writers both shew that in following out their process they obtain *two* formulæ for δs, by performing the operations in different orders, and these two formulæ can only be reconciled by supposing that δx is a function of x only, and δy a function of y only. They proceed thus

$$\delta s = \delta\,\frac{dp}{dy} = \frac{d\delta p - s\,d\delta y}{dy},$$

and

$$\frac{d\delta p}{dy} = \frac{d^2\delta z}{dy\,dx} - s\,\frac{d\delta x}{dx} - p\,\frac{d^2\delta x}{dy\,dx};$$

therefore

$$\delta s = \frac{d^2\delta z}{dy\,dx} - s\,\frac{d\delta x}{dx} - p\,\frac{d^2\delta x}{dy\,dx} - s\,\frac{d\delta y}{dy}.$$

Again, adopting a different order, we have

$$\delta s = \delta\,\frac{dq}{dx} = \frac{d\delta q - s\,d\delta x}{dx},$$

and

$$\frac{d\delta q}{dx} = \frac{d^2\delta z}{dx\,dy} - s\,\frac{d\delta y}{dy} - q\,\frac{d^2\delta y}{dx\,dy};$$

therefore

$$\delta s = \frac{d^2\delta z}{dx\,dy} - s\,\frac{d\delta y}{dy} - q\,\frac{d^2\delta y}{dx\,dy} - s\,\frac{d\delta x}{dx}.$$

These two formulæ for δs contain respectively the essentially different terms $p \cdot \dfrac{d^2 \delta x}{dy\,dx}$ and $q \dfrac{d^2 \delta y}{dx\,dy}$, which can only be made to disappear by supposing that δx does not contain y and that δy does not contain x.

41. The difficulty at which Euler and Lacroix thus arrive is owing to the circumstance that they determine δp and δq erroneously, and repeat their error in determining δs; the correct values will be given hereafter. Strictly speaking it is not absolutely necessary that δx should be a function of x only, and δy of y only in order to make $\dfrac{d^2 \delta x}{dy\,dx}$ and $\dfrac{d^2 \delta y}{dx\,dy}$ vanish; for if δx were a function of x only or of y only $\dfrac{d^2 \delta x}{dy\,dx}$ would vanish, and a similar remark is true with respect to δy. But the supposition that δx is a function of x only and δy of y only is more natural at this point, and is much more convenient for the subsequent processes required in the development of the variation of a double integral. Lacroix seems to intimate on page 778 that there is some loss of generality in imposing the restrictions on δx and δy; this however does not appear to be the case. For let x, y, s be the co-ordinates of any point; and let $x + \delta x$, $y + \delta y$, $s + \delta s$ be the co-ordinates of an adjacent point; then if δx be an arbitrary function of x only, δy an arbitrary function of y only, and δs an arbitrary function of both x and y, we have the power of passing from the point (x, y, z) to an adjacent point in every possible way; that is, our suppositions involve all the generality we require.

42. Lacroix now gives the ordinary development of the variation of a double integral; in so doing he reproduces the error which has been already indicated in Art. 27. He illustrates the whole subject by discussing some of the usual problems; he selects the brachistochrone, the solid of least resistance, the curve which includes a maximum area between itself and its evolute, the integral $\int V\,dx$ where $V = y \int \sqrt{(1 + p^2)}\;dx$, and the brachistochrone in a resisting medium.

43.   Lacroix then gives Euler's method of treating questions of relative maxima and minima; that is, for example, he shews that if we want the maximum or minimum value of $\int u\,dx$ subject to the condition that $\int v\,dx$ shall be constant we must proceed to solve the problem of finding the maximum or minimum of $\int (u + av)\,dx$, where a is a constant.   This part of the subject he illustrates by the problem in which a curve is to be found of given length and area, which by rotation round an axis will generate a maximum or minimum volume.   Lastly he gives some investigations with respect to the problem of discriminating a maximum from a minimum; these are similar to those which we have already noticed in Art. 5.

44.   In the third volume of his work, which was published in 1819, Lacroix has a note on the point which we have noticed in Art. 39.   He gives there the correct forms for δp, δq, ... which had been obtained by Poisson after the publication of the second volume of the *Traité du Calcul Différentiel et du Calcul Intégral*.

45.   On the whole the Calculus of Variations does not seem to have been very successfully expounded by Lacroix, and this is perhaps one of the least satisfactory parts of his great work.   Mr Abbatt, in the preface to his treatise on the subject, speaks thus of it: "In Lacroix's *Traité du Calcul Différentiel et du Calcul Intégral*, Tom. II., we find materials sufficient to form a complete work on Variations; but the subject is treated in a manner so prolix and inelegant, that the reader's taste will scarcely be improved, how much soever his knowledge may be increased by the perusal."

CHAPTER II.

DIRKSEN. OHM.

46. In this Chapter we shall give an account of the works of Dirksen and Ohm. The treatise of Dirksen is entitled *Analytical Exhibition of the Calculus of Variations with the application of it to the determination of Maxima and Minima*, by E. H. Dirksen, Berlin, 1823, (Analytische Darstellung der Variations-rechnung mit Anwendung derselben auf die Bestimmung des Grössten und Kleinsten).

47. Dirksen's book is a small quarto of 243 pages, with a preface of 8 pages; it is very badly and incorrectly printed. In the preface the author says that the *Calculus of Variations* appears to have been neglected, for in elementary works no improvement had been introduced since the time of Euler and Lagrange; he states that he has himself developed the subject from a purely analytical origin; and in conformity with this remark it may be observed that there is no figure in the book.

48. The work is divided into four chapters. The first chapter extends over 32 pages; it is called an *Exhibition of the principles of the Calculus of Variations*. Dirksen takes any function such as $\phi(x, y, z)$ and changes x into $x + k\delta x$, y into $y + k\delta y$, and z into $z + k\delta z$; he then expands the new value of the function in a series proceeding according to ascending powers of k; the coefficient of the first power of k is called the *variation of the first order* of the function, the coefficient of k^2 is called the *variation of the second order* of the function, and so on. In the first chapter the author finds the variations of explicit differential and integral

functions, and of a function which is implicitly determined by means of an unsolved differential equation.

40. The second chapter extends from page 33 to page 73; it is called *Development and Transformation of the variation of the first order of undetermined Integral Formulæ taken between given limits.* Here Dirksen confines himself to the term containing the first power of k in his general expansion, and he gives the ordinary process of integration by parts which separates the variation of an integral into an integrated part and a part still remaining under the sign of integration. He also gives the transformation of a double integral $\iint V dx dy$, supposing the limits of the integrations for both x and y to be constants.

50. The third chapter extends from page 74 to page 200; it is called *Application of the Calculus of Variations to the determination of Maxima and Minima.* The author first considers the maximum or minimum of an explicit function, which is an ordinary problem of the *Differential Calculus.* He then proceeds to the case where the function involves differential coefficients, and he discusses the example given by Lagrange (see Art. 3). Next, he considers undetermined integral formulæ; and with respect to these he investigates the second term of his general expansion in powers of k with the view of discriminating a maximum from a minimum; he uses the method given by Lagrange in the *Théorie des Fonctions Analytiques.*

51. The fourth chapter extends from page 201 to the end; it is called *Examples relating to the determination of the Maximum or Minimum of undetermined Integral Formulæ.* Dirksen states in the preface that these examples are for the most part taken from Euler's *Methodus Inveniendi* ......, but he intimates that the solutions of the examples are in some respects superior to those given by Euler. The examples given by Dirksen are in fact all in Euler; but Dirksen has generally investigated the terms of the second order so as to discriminate a maximum from a minimum, and this gives his solutions an advantage over Euler's. Some of these examples are also discussed in the work of Strauch; it will be useful to point out those which are in Dirksen and which are

not in Strauch; they are the following. The maximum or minimum of the following expressions is required,

$$\int y\,(ax - y^2)\,dx, \qquad\qquad\qquad \text{(Euler, page 39),}$$

$$\int (15a^2x^2y - 15a^2xy + 5a^2y^4 - 3y^2)\,dx, \qquad \text{(Euler, page 40),}$$

$$\int (3ax - 3x^2 - y^2)\,(ax - x^2 - \tfrac{1}{2}xy + y^2)\,dx, \qquad \text{(Euler, page 41),}$$

$$\int \frac{y'\dfrac{d^2y}{dx^2}}{\dfrac{dy}{dx}}\,dx, \qquad\qquad\qquad \text{(Euler, page 61).}$$

Also the maximum or minimum of $\int y^2 dx$ subject to the condition
that $\int yx\,dx$ is constant is found (Euler, page 191). And Dirksen
investigates the shortest line on a spheroid; Euler gave the general
problem of the shortest line on a surface (page 138).

52. On the whole Dirksen's treatise cannot be estimated very
highly, and the inaccuracy of the printing renders it repulsive to a
student. In Ohm's treatise, which we shall next examine, references are made to some unsatisfactory points in Dirksen's work; see
Ohm's *Theory of Maxima and Minima*, pages 6, 11, 18, 50, 53, 55,
62, 74, 84, 115, 119, 233, 250, 292, 313.

53. Ohm's treatise on this subject is entitled *The Theory of
Maxima and Minima*, by Dr Martin Ohm, Berlin. 1825. (Die
Lehre vom Groessten und Kleinsten). This is an octavo volume of
330 pages, with a preface of 18 pages. It may be regarded as
the successor to the work of Dirksen, for Ohm gives frequent references to Dirksen, and corrects some of his errors. Ohm's book is
very correctly printed, but from the highly condensed notation
which he adopts, and from the want of illustrative problems, it is
rather a difficult work for a student.

54. The first 64 pages contain an *Introduction*, in which the
author collects the propositions in Algebra and the Differential and
Integral Calculus, which are especially used in the ordinary theory of
maxima and minima, and in the Calculus of Variations. Thus we
have theorems on the expansion of functions, on differentiating integral expressions with respect to any symbol which they contain,

and on the reductions of certain integral forms by means of integration by parts. This mode of arrangement seems liable to objection, as the various propositions are given apart from their useful applications, and thus they are rendered more difficult and less interesting than they would be if introduced when they were required for immediate service.

55. The portion of the book extending over pages 67—127 is called *Calculus of Variations*. Ohm's view of a variation is similar to that of Euler and Lagrange. (See Art. 22 and Art. 15.) Let V denote any function, and V_s a function which reduces to V when $x = 0$; then V_s is what V becomes by variation, and V_s is supposed developed in a series, so that

$$V_s = V + \delta V \cdot x + \delta^2 V \cdot \frac{x^2}{1 \cdot 2} + \delta^3 V \cdot \frac{x^3}{1 \cdot 2 \cdot 3} + \dots$$

The terms $\delta V, \delta^2 V, \delta^3 V, \dots$ are called *variation-coefficients*, and by Maclaurin's Theorem they are the values of the successive differential coefficients of V when x is supposed zero after the differentiations. The only terms of importance are the first and second variation-coefficients, namely δV and $\delta^2 V$. In this part of the treatise Ohm gives the first and second variation-coefficients of different expressions, some of which involve integrals and some of which do not.

56. The portion of the work extending over pages 131—314 is called the *Theory of Maxima and Minima*. The pages 131—208 contain the theory of maxima and minima, which is given in ordinary treatises on the Differential Calculus. Ohm endeavours to present this part of the subject under a novel aspect, but it does not appear that there is any real extension or improvement of the common methods. The pages 209—244 contain investigations of the maxima and minima of expressions in which *differential coefficients* enter, that is, expressions of the kind exemplified by Lagrange (see Art. 3). This part of Ohm's treatise contains more than had been previously given on this point; the extension however was extremely natural and obvious after the example discussed by Lagrange.

57. We now arrive at the part of Ohm's treatise which is devoted to the maxima and minima of integral expressions. On pages 244—304 Ohm considers expressions which involve single integrals. He takes an integral $\int V dx$, and at first he supposes that V involves only x and y; next he supposes that V involves x, y, and $\frac{dy}{dx}$; next he supposes that V involves x, y, $\frac{dy}{dx}$ and $\frac{d^2y}{dx^2}$; lastly, on page 272 he supposes that V involves x, y, $\frac{dy}{dx}$, $\frac{d^2y}{dx^2}$, ... up to $\frac{d^n y}{dx^n}$. He then takes the case in which V contains besides y another function of x, as z, together with the differential coefficients of y and z.

58. For discriminating between maxima and minima Ohm gives the method which was originally proposed by Legendre, which we have already exemplified in Art. 5. He seems however to consider the results as more certain than they really are, for he omits all reference to the qualifications indicated by Lagrange (see the latter part of Art. 5). Ohm extends this method to the case in which the function under the integral sign involves more than one dependent variable; on page 279 he takes for example $\int V dx$ where V is a function of x, y, z, $\frac{dy}{dx}$, $\frac{d^2y}{dx^2}$ and $\frac{dz}{dx}$.

59. In pages 304—310 we find some investigations with respect to the maxima and minima of multiple integrals. Here for the first time the case is considered in which the limits of the first integration are functions of the other variable. The following is Ohm's process with some change of notation.

Let
$$V = f\left(x, y, z, \frac{dz}{dx}, \frac{dz}{dy}\right),$$
$$U = \int_{x_0}^{x_1} \int_{y_0}^{y_1} V dx dy;$$

the integration in U is supposed to be effected with respect to y first, and the limits y_0 and y_1 may be functions of x. It is required to express δU. With the notation used in Art. 17 we have

$$\delta V = \left(L - \frac{dM}{dx} - \frac{dN}{dy}\right)\delta z + \frac{d}{dx}(M\delta z) + \frac{d}{dy}(N\delta z);$$

therefore $\delta U = \int_{x_0}^{x_1} \int_{y_0}^{y_1} \left(L - \dfrac{dM}{dx} - \dfrac{dN}{dy} \right) \delta z \, dx dy$

$+ \int_{x_0}^{x_1} \int_{y_0}^{y_1} \dfrac{d}{dx} (M\delta z) \, dx dy + \int_{x_0}^{x_1} [(N\delta z)_1 - (N\delta z)_0] \, dx,$

where $(N\delta z)_1$ denotes the value of $N\delta z$ when for y we put y_1, and $(N\delta z)_0$ the value of $N\delta z$ when for y we put y_0. Now

$\int_{y_0}^{y_1} \dfrac{d}{dx} (M\delta z) \, dy = \dfrac{d}{dx} \int_{y_0}^{y_1} M\delta z dy - (M\delta z)_1 \dfrac{dy_1}{dx} + (M\delta z)_0 \dfrac{dy_0}{dx} ;$

thus the term $\int_{x_0}^{x_1} \int_{y_0}^{y_1} \dfrac{d}{dx} (M\delta z) \, dx dy$ gives

$$\left(\int_{y_0}^{y_1} M\delta z dy \right)_{x=x_1} - \left(\int_{y_0}^{y_1} M\delta z dy \right)_{x=x_0}$$

$$- \int_{x_0}^{x_1} (M\delta z)_1 \dfrac{dy_1}{dx} \, dx + \int_{x_0}^{x_1} (M\delta z)_0 \dfrac{dy_0}{dx} \, dx.$$

We have thus the value of δU reduced as much as possible.

60. Pages 811—814 shew how to obtain the variations of functions which are implicitly given by differential equations. The book finishes with an appendix of fourteen pages, in which are given some algebraical expansions which are in fact cases of Taylor's Theorem.

61. There are three other works in which Ohm has touched upon the subject of the Calculus of Variations; these are

System der Mathematik, Band v. Berlin, 1831.

System der Mathematik, Band vii. Berlin, 1833.

Lehrbuch der höhern Mathematik, Band ii. Berlin, 1839.

We shall make some observations on these three works.

62. In the fifth volume of Ohm's *System of Mathematics* the portion of the work devoted to our subject is the eleventh chapter, extending over pages 51—87. The chapter is divided into two

parts; the first is called the *Expansion of polynomial functions in series* and extends over pages 50—81, the second is called *Calculus of Variations* and extends over pages 82—87. The main point of the chapter may be said to be the expansion of a function of $x, y, z, \ldots a, b, c, \ldots$ in powers of x when

$$x = x_0 + x_1 x + x_2 x^2 + \ldots$$
$$a = a_0 + a_1 x + a_2 x^2 + \ldots$$

and similar expressions hold for $y, z, \ldots b, c, \ldots$ There is only a very brief account of the Calculus of Variations, strictly so called, and this account contains nothing of importance.

63. In the seventh Volume of Ohm's *System of Mathematics* there is a chapter on Maxima and Minima, and an Appendix of Examples. The chapter on Maxima and Minima gives a brief sketch of the ordinary portions of the Calculus of Variations; for fuller details Ohm refers to his separate work on the subject, of which we have already given an account in Arts. 53—60. The appendix of problems contains 41 problems and occupies 113 pages; these problems are intended by Ohm to illustrate the separate work to which reference has just been made. The first six of the problems require maxima or minima values of expressions involving a function and its differential coefficients, but not involving integrals. These problems are all reproduced by Strauch in the second volume of his treatise on the subject. The first is given by Strauch on pages 14—16; he ascribes it to Ohm. The second, third, and fourth are given by Strauch on pages 23—27; they consist of the example originally given by Lagrange, and two modifications of it which Strauch ascribes to Ohm. The fifth and sixth problems are ascribed by Strauch to Ohm; Strauch gives them with some extensions on pages 82—89. Ohm's problems from 7 to 17 inclusive consist of different cases of the shortest line that can be drawn in one plane or in free space, with various limiting conditions. The problems from 18 to 20 are respecting the shortest lines that can be drawn on assigned surfaces; Ohm gives the ordinary investigations. The general problem is not treated by Strauch, but he examines in detail the same particular case as Ohm, namely,

that of the shortest line on a sphere. Ohm's remaining problems are all common examples, and are all included in Strauch's second volume, except one which shall be given presently. The problems 21, 22, 31, 32, 33, 34 relate to the brachistochrone and to the curve of greatest final velocity; these are in Strauch, pages 400—454. The problems from 23 to 27 inclusive relate to the curve which is of minimum length and includes a constant area, and the curve of constant length which includes a maximum area; all these problems are in Strauch, pages 476—504. Problems 29 and 30 relate to the surface of minimum area and to the surface of maximum volume with a given area; these problems are in Strauch, pages 616—623. Problem 35 is given by Strauch on pages 454—458. Problem 36 relates to the curve which has the area between itself and its evolute a maximum; it is given by Strauch on pages 289—291. Problem 37 is given by Strauch on pages 584—588. Problem 38 relates to the solid of revolution which has a minimum surface; it is given by Strauch on pages 506, 507. Problem 39 relates to the solid of least resistance; it is given by Strauch on page 399. Problem 40 is given by Strauch on pages 524—527, and problem 41 on pages 527, 528.

64. The solutions of Ohm have not been examined for the present work, as the examples he gives are all discussed in other books. It may be observed that in his first seven problems Ohm investigates the terms of the second order so as to discriminate a maximum from a minimum. From the list given in Art. 63, it will be seen that no problem is contained in Ohm which is not easily accessible in other works except problem 28.

65. Ohm's 28th problem is this; Required the maximum or minimum value of $\int_a^b \dfrac{z}{p}\, dx$, where p stands for $\dfrac{dy}{dx}$, and $z = \int_a^x y\, dx$. His solution is substantially the following.

Here $\dfrac{dz}{dx} = y$; so that $y - \dfrac{dz}{dx} = 0$. Hence we may consider that we have to find the maximum or minimum value of V, where

$$V = \int_a^b \left\{ \frac{z}{p} + \lambda \left(y - \frac{dz}{dx} \right) \right\} dx,$$

λ being a multiplier at present undetermined.　Thus

$$\delta V = \int_a^b \left\{ \frac{\delta z}{p} - \frac{z}{p^3}\, \delta p + \lambda \delta y - \lambda\, \frac{d\delta x}{dx} \right\} dx$$

$$= \int_a^b \left\{ \frac{1}{p} + \frac{d\lambda}{dx} \right\} \delta z\, dx + \int_a^b \left\{ \frac{d}{dx}\left(\frac{z}{p^3} \right) + \lambda \right\} \delta y\, dx$$

$$- \left(\frac{z\delta y}{p^3} \right)_{x=b} + \left(\frac{z\delta y}{p^3} \right)_{x=a} - (\lambda \delta x)_{x=b} + (\lambda \delta x)_{x=a}.$$

Now assume λ such that the coefficient of δz vanishes; that is, assume

$$\frac{1}{p} + \frac{d\lambda}{dx} = 0 \dots\dots\dots\dots\dots\dots\dots\dots (1).$$

Then in order that δV may vanish, we must have the coefficient of δy zero; that is

$$\frac{d}{dx}\left(\frac{z}{p^3} \right) + \lambda = 0 \dots\dots\dots\dots\dots\dots (2).$$

By eliminating λ between (1) and (2) and substituting for z, we obtain ultimately a differential equation of the fourth order for determining y; so that four arbitrary constants occur. These four constants will enable us to make the four terms relating to the limits at present remaining in δV vanish. It does not appear that the differential equation for determining y can be integrated in a finite form.

This example is given in Euler's *Methodus inveniendi* ...... page 102, without however any express indication of the limits of integration.　It is also solved by Dirksen, pages 139—143.

66.　The work of Ohm published in 1839, is noticed by Strauch in the preface to his treatise (page xv).　He says that it is only an abridgment of that published in 1825; it has not been consulted for the present work.

67.　On the whole, with respect to Ohm's works on the subject it may be said that the only one of importance is that published in 1825; and at the time of publication this surpassed all preceding treatises on the subject.　It is however at present only of historical interest, as it is completely superseded by the extensive treatise of Strauch.　Strauch in fact may be considered as the successor of Ohm; a good sketch of Ohm's works will be found in Strauch's preface, pages xiv—xvi.

CHAPTER III.

GAUSS.

68.   On September 28th, 1829, a memoir was communicated by
C. F. Gauss to the Royal Society of Gottingen, entitled *Principia
Generalia Theoriæ Figuræ Fluidorum in Statu Æquilibrii.* The
memoir relates to the theory of Capillary Attraction and demonstrates in a new way some results which had been already obtained
by Laplace.   The memoir is published in the Seventh Volume of
the *Commentationes Societatis Regiæ Scientiarum Gottingensis,* 1833;
it occupies pages 39—88 of the mathematical portion of the volume.
Part of this memoir is devoted to the solution of a problem in the
Calculus of Variations involving the variation of a certain double
integral, *the limits of the integration being also variable;* it is the
earliest example of the solution of such a problem.   Gauss himself
says on page 67, " Sed quum calculus variationum integralium
duplicium pro casu ubi etiam limites tanquam variabiles spectari
debent, hactenus parum excultus sit, hanc disquisitionem subtilem
paullo profundius petere oportet."   We shall give the investigation
of Gauss.

69.   It is not consistent with the scope of the present work to
touch upon the parts of Gauss's memoir which are unconnected with
the Calculus of Variations.   We must refer the student to the
original memoir, and recommend it as important and interesting.
In Liouville's *Journal des Mathématiques,* Vol. xiii., 1848, is a
memoir by M. Bertrand, which is in fact nearly a republication of
that part of the memoir of Gauss which does *not* concern the Calculus of Variations, with some extensions and applications.   That
is to say, M. Bertrand reproduces the physical part of Gauss's

memoir, but substitutes geometrical reasoning instead of the parts which involve the Calculus of Variations. Moreover as we shall see hereafter simpler investigations of the problem in the Calculus of Variations discussed by Gauss have been since given by Pagani and Mainardi, but the interest which belongs to Gauss's method, from the eminence of the author and from the fact of its being the first solution of such a problem, will justify us in reproducing it here.

70. On the first page of his Memoir Gauss has a short note which refers to a problem in the Calculus of Variations. He says, "the greatest attraction which a given homogeneous mass attracting according to the ordinary law can exert on a given particle is to the attraction which a sphere of the same mass would exert on the same particle if placed on its surface as 3 to $\sqrt[3]{25}$." This result may be easily verified; we have to find the form of a solid of given mass so that the attraction upon a particle may be the greatest possible. It is obvious that the solid must be one of revolution, and it may be shewn to be the solid formed by revolving the curve $r' = c' \cos \theta$ about the prime radius. This result is also obtained by Schellbach in Crelle's *Journal fur... Mathematik*, Vol. 41, page 345.

71. In order to facilitate the comprehension of the researches of Gauss we begin with a short account of his notation. Conceive a vessel open at the top containing homogeneous fluid; let ds denote an element of *volume* of this fluid, z the height of this element above a fixed horizontal plane, T the area of the surface of the fluid which is contiguous to the vessel, U the area of the free surface of the fluid, a and β two constant quantities. Then Gauss arrives at the following expression

$$\int z\,ds + (a' - 2\beta')\,T + a'U;$$

this expression he denotes by W, and he has proved that for the fluid to be in equilibrium W must be a *minimum*. Gauss then proceeds to the investigations which occupy the present chapter.

72. It remains to determine the nature of the figure of equilibrium, for which purpose we must find the variation that W experiences when the figure of the space occupied by the fluid undergoes

any infinitely small variation. But since the Calculus of the Variations of double integrals in the case where the limits are also variable has hitherto been little studied, the subject will require careful investigation.

Consider that part of the surface of the fluid which we have denoted by U, and let x, y, z be the co-ordinates of any point of it. We may consider z as a function of the variables x and y, and denote the partial differentials of z in the usual manner, omitting brackets, by

$$\frac{dz}{dx}\, dx, \quad \frac{dz}{dy}\, dy.$$

At the point (x, y, z) suppose a normal to the surface of the fluid drawn outwards, and let ξ, η, ζ be the cosines of the angles between this normal and lines respectively parallel to the axes of x, y, and z. Thus

$$\xi^2 + \eta^2 + \zeta^2 = 1;$$

and

$$\frac{dz}{dx} = -\frac{\xi}{\zeta}, \quad \frac{dz}{dy} = -\frac{\eta}{\zeta}.$$

The boundary of the surface U will be a closed curve which we will denote by P, and which may be supposed described by a point moving always in the same direction, so that the element dP will always be considered positive; also the element dU will always be considered positive. We will denote the cosines of the angles which the direction of dP makes with the co-ordinate axes of x, y, z by X, Y, Z respectively, and in order to remove all ambiguity concerning this direction we shall take it so that a system similar to that of the co-ordinate axes of x, y, z may be formed by the following three lines, namely, the direction of dP, the direction of the normal to dP which touches the surface U and falls within the boundary of it, and the normal to the surface U drawn outwards. Thus it will follow that the cosines of the angles between the second direction and the axes of x, y, z respectively are

$$\eta_1 Z - \zeta_1 Y, \quad \zeta_1 X - \xi_1 Z, \quad \xi_1 Y - \eta_1 X,$$

where ξ_1, η_1, ζ_1, are the values of ξ, η, ζ which belong to the position of the element dP.

73. Let us now suppose the surface U to undergo an indefinitely small mutation. If it were sufficient to consider only those

mutations for which the boundary P remained unchanged, or
always remained in the same vertical surface, it is obvious that
it would only be necessary to ascribe a variation to the vertical
co-ordinate z, and thus the problem would become much simpler.
But we wish to examine the problem in all its generality and
the separate consideration of the change of the limits will be in-
convenient, so that it will be better to ascribe variations to all
three co-ordinates x, y, z. We will suppose therefore that for a
point in the surface whose co-ordinates are x, y, z, another is sub-
stituted whose co-ordinates are $x + \delta x$, $y + \delta y$, $z + \delta z$; and δx, δy,
δz may be considered as undetermined functions of x and y and
indefinitely small. We will now examine the variations of the
different parts of W, beginning with the variation of U.

Let us conceive a triangular element dU of the surface U, and
suppose the co-ordinates of the angular points to be

$$x, \ y, \ z \ ;$$

$$x + dx, \quad y + dy, \quad z + \frac{dz}{dx}\, dx + \frac{dz}{dy}\, dy \ ;$$

$$x + d'x, \quad y + d'y, \quad z + \frac{dz}{dx}\, d'x + \frac{dz}{dy}\, d'y.$$

The double of the area of this triangle is known to be

$$(dx\, d'y - dy\, d'x) \left\{ 1 + \left(\frac{dz}{dx}\right)^2 + \left(\frac{dz}{dy}\right)^2 \right\}^{\frac{1}{2}}.$$

[This follows from the known expression for the area of a triangle in terms of the co-ordinates of its angular points, in conjunc-
tion with the theorem which connects the area of any plane figure
with the area of its projection.]

In the surface obtained by the variation of the first surface we
shall have for the co-ordinates of the points corresponding to the
angular points of dU,

for the first point

$$x + \delta x, \ y + \delta y, \ z + \delta z \ ;$$

for the second point

$$x + dx + \delta x + \frac{d\delta x}{dx}\, dx + \frac{d\delta x}{dy}\, dy.$$

$$y + dy + \delta y + \frac{d\delta y}{dx}\, dx + \frac{d\delta y}{dy}\, dy,$$

$$z + \frac{dz}{dx}\, dx + \frac{dz}{dy}\, dy + \delta z + \frac{d\delta z}{dx}\, dx + \frac{d\delta z}{dy}\, dy;$$

for the third point

$$x + d'x + \delta x + \frac{d\delta x}{dx}\, d'x + \frac{d\delta x}{dy}\, d'y,$$

$$y + d'y + \delta y + \frac{d\delta y}{dx}\, d'x + \frac{d\delta y}{dy}\, d'y,$$

$$z + \frac{dz}{dx}\, d'x + \frac{dz}{dy}\, d'y + \delta z + \frac{d\delta z}{dx}\, d'x + \frac{d\delta z}{dy}\, d'y.$$

The double of the area of this new triangle is found to be

$$(dx\, d'y - dy\, d'x)\, \sqrt{N},$$

where N stands for

$$\left\{ \left(1 + \frac{d\delta x}{dx}\right)\left(1 + \frac{d\delta y}{dy}\right) - \frac{d\delta x}{dy}\,\frac{d\delta y}{dx} \right\}^2$$

$$+ \left\{ \left(1 + \frac{d\delta x}{dx}\right)\left(\frac{dz}{dy} + \frac{d\delta z}{dy}\right) - \frac{d\delta x}{dy}\left(\frac{dz}{dx} + \frac{d\delta z}{dx}\right) \right\}^2$$

$$+ \left\{ \left(1 + \frac{d\delta y}{dy}\right)\left(\frac{dz}{dx} + \frac{d\delta z}{dx}\right) - \frac{d\delta y}{dx}\left(\frac{dz}{dy} + \frac{d\delta z}{dy}\right) \right\}^2.$$

[74.   There are two methods of arriving at this result; we may take the ordinary expression for the area of a triangle in terms of the co-ordinates of its angular points, and substitute the values of the co-ordinates just given. Or we may proceed thus—find the area of the projection of the new triangle on the plane of (x, y) and multiply the result by the secant of the angle of inclination of the triangle to the plane of (x, y): this method is instructive and we will give it in detail.

The area of the projection is best found by imagining for a moment that the origin of co-ordinates has been transferred to the point $x + \delta x$, $y + \delta y$, $z + \delta z$. Thus we obtain for the double of the area of the projection,

$$\left(dx + \frac{d\delta x}{dx}\, dx + \frac{d\delta x}{dy}\, dy\right)\left(d'y + \frac{d\delta y}{dx}\, d'x + \frac{d\delta y}{dy}\, d'y\right)$$

$$- \left(dy + \frac{d\delta y}{dx}\, dx + \frac{d\delta y}{dy}\, dy\right)\left(d'x + \frac{d\delta x}{dx}\, d'x + \frac{d\delta x}{dy}\, d'y\right).$$

The first line gives

$$dx\, d'y \left(1 + \frac{d\delta x}{dx}\right)\left(1 + \frac{d\delta y}{dy}\right) + dx\, d'x \left(1 + \frac{d\delta x}{dx}\right)\frac{d\delta y}{dx}$$

$$+ dy\, d'y \left(1 + \frac{d\delta y}{dy}\right)\frac{d\delta x}{dy} + dy\, d'x \,\frac{d\delta x}{dy}\,\frac{d\delta y}{dx}.$$

The second line may be obtained from the first by interchanging dx with $d'x$ and dy with $d'y$. Thus we have for the double area the expression

$$(dx\, d'y - dy\, d'x)\left\{\left(1 + \frac{d\delta x}{dx}\right)\left(1 + \frac{d\delta y}{dy}\right) - \frac{d\delta x}{dy}\,\frac{d\delta y}{dx}\right\}.$$

We have then to multiply this by the secant of the inclination of the triangle to the plane of (x, y). Now we know that if $x_1,\, y_1,\, z_1$ be the co-ordinates of a point on a surface the corresponding secant is equal to

$$\left\{1 + \left(\frac{dz_1}{dx_1}\right)^2 + \left(\frac{dz_1}{dy_1}\right)^2\right\}^{\frac{1}{2}},$$

where $\left(\frac{dz_1}{dx_1}\right)$ and $\left(\frac{dz_1}{dy_1}\right)$ denote *partial* differential coefficients. The chief point of the present investigation consists in forming these partial differential coefficients correctly. To this we proceed; in forming $\frac{dz_1}{dx_1}$ *we must regard* dy_1 *as zero.* Hence since $x_1,\, y_1,\, z_1$ stand for $x + \delta x,\ y + \delta y,\ z + \delta z$ respectively, and dy_1 is to be zero, we have

$$dx_1 = dx + \frac{d\delta x}{dx}\, dx + \frac{d\delta x}{dy}\, dy,$$

$$0 = dy + \frac{d\delta y}{dx}\, dx + \frac{d\delta y}{dy}\, dy,$$

$$dz_1 = \frac{dz}{dx}\, dx + \frac{dz}{dy}\, dy + \frac{d\delta z}{dx}\, dx + \frac{d\delta z}{dy}\, dy;$$

therefore

$$\left(\frac{dz_i}{dx_i}\right) = \frac{\left(\frac{dz}{dx} + \frac{d\delta z}{dx}\right)\left(1 + \frac{d\delta y}{dy}\right) - \left(\frac{dz}{dy} + \frac{d\delta z}{dy}\right)\frac{d\delta y}{dx}}{\left(1 + \frac{d\delta x}{dx}\right)\left(1 + \frac{d\delta y}{dy}\right) - \frac{d\delta x}{dy}\frac{d\delta y}{dx}}.$$

An analogous expression will be found for $\left(\dfrac{dz_i}{dy_i}\right)$. Thus the required secant is known, and we finally obtain for the double of the required area the result already given

$$(dx\,d'y - d'x\,dy)\sqrt{N}.]$$

75. If we develop the value of N and reject terms of the second order, we have

$$\sqrt{N} = \left\{1 + \left(\frac{dz}{dx}\right)^2 + \left(\frac{dz}{dy}\right)^2\right\}^{\frac{1}{2}} \left\{1 + \frac{L}{1 + \left(\frac{dz}{dx}\right)^2 + \left(\frac{dz}{dy}\right)^2}\right\},$$

where L stands for

$$\frac{d\delta x}{dx}\left\{1 + \left(\frac{dz}{dy}\right)^2\right\} + \frac{d\delta y}{dy}\left\{1 + \left(\frac{dz}{dx}\right)^2\right\}$$

$$- \left(\frac{d\delta x}{dy} + \frac{d\delta y}{dx}\right)\frac{dz}{dx}\frac{dz}{dy} + \frac{d\delta z}{dx}\frac{dz}{dx} + \frac{d\delta z}{dy}\frac{dz}{dy}.$$

Thus the ratio of the first triangle to the second is that of unity to

$$1 + \frac{L}{1 + \left(\frac{dz}{dx}\right)^2 + \left(\frac{dz}{dy}\right)^2},$$

and is therefore independent of the form of the triangle dU. Therefore

$$\delta dU = \frac{L\,dU}{1 + \left(\frac{dz}{dx}\right)^2 + \left(\frac{dz}{dy}\right)^2};$$

this may be written

$$\delta dU = dU\left\{\frac{d\delta x}{dx}(\eta^2 + \zeta^2) + \frac{d\delta y}{dy}(\xi^2 + \zeta^2) - \left(\frac{d\delta x}{dy} + \frac{d\delta y}{dx}\right)\xi\eta\right.$$

$$\left. - \frac{d\delta z}{dx}\xi\zeta - \frac{d\delta z}{dy}\eta\zeta\right\}.$$

76. We shall obtain the variation of the whole surface U by integrating the expression for the variation of the element dU. For this purpose we shall consider separately the two parts of the integral

$$\int dU \left\{ (\eta^2 + \zeta^2) \frac{d\delta x}{dx} - \xi\eta \frac{d\delta y}{dx} - \xi\zeta \frac{d\delta z}{dx} \right\} = A,$$

and

$$\int dU \left\{ (\xi^2 + \zeta^2) \frac{d\delta y}{dy} - \xi\eta \frac{d\delta x}{dy} - \eta\zeta \frac{d\delta z}{dy} \right\} = B.$$

Conceive a plane perpendicular to the axis of y such that the value of y belonging to it is comprised within the limit of the extreme values which y has throughout the surface U. This plane will cut the periphery P in two, or four, or six, ... points of which the co-ordinates parallel to the axis of x may be denoted by x^0, x', x'', ... Similarly the other co-ordinates of these points may be denoted. Also let the surface be cut by a second plane parallel to the former and indefinitely near it, so that its co-ordinate may be denoted by $y + dy$; between these two planes will be found elements of the periphery dP^0, dP', dP'', ... and it will be easily seen that

$$dy = - Y^0 dP^0 = + Y' dP' = - Y'' dP'' = + Y''' dP''' \ldots\ldots$$

If, further, we conceive an infinite number of planes perpendicular to the axis of x, then to every element dx situated between x^0 and x' or between x'' and x''', and so on, will correspond an element dU such that $dU = \dfrac{dx\,dy}{\zeta}$. Hence it follows that the part of the integral A which corresponds to the part of the superficies situated between the planes determined by y and $y + dy$ will be found from the integral

$$dy \int \left\{ \frac{\eta^2 + \zeta^2}{\zeta} \frac{d\delta x}{dx} - \frac{\xi\eta}{\zeta} \frac{d\delta y}{dx} - \xi \frac{d\delta z}{dx} \right\} dx,$$

the integral being taken from $x = x^0$ to $x = x'$, then from $x = x''$ to $x = x'''$, and so on. The above integral, by integration by parts, gives

$$\left\{ \frac{\eta^2 + \zeta^2}{\zeta} \delta x - \frac{\xi\eta}{\zeta} \delta y - \xi\delta z \right\} dy$$

$$- dy \int \left\{ \delta x \frac{d}{dx} \frac{\eta^2 + \zeta^2}{\zeta} - \delta y \frac{d}{dx} \frac{\xi\eta}{\zeta} - \delta z \frac{d\xi}{dx} \right\} dx.$$

Thus we have in the present case

$$\left\{ \frac{(\eta')^2 + (\zeta')^2}{\zeta} \delta x^0 - \frac{\xi^0 \eta^0}{\zeta} \delta y^0 - \xi^0 \delta z^0 \right\} Y^0 dP^0$$

$$+ \left\{ \frac{(\eta')^2 + (\zeta')^2}{\zeta} \delta x' - \frac{\xi \eta'}{\zeta} \delta y' - \xi' \delta x' \right\} Y' dP'$$

$$+ \left\{ \frac{(\eta'')^2 + (\zeta'')^2}{\zeta''} \delta x'' - \frac{\xi'' \eta''}{\zeta''} \delta y'' - \xi'' \delta z'' \right\} Y'' dP''$$

$$+ \ldots \ldots \ldots \ldots$$

$$- \int q dU \left\{ \delta x \frac{d}{dx} \frac{\eta^2 + \zeta^2}{\zeta} - \delta y \frac{d}{dx} \frac{\xi \eta}{\zeta} - \delta z \frac{d\xi}{dx} \right\}.$$

This we may denote by

$$\Sigma \left\{ \frac{\eta^2 + \zeta^2}{\zeta} \delta x - \frac{\xi \eta}{\zeta} \delta y - \xi \delta z \right\} Y dP$$

$$- \int q dU \left\{ \delta x \frac{d}{dx} \frac{\eta^2 + \zeta^2}{\zeta} - \delta y \frac{d}{dx} \frac{\xi \eta}{\zeta} - \delta z \frac{d\xi}{dx} \right\},$$

where the summation extends to all the elements dP which are situated between the planes y and $y + dy$, and the integration to all the elements dU which are situated between the same planes.

Hence the complete integral A is equal to

$$\int \left\{ \frac{\eta^2 + \zeta^2}{\zeta} \delta x - \frac{\xi \eta}{\zeta} \delta y - \xi \delta z \right\} Y dP$$

$$- \int q dU \left\{ \delta x \frac{d}{dx} \frac{\eta^2 + \zeta^2}{\zeta} - \delta y \frac{d}{dx} \frac{\xi \eta}{\zeta} - \delta z \frac{d\xi}{dx} \right\},$$

where the first integral is to extend over the whole periphery P, and the second integral over the whole surface U.

77. In a similar way we may shew that B is equal to

$$\int \left\{ \frac{\xi \eta}{\zeta} \delta x + \eta \delta z - \frac{\xi^2 + \zeta^2}{\zeta} \delta y \right\} X dP$$

$$+ \int q dU \left\{ \delta x \frac{d}{dy} \frac{\xi \eta}{\zeta} + \delta z \frac{d\eta}{dy} - \delta y \frac{d}{dy} \frac{\xi^2 + \zeta^2}{\zeta} \right\}.$$

Let us assume that for any point of the periphery P

$$\{ X \xi \eta + Y (\eta^2 + \zeta^2) \} \delta x - \{ X (\xi^2 + \zeta^2) + Y \xi \eta \} \delta y$$

$$+ (X \eta \zeta - Y \xi \zeta) \delta z = \zeta Q,$$

and also that for any point of the surface U

$$\left(\frac{d}{dy}\frac{\xi\eta}{\zeta} - \frac{d}{dx}\frac{\eta^2+\zeta^2}{\zeta}\right)\zeta\delta x + \left(\frac{d}{dx}\frac{\xi\eta}{\zeta} - \frac{d}{dy}\frac{\xi^2+\zeta^2}{\zeta}\right)\zeta\delta y$$

$$+ \left(\frac{d\xi}{dx} + \frac{d\eta}{dy}\right)\zeta\delta z = V,$$

and we obtain

$$\delta U = \int Q\,dP + \int V\,dU,$$

where the first integral is to extend over the whole periphery P and the second integral over the whole surface U.

78. The expressions given for Q and V admit of remarkable simplification. By using the equation

$$X\xi + Y\eta + Z\zeta = 0,$$

the expression for Q may be put in a symmetrical form; thus

$$Q = (Y\zeta - Z\eta)\,\delta x + (Z\xi - X\zeta)\,\delta y + (X\eta - Y\xi)\,\delta z.$$

In order to simplify V, we observe that since

$$\frac{dz}{dx} = -\frac{\xi}{\zeta} \quad \text{and} \quad \frac{dz}{dy} = -\frac{\eta}{\zeta},$$

it follows that

$$\frac{d}{dy}\frac{\xi}{\zeta} = \frac{d}{dx}\frac{\eta}{\zeta}.$$

Hence

$$\frac{d}{dy}\frac{\xi\eta}{\zeta} = \frac{\xi}{\zeta}\frac{d\eta}{dy} + \eta\frac{d}{dy}\frac{\xi}{\zeta}$$

$$= \frac{\xi}{\zeta}\frac{d\eta}{dy} + \eta\frac{d}{dx}\frac{\eta}{\zeta}.$$

And since

$$\xi^2 + \eta^2 + \zeta^2 = 1,$$

$$\xi\frac{d\xi}{dx} + \eta\frac{d\eta}{dx} + \zeta\frac{d\zeta}{dx} = 0,$$

thus

$$\frac{d}{dx}\frac{\eta^2+\zeta^2}{\zeta} = \eta\frac{d}{dx}\frac{\eta}{\zeta} + \frac{\eta}{\zeta}\frac{d\eta}{dx} + \frac{d\zeta}{dx}$$

$$= \eta\frac{d}{dx}\frac{\eta}{\zeta} - \frac{\xi}{\zeta}\frac{d\xi}{dx}.$$

Substitute these values in the coefficient of δx in V, and that coefficient becomes

$$\xi \left(\frac{d\xi}{dx} + \frac{d\eta}{dy} \right).$$

Similarly the coefficient of δy in V may be transformed into

$$\eta \left(\frac{d\xi}{dx} + \frac{d\eta}{dy} \right).$$

Thus we obtain

$$V = (\xi \delta x + \eta \delta y + \zeta \delta z) \left(\frac{d\xi}{dx} + \frac{d\eta}{dy} \right).$$

79. Before we proceed further, it may be convenient to illustrate the expressions obtained geometrically. We shall refer the various lines of direction which occur to the corresponding points on the surface of a sphere with radius unity described round an arbitrary centre. The directions of the axes of x, y, z will be denoted by the points (1), (2), (3) respectively; the direction of the line which is a normal to the surface and drawn outwards, will be denoted by the point (4); the direction of a line drawn from any point of the surface to the corresponding new point obtained by variation, will be denoted by the point (5). The variation itself which is equal to $\sqrt{(\delta x)^2 + (\delta y)^2 + (\delta z)^2}$, we shall denote by δe and always take it *positive*. The arc joining two points of the spherical surface, as for example, the points (1) and (5) we shall write thus, (1, 5); this arc of course measures a corresponding angle.

Thus we have

$$\delta x = \delta e \cos (1, 5), \quad \delta y = \delta e \cos (2, 5), \quad \delta z = \delta e \cos (3, 5).$$

All the above notation applies to any point on the surface. On its boundary, that is on the periphery P, we have two other directions that require symbols; first, the direction of the element dP which we will denote by the point (6); next, the direction of a line which is normal to dP, and which touches the surface and is drawn so as to fall within P, and this we will denote by the point (7). By hypothesis, the points (6), (7), (4) lie in the same order as the points (1), (2), (3); also (4, 6), (4, 7), (6, 7) subtend right angles, that is, are quadrants. Thus the relations given above in Art. 72 may be written

$$\eta Z - \zeta Y = \cos(1, 7), \quad \zeta X - \xi Z = \cos(2, 7), \quad \xi Y - \eta X = \cos(3, 7).$$

And the equations which determine Q and V may be written

$$Q = -\,\delta e \cos(5, 7)$$

$$V = \quad \delta e \cos(4, 5)\left(\frac{d\xi}{dx} + \frac{d\eta}{dy}\right).$$

Thus Q expresses the transference of any point in the periphery P, from the plane which touches this periphery and is normal to the surface U, and the transference is positive when in a direction outwards from P. The factor $\delta e \cos(4, 5)$ of V expresses the transference of any point of the surface U from the plane touching this surface, and the transference is positive when in a direction outwards from the volume of which U is a boundary.

The other factor of V is also capable of geometrical illustration. For we have

$$\xi = -\,\zeta\frac{dz}{dx}, \qquad \eta = -\,\zeta\frac{dz}{dy},$$

$$\frac{1}{\zeta} = 1 + \left(\frac{dz}{dx}\right)^2 + \left(\frac{dz}{dy}\right)^2.$$

Thus

$$d\zeta = \xi\zeta^2 d\frac{dz}{dx} + \eta\zeta^2 d\frac{dz}{dy},$$

$$\frac{d\xi}{dx} = -\,\zeta\frac{d^2 z}{dx^2} - \frac{dz}{dx}\frac{d\zeta}{dx}$$

$$= -\,\zeta\frac{d^2 z}{dx^2} + \xi^2\zeta\frac{d^2 z}{dx^2} + \xi\eta\zeta\frac{d^2 z}{dx\,dy}$$

$$= -\,\zeta(\eta^2 + \zeta)\frac{d^2 z}{dx^2} + \xi\eta\zeta\frac{d^2 z}{dx\,dy};$$

$$\frac{d\eta}{dy} = -\,\zeta\frac{d^2 z}{dy^2} + \eta^2\zeta\frac{d^2 z}{dy^2} + \xi\eta\zeta\frac{d^2 z}{dx\,dy}$$

$$= -\,\zeta(\xi^2 + \zeta)\frac{d^2 z}{dy^2} + \xi\eta\zeta\frac{d^2 z}{dx\,dy}.$$

Thus
$$\frac{d\xi}{dx} + \frac{d\eta}{dy} =$$

$$-\zeta^3 \left[\frac{d^2z}{dx^2}\left\{1 + \left(\frac{dz}{dy}\right)^2\right\} - 2\frac{d^2z}{dx\,dy}\frac{dz}{dx}\frac{dz}{dy} + \frac{d^2z}{dy^2}\left\{1 + \left(\frac{dz}{dx}\right)^2\right\} \right].$$

This expression is known to be equal to

$$\frac{1}{R} + \frac{1}{R'},$$

where R and R' are the *principal radii of curvature* at the point of the surface under consideration. These quantities are considered positive when the convexity of the surface is turned outwards.

80. A careful examination of the above investigation will shew that throughout it has been assumed that only *one* value of z corresponds to given values of x and y, and that ζ is positive for the whole surface U. Nevertheless the final theorem, namely

$$\delta U = -\int\!\delta e \cos (5,7)\,dP + \int\!\delta e \cos (4,5)\left(\frac{1}{R} + \frac{1}{R'}\right) dU,$$

is true generally, and not limited by the above assumption. If we had wished from the first to have attained this generality it would have been necessary to adopt a different method or to enter into some prolixity. But the result may now be established as follows.

The investigation does not assume that the axis of z is vertical; the situation of the axes is arbitrary, and the truth of the theorem is established for all surfaces such that the points (4) all lie in one hemispherical surface; we may adopt the pole of that hemisphere for (3).

If there be a surface which does not fulfil this condition it may be separated into two or more parts each of which singly does fulfil the condition. Now it will be easily seen that if any surface be separated into two parts, the truth of the theorem for the whole surface follows immediately from its truth for each part. For let the surface U consist of the two parts U' and U'', and let P' be the periphery of U' and P'' the periphery of U''; and further suppose P' and P'' to have the common part P''', so that P' consists of P'''' and P'''' and P'' consists of P''' and P'''''; it is therefore obvious that the periphery of U consists of P'''' and P''''. Thus, we shall have

$$\int \delta e \cos (5, 7) \, dP' = \int \delta e \cos (5, 7) \, dP''' + \int \delta e \cos (5, 7) \, dP''''\,,$$

$$\int \delta e \cos (5, 7) \, dP'' = \int \delta e \cos (5, 7) \, dP''' + \int \delta e \cos (5, 7) \, dP''''\,.$$

It must however be observed that the value of the integral $\int \delta e \cos (5, 7) \, dP'''$, when it is considered as a part of the former expression, is exactly the opposite of its value when considered as a part of the latter expression; for to every point of the line P''', which is to be described in different directions in the two cases, will correspond *opposite* situations of the point (7) and thus opposite values of the factor $\cos (5, 7)$. In addition one of these two parts destroys the other; thus we have

$$\int \delta e \cos (5, 7) \, dP' + \int \delta e \cos (5, 7) \, dP'' = \int \delta e \cos (5, 7) \, dP.$$

Thus since $\delta U = \delta U' + \delta U''$ we obtain for δU a value exactly corresponding to that already given at the beginning of this article, since that formula is supposed to hold for the value of $\delta U'$ and of $\delta U''$.

Lastly, we may observe that the truth of the expression for δU given at the beginning of this article may be shewn by geometrical considerations, and indeed more easily than by the analytical method. But we have adopted the method given above in order to take an opportunity of throwing light upon a subject which has hitherto been little studied, namely, the application of the Calculus of Variations to a double integral with variable limits. The geometrical method we leave to the reader.

[This geometrical method may be seen in a memoir by M. Bertrand in Liouville's *Journal des Mathématiques*, Vol. IX. page 119.]

81. It remains to exhibit the variations which the other terms in W undergo in consequence of a variation of the form of the space s; and first we will consider the variation of the space s.

Resume the two triangles considered in Art. 73, and join corresponding points of the sides so as to form a solid. The base of this solid may be considered to be dU, and its height

$$\xi \delta x + \eta \delta y + \zeta \delta z = \delta e \cos (4, 5)\,;$$

this expression will give the altitude *positive* or negative according as the transposed triangle lies outside or inside the space s, that is, according as the whole solid lies outside or inside the space s. Thus we have

$$\delta s = \int dU \, \delta e \cos (4, 5).$$

Hence it follows that the variation of $\int z \, ds$ will be

$$\int z \, dU \, \delta e \cos (4, 5).$$

With respect to the variation of the quantity T we observe that since P denotes the common boundary of the surfaces T and U, the transpositions of the points in the periphery P must satisfy the condition that the new points should be on the surface of the vessel. It is therefore obvious that by the transposition of the element dP the surface T experiences a variation $\pm dP \delta e \sin (5, 6)$, and speaking generally the sign of this quantity will depend on the sign of the quantity $\cos (4, 5)$. But this variation may be more neatly expressed by introducing a new direction, namely, that of the line which lies in the plane touching the surface of the vessel, which is normal to P, and drawn outwards from the space s. We will denote the point corresponding to this direction by (8), and the variation of the surface T which arises from the transposition of the element dP will be

$$dP \delta e \cos (5, 8).$$

Thus $$\delta T = \int dP \delta e \cos (5, 8),$$

where the sign of the factor $\cos (5, 8)$ will at once decide whether the variation is an increment or a decrement.

As the point (6) is the pole of the great circle which passes through the points (7) and (8), and the point (5) lies in the great circle which passes through the points (6) and (8), the points (5), (7), (8) form a triangle right-angled at (8); thus

$$\cos (5, 7) = \cos (5, 8) \cos (7, 8).$$

Moreover the arc (7, 8) is the measure of the angle between two planes which touch the surface of the space s and the surface of the vessel at their intersection P, the angle being formed by those portions of the planes which include a vacant space. This angle we will denote by i, and thus $180° - i$ will be the angle between those portions of the planes which include the surface s; thus the above equation becomes

$$\cos (5, 7) = \cos (5, 6) \cos i.$$

88. From all the above results we have the following equation for the variation of W,

$$\delta W = \int dU \, \delta e \cos (4, 5) \left\{ z + a^2 \left(\frac{1}{R} + \frac{1}{R'} \right) \right\}$$
$$- \int dP \, \delta e \cos (5, 6) \, (a^2 \cos i - a^2 + 2\beta^2) \, ;$$

the first integral is to extend over all the elements dU of the free part of the surface of the space s, or of the free parts if there are more than one; the latter integral is to extend over all the elements dP of the line or lines which separate that free part or those free parts from the other part or parts contiguous to the surface of the vessel.

Now in the position of equilibrium the value of W ought to be a minimum, and so ought to be incapable of diminution for any indefinitely small change in the figure of the fluid which leaves the volume s unchanged, that is, which makes δs zero. Hence it follows that in the position of equilibrium the figure of the superficies U ought to be such that the variation

$$dU \, \delta e \cos (4, 5) \left\{ z + a^2 \left(\frac{1}{R} + \frac{1}{R'} \right) \right\}$$

should be proportional to the variation δs, that is, to

$$dU \, \delta e \cos (4, 5).$$

Thus we must have

$$z + a^2 \left(\frac{1}{R} + \frac{1}{R'} \right) = \text{constant.}$$

For it is manifest that if this proportion did not hold, the value of W would be capable of diminution by a suitable mutation of the figure of the superficies U, the limit P remaining unchanged.

Gauss then proceeds with the examination of the question of fluid equilibrium.

CHAPTER IV.

POISSON.

83. THE 12th volume of the *Mémoires de l'Académie Royale...* contains a memoir on the Calculus of Variations by M. Poisson. The date of publication of the volume is 1833, but the memoir was presented to the Academy in November 1831. The memoir extends over pages 223—331 of the volume.

Poisson begins with a sketch of the history of the subject; at the end of this sketch he indicates the object of his own memoir as follows: "It will appear singular if we reflect on the attention which has been bestowed on the Calculus of Variations that an essential part of this Calculus is still in a state of imperfection, which renders the solutions of many important problems incomplete. In fact, if the question be to determine the maximum or minimum of a simple integral, the methods which Lagrange has given in the 4th volume of the old series of *Turin Memoirs*, and also in the *Lectures on the Calculus of Functions*, leave nothing to be desired either as to the indefinite equation which is to determine the unknown function or as to the particular equations which must subsist at the limits of the integral. The general method of the Calculus of Variations may be applied also without difficulty to the case of a double or multiple integral in which the limits are fixed and given, so that we have only to obtain the partial differential equation from which the unknown function must be determined. But the case is different when the limits of the double integral are variable and unknown. In the present state of the science we know neither the nature nor even the number of the equations relative to each of the limits, by which these limits are to be determined, so that they may render the integral a maximum or a minimum. Lagrange has considered the question of the variation of a double integral in three places; namely, in the *Miscellanea Taurinensia*, Vol. II. p. 188, in the *Leçons sur le Calcul des Fonctions*, p. 471, of the edition of 1806, and in the *Mécanique Analytique*, second edition, Vol. I. pp. 97 and 148. He has however never investigated in a complete manner the terms of the variation which correspond to the two limits, and he has not formed any of the equations which relate to the limits. This defect in the science deserves the attention of mathematicians. It has been already pointed out by M. Lacroix, in the articles on the Calculus of Variations contained in his treatise on the Differential and Integral Calculus. My object has been to remove this defect, and I believe that I have succeeded in doing so in the memoir which I now submit to the Academy. This memoir contains also some new remarks on the conditions of integrability of differential expressions of any order, and also an expression for the integral under a finite form, by the method of quadratures when these conditions are satisfied."

84. Three remarks may be made on Poisson's statement.

(1) He says that in a double or multiple integral when the limits are fixed and given, there is no difficulty in applying the Calculus of Variations. If by the limits being fixed is meant that the limiting values of the *differential coefficients* which occur are given as well as the limiting values of the variables the remark is obviously true; if however it is meant that only the limiting values of the variables are given the remark seems scarcely correct, for very little appears to have been effected when Poisson wrote. We have seen in Art. 60, that Ohm gives an expression for the variation of a double integral in a particular case, but even there the equations are not given which must hold at the limits.

(2) It is not obvious in the above statement to what part of the treatise of Lacroix Poisson alludes. But from an article by Poisson in the *Bulletin de la Société Philomatique* for 1816, it appears that the allusion is to the part of which we have given an account in Articles 39 and 40.

(3) It is curious that Poisson makes no reference to the memoir of Gauss, which was the subject of the preceding chapter of the present work; it is the more curious because Poisson published a work on Capillary Attraction in 1831, and in the preface he refers to the memoir of Gauss.

85. The memoir of Poisson is divided into two parts; the first is entitled Variations of integrals relative to a single independent variable, and determination of their maxima and minima. The second part is entitled Variations of integrals relative to two independent variables, and determination of their maxima and minima. The first part extends from page 230 to page 286, and the second part from page 286 to the end of the memoir.

In the first part Poisson begins by establishing the ordinary formula for the variation of a single integral; nothing new is obtained but the method is different from the ordinary method. As it may enable the reader more easily to understand Poisson's mode of finding the variation of a double integral, to which we shall hereafter proceed, we will give at full his treatment of the single integral.

86. If K is a function of the variable x and other quantities dependent upon x, we shall represent by K', K'', K''', ... the differential coefficients of K taken with respect to x and to everything which depends upon it; so that we shall have

$$\frac{dK}{dx} = K', \quad \frac{dK'}{dx} = K'', \quad \frac{dK''}{dx} = K''', \quad \dots$$

Let the two limits of an integral with respect to x be denoted by x_0 and x_1, then the values of any quantity H with respect to these limits will be denoted by H_0 for the limit x_0 and by H_1 for the limit x_1.

Let y be a function of the variable x, and according to the notation above adopted we shall have

$$\frac{dy}{dx} = y', \quad \frac{dy'}{dx} = y'', \quad \frac{dy''}{dx} = y''', \quad \dots$$

Suppose V to denote a given function of x, y, y', y'', ... up to the differential coefficient of some determinate order; and let x_0 and x_1 be two constant quantities. Consider the definite integral

$$U = \int_{x_0}^{x_1} V dx.$$

If we regard x and therefore also y as implicit functions of another variable u we can suppose that y', y'', y''', ... have been expressed in terms of the differential coefficients of x and y with respect to u, by means of the ordinary rules for changing the independent variable. Thus V will become a function of x and y and of their differential coefficients with respect to u. Denote by u_0 and u_1 the values of u which correspond to $x = x_0$ and $x = x_1$; thus we shall have

$$U = \int_{u_0}^{u_1} V \frac{dx}{du}\, du.$$

Next suppose that δx and δy are indefinitely small and arbitrary functions of u; without changing u_0 and u_1, put $x + \delta x$ and $y + \delta y$ in the place of x and y under the symbol $\int$. Thus we deduce

$$\delta U = \int_{u_0}^{u_1} \delta V \frac{dx}{du}\, du + \int_{u_0}^{u_1} V \frac{d\delta x}{du}\, du \ \ldots\ldots\ldots\ldots\ (1).$$

The new value of y as a function of x will result from the elimination of u between the values of $x + \delta x$ and $y + \delta y$. [That is, we may put $x + \delta x = X$ and $y + \delta y = Y$; then X and Y are functions of u, and by eliminating u we obtain Y as a function of X.] At the same time the new limits with respect to x of the integral U will be $x_0 + \delta x_0$ and $x_1 + \delta x_1$; and thus although we have not changed the limits u_0 and u_1 the preceding formula will give the complete variation of U both with respect to the form of the function y and also with respect to the limits of the integration.

Now for shortness put

$$\frac{dV}{dx} = M, \quad \frac{dV}{dy} = N, \quad \frac{dV}{dy'} = P, \quad \frac{dV}{dy''} = Q, \ \ldots;$$

we shall have

$$\delta V = M\delta x + N\delta y + P\delta y' + Q\delta y'' + \ldots$$

And suppose

$$\delta y = y'\delta x + \omega;$$

then it will be shewn presently that we shall obtain

$$\delta y' = y''\delta x + \omega',$$
$$\delta y'' = y'''\delta x + \omega'',$$
$$\ldots\ldots\ldots\ldots$$

and generally

$$\delta y^{(m)} = y^{(m+1)}\delta x + \omega^{(m)} \dots\dots\dots\dots\dots (2).$$

Hence

$$\delta V = (M + Ny' + Py'' + Qy''' + \dots)\,\delta x$$
$$+ N\omega + P\omega' + Q\omega'' + \dots$$

The coefficient of δx is the differential coefficient of V with respect to x considering $y, y', y'', \dots$ as functions of x; we denote this by V'. And we have

$$\frac{dV}{du} = V'\frac{dx}{du};$$

thus

$$\delta V\frac{dx}{du} = \frac{dV}{du}\,\delta x + (N\omega + P\omega' + Q\omega'' + \dots)\frac{dx}{du}.$$

Thus equation (1) becomes

$$\delta U = \int_{u_0}^{u_1}\left(\frac{dV}{du}\,\delta x + V\frac{d\delta x}{du}\right)du$$
$$+ \int_{u_0}^{u_1}(N\omega + P\omega' + Q\omega'' + \dots)\frac{dx}{du}\,du.$$

Now

$$\frac{dV}{du}\,\delta x + V\frac{d\delta x}{du} = \frac{d.V\delta x}{du},$$

and

$$\int_{u_0}^{u_1}\frac{d.V\delta x}{du}\,du = V_1\delta x_1 - V_0\delta x_0.$$

If then we transform to the variable x the second integral contained in δU, we shall have

$$\delta U = V_1\delta x_1 - V_0\delta x_0 + \int_{x_0}^{x_1}(N\omega + P\omega' + Q\omega'' + \dots)\,dx.$$

By the process of integration by parts we can remove the differential coefficients $\omega', \omega'', \dots$ from under the integral sign. For we have

$$\int_{x_0}^{x_1} P\omega'\,dx = P_1\omega_1 - P_0\omega_0 - \int_{x_0}^{x_1} P'\omega\,dx,$$

$$\int_{x_0}^{x_1} Q\omega''\,dx = Q_1\omega_1' - Q_0\omega_0' - Q_1'\omega_1 + Q_0'\omega_0 + \int_{x_0}^{x_1} Q''\omega\,dx,$$

and so on.

Thus we conclude finally that

$$\delta U = \Gamma + \int_{x_0}^{x_1} H \, du \, dx \quad \dots\dots\dots\dots\dots\dots \quad (3),$$

where

$$H = N - P' + Q'' - R''' + \dots$$
$$\Gamma = V_1 \delta x_1 - V_0 \delta x_0$$
$$+ (P_1 - Q_1' + R_1'' - \dots)\, \omega_1 - (P_0 - Q_0' + R_0'' - \dots)\, \omega_0$$
$$+ (Q_1 - R_1' + \dots)\, \omega_1' - (Q_0 - R_0' + \dots)\, \omega_0'$$
$$+ (R_1 - \dots)\, \omega_1'' - (R_0 - \dots)\, \omega_0''$$
$$+ \dots\dots$$

87.　It only remains to demonstrate equation (2).
We have

$$y' = \frac{dy}{dx} = \frac{\dfrac{dy}{du}}{\dfrac{dx}{du}}.$$

Put $x + \delta x$ and $y + \delta y$ in place of x and y in this fraction, subtract the original value y' and neglect indefinitely small quantities of the second order; thus

$$\delta y' = \frac{\dfrac{d\delta y}{du}}{\dfrac{dx}{du}} - \frac{\dfrac{dy}{du}\dfrac{d\delta x}{du}}{\left(\dfrac{dx}{du}\right)^2}.$$

But, by hypothesis,

$$\delta y = y'\delta x + \omega ;$$

differentiate with respect to u, thus

$$\frac{d\delta y}{du} = \frac{dy'}{du}\delta x + \frac{d\omega}{du} + y'\,\frac{d\delta x}{du}.$$

Hence we have

$$\delta y' = \frac{\dfrac{dy'}{du}\delta x}{\dfrac{dx}{du}} + \frac{\dfrac{d\omega}{du}}{\dfrac{dx}{du}} + \frac{\left(y'\dfrac{dx}{du} - \dfrac{dy}{du}\right)\dfrac{d\delta x}{du}}{\left(\dfrac{dx}{du}\right)^2} ;$$

and
$$\frac{\dfrac{dy'}{du}}{\dfrac{dx}{du}} = \frac{dy'}{dx} = y'',$$

$$\frac{\dfrac{d\omega}{du}}{\dfrac{dx}{du}} = \omega',$$

$$y'\frac{dx}{du} = \frac{dy}{du};$$

thus the value of $\delta y'$ reduces to
$$\delta y' = y''\delta x + \omega'.$$

Starting from this result and from the equation
$$y'' = \frac{\dfrac{dy'}{du}}{\dfrac{dx}{du}}$$

we shall obtain in like manner
$$\delta y'' = y'''\delta x + \omega'';$$

continuing thus we shall establish equation (2) for any index n.

In equation (3) we may replace ω which is under the integral sign by its value
$$\omega = \delta y - y'\delta x,$$
and in the terms outside the integral sign we may replace $\omega_0, \omega_1, \omega_0', \omega_1', \dots$ by their values
$$\omega_0 = \delta y_0 - y_0'\delta x_0, \quad \omega_0' = \delta y_0' - y_0''\delta x_0, \dots$$
$$\omega_1 = \delta y_1 - y_1'\delta x_1, \quad \omega_1' = \delta y_1' - y_1''\delta x_1, \dots$$

Thus the variation of the integral U will be expressed explicitly in terms of the variations of x and y, and of the variations of the extreme values of $x, y, y', y'', \dots$ up to the differential coefficient of the order next below the highest which is contained in V.

88. We have thus given Poisson's method of establishing the fundamental formula of the Calculus of Variations in the case of a simple integral.

Poisson next shews how this fundamental formula may also be obtained by decomposing the integral U into its indefinitely small elements. This is in fact the old method which was used before the invention of the Calculus of Variations, and it is expounded in Euler's *Methodus inveniendi....* Poisson however extends the old investigation so as to include the terms relative to the *limits* of the integral; this according to Poisson had not been done before.

89. We thus arrive at the end of the fourth section of the memoir. In his fifth section Poisson shews how his results are applied to find the maximum or minimum value of the integral U. He says he will not consider in this memoir the question of the distinction of a maximum from a minimum value. He then makes some remarks on the number of constants which will appear in the solution of the differential equation furnished by the condition of maximum or minimum, and the manner of determining these constants. He draws attention to the obvious fact that the differential equation may be immediately integrated, *once* if $N = 0$, *twice* if $N = 0$ and $P = 0$, and so on. He states that a first integral of the equation can also be obtained when the independent variable does not occur explicitly in V; because then if we consider x as a function of y, this case is analogous to that in which $N = 0$. He shews however that this integral may be found without changing the independent variable in the following manner.

We have

$$dV = Mdx + Ndy + Pdy' + Qdy'' + Rdy''' + \ldots ;$$

here the first term Mdx by hypothesis vanishes; eliminate Ndy by means of the equation

$$N - P' + Q'' - R''' + \ldots = 0,$$

thus

$$dV = Pdy' + P'dy + Qdy'' - Q''dy + Rdy''' + R'''dy + \ldots$$

But the following are identically true:

$$Pdy' + P'dy = d . Py',$$

$$Qdy'' - Q''dy = d (Qy'' - Q'y'),$$

$$Rdy''' + R'''dy = d (Ry''' - R'y'' + R''y')$$

....

Thus

$$dV = d \cdot Py' + d\,(Qy'' - Q'y') + d\,(Ry''' - R'y'' + R''y) + \dots$$

and therefore

$$V = C + Py' + Qy'' - Q'y' + Ry''' - R'y'' + R''y' + \dots$$

where C is an arbitrary constant.

90. In his sixth section Poisson says that the problem of the maximum or minimum of an integral may be decomposed into two parts which may be considered separately. First we may consider that $x_0, y_0, y_0', \dots$ and $x_1, y_1, y_1', \dots$ are given, and proceed to find the value of y in terms of x and the given quantities which makes U a maximum or minimum. The value of y is then to be found from the differential equation

$$N - P' + Q'' - \dots = 0,$$

and the arbitrary constants must be determined by means of the given values of $x_0, y_0, y_0', \dots x_1, y_1, y_1', \dots$ Substitute this value of y and the consequent values of $y', y'', \dots$ in V; then integrate Vdx from $x = x_0$ to $x = x_1$; thus we shall obtain the maximum or minimum value of U, with respect to the form of the function y, in terms of $x_0, y_0, y_0', \dots x_1, y_1, y_1', \dots$. We may then seek for the values of these latter quantities which make U a maximum or minimum.

If we are able to integrate the differential equation and also to obtain the value of $\int_{x_0}^{x_1} Vdx$, then this second part of the problem can be treated by the ordinary rules of the Differential Calculus. Poisson then shews that by the application of these rules we obtain the same conditions as are found by the Calculus of Variations when the limits of integration are varied, and consequently those terms are introduced which have been denoted by the symbol Γ in Article 86.

[91. It is necessary to make some remarks on this suggestion of Poisson's about dividing a problem in the Calculus of Variations into two parts. Suppose we have a problem in the Calculus of Variations, and that for example the differential equation

$$N - P' + Q'' - \dots = 0$$

is the differential equation to a circle. We then according to Poisson's method take the equation to a circle which involves three arbitrary constants, and substituting the value of y in terms of x in V we integrate $\int_{x_0}^{x_1} V\,dx$; then by ordinary Differential Calculus we investigate the values which must be given to the three arbitrary constants in order to make the last integral a maximum or minimum. If suitable values cannot be determined we conclude that a curve having the proposed maximum or minimum property cannot be found. But even if suitable values can be found we have no right to conclude that a circle *does* possess the proposed maximum or minimum property; because we do not compare a circle with *any* adjacent curve in the latter part of this method, but only one circle with another circle. To determine whether a circle *does* possess the proposed maximum or minimum property we must proceed as in Article 5, or in some similar way. In fact Poisson's method will be unobjectionable if we know *a priori* that a curve having the required maximum or minimum property must exist; but it will not be valid to prove that we have found such a curve when we do *not* know *a priori* that the curve must exist.]

92. In his seventh section Poisson gives the usual extension of his preceding results to the case in which V contains *two* dependent variables y and z and their differential coefficients with respect to the independent variable x.

We will give Poisson's result, because it explains the notation which he continues to use in the next section. Let V denote a function of x, y, z and the differential coefficients of y and z with respect to x; also let

$$U = \int_{x_0}^{x_1} V\,dx,$$

then $\qquad \delta U = \Gamma + \int_{x_0}^{x_1} \left\{ H\,(\delta y - y'\delta x) + K\,(\delta z - z'\delta x) \right\}\,dx,$

where Γ denotes that part of the variation of U which is free from the integral sign.

93. We now proceed to Poisson's eighth section.

In a certain case a relation exists between the quantities H and K, which may be obtained in the following manner.

The case is that in which the variable x does not occur explicitly in V, and when we have moreover

$$V = Wz';$$

W being a given function of y and z which contains likewise

$$\frac{dy}{dz}, \quad \frac{d\frac{dy}{dz}}{dz}, \ldots\ldots$$

that is, the quantities

$$\frac{y'}{z'}, \quad \frac{z'y'' - y'z''}{z'^3}, \ldots\ldots$$

which we will denote by t', t'', ... We shall have then

$$U = \int_{x_0}^{x_1} Wz'\,dx = \int_{z_0}^{z_1} W\,dz.$$

Now by means of the last expression for U, we may exhibit the variation of U by the formula (8) of Art. 86, putting z and W in place of x and V, and t', t'', ... in place of y', y'', ... The second term of δU will therefore be of the form

$$\int_{x_0}^{x_1} G\left(\delta y - t'\delta z\right)\,dz,$$

or, which is the same thing,

$$\int_{x_0}^{x_1} G\left(z'\delta y - y'\delta z\right)\,dx;$$

G being a factor which is independent of δy and δz. In order that this may coincide with the second term of the value of δU in the preceding article we must have

$$H\left(\delta y - y'\delta x\right) + K\left(\delta z - z'\delta x\right) = G\left(z'\delta y - y'\delta z\right).$$

This equation resolves itself into

$$H = Gz', \quad K = -Gy', \quad Hy' + Kz' = 0;$$

these results we obtain by equating the coefficients of δx, δy, δz. The third of these results may also be obtained by eliminating G between the other two, and it expresses the relation between H and K which was to be obtained.

[94. The preceding article is clear; in what follows there may be some difficulty. Poisson proceeds thus. In the general case where V is any function of x, y, y', y'', ... z, z' z'', ... let us suppose x an implicit function of another independent variable u, and let us replace therefore y', y'', ... z', z'', ... by

$$\frac{y'}{x'}, \quad \frac{x'y'' - y'x''}{x'^3}, \quad \ldots\ldots \frac{z'}{x'}, \quad \frac{x'z'' - z'x''}{x'^3}, \quad \ldots$$

and Vdx by $Vx'du$. Let us denote relatively to x, x', x'', ... by X the quantity analogous to H and K, then we shall find that these quantities are connected by the identity

$$Xx' + Hy' + Kz' = 0.$$

Reciprocally when a given function of x, x', x'', ... y, y', y'', ... z, z', z'', ... satisfies this equation it will be reducible to the form Vx'; so that without changing its value we can put $x'=1$, $x''=0$, ..., and regard y and z in the given function as functions of x.

It may be remarked here in the first place, that the last sentence, *reciprocally when &c.* is all that is new. Lagrange had given the other part repeatedly; he appears to have thought it very important. See *Miscel. Taur.* Vol. II. page 183, and Vol. IV. page 177; also *Leçons sur le Calcul des Fonctions*, page 412, and page 456. Lacroix also gave the theorem *Calc. Diff. et Int.* Vol. II. page 763. In the next place, there is a little difficulty as to Poisson's notation, so that it is necessary to examine the point in detail. Let V denote a function of x, y, z, and the differential coefficients of y and z with respect to x. Transform these differential coefficients into differential coefficients with respect to a new independent variable u, so that V may be transformed into a function of x, y, z and the differential coefficients of these variables with respect to u; we will denote the transformed function by v. Then put

$$U = \int V dx = \int V \frac{dx}{du} du = \int v \frac{dx}{du} du.$$

We have now two modes of expressing δU; we shall confine ourselves to the unintegrated part. This may be written thus

$$\int \left\{ Y \left(\delta y - \frac{dy}{dx} \delta x \right) + Z \left(\delta z - \frac{dz}{dx} \delta x \right) \right\} dx,$$

or thus

$$\int \left\{ A \left(\delta x - \frac{dx}{du}\,\delta u\right) + B \left(\delta y - \frac{dy}{du}\,\delta u\right) + C \left(\delta z - \frac{dz}{du}\,\delta u\right) \right\} du.$$

Here Y and Z are obtained in the ordinary way from V; and A, B, C are obtained in a similar way from $v\dfrac{dx}{du}$.

By comparing the two results, remembering that the integration in the first is with respect to x, and in the second with respect to u, we obtain

$$Y\frac{dx}{du} = B, \quad Z\frac{dx}{du} = C,$$

$$\left(Y\frac{dy}{dx} + Z\frac{dz}{dx}\right)\frac{dx}{du} = -A,$$

$$A\frac{dx}{du} + B\frac{dy}{du} + C\frac{dz}{du} = 0.$$

The last result will also follow from the first three by eliminating Y and Z.

The last result must be what Poisson denotes by

$$Xx' + Hy' + Kz' = 0;$$

his notation is objectionable however, because he had previously used H and K for what we denote by Y and Z.

Next let us consider the reciprocal theorem which Poisson enunciates. Let ϕ denote any function of $x,\ x',\ x'',\ \ldots\ y,\ y',\ y'',\ \ldots$ $z,\ z',\ z'',\ \ldots$ which satisfies the condition

$$Ax' + By' + Cz' = 0.$$

Transform the independent variable from u to x and let $\psi\dfrac{dx}{du}$ be what ϕ becomes; the assertion then is that ψ will be free from u, that is, ψ will not contain $\dfrac{du}{dx}$, $\dfrac{d^2u}{dx^2}$, $\ldots$ To prove this we observe that if ψ did contain such terms we should have, considering only the unintegrated part of the variation, a result of this form

$$\delta \int \psi\, dx = \int \left\{ J \left(\delta u - \frac{du}{dx}\,\delta x\right) + Y \left(\delta y - \frac{dy}{dx}\,\delta x\right) + Z \left(\delta z - \frac{dz}{dx}\,\delta x\right) \right\} dx.$$

5

But again taking the unintegrated part of the variation

$$\delta \int \phi \, du = \int \left\{ A \left(\delta x - \frac{dx}{du} \delta u \right) + B \left(\delta y - \frac{dy}{du} \delta u \right) + C \left(\delta z - \frac{dz}{du} \delta u \right) \right\} du.$$

Now by supposition $\int \psi \, dx = \int \psi \frac{dx}{du} du = \int \phi \, du$, and therefore the variations of the two expressions must coincide. But δu disappears from $\delta \int \phi \, du$, because by supposition

$$A \frac{dx}{du} + B \frac{dy}{du} + C \frac{dz}{du} = 0.$$

Hence δu must disappear from $\delta \int \psi \, dx$; and thus the terms $\frac{du}{dx}, \frac{d^2 u}{dx^2}, \dots$ cannot occur in ψ.

This proves Poisson's statement, but there appears an exception to it which he has not noticed. The terms $\frac{du}{dx}, \frac{d^2 u}{dx^2}, \dots$ might occur in ψ provided they occurred in such a manner that $J = 0$; for then δu would disappear from $\delta \int \psi \, dx$.]

95. In his ninth section Poisson alludes to the case where V is a function of x, y, z and the differential coefficients of y and z with respect to x; these functions and differential coefficients being connected by an equation $L = 0$. He gives the ordinary method of treatment by means of an arbitrary multiplier. He has here a slight mistake, for he says, "having regard to the equation $dV = 0$, &c." Now there is no such relation as $dV = 0$; thus the expressions for δV which follow are incorrect because the term $\frac{dV}{dx} \delta x$ is omitted, where $\frac{dV}{dx}$ means the complete differential coefficient of V with respect to x; (see Poisson's second section). The final expression for δU is however correct.

96. Poisson's next three sections are devoted to the subject of the conditions of integrability of functions; it will be sufficient here to state what Poisson proves. Let V be a function of $x, y, y', y'', \dots$ which satisfies identically the relation

$$N - P' + Q'' - R''' + \dots = 0,$$

then V is integrable *per se*. This Poisson proves by exhibiting the integral under the form

$$\int V dx = \int F(x, 0, 0, 0, \ldots)\, dx + \int_0^1 \chi(u)\, du\,;$$

here $F(x, 0, 0, 0, \ldots)$ denotes what V becomes when in it we put $y, y', y'', \ldots$ all zero, and $\chi(u)$ is a complicated function of $u, x, y, y', y'', \ldots$ The integration in $\int_0^1 \chi(u)\, du$ is to be made on the supposition that every thing is constant except u. Next Poisson supposes V a function of $x, y, y', y'', \ldots z, z', z'', \ldots$ Let the equation

$$N - P' + Q'' - R''' + \ldots = 0$$

be denoted by $H = 0$, and let a similar equation with respect to z be denoted by $K = 0$; then Poisson proves that if $H = 0$ be identically true, and $K = 0$ be true when $y = 0$ whatever z may be, then $\int V dx$ can be expressed in a form analogous to that just given. Two forms can be given to the result according to the order in which we consider y and z. By comparing these two forms Poisson obtains an equation which must hold; also he infers that if one of the two equations $H = 0$, $K = 0$, be identically true and the other true when one of the variables is zero for all values of the other variable, then both equations are identically true. These two results are verified in an example.

07. Poisson's next three sections contain some remarks on the questions in which one expression is to have a maximum or minimum value while another is to have a constant value, those questions in fact from which the name of *isoperimetrical* problems was obtained and applied to the problems of the Calculus of Variations; Poisson compares the different considerations which have been used in the solution of such problems.

08. In his sixteenth and seventeenth sections Poisson adverts to the problem in which a *closed* curve is to be found which possesses some maximum or minimum property. If we suppose that the function V does not contain the limiting values of x, y or the differential coefficients of y, then the term Γ of the fundamental

formula (Art. 86) will be of the form $\zeta_1 - \zeta_0$, where ζ_1 and ζ_0 are the values which a certain function assumes at the two limits. Now when the problem refers to a plane curve we can use the polar co-ordinates r and θ, and if the curve is *closed* we can put the origin within the figure; then the limiting values of θ may be denoted by 0 and 2π. Thus if the angle θ is only involved through the *trigonometrical functions*, as these functions have the same value for the values 0 and 2π of the angle we obtain $\zeta_1 = \zeta_0$. Therefore Γ vanishes. And the same result follows for a curve of double curvature.

Thus in questions relating to closed curves the equations which depend on the limits of the integral disappear and the arbitrary constants introduced by the integration remain indeterminate.

99. For example; required to determine a plane closed curve of given perimeter which shall include a maximum area.

Let l denote the given perimeter; then with the usual notation

$$\int_0^{2\pi} \sqrt{r^2 + \left(\frac{dr}{d\theta}\right)^2}\, d\theta = l.$$

The integral which is to be a relative maximum, is

$$\frac{1}{2}\int_0^{2\pi} r^2 d\theta.$$

Let a denote an undetermined constant; put

$$V = \frac{1}{2}\, r^2 + a\sqrt{r^2 + \left(\frac{dr}{d\theta}\right)^2}, \quad U = \int_0^{2\pi} V d\theta,$$

then U is the integral which is to be an absolute maximum.

The quantities x, y, y' of the fundamental formula are now replaced by θ, r, r' respectively; thus

$$N = \frac{dV}{dr} = r + \frac{ar}{\sqrt{r^2 + r'^2}},$$

$$P = \frac{dV}{dr'} = \frac{ar'}{\sqrt{r^2 + r'^2}}.$$

The other quantities Q, R, ... (Art. 86) are zero, and the fundamental equation becomes

$$N - \frac{dP}{d\theta} = 0.$$

Thus
$$dV = Ndr + Pdr'$$
$$= \frac{dP}{d\theta}\,dr + Pdr'.$$

Integrate and denote the arbitrary constant by c; thus
$$V = Pr' + c.$$

Substitute in this equation the values of V and P, and solve it with respect to $\dfrac{d\theta}{dr}$; thus

$$\frac{d\theta}{dr} = \frac{r^2 - 2c}{r\sqrt{4a^2 r^2 - (r^2 - 2c)^2}}.$$

This may be integrated as follows

$$\theta = \int \frac{\left(1 - \dfrac{2c}{r^2}\right)dr}{\sqrt{4a^2 + 8c - \left(r + \dfrac{2c}{r}\right)^2}} = \int \frac{dz}{\sqrt{4a^2 + 8c - z^2}},$$

where $z = r + \dfrac{2c}{r}$.

Therefore
$$\theta + A = \sin^{-1}\frac{z}{\sqrt{4a^2 + 8c}},$$

where A is a constant. Hence

$$r + \frac{2c}{r} = \sqrt{4a^2 + 8c}\,\sin(\theta + A).$$

We may write the equation

$$r^2 - 2r\sqrt{a^2 + 2c}\,\sin(\theta + A) + 2c = 0.$$

This is the equation to a circle of which the radius is a; thus a is determined since the perimeter of the curve is given. The constants A and c are indeterminate; it is obvious that they depend on the *position* of the circle and have no influence on its area or perimeter.

If the curve instead of being *closed* were required to pass through two fixed points and the arc between those points were of a given length, then the three constants would all be determined.

For we should have two equations arising from the fact of the circle passing through the two given points and one arising from the given length.

[The mode of integration in the above solution is more simple than that used by Poisson.]

100. We now arrive at the second part of Poisson's memoir which is entitled Variations of integrals relative to two independent variables, and determination of their maxima and minima. This forms by far the most important portion of the memoir; it extends from page 286 to the end.

101. In the eighteenth section Poisson explains the notation to be used. The variables are denoted by x and y. Suppose K any function of x and y and of other quantities which depend on them; then K' denotes the differential coefficient of K with respect to x and to every thing which depends on x; and $K_{,}$ denotes the differential coefficient of K with respect to y and to every thing which depends on y. And so generally accents above indicate differentiation with respect to x, and accents below indicate differentiation with respect to y. Thus

$$\frac{dK}{dx} = K', \quad \frac{dK}{dy} = K_{,}, \quad \frac{d'K}{dx^2} = K'', \quad \frac{d^2K}{dx\,dy} = K'_{,}, \quad \frac{d^2K}{dy^2} = K_{,,},$$

and so on.

The limits known or unknown of a double integral,

$$\iint K\,dx\,dy,$$

will not be indicated. If this double integral extends over a zone of a surface comprised between two closed curves which will generally be curves of double curvature, then x, y, z may denote the co-ordinates of any point of the surface, and the limits of the integration will depend upon the projections on the plane of (x, y) of these curves. In order to indicate what a quantity becomes at the first limit we shall enclose it in parentheses, and to indicate what it becomes at the second we shall enclose it in square brackets. Thus of the following simple integrals,

$$\left(\int K dx\right), \quad \left(\int K dy\right), \quad \left[\int K dx\right], \quad \left[\int K dy\right],$$

the first two belong to the interior curve and are to be taken throughout its entire length, and the last two belong to the exterior curve and are to be taken throughout its entire length. The equations to these curves we will denote for the present by $A = 0$, and $B = 0$.

[Poisson however does not keep to the meaning of the symbols which he gives here; hereafter he really uses the square brackets for points on the upper portion of a curve and the parentheses for points on the lower portion of that curve.]

If we replace x and y by functions of two other independent variables u and v, then z will also become a function of u and v. Substitute these values of x and y in the equations to the limiting curves $A = 0$ and $B = 0$; we thus obtain two equations $C = 0$ and $D = 0$, which determine the limits of the integration relative to u and v. Conversely the equation to the surface will be obtained by eliminating u and v between the values of x, y, z; and the equations $A = 0$, $B = 0$, of the limiting curves in terms of x and y will be found by eliminating u and v between the values of x and y, and the equations $C = 0$ and $D = 0$.

Now let us denote by δx, δy, δz arbitrary indefinitely small functions of u and v; and suppose that x, y, z become respectively $x + \delta x$, $y + \delta y$, $z + \delta z$. Then the equation to the new surface will be found by eliminating u and v between the values of $x + \delta x$, $y + \delta y$, $z + \delta z$; so that its form will differ in an infinitesimal but perfectly arbitrary manner from the form of the original surface. At the same time if the equations $C = 0$ and $D = 0$ have not been changed, the equations to the new limiting curves will result from the elimination of u and v between the values of $x + \delta x$ and $y + \delta y$, and these equations $C = 0$ and $D = 0$. Hence these curves will differ in an infinitesimal but perfectly arbitrary manner from the primitive limiting curves which were given by $A = 0$ and $B = 0$. Thus by varying x, y, z without varying the limits relative to u and v, the zone of surface over which the double integral extends undergoes an arbitrary variation both in its form and its boundaries.

102. In his nineteenth section Poisson gives some important formulae in variations. Suppose z a function of x and y, and let

V be a given function of x, y, z, z', $z_{,}$, z'', $z_{,}'$, $z_{,,}$, ... Denote the complete differential of V thus

$$dV = Ldx + Mdy + Ndz + Pdz' + Qdz_{,}$$
$$+ Rdz'' + Sdz_{,}' + Tdz_{,,} + \ldots\ldots$$

so that L, M, N, P, ... are the partial differential coefficients of V with respect to x, y, z, z', ... The complete variation δV of V may be obtained from dV by changing d into δ; and if we regard δx, δy, δz as functions of x and y which are arbitrary and independent of each other, we shall have to form the corresponding expressions for $\delta z'$, $\delta z_{,}$, $\delta z''$, $\delta z_{,}'$, ...

Consider x and y and consequently z as implicit functions of two other independent variables u and v. Differentiate z with respect to u and v; thus

$$\frac{dz}{du} = z'\frac{dx}{du} + z_{,}\frac{dy}{du},$$

$$\frac{dz}{dv} = z'\frac{dx}{dv} + z_{,}\frac{dy}{dv}.$$

From these we obtain

$$z' = \frac{1}{\zeta}\left(\frac{dz}{du}\frac{dy}{dv} - \frac{dz}{dv}\frac{dy}{du}\right),$$

$$z_{,} = \frac{1}{\zeta}\left(\frac{dz}{dv}\frac{dx}{du} - \frac{dz}{du}\frac{dx}{dv}\right),$$

where
$$\zeta = \frac{dx}{du}\frac{dy}{dv} - \frac{dx}{dv}\frac{dy}{du}.$$

Now if we represent by δx, δy, δz three arbitrary and indefinitely small functions of u and v, we may suppose without varying u and v that x, y, z become simultaneously $x + \delta x$, $y + \delta y$, $z + \delta z$. If we differentiate relatively to the characteristic δ the preceding value of z' and make use of the value of $z_{,}$, we obtain

$$\delta z' = \frac{1}{\zeta}\left(\frac{dy}{dv}\frac{d\delta z}{du} - \frac{dy}{du}\frac{d\delta z}{dv}\right)$$

$$- \frac{z'}{\zeta}\left(\frac{dy}{dv}\frac{d\delta x}{du} - \frac{dy}{du}\frac{d\delta x}{dv}\right)$$

$$- \frac{z_{,}}{\zeta}\left(\frac{dy}{dv}\frac{d\delta y}{du} - \frac{dy}{du}\frac{d\delta y}{dv}\right).$$

But we may also consider u and v and consequently δx, δy, δz as functions of x and y; then we have

$$\frac{d\delta x}{du} = \frac{d\delta x}{dx}\frac{dx}{du} + \frac{d\delta x}{dy}\frac{dy}{du},$$

$$\frac{d\delta x}{dv} = \frac{d\delta x}{dx}\frac{dx}{dv} + \frac{d\delta x}{dy}\frac{dy}{dv},$$

$$\frac{d\delta y}{du} = \frac{d\delta y}{dx}\frac{dx}{du} + \frac{d\delta y}{dy}\frac{dy}{du},$$

$$\frac{d\delta y}{dv} = \frac{d\delta y}{dx}\frac{dx}{dv} + \frac{d\delta y}{dy}\frac{dy}{dv},$$

$$\frac{d\delta z}{du} = \frac{d\delta z}{dx}\frac{dx}{du} + \frac{d\delta z}{dy}\frac{dy}{du},$$

$$\frac{d\delta z}{dv} = \frac{d\delta z}{dx}\frac{dx}{dv} + \frac{d\delta z}{dy}\frac{dy}{dv}.$$

From these we obtain

$$\frac{dy}{dv}\frac{d\delta x}{du} - \frac{dy}{du}\frac{d\delta x}{dv} = \zeta\frac{d\delta x}{dx},$$

$$\frac{dy}{dv}\frac{d\delta y}{du} - \frac{dy}{du}\frac{d\delta y}{dv} = \zeta\frac{d\delta y}{dx},$$

$$\frac{dy}{dv}\frac{d\delta z}{du} - \frac{dy}{du}\frac{d\delta z}{dv} = \zeta\frac{d\delta z}{dx}.$$

By means of these values that of $\delta z'$ becomes

$$\delta z' = \frac{d\delta z}{dx} - z'\frac{d\delta x}{dx} - z_{,}\frac{d\delta y}{dx}.$$

For shortness put

$$\delta z - z'\delta x - z_{,}\delta y = \omega,$$

thus

$$\delta z' = z''\delta x + z_{,}'\delta y + \omega'.$$

In the same manner it may be shewn that

$$\delta z_{,} = z_{,}'\delta x + z_{,,}\delta y + \omega_{,}.$$

These simple expressions for $\delta z'$ and $\delta z_{,}$ are, as we see, independent of any particular relation which may be established between x and y and the auxiliary variables u and v.

We can easily deduce expressions for $\delta z''$, $\delta z_{,}'$, $\delta z_{,,}$, ...

For since $\dfrac{d\omega}{dx} = \omega'$ and $\dfrac{d\omega}{dy} = \omega_{,}$, we have by putting its value for ω

$$\left.\begin{aligned}
\delta z' - z''\delta x - z_{,}'\delta y &= \frac{d\,(\delta z - z'\delta x - z_{,}\delta y)}{dx}, \\[2ex]
\delta z_{,} - z_{,}'\delta x - z_{,,}\delta y &= \frac{d\,(\delta z - z'\delta x - z_{,}\delta y)}{dy}.
\end{aligned}\right\} \quad \ldots\ldots\ldots (1)$$

These equations hold for any function z of x and y, so that we may substitute successively z', $z_{,}$, z'', ... in place of z. Put z' in place of z in the first of equations (1), thus

$$\delta z'' - z'''\delta x - z_{,}''\delta y = \frac{d\,(\delta z' - z''\delta x - z_{,}'\delta y)}{dx}.$$

But by differentiating the same equation with respect to x, we obtain

$$\frac{d\,(\delta z' - z''\delta x - z_{,}'\delta y)}{dx} = \frac{d^{2}\omega}{dx^{2}};$$

thus

$$\delta z'' - z'''\delta x - z_{,}''\delta y = \omega''.$$

Similarly if we put $z_{,}$ in place of z in the second of equations (1), we shall obtain

$$\delta z_{,,} - z_{,,}'\delta x - z_{,,,}\delta y = \omega_{,,}.$$

Again, put z' in place of z in the second of equations (1); thus

$$\delta z_{,}' - z_{,}''\delta x - z_{,,}'\delta y = \frac{d\,(\delta z' - z''\delta x - z_{,}'\delta y)}{dy}.$$

By differentiating the first of equations (1) with respect to y, we obtain

$$\frac{d\,(\delta z' - z''\delta x - z_{,}'\delta y)}{dy} = \frac{d^{2}\omega}{dx\,dy};$$

therefore

$$\delta z_{,}' - z_{,}''\delta x - z_{,,}'\delta y = \omega_{,}'.$$

It is easy to see that by continuing this process we shall obtain for all values of the indices m and n

$$\delta z_{(n)}^{(m)} = z_{(n)}^{(m+1)}\,\delta x + z_{(n+1)}^{(m)}\,\delta y + \omega_{(n)}^{(m)}.$$

This result Poisson says he had arrived at on a former occasion and had used in explaining a difficulty in the *Mécanique Analytique*. See *Bulletin de la Société Philomatique* année 1816, page 82.

[These formulæ supply the corrections of the errors indicated in Arts. 39—41.]

By means of the general formula proved above the variation of V takes the form

$$\delta V = (L + Nz' + Pz'' + Qz_{,}' + Rz'' + Sz_{,}'' + Tz_{,,}' + \ldots)\, \delta x$$
$$+ (M + Nz_{,} + Pz_{,}' + Qz_{,,} + Rz_{,}'' + Sz_{,,}' + Tz_{,,,} + \ldots)\, \delta y$$
$$+ N\omega + P\omega' + Q\omega_{,} + R\omega'' + S\omega_{,}' + T\omega_{,,} + \ldots$$

or, which is the same thing,

$$\delta V = V'\delta x + V_{,}\delta y + N\omega + P\omega' + Q\omega_{,}$$
$$+ R\omega'' + S\omega_{,}' + T\omega_{,,} + \ldots\ldots\ldots\ldots\ldots(2).$$

103. The twentieth section contains some reductions of the variation of a double integral. Consider the definite integral

$$U = \iint V\, dx\, dy.$$

By the known rules for the transformation of double integrals, if we consider x and y as functions of two other variables u and v, we must put

$$dx\, dy = \left(\frac{dx}{du}\, \frac{dy}{dv} - \frac{dx}{dv}\, \frac{dy}{du} \right) du\, dv;$$

so that we have

$$U = \iint V \left(\frac{dx}{du}\, \frac{dy}{dv} - \frac{dx}{dv}\, \frac{dy}{du} \right) du\, dv.$$

Now put $x + \delta x$, $y + \delta y$, $z + \delta z$ in place of x, y, z under the integral sign. From what was said above it will be sufficient that δx, δy, δz should be arbitrary functions of u and v, and it will not be necessary to vary the limits relative to u and v in order that the integral U may vary in the most general manner both with respect to the limits relative to x and y, and with respect to the form of the function z. The complete variation of U will then be

$$\delta U = \iint \left(\frac{dx}{du}\, \frac{dy}{dv} - \frac{dx}{dv}\, \frac{dy}{du} \right) \delta V\, du\, dv$$

$$+ \iint \left(\frac{dx}{du}\, \frac{d\delta y}{dv} - \frac{dx}{dv}\, \frac{d\delta y}{du} + \frac{dy}{dv}\, \frac{d\delta x}{du} - \frac{dy}{du}\, \frac{d\delta x}{dv} \right) V\, du\, dv.$$

But by the formulæ of the preceding article we have

$$\frac{dx}{du}\frac{d\delta y}{dv} - \frac{dx}{dv}\frac{d\delta y}{du} = \left(\frac{dx}{du}\frac{dy}{dv} - \frac{dx}{dv}\frac{dy}{du}\right)\frac{d\delta y}{dy},$$

$$\frac{dy}{dv}\frac{d\delta x}{du} - \frac{dy}{du}\frac{d\delta x}{dv} = \left(\frac{dx}{du}\frac{dy}{dv} - \frac{dx}{dv}\frac{dy}{du}\right)\frac{d\delta x}{dx}.$$

Hence

$$\delta U = \iint\left(\delta V + V\frac{d\delta x}{dx} + V\frac{d\delta y}{dy}\right)\left(\frac{dx}{du}\frac{dy}{dv} - \frac{dx}{dv}\frac{dy}{du}\right)du\,dv,$$

that is, by restoring the variables x and y

$$\delta U = \iint\left(\delta V + V\frac{d\delta x}{dx} + V\frac{d\delta y}{dy}\right)dx\,dy.$$

In this formula the limits are the same as those of U. Now substitute the value of δV given by equation (2), and observe that

$$V'\delta x + V\frac{d\delta x}{dx} = \frac{d\cdot V\delta x}{dx},$$

$$V'\delta y + V\frac{d\delta y}{dy} = \frac{d\cdot V\delta y}{dy};$$

thus

$$\delta U = \left[\int V'\delta x\,dy\right] - \left(\int V\delta x\,dy\right)$$

$$+ \left[\int V'\delta y\,dx\right] - \left(\int V\delta y\,dx\right)$$

$$+ \iint(N\omega + P\omega' + Q\omega_{,} + R\omega'' + S\omega_{,}' + T\omega_{,,} + \ldots)dx\,dy \ldots\ldots (3).$$

By the method of integration by parts we may remove the differential coefficients of ω from under the double integral sign. For

$$\iint P\omega'\,dx\,dy = \left[\int P\omega\,dy\right] - \left(\int P\omega\,dy\right) - \iint P'\omega\,dx\,dy,$$

$$\iint Q\omega_{,}\,dx\,dy = \left[\int Q\omega\,dx\right] - \left(\int Q\omega\,dx\right) - \iint Q_{,}\omega\,dx\,dy.$$

By two successive integrations we have

$$\iint R\omega'' \, dx \, dy = \left[\int R\omega' \, dy \right] - \left(\int R\omega' \, dy \right)$$

$$- \left[\int R'\omega \, dy \right] + \left(\int R'\omega \, dy \right) + \iint R''\omega \, dx \, dy,$$

$$\iint T\omega_{,,} \, dx \, dy = \left[\int T\omega_{,} \, dx \right] - \left(\int T\omega_{,} \, dx \right)$$

$$- \left[\int T_{,}\omega \, dx \right] + \left(\int T_{,}\omega \, dx \right) + \iint T_{,,}\omega \, dx \, dy.$$

By integrating first with respect to y and then with respect to x we obtain

$$\iint S\omega_{,}' \, dx \, dy = \left[\int S\omega' \, dx \right] - \left(\int S\omega' \, dx \right)$$

$$- \left[\int S_{,}\omega \, dy \right] + \left(\int S_{,}\omega \, dy \right) + \iint S_{,}'\omega \, dx \, dy;$$

by performing the integrations in the reverse order, we obtain

$$\iint S\omega_{,}' \, dx \, dy = \left[\int S\omega_{,} \, dy \right] - \left(\int S\omega_{,} \, dy \right)$$

$$- \left[\int S'\omega \, dx \right] + \left(\int S'\omega \, dx \right) + \iint S_{,}'\omega \, dx \, dy.$$

For the sake of symmetry we may use the half sum of these equivalent expressions, that is

$$\iint S\omega_{,}' \, dx \, dy = \tfrac{1}{2} \left[\int S\omega' \, dx \right] + \tfrac{1}{2} \left[\int S\omega_{,} \, dy \right] - \tfrac{1}{2} \left(\int S\omega_{,}' \, dx \right) - \tfrac{1}{2} \left(\int S\omega_{,} \, dy \right)$$

$$- \tfrac{1}{2} \left[\int S_{,}\omega \, dy \right] - \tfrac{1}{2} \left[\int S'\omega \, dx \right] + \tfrac{1}{2} \left(\int S_{,}\omega \, dy \right) + \tfrac{1}{2} \left(\int S'\omega \, dx \right)$$

$$+ \iint S_{,}'\omega \, dx \, dy.$$

The subsequent terms in the last part of the formula (3) may be transformed in a similar manner. Thus the expression for δU will become finally

$$\delta U = \Gamma + \iint H\omega \, dx \, dy \, \ldots\ldots\ldots\ldots\ldots\ldots (4),$$

where for shortness,

$$H = N - P' - Q_{,} + R'' + S'_{,} + T_{,,} - \ldots$$

$$\Gamma = \left[\int V \delta x\, dy\right] - \left(\int V \delta x\, dy\right) + \left[\int V \delta y\, dx\right] - \left(\int V \delta y\, dx\right)$$

$$+ \left[\int P\omega\, dy + \int Q\omega\, dx - \int R'\omega\, dy - \frac{1}{2}\int S_{,}\omega\, dy - \frac{1}{2}\int S'\omega\, dx - \int T_{,}\omega\, dx + \ldots\right]$$

$$- \left(\int P\omega\, dy + \int Q\omega\, dx - \int R'\omega\, dy - \frac{1}{2}\int S_{,}\omega\, dy - \frac{1}{2}\int S'\omega\, dx - \int T_{,}\omega\, dx + \ldots\right)$$

$$+ \left[\int R\omega'\, dy + \frac{1}{2}\int S\omega'\, dx + \int T\omega_{,}\, dx + \frac{1}{2}\int S\omega_{,}\, dy - \ldots\right]$$

$$- \left(\int R\omega'\, dy + \frac{1}{2}\int S\omega'\, dx + \int T\omega_{,}\, dx + \frac{1}{2}\int S\omega_{,}\, dy - \ldots\right)$$

$$+ \ldots\ldots\ldots\ldots\ldots\ldots\ldots\ldots\ldots\ldots\ldots\ldots$$

The two expressions which have been found for $\iint S\omega_{,}'\, dx\, dy$ must be identically equal; hence we have

$$\left[\int S\omega'\, dx\right] - \left(\int S\omega'\, dx\right) - \left[\int S_{,}\omega\, dy\right] + \left(\int S_{,}\omega\, dy\right)$$

$$= \left[\int S\omega_{,}\, dy\right] - \left(\int S\omega_{,}\, dy\right) - \left[\int S'\omega\, dx\right] + \left(\int S'\omega\, dx\right).$$

This may be written

$$\left[\int \left(S\omega' + S'\omega\right) dx\right] - \left(\int \left(S\omega' + S'\omega\right) dx\right)$$

$$= \left[\int \left(S\omega_{,} + S_{,}\omega\right) dy\right] - \left(\int \left(S\omega_{,} + S_{,}\omega\right) dy\right) \ldots\ldots\ldots\ldots (5).$$

This will be verified presently (see Art. 106). We may observe here that $S\omega' + S'\omega$ is the partial differential coefficient of $S\omega$ with respect to x *before* substituting the value of y obtained from one of the limiting equations. But the value of $(S\omega' + S'\omega)\, dx$ *after* we substitute for y its value is no longer a complete differential with respect to x and thus cannot be integrated immediately. Similar remarks apply to the term $(S\omega_{,} + S_{,}\omega)\, dy$.

[This remark guards against the error indicated in Art. 27.]

104. The twenty-first section. For U to be a maximum or minimum we must have $\delta U = 0$. The double integral included in equation (4) cannot be reduced to simple integrals because ω is an arbitrary function of x and y; it will therefore be necessary that the two parts of this formula should separately vanish. Thus we obtain

$$\Gamma = 0, \quad H = 0,$$

for the equations which must be satisfied in order that the double integral which we are considering should have a maximum or minimum value. The second equation will serve to find z in terms of x and y; this equation will be in general a partial differential equation of the order $2n$ if V be of the order n. The first equation will decompose into others the number and nature of which in the different cases which may occur we will investigate in the subsequent articles. This is the most delicate part of the question.

The preceding analysis may be extended without difficulty to triple and quadruple integrals, &c. In the case of a triple integral, for example, we shall obtain for the variation an expression analogous to that in equation (4); this expression will consist of a triple integral, and of another part containing only double integrals which relate to the limits of the triple integral we are considering. We might also suppose that the quantity under the triple integral sign involves unknown functions of the independent variables, and that these functions are independent, or that they are connected by given partial differential equations. We shall not stop to consider these questions, since they present no new difficulties and no useful applications.

The determination of the *relative* maxima or minima of multiple integrals can be reduced to the determination of *absolute* maxima or minima by the method of the thirteenth section, which is obviously applicable whatever may be the number of the independent variables. Thus, for example, if the first of the double integrals

$$\iint V\,dx\,dy, \quad \iint T\,dx\,dy, \quad \iint W\,dx\,dy, \dots$$

is to be a maximum or minimum, and at the same time the others are to have given values, the problem amounts to investigating the absolute maximum or minimum value of

$$\iint (V + aT + bW + \&c.)\, dx\, dy;$$

where a, b, ... are unknown constants which must be determined by means of the given values of the integrals. We suppose here that these integrals and the first integral are all taken between the same limits.

105. The twenty-second section. [The results from this point to the end of the memoir were not known before the publication of the memoir.] Let us now examine the equations relative to the limits of U which are necessary for the maximum or minimum of this double integral, and which must be deduced from the condition $\Gamma = 0$.

In order to render the reasoning easier to follow, we will suppose that x, y, z are the rectangular co-ordinates of any point of the surface determined by $H = 0$, and that the integral U corresponds to a zone of this surface comprised between two closed curves which will be given or which will have to be determined. Let ABC be the projection of the exterior curve upon the plane of (x, y), and DEF that of the interior curve upon the same plane (see fig. 2). The integral relative to x and y which δU represents will extend to all the elements $dx\, dy$ of the plane area intercepted between these two curves. It may however also be considered to represent the excess of a double integral extended to all the elements of area enclosed by the curve ABC over the same double integral extended to all the elements of area enclosed by the curve DEF. Now δU reduces to Γ since by supposition $H = 0$; and $\Gamma = \Gamma''' - \Gamma'''$ where Γ''' denotes that part of δU which arises from the area bounded by ABC and Γ''' that which arises from the area bounded by DEF. Since these two limits ABC and DEF are in general independent of each other, the equation $\Gamma = 0$ will decompose into two others, namely,

$$\Gamma''' = 0, \quad \Gamma''' = 0.$$

It will be sufficient to consider one of these; the other will be of the same form and susceptible of the same transformations.

We had in the twentieth section the equation

$$\iint \frac{d . V \delta y}{dy}\, dx\, dy = \left[\int V \delta y\, dx \right] - \left(\int V' \delta y\, dx \right).$$

[It has been already intimated in a remark on Art. 101, that Poisson does not use his symbols in the sense which he assigned to them; the terms in square brackets refer to the upper portions of a curve, and those in parentheses refer to the lower portions of the same curve.]

If this double integral relates to the area ABC, the integration relative to y which has been effected, is to be extended from one to the other of the two ordinates PM and PM', which correspond to the same abscissa x. We will suppose that it is extended from the smaller ordinate PM' to the greater PM; that is, we consider the variable y to increase and so dy to be positive. As the element of area $dx\, dy$ is essentially positive, it follows that dx must be regarded as positive in the two simple integrals which are indicated. The first will correspond to the part AMB of the curve ABC and the second to the part $AM'B$ supposing that A and B are the two points of the curve where the tangents are parallel to the axis of y. Let s denote the length of an arc of the curve ABC measured from any fixed point of the curve up to the point M, and let l be the complete perimeter of the curve. Then we shall consider s to increase from $s = 0$ to $s = l$, and thus the differential ds to be positive. Let β be the angle comprised between the exterior normal MN and the produced part of the ordinate PM. Since dx is the projection of ds on the axis of x, we shall have

$$dx = \pm \cos \beta\, ds;$$

the upper or lower sign must be taken according as $\cos \beta$ is positive or negative. But the angle β is acute in all the part AMB of the curve ABC and obtuse in all the part $AM'B$; hence we shall have

$$dx = \cos \beta\, ds$$ throughout the extent of the integral $\left[\int V \delta y\, dx \right]$, and

$$dx = - \cos \beta\, ds$$ throughout the extent of the integral $\left(\int V \delta y\, dx \right).$

Hence we conclude that their difference will reduce to a single integral relative to s which will extend throughout the whole curve; that is, we shall have

$$\left[\int V \delta y\, dx\right] - \left(\int V \delta y\, dx\right) = \int_0^1 V \cos \beta\, \delta y\, ds.$$

Similarly we shall have

$$\left[\int V \delta x\, dy\right] - \left(\int V \delta x\, dy\right) = \int_0^1 V \cos \alpha\, \delta x\, ds,$$

where α denotes the angle which the exterior normal MN makes with the produced part of the abscissa of the point M. By similar reasoning we may reduce to a single integral each of the differences of two homologous integrals of which the expression Γ is composed. Thus the equation $\Gamma^{(4)} = 0$ will be transformed into the following:

$$\int_0^1 V\left(\cos \alpha\, \delta x + \cos \beta\, \delta y\right) ds$$

$$+ \int_0^1 \left[\left(P - R' - \frac{1}{2} S_, + \ldots\right) \cos \alpha + \left(Q - T_, - \frac{1}{2} S' + \ldots\right) \cos \beta\right] \omega\, ds$$

$$+ \int_0^1 \left(R \cos \alpha + \frac{1}{2} S \cos \beta - \ldots\right) \omega'\, ds$$

$$+ \int_0^1 \left(T \cos \beta + \frac{1}{2} S \cos \alpha - \ldots\right) \omega_,\, ds$$

$$+ \ldots = 0. \dots\dots\dots\dots\dots\dots\dots\dots\dots\dots\dots\dots\dots\dots\dots\dots\dots \text{(6).}$$

The figure supposes that each line parallel to the axis of y meets the closed curve ABC in only two points; but this transformation of the equation $\Gamma^{(4)} = 0$ would still hold if the number of intersections, which must be even, were greater than two; we should then take successively for the two ordinates PM and PM' which correspond to the same abscissa, those of the first and second intersection, those of the third and fourth, and so on.

106. In his twenty-third section Poisson verifies equation (5) of the twentieth section.

In fact, as we have just seen, the part of this equation which belongs to the exterior curve is the same thing as

$$\int_0^1 \left(\frac{d \cdot S\omega}{dx}\right) \cos \beta\, ds = \int_0^1 \left(\frac{d \cdot S\omega}{dy}\right) \cos \alpha\, ds,$$

where the parentheses denote that each partial differential coefficient is taken with respect to one of the variables x or y before we substitute in $\delta\omega$ the value of the other variable deduced from the equation to the curve ABC. If we differentiate with respect to x after substituting the value of y, we have

$$\frac{d \cdot \delta\omega}{dx} = \left(\frac{d \cdot \delta\omega}{dx}\right) + \left(\frac{d \cdot \delta\omega}{dy}\right)\frac{dy}{dx},$$

and since $\quad \dfrac{d \cdot \delta\omega}{ds} = \dfrac{d \cdot \delta\omega}{dx}\dfrac{dx}{ds} = \dfrac{d \cdot \delta\omega}{dx}\cos\beta,$

it follows that

$$\int_0^l \left(\frac{d \cdot \delta\omega}{dx}\right)\cos\beta\, ds = \int_0^l \frac{d \cdot \delta\omega}{ds}\, ds - \int_0^l \left(\frac{d \cdot \delta\omega}{dy}\right)\frac{dy}{dx}\cos\beta\, ds.$$

Now $\quad\displaystyle\int \frac{d \cdot \delta\omega}{ds}\, ds = \delta\omega + \text{constant};$

and since $\delta\omega$ has the same value at the two limits $s = 0$ and $s = l$ which belong to the same point of the closed curve ABC, it follows that

$$\int_0^l \frac{d \cdot \delta\omega}{ds}\, ds = 0.$$

Hence the equation reduces to

$$\int_0^l \left(\frac{d \cdot \delta\omega}{dx}\right)\cos\beta\, ds = -\int_0^l \left(\frac{d \cdot \delta\omega}{dy}\right)\frac{dy}{dx}\cos\beta\, ds.$$

By help of this result we see that the equation which we are to verify may be written thus,

$$\int_0^l \left(\frac{d \cdot \delta\omega}{dy}\right)\left\{\frac{dy}{dx}\cos\beta + \cos\alpha\right\} ds = 0.$$

But if a and b denote the angles which the tangent at any point M of the curve ABC makes with the axes of x and y, we can take in this equation where the differentials dx and dy may be positive or negative,

$$dx = \cos a\, ds, \quad dy = \cos b\, ds.$$

Thus the equation is transformed into the following:

$$\int_0^1 \left(\frac{d \cdot \delta\omega}{dy}\right) \left\{ \cos\alpha \cos a + \cos\beta \cos b \right\} \frac{ds}{\cos a} = 0;$$

this result is obviously true since the factor $\cos\alpha \cos a + \cos\beta \cos b$ is the cosine of the angle comprised between the tangent and the normal at the same point M of the curve ABC, and is therefore equal to zero. It is evident this verification applies in the same way to the part of equation (5) which belongs to the interior curve.

107.　In his twenty-fourth section Poisson 'effects some transformations of the equation (6) of Art. 105.　The applications of the preceding formulæ to geometry and mechanics relate to problems where the function V depends on the inclination of tangent planes and on the magnitude of radii of curvature.　In order then to avoid useless complication, we will suppose that the highest differential coefficient contained in V is of the second order.　In this case the equation $H = 0$ involves partial differential coefficients of the fourth order, and the first member of equation (6) is reduced to its first four terms.　But in order to be able to deduce from this equation (6) the conditions relative to the second limit of U, it is necessary to transform its third and fourth terms, and to reduce the three variations ω, ω', and ω_i to two only.

All the terms of equation (6) are integrals relative to the arc s of the curve ABC, where s is the independent variable and ds is constant and positive.　Under the integral sign s is regarded as a function of x and y, which is obtained from the equation to the required surface, that is, from the complete integral of the equation $H = 0$. The variables x and y are implicitly supposed to be functions of s determined by the equation, known or unknown, of the curve ABC. Thus by differentiating ω with respect to s, we have

$$\frac{d\omega}{ds} = \omega' \frac{dx}{ds} + \omega_i \frac{dy}{ds};$$

hence since $dx^2 + dy^2 = ds^2$, we may write

$$\omega' = \frac{dx}{ds} \frac{d\omega}{ds} - \theta \frac{dy}{ds}, \quad \omega_i = \frac{dy}{ds} \frac{d\omega}{ds} + \theta \frac{dx}{ds},$$

where θ is an indeterminate variation.

The differentials dx and dy are as in the preceding article capable of changing sign in the course of the integration, that is, as we proceed from point to point of the curve ABC. Since the angles α and β relate to the exterior part of the normal MN it is easy to see that we shall have at any point M,

$$\cos\alpha = -\frac{dy}{ds}, \quad \cos\beta = \frac{dx}{ds}.$$

Substitute these values and those of ω' and ω, in equation (6), and it becomes

$$\int_0^{\cdot} V\left(\frac{dx}{ds}\,\delta y - \frac{dy}{ds}\,\delta x\right) ds$$

$$+\int_0^l \left[\left(Q - T_{,} - \tfrac{1}{2}S'\right)\frac{dx}{ds} - \left(P - R' - \tfrac{1}{2}S_{,}\right)\frac{dy}{ds}\right]\omega\, ds$$

$$+\int_0^l \left(T - R\right)\frac{dx}{ds}\,\frac{dy}{ds}\,\frac{d\omega}{ds}\, ds$$

$$+\int_0^l \left[R\left(\frac{dy}{ds}\right)^{\!\cdot} + T\left(\frac{dx}{ds}\right)^{\!\cdot} - S\frac{dx}{ds}\,\frac{dy}{ds}\right]\theta\, ds$$

$$+\tfrac{1}{2}\int_0^l S\left[\left(\frac{dx}{ds}\right)^{\!\cdot} - \left(\frac{dy}{ds}\right)^{\!\cdot}\right]\frac{d\omega}{ds}\, ds = 0.$$

[By some accident Poisson himself omits the last line; the error is noticed by Björling. In consequence of this omission two of Poisson's subsequent formulæ in this section are incorrect; the necessary alterations have accordingly been made.]

By integration by parts we have

$$\int_0^l (T - R)\frac{dx}{ds}\,\frac{dy}{ds}\,\frac{d\omega}{ds}\, ds$$

$$= \int_0^l \left[\left(\frac{dR}{ds} - \frac{dT}{ds}\right)\frac{dx}{ds}\,\frac{dy}{ds} + (R - T)\frac{dx\, d'y + dy\, d'x}{ds^2}\right]\omega\, ds;$$

for the terms outside the integral sign vanish since they are the difference of two values of the same quantity, one relating to the limit $s = 0$, and the other to the limit $s = l$, that is to the *same* point of the closed curve ABC. [Similar treatment may be applied to the term which Poisson omits.] Moreover

$$\frac{dR}{ds} = R'\frac{dx}{ds} + R_,\frac{dy}{ds}, \quad \frac{dT}{ds} = T'\frac{dx}{ds} + T_,\frac{dy}{ds}, \quad \frac{dS}{ds} = S'\frac{dx}{ds} + S_,\frac{dy}{ds}.$$

Let us suppose for shortness that

$$P - \frac{1}{2}S_, - R'\left(1 + \frac{dx^2}{ds^2}\right) + T'\frac{dx^2}{ds^2} + (T - R)\frac{d^2x}{ds^2}$$
$$- \frac{1}{2}S'\frac{dx}{ds}\frac{dy}{ds} - \frac{1}{2}S_,\frac{dy^2}{ds^2} - S\frac{d^2y}{ds^2} = X,$$

$$Q - \frac{1}{2}S' - T_,\left(1 + \frac{dy^2}{ds^2}\right) + R_,\frac{dy^2}{ds^2} + (R - T)\frac{d^2y}{ds^2}$$
$$- \frac{1}{2}S'\frac{dx^2}{ds^2} - \frac{1}{2}S_,\frac{dx}{ds}\frac{dy}{ds} - S\frac{d^2x}{ds^2} = Y,$$

$$R\frac{dy^2}{ds^2} - S\frac{dx}{ds}\frac{dy}{ds} + T\frac{dx^2}{ds^2} = Z.$$

[The value of Z agrees with Poisson's; those of X and Y differ since Poisson omits the last three terms of each.]

Thus equation (6) finally becomes

$$\int_0^1 V\left(\frac{dx}{ds}\delta y - \frac{dy}{ds}\delta x\right) ds + \int_0^1 \left(Y\frac{dx}{ds} - X\frac{dy}{ds}\right)\omega ds$$
$$+ \int_0^1 Z\theta\, ds = 0 \dots\dots\dots\dots\dots\dots (7);$$

and this is the simplest form it can take.

108. The twenty-fifth section relates to the case in which some condition is given. In the problems to which this equation can be applied, it will sometimes happen that the length of the exterior curve to which it relates is to have a given value; or more generally that one or more integrals taken throughout this length are to have given values. It will be sufficient to consider one of these integrals; for similar remarks would apply to the others. For greater simplicity we will suppose that the differential function which occurs under the sign of integration is only of the first order.

At any point of the exterior curve then, let

$$\frac{dx}{ds} = x', \quad \frac{dy}{ds} = y';$$

let W denote a given function of x, y, z, x', y', and suppose that
$$\int W\,ds = \sigma\,;$$
σ being a given constant, and the integral extending throughout this curve, so that it is the same thing as $\int_0^1 W\dfrac{ds}{ds}\,ds$. In order to introduce this condition it will be sufficient according to the remark in the thirteenth section to add to U the integral $\int W\,ds$ multiplied by an undetermined constant which we will denote by c. Thus the first member of equation (7) is augmented by the term $c\,\delta\int W\,ds$.

Now if we put
$$\frac{dW}{dx}=\mu,\qquad \frac{dW}{dy}=\nu,\qquad \frac{dW}{dx'}=m,\qquad \frac{dW}{dy'}=n,$$
this term has for its value
$$c\int\left[\left(\mu-\frac{dm}{ds}\right)(\delta x-x'\delta z)+\left(\nu-\frac{dn}{ds}\right)(\delta y-y'\delta z)\right]ds\,;$$
considering x and y as functions of z in the formula of the seventh section (Art. 92) and observing that the part outside the integral sign vanishes because the curve which we are considering is a closed curve.

Suppose that this curve is to lie on a surface which we will denote by the differential equation
$$dz = p\,dx + q\,dy,$$
where p and q are given functions of x, y and z. We shall see presently (Art. 114) how the case of a curve unrestricted is comprised in the present. The co-ordinates x, y, z of any point in this curve, and also the varied co-ordinates $x+\delta x$, $y+\delta y$, $z+\delta z$ must satisfy the equation to the given surface; we may therefore differentiate that equation relatively to the characteristic δ; thus we shall have
$$\delta z = p\,\delta x + q\,\delta y$$
as well as
$$dz = p\,dx + q\,dy.$$

Hence
$$\delta x - x'\delta z = q\left(\frac{dy}{dz}\,\delta x - \frac{dx}{dz}\,\delta y\right),$$
$$\delta y - y'\delta z = p\left(\frac{dx}{dz}\,\delta y - \frac{dy}{dz}\,\delta x\right).$$

If then, for abbreviation, we put

$$\mu - \frac{dm}{dz} = h, \quad \nu - \frac{dn}{dz} = k,$$

the term which is to be added to equation (7) becomes

$$c \int_{_s}^{'} (kp - hq) \left(\frac{dx}{ds} \delta y - \frac{dy}{ds} \delta x \right) ds.$$

Thus it has the same form as the first term of this equation; consequently in order to introduce the condition that the integral $\int W dz$ is to have a constant value, we have only to change in equation (7) V into $V + c\,(kp - hq)$. The constant o will have to be determined in every case from the value σ of the integral $\int W dz$.

109. The twenty-sixth section. Let us now observe the results which may be deduced from equation (7) thus modified if necessary. Let us put

$$\frac{dx}{ds} \delta y - \frac{dy}{ds} \delta x = \cos \alpha\, \delta x + \cos \beta\, \delta y = e,$$

$$\omega = \delta z - z'\delta x - z_{,}\delta y = \phi \sqrt{1 + z'^{\,2} + z_{,}^{\,2}}.$$

The point M of the curve ABC whose co-ordinates are x and y being transferred to the position indicated by the co-ordinates $x + \delta x$ and $y + \delta y$, we see by the value of e that this variation denotes the displacement of M projected on the normal MN. The cosines of the angles which the normal to the required surface at the point (x, y, z) makes with the co-ordinate axes are respectively

$$-\frac{z'}{\sqrt{1 + z'^{\,2} + z_{,}^{\,2}}}, \quad -\frac{z_{,}}{\sqrt{1 + z'^{\,2} + z_{,}^{\,2}}}, \quad \frac{1}{\sqrt{1 + z'^{\,2} + z_{,}^{\,2}}}.$$

Thus the variation ϕ is the projection on this normal of the displacement of this point (x, y, z) when its co-ordinates become $x + \delta x$, $y + \delta y$ and $z + \delta z$; and in equation (7) this displacement belongs to any point of the exterior curve. As to the third arbitrary variation contained in equation (7), namely θ, this depends on the change of inclination experienced by the tangent plane to

the required surface at any point of the exterior curve. [In fact
we have from the equations in which θ first occurred

$$\theta = \omega_{,}\frac{dx}{ds} - \omega'\frac{dy}{ds};$$

and if we insert the values of $\omega_{,}$ and ω' from Art. 102 we have

$$\theta = (\delta z_{,} - \varepsilon_{,}'\delta x - \varepsilon_{,,}\delta y)\frac{dx}{ds} - (\delta z' - \varepsilon''\delta x - \varepsilon_{,}'\delta y)\frac{dy}{ds}.$$

Thus θ involves $\delta z_{,}$ and $\delta z'$ and is thus connected with the
change of inclination of the tangent plane.]

Now if the second limit of U is not restrained by any given
condition, the three variations ε, ϕ, θ will be completely arbitrary
and independent; hence in order that equation (7) may subsist it
will be necessary that the coefficients of these variations under the
integral sign should be separately zero. Thus we shall obtain
three equations,

$$V = 0, \quad Y\frac{dx}{ds} - X\frac{dy}{ds} = 0, \quad Z = 0 \dotfill (8).$$

When the second limit of U has to satisfy some given con-
ditions the three variations ε, ϕ, θ are no longer independent; then
the equations (8) or at least one or two of them will not hold and
must be replaced by others. The following are the principal cases
which may arise. [Five cases are considered which will occupy the
following five articles, extending to the end of Poisson's twenty-
sixth section.] .

110. Suppose that the exterior curve is fixed and given, and
let us represent its two equations by

$$f(x, y, z) = 0, \quad F(x, y, z) = 0 \dotfill (9).$$

From the signification of ε and ϕ it follows that these quantities
now vanish; thus the first two terms of equation (7) disappear.
The first two equations of (8) will now no longer be necessary and
they will be replaced by the equations (9).

Let us further suppose that the required surface is to touch
throughout the perimeter of the exterior curve a fixed and given
surface, as for example the surface which has for its equation

$F(x, y, z) = 0$, and the differential equation of which we will represent by

$$dz = pdx + qdy.$$

It will be necessary on account of this contact that

$$p = z', \quad q = z_{,}$$

for every point of the exterior curve. These however are not *two* new independent equations; for since the curve is already the intersection of the required surface and the given surface, the differential dz taken along its direction has the same value whether it be obtained from the equation to the first surface or from the equation to the second surface; thus we have already the relation

$$pdx + qdy = z'dx + z_{,}dy;$$

and by means of this relation one of the equations $p = z'$ and $q = z_{,}$ is a consequence of the other.

On the other hand the variation ϕ and consequently ω will be zero, not only for all the points of the exterior curve, but also for all those of an indefinitely narrow zone of which this curve forms part; we may therefore differentiate the equation $\omega = 0$ along the direction of this curve and along any other direction; thus we shall have throughout the whole perimeter of the curve

$$\frac{d\omega}{dz} = 0, \quad \omega' = 0, \quad \omega_{,} = 0;$$

thus the quantity θ which occurs in the twenty-fourth section vanishes, and the third term of equation (7) vanishes.

Thus in this first case the three variations ϵ, ϕ, θ being zero, the equation (7) vanishes; the equations (8) which were deduced from (7) do not hold, and they must be replaced by the equations (9) which will be given in each particular problem, and by one of the equations $p = z'$, $q = z_{,}$.

111.   Suppose that the exterior curve is fixed and given, so that $\epsilon = 0$ and $\omega = 0$, and suppose that the second limit of U is not restrained by any other condition. The equation $\omega = 0$ can now be differentiated only along the direction of the given curve; we have then

$$\frac{d\omega}{ds} = 0, \quad \omega' = -\theta \frac{dy}{ds}, \quad \omega_, = \theta \frac{dx}{ds};$$

the factor θ remains indeterminate, and we must have $Z = 0$ in order to satisfy equation (7) which now consists of only its third term.

In this second case the third of the equations (8) holds, and the other two are replaced, as in the first case, by the two given equations of the exterior curve.

112. If this curve is not fixed but only constrained to lie on a given surface which is determined by the equation

$$F(x, y, z) = 0 \dots\dots\dots\dots\dots\dots\dots\dots\dots(10),$$

then the co-ordinates x, y, z and also $x + \delta x$, $y + \delta y$, $z + \delta z$ must satisfy this equation. We may therefore differentiate with respect to the characteristic δ; thus if we represent the ordinary differential equation by

$$dz = pdx + qdy,$$

we shall also have simultaneously

$$\delta z = p\delta x + q\delta y.$$

Hence the variation ω will be given by the equation

$$\omega = (p - z') \, \delta x + (q - z_,) \, \delta y.$$

Suppose moreover that the required surface is to touch the given surface throughout the perimeter of the exterior curve. We shall have the two relations $p = z'$ and $q = z_,$, one of which is a consequence of the other, as we have shewn in the first case. These relations will make ω vanish for all points in an indefinitely narrow zone comprising the exterior curve; hence as in the first case we conclude that $\theta = 0$. Since the variations ω and θ are zero the equation (7) is reduced to its first term; and in order that it may hold whatever may be the value of the indeterminate variation ϵ we must have $V = 0$; or rather

$$V + c \, (kp - hq) = 0 \dots\dots\dots\dots\dots\dots\dots(11),$$

if we suppose, as before, that the value of a certain integral $\int W ds$ is given.

Thus in this third case the equations (8) are replaced by the equations (10) and (11) together with one of the two relations $p = z'$ and $q = z_,$.

113. Suppose that the exterior curve is still constrained to lie on the surface determined by equation (10), but that the tangent plane to the required surface is *not* subject to any restriction throughout the perimeter of the exterior curve; the expression for ϖ given in the preceding case will still hold, but there will be no resulting limitation for the quantity θ, which will remain altogether arbitrary and independent of δx and δy; the coefficient of θ in equation (7), that is Z, must therefore be zero. Substitute the expression for ϖ in this equation and it will become

$$\int_{_\bullet}^{^t}\left[\left(Y\frac{dx}{ds} - X\frac{dy}{ds}\right)(p-s') - V\frac{dy}{ds}\right]\delta x\,ds$$

$$+\int_{_\bullet}^{^t}\left[\left(Y\frac{dx}{ds} - X\frac{dy}{ds}\right)(q-s_,) + V\frac{dx}{ds}\right]\delta y\,ds = 0.$$

But as the two variations δx and δy are arbitrary and independent their coefficients must be separately zero; if we add then to V the part which arises from supposing the integral $\int W ds$ to have a given value we shall obtain

$$\left(Y\frac{dx}{ds} - X\frac{dy}{ds}\right)(p-s') = \left[V + c\,(kp - hq)\right]\frac{dy}{ds},$$

$$\left(X\frac{dy}{ds} - Y\frac{dx}{ds}\right)(q-s_,) = \left[V + c\,(kp - hq)\right]\frac{dx}{ds}.$$

But one of these equations is a consequence of the other; for if we multiply them crosswise and suppress the factor common to the two products we obtain

$$(p - s')\,dx = (s_, - q)\,dy;$$

and this equation, as we have seen in the first case, follows from the fact that the required surface and the given surface intersect in the exterior curve which we are considering. These equations may be written in the following manner

$$Y\,(p - s')\,dx = \left[X\,(p - s') + V + c\,(kp - q\lambda)\right]dy,$$

$$X\,(q - s_,)\,dy = \left[Y\,(q - s_,) + V + c\,(kp - qh)\right]dx;$$

multiply these equations and reduce, thus we obtain

$$V + c\,(kp - qh) + X\,(p - s') + Y\,(q - s_,) = 0\ldots\ldots\ldots(12).$$

Thus in this fourth case the third of equations (8) holds, and the two others will be replaced by equation (12) together with that of the given surface of which the differential equation is represented by $dz = pdx + qdy$.

114. Lastly, suppose that the tangent plane to the required surface may vary arbitrarily throughout the perimeter of the exterior curve, and that this curve is not constrained to remain upon a given surface. The equation $Z = 0$ will still hold. We may write equation (12) in the form

$$V' + c(kz' - hz_i) + (X + ck)(p - z') + (Y - ch)(q - z_i) = 0;$$

multiply by dx, and put $(z_i - q)\,dy$ for $(p - z')\,dx$; thus we have

$$[V' + c(kz' - hz_i)]\,dx + [Ydx - Xdy - c(hdx + kdy)](q - z_i) = 0.$$

But the quantity q is altogether arbitrary, since now the surface which had for its differential equation $dz = pdx + qdy$ is not given; the preceding equation must therefore separate into two, and connecting them with $Z = 0$ we shall have for the three equations belonging to this fifth and last case

$$\left.\begin{array}{l} V + c(kz' - hz_i) = 0, \\ Ydx - Xdy - c(hdx + kdy) = 0, \\ Z = 0. \end{array}\right\} \quad\ldots\ldots\ldots\ldots\ldots (13).$$

These equations coincide, as they should do, with the equations (8), when we put $c = 0$; this amounts to suppressing the condition relative to a given value of the integral $\int Wds$; so that now there is no longer any given condition by which the second limit of U is restricted.

115. The twenty-seventh section. The reasoning already given applies equally to the first limit of U; and by the details which have just been given we see that the conditions of a maximum or minimum of this double integral consist in this, that for each limit the required surface must satisfy simultaneously three known equations which will either be directly given, or which may be formed for the different cases which can occur in the manner we have explained. These two systems of three equations will serve

for the determination of the four arbitrary functions involved in the complete integral of the equation $H = 0$.

When the differential function V is only of the first order we shall also have

$$R = 0, \quad S = 0, \quad T = 0;$$

the partial differential equation $H = 0$ will not be of a higher order than the second; we shall have

$$X = P, \quad Y = Q, \quad Z = 0;$$

and the equations of the preceding article will simplify and will reduce to two for each limit of U.

If we wish to apply the formulæ of the preceding article to the case of a single integral, we must suppose that the quantity V is a function only of x, s, s', s''; hence we shall have

$$Q = 0, \quad S = 0, \quad T = 0.$$

It will be necessary at the same time that the zone of the required surface to which the integral U will belong, should be comprised between two planes parallel to that of (y, z). The curve ABC will then reduce to two straight lines parallel to the axis of y, the limits of two oval curves of which one dimension is indefinitely increased; and as in the equations with which we are concerned the differentials of x and y relate to this curve and the differential ds is supposed constant, we must put

$$dx = 0, \quad d^2x = 0, \quad dy = ds, \quad d^2y = 0.$$

The condition relative to the length will no longer hold, so that we also must suppress the terms which thence arise, that is, put $c = 0$. Under these circumstances the equations of the twenty-sixth section will coincide in all cases with those which would be derived from the fifth case (Art. 114), observing that the quantities which were represented by y and Q in that section are now represented by s and R, and that the function V being supposed of the second order, the quantities R, S, &c. of that section are zero. This coincidence would supply, if that were needful, a confirmation of our analysis with respect to double integrals.

116. In his twenty-eighth section Poisson makes some remarks on the mode in which the arbitrary functions are to be determined

in some problems. There are particular problems in which the
curve which forms the inner boundary of the required surface according to the hypothesis of the twenty-second section (Art. 105) does
not exist, and in which consequently the conditions relative to this
curve must be replaced by others, in order that the arbitrary functions which are involved in the general integral of the equation
$H = 0$ may not remain undetermined, and that these problems may
be completely solved.

This circumstance might occur, for example, in the question
where we have to find a surface of which the area should be a
minimum between certain limits. The equation $H = 0$ is then a
partial differential equation of the second order, and its integral
involving two arbitrary functions is known in a finite form. Now
if the minimum area is to be a zone included between two given
curves, we see that these two curves through which the required
surface is to pass will theoretically serve to determine the two
arbitrary functions which occur in the equation to the surface, that
is, in the integral of the equation $H = 0$, the only difficulty being
that which arises from the complicated form of this integral. We
see too that these two curves might be exchanged for other pairs
of conditions. But if we require that the minimum area should be
all that portion of the surface which is bounded by the exterior
curve, it seems then that the integral of the equation $H = 0$ will
have a greater degree of generality than the problem, and that the
given curve will not be sufficient for the determination of the two
arbitrary functions.

117. In order to remove this apparent indeterminateness, suppose we exchange the rectangular co-ordinates x and y for polar co-
ordinates r and θ, where r is the radius vector and θ the angle which
r makes with a fixed line drawn through the origin in the plane of
(x, y). Put the origin within the boundary formed by the projection DEF of the interior curve (Art. 105) when such curve exists.

Let
$$r = f(\theta), \quad s = \phi(\theta),$$
be the two equations of this curve; and
$$r = F(\theta), \quad s = \Phi(\theta),$$
those of the exterior curve of which ABC is the projection.

For the zone of minimum area the values of r will extend from $r = f(\theta)$ to $r = F(\theta)$, and those of θ from $\theta = 0$ to $\theta = 2\pi$, and the arbitrary functions which occur in the integral of $H = 0$ must be determined so that z should become $\phi(\theta)$ and $\Phi(\theta)$ for $r = f(\theta)$ and $r = F(\theta)$ respectively. Outside the zone, that is, for values of r less than $f(\theta)$ or greater than $F(\theta)$ whatever θ may be, the ordinate z will be subject to no limitation and can become infinite. But if the minimum area is to be all that portion of the surface the projection of which is bounded by the curve ABC, the values of r will extend from $r = 0$ to $r = F(\theta)$ for every value of θ, and throughout this extent the ordinate z must be finite. We shall therefore suppress in this case that portion of the integral of $H = 0$ which would become infinite when $r = 0$; and the integral thus modified will be reduced to the degree of generality which the problem has; so that the single condition that z should be equal to $\Phi(\theta)$ when r is equal to $F(\theta)$ will suffice for completing the solution of the problem.

Thus the solution of the question of the minimum area and of similar questions, separates into two problems which are quite distinct so far as relates to the determination of the arbitrary functions. I only here indicate this distinction which I will take up on another occasion.

If the required surface is closed on all sides, so that for example we have to find the surface of greatest area which incloses a given volume, the conditions for this relative maximum will not furnish any equation suitable for determining the two arbitrary functions which the complete integral of the equation $H = 0$ when applied to this problem will involve. It is by means of other considerations that this integral must be reduced so as to contain only three arbitrary constants, namely the three co-ordinates of the centre of the sphere which solves the problem; the radius of the sphere will be determined by means of the given volume. I propose to consider this particular question in another memoir.

[It does not appear that Poisson ever returned to the two problems which he proposed in the above section to consider at a future period.]

118. In the remaining three sections of the memoir Poisson discusses an example. In an addition to the work entitled *Methodus inveniendi lineas….* Euler determines the figure of the elastic lamina, properly so called, by means of a principle communicated to him by Daniel Bernouilli, namely, that the integral $\int \frac{ds}{\rho}$ taken throughout the length of the curve should be less than for any other curve of the same length; ds being the differential element of the sought curve and ρ its radius of curvature. In order to give an example of the employment of the preceding formulæ, we will extend this principle by induction to the figure of equilibrium of an elastic lamina which is curved in every direction and the points of which are not acted on by any given force. Thus denoting by ρ and ξ the two principal radii of curvature at any point of this surface, or more generally the radii of curvature of two normal sections at right angles, and by $d\sigma$ the differential element of the surface, we shall suppose that among all surfaces of the same area the elastic surface is that which gives a minimum value to the integral $\iint \left(\frac{1}{\rho} + \frac{1}{\xi} \right)^2 d\sigma$. [This is what Poisson says, but he really takes the integral $\iint \left(\frac{1}{\rho} + \frac{1}{\xi} \right)^2 dx\, dy$; the two however coincide to the order of approximation which he finally preserves.]

By the theory of the curvature of surfaces we know that the sum $\frac{1}{\rho} + \frac{1}{\xi}$ has the same value for every pair of normal sections at right angles passing through the same point. With the notation already adopted, we have

$$\frac{1}{\rho} + \frac{1}{\xi} = \frac{(1 + z_{,}^{2})\, z'' - 2z' z_{,} z_{,}' + (1 + z'^{2})\, z_{,,}}{(1 + z'^{2} + z_{,}^{2})^{\frac{3}{2}}},$$

or, which is the same thing,

$$\frac{1}{\rho} + \frac{1}{\xi} = u' + v_{,}$$

where

$$u = \frac{z'}{\sqrt{1 + z'^{2} + z_{,}^{2}}}, \qquad v = \frac{z_{,}}{\sqrt{1 + z'^{2} + z_{,}^{2}}}.$$

We have also

$$d\sigma = \sqrt{1 + z'^2 + z_,^2}\, dx\, dy.$$

Let c denote an undetermined constant, and put

$$V = (u' + v_,)^2 + 2c\sqrt{1 + z'^2 + z_,^2};$$

then the question amounts to making the integral $\iint V dx\, dy$ an absolute minimum.   (See Art. 104.)

The quantity N of the nineteenth section (Art. 102) will be zero, and P, Q, R, S, T, will have for values

$$P = 2\,(u' + v_,)\left(\frac{du'}{dz'} + \frac{dv_,}{dz'}\right) + 2cu,$$

$$Q = 2\,(u' + v_,)\left(\frac{du'}{dz_,} + \frac{dv_,}{dz_,}\right) + 2cv,$$

$$R = 2\,(u' + v_,)\left(\frac{du'}{dz''} + \frac{dv_,}{dz''}\right),$$

$$S = 2\,(u' + v_,)\left(\frac{du'}{dz_,} + \frac{dv_,}{dz_,}\right),$$

$$T = 2\,(u' + v_,)\left(\frac{du'}{dz_{,,}} + \frac{dv_,}{dz_{,,}}\right).$$

It will be sufficient to substitute these values and their first and second differential coefficients with respect to x and y in the equation $H = 0$ of the twenty-first section (Art. 104), in order to obtain the indefinite equation to the elastic surface; this equation will be a partial differential equation of the fourth order. We must also substitute these same quantities in the equations of the twenty-sixth section, in order to obtain the equations relative to the perimeter of the elastic surface in all the cases which can occur.

We will confine ourselves to writing these equations for the case where the elastic surface differs but little from a plane figure parallel to the plane of x and y; and we shall neglect consequently the terms in V of the fourth degree with respect to partial differential coefficients of z. Thus the values of P, Q, ... and therefore the equations in question will be exact as far as quantities of the third order.

Thus we have, simply

$$V = (z'' + z_{,,})^2 + 2c + c\,(z'^2 + z_{,}^2),$$

from which we obtain

$$N = 0, \quad P = 2cz', \quad Q = 2cz_{,}, \quad R = T = 2\,(z'' + z_{,,}), \quad S = 0;$$

thus the equation $H = 0$ will become

$$z'''' + 2z_{,,}'' + z_{,,,,} - c\,(z'' + z_{,,}) = 0.$$

If we denote by ζ a new variable, we may replace this equation by the following system of two equations of the second order:

$$z'' + z_{,,} = \zeta, \quad \zeta'' + \zeta_{,,} = c\zeta \quad\ldots\ldots\ldots\ldots\ldots\ldots\ldots (a).$$

In consequence of these values of R, S, T, the quantity Z of the twenty-fourth section (Art. 107) will be equal to 2ζ. In order to fix our ideas, I will suppose that the limits of the elastic surface in equilibrium are curves fixed and given, but that the tangent plane to this surface is not restricted by any condition throughout the perimeters of these curves; hence it will follow from the second case of the twenty-sixth section (Art. 111), that we must combine with the two equations of each limiting curve the equation $Z = 0$ or $\zeta = 0$, in order to form the two systems of simultaneous equations, which with the given area of the elastic lamina will serve to determine the constant c and the arbitrary functions contained in the integrals of equations (a). The area of the lamina cannot differ much from that of its projection on the plane of x and y; denote the area of the projection by λ, and that of the lamina by $\lambda\,(1 + g)$ so that g is a very small positive fraction; we shall have

$$\lambda\,(1 + g) = \iint \sqrt{1 + z'^2 + z_{,}^2}\; dx\,dy,$$

or to that order of approximation which we have adopted

$$\lambda g = \frac{1}{2} \iint (z'^2 + z_{,}^2)\, dx\,dy \quad\ldots\ldots\ldots\ldots\ldots\ldots (b).$$

119. We may give another form to the equations (a) and (b) by changing the rectangular co-ordinates into polar co-ordinates. Let r be the radius vector of the projection of any point of the

surface upon the plane of x and y, and θ the angle which this radius makes with the axis of x, so that

$$x = r \cos \theta, \quad y = r \sin \theta.$$

The ordinate z will become a function of r and θ, and we shall have

$$\frac{dz}{dr} = z' \cos \theta + z_, \sin \theta,$$

$$\frac{dz}{d\theta} = z_, r \cos \theta - z' r \sin \theta;$$

hence

$$z' = \frac{dz}{dr} \cos \theta - \frac{dz}{d\theta} \frac{\sin \theta}{r},$$

$$z_, = \frac{dz}{dr} \sin \theta + \frac{dz}{d\theta} \frac{\cos \theta}{r};$$

and as the element $dx\,dy$ will be replaced by $r\,dr\,d\theta$, the equation (b) will become

$$\lambda g = \frac{1}{2} \iint \left\{ \left(\frac{dz}{dr} \right)^2 + \frac{1}{r^2} \left(\frac{dz}{d\theta} \right)^2 \right\} r\,dr\,d\theta \dots\dots\dots\dots (c).$$

If we put z' in the place of z in the value of z', we shall have

$$z'' = \frac{dz'}{dr} \cos \theta - \frac{dz'}{d\theta} \frac{\sin \theta}{r};$$

by differentiating the value of z' in succession with respect to r and θ, we obtain

$$\frac{dz'}{dr} = \frac{d^2z}{dr^2} \cos \theta - \frac{d^2z}{dr\,d\theta} \frac{\sin \theta}{r} + \frac{dz}{d\theta} \frac{\sin \theta}{r^2},$$

$$\frac{dz'}{d\theta} = \frac{d^2z}{dr\,d\theta} \cos \theta - \frac{d^2z}{d\theta^2} \frac{\sin \theta}{r} - \frac{dz}{dr} \sin \theta - \frac{dz}{d\theta} \frac{\cos \theta}{r};$$

hence

$$z'' = \frac{d^2z}{dr^2} \cos^2 \theta - 2 \frac{d^2z}{dr\,d\theta} \frac{\sin \theta \cos \theta}{r} + \frac{d^2z}{d\theta^2} \frac{\sin^2 \theta}{r^2}$$

$$+ \frac{dz}{dr} \frac{\sin^2 \theta}{r} + 2 \frac{dz}{d\theta} \frac{\sin \theta \cos \theta}{r^2}.$$

We shall find in the same way that

$$s_{,,} = \frac{d^2 s}{dr^2} \sin^2 \theta + 2 \frac{d^2 s}{dr\, d\theta} \frac{\sin \theta \cos \theta}{r} + \frac{d^2 s}{d\theta^2} \frac{\cos^2 \theta}{r^2}$$
$$+ \frac{ds}{dr} \frac{\cos^2 \theta}{r} - 2 \frac{ds}{d\theta} \frac{\sin \theta \cos \theta}{r^2}.$$

The same transformations will apply to the differential coefficients ζ'' and $\zeta_{,,}$; thus the equations (c) will be changed into the following:

$$\left. \begin{array}{l} \dfrac{d^2 s}{dr^2} + \dfrac{1}{r} \dfrac{d^2 s}{d\theta^2} + \dfrac{1}{r} \dfrac{ds}{dr} = \zeta \\[2ex] \dfrac{d^2 \zeta}{dr^2} + \dfrac{1}{r} \dfrac{d^2 \zeta}{d\theta^2} + \dfrac{1}{r} \dfrac{d\zeta}{dr} = c\zeta \end{array} \right\} \quad \dots\dots\dots\dots (d).$$

From the hypothesis of the preceding article and the supposition that the exterior and interior curves which bound the required surface are determined by the same equations as those in the twenty-eighth section (Art. 117), it follows that the value of s which we shall obtain by the integration of equations (d) must satisfy simultaneously the three equations

$$r = F(\theta), \quad s = \Phi(\theta), \quad \zeta = 0 \dots\dots\dots\dots (e)$$

relative to the exterior limit of the surface, and must satisfy simultaneously the three equations

$$r = f(\theta), \quad s = \phi(\theta), \quad \zeta = 0 \dots\dots\dots\dots (f)$$

relative to the interior limit. In the most usual case this second limit will not exist; according to what has been explained above we shall then replace the equations (f) by the condition that the value of s, which corresponds to $r = 0$, shall not become infinite; and the same must hold with respect to ζ, since we have supposed in the preceding article that the partial differential coefficients of s, and therefore ζ, are very small quantities through the whole extent of surface which we are considering. In order that there may not remain any doubt on this last case I will complete the investigation on the simplest hypothesis, namely, supposing that the elastic lamina is circular and that its figure of equilibrium is that of a surface of revolution.

120. If we take the axis of the surface for that of z, the quantities ζ and z will be independent of θ, and the equations (d) will reduce to

$$\frac{d^2z}{dr^2} + \frac{1}{r}\frac{dz}{dr} = \zeta, \quad \frac{d^2\zeta}{dr^2} + \frac{1}{r}\frac{d\zeta}{dr} = c\zeta \dots\dots\dots\dots (g).$$

Let a denote the given radius of the projection of the lamina on the plane of the co-ordinates r and θ; we shall have $\lambda = \pi a^2$. [It does not appear why a is said to be *given*.] The double integral contained in equation (c) will extend from $\theta = 0$ and $r = 0$ to $\theta = 2\pi$ and $r = a$, and this equation will become

$$g = \tfrac{1}{2}\beta^2,$$

where β denotes the value of $\dfrac{dz}{dr}$ when $r = a$, or in other words the inclination of the tangent plane of the lamina to the plane of projection at any point of the perimeter. When this inclination is given we can immediately deduce the value of $1 + g$, which is the ratio of the area of the lamina to the area of its projection; and reciprocally. [It is difficult to comprehend this equation $g = \tfrac{1}{2}\beta^2$; the equation (c) is

$$\lambda g = \frac{1}{2}\int_0^a\int_0^{2\pi}\left(\frac{dz}{dr}\right)^2 r\,dr\,d\theta = \pi\int_0^a\left(\frac{dz}{dr}\right)^2 r\,dr.$$

Poisson seems to put this $= \pi\left(\dfrac{dz}{dr}\right)^2\displaystyle\int_0^a r\,dr$, which is not justifiable. However he only refers to this equation once again, see page 104. Moreover if he takes β as *given* he has no right to the equation $\zeta = 0$ at the limit; see the first case of the twenty-sixth section, Art. 110.] We may suppose that the plane of the co-ordinates r and θ is that of the boundary of the lamina; the equations (e) will then be

$$r = a, \quad z = 0, \quad \zeta = 0 \dots\dots\dots\dots\dots (\lambda).$$

According to what I have found in another memoir (*Journal de l'Ecole Polytechnique* 19ᵉ *cahier*, page 475) the complete integral of the second equation (g) is

$$\zeta = a\int_0^\pi e^{-r\sqrt{c}\cos\omega}\,d\omega + b\int_0^\pi e^{-r\sqrt{c}\cos\omega}\log(r\sin^2\omega)\,d\omega;$$

where a and b are two arbitrary constants, and e the base of the Napierian logarithms. It is indeed easy to verify that this value of ζ satisfies the second equation (g); for we deduce immediately

$$\frac{d^2\zeta}{dr^2} + \frac{1}{r}\frac{d\zeta}{dr} = ac\int_0^\pi e^{-r\sqrt{c}\sin\omega}\cos^2\omega\, d\omega - \frac{a\sqrt{c}}{r}\int_0^\pi e^{-r\sqrt{c}\sin\omega}\cos\omega\, d\omega$$

$$+ bc\int_0^\pi e^{-r\sqrt{c}\sin\omega}\cos^2\omega\log(r\sin^2\omega)\, d\omega$$

$$- \frac{b\sqrt{c}}{r}\int_0^\pi e^{-r\sqrt{c}\sin\omega}\cos\omega\log(r\sin^2\omega)\, d\omega$$

$$- \frac{2b\sqrt{c}}{r}\int_0^\pi e^{-r\sqrt{c}\sin\omega}\cos\omega\, d\omega.$$

By integration by parts we have

$$\frac{\sqrt{c}}{r}\int_0^\pi e^{-r\sqrt{c}\sin\omega}\cos\omega\, d\omega = -c\int_0^\pi e^{-r\sqrt{c}\sin\omega}\sin^2\omega\, d\omega;$$

$$\frac{\sqrt{c}}{r}\int_0^\pi e^{-r\sqrt{c}\sin\omega}\cos\omega\log(r\sin^2\omega)\, d\omega = -\frac{2\sqrt{c}}{r}\int_0^\pi e^{-r\sqrt{c}\sin\omega}\cos\omega\, d\omega$$

$$- c\int_0^\pi e^{-r\sqrt{c}\sin\omega}\sin^2\omega\log(r\sin^2\omega)\, d\omega.$$

Thus the preceding equation is reduced to

$$\frac{d^2\zeta}{dr^2} + \frac{1}{r}\frac{d\zeta}{dr} = ac\int_0^\pi e^{-r\sqrt{c}\sin\omega}\, d\omega + bc\int_0^\pi e^{-r\sqrt{c}\sin\omega}\log(r\sin^2\omega)\, d\omega;$$

and this coincides with the second equation (c) by reason of the value of ζ

I put $b = 0$ and suppress the second term of the value of ζ; otherwise ζ would become very large near the centre of the lamina and infinite at the centre itself. We have then simply

$$\zeta = a\int_0^\pi e^{-r\sqrt{c}\sin\omega}\, d\omega,$$

or, which is the same thing,

$$\zeta = a\int_0^{\frac{\pi}{2}} e^{-r\sqrt{c}\sin\omega}\, d\omega + a\int_0^{\frac{\pi}{2}} e^{r\sqrt{c}\sin\omega}\, d\omega.$$

By reason of the third equation (h) we shall have

$$\int_{\scriptscriptstyle 0}^{\scriptscriptstyle \frac{\pi}{2}} e^{-a\sqrt{i}\cos\omega}\, d\omega + \int_{\scriptscriptstyle 0}^{\scriptscriptstyle \frac{\pi}{2}} e^{a\sqrt{i}\cos\omega}\, d\omega = 0;$$

and if we replace $a\alpha^2$ by another constant $-\gamma^2$, we shall have for determining γ the equation

$$\int_{\scriptscriptstyle 0}^{\scriptscriptstyle \frac{\pi}{2}} \cos(\gamma\cos\omega)\, d\omega = 0 \ \dots\dots\dots\dots\dots\dots \ (i).$$

The value of ζ will become

$$\zeta = a\int_{\scriptscriptstyle 0}^{\scriptscriptstyle \frac{\pi}{2}} \cos\frac{\gamma r\cos\omega}{a}\, d\omega,$$

where $\dfrac{a}{2}$ is put instead of a. I substitute this value in the first equation (g); then integrating we have

$$\frac{ds}{dr} = \frac{a\alpha}{\gamma}\int_{\scriptscriptstyle 0}^{\scriptscriptstyle \frac{\pi}{2}} \sin\frac{\gamma r\cos\omega}{a}\frac{d\omega}{\cos\omega} - \frac{a\alpha^2}{\gamma^2 r}\int_{\scriptscriptstyle 0}^{\scriptscriptstyle \frac{\pi}{2}}\left(1 - \cos\frac{\gamma r\cos\omega}{a}\right)\frac{d\omega}{\cos^2\omega} + \frac{C}{r};$$

C being the arbitrary constant. In order that $\dfrac{ds}{dr}$ should not become very large for very small values of r, and infinite for $r = 0$, we must have $C = 0$. For $r = a$ we shall therefore have

$$\beta = \frac{a\alpha}{\gamma}\int_{\scriptscriptstyle 0}^{\scriptscriptstyle \frac{\pi}{2}} \sin(\gamma\cos\omega)\frac{d\omega}{\cos\omega} - \frac{a\alpha}{\gamma^2}\int_{\scriptscriptstyle 0}^{\scriptscriptstyle \frac{\pi}{2}} [1 - \cos(\gamma\cos\omega)]\frac{d\omega}{\cos^2\omega};$$

this equation will serve to determine the constant a, from the known value of β or $\sqrt{2g}$. Integrate again, and denote the arbitrary constant by f; thus we shall have for the equation to the required surface

$$s = f + \frac{a\alpha^2}{\gamma^2}\int_{\scriptscriptstyle 0}^{\scriptscriptstyle \frac{\pi}{2}}\left(1 - \cos\frac{\gamma r\cos\omega}{a}\right)\frac{d\omega}{\cos^2\omega}$$

$$- \frac{a\alpha^2}{\gamma^2}\int_{\scriptscriptstyle 0}^{\scriptscriptstyle \frac{\pi}{2}}\left[\int\left(1 - \cos\frac{\gamma r\cos\omega}{a}\right)\frac{dr}{r}\right]\frac{d\omega}{\cos^2\omega}.$$

If we suppose that the integral with respect to r which is indicated in the last term of this formula begins with r, the constant

f will be the sagitta of this surface, that is to say, the value of the ordinate z corresponding to its centre, that is, to $r = 0$. From the second equation (h) the value of f will be

$$f = \frac{a a^2}{\gamma^2} \int_0^{\frac{\pi}{2}} \left[\int_0^a \left(1 - \cos \frac{\gamma r \cos \omega}{a} \right) \frac{dr}{r} \right] \frac{d\omega}{\cos^2 \omega}$$

$$- \frac{a a^2}{\gamma^2} \int_0^{\frac{\pi}{2}} [1 - \cos (\gamma \cos \omega)] \frac{d\omega}{\cos^2 \omega} .$$

We can replace by convergent series the definite integrals which occur in these different formulæ. In this manner the equation (i) will become

$$1 - \gamma^2 + \frac{\gamma^4}{(1 \cdot 2)^2} - \frac{\gamma^6}{(1 \cdot 2 \cdot 3)^2} + \ldots = 0 \ldots\ldots\ldots\ldots (k),$$

where 2γ has been put for γ. The values of γ^2 which can be deduced from this equation are known to be infinite in number, and all real and positive; the least of them is, very nearly,

$$\gamma^2 = 1{\cdot}46796491.$$

This number, which occurs in several problems, has been calculated by M. Largeteau, secretary of the *Bureau des longitudes*. [Poisson gives no reference with respect to the roots of the equation just considered; the statements are proved in the memoir by Fourier entitled *Théorie du Mouvement de la Chaleur*. *Mém. de l'Acad.* Tome IV. 1819, 1820, page 432.]

We shall have at the same time

$$\zeta = \frac{\pi a}{2} \left\{ 1 - \frac{\gamma^2 r^2}{a^2} + \frac{\gamma^4 r^4}{(1 \cdot 2)^2 a^4} - \frac{\gamma^6 r^6}{(1 \cdot 2 \cdot 3)^2 a^6} + \ldots \right\},$$

$$\frac{ds}{dr} = \frac{\pi a r}{4} \left\{ 1 - \frac{\gamma^2 r^2}{2 a^2} + \frac{\gamma^4 r^4}{3 (1 \cdot 2)^2 a^4} - \frac{\gamma^6 r^6}{4 (1 \cdot 2 \cdot 3)^2 a^6} + \ldots \right\},$$

$$s = f + \frac{\pi a r^2}{8} \left\{ 1 - \frac{\gamma^2 r^2}{4 a^2} + \frac{\gamma^4 r^4}{9 (1 \cdot 2)^2 a^4} - \frac{\gamma^6 r^6}{16 (1 \cdot 2 \cdot 3)^2 a^6} + \ldots \right\}.$$

The equations on which the values of a and f depend will be

$$\beta = \frac{\pi a a}{4}\left\{1 - \frac{\gamma^2}{2} + \frac{\gamma^4}{3\,(1\,.\,2)^2} - \frac{\gamma^6}{4\,(1\,.\,2\,.\,3)^2} + \cdots\right\},$$

$$0 = f + \frac{\pi a a^2}{8}\left\{1 - \frac{\gamma^2}{4} + \frac{\gamma^4}{9\,(1\,.\,2)^2} - \frac{\gamma^6}{16\,(1\,.\,2\,.\,3)^2} + \cdots\right\};$$

$$\left[\text{that is, } f + \frac{\pi a a^2}{8\gamma^2} = 0 \text{ by } (k)\right];$$

this shews that *ceteris paribus* the sagitta f will be proportional to the radius of the lamina a; if we take the smallest value of γ^2 we shall have

$$f = - a\beta\,(1\cdot 60197).$$

For this value of γ^2 the ordinate z will have the same sign as f throughout the lamina; and there will be no sinuosity in the lamina; hence, disregarding the sign, z will decrease continually from the centre to the perimeter; and thus it is that f has the contrary sign to β.

[We have to shew here that $\dfrac{dz}{dr}$ cannot be zero for the smallest value of γ^2 except when $r = 0$. Let $F(\gamma)$ denote the left-hand member of equation (k), so that

$$F(\gamma) = 1 - \gamma^2 + \frac{\gamma^4}{(1\,.\,2)^2} - \frac{\gamma^6}{(1\,.\,2\,.\,3)^2} + \cdots,$$

then

$$F'(\gamma) = - 2\gamma\left\{1 - \frac{\gamma^2}{2} + \frac{\gamma^4}{3\,(1\,.\,2)^2} - \cdots\right\}.$$

Hence if $\dfrac{dz}{dr}$ could vanish for a value of r between 0 and a, we should have $F'(\gamma) = 0$ for a value of γ^2 less than $1\cdot 46796491$. But this is impossible for

$$F(\gamma) = \frac{2}{\pi}\int_0^{\frac{\pi}{2}} \cos\,(2\gamma \cos \omega)\, d\omega,$$

$$F'(\gamma) = - \frac{4}{\pi}\int_0^{\frac{\pi}{2}} \sin\,(2\gamma \cos \omega)\, \cos \omega\, d\omega;$$

and $F'(\gamma)$ is certainly negative so long as $2\gamma \cos \omega$ is less than π, and is therefore negative if γ^2 lies between 0 and $1\cdot 4679649$.

We may add that the equation $F'(\gamma) = 0$ will have real roots, namely, a root between each consecutive pair of roots of $F(\gamma) = 0$; this will be useful to remember in reading Poisson's next paragraph.]

If we substitute successively in the expression for s different values of γ^2 derived from equation (k) we shall obtain as many different figures of equilibrium of the circular lamina. Their number will be infinite like that of the figures of the ordinary lamina which is curved in only one direction; and the number of their sinuosities will augment more and more with the value of γ^2 which is used. This number will be zero, as just stated, and there will be no inflexion of the lamina, for the smallest value of γ^2. In all cases the inclination of the tangent plane will be zero at the centre of the lamina; for from the value of s we have $\dfrac{ds}{dr} = 0$ when $r = 0$.

121. Here Poisson's memoir closes. The last eleven pages of the memoir have been spent on a problem which is only a case of a single integral. It may be useful then to give a solution of the problem in a simpler form than Poisson's.

Let Os, Or be two axes at right angles and suppose a surface formed by the revolution of a curve round the axis of s. (See figure 8.) The principal radii of curvature at any point of a surface of revolution are the radius of curvature of the generating curve and the length of the normal at the point between the point and the axis of revolution. Denote these by ρ_1 and ρ_2; then

$$\frac{1}{\rho_1} = \frac{\dfrac{d^2s}{dr^2}}{\left\{1 + \left(\dfrac{ds}{dr}\right)^2\right\}^{\frac{3}{2}}}, \quad \frac{1}{\rho_2} = \frac{\dfrac{ds}{dr}}{r\left\{1 + \left(\dfrac{ds}{dr}\right)^2\right\}^{\frac{1}{2}}}.$$

The expression which we have to make a minimum is

$$2\pi \int \left\{\left(\frac{1}{\rho_1} + \frac{1}{\rho_2}\right)^2 + 2c\right\} \left\{1 + \left(\frac{ds}{dr}\right)^2\right\}^{\frac{1}{2}} r\,dr.$$

If we adopt the approximation of Poisson, that is, if we reject terms of the fourth degree, we get

$$2\pi \int \left\{ \left(\frac{d^2s}{dr^2} + \frac{1}{r}\frac{dz}{dr}\right)^2 + 2c + c\left(\frac{ds}{dr}\right)^2 \right\} r\,dr.$$

Thus we may put

$$V = \left\{ \left(\frac{d^2s}{dr^2} + \frac{1}{r}\frac{ds}{dr}\right)^2 + 2c + c\left(\frac{ds}{dr}\right)^2 \right\} r,$$

or $$V = \left\{ \left(\frac{dp}{dr} + \frac{p}{r}\right)^2 + 2c + cp^2 \right\} r,$$

where $p = \dfrac{ds}{dr}$; and we have to make $\int V dr$ a minimum. By ordinary rules then we have

$$2\left(\frac{dp}{dr} + \frac{p}{r}\right) + 2cpr - 2\frac{d}{dr}\left(r\frac{dp}{dr} + p\right) = 0,$$

thus $$cp - \frac{d}{dr}\left(\frac{dp}{dr} + \frac{p}{r}\right) = 0,$$

therefore $$cs - \frac{dp}{dr} - \frac{p}{r} = \text{a constant} = C',$$

or $$\frac{d^2s}{dr^2} + \frac{1}{r}\frac{ds}{dr} = cs - C'.$$

Now put $$s - \frac{C'}{c} = v;\ \text{thus}$$

$$\frac{d^2v}{dr^2} + \frac{1}{r}\frac{dv}{dr} = cv.$$

Hence assuming Poisson's integral of this differential equation we get the value of v; and thus finally

$$s = A\int_0^\pi e^{-r\sqrt{c}\cos\omega}\,d\omega + B\int_0^\pi e^{-r\sqrt{c}\cos\omega}\log (r\sin^2\omega)\,d\omega + C,$$

where A, B, C are arbitrary constants.

The integrated part of $\delta \int V dr$ is

$$V \delta r + 2 \left(r \frac{dp}{dr} + p \right) \left(\delta p - \frac{dp}{dr} \delta r \right).$$

We have now to determine the constants A, B, C and c.

We may obviously give C any value we like, for this amounts to pushing the surface along the axis of z without making any change in the value of any element of $\int V dr$. Suppose then

$$C = 0.$$

Now by hypothesis the area is given, that is, to our order of approximation the value of the integral

$$2\pi \int \left\{ 1 + \frac{1}{2} \left(\frac{dz}{dr} \right)^2 \right\} r \, dr,$$

extended over all admissible values of r is given. Let us suppose with Poisson, that the boundary of the surface is a circle of radius a; then

$$2\pi \int_0^a \left\{ 1 + \frac{1}{2} \left(\frac{dz}{dr} \right)^2 \right\} r \, dr = \text{a given finite quantity.}$$

Now unless $B = 0$ this integral will be infinite and therefore cannot be equal to a given finite quantity. We must therefore have $B = 0$, and then the fact of the area being given supplies a condition for determining A in terms of c. We must examine the integrated part of the variation. Since the limits of r are fixed, namely 0 and a, the variation δr is zero at both limits. Also $r \frac{dp}{dr} + p = 0$ when $r = 0$; thus to make the integrated part vanish all that is necessary is that $r \frac{dp}{dr} + p$ should vanish when $r = a$. This, by reduction as in Poisson, leads to

$$\int_0^a e^{-c\sqrt{c}\,\omega} \cdot \omega \, d\omega = 0,$$

and shews that c must really be a negative quantity; from this equation c must be found in terms of a.

The results of this solution are thus the same as those of Poisson's if we omit that statement of his that $\dfrac{ds}{dr}$ is *given* at the limit. If $\dfrac{ds}{dr}$ were given at the limit the integrated part of $\delta\!\int V dr$ would all vanish; and instead of the equation

$$\int_{0}^{\pi} e^{-a\sqrt{c}\cos\omega}\, d\omega = 0,$$

for determining c we should have

$$-A \int_{0}^{\pi} e^{-a\sqrt{c}\cos\omega}\, \sqrt{c}\cos\omega\, d\omega = \beta,$$

where β is the given value of $\dfrac{ds}{dr}$ when $r = a$. The constant a in Poisson's solution ought to be found from the circumstance of the area being given.

It should be observed that some of Poisson's expressions might be put in a simpler form than he has adopted. For from the values of ζ and s at the bottom of page 105 we see that

$$s = f + \frac{a^2}{6\gamma^2}(\pi a - 2\zeta).$$

This might also be obtained from equations (g); for they will give

$$\frac{d^2(\zeta - cs)}{dr^2} + \frac{1}{r}\,\frac{d(\zeta - cs)}{dr} = 0,$$

and by integrating and determining the constants we shall obtain the above value of s. And with that value of s we can give simpler forms for $\dfrac{ds}{dr}$, β, s, and f, in terms of a definite integral, than those on pages 104 and 105.

CHAPTER V.

OSTROGRADSKY.

122. On the 24th of January 1834, a memoir was communicated by M. Ostrogradsky to the Academy of Sciences of St Petersburg, entitled *Mémoire sur le Calcul des Variations des Intégrales multiples*. This memoir is published in the sixth series of the memoirs of the Academy of St Petersburg; the volume is dated 1838, and is called the *third* volume of the section comprising the mathematical, physical, and natural sciences; it is also called the *first* volume of a section including only the mathematical and physical sciences. The memoir occupies twenty-four pages. The memoir is also published in *Crelle's Journal*, Vol. xv.

We shall give here the whole of Ostrogradsky's memoir; its object will be seen from the introductory paragraphs. Ostrogradsky confirms some of the results obtained by Poisson which have been given in the preceding chapter of the present work; and he points out the error of Euler and Lacroix which has been alluded to in Articles 39 and 40. We now proceed to the memoir.

123. The application of the method of variations to functions which comprise integrals with respect to only one variable may be considered perfect with respect both to simplicity and to generality. But this is far from being the case when we have to obtain the variation of a multiple integral which involves different variables. Certain questions relating to this case seem to require more generality than is possessed by the Calculus of Variations as Lagrange has exhibited it. This might lead us to believe that the principles of that great mathematician have not been suitably applied, or that the principles themselves are not always sufficient.

It is doubtless for this reason that M. Poisson, in a memoir which he read to the Academy of Sciences at Paris, on November 10th, 1831, thought it necessary to add to the principles of the Calculus of Variations which were established by Lagrange, a sort of new principle, which consists in regarding the independent variables of the question as functions of other auxiliary variables. The latter disappear of themselves in the course of the investigation; but by making use of them in the case of two independent variables x and y, M. Poisson has not been compelled to consider the variation δx as a function of x only, and the variation δy as a function of y only; a limitation which all mathematicians who have investigated the variation of the partial differential coefficients of a function of two variables have been in some way forced to make by the nature of their process.

Nevertheless the supposition that δx is independent of y, and that δy is independent of x, seems to follow from the most simple and elementary principles of the differential calculus; and so long as it remains unproved that these principles are insufficient or that an inaccurate application has been made of them, it would be a question whether the formulæ given by M. Poisson for the variation of the partial differential coefficients of a function of two variables ought to be preferred to those of Euler and other mathematicians which have the same object. It is true that the latter are a particular case of the former; but perhaps this particular case is that which must always exist.

We now decide this question in favour of the formulæ of M. Poisson. We shall shew that the mathematicians who have treated of the variation of double integrals, including Euler himself, have not differentiated the partial differential coefficients of the principal variable with regard to the symbol δ correctly. But at the same time it will be seen that the introduction of auxiliary variables into this kind of question is not necessary. The memoir of M. Poisson on the Calculus of Variations will always be cited in the history of differential analysis. There for the first time was given the complete variation of a double integral; it is deduced from the consideration of auxiliary variables. But it is quite possible to restrict ourselves to the principles of the immortal author of the

Mécanique Analytique; for those principles combine extreme simplicity with all the necessary generality.

We will first point out the inaccuracy which has escaped the notice of mathematicians who have investigated the variation of the partial differential coefficients of a function of two variables; and we will then indicate a method for finding the variation of any multiple integral.

124. Let us denote by z any function of the two independent variables x and y; and put $\frac{dz}{dx} = z'$, $\frac{dz}{dy} = z_{,}$, $\frac{d^2z}{dx^2} = z''$, $\frac{d^2z}{dx\,dy} = z_{,}'$, $\frac{d^2z}{dy^2} = z_{,,}$, and so on. Then let us give to the quantities x, y, z, respectively, the simultaneous increments δx, δy, δz, which we will regard as indefinitely small arbitrary functions of x and y; in consequence of these increments the quantities z', $z_{,}$, z'', ... will become respectively $z' + \delta z'$, $z_{,} + \delta z_{,}$, $z'' + \delta z''$, ...; we propose then to determine the variations $\delta z'$, $\delta z_{,}$, $\delta z''$, ...

Consider first $\delta z'$. Since $z' = \frac{dz}{dx}$ it was supposed that in order to obtain $\delta z'$ it was necessary to differentiate in the common way the quantity $\frac{dz}{dx}$ with respect to δ; and this gave the inaccurate result $\delta z' = \frac{d\delta z}{dx} - z'\frac{d\delta x}{dx}$. [See Art. 39.] In order to discover the source of this error we have only to ascend to the origin of the quantity $\delta z'$; let us denote for an instant $x + \delta x$, $y + \delta y$, $z + \delta z$, respectively by X, Y, Z; we shall then have obviously

$$z' + \delta z' = \frac{dZ}{dX},$$

and

$$\delta z' = \frac{dZ}{dX} - z'.$$

The partial differential coefficient z' is taken on the supposition that y is invariable; and the partial differential coefficient $\frac{dZ}{dX}$ on the supposition that Y is invariable, that is, on the supposition that $y + \delta y$ is invariable.   But it was supposed that the differential coefficients z' and $\dfrac{dZ}{dX}$ were both obtained on the same supposition, namely, that $dy = 0$; and this is the inaccuracy to which we have referred.

Restore for X, Y, Z their values $x + \delta x$, $y + \delta y$, $z + \delta z$.   We shall obtain

$$\delta z' = \frac{d\,(z + \delta z)}{d\,(x + \delta x)} - z' = \frac{d\,(z + \delta z) - z'\,d\,(x + \delta x)}{d\,(x + \delta x)};$$

the differentials $d\,(z + \delta z)$ and $d\,(x + \delta x)$ are to be taken on the supposition that $d\,(y + \delta y) = 0$.

But $\qquad d\,(z + \delta z) = \left(z' + \dfrac{d\delta z}{dx}\right) dx + \left(z_, + \dfrac{d\delta z}{dy}\right) dy,$

$$d\,(x + \delta x) = \left(1 + \frac{d\delta x}{dx}\right) dx + \frac{d\delta x}{dy}\, dy,$$

$$d\,(y + \delta y) = \frac{d\delta y}{dx}\, dx + \left(1 + \frac{d\delta y}{dy}\right) dy;$$

substitute these values of $d\,(z + \delta z)$ and $d\,(x + \delta x)$ in the last value of $\delta z'$; we shall obtain

$$\delta z' = \frac{\left(\dfrac{d\delta z}{dx} - z'\dfrac{d\delta x}{dx}\right) dx + \left(z_, + \dfrac{d\delta z}{dy} - z'\dfrac{d\delta x}{dy}\right) dy}{\left(1 + \dfrac{d\delta x}{dx}\right) dx + \dfrac{d\delta x}{dy}\, dy};$$

and at the same time

$$0 = \frac{d\delta y}{dx}\, dx + \left(1 + \frac{d\delta y}{dy}\right) dy.$$

Eliminating dx and dy, we have

$$\delta z' = \frac{\left(\dfrac{d\delta z}{dx} - z'\dfrac{d\delta x}{dx} - z_,\dfrac{d\delta y}{dx}\right)\left(1 + \dfrac{d\delta y}{dy}\right) - \left(\dfrac{d\delta z}{dy} - z'\dfrac{d\delta x}{dy} - z_,\dfrac{d\delta y}{dy}\right)\dfrac{d\delta y}{dx}}{\left(1 + \dfrac{d\delta x}{dx}\right)\left(1 + \dfrac{d\delta y}{dy}\right) - \dfrac{d\delta x}{dy}\dfrac{d\delta y}{dx}}.$$

And from this by including only small terms of the first order we have

$$\delta z' = \frac{d\delta z}{dx} - z' \frac{d\delta x}{dx} - z_, \frac{d\delta y}{dx}.$$

If we compare this value $\delta z'$ with the former, namely,

$$\delta z' = \frac{d\delta z}{dx} - z' \frac{d\delta x}{dx},$$

we see that by assuming $dy = 0$ instead of $d(y + \delta y) = 0$, we suppress in $\delta z'$ the term $z_, \frac{d\delta y}{dx}$ which is of the same order of magnitude as $\delta z'$, and which by the principles of the Differential Calculus ought to be retained.

Suppose that the quantity δy is independent of x; we shall have $\frac{d\delta y}{dx} = 0$, and $\delta z' = \frac{d\delta z}{dx} - z' \frac{d\delta x}{dx}$, which is the result obtained by differentiating in the ordinary way the quantity $\frac{dz}{dx}$ with respect to δ. And it is easy to see that on the hypothesis $\frac{d\delta y}{dx} = 0$ the common differentiation is allowable; for since then $d(y + \delta y) = \left(1 + \frac{d\delta y}{dy}\right) dy$, if we put $d(y + \delta y) = 0$, we have obviously $dy = 0$; then in the expression $\delta z' = \frac{d(z + \delta z)}{d(x + \delta x)} - z'$, the partial differential coefficients z' and $\frac{d(z + \delta z)}{d(x + \delta x)}$ are both formed on the same supposition, namely, that $dy = 0$.

It is evident that

$$\delta z' = \frac{d\delta z}{dx} - z' \frac{d\delta x}{dx} - z_, \frac{d\delta y}{dx} = z'' \delta x + z_,' \delta y + \frac{d(\delta z - z' \delta x - z_, \delta y)}{dx}.$$

We shall obtain in the same manner

$$\delta z_, = z_,' \delta x + z_{,,} \delta y + \frac{d(\delta z - z' \delta x - z_, \delta y)}{dy}.$$

For the differential coefficients of the second order we have

$$\delta z'' = \frac{d\,(z' + \delta z')}{d\,(x + \delta x)} - z'',$$

$$\delta z_{,}' = \frac{d\,(z' + \delta z')}{d\,(y + \delta y)} - z_{,}' = \frac{d\,(z_{,} + \delta z_{,})}{d\,(x + \delta x)} - z_{,}',$$

$$\delta z_{,,} = \frac{d\,(z_{,} + \delta z_{,})}{d\,(y + \delta y)} - z_{,,}.$$

Then we shall obtain the variations $\delta z''$, $\delta z_{,}'$, $\delta z_{,,}$ by changing z into z' or $z_{,}$ in the values of $\delta z'$ and $\delta z_{,}$.   Thus we shall have

$$\delta z'' = z'''\delta x + z_{,}''\delta y + \frac{d\,(\delta z' - z''\delta x - z_{,}'\delta y)}{dx},$$

$$\delta z_{,}' = z_{,}''\delta x + z'_{,,}\delta y + \frac{d\,(\delta z' - z''\delta x - z_{,}'\delta y)}{dy},$$

$$\delta z_{,}' = z_{,}''\delta x + z'_{,,}\delta y + \frac{d\,(\delta z_{,} - z_{,}'\delta x - z_{,,}\delta y)}{dx},$$

$$\delta z_{,,} = z'_{,,}\delta x + z_{,,,}\delta y + \frac{d\,(\delta z_{,} - z_{,}'\delta x - z_{,,}\delta y)}{dy}.$$

Therefore

$$\delta z'' = z'''\delta x + z_{,}''\delta y + \frac{d^2\,(\delta z - z'\delta x - z_{,}\delta y)}{dx^2},$$

$$\delta z_{,}' = z_{,}''\delta x + z'_{,,}\delta y + \frac{d^2\,(\delta z - z'\delta x - z_{,}\delta y)}{dx\,dy},$$

$$\delta z_{,,} = z'_{,,}\delta x + z_{,,,}\delta y + \frac{d^2\,(\delta z - z'\delta x - z_{,}\delta y)}{dy^2}.$$

And similarly we can find the variations of the differential coefficients of the higher orders.

[These results agree with Poisson's; see Art. 102.]

125. The preceding method shews sufficiently how by direct application of the characteristic δ to the partial differential coefficients z', $z_{,}$, z'', ... we can find the variations of these differential coefficients. But it is better to seek the variations $\delta z'$, $\delta z_{,}$, $\delta z''$, ... by the use of total differentials.

In order to consider the subject with due generality, let us designate by u a function of as many quantities x, y, z, ... as we please, and suppose that the variable u and the independent quantities x, y, z, ... receive simultaneously the increments δu, δx, δy, δz, ... which we shall consider as arbitrary functions of all the independent variables.

In order to find the variations

$$\delta \frac{du}{dx}, \ \delta \frac{du}{dy}, \ \delta \frac{du}{dz}, \ ...$$

due to the increments δu, δx, δy, δz, ... let us take the fundamental equation

$$\delta du = d\delta u \,;$$

put for $d\delta u$ its value

$$\frac{d\delta u}{dx} dx + \frac{d\delta u}{dy} dy + \frac{d\delta u}{dz} dz + ...,$$

and for du its value

$$\frac{du}{dx} dx + \frac{du}{dy} dy + \frac{du}{dz} dz + ... \,;$$

develop δdu, that is,

$$\delta \left(\frac{du}{dx} dx + \frac{du}{dy} dy + \frac{du}{dz} dz + ... \right),$$

in the following manner;

$$\delta du = \left(\delta \frac{du}{dx} + \frac{du}{dx} \frac{d\delta x}{dx} + \frac{du}{dy} \frac{d\delta y}{dx} + \frac{du}{dz} \frac{d\delta z}{dx} + ... \right) dx$$

$$+ \left(\delta \frac{du}{dy} + \frac{du}{dx} \frac{d\delta x}{dy} + \frac{du}{dy} \frac{d\delta y}{dy} + \frac{du}{dz} \frac{d\delta z}{dy} + ... \right) dy$$

$$+ \left(\delta \frac{du}{dz} + \frac{du}{dx} \frac{d\delta x}{dz} + \frac{du}{dy} \frac{d\delta y}{dz} + \frac{du}{dz} \frac{d\delta z}{dz} + ... \right) dz$$

$$+ ... \,;$$

Now equate the coefficients of the arbitrary quantities dx, dy, dz, ... and we have

$$\delta\frac{du}{dx} = \frac{d\delta u}{dx} - \frac{du}{dx}\frac{d\delta x}{dx} - \frac{du}{dy}\frac{d\delta y}{dx} - \frac{du}{dz}\frac{d\delta z}{dx} - \dots,$$

$$\delta\frac{du}{dy} = \frac{d\delta u}{dy} - \frac{du}{dx}\frac{d\delta x}{dy} - \frac{du}{dy}\frac{d\delta y}{dy} - \frac{du}{dz}\frac{d\delta z}{dy} - \dots,$$

$$\delta\frac{du}{dz} = \frac{d\delta u}{dz} - \frac{du}{dx}\frac{d\delta x}{dz} - \frac{du}{dy}\frac{d\delta y}{dz} - \frac{du}{dz}\frac{d\delta z}{dz} - \dots,$$

$$\dots\dots\dots\dots\dots\dots\dots\dots\dots$$

It is easy to give to these expressions the following form;

$$\delta\frac{du}{dx} = \frac{d^2u}{dx^2}\,\delta x + \frac{d^2u}{dx\,dy}\,\delta y + \frac{d^2u}{dx\,dz}\,\delta z + \dots$$
$$+ \frac{d\left(\delta u - \dfrac{du}{dx}\delta x - \dfrac{du}{dy}\delta y - \dfrac{du}{dz}\delta z - \dots\right)}{dx},$$

$$\delta\frac{du}{dy} = \frac{d^2u}{dx\,dy}\,\delta x + \frac{d^2u}{dy^2}\,\delta y + \frac{d^2u}{dy\,dz}\,\delta z + \dots$$
$$+ \frac{d\left(\delta u - \dfrac{du}{dx}\delta x - \dfrac{du}{dy}\delta y - \dfrac{du}{dz}\delta z - \dots\right)}{dy},$$

$$\delta\frac{du}{dz} = \frac{d^2u}{dx\,dz}\,\delta x + \frac{d^2u}{dy\,dz}\,\delta y + \frac{d^2u}{dz^2}\,\delta z + \dots$$
$$+ \frac{d\left(\delta u - \dfrac{du}{dx}\delta x - \dfrac{du}{dy}\delta y - \dfrac{du}{dz}\delta z - \dots\right)}{dz},$$

$$\dots\dots\dots\dots\dots\dots\dots\dots\dots\dots\dots\dots$$

For abbreviation put

$$\delta u = \frac{du}{dx}\,\delta x + \frac{du}{dy}\,\delta y + \frac{du}{dz}\,\delta z + \dots + Du;$$

thus

$$\delta\frac{du}{dx} = \frac{d^2u}{dx^2}\,\delta x + \frac{d^2u}{dx\,dy}\,\delta y + \frac{d^2u}{dx\,dz}\,\delta z + \dots + \frac{d\,Du}{dx},$$

$$\delta \frac{du}{dy} = \frac{d^2u}{dx\,dy}\,\delta x + \frac{d^2u}{dy^2}\,\delta y + \frac{d^2u}{dy\,dz}\,\delta z + \ldots + \frac{d\,Du}{dy},$$

$$\delta \frac{du}{dz} = \frac{d^2u}{dx\,dz}\,\delta x + \frac{d^2u}{dy\,dz}\,\delta y + \frac{d^2u}{dz^2}\,\delta z + \ldots + \frac{d\,Du}{dz},$$

. . . .

We may remark that the terms which do not involve Du in the preceding formulæ are the ordinary differentials of the quantities $u,\ \dfrac{du}{dx},\ \dfrac{du}{dy},\ \dfrac{du}{dz},\ \ldots$ considered as functions of $x,\ y,\ z,\ \ldots$ and supposing that the differentials of $x,\ y,\ z,\ \ldots$ are $\delta x,\ \delta y,\ \delta z,\ \ldots$ If then we denote by the symbol Δ the differential of a function of $x,\ y,\ z,\ \ldots$ due to the increments $\delta x,\ \delta y,\ \delta z,\ \ldots$ we shall have

$$\delta u = \Delta u + Du,$$

$$\delta \frac{du}{dx} = \Delta \frac{du}{dx} + \frac{d\,Du}{dx},$$

$$\delta \frac{du}{dy} = \Delta \frac{du}{dy} + \frac{d\,Du}{dy},$$

$$\delta \frac{du}{dz} = \Delta \frac{du}{dz} + \frac{d\,Du}{dz},$$

. . . .

It is not difficult to find the variations of the higher differential coefficients $\dfrac{d^2u}{dx^2},\ \dfrac{d^2u}{dx\,dy},\ \ldots$; it may be easily seen that we shall have generally,

$$\delta \frac{d^ru}{dx^l\,dy^m\,dz^n\ldots} = \Delta \frac{d^ru}{dx^l\,dy^m\,dz^n\ldots} + \frac{d^r\,Du}{dx^l\,dy^m\,dz^n\ldots}.$$

[The method of this Article appears less clear than that in Art. 124; there is a want of *definition* of what is meant by such a symbol as $\delta \dfrac{du}{dx}$. In the first method definition is given and consequences deduced from it; the formulæ given in the present Article may be obtained by the first method. An additional advantage in the first method is, that we can see more easily to what order of approximation the results are true.]

120. What has now been given will suffice for finding the variation of a function U which involves u, x, y, z, ... and the differential coefficients of u with respect to the variables. We have only to take the differential of U supposing that all the quantities x, y, z, ... u, $\dfrac{du}{dx}$, ... receive their variations denoted by the symbol δ. But since the variations of each of the quantities u, $\dfrac{du}{dx}$, ... is composed of two indefinitely small quantities, we may by the principles of the Differential Calculus augment x, y, z, ... by δx, δy, δz, ... and give to u, $\dfrac{du}{dx}$, ... at first only the former parts of their variations, namely Δu, $\Delta \dfrac{du}{dx}$, ... Thus we shall obtain an increment for U which will form the first part of the variation δU. Then without changing x, y, z, ... we can augment u and its differential coefficients by the second part of their variations Du, $\dfrac{d\,Du}{dx}$, ... ; the increment which the function U will in consequence receive will form the second part of the variation of U.

The first part of the variation δU will evidently be

$$\frac{dU}{dx}\,\delta x + \frac{dU}{dy}\,\delta y + \frac{dU}{dz}\,\delta z + \dots,$$

where $\dfrac{dU}{dx}$ means the *complete* differential coefficient of U with respect to x, and $\dfrac{dU}{dy}$ the *complete* differential coefficient with respect to y, and so on. Let us denote by DU the second part of the variation δU; this part is due to the increment Du of the quantity u, this increment being ascribed to u wherever it occurs in U. We shall then have

$$\delta U = \frac{dU}{dx}\,\delta x + \frac{dU}{dy}\,\delta y + \frac{dU}{dz}\,\delta z + \dots + DU.$$

We abstain from writing the development of the differential DU.

127. Let us now proceed to find the variation of the definite integral

$$V = \int U\,dx\,dy\,dz\,\ldots$$

taken for all the values of x, y, z ... which satisfy the inequality

$$L < 0,$$

L being a function of x, y, z, ...

The variation of the integral $\int U\,dx\,dy\,dz$ ... is obviously equal to the sum of the variations of all its differential elements; thus in order to obtain δV we have only to take the integral of the variation $\delta(U\,dx\,dy\,dz\,\ldots)$; this will give

$$\delta V = \int \delta(U\,dx\,dy\,dz\,\ldots).$$

But by the principle of the Differential Calculus

$$\delta(U\,dx\,dy\,dz\,\ldots) = \delta U\,dx\,dy\,dz\,\ldots + U\delta(dx\,dy\,dz\,\ldots);$$

thus by the preceding article

$$\delta(U\,dx\,dy\,dz\,\ldots) = \left(\frac{dU}{dx}\delta x + \frac{dU}{dy}\delta y + \frac{dU}{dz}\delta z + \ldots\right)dx\,dy\,dz\,\ldots$$
$$+ U\delta(dx\,dy\,dz\,\ldots) + DU\,dx\,dy\,dz\,\ldots$$

Therefore

$$\delta V = \int \left\{\frac{dU}{dx}\delta x + \frac{dU}{dy}\delta y + \frac{dU}{dz}\delta z + \ldots + U\frac{\delta(dx\,dy\,dz\,\ldots)}{dx\,dy\,dz\,\ldots}\right\}dx\,dy\,dz\,\ldots$$
$$+ \int DU\,dx\,dy\,dz\,\ldots$$

We shall presently prove that

$$\delta(dx\,dy\,dz\,\ldots) = \left(\frac{d\delta x}{dx} + \frac{d\delta y}{dy} + \frac{d\delta z}{dz} + \ldots\right)dx\,dy\,dz\,\ldots;$$

hence it will follow that

$$\delta V = \int \left\{\frac{d(U\delta x)}{dx} + \frac{d(U\delta y)}{dy} + \frac{d(U\delta z)}{dz} + \ldots\right\}dx\,dy\,dz\,\ldots$$
$$+ \int DU\,dx\,dy\,dz\,\ldots$$

The differential coefficient $\dfrac{d(U\delta x)}{dx}$ is *total* with respect to x, and $\dfrac{d(U\delta y)}{dy}$ is *total* with respect to y, and so on.

128.　We will now investigate the variation $\delta\,(dx\,dy\,dz\,...)$. Suppose $x + \delta x = X$, $y + \delta y = Y$, $z + \delta z = Z$, $...$; we shall have

$$\delta\,(dx\,dy\,dz\,...) = dX\,dY\,dZ\,... - dx\,dy\,dz\,...$$

The quantities X, Y, Z... are functions of x, y, z,...; to obtain dX we have only to differentiate X in the ordinary way and suppose Y, Z, ... constant. Thus

$$dX = \frac{dX}{dx}\,dx + \frac{dX}{dy}\,dy + \frac{dX}{dz}\,dz + ...,$$

$$0 = \frac{dY}{dx}\,dx + \frac{dY}{dy}\,dy + \frac{dY}{dz}\,dz + ...,$$

$$0 = \frac{dZ}{dx}\,dx + \frac{dZ}{dy}\,dy + \frac{dZ}{dz}\,dz + ...,$$

$$..$$

From these we shall derive

$$dX = \frac{S\left(\dfrac{dX}{dx}\cdot\dfrac{dY}{dy}\cdot\dfrac{dZ}{dz}\,...\right)dx}{S\left(\dfrac{dY}{dy}\cdot\dfrac{dZ}{dz}\,...\right)}.$$

We have followed the notation of M. Cauchy, and denoted by

$$S\,(a,\,b,\,c\,...\,)$$

the result of eliminating the quantities p, q, r, ... which satisfy the equations

$$0 = ap + a_1 q + a_2 r + ...,$$
$$0 = bp + b_1 q + b_2 r + ...,$$
$$0 = cp + c_1 q + c_2 r + ...,$$
$$......................$$

We suppose that the term $ab_1 c_2 ...$ in the result is taken with the positive sign.

To obtain dY we must differentiate Y and suppose

$$dX = 0,\quad dZ = 0, ...;$$

that is, $dx = 0$, $dZ = 0$, ...; thus

$$dY = \frac{dY}{dy}\, dy + \frac{dY}{dz}\, dz + \ldots$$

$$0 = \frac{dZ}{dy}\, dy + \frac{dZ}{dz}\, dz + \ldots$$

$$\ldots\ldots\ldots\ldots\ldots\ldots\ldots\ldots$$

whence
$$dY = \frac{S\left(\frac{dY}{dy} \cdot \frac{dZ}{dz} \ldots\right) dy}{S\left(\frac{dZ}{dz} \ldots\right)}.$$

We shall obtain in the same manner

$$dZ = \frac{S\left(\frac{dZ}{dz} \ldots\right) dz}{S(\ldots)},$$

and so on. The denominator of the last differential will be unity; for if, for example, Z were the last variable, we should have had

$$dZ = \frac{dZ}{dz}\, dz.$$

Now form the product $dX \cdot dY \cdot dZ \ldots$; we have

$$dX \cdot dY \cdot dZ \ldots = S\left(\frac{dX}{dx} \cdot \frac{dY}{dy} \cdot \frac{dZ}{dz} \ldots\right) dx\, dy\, dz \ldots;$$

therefore

$$\delta\,(dx\, dy\, dz \ldots) = \left\{ S\left(\frac{dX}{dx} \cdot \frac{dY}{dy} \cdot \frac{dZ}{dz} \ldots\right) - 1 \right\} dx\, dy\, dz \ldots$$

The principles of Differential Analysis require that in calculating the coefficient

$$S\left(\frac{dX}{dx} \cdot \frac{dY}{dy} \cdot \frac{dZ}{dz} \ldots\right) - 1$$

we should take account only of infinitely small quantities of the first order, because $\dfrac{\delta\,(dx\, dy\, dz \ldots)}{dx\, dy\, dz \ldots}$ is an indefinitely small quantity of the first order. But except the term $\dfrac{dX}{dx} \cdot \dfrac{dY}{dy} \cdot \dfrac{dZ}{dz} \ldots$ all the terms in $\delta\left(\dfrac{dX}{dx} \cdot \dfrac{dY}{dy} \cdot \dfrac{dZ}{dz} \ldots\right)$ are of the second order at least; thus the following is true as far as quantities of the first order:

$$\delta\left(\frac{dX}{dx} \cdot \frac{dY}{dy} \cdot \frac{dZ}{dz} \ldots\right) = \frac{dX}{dx} \cdot \frac{dY}{dy} \cdot \frac{dZ}{dz} \ldots$$

Hence $\quad \delta\,(dx\,dy\,dz\ldots) = \left(\dfrac{dX}{dx}\dfrac{dY}{dy}\dfrac{dZ}{dz} \ldots - 1\right) dx\,dy\,dz \ldots$

Restore for X, Y, Z, ... their values $x + \delta x$, $y + \delta y$, $z + \delta z$, ...; we shall then have

$$\delta\,(dx\,dy\,dz\ldots) = \left\{\left(1 + \frac{d\delta x}{dx}\right)\left(1 + \frac{d\delta y}{dy}\right)\left(1 + \frac{d\delta z}{dz}\right) \ldots - 1\right\} dx\,dy\,dz \ldots$$

Therefore retaining only small quantities of the first order

$$\delta\,(dx\,dy\,dz\ldots) = \left(\frac{d\delta x}{dx} + \frac{d\delta y}{dy} + \frac{d\delta z}{dz} + \ldots\right) dx\,dy\,dz \ldots$$

[This result may be simply found as follows; suppose for example three variables, and take the equations

$$dX = \frac{dX}{dx} dx + \frac{dX}{dy} dy + \frac{dX}{dz} dz,$$

$$0 = \frac{dY}{dx} dx + \frac{dY}{dy} dy + \frac{dY}{dz} dz,$$

$$0 = \frac{dZ}{dx} dx + \frac{dZ}{dy} dy + \frac{dZ}{dz} dz,$$

The second and third equations shew that dy and dz are of the second order compared with dx; for $\dfrac{dY}{dx}$ and $\dfrac{dZ}{dx}$ are indefinitely small while $\dfrac{dY}{dy}$ and $\dfrac{dZ}{dz}$ are finite. Hence if we reject terms of the *third* order

$$dX = \frac{dX}{dx} dx.$$

Similar equations hold for dY and dZ; therefore

$$dX\,dY\,dZ = \frac{dX}{dx} \cdot \frac{dY}{dy} \cdot \frac{dZ}{dz} dx\,dy\,dz$$

where terms of the second order are rejected.   Thus

$$\delta\,(dx\,dy\,dz) = \left\{\left(1 + \frac{d\delta x}{dx}\right)\left(1 + \frac{d\delta y}{dy}\right)\left(1 + \frac{d\delta z}{dz}\right) - 1\right\}\,dx\,dy\,dz.$$

With respect to some of the points suggested by this article the student is referred to Chapter XI. of the Treatise on the Integral Calculus.]

129.   Before proceeding further we will determine the limits of the variables x, y, z ... in the integral

$$\int U\,dx\,dy\,dz\,...$$

when extended to all the values of x, y, z ... which satisfy the inequality $L < 0$ so that at the limits of the integral we have $L = 0$. We propose to integrate first with respect to x, then with respect to y, then with respect to z, and so on.

Assume that the equation $L = 0$ when solved with respect to x gives only two values for this variable x_0 and x_1.   These values are the limits of the variable x, and supposing that the function L continues negative for values of x comprised between x_0 and x_1, we must integrate the expression

$$\int U\,dx\,dy\,dz\,...$$

from $x = x_0$ to $x = x_1$, supposing x_0 less than x_1.   As to the quantities y, z, ... we must ascribe to them all values which allow x_0 and x_1 to be real, and we must exclude all values which make x_0 and x_1 imaginary; but in passing from real to imaginary values the roots x_0 and x_1 become equal, as we know from the theory of equations; therefore at the limits of y, z, ... we shall have simultaneously

$$L = 0, \quad \frac{dL}{dx} = 0.$$

If we eliminate x between these two equations we shall obtain an equation in y, z, ...; this equation we will suppose gives two values of y, say y_0 and y_1, which will be the limits between which we must integrate $\int U\,dx\,dy\,dz\,...$ with respect to y; we take the integral from the less of the two values y_0 and y_1 to the greater.

We shall arrive at the same result in the following manner; after having integrated with respect to x we ought to integrate with respect to y obviously from the least to the greatest value of this variable, supposing x and y connected by the equation $L = 0$, and considering $z, \ldots$ as constant; differentiating on this hypothesis we have

$$0 = \frac{dL}{dx} + \frac{dL}{dy} \frac{dy}{dx};$$

in order that y may be a maximum we must have $\frac{dy}{dx} = 0$, and this gives to determine the limit of y the equation $\frac{dL}{dx} = 0$; this coincides with the result already found.

To obtain the limits with respect to z we must treat the equation which results by eliminating x between $L = 0$ and $\frac{dL}{dx} = 0$ precisely as we have already treated the equation $L = 0$. But we may suppose that this result of the elimination of the variable x between $L = 0$ and $\frac{dL}{dx} = 0$ is the equation $L = 0$, in which we put for x its value found from $\frac{dL}{dx} = 0$. In order then to find the limits of z we must differentiate the equation $L = 0$ with respect to y, considering x as a function of y; this will give

$$\frac{dL}{dy} + \frac{dL}{dx} \frac{dx}{dy} = 0,$$

and therefore $\frac{dL}{dy} = 0$ since $\frac{dL}{dx} = 0$. By eliminating y between $L = 0$ and $\frac{dL}{dy} = 0$ we shall obtain an equation which will furnish the limits for z. By proceeding in this way we shall find the limits for all the variables which occur in the integral

$$\int U \, dx \, dy \, dz \ldots$$

Thus we have the following conclusion; the limits of x are given immediately by the solution of the equation $L = 0$ with respect to x; the limits of y are determined by solving with respect to y the equation which results from the elimination of x between $L = 0$ and $\dfrac{dL}{dx} = 0$; the limits of z are determined by solving with respect to z the equation which results from the elimination of x and y between

$$L = 0, \ \frac{dL}{dx} = 0, \ \frac{dL}{dy} = 0;$$

and so on.

We have supposed that the equations relative to the limits of the integral

$$\int U\, dx\, dy\, dz \ ...$$

give only two values for each of the quantities $x, y, z, ...$ but it would be easy, from what has been given, to treat the case where the equations have more than two roots. The number of limiting values for each variable $x, y, z, ...$ including if necessary infinite values, must be an *even* number.

130. We now return to the variation

$$\delta V = \int\!\!\int \left\{ \frac{d\,(U\delta x)}{dx} + \frac{d\,(U\delta y)}{dy} + \frac{d\,(U\delta z)}{dz} + ... \right\}\, dx\, dy\, dz \ ...$$
$$+ \int D U\, dx\, dy\, dz \ ...;$$

for shortness put $U\delta x = P, \ U\delta y = Q, \ U\delta z = R, ...;$ we shall have then

$$\delta V = \int \left(\frac{dP}{dx} + \frac{dQ}{dy} + \frac{dR}{dz} + ... \right) dx\, dy\, dz \ ... \ + \int D U\, dx\, dy\, dz \ ....$$

Consider first the part

$$\int \left(\frac{dP}{dx} + \frac{dQ}{dy} + \frac{dR}{dz} + ... \right) dx\, dy\, dz \ ...$$

of the preceding variation; suppose that x_1 is the greater of the two values x_0 and x_1 which are obtained by solving the equation $L = 0$ with respect to x. We have

$$\int \frac{dP}{dx}\, dx\, dy\, dz \ ... \ = \int (P_1 - P_0)\, dy\, dz \ ...$$

By P_1 we denote the value of P when x_1 is put in it for x, and by P_0 the value of P when x_0 is put in it for x.

Since the function L has a positive value before it vanishes when $x = x_0$, and a negative value before it vanishes when $x = x_1$, it follows that the differential coefficient $\dfrac{dL}{dx}$ is negative for $x = x_0$, and is positive for $x = x_1$; therefore if we take the radical $\sqrt{\left(\dfrac{dL^2}{dx^2}\right)}$ positively we shall have

$$- P_0 = \frac{P\dfrac{dL}{dx}}{\sqrt{\left(\dfrac{dL^2}{dx^2}\right)}} \qquad \text{when } x = x_0,$$

$$P_1 = \frac{P\dfrac{dL}{dx}}{\sqrt{\left(\dfrac{dL^2}{dx^2}\right)}} \qquad \text{when } x = x_1.$$

Substitute these values in the equation

$$\int \frac{dP}{dx}\, dx\, dy\, dz \ldots \quad = \int (P_1 - P_0)\, dy\, dz \ldots ,$$

and we shall have

$$\int \frac{dP}{dx}\, dx\, dy\, dz \ldots \quad = \int \frac{P\dfrac{dL}{dx}}{\sqrt{\left(\dfrac{dL^2}{dx^2}\right)}}\, dy\, dz \ldots ,$$

the integral on the right-hand side includes only those values of x, y, z, ... which satisfy the equation $L = 0$.

In the same way we shall obtain

$$\int \frac{dQ}{dy}\, dx\, dy\, dz \ldots \quad = \int \frac{Q\dfrac{dL}{dy}}{\sqrt{\left(\dfrac{dL^2}{dy^2}\right)}}\, dx\, dz \ldots ,$$

$$\int \frac{dR}{dz}\, dx\, dy\, dz \ldots \quad = \int \frac{R\dfrac{dL}{dz}}{\sqrt{\left(\dfrac{dL^2}{dz^2}\right)}}\, dx\, dy \ldots$$

Thus,

$$(A) \qquad \int \left(\frac{dP}{dx} + \frac{dQ}{dy} + \frac{dR}{dz} + \ldots \right) dx\, dy\, dz \ldots$$

$$= \int \frac{P \frac{dL}{dx}}{\sqrt{\left(\frac{dL}{dx^2}\right)}} dy\, dz \ldots \quad + \int \frac{Q \frac{dL}{dy}}{\sqrt{\left(\frac{dL}{dy^2}\right)}} dx\, dz \ldots$$

$$+ \int \frac{R \frac{dL}{dz}}{\sqrt{\left(\frac{dL}{dz^2}\right)}} dx\, dy \ldots + \ldots$$

The integrals on the right-hand side must be taken for those values of x, y, z, ... which satisfy the equation $L = 0$. Consider two of these integrals, for example,

$$\int \frac{P \frac{dL}{dx}}{\sqrt{\left(\frac{dL}{dx^2}\right)}} dy\, dz \ldots \quad \text{and} \quad \int \frac{Q \frac{dL}{dy}}{\sqrt{\left(\frac{dL}{dy^2}\right)}} dx\, dz \ldots ;$$

from the preceding article we may easily see that their limits with respect to z, ... are the same; further we have

$$\frac{dL}{dx} dx + \frac{dL}{dy} dy = 0$$

for all the elements of these integrals in which the variables z, ... remain the same; so that the differentials $\frac{dL}{dx} dx$ and $\frac{dL}{dy} dy$ are equal, neglecting the sign. Thus if we take the increments dx and dy positively and also the radicals, we have

$$\frac{dy}{\sqrt{\left(\frac{dL}{dx^2}\right)}} = \frac{dx}{\sqrt{\left(\frac{dL}{dy^2}\right)}},$$

and therefore multiplying by dz ...,

$$\frac{dy\, dz \ldots}{\sqrt{\left(\frac{dL}{dx^2}\right)}} = \frac{dx\, dz \ldots}{\sqrt{\left(\frac{dL}{dy^2}\right)}}.$$

It is easy to deduce that in general we shall have

$$\frac{dy\,ds\ldots}{\sqrt{\left(\frac{dL^2}{dx^2}\right)}} = \frac{dx\,dz\ldots}{\sqrt{\left(\frac{dL^2}{dy^2}\right)}} = \frac{dx\,dy\ldots}{\sqrt{\left(\frac{dL^2}{dz^2}\right)}} = \ldots.$$

Hence, if for shortness we put

$$ds = \sqrt{(dy^2\,dz^2\ldots + dx^2\,dz^2\ldots + dx^2\,dy^2\ldots + \ldots)},$$

$$\frac{dy\,dz\ldots}{\sqrt{\left(\frac{dL^2}{dx^2}\right)}} = \frac{dx\,dz\ldots}{\sqrt{\left(\frac{dL^2}{dy^2}\right)}} = \frac{dx\,dy\ldots}{\sqrt{\left(\frac{dL^2}{dz^2}\right)}} = \ldots$$

$$= \frac{ds}{\sqrt{\left(\frac{dL^2}{dx^2} + \frac{dL^2}{dy^2} + \frac{dL^2}{dz^2} + \ldots\right)}}.$$

By means of these equalities, equation (A) will become

$$(\text{B})\ldots \int\left(\frac{dP}{dx} + \frac{dQ}{dy} + \frac{dR}{dz} + \ldots\right) dx\,dy\,dz\ldots$$

$$= \int \frac{\left(P\frac{dL}{dx} + Q\frac{dL}{dy} + R\frac{dL}{dz} + \ldots\right) ds}{\sqrt{\left(\frac{dL^2}{dx^2} + \frac{dL^2}{dy^2} + \frac{dL^2}{dz^2} + \ldots\right)}}.$$

We may, in order to facilitate the integration of the differential

$$\frac{\left(P\frac{dL}{dx} + Q\frac{dL}{dy} + R\frac{dL}{dz} + \ldots\right) ds}{\sqrt{\left(\frac{dL^2}{dx^2} + \frac{dL^2}{dy^2} + \frac{dL^2}{dz^2} + \ldots\right)}},$$

instead of the variables x, y, z, ... connected by the equation $L = 0$ introduce other variables a, b, c, ... which are independent.

We must transform by the usual method all the elements $dy\,dz\ldots$, $dx\,dz\ldots$, $dx\,dy\ldots$, into elements proportional to the product $da\,db\ldots$; we shall have such results as $dy\,dz\ldots = A\,da\,db\ldots$, $dx\,dz\ldots = B\,da\,db\ldots$, $dx\,dy\ldots = C\,da\,db\ldots$, where A, B, C,..., are finite functions of a, b, ...; thus

$$ds = da\,db\ldots \sqrt{(A^2 + B^2 + C^2 + \ldots)}.$$

. If for example we wish to integrate with respect to the variables y, z, ... we must observe with respect to the elements $dx\,dz$ ..., $dx\,dy$ ..., ... that we must take the differential of the variable x in the first considering y alone as variable, in the second considering z alone as variable, and so on; hence

$$dx\,dz\,... = \frac{dx}{dy}\,dy\,dz\,...,\quad dx\,dy\,... = \frac{dx}{dz}\,dy\,dz\,...,\,...;\ \text{thus}$$

$$dz = dy\,dz\,...\sqrt{\left(1 + \frac{dx^2}{dy^2} + \frac{dx^2}{dz^2} + ...\right)}$$

$$= dy\,dz\,...\frac{\sqrt{\left(\frac{dL^2}{dx^2} + \frac{dL^2}{dy^2} + \frac{dL^2}{dz^2} + ...\right)}}{\sqrt{\left(\frac{dL^2}{dx^2}\right)}},$$

so that

$$(C)\ ...\int\left(\frac{dP}{dx} + \frac{dQ}{dy} + \frac{dR}{dz} + ...\right)dx\,dy\,dz\,...$$

$$= \int\frac{\left(P\frac{dL}{dx} + Q\frac{dL}{dy} + R\frac{dL}{dz} + ...\right)dy\,dz\,...}{\sqrt{\left(\frac{dL^2}{dx^2}\right)}}.$$

In the formula (B) restore for P, Q, R, ... their values $U\delta x$, $U\delta y$, $U\delta z$, ...; we shall then have

$$\int\left\{\frac{d\,(U\delta x)}{dx} + \frac{d\,(U\delta y)}{dy} + \frac{d\,(U\delta z)}{dz} + ...\right\}dx\,dy\,dz\,....$$

$$= \int\frac{U\left(\frac{dL}{dx}\delta x + \frac{dL}{dy}\delta y + \frac{dL}{dz}\delta z + ...\right)ds}{\sqrt{\left(\frac{dL^2}{dx^2} + \frac{dL^2}{dy^2} + \frac{dL^2}{dz^2} + ...\right)}},$$

that is,

$$\int\left\{\frac{d\,(U\delta x)}{dx} + \frac{d\,(U\delta y)}{dy} + \frac{d\,(U\delta z)}{dz} + ...\right\}dx\,dy\,dz\,....$$

$$= \int\frac{U\delta L\,ds}{\sqrt{\left(\frac{dL^2}{dx^2} + \frac{dL^2}{dy^2} + \frac{dL^2}{dz^2} + ...\right)}};$$

and therefore

$$\delta V = \int \frac{U\delta L\, ds}{\sqrt{\left(\dfrac{dL^2}{dx^2} + \dfrac{dL^2}{dy^2} + \dfrac{dL^2}{dz^2} + \dots\right)}} + \int D U\, dx\, dy\, dz \dots.$$

131.   We now proceed to indicate the reductions to be made in the term $\int D U\, dx\, dy\, dz \dots$ of the variation δV; these reductions consist in making as many as possible of the partial differential coefficients of the quantity Du disappear under the integral sign.

By means of the formula (B) of the preceding article it will be easy to replace the integral $\int D U\, dx\, dy\, dz \dots$ by the sum of the two integrals $\int WDu\, dx\, dy\, dz \dots$ and $\int \Theta\, ds$, the first of which like $\int D U\, dx\, dy\, dz \dots$ relates to all the values of $x,\ y,\ z, \dots$ which satisfy the inequality $L < 0$, and the second of which comprises only those values of the variables which satisfy the equation $L = 0$. The function W does not include the variation Du; on the other hand, the function Θ does include it as well as its partial differential coefficients with respect to $x,\ y,\ z, \dots$; the differential ds is the same as in the preceding section; that is,

$$ds = \sqrt{(dy^2 dz^2 \dots + dz^2 dx^2 \dots + dx^2 dy^2 \dots + \dots)}.$$

Thus we shall have

$$\int D U\, dx\, dy\, ds \dots = \int WDu\, dx\, dy\, ds \dots + \int \Theta\, ds;$$

and therefore

$$\delta V = \int WDu\, dx\, dy\, ds \dots + \int \frac{U\delta L\, ds}{\sqrt{\left(\dfrac{dL^2}{dx^2} + \dfrac{dL^2}{dy^2} + \dfrac{dL^2}{dz^2} + \dots\right)}} + \int \Theta\, ds.$$

The integrals $\int WDu\, dx\, dy\, dz \dots$

and $$\int \frac{U\delta L\, ds}{\sqrt{\left(\dfrac{dL^2}{dx^2} + \dfrac{dL^2}{dy^2} + \dfrac{dL^2}{dz^2} + \dots\right)}}$$

are not susceptible of any reduction, but the integral $\int \Theta\, ds$ may be still reduced.

To effect the reduction of $\int \Theta ds$, we must first of all replace the variables x, y, z, ... which are connected by the equation $L = 0$ by other quantities a, b, ... which are independent. The number of these quantities a, b, ... must be one less than the number of the original variables x, y, z, ...

Now considering x, y, z, ... as functions of a, b, ... let us transform the element ds into an element proportional to the product $da\, db\,...$; we shall thus obtain

$$ds = K\, da\, db\, ...$$

where K is a finite function of a, b, ... Let us also transform the differential coefficients $\dfrac{dDu}{dx}$, $\dfrac{dDu}{dy}$, $\dfrac{dDu}{dz}$, ... $\dfrac{d^2Du}{dx^2}$, $\dfrac{d^2Du}{dx\,dy}$, ... into $\dfrac{dDu}{da}$, $\dfrac{dDu}{db}$, ... $\dfrac{d^2Du}{da^2}$, $\dfrac{d^2Du}{da\,db}$, ...; we shall have for this end

$$\frac{dDu}{da} = \frac{dDu}{dx}\frac{dx}{da} + \frac{dDu}{dy}\frac{dy}{da} + \frac{dDu}{dz}\frac{dz}{da} + ...$$

$$\frac{dDu}{db} = \frac{dDu}{dx}\frac{dx}{db} + \frac{dDu}{dy}\frac{dy}{db} + \frac{dDu}{dz}\frac{dz}{db} + ...$$

$$............................$$

$$\frac{d^2Du}{da^2} = \frac{d^2Du}{dx^2}\frac{dx^2}{da^2} + 2\frac{d^2Du}{dx\,dy}\frac{dx}{da}\frac{dy}{da} + ...$$

$$\frac{d^2Du}{da\,db} = \frac{d^2Du}{dx^2}\frac{dx}{da}\frac{dx}{db} + \frac{d^2Du}{dx\,dy}\left(\frac{dx}{da}\frac{dy}{db} + \frac{dx}{db}\frac{dy}{da}\right) + ...$$

$$............................$$

But since the preceding equations are not enough to obtain the value of all the quantities $\dfrac{dDu}{dx}$, $\dfrac{dDu}{dy}$, $\dfrac{dDu}{dz}$, ... $\dfrac{d^2Du}{dx^2}$, $\dfrac{d^2Du}{dx\,dy}$, ... some of these differential coefficients will remain indeterminate; the others can be expressed in terms of these and of the quantities $\dfrac{dDu}{da}$, $\dfrac{dDu}{db}$, ... $\dfrac{d^2Du}{da^2}$, $\dfrac{d^2Du}{da\,db}$, ... Instead of considering some of the differential coefficients $\dfrac{dDu}{dx}$, $\dfrac{dDu}{dy}$, $\dfrac{dDu}{dz}$, ... $\dfrac{d^2Du}{dx^2}$,

$\dfrac{d^2 Du}{dxdy}, \dots$ as indeterminate, it is convenient, for the sake of symmetry, to introduce as many linear functions $p, q, r, \dots$ of $\dfrac{dDu}{dx}$, $\dfrac{dDu}{dy}, \dfrac{dDu}{dz}, \dots \dfrac{d^2 Du}{dx^2}, \dfrac{d^2 Du}{dxdy}, \dots$ as will be necessary in order to express all the quantities $\dfrac{dDu}{dx}, \dfrac{dDu}{dy}, \dfrac{dDu}{dz}, \dots \dfrac{d^2 Du}{dx^2}, \dfrac{d^2 Du}{dxdy}, \dots$ in terms of $p, q, r, \dots, \dfrac{dDu}{da}, \dfrac{dDu}{db}, \dots \dfrac{d^2 Du}{da^2}, \dfrac{d^2 Du}{da\,db}, \dots$, and it will be the quantities $p, q, r, \dots$ which will remain arbitrary.

But the introduction of the quantities $p, q, r, \dots$ amounts to imagining among the variables $a, b, \dots$ one variable more ω; thus the number of quantities $\omega, a, b, \dots$ is equal to that of the variables $x, y, z, \dots$. Considering then $x, y, z, \dots$ as functions of $\omega, a, b, \dots$ we have the equations

$$\frac{dDu}{d\omega} = \frac{dDu}{dx}\frac{dx}{d\omega} + \frac{dDu}{dy}\frac{dy}{d\omega} + \frac{dDu}{dz}\frac{dz}{d\omega} + \dots,$$

$$\frac{dDu}{da} = \frac{dDu}{dx}\frac{dx}{da} + \frac{dDu}{dy}\frac{dy}{da} + \frac{dDu}{dz}\frac{dz}{da} + \dots,$$

$$\frac{dDu}{db} = \frac{dDu}{dx}\frac{dx}{db} + \frac{dDu}{dy}\frac{dy}{db} + \frac{dDu}{dz}\frac{dz}{db} + \dots,$$

$$\dots\dots\dots\dots\dots\dots\dots\dots$$

$$\frac{d^2 Du}{d\omega^2} = \frac{d^2 Du}{dx^2}\frac{dx^2}{d\omega^2} + 2\frac{d^2 Du}{dxdy}\frac{dx}{d\omega}\frac{dy}{d\omega} + \dots,$$

$$\frac{d^2 Du}{da\,d\omega} = \frac{d^2 Du}{dx^2}\frac{dx}{d\omega}\frac{dx}{da} + \frac{d^2 Du}{dxdy}\left(\frac{dx}{d\omega}\frac{dy}{da} + \frac{dx}{da}\frac{dy}{d\omega}\right) + \dots$$

$$\dots\dots\dots\dots\dots\dots\dots\dots$$

There will be as many of these equations as are necessary in order to express $\dfrac{dDu}{dx}, \dfrac{dDu}{dy}, \dfrac{dDu}{dz}, \dots \dfrac{d^2 Du}{dx^2}, \dfrac{d^2 Du}{dxdy}, \dots$ in terms of $\dfrac{dDu}{d\omega}$, $\dfrac{dDu}{da}$, $\dfrac{dDu}{db}$, ... $\dfrac{d^2Du}{d\omega^2}$, $\dfrac{d^2Du}{d\omega\,da}$, ...; but as the variable ω really does not exist we must look upon the differential coefficients $\dfrac{dx}{d\omega}$, $\dfrac{dy}{d\omega}$, $\dfrac{dz}{d\omega}$, ... as quantities which we may assume at our pleasure so as to simplify the expression of $\dfrac{dDu}{dx}$, $\dfrac{dDu}{dy}$, $\dfrac{dDu}{dz}$, ... $\dfrac{d^2Du}{dx^2}$, $\dfrac{d^2Du}{dx\,dy}$, ... The differential coefficients $\dfrac{dDu}{d\omega}$, $\dfrac{d^2Du}{d\omega^2}$, ... remain entirely indeterminate.

Having expressed the differential coefficients

$$\frac{dDu}{dx}, \quad \frac{dDu}{dy}, \quad \frac{dDu}{dz}, \quad \cdots \quad \frac{d^2Du}{dx^2}, \quad \frac{d^2Du}{dx\,dy}, \quad \cdots$$

in terms of

$$\frac{dDu}{d\omega}, \quad \frac{dDu}{da}, \quad \frac{dDu}{db}, \quad \cdots \quad \frac{d^2Du}{d\omega^2}, \quad \frac{d^2Du}{d\omega\,da}, \quad \cdots$$

we must put these values in the integral

$$\int \Theta\, ds = \int \Theta K\, da\, db \dots .$$

Then by making use of the formula (B) and putting for shortness

$$ds' = \sqrt{(db^2 \dots + da^2 \dots + \dots)}$$

we can replace the integral $\int \Theta K\, da\, db \dots$ by the sum

$$\int \left(PDu + Q\frac{dDu}{d\omega} + R\frac{d^2Du}{d\omega^2} + \dots \right) da\, db \dots + \int \Phi\, ds'.$$

The first of these integrals is not susceptible of reduction; the second may be reduced in the same way as $\int \Theta\, ds$.

Thus we shall have

$$\delta V = \int WDu\, dx\, dy\, dz \dots + \int \frac{U\delta L\, ds}{\sqrt{\left(\dfrac{dL^2}{dx^2} + \dfrac{dL^2}{dy^2} + \dfrac{dL^2}{dz^2} + \dots\right)}}$$

$$+ \int \left(PDu + Q\frac{dDu}{d\omega} + R\frac{d^2Du}{d\omega^2} + \dots \right) da\, db \dots + \int \Phi\, ds'.$$

We may treat the integral $\int \Phi ds'$ as we treated $\int \Theta ds$; we may decompose it into two integrals, the first of which is completely reduced, and the second is susceptible of reduction; proceeding in this way we shall exhaust the reductions which can be effected in the integrals, and thus the variation δV will be in the proper shape for applications.

132. Since the integral $\int \Theta ds$ of the preceding article relates to the values of $x, y, z, \dots$ which satisfy the equation $L = 0$, we may consider one of these quantities as a function of all the others, and the latter as independent. Suppose, for example, that we consider x to be a function of $y, z, \dots$; we shall have (by Article 130)

$$ds = \frac{\sqrt{\left(\dfrac{dL^2}{dx^2} + \dfrac{dL^2}{dy^2} + \dfrac{dL^2}{dz^2} + \dots\right)}}{\sqrt{\left(\dfrac{dL^2}{dx^2}\right)}} \, dy \, dz \dots ;$$

put for shortness

$$\frac{\Theta \sqrt{\left(\dfrac{dL^2}{dx^2} + \dfrac{dL^2}{dy^2} + \dfrac{dL^2}{dz^2} + \dots\right)}}{\sqrt{\left(\dfrac{dL^2}{dx^2}\right)}} = \Psi,$$

we shall have

$$\int \Theta ds = \int \Psi \, dy \, dz \dots .$$

We shall obtain the equation relative to the limits of $y, z, \dots$ by eliminating x between $L = 0$ and $\dfrac{dL}{dx} = 0$.

The function Ψ contains the partial differential coefficients

$$\frac{dDu}{dx}, \quad \frac{dDu}{dy}, \quad \frac{dDu}{dz}, \quad \dots \quad \frac{d^2Du}{dx^2}, \quad \frac{d^2Du}{dxdy}, \quad \dots$$

taken relatively to $x, y, z, \dots$ on the hypothesis that these variables are all independent; but after the differentiation we must put for x its value furnished by the equation $L = 0$. It is advisable to eliminate these partial differential coefficients as far as possible; to this end considering x as a function of $y, z, \ldots$ we shall have

$$\frac{dDu}{dy} = \left(\frac{dDu}{dy}\right) + \left(\frac{dDu}{dx}\right)\frac{dx}{dy},$$

$$\frac{dDu}{dz} = \left(\frac{dDu}{dz}\right) + \left(\frac{dDu}{dx}\right)\frac{dx}{dz},$$

$$\cdots\cdots\cdots\cdots\cdots\cdots\cdots\cdots$$

$$\frac{d\left(\frac{dDu}{dx}\right)}{dy} = \left(\frac{d^2Du}{dxdy}\right) + \left(\frac{d^2Du}{dx^2}\right)\frac{dx}{dy},$$

$$\frac{d\left(\frac{dDu}{dx}\right)}{dz} = \left(\frac{d^2Du}{dxdz}\right) + \left(\frac{d^2Du}{dx^2}\right)\frac{dx}{dz},$$

$$\cdots\cdots\cdots\cdots\cdots\cdots\cdots\cdots$$

$$\frac{d^2Du}{dy^2} = \left(\frac{d^2Du}{dy^2}\right) + 2\left(\frac{d^2Du}{dxdy}\right)\frac{dx}{dy} + \left(\frac{d^2Du}{dx^2}\right)\frac{dx^2}{dy^2} + \left(\frac{dDu}{dx}\right)\frac{d^2x}{dy^2},$$

$$\frac{d^2Du}{dydz} = \left(\frac{d^2Du}{dydz}\right) + \left(\frac{d^2Du}{dxdy}\right)\frac{dx}{dz} + \left(\frac{d^2Du}{dxdz}\right)\frac{dx}{dy}$$
$$+ \left(\frac{d^2Du}{dx^2}\right)\frac{dx}{dy}\frac{dx}{dz} + \left(\frac{dDu}{dx}\right)\frac{d^2x}{dydz},$$

$$\frac{d^2Du}{dz^2} = \left(\frac{d^2Du}{dz^2}\right) + 2\left(\frac{d^2Du}{dxdz}\right)\frac{dx}{dz} + \left(\frac{d^2Du}{dx^2}\right)\frac{dx^2}{dz^2} + \left(\frac{dDu}{dx}\right)\frac{d^2x}{dz^2}.$$

$$\cdots\cdots\cdots\cdots\cdots\cdots\cdots\cdots ;$$

the brackets indicate partial differential coefficients of Du taken on the supposition that $x, y, z, \ldots$ are independent.

From the preceding equations we deduce the following, putting for abbreviation v for $\left(\frac{dDu}{dx}\right)$ and $\left(\frac{dv}{dx}\right)$ for $\left(\frac{d^2Du}{dx^2}\right)$

$$\left(\frac{dDu}{dy}\right) = \frac{dDu}{dy} - v\frac{dx}{dy},$$

$$\left(\frac{dDu}{dz}\right) = \frac{dDu}{dz} - v\frac{dx}{dz},$$

$$\cdots\cdots\cdots\cdots\cdots\cdots$$

$$\left(\frac{d^2 Du}{dx\,dy}\right) = \frac{dv}{dy} - \left(\frac{dv}{dx}\right)\frac{dx}{dy},$$

$$\left(\frac{d^2 Du}{dx\,dz}\right) = \frac{dv}{dz} - \left(\frac{dv}{dx}\right)\frac{dx}{dz},$$

$$\cdots\cdots\cdots\cdots\cdots\cdots\cdots$$

$$\left(\frac{d^2 Du}{dy^2}\right) = \frac{d^2 Du}{dy^2} - 2\frac{dv}{dy}\frac{dx}{dy} + \left(\frac{dv}{dx}\right)\frac{dx^2}{dy^2} - v\frac{d^2 x}{dy^2},$$

$$\left(\frac{d^2 Du}{dy\,dz}\right) = \frac{d^2 Du}{dy\,dz} - \frac{dv}{dy}\frac{dx}{dz} - \frac{dv}{dz}\frac{dx}{dy} + \left(\frac{dv}{dx}\right)\frac{dx}{dy}\frac{dx}{dz} - v\frac{d^2 x}{dz\,dy},$$

$$\left(\frac{d^2 Du}{dz^2}\right) = \frac{d^2 Du}{dz^2} - 2\frac{dv}{dz}\frac{dx}{dz} + \left(\frac{dv}{dx}\right)\frac{dx^2}{dz^2} - v\frac{d^2 x}{dz^2}.$$

Put for $\dfrac{dx}{dy},\ \dfrac{dx}{dz},\ \cdots\ \dfrac{d^2 x}{dy^2},\ \dfrac{d^2 x}{dy\,dz},\ \dfrac{d^2 x}{dz^2},\ \cdots$

their values found from the equation $L=0$; thus

$$\frac{dL}{dx}\left(\frac{dDu}{dy}\right) = \frac{dL}{dx}\frac{dDu}{dy} + v\frac{dL}{dy},$$

$$\frac{dL}{dx}\left(\frac{dDu}{dz}\right) = \frac{dL}{dx}\frac{dDu}{dz} + v\frac{dL}{dz},$$

$$\cdots\cdots\cdots\cdots\cdots\cdots\cdots$$

$$\frac{dL}{dx}\left(\frac{d^2 Du}{dx\,dy}\right) = \frac{dL}{dx}\frac{dv}{dy} + \frac{dL}{dy}\left(\frac{dv}{dx}\right),$$

$$\frac{dL}{dx}\left(\frac{d^2 Du}{dx\,dz}\right) = \frac{dL}{dx}\frac{dv}{dz} + \frac{dL}{dz}\left(\frac{dv}{dx}\right),$$

$$\cdots\cdots\cdots\cdots\cdots\cdots\cdots$$

$$\frac{dL^2}{dx^2}\left(\frac{d^2 Du}{dy^2}\right) = \frac{dL}{dx}\left\{\frac{dL^2}{dx^2}\frac{d^2 Du}{dy^2} + 2\frac{dL}{dx}\frac{dL}{dy}\frac{dv}{dy} + \frac{dL^2}{dy^2}\left(\frac{dv}{dx}\right)\right\}$$
$$+ v\left\{\frac{dL^2}{dx^2}\frac{d^2 L}{dy^2} - 2\frac{dL}{dx}\frac{dL}{dy}\frac{d^2 L}{dx\,dy} + \frac{dL^2}{dy^2}\frac{d^2 L}{dx^2}\right\},$$

$$\frac{dL^2}{dx^2}\left(\frac{d^2 Du}{dy\,dz}\right) = \frac{dL}{dx}\left\{\frac{dL^2}{dx^2}\frac{d^2 Du}{dy\,dz} + \frac{dL}{dx}\frac{dL}{dz}\frac{dv}{dy} + \frac{dL}{dx}\frac{dL}{dy}\frac{dv}{dz} + \frac{dL}{dy}\frac{dL}{dz}\left(\frac{dv}{dx}\right)\right\}$$
$$+ v\left\{\frac{dL^2}{dx^2}\frac{d^2 L}{dy\,dz} - \frac{dL}{dx}\frac{dL}{dz}\frac{d^2 L}{dx\,dy} - \frac{dL}{dx}\frac{dL}{dy}\frac{d^2 L}{dx\,dz} + \frac{dL}{dy}\frac{dL}{dz}\frac{d^2 L}{dx^2}\right\},$$

$$\frac{dL'}{dx^2}\left(\frac{d^m Du}{dz^2}\right) = \frac{dL}{dx}\left\{\frac{dL'}{dx^2}\frac{d^m Du}{dz^2} + 2\frac{dL}{dx}\frac{dL}{dz}\frac{dv}{dz} + \frac{dL'}{dz^2}\left(\frac{dv}{dx}\right)\right\}$$

$$+ v\left\{\frac{dL'}{dx^2}\frac{d^m L}{dz^2} - 2\frac{dL}{dx}\frac{dL}{dz}\frac{d^m L}{dx\,dz} + \frac{dL'}{dx^2}\frac{d^m L}{dx^2}\right\},$$

Substitute these values in

$$\int \Theta\, ds = \int \Psi\, dy\, dz \dots$$

and use the formula (C) of Art. 130; thus we replace the integral $\int \Psi dy dz$ ... by the sum of two integrals, namely,

$$\int\left\{PDu + Q\left(\frac{dDu}{dx}\right) + R\left(\frac{d^m Du}{dx^2}\right) + \dots\right\} dy\, dz \dots + \int \Phi\, ds \dots;$$

the first of these integrals is completely reduced, the second is still susceptible of reduction. The second integral is with respect to the variables z, ... ; its limits depend on the equation which will be obtained by eliminating x and y between

$$L = 0, \quad \frac{dL}{dx} = 0, \quad \frac{dL}{dy} = 0.$$

In fact this integral resembles the integral $\int \Psi\, dy\, dz$ ... and may be treated in the same way.

We have merely indicated the transformations which must be applied to the portion $\int D U\, dx\, dy\, dz$ ... of the variation δV; because since these transformations reduce to integration by parts they belong to the Integral Calculus rather than to the method of variations. It is true that one of the fundamental principles of this method consists in removing as much as possible the differential coefficients of the variations which occur under the integral sign; but the calculus of variations only indicates this operation and refers the execution of it to the Integral Calculus.

CHAPTER VI.

DELAUNAY.

183. THE Academy of Sciences at Paris proposed the following as the subject of competition for their great mathematical prize in 1842; To find the limiting equations which must be combined with the indefinite equations in order to determine completely the maxima and minima of multiple integrals, the formulæ to be applied to triple integrals.

Four memoirs were sent in which were examined by MM. Liouville, Sturm, Poinsot, Duhamel, and Cauchy. The prize was awarded to M. Sarrus, and honourable mention was made of M. Delaunay.

With respect to M. Sarrus the judges said that, by the aid of a new symbol, which he calls a sign of substitution, he has established elegant and general formulæ which furnish, under a convenient form, the variations of multiple integrals and enable us to apply in all cases the process of integration by parts; he has thus contributed in a remarkable manner to the improvement of analysis, and deserves the great prize for mathematics.

With respect to M. Delaunay the judges said that, although he has not given to his processes all the generality which could be desired, yet he deserves honourable mention on account of the elegance of his formulæ, especially by reason of the applications which he has made of them, and his researches upon the distinction of maxima and minima.

(*Comptes Rendus*, Vol. XVIII. page 315.)

We shall give an account of the memoir of Delaunay in the present chapter, and of the memoir of Sarrus in the next chapter.

134. The memoir on the Calculus of Variations, by M. Charles Delaunay, was published in the 29th Cahier of the *Journal de l'Ecole Polytechnique*, which is dated 1843. The memoir extends over pages 37—120. Some introductory observations are given in the first seven pages. Delaunay refers to the method which was used in the solution of problems in the Calculus of Variations by those who first studied the subject; these writers considered any proposed integral as the sum of an indefinitely large number of terms depending on the values of the ordinates of the different points of a curve, and they investigated the change produced in the sum by varying one or more of the ordinates. By this method they obtained the differential equation of the required curve, but they did not obtain the equations which must hold at the limits. It was first shewn by Poisson in his memoir, which was presented to the Academy of Sciences in 1831, that the old method could be made to furnish the equations which must hold at the limits as well as the general differential equation.

The method of Lagrange gives the terms which exist at the limits in the case of a double or multiple integral, but not in a convenient form; they require transforming so as to shew how many arbitrary variations they involve, and to put them in a convenient shape for application. Poisson led the way in these researches, by giving in the memoir already cited the terms at the limits in the case of a double integral. Delaunay concludes his introductory observations with the following sentences. The Academy having proposed for competition the question of determining the terms at the limits for multiple integrals, I have investigated the subject, and I present this memoir as the result of my researches, which I hope leaves nothing to be desired. After my task was completely finished, I became acquainted with a memoir by M. Ostrogradsky, in which he overcomes the principal difficulties of the question proposed by the Academy; and his method is nearly the same as mine. But he stops there, and does not deduce from his method the formulæ which may be used in applications. M. Ostrogradsky and myself have taken for a guide in our researches the memoir of M. Poisson; the coincidence of our results proves then only one thing, and that is that the course had been so well traced out by the illustrious French mathematician, that it was impossible to wander from it, and thus to him must belong the merit of the subsequent discoveries. [The memoir by M. Ostrogradsky, to which allusion is made, is that which we have given in Chapter V.]

135. The first part of the memoir is called *variation of a definite integral*; it extends over pages 43—79. Delaunay's investigations apply to *multiple* integrals; his method will be sufficiently illustrated by the case of a *triple* integral, to which we shall confine ourselves, and we shall not use exactly the same notation as Delaunay.

Let there be a definite triple integral

$$\iiint dx\, dy\, dz\, K,$$

in which K is supposed a function of x, y, z, u, $\dfrac{du}{dx}$, $\dfrac{du}{dy}$, $\dfrac{du}{dz}$, $\dfrac{d^2u}{dx^2}$, $\dfrac{d^2u}{dx\,dy}$, $\ldots\ldots\ldots$

The integration is supposed to extend over all the values of x, y, and z which render a certain function $f(x, y, z)$ negative. We shall denote the triple integral by U.

If we put a given function of x, y, z in the place of u, and if $f(x, y, z)$ be a known function, then U can be calculated. It will be necessary to effect successive integrations, and to take each integral between appropriate limits, and these can be determined in the following manner.

The order of the successive integrations being arbitrary, we can suppose that we integrate first with respect to z, then with respect to y, and then with respect to x. In the first integration y and x are regarded as constants, and the integration with respect to z extends over all the values of z which render $f(x, y, z)$ negative; so that we must take for limits the values of z which satisfy

$$f(x, y, z) = 0\ldots\ldots\ldots\ldots\ldots\ldots\ldots\ldots\ldots\ldots\ldots(1).$$

The result of the first integration will be a known function of x and y and will form the element of a new integral with respect to these variables, and this integral must extend over all the values of x and y which make the values of z found from (1) real. These limiting values of x and y then are such that if we give one of them a suitable indefinitely small change the roots of (1) pass from real values to imaginary values. The limiting values of x and y must therefore be such as to introduce *equal roots* into (1), so that (1) must have some roots in common with the derived equation relative to z.

The limiting values of x and y must therefore satisfy the equation

$$f_1(x, y) = 0 \dots\dots\dots\dots\dots\dots\dots(2),$$

which is obtained by eliminating z between

$$f(x, y, z) = 0 \text{ and } \frac{df(x, y, z)}{dz} = 0.$$

If the sign of the left-hand member of (2) has been properly chosen we may say that the new definite integral must extend over all the values of x and y which render $f_1(x, y)$ negative.

There is no difficulty in determining the limits of the integrations which remain to be effected. For by proceeding as before we find that we must integrate with respect to y considering. x constant, and then the limits of y are given by (2). Lastly the limits of x are given by the equation

$$f_2(x) = 0 \dots\dots\dots\dots\dots\dots\dots (3),$$

which is obtained by eliminating y between

$$f_1(x, y) = 0 \text{ and } \frac{df_1(x, y)}{dy} = 0.$$

Suppose that the equation (1) gives only two values of z, and denote them by z_0 and z_1; suppose that equation (2) gives only two values of y, and denote them by y_0 and y_1; suppose that equation (3) gives only two values of x, and denote them by x_0 and x_1. Then the definite triple integral may be thus written with the limits expressed,

$$U = \int_{x_0}^{x_1} dx \int_{y_0}^{y_1} dy \int_{z_0}^{z_1} dz\, K.$$

Here z_0 and z_1 are functions of x and y; y_0 and y_1 are functions of x; x_0 and x_1 are constants.

If any of the equations (1), (2), (3) give more than two values of the unknown quantity with respect to which it is to be solved, then in order to express the limits of the integrations it will be necessary to decompose U into several definite integrals, and the limits for these integrals will be determined by the equations (1), (2), (3). This decomposition of U presents no difficulty, and we will not delay upon it; we shall reason hereafter on the supposition that each equation (1), (2), (3) has two roots, and it will be easy if necessary to modify this supposition.

136. Suppose that after having given to u a particular value in terms of x, y, z, we augment the value of u corresponding to each system of values of x, y, z by an indefinitely small quantity; or, which comes to the same thing, suppose that we augment the general expression for u in terms of x, y, z by an arbitrary indefinitely small function δu of the quantities x, y, z. Suppose moreover that we give an indefinitely small variation to the function $f(x, y, z)$. By these changes the triple integral U will assume a new value which differs by an indefinitely small quantity from its original value; this indefinitely small difference we shall now calculate.

The part depending upon the variation of K is easily expressed by well-known methods. If p denote any of the quantities u, $\dfrac{du}{dx}$, $\dfrac{du}{dy}$, ... then the corresponding term in the variation of K is $\dfrac{dK}{dp}\,\delta p$.

137. The only part of δU to which we need give special attention is that which arises from the variation of the limits of the integrations. The part of δU which arises from the variation of the limits of z is obviously

$$\int_{x_0}^{x_1} dx \int_{y_0}^{y_1} dy\, K_1\, \delta z_1 - \int_{x_0}^{x_1} dx \int_{y_0}^{y_1} dy\, K_0\, \delta z_0,$$

where K_1 and K_0 represent what K becomes when we put z_1 and z_0 respectively for z.

To obtain the terms arising from the variation of the limits y_1 and y_0 we must in the integral $\int_{z_0}^{z_1} dz\, K$ replace y by y_1 and y_0 respectively, then multiply the first result by δy_1 and the second by δy_0 and subtract the second product from the first, and finally integrate with respect to x between the limits x_0 and x_1.

But when $y = y_1$ and also when $y = y_0$ the limits z_1 and z_0 become equal, so that the integral $\int_{z_0}^{z_1} dz\, K$ vanishes; thus the terms in δU which arise from the variation of y_0 and y_1 are zero. Similarly δU will not contain any term arising from the variation of x_0 and x_1. Thus

$$\delta U = \int_{x_0}^{x_1} dx \int_{y_0}^{y_1} dy \int_{z_0}^{z_1} dz\, \Sigma\, \frac{dK}{dp}\, \delta p$$

$$+ \int_{x_0}^{x_1} dx \int_{y_0}^{y_1} dy\, K_1\, \delta z_1 - \int_{x_0}^{x_1} dx \int_{y_0}^{y_1} dy\, K_0\, \delta z_0.$$

138. A remark may be made with respect to the result just obtained, namely, that it is only the variation of the limits of the *first* integration which gives rise to a term in δU. The student may easily provide himself with a geometrical illustration; suppose that $f(x, y, z)$ is $\frac{x^2}{a^2} + \frac{y^2}{b^2} + \frac{z^2}{c^2} - 1$, so that the triple integral extends throughout the interior of a certain ellipsoid. Let the value of $f(x, y, z)$ be changed by variation into

$$\frac{x^2}{a^2} + \frac{y^2}{b^2} + \frac{z^2}{c^2} - (1 + \mu)^2,$$

where μ may be supposed indefinitely small, so that the varied triple integral extends throughout the interior of a new ellipsoid which is similar to the former and similarly situated and concentric with it. Then the part of δU which arises from the variation of y_0 and y_1 will be easily seen to be, not absolutely zero, but, an indefinitely small quantity, which may be called of the *second* order if that part which arises from the variation of z_0 and z_1 be called of the *first* order. Also that part of δU which arises from the variation

10

of z_0 and z_1 will be an indefinitely small quantity which may be called of the *third* order.

Thus it will be observed that by supposing the triple integral U to be extended over all the values of x, y, z which render $f(x, y, z)$ negative, the variation δU is free from any terms arising from the variation of the limits of the integrals except those which arise from the variation of the limits of the first integration. This simplicity however is obtained by a corresponding loss of generality in the results. The most general supposition would be that the limits z_0 and z_1 are any arbitrary functions of x and y, that y_0 and y_1 are any arbitrary functions of x, and that x_0 and x_1 are any constants; so that no mention would be made of the function $f(x, y, z)$. One of the great merits of the memoir of Sarrus is that it treats the problem in this most general sense; it will be remembered that Ostrogradsky had adopted the same limitation as Delaunay. (See Art. 129.) And in Poisson's researches on the variation of a double integral the same limitation occurs, for the integrations are supposed to extend over an area bounded by a closed curve. (See Art. 105.)

139. We resume the consideration of the value of δU given in Art. 137. The last two terms in the value of δU are united by Delaunay by means of a new notation, which he considers to possess some advantage over that hitherto used; in order to explain it he says he must enter into some details.

Let $\iint dx\,dy\,\lambda$ be a double integral which extends over all the points in the plane of (x, y) comprised within the interior of the closed curve $AmBn$ (see fig. 4). Let y_0 and y_1 represent the ordinates of the curve which correspond to any abscissa x; let x_0 and x_1 be the extreme abscissae Oa and Ob. Then the double integral may be expressed thus,

$$\int_{x_0}^{x_1} dx \int_{y_0}^{y_1} dy\,\lambda.$$

Now suppose we have found the indefinite integral H of λdy, and let H_1 and H_0 represent what H becomes when we substitute y_1 and y_0 respectively for y. Then we have

$$\int_{x_0}^{x_1} dx \int_{y_0}^{y_1} dy\,\lambda = \int_{x_0}^{x_1} H_1\,dx - \int_{x_0}^{x_1} H_0\,dx.$$

Now suppose that a point starts from A and moves round the curve $AmBn$ in the direction indicated by the arrows and finally returns to A. Let dx denote the space traversed by this point in the direction of the axis of x in any indefinitely small time, and let y be the variable ordinate of the point. Then the integral $\int dx\, H$ taken during the time the moving point describes the portion AmB will form the first part of the integral $\int\int dx\, dy\, h$, namely,

$$\int_{x_0}^{x_1} H_1\, dx;$$

and this same integral taken during the time the moving point describes the portion BnA will form the second part of the integral $\int\int dx\, dy\, h$, namely,

$$-\int_{x_0}^{x_1} H_0\, dx;$$

for in this second part of the motion dx is constantly negative. We may then express the integral $\int\int dx\, dy\, h$ completely by $\int dx\, H$ extended throughout the motion of the moving point, that is, from its departure from A until its return to the same point; this will be indicated by the notation

$$\int_{(x)}^{(x)} dx\, H.$$

Besides the advantage of uniting in a single term the two terms which were required to represent the value of $\int\int dx\, dy\, h$, the proposed notation has another advantage; for we can express by a single term the integral $\int\int dx\, dy\, h$ in the case in which the limiting curve can be intersected in more than two points by a line parallel to the axis of y, as may be easily seen.

140.   In the last two terms of the value found for δU (see Art. 137), we may consider the quantities $K_1 \delta z_1$ and $-K_0 \delta z_0$ as forming the two parts of a definite integral taken with respect to z between the limits z_0 and z_1. We may therefore, by Art. 139, put

$$\int_{y_0}^{y_1} dy\, K_1\, \delta z_1 - \int_{y_0}^{y_1} dy\, K_0\, \delta z_0 = \int_{(y)}^{(y)} dy\, K\, \delta z;$$

thus

$$\delta U = \int_{x_0}^{x_1} dx \int_{y_0}^{y_1} dy \int_{z_0}^{z_1} dz \, \Sigma \, \frac{dK}{dp} \delta p$$

$$+ \int_{x_0}^{x_1} dx \int_{(y)}^{(y)} dy \, K \delta z \,;$$

the z which enters into the K of the last line is a function of x and y determined from the equation $f(x, y, z) = 0.$.

141.   We must now transform the terms in the first part of δU by means of integration by parts. This part of Delaunay's memoir is treated by him with great generality; his method will be easily understood from a simple example which we will take.

Let p stand for $$\frac{d^3 u}{dx \, dy \, dz} \,,$$

and M for $$\frac{dK}{dp} \,,$$

then we have in the first part of δU the term

$$\int_{x_0}^{x_1} dx \int_{y_0}^{y_1} dy \int_{z_0}^{z_1} dz \, M \frac{d^3 \delta u}{dx \, dy \, dz} \,,   .$$

and we will take this term and reduce it by integration by parts.

By one integration by parts the term becomes

$$\int_{x_0}^{x_1} dx \int_{(y)}^{(y)} dy \, M \frac{d^2 \delta u}{dx \, dy} - \int_{x_0}^{x_1} dx \int_{y_0}^{y_1} dy \int_{z_0}^{z_1} dz \, \frac{dM}{dz} \frac{d^2 \delta u}{dx \, dy} \,,$$

where in the first term the notation is used which was explained in Art. 139.

If we effect two more integrations by parts in the second of the above two expressions we shall easily see that we shall finally obtain in the indefinite part of the variation δU the term

$$- \int_{x_0}^{x_1} dx \int_{y_0}^{y_1} dy \int_{z_0}^{z_1} dz \, \frac{d^3 M}{dx \, dy \, dz} \delta u \,;$$

we shall also have some limiting terms. The limiting terms it is not as yet easy to write explicitly, because the limits of the respective integrations will not be the same as those we have hitherto used, since the *order* of the integrations becomes changed. In fact to reduce the term

$$\int_{z_0}^{z_1} dx \int_{y_0}^{y_1} dy \int_{z_0}^{z_1} dz \, \frac{dM}{dz} \frac{d'\delta u}{dx\,dy}$$

as much as possible by integration by parts, we must begin by integrating with respect to x or y and not with respect to z, as we have hitherto supposed. But it will introduce confusion if we use different limits, and thus such a transformation is required of the terms at the limits as will allow the integrations to be all performed in the same order. This transformation, as Delaunay says, formed one of the principal difficulties of the problem, and he considers that he has accomplished it with all the simplicity desirable. He adds that Ostrogradsky had arrived at the same mode of transformation as a particular case of a more general method, this particular case being however the simplest that could be derived from it. See formula (C) of Art. 130.

142. Let for example $\iint N \, dy \, dz$ be a term which has arisen from an integration by parts with respect to x and in which we have not yet taken account of the limits between which the integral is to extend, so that N is a function of x, y, and z. In order to determine the limits we must deduce from the equation $f(x, y, z) = 0$ the values of x in terms of y and z; suppose we thus obtain two values of x, which we may denote by x'' and x', and let N'' and N' denote what N becomes when x'' and x' are respectively put for x; then the integral may be denoted by $\iint (N'' - N') \, dy \, dz$, and it is to extend over all values of y and z which make the values of x found from $f(x, y, z) = 0$ real. We want now to transform this double integral so that it shall extend between the old limits; and we shall now shew that it may be put in the form

$$\int_{z_0}^{z_1} dz \int_{y_0}^{y_1} dy\, M, \quad \text{where } M = N \frac{\dfrac{df}{dx}}{\dfrac{df}{dy}},$$

and z_0 and z_1 are the same quantities as have been throughout denoted by these symbols.

For any assigned value of y the equation $f(x, y, z) = 0$, may be regarded as the equation to a plane closed curve AmB of which the variable co-ordinates are x and z. (See figure 5.) Thus in the double integral we are considering, $\iint dy\,dz\,N$, if we integrate with respect to z we must extend the integral to all values of z which allow us to deduce from the equation $f(x, y, z) = 0$ real values of x, that is, the limits of z must be Oa and On. But by Art. 189,

$$\int_{Oa}^{On} (N'' - N')\,dz = \int_{(Oa)}^{(On)} N\,dz.$$

Thus $\iint N\,dy\,dz$ takes the form

$$\int dy \int_{(Oa)}^{(On)} N\,dz.$$

The symbol $\displaystyle\int_{(Oa)}^{(On)} N\,dz$ indicates an integral taken throughout the motion of a point which starts from A and returns to A again after moving round the curve in the order of the outside arrows. But if we suppose a second point to start from B and to move round the curve in the order of the inside arrows and return to B the symbol $\displaystyle\int_{(OB)}^{(OB)} N\,dz$ would indicate an integral taken throughout the second motion. But dz and dx being the increments of z and x which correspond to the instants when the moving point is traversing in opposite directions the same element of the curve, we have obviously

$$dz = -\frac{dz}{dx}\,dx,$$

where $\dfrac{dz}{dx}$ is the differential coefficient of z with respect to x deduced from $f(x, y, z) = 0$. Thus

$$\int_{(Oa)}^{(On)} dz\,N = -\int_{(OB)}^{(OB)} dx\,\frac{dz}{dx}\,N.$$

Therefore the double integral we are considering becomes

$$-\int dy \int_{(On)}^{(OB)} dx\,\frac{dz}{dx}\,N.$$

It must be observed that in N in the last expression z is to be considered a function of x and not x of z. This definite integral extends over all the values of x and y which allow of real values of z being found from $f(x, y, z) = 0$, as is easy to see; and as the order of integration may be changed at pleasure, we may take that which has already been adopted in Art. 135. Thus we have finally

$$\iint N\, dy\, dz, \text{ that is, } \iint (N'' - N')\, dy\, dz$$

$$= -\int_{x_0}^{x_1} dx \int_{(y)}^{(y)} dy\, \frac{dz}{dx}\, N = \int_{x_0}^{x_1} dx \int_{(y)}^{(y)} dy\, M,$$

where
$$M = N \frac{\dfrac{df}{dx}}{\dfrac{df}{dz}}. \quad .$$

143. We shall not reproduce the extremely general formulæ which Delaunay now gives with respect to multiple integrals, which extend over pages 69—73 of his memoir. His method will be sufficiently illustrated if we give in detail the investigations of the variations of a double integral and of a triple integral, in which we shall suppose that no differential coefficient of a higher order than the second occurs in the proposed expression. Let us then consider first the variation of a double integral.

Let
$$U = \int_{x_0}^{x_1} dx \int_{y_0}^{y_1} dy\, V.$$

Let V be a function of x, y, u, $\dfrac{du}{dx}$, $\dfrac{du}{dy}$, $\dfrac{d^2u}{dx^2}$, $\dfrac{d^2u}{dy^2}$ and $\dfrac{d^2u}{dx\, dy}$; and let the variation of U be required arising from a variation in u and a variation in the limits of the integrations.

The partial differential coefficient of V with respect to $\dfrac{du}{dx}$ will be denoted by V_x, that with respect to $\dfrac{du}{dy}$ by V_y, that with respect to $\dfrac{d^2u}{dx^2}$ by V_{xx}, and so on.

Then, as in Art. 140,

$$\delta U = \int_{x_0}^{x_1} dx \int_{y_0}^{y_1} dy\, \delta V + \int_{(x)}^{(x)} dx\, V \delta y.$$

Now, $\delta V = \dfrac{dV}{du}\delta u + V_x \delta \dfrac{du}{dx} + V_y \delta \dfrac{du}{dy} + V_{xx}\delta \dfrac{d^2 u}{dx^2}$

$$+ V_{xy}\,\delta \frac{d^2 u}{dx\,dy} + V_{yy}\,\delta \frac{d^2 u}{dy^2}$$

$$= \frac{dV}{du}\delta u + V_x \frac{d\delta u}{dx} + V_y \frac{d\delta u}{dy} + V_{xx}\frac{d^2 \delta u}{dx^2} + V_{xy}\frac{d^2 \delta u}{dx\,dy} + V_{yy}\frac{d^2 \delta u}{dy^2};$$

thus there are six terms in δV; and we shall consider how these six terms will appear in δU.

The first term is not susceptible of reduction.

The second term is $\iint dx\,dy\, V_x \dfrac{d\delta u}{dx};$

by Art. 142 this gives

$$-\int_{(x)}^{(x)} dx\, \frac{dy}{dx}\, V_x \delta u - \iint dx\,dy\, \frac{dV_x}{dx}\,\delta u.$$

The third term is $\iint dx\,dy\, V_y \dfrac{d\delta u}{dy};$

this gives $\qquad \displaystyle \int_{(x)}^{(x)} dx\, V_y \delta u - \iint dx\,dy\, \frac{dV_y}{dy}\,\delta u.$

The fourth term is $\iint dx\,dy\, V_{xx}\dfrac{d^2 \delta u}{dx^2};$

by one integration by parts this gives

$$-\int_{(x)}^{(x)} dx\, \frac{dy}{dx}\, V_{xx}\frac{d\delta u}{dx} - \iint dx\,dy\, \frac{dV_{xx}}{dx}\,\frac{d\delta u}{dx};$$

and by a second integration by parts we obtain

$$-\int_{(x)}^{(x)} dx\, \frac{dy}{dx}\, V_{xx}\frac{d\delta u}{dx} + \int_{(x)}^{(x)} dx\, \frac{dy}{dx}\,\frac{dV_{xx}}{dx}\,\delta u + \iint dx\,dy\, \frac{d^2 V_{xx}}{dx^2}\,\delta u.$$

The fifth term is $\iint dx\,dy\, V_{xy} \dfrac{d^2\delta u}{dx\,dy}$;

by integrating by parts with respect to y we get

$$\int_{(x)}^{(x)} dx\, V_{xy} \frac{d\delta u}{dx} - \iint dx\,dy\, \frac{dV_{xy}}{dy} \frac{d\delta u}{dx};$$

by a second integration by parts we obtain

$$\int_{(x)}^{(x)} dx\, V_{xy} \frac{d\delta u}{dx} + \int_{(x)}^{(x)} dx\, \frac{dy}{dx} \frac{dV_{xy}}{dy}\, \delta u + \iint dx\,dy\, \frac{d^2 V_{xy}}{dx\,dy}\, \delta u.$$

The sixth term is $\iint dx\,dy\, V_{yy} \dfrac{d^2\delta u}{dy^2}$;

by one integration by parts this gives

$$\int_{(x)}^{(x)} dx\, V_{yy} \frac{d\delta u}{dy} - \iint dx\,dy\, \frac{dV_{yy}}{dy} \frac{d\delta u}{dy};$$

by a second integration by parts we obtain

$$\int_{(x)}^{(x)} dx\, V_{yy} \frac{d\delta u}{dy} - \int_{(x)}^{(x)} dx\, \frac{dV_{yy}}{dy}\, \delta u + \iint dx\,dy\, \frac{d^2 V_{yy}}{dy^2}\, \delta u.$$

Then by collecting the terms we have

$$\delta U = \iint dx\,dy \left(\frac{dV}{du} - \frac{dV_x}{dx} - \frac{dV_y}{dy} + \frac{d^2 V_{xx}}{dx^2} + \frac{d^2 V_{xy}}{dx\,dy} + \frac{d^2 V_{yy}}{dy^2} \right) \delta u$$

$$+ \int_{(x)}^{(x)} dx \left(- \frac{dy}{dx} V_x + V_y + \frac{dy}{dx} \frac{dV_{xx}}{dx} + \frac{dy}{dx} \frac{dV_{xy}}{dy} - \frac{dV_{yy}}{dy} \right) \delta u$$

$$+ \int_{(x)}^{(x)} dx \left(- \frac{dy}{dx} V_{xy} \frac{d\delta u}{dx} + V_{xy} \frac{d\delta u}{dx} + V_{yy} \frac{d\delta u}{dy} \right)$$

$$+ \int_{(x)}^{(x)} dx\, V \delta y.$$

In this formula $\dfrac{dy}{dx}$ is to be found from the equation $f(x, y) = 0$, which determines the limits of integrations.

It will be seen that in the third line of the value of δU we have $\dfrac{d\delta u}{dx}$ and $\dfrac{d\delta u}{dy}$, both occurring under the integral sign; we shall now shew that the former symbol may be expressed in terms of the latter.

At the limits of the integration y is a function of x determined by $f(x, y) = 0$; let $\dfrac{D\,\delta u}{dx}$ denote the complete differential co-efficient of δu with respect to x, obtained *after* we have put for y its value; thus at the limit

$$\frac{D\,\delta u}{dx} = \frac{d\,\delta u}{dx} + \frac{d\,\delta u}{dy}\frac{dy}{dx}.$$

Therefore

$$\frac{d\,\delta u}{dx} = \frac{D\,\delta u}{dx} - \frac{d\,\delta u}{dy}\frac{dy}{dx}.$$

By substituting this value of $\dfrac{d\,\delta u}{dx}$ the third line of δU becomes

$$\int_{(x)}^{(x)}dx\left\{V_x + \left(\frac{dy}{dx}\right)'V_y - V_y\frac{dy}{dx}\right\}\frac{d\,\delta u}{dy} + \int_{(x)}^{(x)}dx\left\{V_x - \frac{dy}{dx}V_y\right\}\frac{D\,\delta u}{dx}.$$

The latter part may be integrated with respect to x by parts; the integrated part will vanish because the limits coincide; we shall thus have

$$\int_{(x)}^{(x)}dx\left\{V_x - \frac{dy}{dx}V_y\right\}\frac{D\,\delta u}{dx} = -\int_{(x)}^{(x)}dx\,\delta u\frac{D}{dx}\left(V_x - \frac{dy}{dx}V_y\right),$$

and $\dfrac{D}{dx}\left(V_x - \dfrac{dy}{dx}V_y\right)$ here means the differential coefficient with respect to x supposing y a function of x found from $f(x,y) = 0$; so that

$$\frac{D}{dx}\left(V_x - \frac{dy}{dx}V_y\right) = \frac{dV_x}{dx} + \frac{dV_x}{dy}\frac{dy}{dx}$$

$$-\frac{d^2y}{dx^2}V_y - \frac{dy}{dx}\frac{dV_y}{dx} - \left(\frac{dy}{dx}\right)'\frac{dV_y}{dy}.$$

Thus finally

$$\delta U = \iint dx\,dy \left(\frac{dV}{du} - \frac{dV_x}{dx} - \frac{dV_y}{dy} + \frac{d^2 V_{xx}}{dx^2} + \frac{d^2 V_{xy}}{dx\,dy} + \frac{d^2 V_{yy}}{dy^2} \right) \delta u$$

$$+ \int_{(x)}^{x_1} dx \left\{ V_y - \frac{dy}{dx} V_x + \frac{d^2 y}{dx^2} V_{xx} + 2\frac{dy}{dx}\frac{dV_{xx}}{dx} - \frac{dV_{xy}}{dx} - \frac{dV_{yy}}{dy} \right.$$

$$\left. + \left(\frac{dy}{dx}\right)^2 \frac{dV_{xx}}{dy} \right\} \delta u$$

$$+ \int_{(x)}^{x_1} dx \left\{ V_{yy} + \left(\frac{dy}{dx}\right)^2 V_{xx} - V_{xy}\frac{dy}{dx} \right\} \frac{d\delta u}{dy} + \int_{(x)}^{x_1} dx\, V \delta y.$$

144. We shall now give the variation of a triple integral.

Let $\quad U = \iiint dx\,dy\,dz\, V,\quad$ that is $\displaystyle\int_{x_0}^{x_1} dx \int_{y_0}^{y_1} dy \int_{z_0}^{z_1} dz\, V.$

V is supposed to contain x, y, z, u, and the partial differential coefficients of u with respect to x, y, z, up to the second order inclusive.

Here $\quad \delta U = \iiint dx\,dy\,dz\, \delta V + \displaystyle\int_{x_0}^{x_1} dx \int_{(y)}^{(y)} dy\, V\delta z;$

$$\delta V = \frac{dV}{du}\delta u + V_x \frac{d\delta u}{dx} + V_y \frac{d\delta u}{dy} + V_z \frac{d\delta u}{dz}$$

$$+ V_{xx}\frac{d^2\delta u}{dx^2} + V_{yy}\frac{d^2\delta u}{dy^2} + V_{zz}\frac{d^2\delta u}{dz^2} + V_{xy}\frac{d^2\delta u}{dx\,dy} + V_{xz}\frac{d^2\delta u}{dx\,dz} + V_{yz}\frac{d^2\delta u}{dy\,dz}\,.$$

There will thus be ten terms in δU arising from δV.

The first term is susceptible of no transformation.

The second term is

$$\iiint dx\,dy\,dz\, V_x \frac{d\delta u}{dx};$$

by integration by parts this gives

$$-\int_{x_0}^{x_1} dx \int_{(y)}^{(y)} dy \frac{dz}{dx} V_x \delta u - \iiint dx\,dy\,dz \frac{dV_x}{dx}\delta u.$$

The third term is

$$\iiint dx\,dy\,dz\; V_{s}\,\frac{d\delta u}{dy}\,;$$

by integration by parts this gives

$$-\iint dx\,dy\,\frac{dz}{dy}\,V_{s}\,\delta u - \iiint dx\,dy\,dz\,\frac{dV_{s}}{dy}\,\delta u,$$

where we have put $\iint dx\,dy$ instead of $\int_{x_{0}}^{x_{1}} dx \int_{(y)}^{(y)} dy$, and this abbreviation we shall continue to use.

The fourth term is

$$\iiint dx\,dy\,dz\; V_{s}\,\frac{d\delta u}{dz}\,;$$

by integration by parts this gives

$$\iint dx\,dy\; V_{s}\,\delta u - \iiint dx\,dy\,dz\,\frac{dV_{s}}{dz}\,\delta u.$$

The fifth term is

$$\iiint dx\,dy\,dz\; V_{xx}\,\frac{d^{2}\delta u}{dx^{2}}\,;$$

by one integration by parts this gives

$$-\iint dx\,dy\,\frac{dz}{dx}\,V_{xx}\,\frac{d\delta u}{dx} - \iiint dx\,dy\,dz\,\frac{dV_{xx}}{dx}\,\frac{d\delta u}{dx}\,;$$

by a second integration by parts we obtain

$$-\iint dx\,dy\,\frac{dz}{dx}\,V_{xx}\,\frac{d\delta u}{dx} + \iint dx\,dy\,\frac{dz}{dx}\,\frac{dV_{xx}}{dx}\,\delta u + \iiint dx\,dy\,dz\,\frac{d^{2}V_{xx}}{dx^{2}}\,\delta u.$$

The sixth term is

$$\iiint dx\,dy\,dz\; V_{yy}\,\frac{d^{2}\delta u}{dy^{2}}\,;$$

by one integration by parts this gives

$$-\iint dx\,dy\,\frac{dz}{dy}\,V_{yy}\,\frac{d\delta u}{dy} - \iiint dx\,dy\,dz\,\frac{dV_{yy}}{dy}\,\frac{d\delta u}{dy}\,;$$

by a second integration by parts we obtain

$$-\iint dx\,dy\,\frac{dz}{dy}\,V_{xy}\,\frac{d\delta u}{dy} + \iint dx\,dy\,\frac{dz}{dy}\frac{dV_{xy}}{dy}\,\delta u + \iiint dx\,dy\,dz\,\frac{d^{2}V_{xy}}{dy^{2}}\,\delta u.$$

The seventh term is

$$\iiint dx\,dy\,dz\,V_{xx}\,\frac{d^{2}\delta u}{dx^{2}}\,;$$

by two integrations by parts this gives

$$\iint dx\,dy\,V_{xx}\,\frac{d\delta u}{dx} - \iint dx\,dy\,\frac{dV_{xx}}{dx}\,\delta u + \iiint dx\,dy\,dz\,\frac{d^{2}V_{xx}}{dx^{2}}\,\delta u.$$

The eighth term is

$$\iiint dx\,dy\,dz\,V_{xy}\,\frac{d^{2}\delta u}{dx\,dy}\,;$$

by one integration by parts this gives

$$-\iint dx\,dy\,\frac{dz}{dx}\,V_{xy}\,\frac{d\delta u}{dy} - \iiint dx\,dy\,dz\,\frac{dV_{xy}}{dx}\,\frac{d\delta u}{dy}\,;$$

by a second integration by parts we obtain

$$-\iint dx\,dy\,\frac{dz}{dx}\,V_{xy}\,\frac{d\delta u}{dy} + \iint dx\,dy\,\frac{dz}{dy}\frac{dV_{xy}}{dx}\,\delta u + \iiint dx\,dy\,dz\,\frac{d^{2}V_{xy}}{dx\,dy}\,\delta u.$$

The ninth term is

$$\iiint dx\,dy\,dz\,V_{xz}\,\frac{d^{2}\delta u}{dx\,dz}\,;$$

by one integration by parts this gives

$$\iint dx\,dy\,V_{xz}\,\frac{d\delta u}{dx} - \iiint dx\,dy\,dz\,\frac{dV_{xz}}{dz}\,\frac{d\delta u}{dx}\,;$$

by a second integration by parts we obtain

$$\iint dx\,dy\,V_{xz}\,\frac{d\delta u}{dx} + \iint dx\,dy\,\frac{dz}{dx}\frac{dV_{xz}}{dz}\,\delta u + \iiint dx\,dy\,dz\,\frac{d^{2}V_{xz}}{dx\,dz}\,\delta u.$$

The tenth term is

$$\iiint dx\,dy\,dz\,V_{yz}\,\frac{d^{2}\delta u}{dy\,dz}\,;$$

. by two integrations by parts this gives

$$\iint dx\, dy\; V_{\varpi}\frac{d\delta u}{dy} + \iint dx\, dy\; \frac{dz}{dy}\frac{dV_{\varpi}}{dz}\delta u + \iiint dx\, dy\, dz\; \frac{d^2 V}{dy\, dz}\delta u.$$

In these formulæ $\dfrac{dz}{dx}$ and $\dfrac{dz}{dy}$ are to be found from the equation determining the limits which is supposed to be given, $f(x,\, y,\, z)=0$, (see Art. 135). We shall put p for $\dfrac{dz}{dx}$ and q for $\dfrac{dz}{dy}$.

$$\begin{aligned}
\text{Thus}\quad \delta U = \iiint & dx\, dy\, dz\left\{\frac{dV}{du} - \frac{dV_x}{dx} - \frac{dV_y}{dy} - \frac{dV_z}{dz}\right.\\
& \left. + \frac{d^2 V_{xx}}{dx^2} + \frac{d^2 V_{yy}}{dy^2} + \frac{d^2 V_{zz}}{dz^2} + \frac{d^2 V_{xy}}{dx\, dy} + \frac{d^2 V_{xz}}{dx\, dz} + \frac{d^2 V_{yz}}{dy\, dz}\right\}\delta u\\
& + \iint dx\, dy\left\{-p V_x - q V_y + V_z\right.\\
& \left. + p\frac{dV_{xx}}{dx} + q\frac{dV_{yy}}{dy} - \frac{dV_{zz}}{dz} + q\frac{dV_{xy}}{dz} + p\frac{dV_{yz}}{dz} + q\frac{dV_{xz}}{dz}\right\}\delta u\\
& + \iint dx\, dy\left\{-p V_{xx} + V_{xz}\right\}\frac{d\delta u}{dx}\\
& + \iint dx\, dy\left\{-q V_{yy} - p V_{yz} + V_{yz}\right\}\frac{d\delta u}{dy}\\
& + \iint dx\, dy\left\{V_{zz}\right\}\frac{d\delta u}{dz}\\
& + \iint dx\, dy\; V\delta z.
\end{aligned}$$

Here are six different terms in δU; the first involves a triple integral; the second a double integral in which δu occurs; the third, fourth, and fifth double integrals in which $\dfrac{d\delta u}{dx}$, $\dfrac{d\delta u}{dy}$, $\dfrac{d\delta u}{dz}$, respectively occur; the sixth a double integral in which δz occurs. In all the double integrals z is supposed a function of x and y determined by $f(x,\, y,\, z) = 0$. The third and fourth terms will now be modified so as to get rid of $\dfrac{d\delta u}{dx}$ and $\dfrac{d\delta u}{dy}$.

If as before $\dfrac{D\,\delta u}{dx}$ denote the differential coefficient of δu with respect to x *after* the value of z has been substituted, we have at the limits

$$\frac{D\,\delta u}{dx} = \frac{d\,\delta u}{dx} + p\,\frac{d\,\delta u}{dz}.$$

Similarly
$$\frac{D\,\delta u}{dy} = \frac{d\,\delta u}{dy} + q\,\frac{d\,\delta u}{dz}.$$

Therefore at the limits, as on page 154,

$$\iint dx\,dy \left\{ - p\,V_{x} + V_{x} \right\} \frac{d\,\delta u}{dx} =$$

$$\iint dx\,dy\, \delta u\, \frac{D}{dx}\left(p\,V_{x} - V_{x} \right) + \iint dx\,dy \left(p^{2}V_{x} - p\,V_{x} \right)\frac{d\,\delta u}{dz} ;$$

$$\iint dx\,dy \left\{ - q\,V_{y} - p\,V_{x} + V_{y} \right\} \frac{d\,\delta u}{dy} =$$

$$\iint dx\,dy\, \delta u\, \frac{D}{dy}\left(q\,V_{y} + p\,V_{x} - V_{y} \right) + \iint dx\,dy \left(q^{2}V_{y} + pq\,V_{x} - q\,V_{y} \right)\frac{d\,\delta u}{dz}.$$

Thus δU finally consists of the following terms:

the part involving the triple integral;

the term $\iint dx\,dy\, V\delta z$;

the term $\iint dx\,dy \left\{ V_{x} - p\,V_{x} - q\,V_{y} + p^{2}V_{x} + q^{2}V_{y} + pq\,V_{x} \right\}\frac{d\,\delta u}{dz}$;

and a term $\iint dx\,dy\, M\delta u,$

where $M = V_{u} - p\,V_{x} - q\,V_{y}$

$$+ p\,\frac{d\,V_{x}}{dx} + q\,\frac{d\,V_{y}}{dy} - \frac{d\,V_{x}}{dz} + q\,\frac{d\,V_{y}}{dx} + p\,\frac{d\,V_{x}}{dz} + q\,\frac{d\,V_{y}}{dz}$$

$$+ \frac{D}{dx}\left(p\,V_{x} - V_{x} \right) + \frac{D}{dy}\left(q\,V_{y} + p\,V_{x} - V_{y} \right).$$

Also $\dfrac{D}{dx}\left(pV_{xz} - V_{zx}\right) = rV_{xz} + p\dfrac{dV_{xz}}{dx} + p'\dfrac{dV_{xz}}{dz} - \dfrac{dV_{zx}}{dx} - p\dfrac{dV_{zx}}{dz}$,

$\dfrac{\dot{D}}{dy}\left(qV_{yz} + pV_{xy} - V_{zy}\right) = tV_{yz} + q\dfrac{dV_{yz}}{dy} + q'\dfrac{dV_{yz}}{dz} - \dfrac{dV_{zy}}{dy} - q\dfrac{dV_{zy}}{dz}$

$$+ sV_{xy} + p\dfrac{dV_{xy}}{dy} + pq\dfrac{dV_{xy}}{dz},$$

where $r = \dfrac{d^2z}{dx^2}$, $s = \dfrac{d^2z}{dx\,dy}$, $t = \dfrac{d^2z}{dy^2}$;

these being all supposed found from $f(x, y, z) = 0$.

Thus $M = V_z - pV_x - qV_y$

$$+ 2p\dfrac{dV_{xz}}{dx} + 2q\dfrac{dV_{yz}}{dy} - \dfrac{dV_{zz}}{dz} + p'\dfrac{dV_{xz}}{dz} + q'\dfrac{dV_{yz}}{dz}$$

$$+ q\dfrac{dV_{yz}}{dx} + p\dfrac{dV_{xy}}{dy} + pq\dfrac{dV_{xy}}{dz} - \dfrac{dV_{zx}}{dx} - \dfrac{dV_{zy}}{dy} + rV_{xz} + sV_{xy} + tV_{yy}.$$

145. The second section of Delaunay's memoir is entitled *conditions that a definite integral may be a maximum or a minimum; distinction between a maximum and a minimum.* This section extends over pages 79—97.

Delaunay makes some remarks on problems of relative maxima and minima, and he arrives at a result which requires examination. Consider the integral $\int K\,dx$ where K is supposed to contain different unknown functions y, z, ... and their differential coefficients with respect to x. Suppose that this integral is to be a maximum or minimum at the same time that a relation $\phi = 0$ is to hold between the functions and their differential coefficients. Delaunay then supposes that as usual we proceed to find the maximum or minimum of $\int(K + m\phi)\,dx$, where m is some function of x at present undetermined. Delaunay considers that there will be different cases in this problem according as the differential coefficients which occur in ϕ are, or are not, of a higher order than those which occur in K. If, for example, the highest differential coefficient which occurs in ϕ is *one* order higher than the highest which occurs in K, Delaunay arrives at the result that at each limit of the integration we must have $m = 0$; if the highest differential coefficient which occurs in ϕ is *two* orders higher than the highest which occurs in K, Delaunay arrives at the result that at each limit of the integration we must have $m = 0$ and $\dfrac{dm}{dx} = 0$.

146. Without going into detail on the subject we will indicate two objections to Delaunay's conclusions.

First. Suppose, for example, that K involves differential coefficients up to the second order inclusive, and that ϕ involves differential coefficients up to the fourth order inclusive. Let x_0 and x_1 denote the limits of the integration, and suppose that $x_1 - x_0$ is divided into n equal parts; and put $x_1 - x_0 = nh$. Then Delaunay says that the relation $\phi = 0$ is meant to hold for the following values of x, when n is supposed large enough :

$$x_0 + 3h, \ x_0 + 4h, \dots, \ x_0 + (n-4)h, \ x_0 + (n-3)h;$$

that is to say, it is not meant to hold for the values

$$x_0, \ x_0 + h, \ x_0 + 2h, \ x_1, \ x_1 - h, \ x_1 - 2h.$$

For ϕ involves differential coefficients of the fourth order, and such differential coefficients may be supposed to depend upon four consecutive values of x; so that if for example we suppose $\phi = 0$ to hold when $x = x_1 - 2h$, a value $x_1 + h$ would be involved in ϕ, which lies beyond the limits of our integration. The reply is simple; the proposer of a problem may attach his own meaning to his conditions; he may say that ϕ is to be zero for all values of x within the limits x_0 and x_1, or he may say that ϕ is to be zero for all values of x within the limits $x_0 + 3h$ and $x_1 - 3h$. Thus Delaunay's investigations do in effect attach one of two possible meanings to a certain condition, but probably not the meaning which would generally be attached to such a condition.

Secondly. Let us now take Delaunay's own view of the meaning of the condition and examine if his conclusions hold. We have then the following problem: $\int_{x_0}^{x_1} K dx$ is to be a maximum or a minimum while the condition $\phi = 0$ is to hold for all values of x comprised between ξ_0 and ξ_1, where ξ_0 and ξ_1 lie themselves between x_0 and x_1. In Delaunay's problem the difference between

11

x_0 and ξ_0 is infinitesimal, and so is the difference between ξ_1 and x_1, but we need not restrict ourselves with this limitation. We have then to make the variation of the following expression zero :

$$\int_{x_0}^{\xi_0} K dx + \int_{\xi_0}^{\xi_1} (K + m\phi)\, dx + \int_{\xi_1}^{x_1} K dx.$$

The variation as usual will consist of two parts, an integrated part and a part still remaining under the sign of integration. To make the latter part vanish we must take a solution which leads to discontinuity in the form of our functions; that is, a certain equation or certain equations will be obtained which must hold between the limits x_0 and ξ_0 and also between the limits ξ_1 and x_1, and a certain other equation or certain other equations will be obtained which must hold between the limits ξ_0 and ξ_1. There will be no objection to this discontinuity in form provided we can also make the integrated part of the variation vanish; this we must now consider. The integrated part which occurs at the lower limit of $\delta \int_{x_0}^{\xi_0} K dx$ and the integrated part which occurs at the upper limit of $\delta \int_{\xi_1}^{x_1} K dx$ may be made to vanish in the usual way by a proper disposal of the constants which occur in the integral of the differential equation obtained by making $\delta \int K dx = 0$. The integrated part which occurs at the lower limit of $\delta \int_{\xi_0}^{\xi_1} (K + m\phi)\, dx$ will partly unite with that which occurs at the upper limit of $\delta \int_{x_0}^{\xi_0} K dx$; and the integrated part which occurs at the upper limit of $\delta \int_{\xi_0}^{\xi_1} (K + m\phi)\, dx$ will partly unite with that which occurs at the lower limit of $\delta \int_{\xi_1}^{x_1} K dx$. Theoretically the complete set of terms at the limit ξ_0 and the complete set of terms at the limit ξ_1 can be made to vanish by a proper disposal of the constants which occur in the integral of the differential equation obtained by making

$$\delta \int (K + m\phi)\, dx = 0.$$

We must now examine some of these terms more particularly. We have already supposed y to denote one of the variables which occur in K; put

$$\frac{dy}{dx} = p, \quad \frac{d^2y}{dx^2} = q, \quad \frac{d^3y}{dx^3} = r, \quad \frac{d^4y}{dx^4} = s.$$

Then among the terms of the integrated part we shall have

$$\frac{dm\phi}{ds}\,(\delta r - s\delta x) + \left(\frac{dm\phi}{dr} - \frac{d}{dx}\,\frac{dm\phi}{ds}\right)(\delta q - r\delta x),$$

and δr and δq will not occur elsewhere among the integrated terms. And as m is supposed a function of x only we have

$$\frac{dm\phi}{ds} = m\,\frac{d\phi}{ds}, \quad \frac{dm\phi}{dr} = m\,\frac{d\phi}{dr}.$$

Thus δr and δq will disappear from the integrated part if we have, at the limits ξ_0 and ξ_1,

$$m\,\frac{d\phi}{ds} = 0 \quad \text{and} \quad m\,\frac{d\phi}{dr} - \frac{d}{dx}\,m\,\frac{d\phi}{ds} = 0.$$

The last relations are satisfied if at both the limits we have

$$m = 0 \quad \text{and} \quad \frac{dm}{dx} = 0 \dots\dots\dots\dots\dots\dots\dots\dots(1)$$

as Delaunay states; but they are *also satisfied* if at both limits

$$\frac{d\phi}{ds} = 0 \quad \text{and} \quad \frac{d\phi}{dr} - \frac{d}{dx}\,\frac{d\phi}{ds} = 0 \dots\dots\dots\dots\dots (2).$$

Moreover if r and q are to have *given* values at the limits ξ_0 and ξ_1, then δr and δq are themselves zero at these limits, and then neither (1) nor (2) need hold.

We conclude then that Delaunay's results are not necessarily true even for the special meaning which he attaches to the condition $\phi = 0$.

We shall presently consider a problem which will illustrate the preceding remarks; see Art. 159. Mr Jellett has indicated his dissent from Delaunay's conclusions; see his *Calculus of Variations*, page 362.

147. Delaunay makes some remarks on the distinction between maxima and minima values of an integral in the following words. Legendre was the first who considered this question, but he only applied his method to simple integrals. Lagrange modified the method, and Jacobi rendered it as complete as possible by reducing the investigations which it requires to the general process of integration by parts. But neither of them I believe attempted to extend the method to multiple integrals. In examining this question I have found that the generalisation of Legendre's method presents no difficulty, at least if his steps are followed. But the generalisation of the completeness which Jacobi has given to the method appears to me to present great difficulties, and I shall not enter upon it.

Delaunay then extends Legendre's method to a double integral; he confines himself to the case in which no differential coefficients of a higher order than the second occur in the integral which is to be made a maximum or minimum. The problem which Delaunay considers had been previously solved by Brunacci, who had arrived at the same results as Delaunay gives. The investigation is reproduced by Mr Jellett in his *Calculus of Variations*, pages 269—272.

Jacobi's additions to Legendre's method will be explained hereafter; and we shall see that the investigations of Jacobi have been generalised so as to apply to multiple integrals.

148. The third section of Delaunay's memoir is entitled *application of the preceding theories to some examples;* this section extends over pages 97—120, and contains four examples.

The first example is to find the curve which has a constant curvature and has a maximum or minimum length between two points. Delaunay intimates that this example is to bear upon the results given in Art. 145.

Let x, y, z be the rectangular co-ordinates of any point in the sought line; x_0 and x_1 the abscissae of the extreme points. Take x as the independent variable and use the ordinary notation for differential coefficients; then the length of the curve is

$$\int_{x_0}^{x_1} \sqrt{(1 + y'^2 + z'^2)}\, dx,$$

which is to be a maximum or minimum; and

$$\frac{\sqrt{(y''^2 + z''^2 + (z'y'' - y'z'')^2)}}{(1 + y'^2 + z'^2)^{\frac{3}{2}}}$$

is the reciprocal of the radius of curvature which is to have a constant value; this constant value we shall denote by $\frac{1}{\rho}$.

Thus we proceed in the usual way to make $\int_{x_0}^{x_1} V dx$ a maximum or minimum, where

$$V = \sqrt{(1 + y'^2 + z'^2)} + m \left[\frac{\sqrt{(y''^2 + z''^2 + (z'y'' - y'z'')^2)}}{(1 + y'^2 + z'^2)^{\frac{3}{2}}} - \frac{1}{\rho} \right].$$

By the ordinary principles of the subject we have the following equations as necessary for the existence of a maximum or minimum:

$$\frac{d}{dx}\frac{dV}{dy'} - \frac{d^2}{dx^2}\frac{dV}{dy''} = 0,$$

$$\frac{d}{dx}\frac{dV}{dz'} - \frac{d^2}{dx^2}\frac{dV}{dz''} = 0.$$

Therefore by integration

$$\frac{dV}{dy'} - \frac{d}{dx}\frac{dV}{dy''} = a \quad\ldots\ldots\ldots\ldots\ldots\ldots\ldots (1),$$

$$\frac{dV}{dz'} - \frac{d}{dx}\frac{dV}{dz''} = \beta \quad\ldots\ldots\ldots\ldots\ldots\ldots\ldots (2),$$

where a and β are two arbitrary constants.

The solution of the problem then depends on equations (1) and (2) together with

$$\frac{\sqrt{(y''^2 + z''^2 + (z'y'' - y'z'')^2)}}{(1 + y'^2 + z'^2)^{\frac{3}{2}}} - \frac{1}{\rho} = 0 \quad\ldots\ldots\ldots\ldots (3).$$

This is as far as Delaunay carries the general solution; he adds the following remark. Since it is impossible to obtain the general solution we may inquire if the circle which is the only plane curve of constant curvature satisfies all the conditions; on trial we shall find that the equations (1), (2), (3) are satisfied when we establish the following relations between x, y, z and m;

$$z = ay + bx + c \dots\dots\dots (4),$$

$$\rho = \frac{[1 + b^2 + 2aby' + (1 + a^2) y'^2]^{\frac{3}{2}}}{y'' \surd(1 + a^2 + b^2)} \dots\dots (5),$$

$$m = \rho \left\{ \surd(1 + y'^2 + z'^2) - ay' - \beta z' - \frac{\beta - a\alpha}{b} \right\} \dots\dots (6).$$

And hence he infers that the circle is a solution of the problem.

149. This problem will lead us into a long discussion; we shall begin by carrying the *general* solution a little further in Delaunay's notation. We shall obtain two first integrals of the equations (1) and (2); for this purpose it will be necessary to develope these equations (1) and (2).

Let μ stand for

$$\surd[y'^2 + z'^2 + (z'y'' - y'z'')^2] \text{ and } \frac{ds}{dx} \text{ for } \surd(1 + y'^2 + z'^2),$$

so that s is the length of the curve measured from some fixed point up to the point (x, y, z); then we shall find that

$$\frac{dV}{dy'} = \frac{y'}{\frac{ds}{dx}} - \frac{mz''(z'y'' - y'z'')}{\mu \left(\frac{ds}{dx}\right)^3} - \frac{3m\mu y'}{\left(\frac{ds}{dx}\right)^4},$$

$$\frac{dV}{dy''} = \frac{m}{\mu \left(\frac{ds}{dx}\right)^3} \left\{ y'' + z'(z'y'' - y'z'') \right\},$$

$$\frac{dV}{dz'} = \frac{z'}{\frac{ds}{dx}} + \frac{my''(z'y'' - y'z'')}{\mu \left(\frac{ds}{dx}\right)^3} - \frac{3m\mu z'}{\left(\frac{ds}{dx}\right)^4},$$

$$\frac{dV}{dz''} = \frac{m}{\mu \left(\frac{ds}{dx}\right)^3} \left\{ z'' - y'(z'y'' - y'z'') \right\}.$$

Multiply equation (1) by y'' and equation (2) by z'' and add; thus

$$\alpha y'' + \beta z'' = \frac{y'y'' + z'z''}{\dfrac{ds}{dx}} - \frac{3m\mu\,(y'y'' + z'z'')}{\left(\dfrac{ds}{dx}\right)^{5}} - y''\frac{d}{dx}\frac{dV}{dy''} - z''\frac{d}{dx}\frac{dV}{dz''}$$

$$= \frac{y'y'' + z'z''}{\dfrac{ds}{dx}} - \frac{3m\,(y'y'' + z'z'')}{\rho\left(\dfrac{ds}{dx}\right)^{5}} - y''\frac{d}{dx}\frac{dV}{dy''} - z''\frac{d}{dx}\frac{dV}{dz''};$$

and

$$y''\frac{d}{dx}\frac{dV}{dy''} + z''\frac{d}{dx}\frac{dV}{dz''} = \frac{d}{dx}\left(y''\frac{dV}{dy''} + z''\frac{dV}{dz''}\right) - y'''\frac{dV}{dy''} - z'''\frac{dV}{dz''}$$

$$= \frac{d}{dx}\frac{m}{\rho} - y'''\frac{dV}{dy''} - z'''\frac{dV}{dz''};$$

and

$$y'''\frac{dV}{dy''} + z'''\frac{dV}{dz''} = \frac{m}{\mu\left(\dfrac{ds}{dx}\right)}\left\{y''y'' + z''z'' + (z'y'' - y'z'')(z'y'' - y'z'')\right\}$$

$$= \frac{m}{\mu\left(\dfrac{ds}{dx}\right)}\frac{\mu\,d\mu}{dx} = \frac{m}{\rho\mu}\frac{d\mu}{dx};$$

thus

$$\alpha y'' + \beta z'' = \frac{y'y'' + z'z''}{\dfrac{ds}{dx}} - \frac{m}{\rho}\left\{\frac{3\,(y'y'' + z'z'')}{\left(\dfrac{ds}{dx}\right)^{5}} - \frac{1}{\mu}\frac{d\mu}{dx}\right\} - \frac{d}{dx}\frac{m}{\rho}$$

$$= \frac{y'y'' + z'z''}{\dfrac{ds}{dx}} - \frac{d}{dx}\frac{m}{\rho},$$

since $\quad\dfrac{3\,(y'y'' + z'z'')}{\left(\dfrac{ds}{dx}\right)^{5}} - \dfrac{1}{\mu}\dfrac{d\mu}{dx} = 0$ by (3).

Therefore by integration

$$\alpha y' + \beta z' + \gamma = \sqrt{(1 + y'^2 + z'^2)} - \frac{m}{\rho},$$

where γ is an arbitrary constant. Thus

$$m = \rho\left[\sqrt{(1 + y'^2 + z'^2)} - \alpha y' - \beta z' - \gamma\right] \quad\ldots\ldots\ldots\ldots (7).$$

Again, by ordinary transformations the values obtained for $\frac{dV}{dy''}$ and $\frac{dV}{dz''}$ may be written thus:

$$\frac{dV}{dy''} = \frac{m}{\mu}\frac{d^2y}{ds^2}\frac{ds}{dx}, \quad \frac{dV}{dz''} = \frac{m}{\mu}\frac{d^2z}{ds^2}\frac{ds}{dx}.$$

Multiply equation (1) by $\frac{dz}{ds}$ and (2) by $\frac{dy}{ds}$ and subtract; thus

$$\alpha\frac{dz}{ds} - \beta\frac{dy}{ds}$$

$$= \frac{m(y'y''+z'z'')(y'z''-z'y'')}{\mu\left(\frac{ds}{dx}\right)^4} - \frac{dz}{ds}\frac{d}{dx}\frac{m}{\mu}\frac{d^2y}{ds^2}\frac{ds}{dx} + \frac{dy}{ds}\frac{d}{dx}\frac{m}{\mu}\frac{d^2z}{ds^2}\frac{ds}{dx}$$

$$= \frac{m\frac{d^2s}{dx^2}(y'z''-z'y'')}{\mu\left(\frac{ds}{dx}\right)^3} + \frac{d}{dx}\frac{m}{\mu}\frac{ds}{dx}\left(\frac{dy}{ds}\frac{d^2z}{ds^2} - \frac{dz}{ds}\frac{d^2y}{ds^2}\right);$$

and $y'z'' - z'y'' = \left(\frac{ds}{dx}\right)^3\left(\frac{dy}{ds}\frac{d^2z}{ds^2} - \frac{dz}{ds}\frac{d^2y}{ds^2}\right)$; thus

$$\alpha\frac{dz}{ds} - \beta\frac{dy}{ds} = \frac{m}{\mu}\frac{d^2s}{dx^2}\left(\frac{dy}{ds}\frac{d^2z}{ds^2} - \frac{dz}{ds}\frac{d^2y}{ds^2}\right) + \frac{d}{dx}\frac{m}{\mu}\frac{ds}{dx}\left(\frac{dy}{ds}\frac{d^2z}{ds^2} - \frac{dz}{ds}\frac{d^2y}{ds^2}\right)$$

$$= \frac{dx}{ds}\frac{d}{dx}\frac{m}{\mu}\left(\frac{ds}{dx}\right)^2\left(\frac{dy}{ds}\frac{d^2z}{ds^2} - \frac{dz}{ds}\frac{d^2y}{ds^2}\right).$$

Divide by $\frac{dx}{ds}$ and then integrate; thus

$$\alpha z - \beta y + C = \frac{m}{\mu}\left(\frac{ds}{dx}\right)^2\left(\frac{dy}{ds}\frac{d^2z}{ds^2} - \frac{dz}{ds}\frac{d^2y}{ds^2}\right) \quad\text{............ (8)},$$

where C is an arbitrary constant.

And, since $\frac{m}{\mu}\left(\frac{ds}{dx}\right)^2\left(\frac{dy}{ds}\frac{d^2z}{ds^2} - \frac{dz}{ds}\frac{d^2y}{ds^2}\right) = \frac{m}{\mu}\frac{y'z''-z'y''}{\frac{ds}{dx}}$

$$= \frac{\rho m(y'z''-z'y'')}{(1+y'^2+z'^2)^{\frac{1}{2}}},$$

we may write equation (8) thus:

$$\alpha z - \beta y + C = \frac{\rho m \,(y' z'' - z' y'')}{(1 + y'^2 + z'^2)^{\frac{3}{2}}} \quad \ldots\ldots\ldots\ldots\ldots\ldots \text{(9)}.$$

Equations (7) and (9) are the integrals it was proposed to obtain; the problem is thus reduced to depend upon the solution of equations (3), (7) and (9). The value of m from (7) may be substituted in (9) and the result will, with equation (3), constitute two simultaneous differential equations of the second order for determining the required curve.

150. We have not yet verified Delaunay's statement that equations (4), (5) and (6) give *a* solution of the problem; we shall arrive at this result most easily by arranging the whole solution of the problem as far as it can be completed in a symmetrical manner. Take the arc s for the independent variable; then we have

$$\left(\frac{dx}{ds}\right)^2 + \left(\frac{dy}{ds}\right)^2 + \left(\frac{dz}{ds}\right)^2 - 1 = 0, \quad \left(\frac{d^2x}{ds^2}\right)^2 + \left(\frac{d^2y}{ds^2}\right)^2 + \left(\frac{d^2z}{ds^2}\right)^2 - \frac{1}{\rho^2} = 0,$$

and subject to these conditions we have to make $\int_{s_0}^{s_1} ds$ a maximum or a minimum. We may then in the usual way consider that we have to make $\int_{s_0}^{s_1} V ds$ a maximum or a minimum, where

$$V = 1 + \frac{\lambda}{2}\left\{\left(\frac{dx}{ds}\right)^2 + \left(\frac{dy}{ds}\right)^2 + \left(\frac{dz}{ds}\right)^2 - 1\right\} + \frac{\lambda'}{2}\left\{\left(\frac{d^2x}{ds^2}\right)^2 + \left(\frac{d^2y}{ds^2}\right)^2 + \left(\frac{d^2z}{ds^2}\right)^2 - \frac{1}{\rho^2}\right\}.$$

Here $\dfrac{\lambda}{2}$ and $\dfrac{\lambda'}{2}$ denote functions of s at present undetermined.

Hence in the usual way we obtain as the necessary equations for a maximum or a minimum,

$$\left.\begin{aligned}
\frac{d^2}{ds^2}\,\lambda'\,\frac{d^2x}{ds^2} - \frac{d}{ds}\,\lambda\,\frac{dx}{ds} &= 0 \\[4pt]
\frac{d^2}{ds^2}\,\lambda'\,\frac{d^2y}{ds^2} - \frac{d}{ds}\,\lambda\,\frac{dy}{ds} &= 0 \\[4pt]
\frac{d^2}{ds^2}\,\lambda'\,\frac{d^2z}{ds^2} - \frac{d}{ds}\,\lambda\,\frac{dz}{ds} &= 0
\end{aligned}\right\} \quad \ldots\ldots\ldots\ldots\ldots \text{(10)}.$$

Therefore by integration

$$
\left.\begin{aligned}
\frac{d}{ds}\lambda'\frac{d'x}{ds'}-\lambda\frac{dx}{ds}&=a\\[4pt]
\frac{d}{ds}\lambda'\frac{d'y}{ds'}-\lambda\frac{dy}{ds}&=b\\[4pt]
\frac{d}{ds}\lambda'\frac{d'z}{ds'}-\lambda\frac{dz}{ds}&=c
\end{aligned}\right\}\quad\ldots\ldots\ldots\ldots\ldots\ldots\ (11).
$$

Multiply the first of equations (11) by $\frac{dy}{ds}$ and the second by $\frac{dx}{ds}$ and subtract; thus

$$
\left(\frac{dy}{ds}\frac{d'x}{ds'}-\frac{dx}{ds}\frac{d'y}{ds'}\right)\frac{d\lambda'}{ds}+\left(\frac{dy}{ds}\frac{d'x}{ds'}-\frac{dx}{ds}\frac{d'y}{ds'}\right)\lambda'=a\frac{dy}{ds}-b\frac{dx}{ds}.
$$

By integration we deduce the first of the following three equations, and the other two may be obtained in a similar manner,

$$
\left.\begin{aligned}
\lambda'\left(\frac{dy}{ds}\frac{d'z}{ds'}-\frac{dx}{ds}\frac{d'y}{ds'}\right)&=ay-bx+f\\[4pt]
\lambda'\left(\frac{dx}{ds}\frac{d'z}{ds'}-\frac{dz}{ds}\frac{d'x}{ds'}\right)&=cx-az+f'\\[4pt]
\lambda'\left(\frac{dz}{ds}\frac{d'y}{ds'}-\frac{dy}{ds}\frac{d'z}{ds'}\right)&=bz-cy+f''
\end{aligned}\right\}\quad\ldots\ldots\ldots\ldots(12).
$$

In these equations $f,\,f'$, and f'' are arbitrary constants. This method of solution is given by Mr Jellett; see his *Calculus of Variations*, page 195.

151. We have not yet considered the integrated part of the variation. We suppose that the extreme points of the curve are fixed. Then with the notation of Art. 149 the integrated part of the variation will consist of

$$
\frac{dV}{dy'}\,\delta y'+\frac{dV}{dz''}\,\delta z'.
$$

If we suppose that there is no restriction on the tangents at the limiting points, then since $\delta y'$ and $\delta z'$ are independent, we must have $\frac{dV}{dy''}=0$ and $\frac{dV}{dz''}=0$ at both the limits in order that the integrated part of the variation may vanish. Hence from the known expressions for $\dfrac{dV}{dy''}$ and $\dfrac{dV}{dz''}$ we must either have $m=0$ at both limits, or else we must have simultaneously

$$y'' + z'(z'y'' - y'z'') = 0, \quad \text{and} \quad z'' - y'(z'y'' - y'z'') = 0,$$

at one limit or at both limits. But the latter equations are not admissible, for they lead by squaring and adding to

$$y''^2 + z''^2 + (y'^2 + z'^2)(z'y'' - y'z'')^2 + 2(z'y'' - y'z'')^2 = 0,$$

and this would make that expression vanish which is always equal to the constant $\dfrac{1}{\rho}$ by hypothesis.

152. Let us now examine the form of the integrated part when we adopt the method of solution given in Art. 150.

The integrated part consists of the following terms;

first, $\Gamma\delta s$,

secondly, $\left(\lambda \dfrac{dx}{ds} - \dfrac{d}{ds}\lambda'\dfrac{d^2x}{ds^2}\right)\left(\delta x - \dfrac{dx}{ds}\delta s\right)$ together with two similar terms in y and z,

thirdly, $\lambda'\dfrac{d^2x}{ds^2}\left(\delta\dfrac{dx}{ds} - \dfrac{d^2x}{ds^2}\delta s\right)$ together with two similar terms in y and z.

Since the extreme points are supposed fixed δx, δy, and δz vanish; hence by using equations (11) we obtain for the integrated part

$$\left(V + a\dfrac{dx}{ds} + b\dfrac{dy}{ds} + c\dfrac{dz}{ds} - \dfrac{\lambda}{\rho}\right)\delta s + \lambda'\left(\dfrac{d^2x}{ds^2}\delta\dfrac{dx}{ds} + \dfrac{d^2y}{ds^2}\delta\dfrac{dy}{ds} + \dfrac{d^2z}{ds^2}\delta\dfrac{dz}{ds}\right),$$

where it is to be observed that $V=1$.

It will now be convenient to determine λ'; for this purpose multiply equations (11) by $\dfrac{d^2x}{ds^2}$, $\dfrac{d^2y}{ds^2}$, $\dfrac{d^2z}{ds^2}$, respectively, and add; thus

$$\frac{1}{\rho^2}\frac{d\lambda'}{ds} = a\frac{d^2x}{ds^2} + b\frac{d^2y}{ds^2} + c\frac{d^2z}{ds^2};$$

therefore
$$\frac{\lambda'}{\rho} = a\,\frac{dx}{ds} + b\,\frac{dy}{ds} + c\,\frac{dz}{ds} + \text{a constant};$$

and in order that the coefficient of δs in the integrated part of the variation may vanish this constant must equal unity, so that

$$\frac{\lambda'}{\rho} = 1 + a\,\frac{dx}{ds} + b\,\frac{dy}{ds} + c\,\frac{dz}{ds}.$$

In order that the rest of the integrated part of the variation may vanish it may be shewn as in Art. 151 that λ' must vanish at both limits of the integration; this is proved by Mr Jellett on page 197 of his work.

The value of λ may also be found; for this purpose multiply equations (11) by $\frac{dx}{ds}$, $\frac{dy}{ds}$, $\frac{dz}{ds}$, respectively, and add; thus

$$\lambda = \lambda'\left(\frac{dx}{ds}\,\frac{d^2x}{ds^2} + \frac{dy}{ds}\,\frac{d^2y}{ds^2} + \frac{dz}{ds}\,\frac{d^2z}{ds^2}\right) - a\,\frac{dx}{ds} - b\,\frac{dy}{ds} - c\,\frac{dz}{ds}$$

$$= -\frac{\lambda'}{\rho} - a\,\frac{dx}{ds} - b\,\frac{dy}{ds} - c\,\frac{dz}{ds} = 1 - \frac{2\lambda'}{\rho}.$$

153. Now return to equations (12) of Art. 150 and remember the result just mentioned that λ' vanishes at both limits of the integration. Take the origin of co-ordinates at one of the fixed points; then since we have simultaneously $x = 0$, $y = 0$, $z = 0$, $\lambda' = 0$, it follows that $f = 0$, $f' = 0$, $f'' = 0$; multiply equations (12) by $\frac{dz}{ds}$, $\frac{dy}{ds}$, $\frac{dx}{ds}$, respectively, and add; thus we obtain

$$(ay - bx)\,\frac{dz}{ds} + (cx - az)\,\frac{dy}{ds} + (bz - cy)\,\frac{dx}{ds} = 0,$$

or
$$a\left(y\,\frac{dz}{ds} - z\,\frac{dy}{ds}\right) + b\left(z\,\frac{dx}{ds} - x\,\frac{dz}{ds}\right) + c\left(x\,\frac{dy}{ds} - y\,\frac{dx}{ds}\right) = 0.$$

This equation may be integrated by assuming

$$y = ux, \quad z = vx;$$

it leads to
$$ay - bx = n\,(az - cx),$$

where n is a constant; this is the equation to a plane passing through the origin. Thus the required curve is a plane curve, and as a circle is the only plane curve of constant curvature, we obtain a circle as the required solution.

154. The preceding article is due to Mr Jellett; it will be seen that it adds something to the result enunciated by Delaunay; for Delaunay stated that a circle is *a* solution of the problem, while Mr Jellett shews that if there is no restriction on the tangents at the extreme points the required curve must be a plane curve and therefore a circle.

Some further remarks however are necessary here. The proposed problem may be understood in two senses; for we may be required to find a curve of maximum or minimum length while the curvature has *some* constant value, or we may be required to find a curve of maximum or minimum length while the curvature has an *assigned* constant value.

In the first case, when the curvature is merely required to be constant, we may take ρ as large as we please, and thus the solution will degenerate into the straight line joining the two given points. Let us next consider the second case, in which the curve must have an *assigned* constant curvature; it might then be impossible to draw an arc of a circle so as to have a given curvature and to pass through two given points, and in fact this could not be done if the given points are at a greater distance than the diameter of a circle which has the assigned curvature. It becomes a question then, what the solution of the problem is in such a case where the distance of the given points is too great to allow of their being connected by an arc of a circle. We shall shew that the problem is solved by a set of arcs of the required curvature.

Let A and D be the two fixed points (see figure 6).

Let ACD, DEF, FGB be three equal arcs of the assigned curvature, and let them be placed so as to have a common tangent at the points of junction D and F; then we shall shew that the curve $ACDEFGB$ constitutes a solution of the problem under consideration.

For let us suppose the quantity $s_1 - s_0$ divided into three parts $s_1 - \sigma_1$, $\sigma_1 - \sigma_0$, $\sigma_0 - s_0$; then

$$\int_{s_0}^{s_1} V ds = \int_{s_0}^{\sigma_0} V ds + \int_{\sigma_0}^{\sigma_1} V ds + \int_{\sigma_1}^{s_1} V ds,$$

and the variation of the left-hand member will be zero if the variation of the right-hand member be so.

Now consider $\delta \int_{s_0}^{\sigma_0} V ds$. The part of this which remains under the sign of integration vanishes when equations (12) are satisfied. And by proceeding as in Art. 152 it appears that if λ' vanishes at both limits the integrated part at the *lower* limit will entirely vanish and the integrated part at the *upper* limit will reduce to

$$- (a \delta x + b \delta y + c \delta z) \, ;$$

this term remains because the upper limit is now not a fixed point. The term just exhibited is destroyed by a similar term which occurs at the lower limit of $\delta \int_{\sigma_0}^{\sigma_1} V ds$, if a, b, c retain the same values.

In this way we see that we shall have

$$\delta \int_{s_0}^{\sigma_0} V ds + \delta \int_{\sigma_0}^{\sigma_1} V ds + \delta \int_{\sigma_1}^{s_1} V ds = 0$$

for the system of arcs in figure 6, provided that a, b, c *retain the same values* for all the arcs.

It will be remembered that by Art. 152,

$$\lambda' = \rho' \left(1 + a \frac{dx}{ds} + b \frac{dy}{ds} + c \frac{ds}{ds} \right) \dots\dots\dots\dots (13) \, ;$$

moreover the common tangent at D makes the same angle with AB as the tangent at B, and the common tangent at F makes the same angle with AB as the tangent at A; thus if a, b, c retain the same values throughout the arcs, λ' vanishes at F and B if it vanishes at A and D.

Thus all that we have to do is to shew that equations (12) are true for all the arcs in figure 6 while a, b, c retain the same values throughout, and λ' has the value given in (13). That is, in effect we have to shew that equations (12) and (13) are true for a circle of radius ρ without imposing any restriction on the co-ordinates of its centre which it may be impossible to fulfil.

Since the direction of the axes is in our power, let us suppose that A is the origin, AD the direction of the axis of x, and the plane of the arcs the plane of (x, y). Then $z = 0$; thus we must have $f = 0$, $f' = 0$, $f'' = 0$, $c = 0$ in (12), so that these equations reduce to

$$\lambda'\left(\frac{dy}{ds}\frac{d^2x}{ds^2} - \frac{dx}{ds}\frac{d^2y}{ds^2}\right) = ay - bx \quad \dotsc \quad (14),$$

where

$$\lambda' = \rho^2\left(1 + a\frac{dx}{ds} + b\frac{dy}{ds}\right) \quad \dotsc \quad (15).$$

Now let $(x - h)^2 + (y - k)^2 = \rho^2$ be the equation to the circle of which the first arc ACD is a portion; and suppose that the axis of y is taken so that k is positive. We shall have

$$(x - h)\frac{dx}{ds} + (y - k)\frac{dy}{ds} = 0,$$

and

$$\left(\frac{dx}{ds}\right)^2 + \left(\frac{dy}{ds}\right)^2 = 1;$$

from these we deduce

$$\frac{dx}{ds} = \pm\frac{y - k}{\rho}, \quad \frac{dy}{ds} = \mp\frac{x - h}{\rho} \quad \dotsc \quad (16);$$

and supposing that s increases with x so that $\dfrac{dx}{ds}$ is positive we must take the *lower* signs;

then

$$\frac{d^2x}{ds^2} = -\frac{1}{\rho}\frac{dy}{ds} = -\frac{x - h}{\rho^2},$$

$$\frac{d^2y}{ds^2} = \frac{1}{\rho}\frac{dx}{ds} = -\frac{y - k}{\rho^2}.$$

Thus that (14) and (15) may be true, we require that

$$-\rho^2\left(1 - a\frac{y - k}{\rho} + b\frac{x - h}{\rho}\right)\frac{1}{\rho} = ay - bx,$$

so that

$$1 + \frac{ak - bh}{\rho} = 0 \quad \dotsc \quad (17),$$

is the only relation between the constants.

Now we have already supposed that λ' vanishes both at A and D; at these points $\dfrac{dx}{ds}$ has the same value while $\dfrac{dy}{ds}$ has values numerically equal but of opposite sign.

We must therefore have $b = 0$, so that (17) reduces to

$$1 + \frac{ak}{\rho} = 0.$$

Now suppose h' and k' the co-ordinates of the centre of the circle of which the second arc DEF is a portion. Proceeding as before we shall find that we must now use the *upper* signs in the equations which replace (16), and we shall finally arrive at

$$1 - \frac{ak'}{\rho} = 0.$$

Thus k and k' are equal in magnitude and of opposite sign, and this is the only condition necessary to ensure that equations (14) and (15) shall hold for both arcs with the same values of the constants a and b; and this condition *is* satisfied by the figure.

The relation expressed by $1 + \dfrac{ak}{\rho} = 0$, or $1 - \dfrac{ak'}{\rho} = 0$, is in fact the same as that which must hold in order that λ' may vanish at A and D.

We have supposed in the figure *three* arcs, but it is obvious that the reasoning we have used will apply whatever may be the number of arcs; and as we may make this number as great as we please, we can finally obtain a curved line which differs in length by as small a quantity as we please from the straight line AB.

Thus when the curvature is to have an *assigned* constant value, the solution will, as in the former case, coincide practically with the straight line which joins the two given points.

155. In the preceding four articles we have supposed that there is no restriction on the tangents at the extreme points. If the directions of the tangents at the extreme points are given, it will no longer be necessary, as in Art. 152, that λ' should

vanish at both limits. If the tangents at the extreme points are equally inclined to the straight line which joins the extreme points, and if also the two tangents and the straight line are in the same plane, then if the value of the curvature is not assigned, it will be possible to satisfy the conditions of the problem by a series of circular arcs as in Art. 154; and if the value of the curvature is assigned, it will be possible to satisfy the conditions of the problem by such an arc or such a series of arcs, if the distance of the extreme points and the magnitude of the radius of curvature and the directions of the tangents have been given suitably, but not otherwise. But no solution has hitherto been given for the general problem when the directions of the tangents at the extreme points are assigned in a perfectly arbitrary manner.

156. We will shew that in certain cases a helix may be the solution of the problem. For suppose in equations (12) that

$$a = 0, \ b = 0, \ f = 0, \ f'' = 0;$$

assume
$$x = h \cos \theta, \ y = h \sin \theta, \ z = k\theta;$$

thus
$$\frac{ds}{d\theta} = \sqrt{(h^2 + k^2)},$$

and
$$\frac{dx}{ds} = -\frac{y}{\sqrt{(h^2 + k^2)}}, \quad \frac{dy}{ds} = \frac{x}{\sqrt{(h^2 + k^2)}}, \quad \frac{dz}{ds} = \frac{k}{\sqrt{(h^2 + k^2)}},$$

$$\frac{d^2x}{ds^2} = -\frac{x}{h^2 + k^2}, \quad \frac{d^2y}{ds^2} = -\frac{y}{h^2 + k^2}, \quad \frac{d^2z}{ds^2} = 0,$$

$$\lambda' = \rho^2 \left(1 + c\,\frac{dz}{ds}\right) = \rho^2 \left\{1 + \frac{ck}{\sqrt{(h^2 + k^2)}}\right\}.$$

The first of equations (12) when these values are substituted becomes

$$\rho^2 \left\{1 + \frac{ck}{\sqrt{(h^2 + k^2)}}\right\} \frac{h^2}{(h^2 + k^2)^2} = -f \ \ldots\ldots\ldots\ (18),$$

and the other two become

$$\rho^2 \left\{1 + \frac{ck}{\sqrt{(h^2 + k^2)}}\right\} \frac{k}{(h^2 + k^2)^2} = c \ \ldots\ldots\ldots\ (19).$$

And $\rho = \frac{h^2 + k^2}{h}$; thus from (19) we shall obtain

$$k\sqrt{(h^2 + k^2)} = c\,(h^2 - k^2) \ \ldots\ldots\ldots\ldots\ldots\ (20);$$

and from (18)

$$-f = \frac{ch'}{k} = \frac{h'(h'+k')^{\frac{1}{2}}}{h'-k'} \quad\dots\dots\dots\dots\dots\dots \text{(21)}.$$

It appears from (20) and (21) that we cannot have $h = k$, and with this exception a helix may be a solution of the problem.

157.   We will now return to Delaunay's notation.   It may be shewn by performing some ordinary transformations that the equations (1) and (2) may be written thus:

$$\frac{dy}{ds}\left(1 - \frac{2m}{\rho}\frac{dx}{ds}\right) - \frac{d}{ds}\left(m\rho\frac{dx}{ds}\frac{d^2y}{ds^2}\right) = a,$$

$$\frac{dz}{ds}\left(1 - \frac{2m}{\rho}\frac{dx}{ds}\right) - \frac{d}{ds}\left(m\rho\frac{dx}{ds}\frac{d^2z}{ds^2}\right) = \beta.$$

These coincide with the second and third of equations (11) by supposing

$$a = -b, \quad \beta = -c, \quad m\rho\frac{dx}{ds} = \lambda', \text{ and } 1 - \frac{2m}{\rho}\frac{dx}{ds} = \lambda,$$

that is

$$\lambda = 1 - \frac{2\lambda'}{\rho^2}.$$

And the equation (7) may be written

$$m\frac{dx}{ds} = \rho\left\{1 - a\frac{dy}{ds} - \beta\frac{dz}{ds} - \gamma\frac{dx}{ds}\right\},$$

and thus the value of $m\rho\frac{dx}{ds}$ coincides with that found for λ' in Art. 152, by supposing $\gamma = -a$.

From equations (1), (2) and (7) in the form in which they are here given, we can deduce an equation coincident with the first of equations (11); so that the two solutions agree, as of course they should.

Now in Art. 153 we obtained as the result of the symmetrical solution that in the case in which the tangents at the limiting points are unrestricted the required curve must be a plane curve, and that the plane of the curve must contain the line

$$\frac{x}{a} = \frac{y}{b} = \frac{z}{c}.$$

If this result be transformed into Delaunay's notation it leads to this conclusion; the plane determined by $z = ay + bx + c$ in his notation must contain the line determined by $\dfrac{x}{-\gamma} = \dfrac{y}{-a} = \dfrac{z}{-\beta}$ in his notation. For this to be the case we must have $\gamma = \dfrac{\beta - a\alpha}{b}$. This agrees with equation (6) and verifies Delaunay's conclusion; but it is not obvious in what way he arrived at it.

158. It must be observed that Delaunay does not treat the integrated part of the variation as we have done in Art. 151; he considers that in virtue of his previous remarks we must always have $m = 0$ at the limits of the integration. But if $m = 0$ at the limits the curve is necessarily a plane curve, as appears in Art. 153; and this is obviously impossible when the tangents at the limits are so assigned that they do not lie in one plane. This furnishes additional evidence against Delaunay's views.

Moreover this problem affords a good illustration of the remarks made in the first part of Art. 146; for when the condition is given that the curvature of the required curve is to be constant the natural meaning of this condition would be that at *every* point of the curve *up to and including the limiting points* the radius of curvature is to be constant.

159. The next problem considered is to find a surface of minimum area, the required surface being supposed to be bounded by a curve lying on a given surface. The problem had been considered originally by Lagrange, in the case in which the bounding curve was supposed fixed; see Art. 18. Delaunay arrives at the known result that the required surface must be one that has at every point the sum of its two principal radii of curvature zero. Delaunay shews moreover from the equation which holds at the limits that the required surface must cut the given surface at right angles at every point of the curve of intersection of the two surfaces. Delaunay then generalizes his results by considering the multiple integral

$$\int \ldots \iiint du \ldots dv\,dx\,dy \; \sqrt{\left\{ 1 + \left(\frac{dz}{du}\right)^{2} + \ldots + \left(\frac{dz}{dv}\right)^{2} + \left(\frac{dz}{dx}\right)^{2} + \left(\frac{dz}{dy}\right)^{2} \right\}}.$$

160. The next problem is to find the surface which has a given area and bounds a maximum volume; that is, z must be determined such a function of x and y as will make $\iint dx\, dy\, z$ a maximum, while

$$\iint dx\, dy\, \sqrt{\left\{ 1 + \left(\frac{dz}{dx}\right)^2 + \left(\frac{dz}{dy}\right)^2 \right\}}$$

is to be constant. This problem was originally considered by Lagrange; see Strauch, Vol. II. page 623.

Delaunay obtains as the result that the required surface must be such that at every point the sum of its two principal curvatures must be constant. He supposes that the required surface is to be bounded by a curve lying on a given surface, and he gives a geometrical interpretation of the equation which he finds must hold at the bounding curve. He then generalizes his results by taking the case in which

$$\int \cdots \iiint du \cdots dv\, dx\, dy\, z$$

is to be a maximum, while

$$\int \cdots \iiint du \cdots dv\, dx\, dy\, \sqrt{\left\{ 1 + \left(\frac{dz}{du}\right)^2 + \cdots + \left(\frac{dz}{dv}\right)^2 + \left(\frac{dz}{dx}\right)^2 + \left(\frac{dz}{dy}\right)^2 \right\}}$$

is to be constant.

161. Delaunay makes some further investigations respecting the surface which includes a maximum volume with a given area. He says that of all closed surfaces the sphere was known to be that which included the greatest volume under a given surface, but that this result had not yet been deduced from the equations furnished by the Calculus of Variations. He tried the question in another way, and although he did not succeed in arriving at a complete solution he gives his results. The problem considered is the following; it is required to join by a surface of given area two curves of given length situated in two parallel planes, in such a manner that the included volume may be a maximum. The differential equations to which the problem leads are then given, and, assuming that the required surface will be a surface of revolution, it is proved that it must be a sphere. The problem is

given by Mr Jellett, with some additional remarks on the last of the limiting equations; see his *Calculus of Variations*, pages 282—286.

162. The last example considered by Delaunay is the variation of the following expression which occurs in the theory of heat,

$$\iiint dx\,dy\,dz\,k \left[\left(\frac{dV}{dx}\right)^{2} + \left(\frac{dV}{dy}\right)^{2} + \left(\frac{dV}{dz}\right)^{2}\right]$$

$$+ \iint dx\,dy\,h\,V^{2} \sqrt{\left\{1 + \left(\frac{dz}{dx}\right)^{2} + \left(\frac{dz}{dy}\right)^{2}\right\}}.$$

In concluding our account of Delaunay's memoir it may be observed that the examples, although interesting in themselves, do not throw much light on the precise point which according to the announcement of the Academy of Sciences required illustration, namely, the equations which must hold at the limits of the integrations; see Art. 133. And there is very little that can be considered as an application to triple integrals which was specially indicated. From the fact that the judges drew attention to Delaunay's researches on the distinction of maxima and minima, it may be inferred that they, as well as Delaunay himself, were not aware that he had been anticipated by Brunacci on this point.

CHAPTER VII.

SARRUS.

163. WE have already stated that the prize offered by the Academy of Sciences of Paris for an essay on the Calculus of Variations was awarded to M. Sarrus; see Art. 133. We now proceed to give an account of the memoir which obtained the prize.

This memoir is entitled *Recherches sur le Calcul des Variations;* it is published in the tenth volume of the memoirs of the *Savants Étrangers*, and the date of publication is 1846.

164. The memoir consists of 127 quarto pages. It is divided into five chapters. The first chapter is chiefly occupied with formulæ for differentiating integral expressions with respect to any parameter which they may involve; the second chapter applies these formulæ so as to obtain the variation of a multiple integral in an undeveloped form; the third chapter developes this variation and shews how many equations must be satisfied in order that the variation may be zero; the fourth chapter gives special development of the formulæ in the case of triple integrals; the fifth chapter applies the formulæ to three examples.

The memoir is extremly interesting and valuable, and contains a complete solution of the question proposed by the Academy. The formulæ which are obtained are rather complicated, but this can hardly be avoided in the subject. The memoir is probably the most important original contribution to the Calculus of Variations which has been made during the present century.

165. The investigations of Sarrus apply to multiple integrals of any order, and some doubt has been felt with respect to the best method of giving an account of them. We shall confine ourselves to the case of a *triple* integral, because it appears that

no abridgement could render adequate justice to the general results given by Sarrus, and it would be almost impossible to comprise some of the more complicated formulæ within the breadth of an octavo page. We may hope to succeed in giving an intelligible specimen of the investigations of Sarrus by taking the case of a triple integral; and we must refer the student who wishes to appreciate the full merit of the author to the original memoir.

We shall not therefore give an analysis of the memoir article by article, nor shall we adopt the notation of the author. Sarrus uses the symbols x_1, x_2, x_3, ... for the independent variables; the lower *limiting* values of the variables are denoted by a single accent, as x_1', x_2', x_3', ... and the upper *limiting* values of the variables are denoted by two accents as x_1'', x_2'', x_3'', ... We shall use x, y, s as independent variables, and shall denote as we have done heretofore the lower *limiting* values by the suffix 0 and the upper *limiting* values by the suffix 1. The unavoidable complexity of the notation in the original memoir has led there to numerous misprints, which however are not of great importance.

106. We shall use then the following notation; by the expression $\int dx \int dy \int dzu$ we denote a triple integral; we suppose that u is a function of the independent variables x, y, s, and of any dependent variable or variables, and differential coefficients with respect to x, y, and s. The integration in the triple integral is supposed to be performed, first with respect to s from the limit z_0 to the limit z_1, next with respect to y from the limit y_0 to the limit y_1, lastly with respect to x from the limit x_0 to the limit x_1. It follows from the nature of definite integration that the limits z_0 and z_1 will not be functions of s, but may be functions of x and y; the limits y_0 and y_1 will not be functions of y or z, but may be functions of x; and the limits x_0 and x_1 will not be functions of x or y or s.

The limits of the integrations being thus distinctly stated we shall not express them in our formulæ; but they must always be *understood*. No confusion or difficulty will arise from our not explicitly introducing the limits because we shall never have occasion to use any indefinite integral, and we shall not make any change in

the *order* of the integrations.   Also when we have occasion to use
a single or double integral involving respectively one or two of the
variables x, y, z, we shall not express the limits, but they must be
understood.   This omission of the limits in our integrals may at
first be a little perplexing to the student, but it is strongly recommended by the simplification thus effected in the formulæ.

167.   The symbol 7 will be employed in the following manner.
Suppose u any function which involves a quantity p; if in u we
change p into q we obtain a result which we shall denote by

$$7_p^q u.$$

This symbol is the one which Sarrus himself employs; he calls it
a *sign of substitution*.   The use of this symbol will lead us to expressions of the following forms,

$$7_x^{x_0} 7_y^{y_0} u, \quad 7_x^{x_0} 7_y^{y_0} 7_z^{z_0} u, \quad \int dx\, 7_y^{y_0} u, \quad \int dx \int dy\, 7_z^{z_0} u,$$

$$7_x^{x_0} \int dy\, u, \quad 7_x^{x_0} 7_y^{y_0} \int dz\, u;$$

these expressions do not require any explanation.

This notation is certainly one of the great merits of the memoir,
and in this respect nothing has probably been suggested which is
of so much service to the Calculus of Variations as this sign of
substitution since Lagrange introduced the symbol δ.

168.   We shall now shew how to differentiate an integral
expression with respect to any parameter which it may involve;
the formula is well known, but it may be interesting to see the
method of Sarrus, and to exhibit the result by means of the
symbol 7.

Let $F(t, x)$ denote any function of the parameter t, the variable
x, and other variables if required.   Put

$$\frac{dF(t, x)}{dt} = \phi(t, x) \quad \dotfill \quad (1),$$

$$\frac{dF(t, x)}{dx} = \psi(t, x) \quad \dotfill \quad (2);$$

we have then identically

$$\frac{d\phi(t, x)}{dx} = \frac{d\psi(t, x)}{dt} \quad\dots\dots\dots\dots\dots\dots\dots (3).$$

Let x_0 and x_1 denote particular values of x; then

$$\frac{d\left[F(t, x_1) - F(t, x_0)\right]}{dt} = \phi(t, x_1) - \phi(t, x_0)$$

$$+ \frac{dx_1}{dt}\,\psi(t, x_1) - \frac{dx_0}{dt}\,\psi(t, x_0) \quad\dots\dots\dots (4).$$

But from (2) and (3) by integrating with respect to x, we obtain

$$F(t, x_1) - F(t, x_0) = \int dx\,\psi(t, x),$$

$$\phi(t, x_1) - \phi(t, x_0) = \int dx\,\frac{d\psi(t, x)}{dt}.$$

Substitute these values in (4); we thus obtain

$$\frac{d}{dt}\int dx\,\psi(t, x) = \int dx\,\frac{d\psi(t, x)}{dt} + \frac{dx_1}{dt}\,\psi(t, x_1) - \frac{dx_0}{dt}\,\psi(t, x_0).$$

Now put u for $\psi(t, x)$ for shortness; then the last result may be expressed thus:

$$\frac{d}{dt}\int dx\,u = \int dx\,\frac{du}{dt} + \frac{dx_1}{dt}\,\rceil_x^{x_1} u - \frac{dx_0}{dt}\,\rceil_x^{x_0} u,$$

where u may denote any function whatever.

It will be observed that in accordance with the remark in Art. 166, the limits of the integrals are not expressed, but they must be understood.

109. We now proceed to differentiate a *double* integral with respect to any parameter which it may involve.

We have seen that if u be any function whatever,

$$\frac{d}{dt}\int dx\,u = \int dx\,\frac{du}{dt} + \frac{dx_1}{dt}\,\rceil_x^{x_1} u - \frac{dx_0}{dt}\,\rceil_x^{x_0} u;$$

186 BABBL'S.

in this formula change u into $\int dy\, u$; thus

$$\frac{d}{dt}\int dx\int dy\, u = \int dx\, \frac{d}{dt}\int dy\, u + \frac{dx_1}{dt} T_x^{x_1}\int dy\, u - \frac{dx_0}{dt} T_x^{x_0}\int dy\, u,$$

and as in the preceding article

$$\frac{d}{dt}\int dy\, u = \int dy\, \frac{du}{dt} + \frac{dy_1}{dt} T_y^{y_1} u - \frac{dy_0}{dt} T_y^{y_0} u;$$

hence by substitution we obtain

$$\frac{d}{dt}\int dx\int dy\, u = \int dx\int dy\, \frac{du}{dt} + \int dx\, \frac{dy_1}{dt} T_y^{y_1} u - \int dx\, \frac{dy_0}{dt} T_y^{y_0} u$$
$$+ \frac{dx_1}{dt} T_x^{x_1}\int dy\, u - \frac{dx_0}{dt} T_x^{x_0}\int dy\, u.$$

170. We now proceed to differentiate a *triple* integral with respect to any parameter which it may involve.

In the result of the preceding article change u into $\int dz\, u$; thus

$$\frac{d}{dt}\int dx\int dy\int dz\, u = \int dx\int dy\, \frac{d}{dt}\int dz\, u$$
$$+ \int dx\, \frac{dy_1}{dt} T_y^{y_1}\int dz\, u - \int dx\, \frac{dy_0}{dt} T_y^{y_0}\int dz\, u$$
$$+ \frac{dx_1}{dt} T_x^{x_1}\int dy\int dz\, u - \frac{dx_0}{dt} T_x^{x_0}\int dy\int dz\, u.$$

Now transform the first term on the right-hand side by Art. 168; thus

$$\frac{d}{dt}\int dx\int dy\int dz\, u = \int dx\int dy\int dz\, \frac{du}{dt}$$
$$+ \int dx\int dy\, \frac{dz_1}{dt} T_z^{z_1} u - \int dx\int dy\, \frac{dz_0}{dt} T_z^{z_0} u$$
$$+ \int dx\, \frac{dy_1}{dt} T_y^{y_1}\int dz\, u - \int dx\, \frac{dy_0}{dt} T_y^{y_0}\int dz\, u$$
$$+ \frac{dx_1}{dt} T_x^{x_1}\int dy\int dz\, u - \frac{dx_0}{dt} T_x^{x_0}\int dy\int dz\, u.$$

171. We may modify the form of the preceding result. It is evident that if r be independent of p,

$$J{}_p^q\, ur = r\, J{}_p^q\, u\,;$$

now x_0 and x_1 are independent of x, also y_0 and y_1 are independent of y and z, and z_0 and z_1 are independent of x, y, and z. Therefore we can alter the order of some of the symbols which occur in the right-hand member of the result of the preceding article, and exhibit that result thus,

$$\frac{d}{dt}\int dx \int dy \int dz\, u = \int dx \int dy \int dz\, \frac{du}{dt}$$

$$+ \int dx \int dy\, J{}_z^{z_1} u\, \frac{dz_1}{dt} - \int dx \int dy\, J{}_z^{z_0} u\, \frac{dz_0}{dt}$$

$$+ \int dx\, J{}_y^{y_1} \int dz\, u\, \frac{dy_1}{dt} - \int dx\, J{}_y^{y_0} \int dz\, u\, \frac{dy_0}{dt}$$

$$+ J{}_x^{x_1} \int dy \int dz\, u\, \frac{dx_1}{dt} - J{}_x^{x_0} \int dy \int dz\, u\, \frac{dx_0}{dt}\,.$$

172. We will now give some formulæ for differentiating quantities affected with the symbol J which will be useful hereafter.

Let $F(t, \xi)$ denote any function of the parameter t, the variable ξ, and other variables if required. Let $\phi(t, \xi)$ denote the partial differential coefficient of $F(t, \xi)$ with respect to t, and $\psi(t, \xi)$ the partial differential coefficient of $F(t, \xi)$ with respect to ξ; then we have

$$\frac{dF(t, \xi)}{dt} = \phi(t, \xi) + \frac{d\xi}{dt}\psi(t, \xi)\,;$$

now let $u = F(t, x)$; then

$$F(t, \xi) = J{}_x^\xi u,\quad \phi(t, \xi) = J{}_x^\xi \frac{du}{dt},\quad \psi(t, \xi) = J{}_x^\xi \frac{du}{dx}\,;$$

thus we have

$$\frac{d}{dt} J{}_x^\xi u = J{}_x^\xi \frac{du}{dt} + \frac{d\xi}{dt} J{}_x^\xi \frac{du}{dx}\,.$$

Suppose that ξ is independent of x, then by Art. 171,

$$\frac{d\xi}{dt} J{}_x^\xi \frac{du}{dx} = J{}_x^\xi \frac{du}{dx}\frac{d\xi}{dt}\,,$$

and finally

$$\frac{d}{dt}\gamma_x^{\xi} u = \gamma_x^{\xi}\left(\frac{du}{dt}+\frac{du}{dx}\frac{d\xi}{dt}\right) \ldots\ldots\ldots\ldots (1).$$

Now $\int dy\,\dfrac{du}{dy} = \gamma_y^{y_1} u - \gamma_y^{y_0} u$; and if in this we replace u by $\gamma_x^{\zeta} u$ we have

$$\int dy\,\frac{d}{dy}\gamma_x^{\zeta} u = \gamma_y^{y_1}\gamma_x^{\zeta} u - \gamma_y^{y_0}\gamma_x^{\zeta} u.$$

Hence by (1),

$$\int dy\,\gamma_x^{\zeta}\left(\frac{du}{dy}+\frac{du}{dz}\frac{d\zeta}{dy}\right) = \gamma_y^{y_1}\gamma_x^{\zeta} u - \gamma_y^{y_0}\gamma_x^{\zeta} u\,;$$

therefore

$$\int dy\,\gamma_x^{\zeta}\frac{du}{dy} = -\int dy\,\gamma_x^{\zeta}\frac{du}{dz}\frac{d\zeta}{dy} + \gamma_y^{y_1}\gamma_x^{\zeta} u - \gamma_y^{y_0}\gamma_x^{\zeta} u \ldots\ldots\ldots (2).$$

In the applications we shall make of the formula (2) hereafter, ζ will denote either z_0 or z_1.

173. We shall now proceed to use the results already obtained in expressing the variation of a triple integral. Sarrus adopts an idea of a variation which had previously presented itself to Euler and Lagrange; see Arts. 22 and 15.

We consider then that we have a triple integral taken between limits for each of the three integrations; and we use the symbol u to denote the function to be integrated. Now u involves x, y, z, and any function v of x, y, z, together with the differential coefficient of v with respect to x, y, z; also u may involve any other function w of x, y, z, together with the differential coefficients of w with respect to x, y, z; and so on. Now to obtain the variation of the quantity which is denoted by any symbol, we suppose that such a symbol instead of representing a function of x, y, z, or of some of these variables, becomes a function of t also, where t is a new variable which is supposed to enter in a perfectly arbitrary manner; then if the quantity in question be supposed to be differentiated with respect to t, and t made equal to zero after the differentiation, the result is called the variation of that quantity. This idea of a variation had been used by Euler and

Lagrange as we have already intimated, and subsequently by Ohm; see Arts. 22, 15 and 55.

174. In pages 45—47 of his memoir, Sarrus distinguishes between two kinds of variations; and we will now explain this distinction.

Suppose we had such a triple integral as we have considered in the preceding article. We might conceive that the independent variables x, y, z received changes by variation as well as the dependent variables v, w, ... which occur in u. When however the integrations are taken between limits it is unnecessary to suppose that the independent variables themselves receive variations; we obtain sufficient generality by ascribing variations to the dependent variables and to the *limits* of the integrations. When the variation of a function is taken on the supposition that the independent variables themselves do not receive variations, Sarrus calls the variation a *variation tronquée*, and he denotes it thus, $\bar{\delta}$. Then as he supposes his integrals to be taken between limits, he says that he is only concerned with these *variations tronquées*.

175. Now take the result obtained in Art. 171; then if we adopt the idea of a variation explained in Art. 173, and use the symbol $\bar{\delta}$ to denote a variation, we have the following formula:

$$\bar{\delta} \int dx \int dy \int dz\, u = \int dx \int dy \int dz\, \bar{\delta}u$$
$$+ T_x^{x_1} \int dy \int dz\, u\, \bar{\delta}x_1 - T_x^{x_0} \int dy \int dz \int u\, \bar{\delta}x_0$$
$$+ \int dx\, T_y^{y_1} \int dz\, u\, \bar{\delta}y_1 - \int dx\, T_y^{y_0} \int dz\, u\, \bar{\delta}y_0$$
$$+ \int dx \int dy\, T_z^{z_1} u\, \bar{\delta}z_1 - \int dx \int dy\, T_z^{z_0} u\, \bar{\delta}z_0.$$

This gives in an undeveloped form the variation of a triple integral.

176. It is certainly not necessary to verify the preceding result, but it may be interesting to show that it does agree with that

which had been given by previous writers; this Sarrus does in the manner we will now indicate.

According to Sarrus the known formula for the variation of a triple integral is the following:

$$\delta \int dx \int dy \int dz\, u = \int dx \int dy \int dz \left(\delta u - \frac{du}{dx}\delta x - \frac{du}{dy}\delta y - \frac{du}{dz}\delta z \right)$$
$$+ \int dx \int dy \int dz \left(\frac{d\,u\delta x}{dx} + \frac{d\,u\delta y}{dy} + \frac{d\,u\delta z}{dz} \right).$$

Sarrus calls this a *known* formula, but he does not say where it had been demonstrated. He probably had in view such a method as the following:

$$\delta \int dx \int dy \int dz\, u = \iiint \delta\, dx\, dy\, dz\, u$$
$$= \iiint dx\, dy\, dz\, \delta u + \iiint d\delta x\, dy\, dz\, u$$
$$+ \iiint dx\, d\delta y\, dz\, u + \iiint dx\, dy\, d\delta z\, u$$
$$= \iiint dx\, dy\, dz \left(\delta u - \frac{du}{dx}\delta x - \frac{du}{dy}\delta y - \frac{du}{dz}\delta z + \frac{d\,u\delta x}{dx} + \frac{d\,u\delta y}{dy} + \frac{d\,u\delta z}{dz} \right).$$

But it must be observed that before the researches of Poisson the variation even of a double integral had not been investigated, for the case in which the limits were variable, in an intelligible and satisfactory manner. The formula which Sarrus considers to be known will be seen to be analogous to that demonstrated by Poisson for a double integral; for Poisson's result is

$$\delta \iint V dx\, dy = \iint \left(\delta V + V \frac{d\delta x}{dx} + V \frac{d\delta y}{dy} \right),$$

in which the quantity δV is what Sarrus would denote by

$$\delta V - \frac{dV}{dx}\delta x - \frac{dV}{dy}\delta y;$$

see page 76. And the formula agrees also with the general result given by Ostrogradsky; see Art. 127 at the end, where the quantity which Ostrogradsky denotes by Du is what Sarrus would denote by

$$\delta U - \frac{dU}{dx}\delta x - \frac{dU}{dy}\delta y - \frac{dU}{dz}\delta z - \dots$$

177. In order to shew that the formula given by Sarrus agrees with the result which he considers known, we shall require some simple theorems of the Integral Calculus. Let u be any function; then

$$\int dz\,\frac{du}{dz} = T_z^{z_1}u - T_z^{z_0}u\,;$$

therefore $\int dx \int dy \int dz\,\dfrac{du}{dz} = \int dx \int dy\, T_z^{z_1}u - \int dx \int dy\, T_z^{z_0}u \ldots\ldots\ldots\ldots(1).$

Again $\qquad\int dy\,\dfrac{du}{dy} = T_y^{y_1}u - T_y^{y_0}u,$

change u into $\int dz\,u$; thus

$$\int dy\,\frac{d}{dy}\int dz\,u = T_y^{y_1}\int dz\,u - T_y^{y_0}\int dz\,u\,;$$

therefore $\quad\displaystyle\int dy \left\{\int dz\,\frac{du}{dy} + T_z^{z_1}u\,\frac{dz_1}{dy} - T_z^{z_0}u\,\frac{dz_0}{dy}\right\}$

$$= T_y^{y_1}\int dz\,u - T_y^{y_0}\int dz\,u\,;$$

therefore $\quad\displaystyle\int dy \int dz\,\frac{du}{dy} = -\int dy\, T_z^{z_1}u\,\frac{dz_1}{dy} + \int dy\, T_z^{z_0}u\,\frac{dz_0}{dy}$

$$+ T_y^{y_1}\int dz\,u - T_y^{y_0}\int dz\,u \ldots\ldots\ldots\ldots(2)\,;$$

therefore $\displaystyle\int dx \int dy \int dz\,\frac{du}{dy} = -\int dx \int dy\, T_z^{z_1}u\,\frac{dz_1}{dy} + \int dx \int dy\, T_z^{z_0}u\,\frac{dz_0}{dy}$

$$+ \int dx\, T_y^{y_1}\int dz\,u - \int dx\, T_y^{y_0}\int dz\,u \ldots\ldots\ldots(3).$$

Again, by (2) we have

$$\int dx \int dy\,\frac{du}{dx} = -\int dx\, T_y^{y_1}u\,\frac{dy_1}{dx} + \int dx\, T_y^{y_0}u\,\frac{dy_0}{dx}$$

$$+ T_x^{x_1}\int dy\,u - T_x^{x_0}\int dy\,u\,;$$

change u into $\int dz\, u$; thus we shall obtain

$$\int dx \int dy \int dz \frac{du}{dz} = -\int dx \int dy\, T_z^{z_1} u \frac{dz_1}{dx} + \int dx \int dy\, T_z^{z_0} u \frac{dz_0}{dx}$$
$$-\int dx\, T_y^{y_1} \int dz\, u \frac{dy_1}{dx} + \int dx\, T_y^{y_0} \int dz\, u \frac{dy_0}{dx}$$
$$+ T_x^{x_1} \int dy \int dz\, u - T_x^{x_0} \int dy \int dz\, u \dots\dots\dots(4).$$

Now transform $\int dx \int dy \int dz \dfrac{d\, u\delta x}{dx}$ by means of (4),

transform $\qquad\int dx \int dy \int dz \dfrac{d\, u\delta y}{dy}$ by means of (3),

and transform $\quad.\quad\int dx \int dy \int dz \dfrac{d\, u\delta z}{dz}$ by means of (1),

and rearrange the results; we thus obtain from the known formula of Art. 176,

$$\delta \int dx \int dy \int dz\, u = \int dx \int dy \int dz \left(\delta u - \frac{du}{dx}\delta x - \frac{du}{dy}\delta y - \frac{du}{dz}\delta z \right)$$
$$+ T_x^{x_1} \int dy \int dz\, u\delta x - T_x^{x_0} \int dy \int dz\, u\delta x$$
$$+ \int dx\, T_y^{y_1} \int dz\, u \left(\delta y - \frac{dy_1}{dx}\delta x \right) - \int dx\, T_y^{y_0} \int dz\, u \left(\delta y - \frac{dy_0}{dx}\delta x \right)$$
$$+ \int dx \int dy\, T_z^{z_1} u \left(\delta z - \frac{dz_1}{dy}\delta y - \frac{dz_1}{dx}\delta x \right)$$
$$- \int dx \int dy\, T_z^{z_0} u \left(\delta z - \frac{dz_0}{dy}\delta y - \frac{dz_0}{dx}\delta x \right).$$

Now it is obvious that

$$\int dx \int dy\, T_z^{z_1} u\delta z = \int dx \int dy\, T_z^{z_1} u\delta z_1,$$
$$\int dx\, T_y^{y_1} \int dz\, u\delta y = \int dx\, T_y^{y_1} \int dz\, u\delta y_1,$$
$$T_x^{x_1} \int dy \int dz\, u\delta x = T_x^{x_1} \int dy \int dz\, u\delta x_1,$$

and similar equations hold when the suffix 1 is replaced by the suffix 0. Hence we have

$$\delta \int dx \int dy \int dz\, u = \int dx \int dy \int dz \left(\delta u - \frac{du}{dx}\delta x - \frac{du}{dy}\delta y - \frac{du}{dz}\delta z \right)$$

$$+ T_x^{x_1} \int dy \int dz\, u\delta x_1 - T_x^{x_0} \int dy \int dz\, u\delta x_0$$

$$+ \int dx\, T_y^{y_1} \int dz\, u \left(\delta y_1 - \frac{dy_1}{dx}\delta x \right) - \int dx\, T_y^{y_0} \int dz\, u \left(\delta y_0 - \frac{dy_0}{dx}\delta x \right)$$

$$+ \int dx \int dy\, T_z^{z_1} u \left(\delta z_1 - \frac{dz_1}{dy}\delta y - \frac{dz_1}{dx}\delta x \right)$$

$$- \int dx \int dy\, T_z^{z_0} u \left(\delta z_0 - \frac{dz_0}{dy}\delta y - \frac{dz_0}{dx}\delta x \right).$$

Moreover
$$\delta z_1 - \frac{dz_1}{dy}\delta y - \frac{dz_1}{dx}\delta x = \bar{\delta}z_1,$$

$$\delta y_1 - \frac{dy_1}{dx}\delta x = \bar{\delta}y_1,$$

$$\delta x_1 = \bar{\delta}x_1,$$

and similar equations hold when the suffix 1 is replaced by the suffix 0. Also
$$\delta u - \frac{du}{dx}\delta x - \frac{du}{dy}\delta y - \frac{du}{dz}\delta z = \bar{\delta}u.$$

Thus the known formula of Art. 176 has been so transformed as to agree with the formula of Sarrus in Art. 175.

178. After obtaining the general expression given in Art. 175 for the variation of a triple integral, the next step is to shew how by integration by parts as many of the terms which occur in $\bar{\delta}u$ as possible are removed from under the signs of integration. This part of the subject is fully considered by Sarrus; we will give three of his formulæ.

In equation (4) of Art. 177 change u into $u\theta$; thus

$$\int dx \int dy \int dz\, u \frac{d\theta}{dx} = -\int dx \int dy \int dz\, \frac{du}{dx}\theta$$

$$+ T_z^{z_1} \int dy \int dz\, u\theta - T_z^{z_0} \int dy \int dz\, u\theta$$

$$- \int dx\, T_y^{y_1} \int dz\, u\theta \frac{dy_1}{dx} + \int dx\, T_y^{y_0} \int dz\, u\theta \frac{dy_0}{dx}$$

$$- \int dx \int dy\, T_z^{z_1} u\theta \frac{dz_1}{dx} + \int dx \int dy\, T_z^{z_0} u\theta \frac{dz_0}{dx} \quad\ldots\ldots\ldots (1).$$

In equation (3) of Art. 177 change u into $u\theta$; thus

$$\int dx \int dy \int dz\, u \frac{d\theta}{dy} = -\int dx \int dy \int dz\, \frac{du}{dy}\theta$$

$$+ \int dx\, T_y^{y_1} \int dz\, u\theta - \int dx\, T_y^{y_0} \int dz\, u\theta$$

$$- \int dx \int dy\, T_z^{z_1} u\theta \frac{dz_1}{dy} + \int dx \int dy\, T_z^{z_0} u\theta \frac{dz_0}{dy} \quad\ldots\ldots\ldots (2).$$

In equation (1) of Art. 177 change u into $u\theta$; thus

$$\int dx \int dy \int dz\, u \frac{d\theta}{dz} = -\int dx \int dy \int dz\, \frac{du}{dz}\theta$$

$$+ \int dx \int dy\, T_z^{z_1} u\theta - \int dx \int dy\, T_z^{z_0} u\theta \quad\ldots\ldots\ldots\ldots (3).$$

179. In his last chapter Sarrus applies his formulæ to three examples.

The first example is, to determine the surface which with a given area contains the greatest volume.

The third example is, to determine the law of the density of a body of given form and position in order that the integral

$$\int dx \int dy \int dz\, u \frac{d^3v}{dx\,dy\,dz}$$

taken throughout the body may be a maximum or minimum, v being the density at the point (x, y, z) and w a given function of x, y, z, and v.

The discussion of the first example is too long to be conveniently given, and the third will find an appropriate place in the next chapter; the second example we will now consider.

We shall however in future omit the bar from the symbol $\bar{\delta}$. Sarrus has indeed said very little about what he calls a *variation tronquée;* see Art. 174. Perhaps this term and the corresponding symbol $\bar{\delta}$ were only introduced for the purpose of enabling him to compare his formula with the known expression for the variation of a multiple integral as in Art. 177; and no disadvantage would have arisen if the term and symbol had not been introduced into the memoir.

180. The following is the second example given by Sarrus; to determine the law of density of a body of given form, position, and mass, in order that the integral

$$\int dx \int dy \int dz \sqrt{\left\{1 + \left(\frac{dv}{dx}\right)^2 + \left(\frac{dv}{dy}\right)^2 + \left(\frac{dv}{dz}\right)^2\right\}}$$

taken throughout the body may be a minimum, v being the density at the point (x, y, z).

The mass of the body is equal to

$$\int dx \int dy \int dz \, v,$$

and since the mass is to be constant the variation of this expression must be zero. Moreover since the form and position of the body are known the variations of the limits $\delta x_0, \delta x_1, \delta y_0, \delta y_1, \delta z_0, \delta z_1$; are all zero; thus the variation of the mass reduces to

$$\int dx \int dy \int dz \, \delta v,$$

and this must consequently be zero.

Again, put r for $\sqrt{\left\{1 + \left(\frac{dv}{dx}\right)^2 + \left(\frac{dv}{dy}\right)^2 + \left(\frac{dv}{dz}\right)^2\right\}}$; then the variation of the proposed integral is

$$\int dx \int dy \int dz \left\{ \frac{1}{r} \frac{dv}{dx} \frac{d\delta v}{dx} + \frac{1}{r} \frac{dv}{dy} \frac{d\delta v}{dy} + \frac{1}{r} \frac{dv}{dz} \frac{d\delta v}{dz} \right\}.$$

Then by the ordinary theory of *relative* maxima and minima we must have

$$\int dx \int dy \int dz \left\{ c\delta v + \frac{1}{r} \frac{dv}{dx} \frac{d\delta v}{dx} + \frac{1}{r} \frac{dv}{dy} \frac{d\delta v}{dy} + \frac{1}{r} \frac{dv}{dz} \frac{d\delta v}{dz} \right\} = 0,$$

where c is some constant.

Our object now is to transform this equation so as to reduce as much as possible the number of the signs of integration which occur with any term.

We first transform $\int dx \int dy \int dz \, \frac{1}{r} \frac{dv}{dx} \frac{d\delta v}{dx}$ by means of equation (1) of Art. 178; we obtain as the equivalent

$$- \int dx \int dy \int dz \frac{d \cdot \frac{1}{r} \frac{dv}{dx}}{dx} \delta v$$

$$+ \int_{x_0}^{x_1} \int dy \int dz \, \frac{1}{r} \frac{dv}{dx} \delta v - \int_{x_0}^{x_0} \int dy \int dz \, \frac{1}{r} \frac{dv}{dx} \delta v$$

$$- \int dx \int_{y_0}^{y_1} \int dz \, \frac{1}{r} \frac{dv}{dx} \frac{dy_1}{dx} \delta v + \int dx \int_{y_0}^{y_0} \int dz \, \frac{1}{r} \frac{dv}{dx} \frac{dy_0}{dx} \delta v$$

$$- \int dx \int dy \int_{z_0}^{z_1} \frac{1}{r} \frac{dv}{dx} \frac{dz_1}{dx} \delta v + \int dx \int dy \int_{z_0}^{z_0} \frac{1}{r} \frac{dv}{dx} \frac{dz_0}{dx} \delta v.$$

Next we transform $\int dx \int dy \int dz \, \frac{1}{r} \frac{dv}{dy} \frac{d\delta v}{dy}$ by means of equation (2) of Art. 178; we obtain as the equivalent ·

$$- \int dx \int dy \int dz \frac{d \cdot \frac{1}{r} \frac{dv}{dy}}{dy} \delta v$$

$$+ \int dx \int_{y_0}^{y_1} \int dz \, \frac{1}{r} \frac{dv}{dy} \delta v - \int dx \int_{y_0}^{y_0} \int dz \, \frac{1}{r} \frac{dv}{dy} \delta v$$

$$- \int dx \int dy \int_{z_0}^{z_1} \frac{1}{r} \frac{dv}{dy} \frac{dz_1}{dy} \delta v + \int dx \int dy \int_{z_0}^{z_0} \frac{1}{r} \frac{dv}{dy} \frac{dz_0}{dy} \delta v.$$

Lastly, we transform $\int dx \int dy \int dz \, \frac{1}{r} \frac{dv}{dz} \frac{d\,\delta v}{dz}$ by means of equation (3) of Art. 176; we obtain as the equivalent

$$- \int dx \int dy \int dz \, \frac{d \cdot \frac{1}{r} \frac{dv}{dz}}{dz} \, \delta v$$

$$+ \int dx \int dy \; \tau_{z}^{z_1} \frac{1}{r} \frac{dv}{dz} \, \delta v - \int dx \int dy \; \tau_{z}^{z_0} \frac{1}{r} \frac{dv}{dz} \, \delta v.$$

Substitute the equivalents thus obtained in the original equation; the result will be

$$0 = \int dx \int dy \int dz \left(c - \frac{d \cdot \frac{1}{r} \frac{dv}{dx}}{dx} - \frac{d \cdot \frac{1}{r} \frac{dv}{dy}}{dy} - \frac{d \cdot \frac{1}{r} \frac{dv}{dz}}{dz} \right) \delta v$$

$$- \int dx \int dy \; \tau_{z}^{z_1} \left(\frac{1}{r} \frac{dv}{dx} \frac{dz_1}{dx} + \frac{1}{r} \frac{dv}{dy} \frac{dz_1}{dy} - \frac{1}{r} \frac{dv}{dz} \right) \delta v$$

$$+ \int dx \int dy \; \tau_{z}^{z_0} \left(\frac{1}{r} \frac{dv}{dx} \frac{dz_0}{dx} + \frac{1}{r} \frac{dv}{dy} \frac{dz_0}{dy} - \frac{1}{r} \frac{dv}{dz} \right) \delta v$$

$$- \int dx \; \tau_{y}^{y_1} \int dz \left(\frac{1}{r} \frac{dv}{dx} \frac{dy_1}{dx} - \frac{1}{r} \frac{dv}{dy} \right) \delta v$$

$$+ \int dx \; \tau_{y}^{y_0} \int dz \left(\frac{1}{r} \frac{dv}{dx} \frac{dy_0}{dx} - \frac{1}{r} \frac{dv}{dy} \right) \delta v$$

$$+ \tau_{x}^{x_1} \int dy \int dz \, \frac{1}{r} \frac{dv}{dx} \, \delta v$$

$$- \tau_{x}^{x_0} \int dy \int dz \, \frac{1}{r} \frac{dv}{dx} \, \delta v.$$

Hence we must have by the reasoning commonly used in the Calculus of Variations

$$c - \frac{d \cdot \frac{1}{r} \frac{dv}{dx}}{dx} - \frac{d \cdot \frac{1}{r} \frac{dv}{dy}}{dy} - \frac{d \cdot \frac{1}{r} \frac{dv}{dz}}{dz} = 0;$$

this must hold for every point of the body. We have also certain *limiting equations*, six in number, namely,

$$\gamma^{z_1}_{z}\left(\frac{1}{r}\frac{dv}{dz}\frac{dz_1}{dx}+\frac{1}{r}\frac{dv}{dy}\frac{dz_1}{dy}-\frac{1}{r}\frac{dv}{dz}\right)=0,$$

$$\gamma^{z_1}_{z}\left(\frac{1}{r}\frac{dv}{dz}\frac{dy_1}{dx}-\frac{1}{r}\frac{dv}{dy}\right)=0,$$

$$\gamma^{z_1}_{z}\frac{1}{r}\frac{dv}{dx}=0,$$

and three more which can be obtained from these by replacing the suffix 1 by the suffix 0.

181. There are many misprints in the original memoir, as we have already remarked, but they are not likely to give any trouble to a student except perhaps the following. In the third line from the bottom of page 119 are two mistakes; in the first term the factor $\frac{dx_1''}{dx}$ in the notation of Sarrus is omitted, and in the second term the factor $\frac{dx_1'}{dx}$ is omitted. These lead to mistakes in those terms of Art. 155 which are numbered 9, 11, 15, 18, 21, 24; for $\frac{dx_1''}{dx}$ is omitted in 9, 15, 18, and $\frac{dx_1'}{dx}$ is omitted in 11, 21, 24. Moreover in Art. 155 the terms numbered 14, 17, 20, 23 have the wrong signs prefixed; and the terms numbered 30, 32 have in the notation of Sarrus w instead of $\frac{dw}{dx_1}$.

182. Some other remarks may be made for the use of the student of the original memoir.

In his Art. 156 Sarrus interprets the equations which he has obtained in his solution of his third problem. Thus he finds that the equation

$$\frac{dw}{dv}\frac{d^3v}{dx\,dy\,dz}-\frac{d^3w}{dx\,dy\,dz}=0$$

must hold at every point of the body; and besides this certain *limiting equations* must hold. He appears to sum up his results at the bottom of his page 126 where he says, "by combining the different preceding conditions which hold at the limits we see that they reduce to this—*for all points of the surface of the body in question we must have $w = 0$.*" This must be understood to mean that at all points of the surface of the body w must vanish and so must every differential coefficient of w with respect to x, y, z of any order. In other words w must vanish *identically* at every point of the surface of the body.

Moreover the result might perhaps be obtained more simply than in the way which Sarrus has adopted. For he obtains on page 123 as one of the limiting equations, an equation which expressed in our notation is

$$T_z^{z_1} w = 0.$$

The equation is to hold throughout what we may call one of the bounding faces of the body. Now if the equation just written be not an identity it really furnishes an equation to this bounding face; but the body is supposed to be given in form so that the equation to the bounding face is already known; therefore the equation must

be an identity. The only exception is that the equation $T_z^{z_1} w = 0$

might happen to coincide with the known equation to the bounding surface; but it may be shewn that this supposition is inadmissible

by examining the equations from which $T_z^{z_1} w = 0$ was deduced.

Again, in the method of Sarrus he might have observed that when some of his limiting equations are satisfied some other of these equations are *necessarily* satisfied also. Thus on his page 125 he has a sentence which in our notation will read thus; *moreover the fourteenth and fifteenth terms will give*

$$T_y^{z_1} T_z^{z_1} w = 0, \quad T_y^{z_1} T_z^{z_1} \frac{dw}{dx} = 0.$$

This is quite true, but it is not additional to what is already

known; for he has already shewn that $T_z^{z_1} w = 0$, and therefore of

course $T_y^{z_1} T_z^{z_1} w$ must be $= 0$, and he has also shewn that $T_z^{z_1} \frac{dw}{dx} = 0$,

and therefore of course $T_y^{z_1} T_z^{z_1} \frac{dw}{dx}$ must be $= 0$.

We may observe that the misprints which occur in Art. 155 of the memoir of Sarrus do not affect the validity of the inferences which he draws in his Art. 156.

183. As a further illustration of the method of Sarrus we will give in detail the investigation of the variation of a double integral, in which we will suppose that no differential coefficient of a higher order than the second occurs in the proposed expression. We shall require some formulæ in the integral calculus which might be obtained from those we have already given, but for convenience we will investigate them here.

It is obvious that

$$\int dx \frac{du}{dx} = T_x^{x_1} u - T_x^{x_0} u \dots\dots\dots\dots\dots\dots\dots(1);$$

change u into $\int dy\, u$; thus

$$\int dx \frac{d}{dx} \int dy\, u = T_x^{x_1} \int dy\, u - T_x^{x_0} \int dy\, u,$$

that is

$$\int dx \left\{ \int dy \frac{du}{dx} + T_y^{y_1} u \frac{dy_1}{dx} - T_y^{y_0} u \frac{dy_0}{dx} \right\} = T_x^{x_1} \int dy\, u - T_x^{x_0} \int dy\, u,$$

therefore

$$\int dx \int dy \frac{du}{dx} = T_x^{x_1} \int dy\, u - T_x^{x_0} \int dy\, u$$

$$- \int dx\, T_y^{y_1} u \frac{dy_1}{dx} + \int dx\, T_y^{y_0} u \frac{dy_0}{dx};$$

change u into $u\theta$; thus

$$\int dx \int dy\, u \frac{d\theta}{dx} = - \int dx \int dy \frac{du}{dx} \theta$$

$$+ T_x^{x_1} \int dy\, u\theta - T_x^{x_0} \int dy\, u\theta$$

$$- \int dx\, T_y^{y_1} u\theta \frac{dy_1}{dx} + \int dx\, T_y^{y_0} u\theta \frac{dy_0}{dx} \dots\dots\dots\dots\dots(2).$$

Again, in (1) change u into $T_y^{y} u$; thus

$$\int dx \frac{d}{dx} T_y^{y} u = T_x^{x_1} T_y^{y} u - T_x^{x_0} T_y^{y} u,$$

that is,

$$\int dx\, T_y^{y} \frac{du}{dx} + \int dx\, T_y^{y} \frac{du}{dy}\frac{d\eta}{dx} = T_x^{x_1} T_y^{y} u - T_x^{x_0} T_y^{y} u,$$

therefore
$$\int dx\, \gamma_y^x \frac{du}{dx} = \gamma_x^{x_1} \gamma_y^x u - \gamma_x^{x_0} \gamma_y^x u - \int dx\, \gamma_y^x \frac{du}{dy}\frac{d\eta}{dx};$$

change u into $u\theta$, thus

$$\int dx\, \gamma_y^x u \frac{d\theta}{dx} = -\int dx\, \gamma_y^x \frac{du}{dx}\theta + \gamma_x^{x_1}\gamma_y^x u\theta - \gamma_x^{x_0}\gamma_y^x u\theta$$
$$-\int dx\, \gamma_y^x u \frac{d\theta}{dy}\frac{d\eta}{dx} - \int dx\, \gamma_y^x \frac{du}{dy}\theta \frac{d\eta}{dx}\ \dots\dots\dots\dots(3).$$

In the applications we shall have to make of this formula η will be either y_0 or y_1.

Again, it is obvious that

$$\int dy\, \frac{du}{dy} = \gamma_y^{y_1} u - \gamma_y^{y_0} u;$$

change u into $u\theta$, thus

$$\int dy\, u \frac{d\theta}{dy} = -\int dy\, \frac{du}{dy}\theta + \gamma_y^{y_1} u\theta - \gamma_y^{y_0} u\theta.$$

Hence

$$\int dx \int dy\, u \frac{d\theta}{dy} = -\int dx \int dy\, \frac{du}{dy}\theta + \int dx\, \gamma_y^{y_1} u\theta - \int dx\, \gamma_y^{y_0} u\theta \dots(4);$$

and
$$\gamma_x^{\xi} \int dy\, u \frac{d\theta}{dy} = -\gamma_x^{\xi} \int dy\, \frac{du}{dy}\theta + \gamma_x^{\xi}\gamma_y^{y_1} u\theta - \gamma_x^{\xi}\gamma_y^{y_0} u\theta \dots\dots(5).$$

In the applications we shall have to make of the last formula, ξ will be either x_0 or x_1.

184. Let then

$$U = \int_{x_0}^{x_1} \int_{y_0}^{y_1} V\, dx\, dy,$$

where V is supposed a function of

$$x,\ y,\ z,\ \frac{dz}{dx},\ \frac{dz}{dy},\ \frac{d^2z}{dx^2},\ \frac{d^2z}{dx\,dy},\ \frac{d^2z}{dy^2}.$$

In this double integral we suppose that the integration is effected with respect to y first, and the limits y_0 and y_1 may be functions of x. As the limits and the order of integration will continue unchanged throughout the investigation, it will not be necessary to denote the limits explicitly, but they must be always understood.

As in Art. 175 we shall have, using δ instead of $\bar{\delta}$,

$$\delta U = \int dx \int dy\, \delta V + \overline{V}_x^{x_1} \int dy\, V \delta x_1 - \overline{V}_x^{x_0} \int dy\, V \delta x_0$$
$$+ \int dx\, \overline{V}_y^{y_1} V \delta y_1 - \int dx\, \overline{V}_y^{y_0} V \delta y_0.$$

And

$$\delta V = \frac{dV}{dz}\, \delta z + V_z \frac{d\delta z}{dx} + V_\theta \frac{d\delta z}{dy} + V_{zz} \frac{d^2\delta z}{dx^2} + V_m \frac{d^2\delta z}{dx\,dy} + V_n \frac{d^2\delta z}{dy^2},$$

where V_z denotes the differential coefficient of V with respect to $\dfrac{dz}{dx}$, and V_θ denotes the differential coefficient of V with respect to $\dfrac{dz}{dy}$, and V_{zz} that with respect to $\dfrac{d^2z}{dx^2}$, and so on.

Thus $\int dx \int dy\, \delta V$ consists of six terms, and all of these except the first may be developed by means of the formulæ given in Art. 183.

First; the term $\int dx \int dy\, \dfrac{dV}{dz}\, \delta z$ does not admit of any transformation.

Secondly; by equation (2) of Art. 183,

$$\int dx \int dy\, V_z \frac{d\delta z}{dx} = - \int dx \int dy\, \frac{dV_z}{dx}\, \delta z$$
$$+ \overline{V}_x^{x_1} \int dy\, V_z \delta z - \overline{V}_x^{x_0} \int dy\, V_z \delta z$$
$$- \int dx\, \overline{V}_y^{y_1} V_z \delta z\, \frac{dy_1}{dx} + \int dx\, \overline{V}_y^{y_0} V_z \delta z\, \frac{dy_0}{dx}.$$

Thirdly; by equation (4) of Art. 183,

$$\int dx \int dy\, V_\theta \frac{d\delta z}{dy} = - \int dx \int dy\, \frac{dV_\theta}{dy}\, \delta z$$
$$+ \int dx\, \overline{V}_y^{y_1} V_\theta \delta z - \int dx\, \overline{V}_y^{y_0} V_\theta \delta z.$$

Fourthly; by equation (2) of Art. 183,

$$\int dx \int dy\; V_{zz} \frac{d^2 \delta z}{dx^2} = -\int dx \int dy \frac{dV_{zz}}{dx}\frac{d\delta z}{dx}$$

$$+ T_z^{x_1} \int dy\; V_{zz} \frac{d\delta z}{dx} - T_z^{x_0} \int dy\; V_{zz} \frac{d\delta z}{dx}$$

$$- \int dx\; T_y^{y_1} V_{zz} \frac{d\delta z}{dx}\frac{dy_1}{dx} + \int dx\; T_y^{y_0} V_{zz} \frac{d\delta z}{dx}\frac{dy_0}{dx}.$$

Out of the five terms on the right-hand side of this equation, the first and the last two admit of further transformation; by equation (2) of Art. 183,

$$\int dx \int dy\; \frac{dV_{zz}}{dx}\frac{d\delta z}{dx} = -\int dx \int dy \frac{d^2 V_{zz}}{dx^2}\; \delta z$$

$$+ T_z^{x_1} \int dy\; \frac{dV_{zz}}{dx}\; \delta z - T_z^{x_0} \int dy\; \frac{dV_{zz}}{dx}\; \delta z$$

$$- \int dx\; T_y^{y_1} \frac{dV_{zz}}{dx}\; \delta z\; \frac{dy_1}{dx} + \int dx\; T_y^{y_0} \frac{dV_{zz}}{dx}\; \delta z\; \frac{dy_0}{dx};$$

by equation (3) of Art. 183,

$$\int dx\; T_y^{y_1} V_{zz} \frac{d\delta z}{dx}\frac{dy_1}{dx} = -\int dx\; T_y^{y_1}\; \delta z\; \frac{d}{dx}\left(V_{zz}\frac{dy_1}{dx}\right)$$

$$+ T_z^{x_1} T_y^{y_1} V_{zz} \frac{dy_1}{dx}\; \delta z - T_z^{x_0} T_y^{y_1} V_{zz} \frac{dy_1}{dx}\; \delta z$$

$$- \int dx\; T_y^{y_1} \frac{d\delta z}{dy} V_{zz}\left(\frac{dy_1}{dx}\right)^2 - \int dx\; T_y^{y_1}\delta z\; \frac{dy_1}{dx}\frac{d}{dy}\left(V_{zz}\frac{dy_1}{dx}\right);$$

a similar transformation can be made of

$$\int dx\; T_y^{y_0} V_{zz} \frac{d\delta z}{dx}\frac{dy_0}{dx}.$$

Thus we shall get on the whole

$$\int dx \int dy\; V_{zz} \frac{d^2 \delta z}{dx^2} = \int dx \int dy\; \frac{d^2 V_{zz}}{dx^2}\; \delta z$$

$$- T_z^{x_1} \int dy\; \frac{dV_{zz}}{dx}\; \delta z + T_z^{x_0} \int dy\; \frac{dV_{zz}}{dx}\; \delta z$$

$$+\int dx\, T_y^{y_1}\frac{dV_m}{dx}\frac{dy_1}{dx}\,\delta z-\int dx\, T_y^{y_2}\frac{dV_m}{dx}\frac{dy_2}{dx}\,\delta z$$

$$+T_z^{x_1}\int dy\, V_m\frac{d\delta z}{dx}-T_z^{x_0}\int dy\, V_m\frac{d\delta z}{dx}$$

$$+\int dx\, T_y^{y_1}\,\delta z\,\frac{d}{dx}\left(V_m\frac{dy_1}{dx}\right)-\int dx\, T_y^{y_2}\,\delta z\,\frac{d}{dx}\left(V_m\frac{dy_2}{dx}\right)$$

$$-T_z^{x_1}T_y^{y_1}\,V_m\frac{dy_1}{dx}\,\delta z+T_z^{x_0}T_y^{y_1}\,V_m\frac{dy_1}{dx}\,\delta z$$

$$+T_z^{x_1}T_y^{y_2}\,V_m\frac{dy_2}{dx}\,\delta z-T_z^{x_0}T_y^{y_2}\,V_m\frac{dy_2}{dx}\,\delta z$$

$$+\int dx\, T_y^{y_1}\frac{d\delta z}{dy}\,V_m\left(\frac{dy_1}{dx}\right)'-\int dx\, T_y^{y_2}\frac{d\delta z}{dy}\,V_m\left(\frac{dy_2}{dx}\right)'$$

$$+\int dx\, T_y^{y_1}\,\delta z\,\frac{dy_1}{dx}\frac{d}{dy}\left(V_m\frac{dy_1}{dx}\right)-\int dx\, T_y^{y_2}\,\delta z\,\frac{dy_2}{dx}\frac{d}{dy}\left(V_m\frac{dy_2}{dx}\right).$$

It may be observed that as y_1 and y_2 are independent of y

$$\frac{d}{dy}\left(V_m\frac{dy_1}{dx}\right)=\frac{dy_1}{dx}\frac{dV_m}{dy},\text{ and }\frac{d}{dy}\left(V_m\frac{dy_2}{dx}\right)=\frac{dy_2}{dx}\frac{dV_m}{dy}.$$

Fifthly; by equation (2) of Art. 183,

$$\int dx\int dy\, V_m\frac{d^2\delta z}{dx\,dy}=-\int dx\int dy\frac{dV_m}{dx}\frac{d\delta z}{dy}$$

$$+T_z^{x_1}\int dy\, V_m\frac{d\delta z}{dy}-T_z^{x_0}\int dy\, V_m\frac{d\delta z}{dy}$$

$$-\int dx\, T_y^{y_1}\,V_m\frac{d\delta z}{dy}\frac{dy_1}{dx}+\int dx\, T_y^{y_2}\,V_m\frac{d\delta z}{dy}\frac{dy_2}{dx}.$$

The first term on the right-hand side may be transformed by equation (4) of Art. 183, and the second and third terms may be transformed by equation (5) of Art. 183.

Thus we shall get on the whole

$$\int dx\int dy\, V_m\frac{d^2\delta z}{dx\,dy}=\int dx\int dy\frac{d^2V_m}{dx\,dy}\,\delta z$$

$$-\int dx\, T_y^{z_1}\frac{dV_m}{dx}\,\delta z + \int dx\, T_y^{z_0}\frac{dV_m}{dx}\,\delta z$$

$$-T_z^{x_1}\int dy\,\frac{dV_m}{dy}\,\delta z + T_x^{x_0}\int dy\,\frac{dV_m}{dy}\,\delta z$$

$$+T_x^{x_0}T_y^{y_1}V_m\,\delta z - T_z^{x_0}T_y^{y_1}V_m\,\delta z - T_z^{x_1}T_y^{y_0}V_m\,\delta z + T_x^{x_0}T_y^{y_0}V_m\,\delta z$$

$$-\int dx\, T_y^{y_1}V_m\frac{d\delta z}{dy}\frac{dy_1}{dx} + \int dx\, T_y^{y_0}V_m\frac{d\delta z}{dy}\frac{dy_0}{dx}\,.$$

Sixthly; by equation (4) of Art. 193,

$$\int dx\int dy\, V_m\frac{d^2\delta z}{dy^2} = -\int dx\int dy\,\frac{dV_m}{dy}\frac{d\delta z}{dy}$$

$$+\int dx\, T_y^{y_1}V_m\frac{d\delta z}{dy} - \int dx\, T_y^{y_0}V_m\frac{d\delta z}{dy}\,.$$

The first term on the right-hand side may be transformed by equation (4) of Art. 183. Thus we shall get on the whole

$$\int dx\int dy\, V_m\frac{d^2\delta z}{dy^2} = \int dx\int dy\,\frac{d^2V_m}{dy^2}\,\delta z$$

$$-\int dx\, T_y^{y_1}\frac{dV_m}{dy}\,\delta z + \int dx\, T_y^{y_0}\frac{dV_m}{dy}\,\delta z$$

$$+\int dx\, T_y^{y_1}V_m\frac{d\delta z}{dy} - \int dx\, T_y^{y_0}V_m\frac{d\delta z}{dy}\,.$$

We must now collect the results obtained for the various terms occurring in $\int dx\int dy\,\delta V$. Thus on the whole we shall obtain the following as composing the value of $\int dx\int dy\,\delta V$.

First, a double integral, namely,

$$\int dx\int dy\left\{\frac{dV}{dz} - \frac{dV_z}{dx} - \frac{dV_y}{dy} + \frac{d^2V_m}{dx^2} + \frac{d^2V_n}{dx\,dy} + \frac{d^2V_m}{dy^2}\right\}\delta z.$$

Secondly, terms involving integration with respect to y only, namely,

$$T_z^{z_1}\int dy\left\{\left(V_z - \frac{dV_{zz}}{dx} - \frac{dV'_{zy}}{dy}\right)\delta z + V_{zz}\frac{d\delta z}{dx}\right\}$$

$$-T_z^{z_0}\int dy\left\{\left(V_z - \frac{dV_{zz}}{dx} - \frac{dV'_{zy}}{dy}\right)\delta z + V_{zz}\frac{d\delta z}{dx}\right\}.$$

Thirdly, terms involving integration with respect to x only, namely,

$$\int dx\, T_y^{y_1}\left\{\left[-V_z\frac{dy_1}{dx} + V_z + \frac{dV_{zz}}{dx}\frac{dy_1}{dx} + \frac{d}{dx}\left(V_{zz}\frac{dy_1}{dx}\right)\right.\right.$$

$$\left.+\frac{dV_{zz}}{dy}\left(\frac{dy_1}{dx}\right)^2 - \frac{dV_{zy}}{dx} - \frac{dV_{yy}}{dy}\right]\delta z$$

$$\left.+\left[V_{zz}\left(\frac{dy_1}{dx}\right)^2 - V_{zy}\frac{dy_1}{dx} + V_{yy}\right]\frac{d\delta z}{dy}\right\}$$

$$-\int dx\, T_y^{y_0}\left\{\left[-V_z\frac{dy_0}{dx} + V_z + \frac{dV_{zz}}{dx}\frac{dy_0}{dx} + \frac{d}{dx}\left(V_{zz}\frac{dy_0}{dx}\right)\right.\right.$$

$$\left.+\frac{dV_{zz}}{dy}\left(\frac{dy_0}{dx}\right)^2 - \frac{dV_{zy}}{dx} - \frac{dV_{yy}}{dy}\right]\delta z$$

$$\left.+\left[V_{zz}\left(\frac{dy_0}{dx}\right)^2 - V_{zy}\frac{dy_0}{dx} + V_{yy}\right]\frac{d\delta z}{dy}\right\}.$$

Fourthly, terms involving no integral sign, namely,

$$T_z^{z_1}T_y^{y_1}\left\{-V_{zz}\frac{dy_1}{dx} + V_{zy}\right\}\delta z - T_z^{z_1}T_y^{y_0}\left\{-V_{zz}\frac{dy_0}{dx} + V_{zy}\right\}\delta z$$

$$-T_z^{z_0}\int_y^{y_1}\left\{-V_{zz}\frac{dy_1}{dx} + V_{zy}\right\}\delta z + T_z^{z_0}T_y^{y_0}\left\{-V_{zz}\frac{dy_0}{dx} + V_{zy}\right\}\delta z.$$

Besides these there are in δU the four terms

$$T_z^{z_1}\int dy\, V\delta x_1 - T_z^{z_0}\int dy\, V\delta x_0$$

$$+\int dx\, T_y^{y_1}V\delta y_1 - \int dx\, T_y^{y_0}V\delta y_0.$$

185. We have given in the preceding Article the development of the variation of a double integral; we now proceed to consider the relations which must be satisfied in order that the variation may vanish, supposing that no restriction exists with respect to the limits of the integrations.

In order that the part of the variation which involves a double integral may vanish we must have

$$\frac{dV}{dz} - \frac{dV_z}{dx} - \frac{dV_y}{dy} + \frac{d^2V_{zz}}{dz^2} + \frac{d^2V_{zy}}{dx\,dy} + \frac{d^2V_{yy}}{dy^2} = 0;$$

this must hold for all values of x and y comprised within the limits of the integrations.

Next, the term affected with the symbol $I_z^{y_1}\int dy$ must vanish; that is, when $x = x_1$

$$\left(V_z - \frac{dV_{zz}}{dx} - \frac{dV_{zy}}{dy}\right)\delta z + V_{zz}\frac{d\delta z}{dx} + V\delta x_1$$

must vanish for all values of y between y_0 and y_1. And since δz, $\dfrac{d\delta z}{dx}$, and δx_1 are arbitrary we obtain the three equations

$$V_z - \frac{dV_{zz}}{dx} - \frac{dV_{zy}}{dy} = 0, \quad V_{zz} = 0, \quad V = 0;$$

these are to hold when $x = x_1$ for all values of y between y_0 and y_1, so that we may conveniently express them thus,

$$I_z^{y_1}\left(V_z - \frac{dV_{zz}}{dx} - \frac{dV_{zy}}{dy}\right) = 0, \quad I_z^{y_1}V_{zz} = 0, \quad I_z^{y_1}V = 0.$$

Similarly from considering the terms affected with the symbol $I_z^{y_0}\int dy$ we obtain

$$I_z^{y_0}\left(V_z - \frac{dV_{zz}}{dx} - \frac{dV_{zy}}{dy}\right) = 0, \quad I_z^{y_0}V_{zz} = 0, \quad I_z^{y_0}V = 0.$$

Next consider the terms affected with the symbols $\int dx\,I_y^{x_1}$ and $\int dx\,I_y^{x_0}$. We shall obtain in a similar manner six equations, three to hold when $y = y_1$ for all values of x between x_0 and x_1, and three to hold when $y = y_0$ for all values of x between x_0 and x_1. We may write the first three thus,

$$\int_y^{y_1}\left\{- V_x\frac{dy_1}{dx} + V_0 + \frac{dV_m}{dx}\frac{dy_1}{dx} + \frac{d}{dx}\left(V_m\frac{dy_1}{dx}\right)\right.$$
$$\left. + \frac{dV_m}{dy}\left(\frac{dy_1}{dx}\right)^2 - \frac{dV_m}{dx} - \frac{dV_m}{dy}\right\} = 0,$$

$$\int_y^{y_1}\left\{V_m\left(\frac{dy_0}{dx}\right)^2 - V_m\frac{dy_1}{dx} + V_m\right\} = 0,$$

$$\int_y^{y_1} V = 0.$$

The other three are obtained from these by changing y_1 into y_0.

Lastly, the four terms without any integral sign must vanish; thus we obtain four equations which must hold for special values of x and y, namely $x = x_1$ and $y = y_1$, and so on. These equations are

$$\int_x^{x_1}\int_y^{y_1}\left(V_m\frac{dy_1}{dx} - V_m\right) = 0,$$

$$\int_x^{x_1}\int_y^{y_0}\left(V_m\frac{dy_0}{dx} - V_m\right) = 0,$$

$$\int_x^{x_0}\int_y^{y_1}\left(V_m\frac{dy_1}{dx} - V_m\right) = 0,$$

$$\int_x^{x_0}\int_y^{y_0}\left(V_{xc}\frac{dy_0}{dx} - V_m\right) = 0.$$

The equations we have obtained may of course be combined and thus simplified; thus since we have already obtained

$$\int_x^{x_1} V_m = 0 \quad\text{and}\quad \int_x^{x_0} V_m = 0,$$

it follows that the last four equations reduce to

$$\int_x^{x_1}\int_y^{y_1} V_m = 0, \quad \int_x^{x_1}\int_y^{y_0} V_m = 0,$$

$$\int_x^{x_0}\int_y^{y_1} V_m = 0, \quad \int_x^{x_0}\int_y^{y_0} V_m = 0.$$

186.   We may now make some comparison of the results of Article 184 with those obtained in Art. 143 by Delaunay's method.

According to Delaunay's suppositions we have

$$y_1 = y_0 \text{ when } x = x_0, \text{ and also when } x = x_1.$$

In consequence of this a term affected with the symbol $I_y^{y_1} \int dy$ *vanishes* because the *limits* of the integration with respect to y are *equal* when $x = x_1$; similarly, a term affected with the symbol $I_y^{y_0} \int dy$ vanishes.

Hence the variation of the double integral reduces to

$$\int dx \int dy \left\{ \frac{dV}{dz} - \frac{dV'_z}{dx} - \frac{dV_z}{dy} + \frac{d^2 V_{zz}}{dx^2} + \frac{d^2 V_{zy}}{dx\,dy} + \frac{d^2 V_{yy}}{dy^2} \right\} \delta z$$
$$+ \int dx\, I_y^{y_1} \left\{ P_1 \delta z + Q_1 \frac{d\delta z}{dy} + V \delta y_1 \right\}$$
$$- \int dx\, I_y^{y_0} \left\{ P_0 \delta z + Q_0 \frac{d\delta z}{dy} + V \delta y_0 \right\},$$

where

$$P_1 = V_y - V_z \frac{dy_1}{dx} + \frac{dV'_{zz}}{dx} \frac{dy_1}{dx} + \frac{d}{dx}\left(V_{zz} \frac{dy_1}{dx} \right)$$
$$+ \frac{dV_{zy}}{dy}\left(\frac{dy_1}{dx} \right)^2 - \frac{dV_{zy}}{dx} - \frac{dV_{yy}}{dy} \eta,$$

$$Q_1 = V_{zz}\left(\frac{dy_1}{dx} \right)^2 - V_{zy} \frac{dy_1}{dx} + V_{yy},$$

and P_0 and Q_0 are formed from P_1 and Q_1 by changing the suffix 1 wherever it occurs into 0.

This result coincides as it should do with that in Art. 143.

CHAPTER VIII.

CAUCHY.

187. A MEMOIR by Cauchy on the Calculus of Variations is published in the third volume of his *Exercices d'analyse et de Physique Mathématique*, 1844; it extends from page 50 to page 130 of the volume.

This memoir may be described as a reproduction of a portion of the investigations of Sarrus with some difference of notation, and frequent reference is made to Sarrus throughout the memoir. In fact Cauchy himself does not appear to have considered his own memoir as more than a new exhibition of the method of Sarrus; thus he says at the end of his last chapter: The various formulæ obtained in this last paragraph do not differ in substance from those obtained by M. Sarrus. They are however simplified by the notation which we have employed.... Cauchy adds that he will develop the subject in some other memoirs and apply it to the solution of various problems. This design appears however not to have been accomplished.

The memoir published by Cauchy may be considered an evidence of the favourable opinion he held of the method of Sarrus.

188. Cauchy's memoir begins with a few preliminary remarks and is then arranged in nine sections under the following titles. 1. Definitions. Notation. 2. On the continuity of functions and of their variations. General properties of the variations of several variables or functions connected by known equations. 3. General formulæ suitable for furnishing the variations of functions of one or more variables. 4. Properties of the variations of

different orders. 5. On the variation of a simple or multiple
definite integral. 6. On the different forms which may be given
to the variation of a simple or multiple definite integral. 7. Comparison of the formulæ established in the fifth and sixth sections. [The original memoir by mistake has *third* and *fourth*
sections.] Differentiation of a multiple integral relative to any
variable different from those with respect to which the integrations
are performed. 8. On the partial variation which for a simple or
definite multiple integral corresponds to variations in the form of
the functions which occur under the integral sign. 9. On the reductions which can be effected by integration by parts in the variation of a simple or multiple definite integral.

189. The first four sections are very diffuse, but contain nothing
new or important. In the fifth section a formula is obtained for the
variation of a definite multiple integral which, as Cauchy remarks,
is precisely the same as that obtained by Sarrus; it is the formula
which we have already given in the case of a triple integral; see
Art. 175. In his sixth section Cauchy gives an independent demonstration of that formula for the variation of a multiple integral
which, according to Sarrus, was known before he published his
method; see Art. 176. We will exemplify Cauchy's demonstration by applying it to the case of a triple integral.

190. We have to prove the following formula:

$$\delta \int dx \int dy \int dz\, u = \int dx \int dy \int dz \left(\delta u - \frac{du}{dx} \delta x - \frac{du}{dy} \delta y - \frac{du}{dz} \delta z \right)$$

$$+ \int dx \int dy \int dz \left(\frac{d\, u\delta x}{dx} + \frac{d\, u\delta y}{dy} + \frac{d\, u\delta z}{dz} \right).$$

By $\int dx \int dy \int dz\, u$, as formerly explained, we understand a triple
integral in which we have first to integrate with respect to z from z_0
to z_1, then with respect to y from y_0 to y_1, and lastly with respect
to x from x_0 to x_1.

Now let $X = x + \delta x$, $Y = y + \delta y$, $Z = z + \delta z$, where δx, δy, δz
are indefinitely small arbitrary functions of x, y, z. Let U denote

what u becomes when x, y, z, are changed into X, Y, Z, respectively, and also any function of x, y, z, involved in u, receives an indefinitely small arbitrary increment. Then the varied value of the triple integral is

$$\int dX \int dY \int dZ \; U;$$

the limits will be found by keeping the same limiting values as before for x, y, z. It is important to observe that since δx, δy, δz are *quite arbitrary* we can obtain all the necessary generality in the varied value of the triple integral by retaining the original limiting values of x, y, and z.

The *variation* of the triple integral will be found by subtracting the original value from the varied value.

Now it is obvious that the complete variation will be obtained by determining separately the parts of the variation which arise from the change of u, x, y, z into U, X, Y, Z, respectively; and when we are considering the change of one of the quantities the others may be supposed to retain their original values; the terms thus neglected are in fact of a higher order than those which are retained. Thus by putting $u + \delta u$ for U we find that the term arising from the variation of u is

$$\int dx \int dy \int dz \; \delta u.$$

Now consider the term which arises from the change of z into Z while the other quantities retain their original values. The integration with respect to z is the *first performed;* hence by the change of z into Z the triple integral is changed into

$$\int dx \int dy \int dz \; u \frac{dZ}{dz},$$

where the limits of x, y, z are the original limits; and $\dfrac{dZ}{dz}$ is the differential coefficient of Z with respect to z only, that is, supposing x and y constant. Now

$$\frac{dZ}{dz} = \frac{d}{dz}(z + \delta z) = 1 + \frac{d\delta z}{dz};$$

thus the term in the variation of the triple integral which arises from the change of z into Z is

$$\int dx \int dy \int dz \, u \, \frac{d\delta z}{dz} \, .$$

The simplicity of this process arises from the fact that the integration with respect to z is the *first performed*.

Now let us consider the part of the variation of the triple integral which arises from the change of y into Y. We may conceive that the order of integration in the original integral is changed so that y is now the variable with respect to which the first integration is performed; we know from the Integral Calculus that this can always be done by making suitable changes in the limits of the integrations. Then as before we shall find that the term in the variation of the triple integral which arises from the change of y into Y is

$$\int dx \int dz \int dy \, u \, \frac{d\delta y}{dy} \, ,$$

the limits being as we have already intimated adjusted to the new order of integration. Now restore the original order of integration; then we obtain for the required term

$$\int dx \int dy \int dz \, u \, \frac{d\delta y}{dy} \, ,$$

where the limits will be the original limits.

Similarly the term in the variation of the triple integral which arises from the change of x into X is

$$\int dx \int dy \int dz \, u \, \frac{d\delta x}{dx} \, ,$$

where the limits are the original limits.

Then by collecting the terms we obtain the whole variation, that is,

$$\delta \int dx \int dy \int dz \, u = \int dx \int dy \int dz \left(\delta u + u \, \frac{d\delta x}{dx} + u \, \frac{d\delta y}{dy} + u \, \frac{d\delta z}{dz} \right) ;$$

this result obviously coincides with that which was proposed to be proved.

This investigation seems more simple than that given by Ostrogradsky; see Arts. 127 and 128. The simplification arises from considering the variables separately instead of simultaneously.

191.   In his seventh section Cauchy shews that the form given for the variation of a multiple integral by Sarrus coincides with the form known before; this Cauchy does in the same way as Sarrus; see Art. 176.

Cauchy proposes a new notation which he strongly recommends. According to the notation of Sarrus we have

$$\int_{x_0}^{x_1} dx \frac{du}{dx} = T_x^{x_1} u - T_x^{x_0} u \; ;$$

Cauchy proposes to express this result thus

$$\int_{x_0}^{x_1} dx \frac{du}{dx} = \left.\;\right]_{x=x_0}^{x=x_1} u.$$

Similarly what Sarrus would express thus

$$T_x^{x_1} T_y^{y_1} u - T_x^{x_0} T_y^{y_1} u - T_x^{x_1} T_y^{y_0} u + T_x^{x_0} T_y^{y_0} u,$$

Cauchy proposes to express thus

$$\left.\;\right]_{x=x_0}^{x=x_1} \left.\;\right]_{y=y_0}^{y=y_1} u.$$

This latter is the form that Cauchy really uses; but apparently by a misprint he gives on his page 100 such a symbol as the following

$$\left.\;\right]_{x_0}^{x_1} \left.\;\right]_{y_0}^{y_1} u.$$

This however seems more convenient than the symbol which Cauchy really uses; and it may be rendered still more commodious by writing it thus

$$\left.\;\right|_{x_0}^{x_1} \left.\;\right|_{y_0}^{y_1} u.$$

To exemplify the use of this notation we may take the general formula for the variation of a double integral which has been given

in Art. 184; that formula expressed by the aid of the new notation
will stand thus,

$$\delta \int dx \int dy \; V =$$

$$\int dx \int dy \left\{ \frac{dV}{dz} - \frac{dV_{\text{\tiny o}}}{dz} - \frac{dV_{\text{\tiny p}}}{dy} + \frac{d^2 V_{\text{\tiny oo}}}{dx^2} + \frac{d^2 V_{\text{\tiny pp}}}{dx\,dy} + \frac{d^2 V_{\text{\tiny qq}}}{dy^2} \right\} \delta z$$

$$+ \left|_{x_0}^{x_1} \int dy \left\{ \left(V_{\text{\tiny o}} - \frac{dV_{\text{\tiny oo}}}{dx} - \frac{dV_{\text{\tiny pp}}}{dy} \right) \delta z + V_{\text{\tiny oo}} \frac{d\delta z}{dx} + V \delta x \right\}\right.$$

$$+ \int dx \left|_{y_0}^{y_1} \left\{ \left[- V_{\text{\tiny o}} \frac{dy}{dx} + V_{\text{\tiny p}} + \frac{dV_{\text{\tiny oo}}}{dx} \frac{dy}{dx} + \frac{d}{dx} \left(V_{\text{\tiny oo}} \frac{dy}{dx} \right) \right.\right.$$

$$\left.\left. + \frac{dV_{\text{\tiny oo}}}{dy} \left(\frac{dy}{dx} \right)^2 - \frac{dV_{\text{\tiny pp}}}{dx} - \frac{dV_{\text{\tiny qq}}}{dy} \right] \delta z \right.$$

$$\left. + \left[V_{\text{\tiny oo}} \left(\frac{dy}{dx} \right)^2 - V_{\text{\tiny pp}} \frac{dy}{dx} + V_{\text{\tiny qq}} \right] \frac{d\delta z}{dy} + V \delta y \right\}$$

$$+ \left|_{x_0}^{x_1} \right|_{y_0}^{y_1} \left(- V_{\text{\tiny oo}} \frac{dy}{dx} + V_{\text{\tiny pp}} \right) \delta z,$$

where it must be observed that $\dfrac{dy}{dx}$ will stand either for $\dfrac{dy_1}{dx}$ or for
$\dfrac{dy_0}{dx}$ as may be required.

Cauchy says on his last page that on speaking to Sarrus respecting this new notation by means of which the difference between
two values of a variable is expressed by a single symbol he learned
that the same idea had occurred to Sarrus himself. Perhaps we
may infer that Sarrus on trial was not satisfied with it as he did
not use it in his memoir.

Cauchy also proposes to use $\left.\vphantom{\int}\right|^{x=\xi} u$ in order to denote what
Sarrus denotes by $I_x^\xi u$; we shall not follow Cauchy on this point
but adhere to the notation of Sarrus. Thus we only use Cauchy's
notation when we have to express the *difference* between two values
of a variable, and we use Sarrus's to express a *single* value of a
variable; there is then no possibility of confusion.

192. Cauchy's eighth section contains nothing new or important. In his ninth section he considers the transformations which are to be made of the expressions by means of integration by parts. This section is illustrated by an example which we will now give in detail.

Let u be an unknown function of x, y, z; let v be a function of x, y, z and $\dfrac{d^3u}{dx\,dy\,dz}$. Let δs denote that part of the variation of the triple integral $\int dx \int dy \int dz \, v$ which arises from the variation of u; then we have

$$\delta s = \int dx \int dy \int dz \, r \, \frac{d^3\delta u}{dx\,dy\,dz} \quad \dotfill \quad (1),$$

where r is the differential coefficient of v with respect to $\dfrac{d^3u}{dx\,dy\,dz}$. The limits of the integrations are supposed to be denoted as heretofore. We propose then to reduce δs by means of integration by parts.

We have $\qquad r\frac{d^3\delta u}{dx\,dy\,dz} = \frac{d}{dx}\, r\,\frac{d^2\delta u}{dy\,dz} - \frac{dr}{dx}\,\frac{d^2\delta u}{dy\,dz}\,$,

thus (1) becomes

$$\delta s = \int dx \int dy \int dz \, \frac{d}{dx}\, r\,\frac{d^2\delta u}{dy\,dz} - \int dx \int dy \int dz \, \frac{dr}{dx}\,\frac{d^2\delta u}{dy\,dz} \quad \dotfill \quad (2).$$

By equation (4) of Art. 177,

$$\int dx \int dy \int dz \, \frac{d}{dx}\, r\,\frac{d^2\delta u}{dy\,dz} = \left|_{x_0}^{x_1}\int dy \int dz \, r\,\frac{d^2\delta u}{dy\,dz}\right.$$

$$-\int dx \, r_y^{y_1} \int dz \, r\,\frac{d^2\delta u}{dy\,dz}\,\frac{dy_1}{dx} + \int dx \, r_y^{y_0} \int dz \, r\,\frac{d^2\delta u}{dy\,dz}\,\frac{dy_0}{dx}$$

$$-\int dx \int dy \, r_z^{z_1} \, r\,\frac{d^2\delta u}{dy\,dz}\,\frac{dz_1}{dx} + \int dx \int dy \, r_z^{z_0} \, r\,\frac{d^2\delta u}{dy\,dz}\,\frac{dz_0}{dx}\,.$$

Thus (2) becomes

$$\delta_s = \left|_{x_0}^{x_1} \int dy \int dz \, r \frac{d^2\delta u}{dy\,dz} - \int dx \int dy \int dz \, \frac{dr}{dx} \frac{d^2\delta u}{dy\,dz}\right.$$

$$- \int dx \left|_{y}^{y_1} \int dz \, r \frac{d^2\delta u}{dy\,dz} \frac{dy_1}{dx} + \int dx \left|_{y}^{y_0} \int dz \, r \frac{d^2\delta u}{dy\,dz} \frac{dy_0}{dx}\right.\right.$$

$$- \int dx \int dy \left|_{z}^{z_1} r \frac{d^2\delta u}{dy\,dz} \frac{dz_1}{dx} + \int dx \int dy \left|_{z}^{z_0} r \frac{d^2\delta u}{dy\,dz} \frac{dz_0}{dx} \right.\right. \dots\dots(3).$$

It will be observed that δu is not differentiated with respect to x in any term of (3).

In equation (2) of Art. 177 change u into $r \frac{d\delta u}{dz}$; thus

$$\int dy \int dz \, r \frac{d^2\delta u}{dy\,dz} = - \int dy \int dz \, \frac{dr}{dy} \frac{d\delta u}{dz}$$

$$- \int dy \left|_{z}^{z_1} r \frac{d\delta u}{dz} \frac{dz_1}{dy} + \int dy \left|_{z}^{z_0} r \frac{d\delta u}{dz} \frac{dz_0}{dy}\right.\right.$$

$$+ \left|_{y_0}^{y_1} \int dz \, r \frac{d\delta u}{dz}.$$

Thus the first term on the right-hand side of (3) becomes

$$\left|_{x_0}^{x_1} \left|_{y_0}^{y_1} \int dz \, r \frac{d\delta u}{dz}\right.\right.$$

$$- \left|_{x_0}^{x_1} \int dy \left|_{z}^{z_1} r \frac{d\delta u}{dz} \frac{dz_1}{dy} + \left|_{x_0}^{x_1} \int dy \left|_{z}^{z_0} r \frac{d\delta u}{dz} \frac{dz_0}{dy}\right.\right.\right.$$

$$- \left|_{x_0}^{x_1} \int dy \int dz \, \frac{dr}{dy} \frac{d\delta u}{dz}.\right.$$

Similarly the second term on the right-hand side of (3) becomes

$$\int dx \left|_{y_0}^{y_1} \int dz \, \frac{dr}{dx} \frac{d\delta u}{dz}\right.$$

$$- \int dx \int dy \left|_{z}^{z_1} \frac{dr}{dx} \frac{d\delta u}{dz} \frac{dz_1}{dy} + \int dx \int dy \left|_{z}^{z_0} \frac{dr}{dx} \frac{d\delta u}{dz} \frac{dz_0}{dy}\right.\right.$$

$$- \int dx \int dy \int dz \, \frac{d^2r}{dx\,dy} \frac{d\delta u}{dz}.$$

The third and fourth terms on the right-hand side of (3) we shall not transform; we proceed to the fifth term.

In equation (2) of Art. 172 change u into $r\frac{d\delta u}{dz}\frac{dz_1}{dx}$, and put z_1 for ζ; then observing that z_1 is independent of z we obtain the following result,

$$\int dy \rceil_z^{z_1} r\frac{d^2\delta u}{dy\,dz}\frac{dz_1}{dx} = -\int dy \rceil_z^{z_1}\frac{d\delta u}{dz}\frac{d}{dy} r\frac{dz_1}{dx}$$

$$+ |_{y_0}^{y_1} \rceil_z^{z_1} r\frac{d\delta u}{dz}\frac{dz_1}{dx} - \int dy \rceil_z^{z_1}\frac{dz_1}{dx}\frac{dz_1}{dy}\frac{d}{dz} r\frac{d\delta u}{dz} \text{.............} (4).$$

Now by equation (1) of Art. 172

$$\rceil_z^{z_1}\frac{d}{dy} r\frac{dz_1}{dx} = \frac{d}{dy}\rceil_z^{z_1} r\frac{dz_1}{dx} - \rceil_z^{z_1}\frac{dz_1}{dx}\frac{dz_1}{dy}\frac{dr}{dz}.$$

Thus a part of the first term on the right-hand side of (4) cancels a part of the third term, and we obtain

$$\int dy \rceil_z^{z_1} r\frac{d^2\delta u}{dy\,dz}\frac{dz_1}{dx} = -\int dy \rceil_z^{z_1}\frac{d\delta u}{dz}\frac{d}{dy}\rceil_z^{z_1} r\frac{dz_1}{dx}$$

$$+ |_{y_0}^{y_1}\rceil_z^{z_1} r\frac{d\delta u}{dz}\frac{dz_1}{dx}$$

$$- \int dy \rceil_z^{z_1} r\frac{d^2\delta u}{dz^2}\frac{dz_1}{dx}\frac{dz_1}{dy}.$$

A similar formula holds when z_1 is changed into z_0.

Thus we obtain

$$\delta s = |_{x_0}^{x_1}|_{y_0}^{y_1}\int dz\, r\frac{d\delta u}{dz}$$

$$- |_{x_0}^{x_1}\int dy \rceil_z^{z_1} r\frac{d\delta u}{dz}\frac{dz_1}{dy} + |_{x_0}^{x_1}\int dy \rceil_z^{z_0} r\frac{d\delta u}{dz}\frac{dz_0}{dy}$$

$$- |_{x_0}^{x_1}\int dy\int dz\frac{dr}{dy}\frac{d\delta u}{dz}$$

$$-\int dx \Big|_{z_0}^{z_1} \int dz \, \frac{dr}{dx}\frac{d\delta u}{dz}$$

$$+\int dx \int dy \, \Big|_{z}^{z_1} \frac{dr}{dx}\frac{d\delta u}{dz}\frac{dz_1}{dy} - \int dx \int dy \, \Big|_{z}^{z_0} \frac{dr}{dx}\frac{d\delta u}{dz}\frac{dz_0}{dy}$$

$$+\int dx \int dy \int dz \, \frac{d^2 r}{dx\,dy}\frac{d\delta u}{dz}$$

$$-\int dx \, \Big|_{z}^{z_1}\int dz \, r\, \frac{d^2\delta u}{dy\,dz}\frac{dy_1}{dx} + \int dx \, \Big|_{z}^{z_0}\int dz \, r\, \frac{d^2\delta u}{dy\,dz}\frac{dy_0}{dx}$$

$$+\int dx \int dy \, \Big|_{z}^{z_1}\frac{d\delta u}{dz}\frac{d}{dy}\Big|_{z}^{z_1} r\, \frac{dz_1}{dz} - \int dx \int dy \, \Big|_{z}^{z_0}\frac{d\delta u}{dz}\frac{d}{dy}\Big|_{z}^{z_0} r\, \frac{dz_0}{dx}$$

$$-\int dx \, \Big|_{z_0}^{z_1}\Big|_{z}^{z_1} r\, \frac{d\delta u}{dz}\frac{dz_1}{dx} + \int dx \, \Big|_{z_0}^{z_1}\Big|_{z}^{z_0} r\, \frac{d\delta u}{dz}\frac{dz_0}{dx}$$

$$+\int dx \int dy \, \Big|_{z}^{z_1} r\, \frac{d^2\delta u}{dz^2}\frac{dz_1}{dx}\frac{dz_1}{dy} - \int dx \int dy \, \Big|_{z}^{z_0} r\, \frac{d^2\delta u}{dz^2}\frac{dz_0}{dx}\frac{dz_0}{dy}.$$

In some of these lines terms occur involving integrations with respect to z and differentiation of δu with respect to z; such terms admit of further reduction.

In the first line we have $\int dz \, r \frac{d\delta u}{dz}$, and

$$\int dz \, r \frac{d\delta u}{dz} = \Big|_{z_0}^{z_1} r\,\delta u - \int dz \, \frac{dr}{dz}\delta u.$$

In the third line we have $\int dz \, \frac{dr}{dy}\frac{d\delta u}{dz}$, and

$$\int dz \, \frac{dr}{dy}\frac{d\delta u}{dz} = \Big|_{z_0}^{z_1}\frac{dr}{dy}\delta u - \int dz \, \frac{d^2 r}{dy\,dz}\delta u.$$

In the fourth line we have $\int dz \, \frac{dr}{dx}\frac{d\delta u}{dz}$, and

$$\int dz \, \frac{dr}{dx}\frac{d\delta u}{dz} = \Big|_{z_0}^{z_1}\frac{dr}{dx}\delta u - \int dz \, \frac{d^2 r}{dx\,dz}\delta u.$$

In the sixth line we have $\int dz\,\dfrac{d^2 r}{dx\,dy}\dfrac{d\delta u}{dz}$, and

$$\int dz\,\frac{d^2 r}{dx\,dy}\frac{d\delta u}{dz} = \Big|_{z_0}^{z_1}\frac{d^2 r}{dx\,dy}\,\delta u - \int dz\,\frac{d^3 r}{dx\,dy\,dz}\,\delta u.$$

In the seventh line we have $\int dz\,r\,\dfrac{d^2\delta u}{dy\,dz}\dfrac{dy_1}{dx}$ and $\int dz\,r\,\dfrac{d^2\delta u}{dy\,dz}\dfrac{dy_0}{dx}$,

and
$$\int dz\,r\,\frac{d^2\delta u}{dy\,dz}\frac{dy_1}{dx} = \Big|_{z_0}^{z_1} r\,\frac{dy_1}{dx}\frac{d\delta u}{dy} - \int dz\,\frac{d\delta u}{dy}\frac{dr}{dz}\frac{dy_1}{dx},$$

$$\int dz\,r\,\frac{d^2\delta u}{dy\,dz}\frac{dy_0}{dx} = \Big|_{z_0}^{z_1} r\,\frac{dy_0}{dx}\frac{d\delta u}{dy} - \int dz\,\frac{d\delta u}{dy}\frac{dr}{dz}\frac{dy_0}{dx}.$$

Thus finally

$$\delta s = \Big|_{x_0}^{x_1}\Big|_{y_0}^{y_1}\Big|_{z_0}^{z_1} r\,\delta u - \Big|_{x_0}^{x_1}\Big|_{y_0}^{y_1}\int dz\,\frac{dr}{dz}\,\delta u$$

$$-\ \Big|_{x_0}^{x_1}\int dy\,\Big|_{z}^{z_1} r\,\frac{d\delta u}{dz}\frac{dz_1}{dy} + \Big|_{x_0}^{x_1}\int dy\,\Big|_{z}^{z_0} r\,\frac{d\delta u}{dz}\frac{dz_0}{dy}$$

$$-\ \Big|_{x_0}^{x_1}\int dy\,\Big|_{z_0}^{z_1}\frac{dr}{dy}\,\delta u + \Big|_{x_0}^{x_1}\int dy\int dz\,\frac{d^2 r}{dy\,dz}\,\delta u$$

$$-\ \int dx\,\Big|_{y_0}^{y_1}\Big|_{z_0}^{z_1}\frac{dr}{dx}\,\delta u + \int dx\,\Big|_{y_0}^{y_1}\int dz\,\frac{d^2 r}{dx\,dz}\,\delta u$$

$$+\ \int dx\int dy\,\Big|_{z}^{z_1}\frac{dr}{dx}\frac{d\delta u}{dz}\frac{dz_1}{dy} - \int dx\int dy\,\Big|_{z}^{z_0}\frac{dr}{dx}\frac{d\delta u}{dz}\frac{dz_0}{dy}$$

$$+\ \int dx\int dy\,\Big|_{z_0}^{z_1}\frac{d^2 r}{dx\,dy}\,\delta u - \int dx\int dy\int dz\,\frac{d^3 r}{dx\,dy\,dz}\,\delta u$$

$$-\ \int dx\,\Big|_{y}^{y_1}\Big|_{z_0}^{z_1} r\,\frac{dy_1}{dx}\frac{d\delta u}{dy} + \int dx\,\Big|_{y}^{y_1}\int dz\,\frac{d\delta u}{dy}\frac{dr}{dz}\frac{dy_1}{dx}$$

$$+\ \int dx\,\Big|_{y}^{y_0}\Big|_{z_0}^{z_1} r\,\frac{dy_0}{dx}\frac{d\delta u}{dy} - \int dx\,\Big|_{y}^{y_0}\int dz\,\frac{d\delta u}{dy}\frac{dr}{dz}\frac{dy_0}{dx}$$

$$+\ \int dx\int dy\,\Big|_{z}^{z_1}\frac{d\delta u}{dz}\frac{d}{dy}\Big|_{z}^{z_1} r\,\frac{dz_1}{dx} - \int dx\int dy\,\Big|_{z}^{z_0}\frac{d\delta u}{dz}\frac{d}{dy}\Big|_{z}^{z_0} r\,\frac{dz_0}{dx}$$

$$-\int dx \left[\;\right]_{y_0}^{y_1}\left[\;\right]_{z}^{z_1} r\,\frac{d\delta u}{dz}\frac{dz_1}{dx} + \int dx \left[\;\right]_{y_1}^{}\left[\;\right]_{z}^{z_0} r\,\frac{d\delta u}{dz}\frac{dz}{dx}$$

$$+\int dx \int dy \left[\;\right]_{z}^{z_1} r\,\frac{d^2\delta u}{dz^2}\frac{dz_1}{dx}\frac{dz_1}{dy} - \int dx \int dy \left[\;\right]_{z}^{z_0} r\,\frac{d^2\delta u}{dz^2}\frac{dz}{dx}\frac{dz_0}{dy}\,.$$

103. As a particular case of the preceding result, Cauchy supposes that $r = 1$. Thus we obtain

$$\delta s = \int dx \int dy \int dz\,\frac{d^3\delta u}{dx\,dy\,dz}$$

$$=\left[\;\right]_{x_0}^{x_1}\left[\;\right]_{y_0}^{y_1}\left[\;\right]_{z_0}^{z_1}\delta u$$

$$-\left[\;\right]_{x_0}^{x_1}\int dy \left[\;\right]_{z}^{z_1}\frac{d\delta u}{dz}\frac{dz_1}{dy} + \left[\;\right]_{x_0}^{x_1}\int dy \left[\;\right]_{z}^{z_0}\frac{d\delta u}{dz}\frac{dz_0}{dy}$$

$$-\int dx \left[\;\right]_{y}^{y_1}\left[\;\right]_{z}^{z_1}\frac{dy_1}{dx}\frac{d\delta u}{dy} + \int dx \left[\;\right]_{y}^{y_0}\left[\;\right]_{z}^{z_1}\frac{dy_0}{dx}\frac{d\delta u}{dy}$$

$$+\int dx \int dy \left[\;\right]_{z}^{z_1}\frac{d\delta u}{dz}\frac{d^2z_1}{dx\,dy} - \int dx \int dy \left[\;\right]_{z}^{z_0}\frac{d\delta u}{dz}\frac{d^2z_0}{dx\,dy}$$

$$-\int dx \left[\;\right]_{y_0}^{y_1}\left[\;\right]_{z}^{z_1}\frac{d\delta u}{dz}\frac{dz_1}{dx} + \int dx \left[\;\right]_{y_0}^{}\left[\;\right]_{z}^{z_0}\frac{d\delta u}{dz}\frac{dz_1}{dx}$$

$$+\int dx \int dy \left[\;\right]_{z}^{z_1}\frac{d^2\delta u}{dz^2}\frac{dz_1}{dx}\frac{dz_1}{dy} - \int dx \int dy \left[\;\right]_{z}^{z_0}\frac{d^2\delta u}{dz^2}\frac{dz_0}{dx}\frac{dz_0}{dy}\,.$$

Of the eleven terms here given Cauchy has omitted the sixth and seventh.

With this particular case Cauchy's memoir terminates.

104. We can now conveniently introduce the third example which Sarrus gives in illustration of his formulæ; see Art. 179. The example is the following; to determine the law of the density of a body of given form and position in order that the integral

$$\int dx \int dy \int dz\; w\,\frac{d^3 v}{dx\,dy\,dz}$$

taken throughout the body may be a maximum or a minimum, v being the density at the point (x, y, z), and w a given function of x, y, z and v.

Since the form and position of the body are given there are no terms in the variation of the triple integral arising from the variation of the *limits*. Thus we have for the variation of the proposed triple integral

$$\int dx \int dy \int dz \; \frac{d^3v}{dx\,dy\,dz}\, \delta w + \int dx \int dy \int dz \; w \, \frac{d^3\delta v}{dx\,dy\,dz}\,.$$

The first of these two terms is equal to

$$\int dx \int dy \int dz \; \frac{d^3v}{dx\,dy\,dz}\, \frac{dw}{dv}\, \delta v;$$

the second developes into the twenty-two terms given as the result of Art. 192 provided in that result we change r into w and u into v. Of these twenty-two terms the twelfth is the only term which involves a triple integral; this must be united with the term just given, so that we obtain

$$\int dx \int dy \int dz \left(\frac{d^3v}{dx\,dy\,dz}\, \frac{dw}{dv} - \frac{d^3w}{dx\,dy\,dz} \right) \delta v.$$

This must vanish by the ordinary principles of the Calculus of Variations; hence

$$\frac{d^3v}{dx\,dy\,dz}\, \frac{dw}{dv} - \frac{d^3w}{dx\,dy\,dz} = 0.$$

This partial differential equation must be solved to find v, the solution of course involving arbitrary functions; and the arbitrary functions must be determined from the limiting equations which we shall now examine.

We may consider the given body to be bounded by six faces. Two of these six faces we will call the *upper* and *lower*; they are determined by the known values of z_1 and z_0 in terms of x and y, and may thus be of any form. Two of the six faces we will call the *front* and *back*; they are determined by the known values of y_1 and y_0 in terms of x, and are therefore cylindrical having their generating lines parallel to the axis of z. The remaining two faces we will call the *right* and *left;* they are determined by the known values of x_1 and x_0, and are therefore planes perpendicular to the axis of x.

In particular cases these six faces would assume particular forms. For example, suppose the given body to be the ellipsoid determined by the equation

$$\frac{x^2}{a^2} + \frac{y^2}{b^2} + \frac{z^2}{c^2} = 1;$$

the *upper* and *lower* boundaries are the portions of the surface of the ellipsoid determined respectively by

$$z = + c\sqrt{\left(1 - \frac{x^2}{a^2} - \frac{y^2}{b^2}\right)}, \text{ and } z = -c\sqrt{\left(1 - \frac{x^2}{a^2} - \frac{y^2}{b^2}\right)};$$

the *front* and *back* boundaries are the portions of the ellipse in the plane of (x, y) determined respectively by

$$y = + b\sqrt{\left(1 - \frac{x^2}{a^2}\right)}, \text{ and } y = -b\sqrt{\left(1 - \frac{x^2}{a^2}\right)};$$

the *right* and *left* boundaries are the points on the axis of x for which $x = a$ and $x = -a$ respectively. Thus in this example two of the six faces degenerate into *curves* and two into *points.*

The eleventh term in the result of Art. 192 gives

$$\int dx \int dy \left|_{z_0}^{z_1} \frac{d^2 w}{dx\,dy}\, \delta v\right.;$$

and in order that this may vanish, since δv is arbitrary, we must have

$$\int_{z_0}^{z_1} \frac{d^2 w}{dx\,dy} = 0, \text{ and } \int_{z_0}^{z_1} \frac{d^2 w}{dx\,dy} = 0.$$

The ninth and seventeenth terms in the result of Art. 192 must be united because they involve the same arbitrary term; thus we get

$$\int dx \int dy \int_{z_0}^{z_1} \frac{d\,\delta v}{dz} \left(\frac{dw}{dx}\frac{dz_1}{dy} + \frac{d}{dy} \int_{z_0}^{z_1} w \frac{dz_1}{dx}\right);$$

and in order that this may vanish, since $\dfrac{d\delta w}{dz}$ is arbitrary, we must have

$$\int_z^{z_1}\left(\frac{dw}{dx}\frac{dz}{dy} + \frac{d}{dy}\int_z^{z_1} w\frac{dz}{dx}\right) = 0,$$

or as we may write it

$$\int_z^{z_1}\left(\frac{dw}{dx}\frac{dz_1}{dy} + \frac{dw}{dy}\frac{dz_1}{dx} + \frac{dw}{dz}\frac{dz_1}{dy}\frac{dz_1}{dx} + w\frac{d^2z_1}{dx\,dy}\right) = 0.$$

The tenth and eighteenth terms in the result of Art. 192 lead to a similar equation with z_2 in the place of z_1.

The twenty-first and twenty-second terms in the result of Art. 192 lead respectively to

$$\int_z^{z_1} w\,\frac{dz_1}{dx}\,\frac{dz_1}{dy} = 0,\qquad \int_z^{z_2} w\,\frac{dz_2}{dx}\,\frac{dz_2}{dy} = 0.$$

We have thus proved that the following equations must hold,

$$\int_z^{z_1}\frac{d^2w}{dx\,dy} = 0,$$

$$\int_z^{z_1}\left(\frac{dw}{dx}\frac{dz_1}{dy} + \frac{dw}{dy}\frac{dz_1}{dx} + \frac{dw}{dz}\frac{dz_1}{dx}\frac{dz_1}{dy} + w\frac{d^2z_1}{dx\,dy}\right) = 0,$$

$$\int_z^{z_1} w\,\frac{dz_1}{dx}\,\frac{dz_1}{dy} = 0.$$

The last of these gives $\int_z^{z_1} w = 0$, for $\dfrac{dz_1}{dx}$ and $\dfrac{dz_1}{dy}$ are independent of z.

The equation $\int_z^{z_1} w = 0$ shews that w must vanish *identically* for all points of the upper boundary. For if w does not vanish identically $w = 0$ must coincide with the known equation to the upper boundary; and then we shall not have the other two of the above three equations satisfied. For from $\int_z^{z_1} w = 0$ we obtain by differentiation

$$\int_z^{z_1}\left(\frac{dw}{dx} + \frac{dw}{dz}\frac{dz_1}{dx}\right) = 0,\quad\text{and}\quad \int_z^{z_1}\left(\frac{dw}{dy} + \frac{dw}{dz}\frac{dz_1}{dy}\right) = 0;$$

and from these combined with the second of the above three equations we deduce

$$\left]_{z_0}^{z_1}\frac{dw}{dx}=0,\quad \left]_{z_0}^{z_1}\frac{dw}{dy}=0,\quad \left]_{z_0}^{z_1}\frac{dw}{dz}=0,$$

and these could not be true if $w=0$ were the equation to a surface; because $\dfrac{dw}{dx}$, $\dfrac{dw}{dy}$, and $\dfrac{dw}{dz}$ can only simultaneously vanish for special *points* on a surface and not for any continuous portion of a surface.

Thus w must vanish identically for all points of the upper boundary. And similarly w must vanish identically for all points of the lower boundary.

The eighth term in the result of Art. 192 gives

$$\int dx \left]_{z_0}^{z_1}\int dz\, \delta v\, \frac{d^2 w}{dx\, dz}.$$

This involves the value of δv for the front and back of the given body. Confining ourselves to the former, we obtain

$$\left]_{z_0}^{z_1}.\frac{d^2 w}{dx\, dz}=0.$$

The fourteenth term in the result of Art. 192 gives

$$\int dx \left]_{y_0}^{y_1}\int dz\, \frac{d\delta v}{dy}\cdot\frac{dy_1}{dx}\cdot\frac{dw}{dz};$$

and from this we obtain

$$\left]_{y_0}^{y_1}\frac{dw}{dz}=0,$$

since the factor $\dfrac{dy_1}{dx}$ is independent of y.

From the last two results we infer that w must vanish identically for all points of the front boundary. For if $\dfrac{dw}{dx}$ be denoted by w' we have

$$\left]_{y_0}^{y_1} w'=0,\quad\text{and}\quad \left]_{z_0}^{z_1}\frac{dw'}{dx}=0;$$

and the first of these equations shews that w' must vanish identically for all points of the front boundary, or else $w' = 0$ must coincide with the known equation to this front boundary; but the latter supposition is inconsistent with the second of the above two equations. Thus w' must vanish identically for all points of the front boundary, and from this and the fact that w vanishes identically for the points common to the front boundary and the upper boundary, we infer that w must vanish identically for all points of the front boundary.

Similarly from the remaining part of the eighth term and the sixteenth term in the result of Art. 192, we conclude that w must vanish identically at every point of the back boundary.

From the sixth term in the result of Art. 192 we obtain

$$\int_{z_0}^{z_1} \frac{d^2 w}{dy\, dz} = 0, \quad \text{and} \quad \int_{z_0}^{z_1} \frac{d^2 w}{dy\, dz} = 0;$$

and from these terms combined with what we already know respecting w we conclude that w must vanish identically at every point of the right and left boundaries of the body.

Thus we conclude from the terms that we have examined, that w must vanish identically at every point of all the bounding faces of the given body; and supposing this to be the case we shall find that the remaining terms in the result of Art. 192 vanish.

195.   We will close this part of the subject by giving the complete development of the variation of a triple integral in the case in which no differential coefficient of a higher order than the first occurs in the proposed expression.

Let then $\iiint V\, dx\, dy\, dz$ denote the proposed triple integral, where V is a function of $x, y, z, u, \dfrac{du}{dx}, \dfrac{du}{dy}, \dfrac{du}{dz}$.

The integration is supposed to be effected first with respect to z from z_0 to z_1, then with respect to y from y_0 to y_1, and then with respect to x from x_0 to x_1.

Let the differential coefficient of V with regard to $\dfrac{du}{dx}$ be denoted by X, the differential coefficient of V with regard to $\dfrac{du}{dy}$ by Y, and the differential coefficient of V with regard to $\dfrac{du}{dz}$ by Z. Thus

$$\delta V = \frac{dV}{du}\,\delta u + X\frac{d\delta u}{dx} + Y\frac{d\delta u}{dy} + Z\frac{d\delta u}{dz}.$$

By Art. 175 we have in the notation of the present chapter

$$\delta \iiint V\,dx\,dy\,dz = \iiint \delta V\,dx\,dy\,dz$$
$$+ \Big|_{x_0}^{x_1}\int dy\int dz\, V\,\delta x + \int dx\,\Big|_{y_0}^{y_1}\int dz\, V\,\delta y + \int dx\int dy\,\Big|_{z_0}^{z_1}\, V\,\delta z.$$

There are four terms in δV giving rise to four terms in

$$\iiint \delta V\,dx\,dy\,dz.$$

The first term is not susceptible of transformation.

The second term is to be transformed by equation (1) of Art. 178; this gives

$$\int dx\int dy\int dz\, X\,\frac{d\delta u}{dx} = -\int dx\int dy\int dz\,\frac{dX}{dx}\,\delta u$$
$$+ \Big|_{x_0}^{x_1}\int dy\int dz\, X\delta u - \int dx\,\Big|_{y_0}^{y_1}\int dz\, X\,\frac{dy}{dx}\,\delta u - \int dx\int dy\,\Big|_{z_0}^{z_1}\, X\,\frac{dz}{dx}\,\delta u.$$

The third term arising from δV is to be transformed by equation (2) of Art. 178; this gives

$$\int dx\int dy\int dz\, Y\,\frac{d\delta u}{dy} = -\int dx\int dy\int dz\,\frac{dY}{dy}\,\delta u$$
$$+ \int dx\,\Big|_{y_0}^{y_1}\int dz\, Y\,\delta u - \int dx\int dy\,\Big|_{z_0}^{z_1}\, Y\,\frac{dz}{dy}\,\delta u.$$

The fourth term arising from δV is to be transformed by equation (3) of Art. 176; this gives

$$\int dx \int dy \int dz\, Z \frac{d\delta u}{dz} = -\int dx \int dy \int dz\, \frac{dZ}{dz}\delta u$$
$$+ \int dx \int dy\, \Big|_{z_0}^{z_1}\, Z\,\delta u.$$

Thus we have finally

$$\delta \iiint V\,dx\,dy\,dz = \iiint \delta u \left(\frac{dV}{du} - \frac{dX}{dx} - \frac{dY}{dy} - \frac{dZ}{dz}\right) dx\,dy\,dz$$
$$+ \Big|_{x_0}^{x_1} \int dy \int dz\, (V\delta x + X\delta u)$$
$$+ \int dx \Big|_{y_0}^{y_1} \int dz\, \left(V\delta y - X\frac{dy}{dx}\delta u + Y\delta u\right)$$
$$+ \int dx \int dy\, \Big|_{z_0}^{z_1} \left(V\delta z - X\frac{dz}{dx}\delta u - Y\frac{dz}{dy}\delta u + Z\delta u\right).$$

Of these terms those affected with the symbols

$$\Big|_{x_0}^{x_1} \int dy \int dz \quad \text{and} \quad \int dx \Big|_{y_0}^{y_1} \int dz$$

vanish when we confine ourselves to the particular case considered by Delaunay, as we have already explained in Art. 186. The remaining terms agree as far as they go with the result given in Art. 144.

CHAPTER IX.

LEGENDRE, BRUNACCI, JACOBI.

196. We are now about to give the history of that part of our subject which relates to the criteria for distinguishing a maximum from a minimum, and for ascertaining when neither a maximum nor a minimum exists.

We have already intimated in Art. 5, that Legendre had arrived at some results on these points, and that Lagrange had shewn that further investigations were required in order to ensure the accuracy of Legendre's conclusions. The requisite investigations were supplied by Jacobi in 1837, and the memoir which Jacobi then published has given rise to an extensive series of commentaries and developments. Before however we proceed to Jacobi's investigations, we will give an analysis of Legendre's memoir and of some others connected with it.

197. Legendre's memoir is entitled *Mémoire sur la manière de distinguer les maxima des minima dans le Calcul des Variations.* It is printed in the volume for 1786 of the *Histoire de l'Académie Royale des Sciences;* this volume is dated 1788. The memoir extends from page 7 to page 37. There is an *Addition* to the memoir on pages 348—351 of the volume for 1787 of the *Histoire …;* this volume is dated 1789.

198. The first investigation in Legendre's memoir is in substance the same as that which we have given in Art. 5. He shews

by the method there used that the problem he is considering may
be reduced to the investigation of the sign of

$$\lambda_1 (\delta y_1)^2 - \lambda_0 (\delta y_0)^2 + \frac{1}{2}\int_{x_0}^{x_1} \frac{d^2f}{dp^2}(\delta p + \Delta \delta y)^2\, dx.$$

In Article 5, we supposed δy_1 and δy_0 to be zero, so that the
part of the above expression free from the integral sign vanishes.
Legendre adopts the following method with respect to the integrated part of the above expression; the value of λ is to be
determined from a differential equation and it will therefore involve an arbitrary constant, and this arbitrary constant may be
supposed to be so taken as to make $\lambda_1 (\delta y_1)^2 - \lambda_0 (\delta y_0)^2$ vanish or
have the same sign as the part of the expression under the in-
tegral sign.

199.   Legendre next considers the case in which the integral
of an expression $f(x, y, p, q)$ is to be a maximum or a minimum,
where $p = \dfrac{dy}{dx}$ and $q = \dfrac{d^2y}{dx^2}$. The investigation is similar to that
already given, and the conclusion is that the result found by the
ordinary processes of the Calculus of Variations will be a maximum if $\dfrac{d^2f}{dq^2}$ is always negative between the limits of the integration, and a minimum if it is always positive.

Legendre then says that it is easy to generalise these results
and to infer that the ordinary processes will give a maximum, if
the second differential coefficient of $f\left(x, y, \dfrac{dy}{dx}, \dfrac{d^2y}{dx^2}, \dots\right)$ with respect to the highest of the quantities $\dfrac{dy}{dx}, \dfrac{d^2y}{dx^2}, \dots$ which it involves is always negative between the limits of the integration,
and a minimum if that second differential coefficient is always
positive.

200.   Legendre next considers the case in which we have to
find the maximum or minimum of $\int f(x, y, p)\, dx$, supposing that
x is susceptible of variation as well as y.   The investigation is

now more complicated than that in Articles 5 and 198; the result however is the same, namely, that there is a maximum or minimum according as $\dfrac{d^2f}{dp^2}$ is constantly negative or constantly positive between the limits of the integration.

201. Legendre next supposes that we have to find the maximum or minimum of $\int f(x, y, p, \phi)\, dx$, where ϕ is to be determined from the differential equation $\dfrac{d\phi}{dx} = \psi$, in which ψ is a known function of x, y, p, and ϕ. The result at which Legendre arrives is wrong, and the correct result was afterwards given by Brunacci.

202. Legendre then illustrates his investigations by some examples. He first considers the case of the solid of least resistance, and he shews that the ordinary result is not necessarily a minimum. He then considers the problem in which among all curves of given length having their extremities in two fixed points, that is required which has its centre of gravity lowest; here his method indicates that the catenary does possess the required property. Then he considers the problem in which a curve of given length is to be drawn between two fixed points, so that the area bounded by the curve, the ordinates of the fixed points, and the axis of abscissæ shall be a maximum or a minimum. He shews that the required curve will in some cases be a circular arc, and in other cases will be composed of a circular arc and one or two straight lines; we shall have occasion to return to this point hereafter. The three examples thus discussed by Legendre form a very interesting and instructive part of his memoir.

Finally Legendre takes the problem of the brachistochrone in which the moving particle is to pass from one given curve to another, starting with an assigned velocity. Then the expression to be made a minimum is

$$\int \frac{\sqrt{(1+p^2)}\, dx}{\sqrt{(y-c+h)}},$$

where h is the height due to the assigned initial velocity, and c is the ordinate of the point at which the motion begins. Legendre takes c and x to be susceptible of variation, as well as y and p, and by a laborious investigation he arrives at the result that the time of motion is necessarily a minimum if the curve described be a cycloid, which meets the two given curves in points where the tangents to those curves are parallel, and which cuts the lower curve at right angles.

203. In the addition to his memoir, Legendre makes some remarks in order to strengthen two points in his conclusions. He says that he has to shew in the first place that the quantities which he supposes determined by differential equations, like the λ of Article 5, are necessarily real; and in the second place that, as we have stated in Art. 198, the arbitrary constants which occur in the solutions of the differential equations can be chosen so as to make the integrated part of the terms of the second order in the variation zero, or of the same sign as the unintegrated part. Accordingly he makes some observations in order to establish these two points.

204. Two remarks may be introduced here. In the first place it must be remembered that all Legendre's investigations are subject to the objection indicated by Lagrange; see Articles 5 and 6. Legendre does not solve the differential equations which he obtains, so that there is no security that the quantities he uses retain always finite values; and Lagrange shewed that in a simple example Legendre's conclusions were not necessarily true. In the second place, in all investigations with the view of distinguishing maxima from minima values, it is of course necessary that we should retain *all* the terms of the second order which can occur in our expressions. Now such formulæ as those of Poisson and Ostrogradsky in Articles 102 and 124 are only true to the *first* order, and consequently cannot be used in any investigation in which we are discriminating between maxima and minima values. This is one of the reasons which render it advisable to avoid giving a variation to the independent variable; see Art. 25. If, for example, we vary y and not x, then we have δp absolutely the

same thing as $\dfrac{d\delta y}{dx}$. If however we vary both y and x, it is shewn in elementary works, as in Art 39, that

$$\delta p = \frac{d\delta y}{dx} - p\,\frac{d\delta x}{dx}\,;$$

this equation however is not accurately true, but only true to the first order. For

$$dy = p\,dx,$$
$$dy + d\delta y = (p + \delta p)\,(dx + d\delta x)\,;$$

therefore

$$\delta p = \frac{d\delta y - p\,d\delta x}{dx + d\delta x} = \left(\frac{d\delta y}{dx} - \frac{p\,d\delta x}{dx}\right)\left(1 + \frac{d\delta x}{dx}\right)^{-1};$$

thus in order to be true to the *second* order we must take

$$\delta p = \left(\frac{d\delta y}{dx} - \frac{p\,d\delta x}{dx}\right)\left(1 - \frac{d\delta x}{dx}\right),$$

and in fact Legendre uses this value of δp on page 15 of his memoir.

205. We have next to consider two memoirs by Brunacci. The first of these is entitled, On the criteria which distinguish maxima from minima in integral expressions; it is published in the *Memorie dell'Istituto Nazionale Italiano*, Vol. 1. part 2. Bologna, 1806. The memoir extends over pages 191—202 of the volume; its object is to correct an error in the memoir which Legendre published in the History of the French Academy for 1786; see Art. 201. Suppose we have the integral $\int V\,dx$ where V involves x, y, $\dfrac{dy}{dx}$, and z, and z is determined by the differential equation $\dfrac{dz}{dx} = Z$, where Z is a function of x, y, $\dfrac{dy}{dx}$, and z. Then Legendre arrives at the following result; $\int V\,dx$ is rendered a maximum or minimum by the ordinary processes according as $\dfrac{d^2 V}{dp^2}$ is constantly negative or constantly positive between the

limits of the integration, where p stands for $\dfrac{dy}{dx}$. Legendre's method is rather obscure and Brunacci follows it; we will here give the investigation in the usual manner, and we shall obtain the same result as Brunacci.

206. Let λ denote a function of x at present undetermined; then we may consider that we have to find the maximum or minimum of

$$\int \left\{ V + \lambda \left(\frac{dz}{dx} - Z \right) \right\} dx,$$

and we will denote this expression by U. .

Now, considering only terms of the first order, we have

$$\delta V = \frac{dV}{dz} \delta z + \frac{dV}{dy} \delta y + \frac{dV}{dp} \delta p = A \delta z + B \delta y + C \delta p \quad \text{say};$$

$$\delta Z = \frac{dZ}{dz} \delta z + \frac{dZ}{dy} \delta y + \frac{dZ}{dp} \delta p = A' \delta z + B' \delta y + C' \delta p \quad \text{say};$$

thus

$$\delta U = \int \left\{ (A - \lambda A') \, \delta z + (B - \lambda B') \, \delta y + (C - \lambda C') \, \delta p + \frac{\lambda \, d\delta z}{dx} \right\} dx.$$

By the usual process of integration by parts we get
$$\delta U = (C - \lambda C') \, \delta y + \lambda \delta z$$

$$+ \int \left\{ A - \lambda A' - \frac{d\lambda}{dx} \right\} \delta z \, dx + \int \left\{ B - \lambda B' - \frac{d}{dx} (C - \lambda C') \right\} \delta y \, dx.$$

Now assume λ such that

$$A - \lambda A' - \frac{d\lambda}{dx} = 0;$$

then, in order that δU may vanish, we must have also

$$B - \lambda B' - \frac{d}{dx} (C - \lambda C') = 0.$$

Between the last two equations we must eliminate λ, and thus we shall obtain a differential equation for determining the required relation between x and y. We now proceed to examine whether U is thus rendered a maximum or a minimum. The terms of the second order in δV are

$$\frac{1}{2}\frac{d^2 V}{dz^2}(\delta z)^2 + \frac{d^2 V}{dz\,dy}\,\delta z\,\delta y + \frac{d^2 V}{dz\,dp}\,\delta z\,\delta p + \frac{1}{2}\frac{d^2 V}{dy^2}(\delta y)^2$$
$$+ \frac{d^2 V}{dy\,dp}\,\delta y\,\delta p + \frac{1}{2}\frac{d^2 V}{dp^2}(\delta p)^2,$$

say $= \frac{1}{2}F(\delta z)^2 + G\,\delta z\,\delta y + \Pi\,\delta z\,\delta p + \frac{1}{2}I(\delta y)^2 + K\,\delta y\,\delta p + \frac{1}{2}L\,(\delta p)^2.$

We shall denote the similar terms in δZ by

$$\frac{1}{2}F'(\delta z)^2 + G'\delta z\,\delta y + \Pi'\delta z\,\delta p + \frac{1}{2}I'(\delta y)^2 + K'\delta y\,\delta p + \frac{1}{2}L'(\delta p)^2.$$

Let $\quad F - \lambda F' = M, \quad G - \lambda G' = N, \quad \Pi - \lambda \Pi' = O,$
$$I - \lambda I' = P, \quad K - \lambda K' = Q, \quad L - \lambda L' = R;$$

then we have to examine the sign of

$$\int\left\{M(\delta z)^2 + 2N\,\delta z\,\delta y + 2O\,\delta z\,\delta p + P(\delta y)^2 + 2Q\,\delta y\,\delta p + R\,(\delta p)^2\right\}dz.$$

Now assume that this expression can be put in the form

$$l\,(\delta y)^2 + m\,\delta y\,\delta z + n\,(\delta z)^2 + \int R\,(\delta p + h\,\delta y + k\,\delta z)^2\,dz;$$

differentiate both sides of the assumed identity, and equate the coefficients of like terms, observing that $\dfrac{d\delta z}{dx}$ can be expressed in terms of δy, δz, and δp, since $\dfrac{d\delta z}{dx} = \delta Z$; thus we shall obtain five equations for determining the five quantities h, k, l, m, n, and three of these five equations are differential equations of the first order. Then we assume, as Legendre does, that by giving suitable values to the arbitrary constants we can make the integrated part $l\,(\delta y)^2 + m\,\delta y\,\delta z + n\,(\delta z)^2$ vanish. Thus finally if R be always negative between the limits of the integration, we obtain a maximum value of U, and if R be always positive between the limits of integration, we obtain a minimum value of U. And

$$R = \frac{d^2 V}{dp^2} - \lambda \frac{d^2 Z}{dp^2}.$$

This is Brunacci's result, and it shews that Legendre's result is wrong. The investigation is of course subject to the exceptions that have been already indicated in Articles 5 and 6.

207. We now pass to Brunacci's second memoir. This is entitled, *Memoir on the criteria which distinguish maxima from minima in double integrals*; it is published in the *Memorie dell' Istituto Nazionale Italiano*, Vol. II. part 2. Bologna, 1810. It extends over pages 121—170.

Brunacci refers to Legendre's memoir on the criteria for distinguishing maxima from minima in single integrals, and his own correction of one of Legendre's results in his former memoir. He states that so far as he knew, no similar investigations had been made with respect to double integrals. He proposes to consider this point; but before doing so, he gives some investigations with respect to single integrals in order to prepare the way. His memoir is divided into twelve sections.

208. In his first section, Brunacci makes a few remarks on the conditions necessary for the existence of a maximum or minimum value of a function. He says that he has proved in his Course of higher analysis, that $\int_a^b f(x)\,dx$ is a positive quantity provided that $f(x)$ is always positive for values of x between $x = a$ and $x = b$, and provided also that the differential coefficients $f'(x)$, $f''(x)$, ... are always finite between the same values. It is obvious however that Brunacci is wrong in saying that it is necessary that the differential coefficients should be finite; it is sufficient that $f(x)$ be always positive. Brunacci repeats this unnecessary restriction elsewhere in his memoir, but it does not affect his results.

209. In his second section Brunacci investigates the conditions

which must subsist in order that $\int \psi \, dx$ may have a maximum or a minimum value, where ψ involves x, y, and $\frac{dy}{dx}$; and he shews how to distinguish between a maximum and a minimum. The investigation is the same as Legendre's; see Art. 198.

In his third section Brunacci supposes that ψ involves x, y, $\frac{dy}{dx}$ and $\frac{d^2y}{dx^2}$, and he investigates the condition that must subsist in order that $\int \psi \, dx$ may have a maximum or a minimum value; and he distinguishes between the two cases. The investigation is similar to that already given; and the result coincides with that found by Legendre, and stated in Art. 199.

210. In his fourth section, Brunacci makes some introductory remarks on the subject of double integrals. He states that a double integral $\iint F(x,y) \, dx \, dy$ taken between definite limits is positive, provided that $F(x,y)$ is positive between the limits of the integrations, and provided also that the partial differential coefficients of $F(x,y)$ with respect to x and y are all finite between those limits. The restriction with respect to the differential coefficients is unnecessary. It is of course quite true that in the questions treated by the Calculus of Variations, such restrictions occur, because certain expansions are effected by Taylor's Theorem; but Brunacci is wrong in saying that these restrictions occur in the simple case indicated above.

211. In his fifth section, Brunacci takes the integral $\iint \psi \, dx \, dy$, where ψ involves x, y, and z, and it is required to determine z as a function of x and y so that the double integral may be a maximum or a minimum. He arrives at the following result; for a maximum or a minimum we must have $\frac{d\psi}{dz} = 0$, and then there will be a maximum or a minimum according as $\frac{d^2\psi}{dz^2}$ is

always negative or always positive between the limits of the
integrations.   For an example he supposes $\psi = \dfrac{x^2 + y^2 + z^2}{xyz}$, and
he obtains as the result $z = \sqrt{(x^2 + y^2)}$.   He then suggests as a
particular case, that the integrations should be taken from
$y = 0$ to $y = ax$, and from $x = 0$ to $x = b$; he does not observe
that for these limits his double integral becomes infinite.

212.   In his sixth section, Brunacci considers the double in-
tegral $\iint \psi \, dx \, dy$, where ψ involves x, y, z, and $\dfrac{dz}{dx}$.   He proceeds
as Legendre does for a single integral and he arrives at the fol-
lowing result; let p denote $\dfrac{dz}{dx}$, then to ensure a maximum the
relation between z and x and y must be such as to make $\dfrac{d^2 \psi}{dp^2}$
always negative between the limits of the integrations, and to
ensure a minimum always positive.   As in Legendre's process, it
is assumed that the quantities which occur always remain finite,
and this condition cannot be tested because a certain differential
relation which occurs is not investigated, but only supposed to be
investigated.   Brunacci takes for an example $\psi = \sqrt{(1 + p^2)}$.

213.   In his seventh section, Brunacci considers the double
integral $\iint \psi \, dx \, dy$, where ψ involves x, y, z, $\dfrac{dz}{dx}$, and $\dfrac{dz}{dy}$.   We
will give in substance the investigation of this case as an example.
Let U denote the proposed double integral, then we require the
maximum or minimum value of U.   The first thing to do is to
investigate the value of δU to the first order and to make it vanish.
The value of δU to the first order has been given in Art. 59;
and by the usual method the value of z in terms of x and y must
be found from the equation

$$L - \frac{dM}{dx} - \frac{dN}{dy} = 0.$$

The arbitrary functions which enter into the value of z must
then be so determined as to make the remaining terms in δU
vanish which are given in Art. 59.

We then proceed to consider the terms of the second order.

Let p denote $\dfrac{ds}{dx}$ and q denote $\dfrac{ds}{dy}$; and let

$$\frac{d^2\psi}{ds^2} = Z, \quad \frac{d^2\psi}{dp^2} = P, \quad \frac{d^2\psi}{dq^2} = Q,$$

$$\frac{d^2\psi}{ds\,dp} = R, \quad \frac{d^2\psi}{ds\,dq} = S, \quad \frac{d^2\psi}{dp\,dq} = T,$$

and $$\delta s = \omega.$$

Then we have to examine the sign of the expression

$$\int_{x_0}^{x_1}\int_{y_0}^{y_1} \left\{ Z\omega^2 + P\left(\frac{d\omega}{dx}\right)^2 + Q\left(\frac{d\omega}{dy}\right)^2 + 2R\omega\frac{d\omega}{dx} \right.$$
$$\left. + 2S\omega\frac{d\omega}{dy} + 2T\frac{d\omega}{dx}\frac{d\omega}{dy} \right\} dx\,dy.$$

Let a and β be two quantities at present undetermined; then the above double integral is identically equal to

$$\int_{x_0}^{x_1}\int_{y_0}^{y_1}\frac{d\omega^2 a}{dx}\,dx\,dy + \int_{x_0}^{x_1}\int_{y_0}^{y_1}\frac{d\omega^2\beta}{dy}\,dx\,dy$$

$$+\int_{x_0}^{x_1}\int_{y_0}^{y_1}\left\{ A\omega^2 + 2B\omega\frac{d\omega}{dx} + 2C\omega\frac{d\omega}{dy} + P\left(\frac{d\omega}{dx}\right)^2 \right.$$
$$\left. + Q\left(\frac{d\omega}{dy}\right)^2 + 2T\frac{d\omega}{dx}\frac{d\omega}{dy} \right\} dx\,dy,$$

where $\quad A = Z - \dfrac{da}{dx} - \dfrac{d\beta}{dy}, \quad B = R - a, \quad C = S - \beta.$

The expression

$$\int_{x_0}^{x_1}\int_{y_0}^{y_1}\frac{d\omega^2\beta}{dy}\,dx\,dy$$

really involves only a *single* integral, because the integration with respect to y can be immediately effected.

The expression

$$\int_{x_0}^{x_1}\int_{y_0}^{y_1}\frac{d\omega^2 a}{dx}\,dx\,dy$$

also really involves only a *single* integral; because we may change the order of integration if we make suitable changes in the limits, and then the integration with respect to x can be immediately effected.

Now consider the double integral. The necessary and sufficient conditions in order that

$$A\omega^2 + 2B\omega\frac{d\omega}{dx} + 2C\omega\frac{d\omega}{dy} + P\left(\frac{d\omega}{dx}\right)^2 + Q\left(\frac{d\omega}{dy}\right)^2 + 2T\frac{d\omega}{dx}\frac{d\omega}{dy}$$

should retain an invariable sign are these,

$$PQ - T^2 \text{ must be positive,}$$

and $(PC - BT)^2$ must be less than $(PQ - T^2)(PA - B^2)$;

and the sign is then positive or negative according as P is positive or negative. (See *Differential Calculus*, Art. 236.)

Now we may suppose that the arbitrary quantities a and β are so taken as to satisfy the condition that

$$(PC - BT)^2 \text{ is less than } (PQ - T^2)(PA - B^2);$$

this condition involves a, β, $\dfrac{da}{dx}$ and $\dfrac{d\beta}{dy}$.

We have then the following result. In order to ensure a minimum we must have P positive and $PQ - T^2$ positive throughout the limits of the integrations. That is, we must have $\dfrac{d^2\psi}{dp^2}$ positive, and also $\dfrac{d^2\psi}{dp^2}\dfrac{d^2\psi}{dq^2} - \left(\dfrac{d^2\psi}{dp\,dq}\right)^2$ positive.

Similarly in order to ensure a maximum we must have P negative and $PQ - T^2$ positive throughout the limits of the integrations; that is, $\dfrac{d^2\psi}{dp^2}$ negative and $\dfrac{d^2\psi}{dp^2}\dfrac{d^2\psi}{dq^2} - \left(\dfrac{d^2\psi}{dp\,dq}\right)^2$ positive.

It will also be necessary that the expression

$$\int_{x_0}^{x_1}\int_{y_0}^{y_1}\left(\frac{d\omega^2 a}{dx} + \frac{d\omega^2 \beta}{dy}\right)dx\,dy$$

should be zero or negative for a maximum, and zero or positive for a
minimum; this condition will be secured for example if δz be zero
at the limits of the integrations, for then the term just given will
vanish.

The whole investigation is of course liable to the objection that
as the values of α and β are not explicitly found we have no means
of ascertaining whether they remain finite throughout the limits of
the integrations.

214. For an example of the preceding investigation Brunacci
supposes $\psi = \left(\dfrac{dz}{dy}\right)^2 - a^2\left(\dfrac{dz}{dx}\right)^2$. In this case he finds that the relation between x, y, and z is to be determined from $\dfrac{d^2z}{dy^2} = a^2\dfrac{d^2z}{dx^2}$,
so that

$$z = \phi(x + ay) + F(x - ay),$$

where ϕ and F denote arbitrary functions. For a particular case he
supposes that the surface denoted by the required relation is to pass
through an oval plane curve determined by the equations

$$y = mx + n, \quad z = \sqrt{(r^2 - x^2)}.$$

He says that then by determining suitably the first arbitrary
function we shall have

$$z = \sqrt{\{M + N(x + ay) + L(x + ay)^2\}} + F(x - ay),$$

where
$$M = \frac{r^2(1 + am)^2 - a^2 n^2}{(1 + am)^2},$$

$$N = \frac{2an}{(1 + am)^2}, \qquad L = -\frac{1}{(1 + am)^2}.$$

But the surface Brunacci thus obtains will *not* pass through the
curve in question if $F(x - ay)$ is still left arbitrary. In continuing
the discussion of this example he arrives at the result that there is
neither a maximum nor a minimum. He says that this ought to be
the case, because as ψ is zero the double integral $\iint \psi \, dx \, dy$ over
assigned limits is also zero. Since he says that ψ is zero, it would
appear that he supposes $F(x - ay) = 0$, for then his surface does
pass through the curve in question and ψ is zero. But then it

is not obvious what he means by saying that there ought to be
neither a maximum nor a minimum, since it is quite possible that
a zero value of a function may be a maximum or a minimum value
of that function.

215. In his eighth section Brunacci supposes that ψ involves
$x,\ y,\ z,\ \dfrac{dz}{dx},\ \dfrac{dz}{dy},\ \dfrac{d^2z}{dx^2},\ \dfrac{d^2z}{dx\,dy}$, and $\dfrac{d^2z}{dy^2}$; and he proceeds in the
same manner as before to determine the conditions necessary in
order that $\iint\psi\,dx\,dy$ may have a maximum or minimum value. He
arrives at the same results as Delaunay afterwards gave in his
memoir; see Art. 147.

216. The remainder of Brunacci's memoir consists of four
sections and is devoted to the investigation of the conditions for a
maximum or minimum of $\iint\psi\,dx\,dy$, when ψ involves $x,\ y,\ z,\ \dfrac{dz}{dx}$,
and $\dfrac{dz}{dy}$, and also another function V, which is determined by
$\dfrac{dV}{dx}=\phi$, where ϕ involves $x,\ y,\ z,\ \dfrac{dz}{dx},\ \dfrac{dz}{dy},\ V$, and $\dfrac{dV}{dy}$. This
case is analogous to that involving only a single integral in which
Brunacci corrected an error of Legendre's. Brunacci's method
does not appear very clear. The ordinary method would be to
investigate the maximum or minimum of

$$\iint\left\{\psi+\lambda\left(\frac{dV}{dx}-\phi\right)\right\}dx\,dy.$$

Then when the usual reductions are effected the variation of
the double integral to the first order would contain under the integral signs two terms, one of the form $A\delta V$, and the other of the
form $B\delta z$. We should then assume λ such as to make $A=0$, and
then it follows that in order that the variation may vanish we must
also have $B=0$. The part of the variation which is of the second
order might then be examined in the ordinary way.

217. Nothing was added to this part of the Calculus of Variations between the publication of Brunacci's second memoir and the

publication of Jacobi's memoir. Lacroix, Dirksen, and Ohm in their respective works explained Legendre's method without any improvements. Ohm seems to have regarded the results as more certain than they really are, for he omits all reference to the qualifications indicated by Lagrange; see Articles 5 and 6. Lacroix does give these on his pages 811—813, and Dirksen on his page 113 notices the limitation that the quantities he introduces must remain finite.

218. We now proceed to Jacobi's memoir. This memoir is entitled, *On the theory of the Calculus of Variations and of differential equations*, by C. G. Jacobi. It was published in the 17th volume of Crelle's Mathematical Journal in 1837. The memoir purports to be an extract from a letter dated November 29th, 1836, addressed to Professor Enke, secretary to the mathematical class of the Academy of Sciences at Berlin. The memoir extends over pages 68—82 of the volume; nine pages relate to the Calculus of Variations and the remainder to the differential equations which occur in Dynamics. A French translation of the memoir appeared in the third volume of Liouville's Journal of Mathematics in 1838.

We confine ourselves to that part of Jacobi's memoir which relates to the Calculus of Variations; for an account of Jacobi's researches on Dynamics the student is referred to Mr Cayley's *Report on the recent progress of Theoretical Dynamics*, in the Report of the British Association for the advancement of Science for 1857.

The remainder of the present chapter consists of a translation of the first nine pages of Jacobi's memoir; it will be seen that Jacobi merely gives the enunciation of results without demonstrations, and we shall afterwards indicate the writers who have supplied the demonstrations.

219. I have succeeded in supplying a great deficiency in the Calculus of Variations. In problems on maxima and minima which depend on this Calculus no general rule is known for deciding whether a solution really gives a maximum or a minimum or neither. It has indeed been shewn that the question amounts to determining whether the integrals of a certain system of differential

equations remain finite throughout the limits of the integral which
is to have a maximum or minimum value. But the integrals of
these differential equations were not known, nor had any other
method been discovered for ascertaining whether they did remain
finite throughout the required interval. I have however discovered
that these integrals can be immediately obtained when we have
integrated the differential equations of the problem under consideration, that is, the differential equations which must be satisfied
in order that the first variation may vanish. In fact, suppose that
by the integration of these differential equations we have obtained
expressions for the required functions involving a certain number
of arbitrary constants, then the partial differential coefficients of
these functions with respect to these arbitrary constants will furnish
the integrals of those new differential equations which we have to
solve in order to determine the criteria for the existence of a maximum or minimum.

220.   Let us consider the simplest case ; let the integral which
is to have a maximum or minimum value be

$$\int f(x, y, y')\, dx,$$

where y' is put for $\dfrac{dy}{dx}$. Then we know that y is to be found from
the differential equation

$$\frac{df}{dy} - \frac{d}{dx}\frac{df}{dy'} = 0.$$

The value of y obtained from this differential equation will contain
two arbitrary constants which I will denote by a and b. The
second variation of the proposed integral is

$$\int \left(\frac{d^2f}{dy'^2} w'^2 + 2\frac{d^2f}{dy\, dy'} w w' + \frac{d^2f}{dy'^2} w'^2 \right) dx,$$

where $w = \delta y$ and $w' = \dfrac{dw}{dx}$.

Now to have the complete criteria for the existence of a maxi-

mum or minimum we must know the complete expression of a
function v which satisfies the differential equation

$$\frac{d^2f}{dy'^2}\left(\frac{d^2f}{dy^2}+\frac{dv}{dx}\right)=\left(\frac{d^2f}{dy\,dy'}+v\right)^2;$$

this may be seen in Lagrange's Theory of Functions or in Dirksen's
Calculus of Variations. (Ohm's Calculus of Variations is not exact
on this point.) The expression for v I find in the following manner.
Let

$$u=\alpha\frac{dy}{da}+\beta\frac{dy}{db},$$

where $\frac{dy}{da}$, $\frac{dy}{db}$ are the partial differential coefficients of y with

respect to the constants a and b which occur in y, and α and β
are new arbitrary constants; then the required expression for v
will be

$$v=-\left(\frac{d^2f}{dy\,dy'}+\frac{1}{u}\frac{d^2f}{dy'^2}\frac{du}{dx}\right),$$

which contains one arbitrary constant, namely, $\frac{\beta}{\alpha}$.

[The differential equation which v must satisfy is the same as
equation (2) of Art. 5, supposing $2\lambda=-v$.]

221. The case in which differential coefficients of a higher
order than the first occur in the expression which is to be a maximum or minimum is more difficult. Let the expression which is
to be a maximum or minimum be

$$\int f(x,\,y,\,y',\,y'')\,dx,$$

where $y'=\frac{dy}{dx}$ and $y''=\frac{d^2y}{dx^2}$. Then we know that y must be found
from the differential equation

$$\frac{df}{dy}-\frac{d}{dx}\frac{df}{dy'}+\frac{d^2}{dx^2}\frac{df}{dy''}=0;$$

thus y will contain four arbitrary constants which may be denoted by a, a_1, a_2, a_3. Also let $\delta y = w$, $\delta y' = w'$, $\delta y'' = w''$; then the second variation will be

$$\int \left(\frac{d^2f}{dy^2} w^2 + 2 \frac{d^2f}{dy\,dy'} ww' + 2 \frac{d^2f}{dy\,dy''} ww'' + \frac{d^2f}{dy'^2} w'^2 \right.$$
$$\left. + 2 \frac{d^2f}{dy'\,dy''} w'w'' + \frac{d^2f}{dy''^2} w''^2 \right) dx.$$

For a maximum or minimum $\dfrac{d^2f}{dy''^2}$ must retain the same sign. But in order to have the complete criteria we must integrate the following system of differential equations, as may be seen in Lagrange's Theory of Functions.

$$\left(\frac{d^2f}{dy^2} + \frac{dv}{dx} \right) \left(\frac{d^2f}{dy''^2} + \frac{dr_2}{dx} + 2v_2 \right) = \left(\frac{d^2f}{dy\,dy''} + v + \frac{dv_1}{dx} \right)^2;$$

$$\frac{d^2f}{dy''^2} \left(\frac{d^2f}{dy'^2} + \frac{dv}{dx} \right) = \left(\frac{d^2f}{dy'\,dy''} + v_1 \right)^2.$$

$$\frac{d^2f}{dy''^2} \left(\frac{d^2f}{dy'^2} + \frac{dv_2}{dx} + 2v_1 \right) = \left(\frac{d^2f}{dy'\,dy''} + v_1 \right)^2.$$

From these three differential equations of the first order, which present a rather complicated appearance, the three functions v, v_1, and r_2 must be determined; and the complete expressions for them will involve three arbitrary constants. I have found the integrals of these differential equations as follows; let

$$u = a \frac{dy}{da} + a_1 \frac{dy}{da_1} + a_2 \frac{dy}{da_2} + a_3 \frac{dy}{da_3},$$

$$u_1 = \beta \frac{dy}{da} + \beta_1 \frac{dy}{da_1} + \beta_2 \frac{dy}{da_2} + \beta_3 \frac{dy}{da_3},$$

so that u and u_1 are linear expressions of the partial differential coefficients of y with respect to the arbitrary constants which it involves. The eight constants a, a_1, a_2, a_3, β, β_1, β_2, β_3 are not entirely arbitrary, for a certain relation must exist between these six quantities $a\beta_1 - a_1\beta$, $a\beta_2 - a_2\beta$, $a\beta_3 - a_3\beta$, $a_1\beta_2 - a_2\beta_1$, $a_2\beta_3 - a_3\beta_2$,

$\alpha_1\beta_2 - \alpha_2\beta_1$, which I will not investigate here. The following then are the general expressions which I have found for v, v_1, v_2;

$$v_2 = -\frac{d^2 f}{dy'\,dy''} - \frac{d^2 f}{dy''^2}\,\frac{u\dfrac{d^n u_1}{dx^n} - u_1\dfrac{d^n u}{dx^n}}{u\dfrac{du_1}{dx} - u_1\dfrac{du}{dx}},$$

$$v_1 = -\frac{d^2 f}{dy\,dy''} + \frac{d^2 f}{dy''^2}\,\frac{\dfrac{du}{dx}\dfrac{d^n u_1}{dx^n} - \dfrac{du_1}{dx}\dfrac{d^n u}{dx^n}}{u\dfrac{du_1}{dx} - u_1\dfrac{du}{dx}},$$

$$v = -\frac{dv_1}{dx} - \frac{d^2 f}{dy\,dy'} - \frac{d^2 f}{dy''^2}\,\frac{\left(u\dfrac{d^n u_1}{dx^n} - u_1\dfrac{d^n u}{dx^n}\right)\left(\dfrac{du}{dx}\dfrac{d^n u_1}{dx^n} - \dfrac{du_1}{dx}\dfrac{d^n u}{dx^n}\right)}{\left(u\dfrac{du_1}{dx} - u_1\dfrac{du}{dx}\right)^2}.$$

An identical equation holds between the six quantities $\alpha\beta_1 - \alpha_1\beta$, $\alpha\beta_2 - \alpha_2\beta$, ..., besides the relation which exists between them, and these quantities occur in v_2, v_1, and v only in the form of ratios, so that they constitute in fact the three arbitrary constants which ought to appear.

222. The general theory when differential coefficients of y of any order occur under the sign of integration may be deduced without difficulty from a remarkable property of a certain class of differential equations. These differential equations of the $2n^{\text{th}}$ order have the form

$$0 = Ay + \frac{d.A_1 y'}{dx} + \frac{d^2.A_2 y''}{dx^2} + \frac{d^3.A_3 y'''}{dx^3} + \dots + \frac{d^n.A_n y^{(n)}}{dx^n} = Y,$$

where $y^{(m)} = \dfrac{d^m y}{dx^m}$, and A, A_1, ... are given functions of x.

Now suppose y to be any integral of the equation $Y = 0$, and put $u = ty$, then will the following expression be integrable,

$$y\left(Au + \frac{d.A_1 u'}{dx} + \frac{d^2.A_2 u''}{dx^2} + \dots + \frac{d^n.A_n u^{(n)}}{dx^n}\right) = yU,$$

where $u^{(m)} = \dfrac{d^m u}{dx^m}$, that is the expression is integrable without knowing t. Moreover the integral is of the same form as Y, only n must be diminished by 1; so that

$$\int y U\, dx = D t' + \frac{d \cdot B_1 t'}{dx} + \frac{d^2 \cdot B_2 t''}{dx^2} + \dots + \frac{d^{n-1} \cdot B_{n-1} t^{(n)}}{dx^{n-1}},$$

where $t^{(n)} = \dfrac{d^n t}{dx^n}$ and $B, B_1, \dots$ might be expressed in terms of y and the functions A and their differential coefficients. The proof of this proposition is not without difficulty. I have found the general expression of the functions B; but it is enough for the present question to shew that $\int y U\, dx$ can be put in the form indicated without there being any need of knowing the functions B themselves.

223. The metaphysic of the results obtained (if I may use a French expression) depends nearly upon the following considerations. The first variation is known to take the form $\int V \delta y\, dx$, where $V = 0$ is the equation to be integrated. The second variation then takes the form $\int \delta V \delta y\, dx$. If then the second variation is to be incapable of changing its sign, it must be incapable of vanishing; so that the equation $\delta V = 0$, which is linear in δy, must have no integral δy which satisfies the conditions to which by the nature of the problem δy is subjected. Thus we see that the equation $\delta V = 0$ plays an important part in these investigations, and we soon perceive its connexion with the differential equations which must be integrated in order to obtain the criteria for maxima and minima. Also we easily see that a partial differential coefficient of y with respect to any constant which occurs in y as the solution of $V = 0$, will be a suitable value of δy for satisfying the differential equation $\delta V = 0$. Thus the general expression for δy as the integral of the equation $\delta V = 0$ will be a linear function of all the partial differential coefficients of y with respect to the constants which it involves.

224. The equation $\delta V = 0$, of which we can thus find the complete integral, can be put in the form of the above equation

$Y = 0$, with δy in the place of y. By means of the properties of equations of this kind, we can by repeated integration by parts transform the expression $\int \delta V \delta y \, dx$ into another, which contains a perfect square under the integral sign; we thus obtain the transformation of the second variation which was always desired.

Take for example the integral considered already

$$\int f(x, y, y', y'') \, dx,$$

and let u and u_1 have the meanings already assigned. δV can be put in the form

$$\delta V = A \delta y + \frac{d \cdot A_1 \delta y'}{dx} + \frac{d^2 \cdot A_2 \delta y''}{dx^2} :$$

and δV will $= 0$ when $\delta y = u$. Now put $\delta y = u \delta y$; then from the general theorem (Art. 222) we have

$$\int \delta V \delta y \, dx = \int u \, \delta V \delta y \, dx$$

$$= \left(B \delta y' + \frac{d \cdot B_1 \delta y''}{dx} \right) \delta y - \int \left(B \delta y' + \frac{d \cdot B_1 \delta y''}{dx} \right) \delta y' \, dx.$$

Denote the last integral by $\int V_1 \delta' y' \, dx$; then the equation $V_1 = 0$ is satisfied when we put $\delta' y = \frac{u_1}{u}$, and therefore $\delta' y' = \frac{u u_1' - u_1 u'}{u^2}$. We can now continue the same method by putting

$$\delta' y' = \frac{u u_1' - u_1 u'}{u^2} \delta'' y;$$

so that by the same general theorem

$$\int V_1 \delta' y' \, dx = \int V_1 \frac{u u_1' - u_1 u'}{u^2} \delta'' y \, dx$$

$$= C \delta'' y' \delta' y - \int C (\delta'' y)^2 \, dx;$$

and this is the last transformation, in which the arbitrary variation occurs under the integral sign only in the form of a square. And it is easily seen that

$$B_1 = u^2 A_n, \quad C = \left(\frac{u u_1' - u_1 u'}{u^2}\right)^2 B_1,$$

and therefore

$$C = \left(\frac{u u_1' - u_1 u'}{u}\right)^2 A_n.$$

Moreover $A_n = \dfrac{d^2 f}{d y''^2}$ so that C has always the same sign as $\dfrac{d^2 f}{d y''^2}$ has, and this sign must be always positive for a minimum and always negative for a maximum. We must moreover examine whether $\delta'' y'$ can become infinite within the limits of integration; this we can ascertain by our knowing the functions u and u_1, and these we know as soon as the complete integral of the equation $V = 0$ is given.

225. Although the analysis just indicated requires a good knowledge of the Integral Calculus, yet the criteria thence obtained for determining whether a solution gives in general a maximum or minimum are very simple. I will consider the case in which we have under the integral sign y and its differential coefficients up to the nth, and where the limiting values of $x, y, y', y'', \dots y^{(n-1)}$ are given. Now the $2n$ arbitrary constants which occur in integrating the differential equation of the $(2n)^{th}$ order are to be determined by means of the given limiting values; but as this involves the solution of equations there will be in general several systems of values for the arbitrary constants, so that several curves may be found which satisfy the same differential equation and the same limiting conditions. Let one of these systems be chosen, and let one limiting point be considered as fixed, and then let us pass from this point along the curve to following points. Now take one of these following points as the second limiting point; then, as stated above, it may happen that through this and the first fixed point a second curve can also be drawn which satisfies the same differential equation as the first curve and has the same limiting values of $y', y'', \dots y^{(n-1)}$. As soon then as by passing along the curve we arrive at a point for which one of the other curves coincides with

it, or as we may say approaches indefinitely near to it, we have reached the boundary up to which or beyond which the integration must not extend if there is to be a maximum or a minimum; but if the integration does not extend up to this boundary there will be a maximum or minimum provided that $\frac{d'f}{[dy^{(n)}]^2}$ retains the same sign between the limits.

220. In order to illustrate this by an example I will consider the principle of least action in the elliptic motion of a planet.

The integral considered in the principle of least action can never be a maximum as Lagrange believed; it will not however always be a minimum, but certain conditions must hold with respect to the limits; these conditions are given by the preceding general rule, and if they are not satisfied the integral will be neither a maximum nor a minimum.

Suppose that the planet begins to move from a where a lies between the perihelion and aphelion, and let the other limit be b, (see fig. 7); let $2A$ be the major axis, f the sun; then we know that the other focus of the ellipse is obtained by the intersection of two circles described from the centres a and b with the radii $2A - af$ and $2A - bf$ respectively. The two intersections of the circles give two solutions of the problem which can only coincide when the circles touch, that is when the line ab passes through the other focus. Thus if we draw the chord aa' through the focus f, then by the general rule (Art. 225), the other limit b must fall between a and a' if the integral which occurs in the principle of least action is really to be a minimum for the ellipse. If b coincides with a' then the second variation of the integral cannot become negative, but it can become zero, so that the variation of the integral is then of the third order, and so may be either positive or negative. If b falls beyond a' then the second variation itself can become negative.

If the starting point a is between the aphelion and the perihelion then the extreme point a' is determined by the chord of the ellipse drawn from a through the sun f, (see figure 8). For if a and a' are the limits we can obtain an infinite number of solutions by the revolution of the ellipse round aa'. If then in the last case the second limit falls beyond a' there will be a *curve of double curvature* between the two given limits for which $\int ds$ is less than it is for the ellipse.

227. I will say a few words on the variation of double integrals; the theory of this subject is susceptible of greater elegance than it has obtained even after the labours of *Gauss* and *Poisson*. In order to give an example of the way in which it seems to me proper to express the variation of a double integral, I will take the simplest case and consider $\delta\iint f(x, y, z, p, q)\, dx\, dy$ where $p = \dfrac{dz}{dx}, \; q = \dfrac{dz}{dy}$. Let w be the variation of z; then will

$$\delta\iint f(x, y, z, p, q)\, dx\, dy = \iint dx\, dy \left(\frac{df}{dz}w + \frac{df}{dp}\frac{dw}{dx} + \frac{df}{dq}\frac{dw}{dy}\right).$$

Now the method employed in single integrals consists in this; the expression under the integral sign is divided into two parts, one of which is multiplied by w and the other is the element of an integral. The first must be put equal to zero under the sign of integration if the variation is to vanish; the second can be integrated and we make the integral vanish. So in like manner I divide the expression under the double integral sign into two parts, one of which is multiplied by w and the other is the element of a double integral as follows; let $u = aw$ and put

$$\frac{df}{dz}w + \frac{df}{dp}\frac{dw}{dx} + \frac{df}{dq}\frac{dw}{dy} = Aw + \frac{du}{dx}\frac{dv}{dy} - \frac{du}{dy}\frac{dv}{dx}.$$

Equate the terms in w, $\dfrac{dw}{dx}$, $\dfrac{dw}{dy}$; thus

$$\frac{df}{dz} = A + \frac{da}{dx}\frac{dv}{dy} - \frac{da}{dy}\frac{dv}{dx}, \quad \frac{df}{dp} = a\frac{dv}{dy}, \quad \frac{df}{dq} = -a\frac{dv}{dx};$$

hence $$A = \frac{df}{dz} - \frac{d}{dx}\frac{df}{dp} - \frac{d}{dy}\frac{df}{dq};$$

if this be put equal to zero we obtain the known partial differential equation, which is here deduced in a perfectly symmetrical manner. The function v must satisfy the equation

$$\frac{df}{dp}\frac{dv}{dx} + \frac{df}{dq}\frac{dv}{dy} = 0.$$

If we put $A = 0$, we have

$$\delta \iint f(x, y, z, p, q)\, dx\, dy = \iint dx\, dy \left(\frac{du}{dx}\frac{dv}{dy} - \frac{du}{dy}\frac{dv}{dx} \right) = \iint dv\, du,$$

and this taken throughout the given limits must vanish. If z is given at the limits w is zero at the limits and therefore also δw, that is, u; therefore $\iint dv\, du$ is zero. If the values of z at the limits are entirely arbitrary v must vanish at the limits, or if $v = 0$ represent the limiting curve the arbitrary functions which occur in the solution of $A = 0$ must be so determined that

$$\frac{df}{dp}\frac{dv}{dx} + \frac{df}{dq}\frac{dv}{dy} = 0, \ \&\text{c.}$$

228. To return to the maximum and minimum; it is to be regretted that so much confusion prevails in the use of these words. Sometimes an expression is said to be a maximum or minimum when all that is meant is that its variation vanishes, sometimes when it really is neither a maximum nor a minimum. Sometimes an expression is said to be a maximum when all that is meant is that it is not a minimum. Thus Poisson says in his treatise on Mechanics that the shortest line on a closed surface between two given points can be a maximum; but it is obvious that by indefinitely small inflexions we can increase the length of any such line however long. In fact the shortest line will only be really a minimum when the general condition laid down is fulfilled (Art. 225); that is, when between the two limiting points of the curve two others cannot be found which can be joined by another such curve indefinitely close to the first. In other cases the shortest line is not indeed a maximum; it is neither a maximum nor a minimum. For surfaces which have at every point opposite curvatures I have demonstrated that the shortest line between any two points is really a minimum.

[By the *shortest line* in the above paragraph is meant the line which is furnished by the ordinary rules of the Calculus of Variations; the investigation of it is given in most treatises on the subject, but these treatises do not determine whether the line *called* the shortest line between two points really *is* the shortest line between those points. Such a line is also called a *geodetic curve*.]

CHAPTER X.

COMMENTATORS ON JACOBI.

229. WE now proceed to give an account of the commentaries and developments which have arisen from Jacobi's memoir.

In the sixth volume of Liouville's Journal of Mathematics, dated 1841, there is an article by V. A. Lebesgue entitled *Memoir on a Formula of Vandermonde's and its application to the demonstration of a Theorem of Jacobi's*. It extends over pages 17—35 of the volume. It begins thus—The principal object of the following pages is in the first place to demonstrate the identical equation

$$y \, \Sigma \, \frac{d^i . A_i \, (ty)^{(i)}}{dx^i} = \Sigma \, \frac{d^i . B_i t^{(i)}}{dx^i} \, ;$$

both the summations are taken from $i = 0$ to $i = n$; $(ty)^i$ denotes $\dfrac{d^i ty}{dx^i}$ and $t^{(i)}$ denotes $\dfrac{d^i t}{dx^i}$; y, t, A_0, A_1, ... A_n denote any functions of x; B_0, B_1, ... B_n are functions of y, A_0, A_1, ... A_n and their differential coefficients. In the second place we propose to find the law of the functions B_0, B_1, ... B_n.

The above words indicate the object of Lebesgue's article. The investigations are rather complicated and difficult to follow; they depend partly upon the knowledge of the *condition of integrability* of a function.

230. In the same volume of Liouville's Journal there is an article by C. Delaunay entitled *Essay on the distinction between maxima and minima in questions which depend upon the Calculus of Variations*. This essay is in fact a commentary upon Jacobi's memoir; it extends over pages 209—237 of the volume.

231. Delaunay first proves the theorem enunciated by Jacobi,
which we have given in Art. 222; Delaunay's proof is somewhat
complicated but perfectly intelligible, and it does not assume a
knowledge of the *condition of integrability* of a function. It may be
observed that the result obtained by Delaunay might be stated
more distinctly than he has himself stated it. He really proves
the following theorem; whatever functions of x the symbols u, y,
A_1, A_2, ... A_n, may denote, it is possible to take b_1, b_2, ... b_n such
functions of x that

$$\Sigma u \frac{d^m A_m \frac{d^m uy}{dx^m}}{dx^m} = \Sigma \frac{d^m b_m \frac{d^m y}{dx^m}}{dx^m} + yu \Sigma \frac{d^m A_m \frac{d^m u}{dx^m}}{dx^m},$$

where the summations denoted by Σ relate to the letter m and
extend from $m = 1$ to $m = n$ both inclusive. Now add $A_0 u^2 y$ to both
sides of this identity, and suppose

$$A_0 u^2 + u \Sigma \frac{d^m A_m \frac{d^m u}{dx^m}}{dx^m} = b_0;$$

then

$$A_0 u^2 y + \Sigma u \frac{d^m A_m \frac{d^m uy}{dx^m}}{dx^m} = b_0 y + \Sigma \frac{d^m b_m \frac{d^m y}{dx^m}}{dx^m} \dots\dots\dots(1).$$

If now u be taken so that $b_0 = 0$ the right-hand member of this
identity is immediately integrable, and by integrating we have

$$\int \left\{ A_0 u^2 y + \Sigma u \frac{d^m A_m \frac{d^m uy}{dx^m}}{dx^m} \right\} dx = \Sigma \frac{d^{m-1} b_m \frac{d^m y}{dx^m}}{dx^{m-1}} \dots\dots\dots\dots(2).$$

Thus Delaunay first establishes the general identity (1) and
then deduces (2) which is Jacobi's theorem enunciated in Art. 222.

This is in fact the same order of demonstration as that chosen
by Lebesgue. Delaunay's demonstration has been adopted in substance by subsequent writers on the Calculus of Variations; see the
works of Jellett, Price, and Stegmann.

It should be observed that in equation (2) since it has been
obtained by an integration an arbitrary constant ought to be

explicitly added to the right-hand side or else supposed to be im
plicitly involved on the left-hand side.

232. Delaunay next proves that δV can be put in the form
which Jacobi gives; see Art. 224. Delaunay then investigates in
full the terms of the second order in the variation for the two cases
which Jacobi specially considers, namely

$$\int f(x, y, y')\, dx \quad \text{and} \quad \int f(x, y, y', y'')\, dx.$$

A mistake occurs in this part of Delaunay's memoir which
should be noticed; it is on his page 222, and has passed from Delaunay into other writers. We will here notice it in the form in
which it appears in Mr Jellett's work, since that will probably be
most accessible to the reader. On page 95 of Mr Jellett's work he
has the following equation

$$\int u\delta\beta\, dx = B_1 \frac{d\delta' y}{dx} + \frac{d\,.\,B_2 \frac{d^2\delta y}{dx^2}}{dx},$$

and he says that any value of δy which makes $\delta\beta = 0$ will also
make

$$B_1 \frac{d\delta' y}{dx} + \frac{d\,.\,B_2 \frac{d^2\delta y}{dx^2}}{dx}$$

vanish; the true inference ought to have been that any value of δy
which makes $\delta\beta = 0$ will make

$$B_1 \frac{d\delta' y}{dx} + \frac{d\,.\,B_2 \frac{d^2\delta y}{dx^2}}{dx}$$

equal to a constant. This constant will not be zero unless a relation is established between the constants which are involved in the
value of δy. That is, in Mr Jellett's notation the four constants
C_1, C_2, C_3, C_4 are not all arbitrary, for such a relation must exist
among them as to satisfy his equation (d) and thus reduce them to
three arbitrary constants; and this should be the case since equation (d) is a differential equation of the third order.

In fact Delaunay by this mistake omitted that part of Jacobi's
memoir which forms the latter part of Art. 221, in which Jacobi

intimates that his results will really involve no more arbitrary constants than they ought; whereas in Delaunay's process there would be too many arbitrary constants.

It is possible that the mistake may have been introduced through Jacobi's statement given in Art. 224 that $V_1 = 0$ is satisfied when we put $\delta'y = \dfrac{u}{u}$; but Jacobi has expressly said a little before that u and u_1 are to have the meanings already assigned, and when u and u_1 were introduced in Art. 221 it was stated that the constants occurring in them were subjected to certain relations.

233. Delaunay next considers the case in which questions of *relative* maxima and minima are proposed. Mr Jellett says on page 363 of his work with reference to this part of Delaunay's memoir, " the reasoning does not appear to me to be quite satisfactory, and the conclusion is far less perfect than in the case of absolute maxima and minima."

234. Delaunay examines four problems as examples of Jacobi's criteria. 1. The shortest line between two points. 2. The brachistochrone. 3. The curve of given length which includes a given area. 4. The curve of given length which has its centre of gravity highest or lowest.

235. Lastly Delaunay demonstrates the statements made by Jacobi respecting three differential equations given in Art. 221. It may be observed that Jacobi's memoir involves two points. We have on the one hand Jacobi's own method of exhibiting the criteria for the maxima or minima values of an integral; this is described by Jacobi in Art. 224, and it is explained by Delaunay in his pages 209—234. On the other hand since the method of Jacobi does solve the problem in question, it may be inferred that his method will really supply the solution of the complicated differential equations on which Legendre had made the problem depend; this is in fact what Jacobi states in Articles 220 and 221, and what Delaunay explains in his pages 234—237. It should be remarked that Delaunay here notices the relations which must exist among the constants, according to Jacobi's observation at the end of Art.

221.   The second point in Jacobi's memoir will thus be seen to belong rather to the subject of differential equations than to that of the Calculus of Variations.

236.   Delaunay's memoir is interesting and valuable and deserves especial attention as being the first which gave a demonstration of the whole of Jacobi's method. We have however not thought it necessary to reproduce the investigations because they have been substantially adopted by writers whose works are readily accessible; see Art. 231.

237.   In the *Journal de l'Ecole Polytechnique*, Cahier 28, 1841, there is an article by M. J. Bertrand entitled, *Demonstration of a theorem of M. Jacobi;* the article extends over pages 276—283. The theorem in question is that given in Art. 222.   Bertrand's article was published in the same year as those of Lebesgue and Delaunay, but whether it preceded them both, or followed them both, or came between them, does not appear.   The proof given by Bertrand depends upon a knowledge of the *condition of integrability* of a function; the proof is valuable, and as it seems possible to present it in a clearer form than Bertrand has done, we shall exhibit it here with some modifications.

238.   Let a_{0}, a_{1}, a_{2}, ... a_{n}, denote any functions of x; let y be any function of x, and let y', y'', ... $y^{(n)}$, denote the successive differential coefficients of y with respect to x.   Then a differential expression of the following form we shall call a differential expression of *Jacobi's form*,

$$a_{0}y + \frac{da_{1}y'}{dx} + \frac{d^{2}a_{2}y''}{dx^{2}} + \frac{d^{3}a_{3}y'''}{dx^{3}} + ... + \frac{d^{n}a_{n}y^{(n)}}{dx^{n}} ;$$

and we shall denote this function of x, y, and the differential coefficients of y, by $\phi(y)$; and $\phi(v)$ will denote what the expression becomes when y is changed to v.

We shall now prove the following theorem; let v be a quantity such that $v\phi(y)$ is an exact differential coefficient, then it is necessary and sufficient that v should satisfy the differential equation $\phi(v) = 0$.

By saying that $v\phi(y)$ is an *exact differential coefficient* we mean that $v\phi(y)$ will result from differentiating with respect to x some function of x, y, and the differential coefficients of y, this function remaining unchanged in form whatever may be the value of y in terms of x.

We have

$$v\phi(y) = v\phi(y) - y\phi(v) + y\phi(v).$$

Now $v\phi(y) - y\phi(v)$ *is* an exact differential coefficient. For consider a pair of terms from this expression, for example

$$v\frac{d^r a_r y^n}{dx^r} - y\frac{d^r a_r v^n}{dx^r};$$

integrate by parts, and we obtain

$$v\frac{d^{r-1} a_r y^n}{dx^{r-1}} - y\frac{d^{r-1} a_r v^n}{dx^{r-1}} - \int\left\{\frac{dv}{dx}\frac{d^{r-1} a_r y^n}{dx^{r-1}} - \frac{dy}{dx}\frac{d^{r-1} a_r v^n}{dx^{r-1}}\right\} dx.$$

The term still under the integral sign may be integrated again by parts; and so on. Then after r integrations by parts we shall have under the integral sign

$$\frac{d^r v}{dx^r} a_r y^n - \frac{d^r y}{dx^r} a_r v^n, \quad \text{that is zero.}$$

Thus the pair of terms is shewn to be an exact differential coefficient by actually finding its integral. Similarly each pair of terms in $v\phi(y) - y\phi(v)$ is an exact differential coefficient, and therefore $v\phi(y) - y\phi(v)$ is an exact differential coefficient.

Since then $v\phi(y) - y\phi(v) + y\phi(v)$ is to be an exact differential coefficient, and $v\phi(y) - y\phi(v)$ is such, $y\phi(v)$ must either be an exact differential coefficient or must vanish. The former cannot be the case, since it is impossible that $y\phi(v)$ can be obtained by differentiating with respect to x any function of y and its differential coefficients whatever y may be; we must therefore have $\phi(v) = 0$.

239. We shall now prove the converse of the preceding theorem, namely the following; if any linear differential expression of an even order has the property that it is made an exact differential coefficient when multiplied by any one of the quantities which

make the differential expression vanish, and by no other multiplier, that differential expression can be put in Jacobi's form.

The proof of this theorem is somewhat indirect.   We first examine the nature of the conditions which must be satisfied in order that a linear differential expression of an even order may be capable of being put in Jacobi's form.

If we develope the expression which we have denoted by $\phi(y)$, we obtain for it

$$a_n \frac{d^n y}{dx^n} + n \frac{da_n}{dx} \frac{d^{n-1}y}{dx^{n-1}} + \left(\frac{n(n-1)}{1.2} \frac{d^2 a_n}{dx^2} + a_{n-1} \right) \frac{d^{n-2}y}{dx^{n-2}}$$

$$+ \left(\frac{n(n-1)(n-2)}{1.2.3} \frac{d^3 a_n}{dx^3} + (n-1) \frac{da_{n-1}}{dx} \right) \frac{d^{n-3}y}{dx^{n-3}} + \dots$$

The chief point to be observed here is that the coefficient a_n does not occur *until* we arrive at the term $\frac{d^n y}{dx^n}$, and then it does occur in the simple form a_n.

Now let any linear differential expression of the order indicated by $2n$ be denoted thus,

$$c_n \frac{d^n y}{dx^n} + c_{n-1} \frac{d^{n-1}y}{dx^{n-1}} + c_{n-2} \frac{d^{n-2}y}{dx^{n-2}} + \dots + c_1 \frac{dy}{dx} + c_0 y;$$

in order that this differential expression may take Jacobi's form the coefficients must agree with those in the developed form of $\phi(y)$. This requires that we should be able to find $a_n, a_{n-1}, a_{n-2}, \dots a_0$, so as to satisfy the following equations;

$$a_n = c_n, \qquad n \frac{da_n}{dx} = c_{n-1},$$

$$\frac{n(n-1)}{1.2} \frac{d^2 a_n}{dx^2} + a_{n-1} = c_{n-2}, \qquad \frac{n(n-1)(n-2)}{1.2.3} \frac{d^3 a_n}{dx^3} + (n-1) \frac{da_{n-1}}{dx} = c_{n-3},$$

. . . .

It will not be necessary for us to do more with respect to these equations than to observe the following two points. The first, third, fifth, ... of these equations will determine successively a_n, $a_{n-1}, a_{n-2}, \dots a_0$, whatever the coefficients $c_n, c_{n-1}, c_{n-2}, \dots c_1, c_0$, may be; and they assign a single definite value to each of the coefficients $a_n, a_{n-1}, \ldots a_0$. The second, fourth, sixth, ... of these equations will then give relations involving $c_{m-1}, c_{m-2}, c_{m-3}, \ldots c_2, c_1$, which these coefficients must fulfil in order that it may be possible for the proposed differential expression to take Jacobi's form.

Now let the differential expression which is under consideration be denoted by $\psi(y)$, and let us examine the nature of the conditions which must be satisfied in order that $v\psi(y)$ may be an exact differential coefficient when v is such that $\psi(v) = 0$ and only then.

In order that $v\psi(y)$ may be an exact differential coefficient it is necessary and sufficient that

$$\frac{d^m c_m v}{dx^m} - \frac{d^{m-1} c_{m-1} v}{dx^{m-1}} + \frac{d^{m-2} c_{m-2} v}{dx^{m-2}} - \ldots\ldots - \frac{dc_1 v}{dx} + c_0 v = 0.$$

This follows from the known *condition for the integrability of a function* which will be given hereafter in this work. It may also be deduced from a known theorem in the differential calculus, namely

$$z \frac{d^r y}{dx^r} = \frac{d^r yz}{dx^r} - r \frac{d^{r-1}}{dx^{r-1}} \left(y \frac{dz}{dx} \right) + \frac{r(r-1)}{1 \cdot 2} \frac{d^{r-2}}{dx^{r-2}} \left(y \frac{d^2 z}{dx^2} \right)$$
$$- \ldots\ldots\ldots\ldots + (-1)^r y \frac{d^r z}{dx^r}.$$

Put $c_r v$ for z and use this theorem to transform every term in $v\psi(y)$; thus we shall find that $v\psi(y)$ consists of a series of terms each of which is an exact differential coefficient together with the term Cy, where

$$C = \frac{d^m c_m v}{dx^m} - \frac{d^{m-1} c_{m-1} v}{dx^{m-1}} + \frac{d^{m-2} c_{m-2} v}{dx^{m-2}} - \ldots\ldots - \frac{dc_1 v}{dx} + c_0 v.$$

Therefore $v\psi(y)$ cannot be an exact differential coefficient unless $C = 0$.

Or we may obtain the result still more simply thus. Integrate by parts the terms of $v\psi(y)$ as much as possible; thus we shall find

$$\int v\psi(y)\, dx = S + \int Cy\, dx,$$

where S represents a series of terms free from the integral sign.

Hence, as before, $v\psi(y)$ cannot be an exact differential coefficient unless $C = 0$.

Now by hypothesis the values of v which make $C = 0$ must be those, and those only, which make $\psi(v) = 0$; and therefore the differential equation $C = 0$ must be identical with the differential equation $\psi(v) = 0$. Hence comparing the coefficients of the various differential coefficients of v we must have the following relations satisfied,

$$c_{2n} = c_{2n},$$

$$2n\frac{dc_{2n}}{dx} - c_{2n-1} = c_{2n-1},$$

$$\frac{2n(2n-1)}{1.2}\frac{d^2c_{2n}}{dx^2} - (2n-1)\frac{dc_{2n-1}}{dx} + c_{2n-2} = c_{2n-2},$$

$$\frac{2n(2n-1)(2n-2)}{1.2.3}\frac{d^3c_{2n}}{dx^3} - \frac{(2n-1)(2n-2)}{1.2}\frac{d^2c_{2n-1}}{dx^2} + (2n-2)\frac{dc_{2n-2}}{dx} - c_{2n-3}$$
$$= c_{2n-3},$$

It will not be necessary for us to do more with respect to these equations than to observe the following two points. The second, fourth, sixth, ... of these equations will determine successively $c_{2n-1}, c_{2n-3}, c_{2n-5}, \ldots c_3, c_1$, in terms of $c_{2n}, c_{2n-2}, c_{2n-4}, \ldots c_2, c_0$; and they assign a single definite value to each of the coefficients $c_{2n-1}, c_{2n-3}, c_{2n-5}, \ldots c_3, c_1$. The first, third, fifth, ... of these equations will then give relations which these quantities must satisfy, and by substituting the values of these quantities the relations will only involve the coefficients with the *even* suffixes. It is however certain that these relations will then be *identically* satisfied; because if they were not it would follow that some necessary conditions must hold among the coefficients with *even* suffixes in order that $v\psi(y)$ may be an exact differential coefficient when v satisfies $\psi(v) = 0$ and only then. But this is impossible; because by the former part of the present article we know that *whatever* the coefficients with *even* suffixes may be, if the others are properly determined, $\psi(y)$ will take Jacobi's form, and therefore $v\psi(y)$ be an exact differential coefficient when v satisfies $\psi(v) = 0$ and only then.

Hence we infer that exactly the same conditions must hold whether we require that $r\psi(y)$ should be an exact differential coefficient when $\psi(v) = 0$ and only then, or whether we require that $\psi(y)$ should be capable of being put in Jacobi's form. For we have proved in the preceding article that when the second of these properties subsists the first follows; and we have proved in the present article that to ensure either the first or the second property, each coefficient with an *odd* suffix must have a single definite value in terms of the coefficients with even suffixes which are themselves arbitrary.

Thus we have proved, as we proposed, the converse of the theorem proved in the preceding article.

240. We shall now prove Jacobi's theorem given in Art. 222.

Let $\phi(ty)$ denote what $\phi(y)$ becomes when ty is put for y; and let Y denote $y\phi(ty) - ty\phi(y)$. Then Y is an exact differential coefficient whatever y may be; this may be shewn in the same manner as that in which it is proved in Art. 238, that $r\phi(y) - y\phi(v)$ is an exact differential coefficient. Let Z stand for the integral of Y and let k be an arbitrary constant.

Suppose $\dfrac{dz}{dx}$ to be a quantity such that $\dfrac{dz}{dx}(Z - k)$ is an exact differential coefficient. We have

$$\int \frac{dz}{dx}(Z-k)\,dx = z(Z-k) - \int z\,\frac{d(Z-k)}{dx}\,dx$$

$$= z(Z-k) - \int zY\,dx\,;$$

thus if $\dfrac{dz}{dx}(Z-k)$ is an exact differential coefficient zY is so also. But

$$zY = yz\left\{\phi(ty) - t\phi(y)\right\},$$

and $\phi(ty) - t\phi(y)$ is of Jacobi's form with respect to u and its differential coefficients, where $u = ty$. Hence, by Art. 238, if zY is an exact differential coefficient, yz must be one of the values of u found from $\phi(u) - \dfrac{u}{y}\phi(y) = 0$, say $yz = u_1$; therefore $\dfrac{dz}{dx} = \dfrac{d}{dx}\left(\dfrac{u_1}{y}\right)$.

Thus the multiplier of $Z - k$ which will make the product an exact differential coefficient is a quantity of which the type is $\dfrac{d}{dx}\left(\dfrac{u_1}{y}\right)$.

We must now indicate some properties of the expression $Z - k$. It will be seen on examination that Y does not contain t itself but only the *differential coefficients* of t; this will also be the case with Z, which is the integral of Y.

For suppose the differential expression Y when arranged according to differential coefficients of t to take the form

$$A_1 \frac{dt}{dx} + A_2 \frac{d^2t}{dx^2} + \dots + A_m \frac{d^m t}{dx^m};$$

then if Z contained t at all it could be only by reason of the term $A_1 t$ entering into Z; and then $\dfrac{dZ}{dx}$ or Y would contain the term $t \dfrac{dA_1}{dx}$. And $\dfrac{dA_1}{dx}$ is a function of y which is at present quite arbitrary, so that $\dfrac{dA_1}{dx}$ cannot be zero. Thus as Y does not contain t but only its differential coefficients, it follows that Z does not contain t but only its differential coefficients.

We may shew that Z does not contain t in another way. If we integrate each pair of terms in Y in the manner given in Art. 238, we find that Z consists of pairs of terms of which the type is

$$(-1)^s \left\{ \frac{d^s y}{dx^s} \frac{d^{m-s} a_r (ty)^{[r]}}{dx^{r-s}} - \frac{d^s (ty)}{dx^s} \frac{d^{m-s} a_r y^{[r]}}{dx^{r-s}} \right\},$$

and on effecting the differentiations we see that t does not occur in this expression but only differential coefficients of t.

If then we put τ for $\dfrac{dt}{dx}$ the expression $Z - k$ will be a differential expression of the order $2n - 2$ with respect to τ and its differential coefficients. And the solutions of $Z - k = 0$ can only be such quantities as render Z constant and therefore Y zero; that is, the values of τ must be those of which the type is $\dfrac{d}{dx}\left(\dfrac{u_1}{y}\right)$.

Thus $Z - k$ is a differential expression such that any multiplier of it which renders the product an exact differential coefficient must be a solution of $Z - k = 0$. Hence, by Art. 239, this differential expression must be capable of being put in Jacobi's form; that is, omitting the arbitrary constant, the integral of $y\phi(ty) - ty\phi(y)$ is of the form

$$b_1\tau + \frac{db_1\tau'}{dc} + \frac{d^2b_2\tau''}{dc^2} + \dots + \frac{d^{n-1}b_n\tau^{(n-1)}}{dx^{n-1}}.$$

If now we suppose y such that $\phi(y) = 0$, we have the integral of $y\phi(ty)$ assuming the above form. This is the theorem enunciated in Art. 222.

241. A remark may be added to obviate a possible misconception of part of the preceding article. The equation $Y = 0$ is of the order $2n - 1$ in τ and its differential coefficients; thus the general solution of it will involve $2n - 1$ arbitrary constants. This general solution would make Z *constant* since it makes $\dfrac{dZ}{dx} = 0$; therefore in order that $Z - k$ may be *zero* a relation must hold among the $2n - 1$ arbitrary constants. Thus in effect we have only $2n - 2$ *arbitrary* constants in the solution of $Z - k = 0$, as of course should be the case. Particular solutions of $Z - k = 0$ will then be obtained by giving particular values to any or all of these arbitrary constants.

242. More than ten years elapsed before another commentator upon Jacobi's memoir appeared. We have next to consider a memoir published by Professor G. Mainardi in the third volume of Tortolini's *Annali di Scienze Mathematiche e Fisiche*, 1852. This memoir is entitled *Researches on the Calculus of Variations;* it occupies pages 149—192 of the volume, and there is an appendix which occupies pages 379—383.

243. Mainardi begins by referring to what had been done by Poisson, Ostrogradsky, Cauchy, Sarrus, Jacobi, Bertrand, Lebesgue and Delaunay; he intimates that the propositions of Jacobi require yet to be more completely developed, and he says that with respect to the criteria which distinguish a maximum from a minimum in

the case of multiple integrals he believes nothing had been added to the remarks of Legendre and Lagrange.

244. Mainardi's memoir is divided into five sections. The first section occupies pages 149—153; this section contains some illustrations of the method which was used by John and James Bernouilli in solving isoperimetrical problems. Poisson in his memoir had referred to this old method, see Arts. 88 and 97; and Mainardi intimates that he will hereafter publish his researches on the comparison of the old and modern methods. He confines himself in this section to shewing how the old method could be made to give the terms relative to the *limits* in the case of a single integral, and how it could be made to give the variation of a double integral.

245. The second section occupies pages 154—171. Mainardi says that in this section he proposes a new method for distinguishing between the maxima and minima values of integrals. Speaking generally this method may be described as Legendre's improved by some additions borrowed from Jacobi. Mainardi considers successively six cases. (1) A single integral involving x, y, and $\frac{dy}{dx}$. (2) A single integral involving x, y, $\frac{dy}{dx}$, and $\frac{d^2y}{dx^2}$. (3) A single integral involving x, y, $\frac{dy}{dx}$, $\frac{d^2y}{dx^2}$, and $\frac{d^3y}{dx^3}$. (4) A double integral involving x, y, z, $\frac{dz}{dx}$, and $\frac{dz}{dy}$. (5) A double integral involving x, y, z, $\frac{dz}{dx}$, $\frac{dz}{dy}$, $\frac{d^2z}{dx^2}$, $\frac{d^2z}{dxdy}$, and $\frac{d^2z}{dy^2}$; he also touches upon the particular case in which the double integral involves only x, y, z, $\frac{dz}{dx}$, $\frac{dz}{dy}$, and $\frac{d^2z}{dxdy}$. (6) A single integral involving x, y, z, $\frac{dy}{dx}$, and $\frac{dz}{dx}$. Of these cases (1) and (4) may be considered to be completely investigated, (2) and (3) nearly completely, and the others only imperfectly. We shall presently give a more detailed account of some of these cases.

246. In his third section Mainardi gives an investigation of Jacobi's theorem enunciated in Art. 222, using, as he says, Bertrand for his guide. This investigation extends over pages 172—179, and then Mainardi indicates briefly the application of the theorem to the Calculus of Variations. Mainardi's proof does not seem so good as Bertrand's; the principal difference consists in replacing the indirect reasoning of Art. 239 by direct reasoning. But a student who had not read Bertrand's proof would find one point of Mainardi's unsatisfactory. For on comparing, as we have done on page 262, the coefficients of the various differential coefficients of v, Mainardi only writes down what we have called the second, fourth, sixth, ... equations; and he says briefly that these include the others; see his page 177 at the top. This amounts to omitting one of the most difficult points in the investigation.

247. In his fourth section Mainardi applies Jacobi's method to a double integral; this section extends over pages 183—185. There is no difficulty in his first case where differential coefficients of the first order only occur; but in his second case where differential coefficients of the second order occur Mainardi himself intimates at the end of the section that he has accomplished very little.

248. The fifth section extends over pages 185—192. In this section Mainardi says that he will collect some applications of the Calculus of Variations which afford ground for some remarks; accordingly he discusses four examples. (1) He gives a theorem on geodetic curves; this amounts to finding the first integral of the equation which determines such a curve for a large class of surfaces. (2) He speaks of Gauss's theory of capillary attraction as affording one of the finest modern applications of the Calculus of Variations; but he thinks that the investigation given by Gauss admits of great simplification. Accordingly Mainardi gives an investigation of the variation of the function which Gauss considered; see Art. 71. Mainardi's investigation is far shorter than that of Gauss, but it would not be very easy to follow unless the student had previously read Poisson's memoir or some equivalent method. (3) Mainardi forms the equation furnished by the Calculus of Variations for the form of a flexible surface which is in equilibrium under the action of gravity; this problem will be

found in Mr Jellett's *Calculus of Variations*, page 323. (4) Mainardi says that Steiner found by a geometrical method an elegant property of the polygon of given perimeter which can be drawn on a given surface so as to have a maximum area. Mainardi infers from the Calculus of Variations that when such a polygon is to be inscribed in a given polygon, the two arcs of the required polygon which meet on a side of the given polygon will there make equal angles with that side. Mainardi gives no reference; a memoir by Steiner will however be found in the sixth volume of Liouville's Journal of Mathematics. Steiner's enunciation of his theorem occurs on page 168, and the enunciation is more explicit than Mainardi's, namely, the two arcs which form a part of the inscribed figure, and meet on the same side of the given figure, either cut it in one point at equal angles or else touch it in two points.

249. We have thus given an outline of the whole memoir, and we shall now return to the second section of it and examine more particularly the method proposed by Mainardi for distinguishing between maxima and minima values. The second section constitutes in fact the most important part of the memoir, and although it will be seen that the investigations are incomplete, they are not without interest and value. The *appendix* to the memoir is devoted to the elucidation of part of the second section, and we shall presently have occasion to refer to it. We may remark that the whole memoir is difficult, and that it is disfigured by extreme inaccuracy of printing.

250. We will first give Mainardi's method for distinguishing a maximum from a minimum in the case of a single integral involving $x, y,$ and $\dfrac{dy}{dx}$.

Let $\int F(x, y, y')\, dx$ denote the integral which is to be a maximum or minimum. Change y into $y + i\omega$, where i is supposed to be an indefinitely small constant quantity and ω an arbitrary function of x. Then expand the new value of $F(x, y, y')$ in a series proceeding according to ascending powers of i; thus the new value of the integral, that is $\int F(x, y + i\omega, y' + i\omega')\, dx$, is equal to

$$\int F(x, y, y')\, dx + I_1 i + I_2 \frac{i^2}{2} + \dots$$

where the terms not expressed involve powers of i higher than the second; and

$$I_1 = \int \left(\frac{dF}{dy}\, \omega + \frac{dF}{dy'}\, \omega' \right) dx,$$

$$I_2 = \int \left(\frac{d^2F}{dy^2}\, \omega^2 + 2\, \frac{d^2F}{dy\, dy'}\, \omega\omega' + \frac{d^2F}{dy'^2}\, \omega'^2 \right) dx.$$

The expression $I_1 i$ constitutes the variation to the first order of the proposed integral; this must vanish, and thus by the usual method we arrive at the equation

$$\frac{dF}{dy} - \frac{d}{dx}\frac{dF}{dy'} = 0 \dots\dots\dots\dots\dots\dots\dots (1).$$

From this equation we must suppose y to be found in terms of x, and when this value of y is used, let

$$\frac{d^2F}{dy^2} = A, \qquad \frac{d^2F}{dy\, dy'} = B, \qquad \frac{d^2F}{dy'^2} = C.$$

We have then to examine the sign of

$$\int (A\omega^2 + 2B\omega\omega' + C\omega'^2)\, dx.$$

Now assume that we have identically

$$A\omega^2 + 2B\omega\omega' + C\omega'^2 = (M\omega^2)' + a\omega^2 + 2b\omega\omega' + c\omega'^2;$$

then we must have

$$a + M' = A, \quad b + M = B, \quad c = C \dots\dots\dots\dots (2).$$

We have thus *three* equations involving the *four* unknown quantities a, b, c, M, so that we are at liberty to make one more supposition respecting them; it is found convenient to introduce another quantity and to make *two* more suppositions.

Let θ denote this new quantity, and suppose

$$a\theta + b\theta' = 0, \text{ and } b\theta + c\theta' = 0 \dots\dots\dots\dots\dots\dots (3);$$

thus (2) and (3) supply five equations for determining five quantities.

From the first two equations of (2) combined with (3) we obtain

hence

$$B\theta + C\theta' = M\theta, \quad A\theta + B\theta' = (M\theta)' \dots\dots\dots\dots(4);$$

$$A\theta + B\theta' - (B\theta + C\theta')' = 0 \dots\dots\dots\dots\dots(5).$$

From this differential equation θ must be determined, and then from the first of equations (4) we have

$$M = \frac{1}{\theta}(B\theta + C\theta');$$

then from equations (2) we must obtain a and b; also it appears from (3) that $ac = b^2$, so that

$$a\omega'^2 + 2b\omega\omega' + c\omega'^2 = c\left(\omega' + \frac{b}{c}\omega\right)^2.$$

Also $c = C$; thus finally

$$\int(A\omega'^2 + 2B\omega\omega' + C\omega'^2)\,dx = M\omega^2 + \int C\left(\omega' + \frac{b}{C}\omega\right)^2 dx,$$

where M has the value just assigned.

Hence if C retains constantly the same sign between the limits of the integration, and $M\omega^2$ either vanishes at the limits or gives rise to a result of the same sign as C, we have in general a maximum or a minimum according as the sign of C is negative or positive.

It may be observed that $\dfrac{b}{C} = \dfrac{B - M}{C} = -\dfrac{\theta'}{\theta}$.

251. The above article contains all that is peculiar to Mainardi, for the differential equation (5) is solved, with the assistance of Jacobi, in the following manner; see Art. 221. Let the value of y found from (1) be denoted by $f(x, \gamma_1, \gamma_2)$, where γ_1 and γ_2 are arbitrary constants; then we shall have

$$\theta = \beta_1 \frac{df}{d\gamma_1} + \beta_2 \frac{df}{d\gamma_2},$$

where β_1 and β_2 are new arbitrary constants; this we shall now prove.

The expression I_1 is the coefficient of t in the expansion of the varied value of the proposed integral $\int F(x, y, \dot{y})\, dx$, and I_1 is the coefficient of $\frac{i^2}{2}$ in the same expansion. We may also say that I_2 is the coefficient of i in the expansion of the varied value of I_1; that is, if in I_1 we change y into $y + i\omega$, and expand in a series proceeding according to ascending powers of i, the term involving i will be found to be $I_2 i$. Now if the limiting values of y are fixed, I_1 will vanish whatever may be the values ascribed to the constants γ_1 and γ_2, so that I_1 will also vanish when γ_1 is changed into $\gamma_1 + \delta\gamma_1$, and γ_2 into $\gamma_2 + \delta\gamma_2$. Thus I_1 vanishes when

$$y = f(x, \gamma_1, \gamma_2),$$

and I_1 also vanishes when y receives the increment

$$\frac{df}{d\gamma_1}\delta\gamma_1 + \frac{df}{d\gamma_2}\delta\gamma_2,$$

where $\delta\gamma_1$ and $\delta\gamma_2$ are indefinitely small; that is, iI_2 vanishes when

$$i\omega = \frac{df}{d\gamma_1}\delta\gamma_1 + \frac{df}{d\gamma_2}\delta\gamma_2,$$

and $\delta\gamma_1$ and $\delta\gamma_2$ are indefinitely small.

Now we may modify the form of I_1 and of I_2 by integration by parts, and thus obtain

$$I_1 = \frac{dF}{d\dot{y}}\,\omega + \int\left(\frac{dF}{dy} - \frac{d}{dx}\frac{dF}{d\dot{y}}\right)\omega\, dx,$$

$$I_2 = \left(\frac{d^2F}{dy\, d\dot{y}}\,\omega + \frac{d^2F}{d\dot{y}^2}\,\omega'\right)\omega$$

$$+ \int\left\{\left(\frac{d^2F}{dy^2}\,\omega + \frac{d^2F}{dy\, d\dot{y}}\,\omega' - \frac{d}{dx}\left(\frac{d^2F}{dy\, d\dot{y}}\,\omega + \frac{d^2F}{d\dot{y}^2}\,\omega'\right)\right)\right\}\omega\, dx.$$

And, as before, if in I_1 we change y into $y + i\omega$ the term involving i in the expansion of the new value of I_1 will be iI_2. Hence we infer that the coefficient of ω under the integral sign in I_2 will vanish when $i\omega = \frac{df}{d\gamma_1}\delta\gamma_1 + \frac{df}{d\gamma_2}\delta\gamma_2$.

But the coefficient of ω under the integral sign in the last form of I_2 is a linear differential expression of the second order in ω, and so the general form of the value of ω which makes this coefficient vanish must be $\beta_1 u_1 + \beta_2 u_2$, where β_1 and β_2 are arbitrary constants and u_1 and u_2 are functions of x. Hence we infer that the value of ω which makes the coefficient of ω under the integral sign in the last form of I_2 vanish, must be

$$\beta_1 \frac{df}{d\gamma_1} + \beta_2 \frac{df}{d\gamma_2}.$$

Thus the value of θ is to be found in the manner already stated.

252. The solution of the differential equation (5) of Art. 250 does in fact constitute one of the most important parts of Jacobi's theory. We have here had occasion to use it in only a simple case, namely that in which equation (5) of Art. 250 is of the second order; the method however is perfectly general whatever be the order of the equation analogous to (5), and we shall have to apply it again. The general process is as follows. With the usual notation the terms of the first order in the variation of an integral will take the form $\int I \delta y\, dx$, excluding the integrated terms. The terms of the second order, with the same exclusion, will take the form $\frac{1}{2} \int \delta V \delta y\, dx$, where

$$\delta V = \frac{dV}{dy} \delta y + \frac{dV}{dy'} \delta y' + \frac{dV}{dy''} \delta y'' + \dots$$

Now suppose that the solution of the equation $V = 0$ is

$$y = f(x, \gamma_1, \gamma_2, \dots),$$

where $\gamma_1, \gamma_2, \dots$ are arbitrary constants. If this value of y be substituted in V the result will be identically zero, so that we may differentiate V with respect to any of the arbitrary constants which occur in f, and the result will still be zero. Let $\frac{df}{d\gamma_1} = u$, then by differentiating V with respect to γ_1 we obtain

$$\frac{dV}{dy} u + \frac{dV}{dy'} u' + \frac{dV}{dy''} u'' + \dots = 0.$$

This shews that $\delta V = 0$ is satisfied by $\delta y = u$; and therefore it will be satisfied by $\delta y = \beta u$, where β is an arbitrary constant. Hence the general solution of $\delta V = 0$ will be

$$\delta y = \beta_1 \frac{df}{d\gamma_1} + \beta_2 \frac{df}{d\gamma_2} + \dots$$

253. Next let the proposed integral, which is to be a maximum or a minimum, involve x, y, $\dfrac{dy}{dx}$ and $\dfrac{d^2y}{dx^2}$.

Let $\int F(x, y, y', y')\, dx$ denote this integral, change as before y into $y + i\omega$, and expand the new value of $F(x, y, y', y'')$ in a series proceeding according to ascending powers of i; then the new value of the integral may be denoted by

$$\int F(x, y, y', y'')\, dx + I_1 i + I_2 \frac{i^2}{2} + \ldots\ldots,$$

where
$$I_1 = \int\left(\frac{dF}{dy}\,\omega + \frac{dF}{dy'}\,\omega' + \frac{dF}{dy''}\,\omega''\right) dx,$$

$$I_2 = \int\left(\frac{d^2F}{dy^2}\,\omega^2 + \frac{d^2F}{dy'^2}\,\omega'^2 + \frac{d^2F}{dy''^2}\,\omega''^2 + 2\,\frac{d^2F}{dy\,dy'}\,\omega\omega'\right.$$
$$\left. + 2\,\frac{d^2F}{dy\,dy''}\,\omega\omega'' + 2\,\frac{d^2F}{dy'\,dy''}\,\omega'\omega''\right) dx.$$

Then as usual I_1 must vanish; this leads to the equation

$$\frac{dF}{dy} - \frac{d}{dx}\frac{dF}{dy'} + \frac{d^2}{dx^2}\frac{dF}{dy''} = 0 \ldots\ldots\ldots\ldots\ldots\ldots(1).$$

From this equation we must suppose y to be found in terms of x, and when this value of y is used let

$$\frac{d^2F}{dy^2} = A, \quad \frac{d^2F}{dy\,dy'} = B, \quad \frac{d^2F}{dy'^2} = C,$$

$$\frac{d^2F}{dy''^2} = G, \quad \frac{d^2F}{dy\,dy''} = H, \quad \frac{d^2F}{dy'\,dy''} = K.$$

We have then to examine the sign of

$$\int \left(A\omega^2 + 2B\omega\omega' + C\omega'^2 + G\omega''^2 + 2H\omega\omega'' + 2K\omega'\omega''\right) dx.$$

Now assume that the expression under the integral sign is identically equal to

$$(M\omega^2 + 2N\omega\omega' + P\omega'^2)'$$
$$+ a\omega^2 + 2b\omega\omega' + c\omega'^2 + g\omega''^2 + 2h\omega\omega'' + 2k\omega'\omega'';$$

then we must have

$$a + M' = A, \quad b + M + N' = B, \quad c + 2N + P' = C,$$
$$g = G, \quad\quad h + N = H, \quad\quad k + P = K, \quad\quad\Big\} \;\dots\dots(2).$$

We have thus *six* equations involving the *nine* unknown quantities M, N, P, a, b, c, g, h, k, so that we are at liberty to make three more suppositions respecting them; it is found convenient to introduce another quantity and to make *four* more suppositions. Let θ denote this new quantity and suppose

$$g\theta'' + k\theta' + h\theta = 0, \quad k\theta'' + c\theta' + b\theta = 0, \quad h\theta'' + b\theta' + a\theta = 0 \dots (3);$$

also suppose
$$c - \frac{k^2}{g} = 0 \dots\dots\dots\dots\dots\dots(4).$$

Thus (2), (3) and (4) supply ten equations for determining ten quantities.

From the equations (2) combined with (3) we obtain

$$G\theta'' + K\theta' + H\theta = N\theta + P\theta',$$

$$\left. \begin{aligned} K\theta'' + C\theta' + D\theta &= M\theta + N\theta' + (N\theta + P\theta')' \\ H\theta'' + D\theta' + A\theta &= (M\theta + N\theta')' \end{aligned} \right\} \;\dots\dots(5).$$

Hence,

$$H\theta'' + D\theta' + A\theta - (K\theta' + C\theta' + D\theta)' + (G\theta'' + K\theta' + H\theta)'' = 0 \dots (6).$$

From this differential equation θ must be determined, and then from equations (2), (3) and (4) the rest of the unknown quantities must be found.

Also since $c - \dfrac{k^2}{g} = 0$, we have

$$a\omega^2 + 2b\omega\omega' + c\omega'^2 + g\omega''^2 + 2h\omega\omega'' + 2k\omega'\omega''$$

$$= g\left(\omega'' + \frac{k\omega' + h\omega}{g}\right)^2 + \left(a - \frac{h^2}{g}\right)\omega^2 + 2\left(b - \frac{hk}{g}\right)\omega\omega';$$

but by eliminating θ'' from equations (3) we obtain

$$(k^2 - gc)\,\theta' + (hk - bg)\,\theta = 0, \quad (hk - bg)\,\theta' + (h^2 - ag)\,\theta = 0,$$

so that since $k^2 - gc = 0$, we have also $hk - bg = 0$, and $h^2 - ag = 0$. Therefore

$$a\omega^2 + 2b\omega\omega' + c\omega'^2 + g\omega''^2 + 2h\omega\omega'' + 2k\omega'\omega''$$

$$= g\left(\omega'' + \frac{k\omega' + h\omega}{g}\right)^2.$$

Also $g = G$; thus finally,

$$\int (A\omega^2 + 2B\omega\omega' + C\omega'^2 + G\omega''^2 + 2\Pi\omega\omega'' + 2K\omega'\omega'') \, dx$$

$$= M\omega^2 + 2N\omega\omega' + P\omega'^2 + \int G\left(\omega'' + \frac{k\omega' + h\omega}{G}\right)^2 dx.$$

Hence if G retains constantly the same sign between the limits of the integration, and the integrated part either vanishes or gives rise to a result of the same sign as G, we have in general a maximum or a minimum according as the sign of G is negative or positive.

254. It remains to shew how to determine the auxiliary quantities a, b, c, h, k, M, N, P, θ which are introduced in the preceding article; for if they are not determined we shall not be able to ascertain whether they remain finite or not between the limits of the integration. The value of θ is determined as before; see Arts. 251 and 252. If we represent the solution of (1) by

$$y = f(x, \gamma_1, \gamma_2, \gamma_3, \gamma_4)$$

where γ_1, γ_2, γ_3, γ_4 are arbitrary constants, we shall have

$$\theta = \beta_1 \frac{df}{d\gamma_1} + \beta_2 \frac{df}{d\gamma_2} + \beta_3 \frac{df}{d\gamma_3} + \beta_4 \frac{df}{d\gamma_4},$$

where β_1, β_2, β_3, β_4 are new arbitrary constants.

It is with respect to the methods which he proposes for determining the remaining auxiliary quantities that Mainardi's investigations are the least satisfactory. He proposes in fact three methods for this purpose.

(1) He intimates obscurely that h and k may be determined thus; let ϕ be a quantity found like θ from the differential equation

(6) of the preceding article, so that ϕ is of the same form as θ but has other arbitrary constants instead of β_1, β_2, β_3 and β_4; then h and k will be determined by the equations

$$G\theta'' + k\theta' + h\theta = 0, \quad G\phi'' + k\phi' + h\phi = 0 \dots\dots\dots (7).$$

Mainardi seems to intimate that if h and k be thus determined and then the remaining auxiliary quantities deduced from such of the equations (2), (3), (4) as may be convenient, the remainder of these equations will be satisfied. See his page 157 at the bottom.

(2) Mainardi however seems to allow that the statements just made require to be proved; and accordingly he proceeds to verify them. With respect to this verification we may observe that it is really a long process, and in consequence of it Mainardi's method loses the apparent simplicity which constitutes its chief recommendation. Moreover in this verification, on the sixth line of his page 168 the right-hand member of his equation should be a constant and not zero as he gives it; this in fact is the same mistake as we have already indicated in Art. 232. Thus h and k cannot be found as Mainardi intimates from equations (7) where the four constants in ϕ and the four constants in θ are all arbitrary; there must be a relation between these constants.

(3) Mainardi returns to the point in the appendix and offers another reason for the statement that h and k are to be found from equations (7). He says the equations (2) of Art. 253 really express the conditions that must hold in order that

$$(A-a)\,\omega^2 + 2(B-b)\,\omega\omega' + (C-c)\,\omega'^2 + (G-g)\,\omega''^2$$
$$+ 2(H-h)\,\omega\omega'' + 2(K-k)\,\omega'\omega''$$

may be an exact differential coefficient. Now when θ is found from equation (6), he says that

$$A\theta^2 + 2D\theta\theta' + C\theta'^2 + G\theta''^2 + 2H\theta\theta' + 2K\theta''\theta'$$

is an exact differential coefficient, and

$$a\theta^2 + 2b\theta\theta' + c\theta'^2 + g\theta''^2 + 2h\theta\theta' + 2k\cdot\theta''\theta'$$

vanishes. Thus

$$(A-a)\,\omega^2 + 2(B-b)\,\omega\omega' + (C-c)\,\omega'^2 + (G-g)\,\omega''^2$$
$$+ 2(H-h)\,\omega\omega'' + 2(K-k)\,\omega'\omega''$$

is an exact differential coefficient when $\omega = \theta$, and when $\omega = \phi$, and therefore the equations (2) must be satisfied when h and k and the remainder of the auxiliary quantities are found in the way proposed. This however is quite unsound; the equations (2) express the conditions that $(A-a)\,\omega^2 + 2\,(B-b)\,\omega\omega' + \ldots$ should be an exact differential coefficient *whatever* ω may be, and to say that this expression is integrable *when* $\omega = \theta$ or $= \phi$ is very different from saying that it is an exact differential coefficient *whatever* ω may be.

255. The student of the original memoir will see that we have not kept to the original notation; that notation is singularly perplexing and the language inaccurate. We will indicate one example of the latter; Mainardi has a term $\left(c - \dfrac{c^2}{f}\right) Y$, and this term vanishes by virtue of the relation $c - \dfrac{c^2}{f} = 0$ which he establishes; but instead of saying that the term vanishes he says that $Y = 0$, which is not the case. This inaccuracy occurs repeatedly.

256. We will now indicate the method which Mainardi gives for distinguishing a maximum from a minimum in the case of a double integral which involves differential coefficients to the first order only.

Let $\iint F(x, y, z, z', z_{,})\,dx\,dy$ denote the double integral which is to be a maximum or a minimum, where z' stands for $\dfrac{dz}{dx}$ and $z_{,}$ for $\dfrac{dz}{dy}$. Change z into $z + i\omega$ where i is supposed to be an indefinitely small constant quantity and ω an arbitrary function of x and y. Then expand the new value of $F(x, y, z, z', z_{,})$ in a series proceeding according to ascending powers of i; thus the new value of the double integral is

$$\iint F(x, y, z, z', z_{,})\,dx\,dy + I_{1}\,i + I_{2}\,\frac{i^2}{2} + \ldots\ldots,$$

where $I_{1} = \iint \left(\frac{dF}{dz}\,\omega + \frac{dF}{dz'}\,\omega' + \frac{dF}{dz_{,}}\,\omega_{,}\right) dx\,dy,$

$$I_2 = \iint\left\{\frac{d^2F}{dz^2}\omega^2 + 2\frac{d^2F}{dz\,dz'}\omega\omega' + 2\frac{d^2F}{dz\,dz_{,}}\omega\omega_{,}\right.$$
$$\left. + \frac{d^2F}{dz'^2}\omega'^2 + 2\frac{d^2F}{dz'\,dz_{,}}\omega'\omega_{,} + \frac{d^2F}{dz_{,}^2}\omega_{,}^2\right\} dx\,dy.$$

The expression I_2 must vanish, and thus in the usual way we arrive at the equation

$$\frac{dF}{dz} - \frac{d}{dx}\frac{dF}{dz'} - \frac{d}{dy}\frac{dF}{dz_{,}} = 0 \text{ .... (1).}$$

From this equation we must suppose z to be found in terms of x and y, and when this value of z is used let

$$\frac{d^2F}{dz^2} = A, \quad \frac{d^2F}{dz\,dz'} = B, \quad \frac{d^2F}{dz\,dz_{,}} = C,$$
$$\frac{d^2F}{dz'^2} = G, \quad \frac{d^2F}{dz'dz_{,}} = H, \quad \frac{d^2F}{dz_{,}^2} = K.$$

We have then to examine the sign of

$$\iint(A\omega^2 + 2B\omega\omega' + 2C\omega\omega_{,} + G\omega'^2 + 2H\omega'\omega_{,} + K\omega_{,}^2)\,dx\,dy.$$

Now assume that the expression under the integral sign is identically equal to

$$(M\omega^2)' + (N\omega^2)_{,} + a\omega^2 + 2b\omega\omega' + 2c\omega\omega_{,} + G\omega'^2 + 2H\omega'\omega_{,} + K\omega_{,}^2;$$

then we must have

$$a + M' + N_{,} = A, \quad b + M = B, \quad c + N = C \text{ ...... (2).}$$

We have thus *three* equations involving the *five* unknown quantities a, b, c, M, N, so that we are at liberty to make two more suppositions respecting them; it is found convenient to introduce another quantity and to make *three* more suppositions.

Let θ be this new quantity and suppose that

$$\left.\begin{aligned} G\theta' + H\theta_{,} + b\theta = 0 \\ H\theta' + K\theta_{,} + c\theta = 0 \\ b\theta' + c\theta_{,} + a\theta = 0 \end{aligned}\right\} \text{ .... (3).}$$

From (2) and (3) we obtain

$$\left.\begin{aligned} G\theta' + H\theta_{,} + D\theta &= M\theta \\ H\theta' + K\theta_{,} + C\theta &= N\theta \\ B\theta' + C\theta_{,} + \Delta\theta &= (M\theta)' + (N\theta)_{,} \end{aligned}\right\} \ldots\ldots\ldots\ldots\ldots\ldots (4);$$

hence

$$B\theta' + C\theta_{,} + A\theta - (G\theta' + H\theta_{,} + D\theta)' - (H\theta' + K\theta_{,} + C\theta)_{,} = 0 \quad (5).$$

From this partial differential equation θ must be found; then from the first and second of equations (4) we obtain M and N, namely,

$$M = \frac{1}{\theta}(G\theta' + H\theta_{,} + D\theta), \quad N = \frac{1}{\theta}(H\theta' + K\theta_{,} + C\theta);$$

and from equations (3) we obtain a, b, and c. Now we have

$$\begin{aligned} &a\omega^2 + 2b\omega\omega' + 2c\omega\omega_{,} + G\omega'^2 + 2H\omega'\omega_{,} + K\omega_{,}^2 \\ &\qquad = G\left(\omega' + \frac{H\omega_{,} + b\omega}{G}\right)^2 \\ &\qquad + \left(K - \frac{H^2}{G}\right)\left(\omega_{,} + \frac{Gc - Hb}{KG - H^2}\omega\right)^2 \\ &\qquad + \left\{a - \frac{b^2}{G} - \frac{(Gc - Hb)^2}{G(KG - H^2)}\right\}\omega^2; \end{aligned}$$

and the coefficient of ω^2 in the last line vanishes, as we shall find by eliminating $\frac{\theta'}{\theta}$ and $\frac{\theta_{,}}{\theta}$ from equations (3).

Hence, finally, we obtain

$$\begin{aligned} &\iint (A\omega^2 + 2B\omega\omega' + 2C\omega\omega_{,} + G\omega'^2 + 2H\omega'\omega_{,} + K\omega_{,}^2)\,dx\,dy \\ &= \iint \left\{\left(\frac{G\theta' + H\theta_{,} + D\theta}{\theta}\omega^2\right)' + \left(\frac{H\theta' + K\theta_{,} + C\theta}{\theta}\omega^2\right)_{,}\right\} dx\,dy \\ &+ \iint \left\{G\left(\omega' + \frac{H\omega_{,} + b\omega}{G}\right)^2 + \left(K - \frac{H^2}{G}\right)\left(\omega_{,} + \frac{Gc - Hb}{KG - H^2}\omega\right)^2\right\} dx\,dy. \end{aligned}$$

The expression in the first of these two lines really involves only a single integral; the expression in the second line is a double integral. In order to ensure that this double integral shall retain the same sign whatever ω may be we must have $K - \dfrac{H^2}{G}$ and G of the same sign; that is, $GK - H^2$ must be positive. Then if $GK - H^2$ is constantly positive throughout the limits of the integration we shall in general have a maximum if G be constantly negative, and a minimum if G be constantly positive. These results agree with those obtained in Art. 213.

257. A value of θ which will satisfy equation (5) of the preceding article may be obtained in the manner explained in Art. 251. Suppose, for example, a solution of (1) obtained which involves two arbitrary constants, and denote it by

$$z = f(x,\ y,\ \gamma_1,\ \gamma_2),$$

where γ_1 and γ_2 are the two arbitrary constants; then the partial differential equation (5) will be satisfied by

$$\theta = \beta_1 \frac{df}{d\gamma_1} + \beta_2 \frac{df}{d\gamma_2},$$

where β_1 and β_2 are arbitrary constants.

258. Thus it will be seen that the investigation given by Mainardi of the question discussed in the preceding two articles may be considered complete, because the values of the auxiliary quantities introduced can be really found. But the investigation is not preferable to another which Mainardi gives and which exactly follows the method given by Jacobi for a single integral. With this other investigation we will close our account of Mainardi's memoir. We will suppose, as is usual in discussing Jacobi's method, that the limiting values of z, $\dfrac{dz}{dx}$ and $\dfrac{dz}{dy}$ are given so that the quantities ω, ω', and $\omega_{,}$ vanish at the limits. With this supposition it will be found that the expression in Art. 256 of which the sign is to be examined may be written thus,

$$\iint \left\{ A\omega + B\omega' + C\omega_{,} - (B\omega + G\omega' + H\omega_{,})' - (C\omega + H\omega' + K\omega_{,})_{,} \right\} \omega\, dx\, dy.$$

We may prove this by integrating

$$\iint (B\omega + G\omega' + H\omega_,)'\,\omega\,dx\,dy \quad\text{and}\quad \iint (C\omega + H\omega' + K\omega_,)_,\,\omega\,dx\,dy$$

each once by parts, and then we shall obtain the same expression as we used in Art. 256. Or we may modify the form of I_1 and then deduce that of I_2 in the manner explained in Art. 251.

Let a stand for $A - B' - C_,$; then the expression of which the sign is to be examined may be written

$$\iint \left\{ a\omega - (G\omega' + H\omega_,)' - (H\omega' + K\omega_,)_, \right\} \omega\,dx\,dy.$$

Let θ be such a quantity that

$$a\theta - (G\theta + \Pi\theta_,)' - (H\theta + K\theta_,)_, = 0,$$

and assume $\omega = u\theta$. The above double integral becomes

$$\iint \left\{ a u\theta - (G u'\theta + G u\theta' + \Pi u_,\theta + \Pi u\theta_,)'\right.$$
$$\left. - (H u'\theta + \Pi u\theta' + K u_,\theta + K u\theta_,)_, \right\} u\theta\,dx\,dy;$$

and this on reduction will be found equal to

$$- \iint \left\{ [(G u' + \Pi u_,)\,\theta^2]' + [(\Pi u' + K u_,)\,\theta^2]_, \right\} u\,dx\,dy.$$

Integrate by parts and omit the terms which vanish at the limits; thus this double integral becomes

$$\iint \left\{ (G u' + H u_,)\,\theta^2 u' + (H u' + K u_,)\,\theta^2 u_, \right\} dx\,dy,$$

that is,

$$\iint \left\{ G u'^2 + 2\Pi u' u_, + K u_,^2 \right\} \theta^2\,dx\,dy.$$

Hence, finally, we have in general a maximum if $GK - \Pi^2$ is positive and G negative throughout the limits of the integrations, and a minimum if $GK - \Pi^2$ is positive and G positive.

The quantity θ may be determined in the manner explained in Art. 257.

259.   In the volume of Tortolini's Mathematical Journal which contains Mainardi's memoir there is a short article on our subject by Professor F. Brioschi.   It is entitled, *On a theorem of Jacobi's relative to the criteria for distinguishing the maxima from the minima values of integrals.*   The article occupies pages 322—326 of the volume.

Brioschi refers to Mainardi's method for distinguishing maxima from minima values, and he says this method is complicated, by the admission of Mainardi himself.   Brioschi then says he will briefly indicate criteria for solving the problem proposed.   Thus the title of the article does not give a correct idea of its contents; for there seems to be no reference to Jacobi's theorem, but instead of that a new method is proposed.

260.   Brioschi does not demonstrate the theorems he enunciates; the theorems themselves are enunciated in the language of *determinants*.   The following example will give some idea of the object of the article.

Consider the expression

$$A\omega^2 + B\omega'^2 + C\omega''^2 + 2E\omega\omega' + 2F\omega\omega'' + 2G\omega'\omega'';$$

this expression can be put in the form

$$C\left(\omega'' + \frac{G\omega' + F\omega}{C}\right)^2 + a(\omega' + \beta\omega)^2 + \gamma\omega^2,$$

where a, β, γ are certain functions of A, B, ... G; we have in fact indicated the values of a, β, γ in Art. 256.   The use of such a transformation is that we can thus see what conditions must hold in order that the original expression may be incapable of changing its sign; if a, γ and C are all of the same sign, or if a and γ are zero, the proposed expression cannot differ in sign from C.   Now the theory of *determinants* furnishes general forms for such coefficients as we have denoted by a and γ whatever be the number of the quantities ω, ω', ω'', ... which occur in the original expression.   It is this part of the theory of determinants which Brioschi introduces; and he indicates its use in the question of distinguishing a maximum from a minimum value of an integral which involves x, y, and z, and the differential coefficients of y and z with respect to x up to those of the nth order. But as we have stated, the results are briefly enunciated without any demonstration.

261. The introduction of the theory of determinants into the subject is an important point, and, as we shall see hereafter, this has been recognized by Hesse and Clebsch. It should be stated that there are intimations of the value of the theory of determinants in Mainardi's memoir, but we have not adverted to them in our account of that memoir, because they are merely intimations which do not in any practical degree affect the nature or value of Mainardi's investigations.

262. On the last page of Brioschi's article there are two observations which may be noticed. The first is historical; Brioschi states that the formulæ for the complete variation of a double integral were given by Bordoni in his treatise on the higher Calculus in 1831, while Poisson's memoir appeared in 1833, and Ostrogradsky's in 1838. Brioschi however refers to the fact that Poisson had himself enunciated his formulæ in 1816. This fact seems to render Brioschi's observation altogether superfluous. Moreover Poisson enunciated his formulæ in 1816 and not in 1818 as Brioschi states; see Art. 102. Also Ostrogradsky's memoir was first published in 1836 in Crelle's Journal, and not in 1838, as Brioschi states.

The second observation is on a mechanical point. Mainardi had applied the Calculus of Variations to determine the form of a flexible surface which is in equilibrium under the action of gravity. Brioschi states that Mainardi's result is only true on the supposition that the tension is constant in every direction round any point of the surface; he says that this follows from the researches of Poisson, Cisa de Gresy and Mossotti. Brioschi gives no references to the places in which these writers have discussed the question, but probably the following are the works he has in view. (1) Poisson's memoir in the *Mémoires de l'Institut* for 1812, entitled *Mémoire sur les surfaces élastiques*. (2) A memoir by Cisa de Gresy in the *Memorie della Reale Accademia delle Scienze di Torino*, Tomo XXIII. 1818, entitled *Considérations sur l'équilibre des surfaces flexibles et inextensibles.* (8) Mossotti's *Lezioni di Meccanica Razionale*, Firenze, 1851.

263. The next memoir we have to consider is by Eisenlohr, entitled Researches on the Calculus of Variations; *Untersuchungen über Variations-rechnung. Inaugural-Dissertation von Dr Friedrich Eisenlohr.* Manheim, 1858. This is a quarto pamphlet of 20 pages.

264. The memoir begins with a few introductory observations; the author says that his object was to give a simple proof of the propositions required in Jacobi's method, and to shew that in a certain case that method might be extended to a double integral. He says that so far as he knew the second variation of a double integral had not yet been considered; on this point Eisenlohr was in error, as appears from Articles 147, 213, and 258.

265. The memoir is divided into eleven sections. The first section contains some remarks on the nature of the Calculus of Variations; and Eisenlohr here objects to the introduction into the subject of such problems as we have considered in Art. 3. In his second section, Eisenlohr gives the ordinary investigation of the variation of a single integral. In his third section, he infers from the result of his preceding section the condition that must hold in order that a given function of x, y, and the differential coefficients of y with respect to x, may be an *exact* differential coefficient. In his fourth section, Eisenlohr distinguishes between the maximum and minimum of $\int f\left(x, y, \dfrac{dy}{dx}\right) dx$; and in effect he verifies the statements of Jacobi in Art. 220. In his fifth section, Eisenlohr distinguishes between the maximum and minimum of $\int f\left(x, y, \dfrac{dy}{dx}, \dfrac{d^2 y}{dx^2}\right) dx$; and in effect he verifies the statements of Jacobi in Art. 221. These investigations in his fourth and fifth sections serve as Eisenlohr says to prove the truth of Jacobi's solutions *a posteriori*, and the length to which they extend shews the necessity for some general method of treatment. Accordingly in his sixth section, Eisenlohr gives his investigation of the fundamental theorems of Art. 222. In his seventh section, he shews

the application of these fundamental theorems to the Calculus of
Variations. In his eighth section, Eisenlohr investigates the maximum or minimum of $\int f(x, y, y', y'') \, dx$, as in Jacobi's process of
Art. 224; Eisenlohr also illustrates Art. 225 of Jacobi's memoir,
in the case where we have to find the maximum or minimum of
$\int f\left(x, y, \dfrac{dy}{dx}\right) dx$. In his ninth section, Eisenlohr gives the ordinary investigation of the variation of a double integral arising
from the variation of the dependent variable; he confines himself
to the case in which no differential coefficient occurs of a higher
order than the first. In his tenth section, Eisenlohr gives a theorem
respecting linear partial differential equations, analogous to that
which he proved in his sixth section. In his eleventh section he
distinguishes between the maximum and minimum value of a
double integral in which no differential coefficient occurs of a
higher order than the first; this investigation is equivalent to that
by Mainardi which we have given in Art. 258.

It may be observed that Eisenlohr is free from that mistake as
to the constants which we have noticed in Arts. 232 and 254.

From the above general account of Eisenlohr's memoir it will be
seen that the only points of novelty which it presents are the proof
of Jacobi's theorems in the sixth section, the application to the Calculus of Variations in the seventh section, and the extension of
Jacobi's theorems in the tenth section; these we shall now give.

266. Eisenlohr says in his sixth section that Jacobi's method
depends upon the following theorem; a differential expression of
the form

$$uy\left\{a_0 uy + \frac{d \cdot a_1 (uy)'}{dx} + \frac{d^2 \cdot a_2 (uy)''}{dx^2} + \dots + \frac{d^n \cdot a_n (uy)^{(n)}}{dx^n}\right\}$$

can always be put in the form

$$y\left\{b_0 y + \frac{d \cdot b_1 y'}{dx} + \frac{d^2 \cdot b_2 y''}{dx^2} + \dots + \frac{d^n \cdot b_n y^{(n)}}{dx^n}\right\}.$$

This theorem was not proved by Jacobi himself; proofs however had been given by Delaunay, Lebesgue, and Bertrand.

Eisenlohr says that Bertrand's proof is the only one that is satisfactory, and that is very long; (*worunter nur der letztere Beweis befriedigend, aber auch sehr weitläufig ist*). Eisenlohr does not say what objection he has against the proofs given by Delaunay and Lebesgue. He then produces his own proof, which he says rests upon the same principles as Bertrand's. Eisenlohr establishes the following theorem. Let there be any linear differential expression which involves x, y, and the differential coefficients of y with respect to x; let it be multiplied by y so that we may denote the product by $yF(x, y, y', y'', ...)$. Now put $y = wz$, where w is any function of x, and subtract the terms which involve z', so that the remainder may be denoted by $zF_1(x, z', z'', ...)$. If then $F_1(x, z', z'', ...)$ is an exact differential coefficient whatever w may be, the expression $yF(x, y, y', y'', ...)$ can be put in the form

$$y\left\{ b_0 y + \frac{d.b_1 y'}{dx} + \frac{d^2.b_2 y''}{dx^2} + ... + \frac{d^a.b_a y^{(a)}}{dx^a} \right\}.$$

We shall denote this form for shortness by $y\Phi(x, y, y', y'', ...)$. Now if $F(x, y, y', y'', ...)$ be linear and of an order not exceeding $2n$ it is obvious that if b_0, b_1, b_2, ... b_a, are properly chosen

$$F(x, y, y', y'', ...) - \Phi(x, y, y', y'', ...)$$

can be made to involve only differential coefficients of y of *odd* orders; that is, we can obtain the identity

$$F(x, y, y', y'', ...) - \Phi(x, y, y', y'', ...) = c_1 y' + c_3 y''' + ... + c_{2n-1} y^{(2n-1)}.$$

(See the commencement of Art. 239.) If then we wish to prove that $F(x, y, y', y'', ...)$ can be put in the form $\Phi(x, y, y', y'', ...)$, we must shew that c_1, c_3, ... c_{2n-1} all vanish.

We suppose it *given* that if in $yF(x, y, y', y'' ...)$ we change y into wz and subtract the terms which involve z' the remainder when divided by z is an exact differential coefficient whatever w may be; and we shall *prove* that $y\Phi(x, y, y', y'', ...)$ possesses the same property. For when we change y into wz in the last expression we obtain a series of terms of which the type is

$$wz \frac{d^r.b_r (wz)^{(m)}}{dx^r},$$

and after subtracting all that involves z^2 we obtain pairs of terms of which the type is

$$wz \frac{d^r . b_r (wz)^m}{dx^r} - wz^2 \frac{d^r . b_r w^m}{dx^r},$$

and thus after dividing by z the type becomes

$$w \frac{d^r . b_r (wz)^m}{dx^r} - wz \frac{d^r . b_r w^m}{dx^r};$$

and this expression is an exact differential coefficient, as we see by the method used in Art. 238 and referred to in Art. 240.

Thus $y\Phi(x, y, y', y'', \ldots)$ does possess the property which by hypothesis $yF(x, y, y', y'', \ldots)$ possesses; hence also

$$y\{F(x, y, y', y'', \ldots) - \Phi(x, y, y', y'', \ldots)\}$$

possesses the property, and therefore so also does the identical equivalent of this expression, namely

$$y\left[c_1 y' + c_2 y''' + \ldots + c_{n-1} y^{(2n-1)}\right].$$

Thus

$$w\left[c_1 (wz)' + c_2 (wz)''' + \ldots + c_{n-1} (wz)^{(2n-1)}\right]$$
$$- wz\left[c_1 w' + c_2 w''' + \ldots + c_{n-1} w^{(2n-1)}\right]$$

is an exact differential coefficient, whatever w may be, or else it is zero. Now apply the theorem in Differential Calculus which we have quoted in Art. 239, to every term in the former part of the last expression, or else integrate by parts as much as possible; we shall thus find that the whole expression consists of terms which are immediately integrable together with a term $- Cwz$, where

$$C = (c_1 w)' + (c_2 w)''' + \ldots + (c_{n-1} w)^{(2n-1)} + c_1 w' + c_2 w''' + \ldots + c_{n-1} w^{(2n-1)}.$$

Now C does not contain z and z is arbitrary, so that Cwz cannot be an exact differential coefficient; we must therefore have $C = 0$. And as C must vanish whatever w may be, the coefficients of the differential coefficients of w which occur in C must separately vanish; thus we shall obtain in succession

$$c_{n-1} = 0, \; c_{n-2} = 0, \; \ldots \; c_2 = 0, \; c_1 = 0.$$

This proves Eisenlohr's theorem. Now to apply this theorem consider the expression

$$uy\left\{a_0 uy + \frac{d.a_1(uy)'}{dx} + \frac{d^2.a_2(uy)''}{dx^2} + \dots + \frac{d^n.a_n(uy)^{(n)}}{dx^n}\right\};$$

change y into wz, subtract the part involving z^2, and divide by z; we thus obtain pairs of terms of which the type is

$$uw\frac{d^r.a_r(uwz)^{(r)}}{dx^r} - uwz\frac{d^r.a_r(uw)^{(r)}}{dx^r}.$$

The last expression is an exact differential coefficient, as we see by the method used in Art. 238 and referred to in Art. 240. Hence by Eisenlohr's theorem it follows that the expression

$$uy\left\{a_0 uy + \frac{d.a_1(uy)'}{dx} + \frac{d^2.a_2(uy)''}{dx^2} + \dots + \frac{d^n.a_n(uy)^{(n)}}{dx^n}\right\},$$

which is of the form $yF(x, y, y', y'', \dots)$, where $F(x, y, y', y'', \dots)$ is linear, can be put in the form

$$y\left\{b_0 y + \frac{d.b_1 y'}{dx} + \frac{d^2.b_2 y''}{dx^2} + \dots + \frac{d^n.b_n y^{(n)}}{dx^n}\right\}.$$

267. The proof in the preceding article is that given by Eisenlohr himself, except that he does not enter into any detail respecting the relation $O = 0$, but merely intimates that it follows from the known *condition of integrability* of a function. It may be remarked that the memoir is not free from misprints and inaccuracies; thus, for example, Eisenlohr uses the words differential *equation* repeatedly, when he means differential *expression*, and he speaks of subtracting the *coefficient* of z^2 when he means subtracting the *terms involving* z^2.

268. In his seventh section Eisenlohr shews that the terms of the second order in the variation of an integral will take the form which Jacobi gives; see Art. 224. The variation to the first order may be denoted by $\int V\delta y\, dx$, where we omit the integrated terms; that is, we suppose the limiting values of x and y, and of the differential coefficients of y to be fixed. Then the

quantity of the second order which we have to examine will be $\int \delta V \delta y \, dx$. We have then to shew that δV is a function of δy and its differential coefficients which can be put in Jacobi's form. This will follow by Eisenlohr's theorem since we shall prove that δV has the following property; in $\delta V \delta y$ change δy into $w \delta z$ where w is any function of x, and subtract the terms involving $(\delta z)^2$, then divide by δz, and the quotient will be an exact differential coefficient whatever w may be.

For suppose that $\int V \delta y \, dx$ becomes $\int V_1 \delta z \, dx$ by the change of y into wz, then by the same change $\int \delta V \delta y \, dx$ must become $\int \delta V_1 \delta z \, dx$, that is, $\delta V \delta y$ becomes $\delta V_1 \delta z$ by the change of δy into $w \delta z$. The part of $\delta V_1 \delta z$ which involves $(\delta z)^2$ is $\dfrac{dV_1}{dz} (\delta z)^2$; hence the expression which is to be shewn to be an exact differential coefficient is

$$\frac{1}{\delta z} \left\{ \delta V \delta y - \frac{dV_1}{dz} (\delta z)^2 \right\},$$

that is, $\delta V_1 - \dfrac{dV_1}{dz} \delta z$.

Now suppose that $\int f(x, z, z', \ldots) \, dx$ represents the integral of which the variation to the first order, excluding the integrated terms, is $\int V_1 \delta z \, dx$; then $V_1 - \dfrac{df}{dz}$ is an exact differential coefficient; and so also is $\delta V_1 - \delta \dfrac{df}{dz}$. Hence we have only to shew that $\delta \dfrac{df}{dz} - \dfrac{dV_1}{dz} \delta z$ is an exact differential coefficient. Now if we develope $\int \delta \dfrac{df}{dz} \, dx$ by the ordinary process of the Calculus of Variations we shall find that we obtain a series of terms free from the integral sign, together with the term

$$\int \left(\frac{df_1}{dz} - \frac{d}{dx} \frac{df_1}{dz'} + \frac{d^2}{dx^2} \frac{df_1}{dz''} - \ldots \right) \delta z \, dz,$$

where f_1 stands for $\frac{df}{dz}$. And the last integral will be found to be $\int \frac{dV_1}{dz} \delta z \, dx$, so that $\delta \frac{df}{dz} - \frac{dV_1}{dz} \delta z$ *is* an exact differential coefficient.

Hence, $\delta V \delta y$ does possess the required property, and therefore by Eisenlohr's theorem δV can be put in Jacobi's form.

209. The following is the theorem which Eisenlohr gives in his tenth section, analogous to that in his sixth section.

Let $F(x, y, z, z', z_1, \ldots)$ be any linear differential expression in z, and its partial differential coefficients with respect to x and y, where as usual accents *above* z indicate differentiations with respect to x, and accents *below* z indicate differentiations with respect to y. Multiply the expression by z, put $z = wt$ where w is any function of x and y, and subtract all the terms which involve t. If every term of the remainder when divided by t is susceptible of at least one integration with respect to x or y whatever w may be, $F(x, y, z, z', z_1, \ldots)$ can be put in the form

$$A_0 z + \frac{d}{dx}(A_1 z' + B_1 z_1) + \frac{d}{dy}(B_1 z' + C_1 z_1)$$

$$+ \frac{d^2}{dx^2}(A_2 z'' + B_2 z_1' + C_2 z_{11}) + \frac{d^2}{dx\,dy}(B_2 z'' + C_2 z_1' + H_2 z_{11})$$

$$+ \frac{d^2}{dy^2}(C_2 z'' + H_2 z_1' + K_2 z_{11})$$

$$+ \ldots\ldots$$

The proof is similar to that in Art. 266. We denote the expression last given by $\Phi(x, y, z, z', z_1, \ldots)$.

Then in the first place we observe that by properly choosing the coefficients $A_0, A_1, B_1, C_1, A_2, \ldots$ we can obtain the following *identity*,

$$z F(x, y, z, z', z_1, \ldots) - z \Phi(x, y, z, z', z_1, \ldots) = z \Psi(x, y, z', z_1, \ldots),$$

where $\Psi(x, y, z', z_1, \ldots)$ is a linear function of the differential coefficients of z of *odd* orders.

In the second place we *prove* that $z \Phi(x, y, z, z', z_1, \ldots)$ possesses the property which by supposition $z F(x, y, z, z', z_1, \ldots)$ possesses.

For change z into wt and subtract all that involves t and then divide by t; we thus obtain terms which may be arranged in pairs, and by pairing them suitably we shall obtain expressions which are integrable either with respect to x or y. For example a part of the result is

$$w\frac{d}{dx}\left\{A_{,}\,(wt)' + B_{,}\,(wt)_{,}\right\} + w\frac{d}{dy}\left\{B_{,}\,(wt)' + C_{,}\,(wt)_{,}\right\}$$
$$-\,wt\frac{d}{dx}\left\{A_{,}w' \quad + B_{,}w_{,} \quad\right\} - wt\frac{d}{dy}\left\{B_{,}w' \quad + C_{,}w_{,} \quad\right\};$$

and we arrange these terms in the following pairs,

$$w\frac{d}{dx}A_{,}\,(wt)' - wt\frac{d}{dx}A_{,}w',$$
$$w\frac{d}{dy}C_{,}\,(wt)_{,} - wt\frac{d}{dy}C_{,}w_{,,}$$
$$w\frac{d}{dx}B_{,}\,(wt)_{,} - wt\frac{d}{dy}B_{,}w',$$
$$w\frac{d}{dy}B_{,}\,(wt)' - wt\frac{d}{dx}B_{,}w_{,};$$

the first of these four expressions is exactly integrable with respect to x and the second with respect to y; the third expression is equal to

$$\frac{d}{dx}wB_{,}\,(wt)_{,} - \frac{d}{dy}wt\,B_{,}w',$$

and the fourth to

$$\frac{d}{dy}wB_{,}\,(wt)' - \frac{d}{dx}wt\,B_{,}w_{,};$$

and thus every term is susceptible of exact integration either with respect to x or y.

The general process which is exemplified in the first and second of these four expressions presents no difficulty; that which is exemplified in the third and fourth of these expressions will be now given.

Let us denote one of the terms in $z\,\Phi(x,\,y,\,z,\,z',\,z_{,}\,\ldots)$ by

$$z\,\frac{d^{m}}{dx^{r}\,dy^{s}}\left(K\,\frac{d^{m}z}{dx^{r}\,dy^{s}}\right).$$

where $r + s = \rho + \sigma = m$; then, as we suppose r not equal to ρ, there will also be the term

$$s \frac{d^m z}{dx^r \, dy^s} \left(K \frac{d^m z}{dx^\rho \, dy^\sigma} \right).$$

Now change z into wt and subtract all that involves t^2, and divide by t. We thus obtain

$$w \frac{d^m}{dx^r \, dy^s} \left(K \frac{d^m wt}{dx^\rho \, dy^\sigma} \right) - wt \frac{d^m}{dx^r \, dy^s} \left(K \frac{d^m w}{dx^\rho \, dy^\sigma} \right),$$

and

$$w \frac{d^m}{dx^r \, dy^s} \left(K \frac{d^m wt}{dx^\rho \, dy^\sigma} \right) - wt \frac{d^m}{dx^r \, dy^s} \left(K \frac{d^m w}{dx^\rho \, dy^\sigma} \right).$$

Now by repeated integration by parts we have

$$\int w \frac{d^m}{dx^r \, dy^s} \left(K \frac{d^m wt}{dx^\rho \, dy^\sigma} \right) dx = S + (-1)^r \int \frac{d^r w}{dx^r} \frac{d^s}{dy^s} \left(K \frac{d^m wt}{dx^\rho \, dy^\sigma} \right) dx,$$

where S represents a series of terms free from the integral sign. Then if we integrate both members of the last equation with respect to y, we shall find that the only term on the right-hand side that remains under the *double* integral sign is

$$(-1)^m \iint \frac{d^m w}{dx^r \, dy^s} K \frac{d^m wt}{dx^\rho \, dy^\sigma} \, dy \, dx.$$

And this term is the only term that will remain under the *double* integral sign when we integrate

$$wt \frac{d^m}{dx^r \, dy^s} \left(K \frac{d^m w}{dx^\rho \, dy^\sigma} \right).$$

Hence the first pair of terms written above is such that it consists of parts which are susceptible of exact integration either with respect to x or y. And the same holds with respect to the second pair of terms. Thus $z \Phi(x, y, z, z', z_{,}, \ldots)$ does possess the property in question.

In the third place it will follow that $z \Psi(x, y, z', z_{,}, \ldots)$ must also possess the property in question or else vanish identically; and from this it will follow that $\Psi(x, y, z', z_{,}, \ldots)$ *does* vanish identically.

If for example $\Psi(x, y, z', z_{,}, \ldots)$ does not involve differential coefficients of a higher order than the third, we should have for $z\Psi(x, y, z', z_{,}, \ldots)$ an expression of the form

$$z\left\{ M_1 z' + M_2 z_{,} + N_1 z''' + N_2 z_{,}'' + N_3 z_{,,}' + N_4 z_{,,,} \right\}.$$

Hence the following expression must be susceptible of integration with respect to x or y, or else vanish identically,

$$w\left\{ M_1 (wt)' + M_2 (wt)_{,} + N_1 (wt)''' + N_2 (wt)_{,}'' + N_3 (wt)'_{,,} + N_4 (wt)_{,,,} \right\}$$
$$- wt\left\{ M_1 w' + M_2 w_{,} + N_1 w''' + N_2 w_{,}'' + N_3 w'_{,,} + N_4 w_{,,,} \right\}.$$

By reducing the terms of the first line by integration by parts with respect to x or y, we arrive at an unintegrated expression of the form Ct where C does not contain t; this must vanish since it cannot be an exact integral with respect to x or y. And as C must vanish whatever w may be, we shall find in succession that N_4, N_3, N_2, N_1, M_2, M_1 must all vanish.

Thus Eisenlohr's theorem is established.

The theorem is applied to the purposes of the Calculus of Variations in a manner similar to the application of the theorem in Eisenlohr's sixth section.

270. The next work we have to consider is by Spitzer, entitled *On the criteria for maxima and minima in problems of the Calculus of Variations.* This work consists of two memoirs which were communicated to the Academy of Sciences at Vienna; the memoirs were published in 1854 in the *Sitzungsberichte* of the Academy. The first memoir extends over pages 1014—1071 of the 12th volume, and the second over pages 41—120 of the 14th volume of the *Sitzungsberichte.*

Spitzer refers in the beginning of his first memoir to the memoirs of Jacobi and Delaunay, which we have already noticed; and then he says, that he has sought to deduce Jacobi's criteria in another manner, and believes that this new way may deserve some consideration.

271. The two memoirs consist altogether of thirty sections, of which thirteen are contained in the first memoir, and the remainder in the second. The first section gives the ordinary

investigation of the terms of the first order in the variation of an
integral which involves x, y, and the differential coefficients of y
with respect to x. The second section gives an investigation of
the terms of the second order in the variation of the integral.
The third section shews how Legendre transformed the terms of
the second order so that the existence of a maximum or minimum
might be recognized; Spitzer writes the equations at full for the
case in which the integral involves only the first differential
coefficient of y, for the case in which it involves both the first
and second differential coefficients of y, and for the case in which
it involves the first second and third differential coefficients of y.
In his fourth section Spitzer makes some remarks on the equations given in his third section; he shews that the equations take
the complicated form that has been indicated in Arts. 220 and 221,
and he says that Jacobi had succeeded in integrating these equations by a refined and difficult analysis, and that he himself had
solved the equations in a much simpler manner. The fifth section contains that part of Jacobi's theory which we have given
in Art. 252. The sixth section indicates briefly the general way
in which Spitzer proposes to solve the problem under discussion. The seventh section contains a complete investigation of the
general criteria for the maximum or minimum of an integral
$\int_{x_0}^{x_1} V dx$, where V involves x, y, and y'. The eighth section contains a discussion of that particular case in which $\dfrac{d^2 V}{dy'^2}$ is zero.
The ninth section contains a complete investigation of the ge-
neral criteria for the maximum or minimum of an integral $\int_{x_0}^{x_1} V dx$
where V involves x, y, y', and y''. The tenth section contains a
discussion of that particular case in which $\dfrac{d^2 V}{dy''^2}$ is zero. The
eleventh section contains a complete investigation of the general
criteria for the maximum or minimum of an integral $\int_{x_0}^{x_1} V dx$
where V involves x, y, y', y'', and y'''. The twelfth and thirteenth
sections contain a discussion of that particular case in which
$\dfrac{d^2 V}{dy'''^2}$ is zero. The fourteenth, fifteenth, and sixteenth sections

contain some additional investigations respecting the particular
cases which are discussed in the eighth, tenth, twelfth, and thirteenth sections. The seventeenth section gives the ordinary investigation of the terms of the first order in the variation of an
integral which involves $x, y, z,$ and the differential coefficients of
y and z with respect to x. The eighteenth section gives an investigation of the terms of the second order in the variation of the
integral. The nineteenth section shews how the terms of the
second order are to be transformed so that the existence of a
maximum or a minimum may be recognised; the necessary equations are given at full for the case in which the differential coefficients which occur do not rise above the first order, and for that
in which they do not rise above the second order. The twentieth
section generalises the theorem given in the fifth section. The
twenty-first and twenty-second sections contain a complete investigation of the general criteria for the maximum or minimum of
an integral $\int_{x_0}^{x_1} V\,dx$ where V involves x, y, z, y' and z'. The remaining sections contain discussions of the particular cases which
occur when V assumes particular forms.

272. Speaking generally we may describe Spitzer's work in
the terms we used with reference to Mainardi's, namely, as Legendre's method improved by additions borrowed from Jacobi;
see Art. 245. Spitzer was acquainted with Mainardi's memoir,
for he refers to it on page 62 of the 14th volume of the *Sitzungsberichte*. The investigations of Spitzer however are much more
complete than those of Mainardi; Spitzer does not shrink from
the labour of working out the solutions of his equations completely. Spitzer was the first who developed completely the
second variation of an integral involving $x, y, y', y'',$ and y'''; the
preceding writers had confined themselves to the case in which
the integral involved only x, y, y' and y''. Spitzer's investigation
of this problem is extremely complex, and occupies twenty large
octavo pages; besides seven more pages which relate to certain
special cases. In fact it seems improbable that any student
would verify the long calculations contained in Spitzer's twelfth
and thirteenth sections, and in his sections comprised between the
twenty-first and thirtieth inclusive.

It should be observed that the memoir is well and correctly printed; some mistakes at the ends of sections 8, 10, and 13 are corrected by the author himself in a note to section 14. A mistake occurs in the second line of page 1032 of the 12th volume of the *Sitzungsberichte*, for the sign of the right-hand side of the equation must be changed; this mistake leads to two more on the same page, and it appears again on page 44 of the 14th volume.

273.　We will now give some specimens of the investigations and conclusions of Spitzer.

In Arts. 250 and 251 we have shewn how in general we may distinguish between the maximum and minimum of $\int_{x_0}^{x_1} V\,dx$, where V involves x, y, and y'. Now suppose for a particular case that $\dfrac{d^2V}{dy'^2} = 0$, then, excluding the integrated terms, the value of I_2 on page 271 will take the form

$$\int\left(\frac{d^2V}{dy^2} - \frac{d}{dx}\frac{d^2V}{dy\,dy'}\right)\omega^2 dx.$$

Thus for a maximum or minimum it is necessary that

$$\frac{d^2V}{dy^2} - \frac{d}{dx}\frac{d^2V}{dy\,dy'}$$

should be respectively constantly negative or constantly positive throughout the limits of the integration.

Since $\dfrac{d^2V}{dy'^2} = 0$, it is obvious that V must be of the form

$$\phi\,(x,\,y) + y'\,\psi\,(x,\,y);$$

thus the differential equation from which y is to be found, namely,

$$\frac{dV}{dy} - \frac{d}{dx}\frac{dV}{dy'} = 0,$$

becomes

$$\frac{d\phi}{dy} + y'\frac{d\psi}{dy} - \frac{d\psi}{dx} - \frac{d\psi}{dy}y' = 0,$$

that is

$$\frac{d\phi}{dy} - \frac{d\psi}{dx} = 0.$$

This gives y as a function of x without any arbitrary constant. Thus, adopting geometrical language, the limiting points between which the required curve is to be drawn cannot be taken arbitrarily; they must lie on the curve determined by $\frac{d\phi}{dy} - \frac{d\psi}{dx} = 0$, or else the problem will be impossible.

In the next place let us suppose that besides $\frac{d^2V}{dy'^2} = 0$, we have also $\frac{d^2V}{dy^2} - \frac{d}{dx}\frac{d^2V}{dy\,dy'} = 0$; Spitzer in his fourteenth section determines what the form of V must then be, in the following manner.

Since $\frac{d^2V}{dy'^2} = 0$, we must have V of the form $f_1(x,y) + y'\,f_2(x,y)$. Now suppose $f_1(x,y)$ and $f_2(x,y)$ expanded in series proceeding according to ascending powers of y, and let

$$f_1(x,y) = A_0 + A_1 y + A_2 y^2 + A_3 y^3 + \dots$$
$$f_2(x,y) = B_0 + B_1 y + B_2 y^2 + B_3 y^3 + \dots$$

Thus
$$\frac{d^2V}{dy^2} = 1.2A_2 + 2.3A_3 y + 3.4A_4 y^2 + \dots$$
$$+ y'(1.2B_2 + 2.3B_3 y + 3.4B_4 y^2 + \dots);$$

$$\frac{d^2V}{dy\,dy'} = B_1 + 2B_2 y + 3B_3 y^2 + 4B_4 y^3 + \dots;$$

$$\frac{d}{dx}\frac{d^2V}{dy\,dy'} = B_1' + 2B_2'y + 3B_3'y^2 + 4B_4'y^3 + \dots$$
$$+ y'(1.2B_2 + 2.3B_3 y + 3.4B_4 y^2 + \dots).$$

And since
$$\frac{d^2V}{dy^2} = \frac{d}{dx}\frac{d^2V}{dy\,dy'},$$
we must have
$$2A_2 = B_1', \quad 3A_3 = B_2', \quad 4A_4 = B_3', \dots$$

Thus
$$V = A_0 + A_1 y + \frac{B_1'}{2}y^2 + \frac{B_2'}{3}y^3 + \frac{B_3'}{4}y^4 + \dots$$
$$+ y'(B_0 + B_1 y + B_2 y^2 + B_3 y^3 + B_4 y^4 + \dots),$$

or
$$V = A_0 + A_1 y + B_0 y' + \left(\frac{B_1}{2}y^2 + \frac{B_2}{3}y^3 + \frac{B_3}{4}y^4 + \dots\right)'.$$

This gives for V the following form,

$$\phi(x) + y\phi_1(x) + y'\phi_2(x) + [\phi_3(x,y)]';$$

or we may express our result without any loss of generality thus,

$$V = y\chi(x) + [\psi(x,y)]'.$$

With this value of V we have

$$\int V dx = \psi(x,y) + \int y\chi(x)\, dx;$$

thus in $\delta\int V dx$ the unintegrated part is $\int\chi(x)\,\delta y\, dx$, and this will not vanish unless $\chi(x)$ vanishes. Then $\int V dx$ is exactly integrable, and its maximum or minimum can be sought by ordinary methods.

274. Besides Spitzer's method, we may use another for finding the form of V in order that we may have

$$\frac{d^2 V}{dy'^2} = 0, \text{ and also } \frac{d V}{dy'} - \frac{d}{dx}\,\frac{d V}{dy dy'} = 0.$$

The latter result is the *condition of integrability* of the function $\frac{dV}{dy}$; so that we must have $\frac{dV}{dy}$ an exact differential coefficient of some function of x and y. Thus

$$\frac{dV}{dy} = [f(x,y)]'.$$

We do not introduce y' into the function $f(x,y)$, because if we did $\frac{dV}{dy}$ would contain y''; and this is impossible, because since $\frac{d^2 V}{dy'^2} = 0$, we know that V is of the form $f_1(x,y) + y' f_2(x,y)$, and so $\frac{dV}{dy}$ does not involve y''.

Thus
$$\frac{dV}{dy} = \frac{df}{dx} + y'\frac{df}{dy},$$

therefore
$$V = \int\frac{df}{dx}\, dy + y'\int\frac{df}{dy}\, dy.$$

Now let $F(x, y)$ be such a function of x and y, that

$$\frac{dF}{dy} = \int \frac{df}{dy}\, dy,$$

so that
$$\frac{dF}{dy} = f(x, y) - \chi_1(x),$$

where $\chi_1(x)$ is an arbitrary function of x.

Then
$$\int \frac{df}{dx}\, dy = \int \left\{ \frac{d^2F}{dx\, dy} + \chi_1{}'(x) \right\} dy = \frac{dF}{dx} + y\chi_1{}'(x) + \chi_2(x),$$

where $\chi_2(x)$ is another arbitrary function of x.

Therefore
$$V = \frac{dF}{dx} + y'\frac{dF}{dy} + y\chi_1{}'(x) + \chi_2(x)$$

$$= \left\{ F(x, y) + \int \chi_2(x)\, dx \right\}' + y\chi_1{}'(x).$$

And this agrees with Spitzer's form of V.

275. We will in the next place show the manner in which Spitzer investigates the criteria for the maximum or minimum of $\int V dx$, where V involves x, y, y' and y''. We have first to find in the ordinary manner the terms of the first order in $\delta \int V dx$ and to make them vanish. Then to distinguish between a maximum and a minimum, we must investigate the sign of

$$\int \left(\frac{d^2V}{dy^2} w^2 + \frac{d^2V}{dy'^2} w'^2 + \frac{d^2V}{dy''^2} w''^2 + 2\frac{d^2V}{dy\, dy'} ww' \right.$$
$$\left. + 2\frac{d^2V}{dy\, dy''} ww'' + 2\frac{d^2V}{dy'\, dy''} w'w'' \right) dx,$$

where w is put for δy.

Suppose
$$W = \frac{dV}{dy} w + \frac{dV}{dy'} w' + \frac{dV}{dy''} w'',$$

then the above expression which we have to examine is equivalent to

$$w \left\{ \frac{dW}{dy'} - \left(\frac{dW}{dy''} \right)' \right\} + w'\frac{dW}{dy''}$$
$$+ \int \left\{ \frac{dW}{dy} - \left(\frac{dW}{dy'} \right)' + \left(\frac{dW}{dy''} \right)'' \right\} w\, dx.$$

The coincidence of the two expressions is easily shewn by integrating $\int \left(\dfrac{d W}{dy'}\right)' w\,dx$ once by parts, and $\int \left(\dfrac{d W}{dy''}\right)'' w\,dx$ twice by parts.

Now assume that these terms of the second order can be put in the form

$$v w^2 + 2 v_1 w w' + v_2 w'^2 + \int \frac{d^2 V}{dy''^2}\,(w'' + \lambda w' + \mu w)^2\,dx,$$

where v, v_1, v_2, λ, and μ are at present undetermined.

In order that this transformation may be possible the following equations must be satisfied:

$$\frac{d^2 V}{dy'^2} = v' + \mu^2 \frac{d^2 V}{dy''^2},$$

$$\frac{d^2 V}{dy'^2} = 2v_1 + v_2' + \lambda^2 \frac{d^2 V}{dy''^2},$$

$$\frac{d^2 V}{dy\,dy'} = v + v_1' + \lambda\mu \frac{d^2 V}{dy''^2},$$

$$\frac{d^2 V}{dy\,dy''} = v_1 + \mu \frac{d^2 V}{dy''^2},$$

$$\frac{d^2 V}{dy'\,dy''} = v_2 + \lambda \frac{d^2 V}{dy''^2}.$$

We may observe that if λ and μ are known the last three of these five equations will find in succession v_2, v_1, and v.

We do not propose to give the long process by which Spitzer solves these equations; we will however briefly indicate the principle on which he proceeds.

Let w_1 denote a value of w or δy which makes the unintegrated terms of the second order in the variation vanish, that is, which makes

$$\frac{d W}{dy} - \left(\frac{d W}{dy'}\right)' + \left(\frac{d W}{dy''}\right)'' = 0 \dots\dots\dots\dots\dots\dots(1);$$

then we may infer that this will make $w'' + \lambda w' + \mu w$ vanish, that is, we shall have

$$u_1'' + \lambda u_1' + \mu u_1 = 0 \dots\dots\dots\dots\dots\dots\dots (2).$$

Similarly, let u_2 be another such value of w or δy, then

$$u_2'' + \lambda u_2' + \mu u_2 = 0 \dots\dots\dots\dots\dots\dots\dots (3).$$

Then from (2) and (3) we can find λ and μ in terms of u_1 and u_2 and their first and second differential coefficients; and when v, v_1, and v_2 are expressed in terms of λ and μ from the last three of the five equations given above, it remains to shew that the first two of these five equations are satisfied.

When the equation (1) is developed it takes the form

$$\frac{d^2 V}{dy'''^2}\, w'''' + 2\left(\frac{d^2 V}{dy'''^2}\right)' w''' + \left\{ 2\,\frac{d^2 V}{dy\,dy''} - \frac{d^2 V}{dy''^2} + \left(\frac{d^2 V}{dy'\,dy''}\right)' + \left(\frac{d^2 V}{dy'''^2}\right)'' \right\} w''$$

$$+ \left\{ 2\left(\frac{d^2 V}{dy\,dy''}\right)' - \left(\frac{d^2 V}{dy''^2}\right)' + \left(\frac{d^2 V}{dy'\,dy''}\right)'' \right\} w'$$

$$+ \left\{ \frac{d^2 V}{dy^2} - \left(\frac{d^2 V}{dy\,dy'}\right)' + \left(\frac{d^2 V}{dy\,dy''}\right)'' \right\} w = 0 \dots\dots\dots\dots (4).$$

This is a differential equation of the fourth order, so that u_1 and u_2 may each involve four arbitrary constants. But practically to find u_1 and u_2 we do not require to solve this differential equation; for we use the principle explained in Art. 252.

Spitzer does shew that when λ and μ are found in the manner indicated, and then v, v_1, and v_2 deduced, the first two of the five equations given above are satisfied, provided a certain relation subsists among the eight constants which occur in u_1 and u_2. This agrees with Jacobi's statements in Art. 221.

Since the above five equations lead by the elimination of λ and μ to three differential equations of the first order for finding v, v_1, and v_2, it follows that if the most general values of these quantities are obtained three arbitrary constants should be involved. And Spitzer shews that the eight constants which occur in u_1 and u_2 do combine in such a manner as to leave finally three independent arbitrary constants in the values of v, v_1, and v_2. This gives a

completeness to the investigations which is desirable, but it is not
absolutely necessary. For all that is required in order that the
proposed transformation of the terms of the second order in the
variation may be effected, is that certain differential equations
should be satisfied; and it would have been of no importance if
the number of arbitrary constants had been less than the extreme
number which the most general solutions would supply.

276. The general results at which Spitzer arrives in the investigations noticed in the preceding article are the same as those
of Jacobi given in Art. 224; but in addition to these he discusses
some particular cases, and these we will now consider.

Suppose then that we have $\dfrac{d^2 V}{dy''^2} = 0$; then V must be of the
form

$$f_1(x, y, y') + y'' f_2(x, y, y').$$

In this case the differential equation in y, which is formed by
equating to zero the terms of the first order in $\delta \int V dx$, is a differential equation of the second order. We will suppose its integral to be $y = \phi(x, a_1, a_2)$.

Now assume that the terms of the second order which we have
to examine can be put in the form

$$v w^2 + 2 v_1 w w' + v_2 w'^2 + \int P(w' + \lambda w)^2 \, dx;$$

and put for shortness

$$\frac{d^2 V}{dy^2} = A, \quad \frac{d^2 V}{dy'^2} = B, \quad \frac{d^2 V}{dy' dy''} = D,$$

$$\frac{d^2 V}{dy \, dy''} = E, \quad \frac{d^2 V}{dy \, dy'} = F.$$

Then we require that

$$A w^2 + B w'^2 + 2 D w' w'' + 2 E w w'' + 2 F w w'$$

$$= (v w^2 + 2 v_1 w w' + v_2 w'^2)' + P(w' + \lambda w)^2.$$

Thus we must have

$$A = v' + P\lambda^2,$$
$$B = 2v_1 + v_2' + P,$$
$$D = v_2,$$
$$E = v_1,$$
$$F = v + v_1' + \lambda P.$$

Now let $u = C_1 \dfrac{d\phi}{du_1} + C_2 \dfrac{d\phi}{du_2}$, where C_1 and C_2 are arbitrary constants; and assume λ such that $u' + \lambda u = 0$; we shall then examine if we can satisfy the above five equations. The third and fourth give immediately $v_1 = E$, $v_2 = D$; then the second and fifth give

$$P = B - 2E - D',$$
$$v = F - E' + \frac{u'}{u}(B - 2E - D');$$

it remains to try if the values thus obtained satisfy

$$A = v' + P\lambda^2.$$

This requires that

$$A = F' - E'' + \frac{u'}{u}(D' - 2E' - D'') + \frac{uu'' - u'^2}{u^2}(B - 2E - D)$$
$$+ \frac{u'^2}{u^2}(B - 2E - D'),$$

that is

$$(A - F' + E'')\,u + u'(2E' + D' - B') + u''(2E + D - B) = 0.$$

This equation is in fact what equation (4) of the preceding article becomes when $\dfrac{d^2V}{dy'^2} = 0$, with u in the place of w; and from Art. 252 we know that the value assigned to u does satisfy it.

Thus the unintegrated part of the terms which we are examining, that is,

$$\int P(w' + \lambda w)^2 \, dx,$$

becomes

$$\int (B - 2E - D)\left(w' - \frac{u'}{u}w\right)^2 dx;$$

hence for a maximum or minimum $B - 2E - D'$ must be respectively negative or positive throughout the limits of the integration.

Next, suppose that we have

$$\frac{d^2 V}{dy''^2} = 0, \text{ and also } \frac{d^2 V}{dy'^2} - 2\,\frac{d^2 V}{dy\,dy''} - \left(\frac{d^2 V}{dy'\,dy''}\right)' = 0.$$

The unintegrated part of the terms of the second order is now

$$\int (A - F' + E'')\,w^2\,dx,$$

and thus for a maximum or minimum $A - F' + E''$ must be respectively negative or positive throughout the limits of the integration.

In this case the equation $\dfrac{d W}{dy} - \left(\dfrac{d W}{dy'}\right)' + \left(\dfrac{d W}{dy''}\right)'' = 0$, is no longer a *differential* equation for finding w, because w'''', w''', w'', and w' disappear from it. This suggests that the equation obtained by putting the terms of the first order in $\delta\!\int V dx$ equal to zero will not be a differential equation in y, but an ordinary equation; and this will be found to be the case.

For Spitzer shews in the same manner as in Art. 273, that the form of V must in this case be

$$\phi\,(x,\,y) + y'\,\psi\,(x,\,y) + [\chi\,(x,\,y,\,y')]',$$

and as in Art. 273, we shall obtain for determining y the equation

$$\frac{d\phi}{dy} - \frac{d\psi}{dx} = 0.$$

Lastly, suppose that we have

$$\frac{d^2 V}{dy''^2} = 0, \qquad \frac{d^2 V}{dy'^2} - 2\,\frac{d^2 V}{dy\,dy''} - \left(\frac{d^2 V}{dy'\,dy''}\right)' = 0,$$

and also

$$\frac{d^2 V}{dy^2} - \left(\frac{d^2 V}{dy\,dy'}\right)' + \left(\frac{d^2 V}{dy\,dy''}\right)'' = 0.$$

Spitzer shews in the same manner as in Art. 273, that the form of V must in this case be

$$y\phi\,(x) + [\psi\,(x,\,y)]' + [\chi\,(x,\,y,\,y')]';$$

thus in $\delta \int V dx$ the unintegrated part is $\int \phi(x)\, \delta y\, dx$, and this will not vanish unless $\phi(x)$ vanishes. Then $\int V dx$ is exactly integrable, and its maximum or minimum can be sought by ordinary methods.

277. We may also obtain the results of the preceding article by another method. Suppose $\dfrac{d^2 V}{dy'^2} = 0$, then the left-hand member of equation (4) of Art. 275 takes the form

$$(2E + D' - B)\, w'' + (2E + D' - B')\, w' + (A - F' + E'')\, w,$$

where A, B, D, E, F have the same meaning as in Art. 276. The above expression may be written thus

$$[(2E + D' - B)\, w']' + (A - F' + E'')\, w,$$

so that we have to determine the sign of

$$\int \left[[(2E + D' - B)\, w']' + (A - F' + E'')\, w \right] w\, dx.$$

Suppose u such a quantity that

$$[(2E + D' - B)\, u']' + (A - F' + E'')\, u = 0.$$

Then the expression which we have to examine may be written

$$\int \left[[(2E + D' - B)\, w']' - [(2E + D' - B)\, u']' \frac{w}{u} \right] w\, dx.$$

Integrate by parts; then the terms remaining under the integral sign will be

$$\int \left[(B - 2E - D')\, w'^2 - (B - 2E - D')\, u' \left(\frac{w^2}{u} \right)' \right] dx,$$

that is, $$\int (B - 2E - D') \left(w' - \frac{u'}{u}\, w \right)^2 dx.$$

This agrees with the result at the bottom of page 303.

278. In his sixteenth section Spitzer examines some exceptional cases which occur in finding the maximum or minimum of

$\int V dx$, when V involves x, y, y', y'', and y'''. He does not here prove that V must have specific forms in certain cases, but he assumes specific forms for V and shews that certain exceptional cases do thence arise. The following four forms for V are examined.

1. $\quad \phi(x, y, y', y'') + y''' \psi(x, y, y', y'')$.

2. $\quad \phi(x, y, y') + y'' \psi(x, y, y') + [\chi(x, y, y', y'')]'$.

3. $\quad \phi(x, y) + y' \psi(x, y) + [\chi_1(x, y, y')]' + [\chi_2(x, y, y', y'')]'$.

4. $\quad y \phi(x) + [\chi_1(x, y)]' + [\chi_2(x, y, y')]' + [\chi_3(x, y, y', y'')]'$.

279. In concluding our account of Spitzer's memoirs, we may state that the most interesting and valuable portion of them consists in the examination of certain special cases in which the general results obtained by Jacobi require to be modified; and these special cases appear to have been examined by no other writer.

280. The next memoir we have to consider is by Otto Hesse; it is entitled, *On the criteria for the maxima and minima of single Integrals.* It was published in the 54th volume of Crelle's Mathematical Journal in 1857, and occupies pages 227—273 of the volume. In the beginning of his memoir Hesse refers to the following authors who have written commentaries on Jacobi's memoir, Lebesgue, Delaunay, Bertrand, Eisenlohr and Spitzer; he makes special mention of Spitzer, and commends his acuteness and industry. It seems probable that Hesse was led to turn his attention to the subject by seeing Spitzer's investigations.

281. The first twenty pages of Hesse's memoir contain investigations of Jacobi's theorems. Although there is little that is substantially new here given, the investigations are well worthy of study from their complete and systematic form.

282. In the next seven pages the result obtained by Jacobi's method is developed by the aid of the theory of determinants, so as to present the unintegrated part of the second variation in a more explicit form than that in which Jacobi leaves it. These

seven pages constitute the most important portion of the memoir; and we will give here the result obtained by Hesse. Suppose that $\int V dx$ is to be a maximum or minimum, where V contains x, y, and the differential coefficients of y up to the nth inclusive. Let z stand for δy; then the terms of the second order which we have to examine can be put in the form $\int \psi (z) z\, dx$. This is proved by Hesse; it is equivalent to the statement in Art. 223, that the terms of the second order can be put in the form $\int \delta V \delta y\, dx$. Now let u, v, w, ... be values of z which satisfy the equation $\psi (z) = 0$; we suppose n of these solutions obtained, and they will be all of the same *form*, but differ in the values of the $2n$ arbitrary constants which each of them involves. Now adopting the usual notation of determinants let

$$\nabla = \begin{vmatrix} u, & u', & u'', & \ldots\ldots & u^{(n)} \\ v, & v', & v'', & \ldots\ldots & v^{(n)} \\ w, & w', & w'', & \ldots\ldots & w^{(n)} \\ \cdots & \cdots & \cdots & \cdots & \cdots \\ \cdots & \cdots & \cdots & \cdots & \cdots \\ z, & z', & z'', & \ldots\ldots & z^{(n)} \end{vmatrix}$$

and

$$\nabla_n = \begin{vmatrix} u, & u', & u'', & \ldots\ldots & u^{(n-1)} \\ v, & v', & v'', & \ldots\ldots & v^{(n-1)} \\ w, & w', & w'', & \ldots\ldots & w^{(n-1)} \\ \cdots & \cdots & \cdots & \cdots & \cdots \\ \cdots & \cdots & \cdots & \cdots & \cdots \end{vmatrix}$$

where accents denote as usual differential coefficients. Thus ∇ is a determinant of the $(n+1)^{th}$ order and ∇_n is a determinant of the nth order. Then Hesse proves that the terms of the second order which we have to examine can be put into the form $\int N \dfrac{\nabla'}{\nabla_n^2} dx$, where N is the second differential coefficient of V with respect to $\dfrac{d^n y}{dx^n}$

Moreover Hesse draws particular attention to the fact that certain relations must hold among the arbitrary constants involved in u, v, w,... See Arts. 221 and 232.

283. The remainder of Hesse's memoir is devoted to the examination of three particular cases, that in which the integral involves x, y, y', that in which the integral involves x, y, y', y'', and that in which the integral involves x, y, y', y'', y'''. These cases are treated very fully, and the relations which hold among the arbitrary constants are completely exhibited. No notice however is taken of the exceptions to the general theory which Spitzer considered; see Arts. 273, 274, 276. In connexion with the first of the three particular cases which he examines, Hesse gives a good discussion of the remarks made by Jacobi relating to the extreme limits which may be assigned to an integral in order to ensure a maximum or a minimum; see Art. 225.

284. The memoir by Hesse forms the most elaborate commentary that has yet appeared on Jacobi's theorems and method. The student who masters this and examines what Spitzer has given on the exceptional cases will not require any further information on the maxima and minima of single integrals which involve one dependent variable. Hesse uses the theory of determinants, but a student who is acquainted with the elements of that subject will not find any serious difficulty in Hesse's memoir.

285. We have next to consider a memoir by A. Clebsch; it is entitled *On the reduction of the second variation to its simplest form*. It was published in the 55th volume of Crelle's Mathematical Journal in 1858, and occupies pages 254—273 of the volume.

This is the first of three memoirs by this writer on the Calculus of Variations. He begins by referring to Jacobi's results, and to the excellent memoir published by Hesse respecting them. He then indicates the points in which Jacobi's results require still to be generalised, namely, that similar investigations should be supplied for the case of a single integral which involves more than one dependent variable, and for the case of a multiple integral, and for the case in which equations are given connecting the variables involved in the integral. The present memoir proposes to supply some of these required investigations. Thus, Clebsch states that the memoir solves the following problem; to reduce the second variation of a single integral so as to make it depend upon the smallest number of variations, the integral involving any number of dependent variables and their differential coefficients to any order, and also any number of equations being given connecting the variables. In addition to the solution of this problem, there is a short section on the subject of multiple integrals, but this is of no great importance; the writer however intimates that at the time of printing he had succeeded in overcoming the difficulties of this part of the subject, and would publish a memoir on it, and in fact the third memoir fulfils this promise.

As an example of his method, Clebsch gives the ordinary case of one dependent variable without any connecting equations, and he arrives at the result obtained by Hesse; see Art. 281.

280. The second memoir by Clebsch is entitled *On those problems in the Calculus of Variations which involve only one independent variable.* It was published in the 55th volume of Crelle's Mathematical Journal in 1858, and occupies pages 335—355 of the volume.

This memoir may be said to consist of two parts. The first part is occupied in proving that the solution of any problem in the Calculus of Variations in which there is only one independent variable may be made to depend on the solution of a certain partial differential equation of the first order. It had been intimated by Jacobi that this proposition was true in a certain case, so that a problem in the Calculus of Variations could be treated in a manner analogous to the treatment of dynamical problems by the methods of Hamilton and Jacobi. Clebsch easily proves the proposition which he enunciates.

The second part of the memoir is occupied in shewing that this mode of treating a problem in the Calculus of Variations presents great advantages in the discussion of the terms of the second order with the view of discriminating between maxima and minima values. This part of the memoir is extremely complicated and requires the reader to possess a good knowledge of the theory of determinants.

287. The third memoir by Clebsch is entitled *On the second variation of Multiple Integrals*. It was published in the 56th volume of Crelle's Mathematical Journal in 1859, and occupies pages 122—148 of the volume.

The object of the memoir is to shew how to discriminate between the maxima and minima values of multiple integrals; like the second memoir by the author it is extremely complicated, and requires the reader to possess a good knowledge of the theory of determinants.

288. We have been compelled to give very brief accounts of the memoirs by Hesse and Clebsch. From the nature of the memoirs it seems impossible to present any abridgement of them or any extract from them which will be easily intelligible; and moreover the memoirs belong rather to the Theory of Determinants than to the Calculus of Variations. As however these memoirs have been published so recently they can be readily obtained, and thus there is less need of a detailed account of them than in the case of works which are more difficult of access.

CHAPTER XI.

ON JACOBI'S MEMOIR.

289. The preceding chapter contains an account in chronological order of the writings of commentators on Jacobi's memoir; the present chapter consists of some miscellaneous articles bearing on certain parts of Jacobi's memoir.

In Art. 228 we have given Jacobi's remarks on the shortest line that can be drawn on a surface; these remarks are connected with those in Art. 225. We have also intimated that some of the commentators on Jacobi's memoir have considered these parts of it; see Arts. 265 and 283. There is a note by J. Bertrand entitled *On the shortest distance between two points on a surface*, which was published in 1855 in the second volume of the third edition of Lagrange's *Mécanique Analytique*, pages 350—352. We will give this note in the next article.

290. When a material point moves on a fixed surface, and has an initial velocity but is acted on by no force, Lagrange proves that its velocity is constant and the curve which it describes is the shortest that can be drawn between two of its points. In order to prove this proposition the illustrious author shews that the variation of the arc $\int ds$ is zero, and therefore there is either a maximum or a minimum; but he says there cannot be a maximum and therefore there must be a minimum. This manner of reasoning is inadmissible, because we know that the variation of an integral may be zero while the integral is neither a maximum nor a minimum. However in the particular case in question Lagrange's statement is exact, as we may shew in a few words.

The differential equation which expresses that the variation of the integral $\int ds$ is zero proves, as is well known, that the osculating plane of the curve is at every point normal to the surface. But if we suppose the two extremities of the arc considered to be indefinitely close, among all the arcs drawn on the surface joining the extremities, the least, that in fact which differs least from the chord, will evidently be the arc which has the least curvature, that is, the arc which has the greatest radius of curvature. But the arcs which unite two points of the surface indefinitely close may be considered as having the same tangent, and therefore, by the well-known theorem of Meunier, that of which the osculating plane is normal to the surface has the greatest radius of curvature, and is consequently the shortest.

The proposition enunciated by Lagrange is exact as we have just seen for any indefinitely small arc, but it would cease to be so if we considered an arc of finite size. There exists a curious theorem on this subject enunciated by Jacobi without demonstration, which gives a general method for determining with respect to every line traced upon a surface and satisfying the conditions of a minimum, the limits between which it is really the shortest line.

Let AMA' be such a line; proceed along this line from the point A which is fixed towards the following points of the curve. If we take one of these points as a second limit it may happen that between this point and the first another curve can be drawn which satisfies the analytical condition for a minimum as well as the first; then the line considered will cease to be a minimum between the point A and the second extremity considered, at a point for which the second line coincides with (se confond) the first.

This theorem has not been demonstrated by the mathematicians who have explained the celebrated letter in which it is enunciated. We think that it will be useful to indicate briefly how it follows from the analysis of Jacobi.

The integral considered being $\int f\left(x,\, y,\, \dfrac{dy}{dx}\right) dx$, the variation takes the form $\int V\, \delta y\, dx$, V being the function which by being equated to zero furnishes by integration the solution of the problem.

That there may be a minimum, the function $\dfrac{d^2f}{dy'^2}$ must remain constantly positive during the limits of integration. This condition will certainly be fulfilled whatever the limits may be, because we have seen that there is always a minimum between any two limits whatever if they are sufficiently close. Besides this we must have according to Jacobi's analysis another condition fulfilled. Let y denote the expression deduced from the equation $V = 0$, then y contains two constants a and b suppose; let α and β be two other constants, and let

$$u = a\,\frac{dy}{da} + \beta\,\frac{dy}{db}.$$

Then the other condition is that it must be possible to take the constants α and β so that the expression

$$-\left(\frac{d^2f}{dy\,dy'} + \frac{1}{u}\,\frac{d^2f}{dy'^2}\,\frac{du}{dx} \right)$$

may not become infinite between the limits of integration, or, which comes to the same thing, u must not vanish between these limits. Hence it is clear that for each value of $\dfrac{\beta}{a}$ if the expression for u becomes zero in two points of the minimum line furnished by the Calculus of Variations, then between these two points we can affirm that the integral is a minimum. Now two such points will possess the property indicated by Jacobi, that is, it will be possible to draw between them two lines indefinitely close, each of which has the minimum property. For we observe that the expression

$$u = a\,\frac{dy}{da} + \beta\,\frac{dy}{db}$$

is the general integral of the linear equation $\delta V = 0$, in which δy is the unknown quantity. (See Jacobi's Memoir.) If then we put instead of y the value $y + u$, where α and β are so chosen as to make u indefinitely small, which is allowable, the expression V

will vanish, because by supposition y makes it vanish and the indefinitely small increment u renders its variation zero.

Thus there are two lines indefinitely close joining the same two points, for which the relation $V = 0$ is fulfilled, that is, two lines which equally satisfy the conditions of minimum.

The proposition thus demonstrated is not identical with that of Jacobi, but it is perhaps allowable to suppose that the illustrious author went a little too far in the rapid sketch which he gave of his results; it is clear, for example, that the conditions found by him are sufficient but not necessary for the existence of a minimum. There is therefore no ground for affirming that the minimum ceases to exist because the *function* u becomes zero; but this would be necessary in order that the enunciation should take the completely affirmative form given above.

We may observe before closing this note that Jacobi's memoir contains the enunciation of another very remarkable theorem ; *if at every point of a surface the two curvatures are in opposite directions the line which satisfies the analytical conditions of a minimum is always really the shortest.* We confine ourselves to recalling this theorem to the attention of mathematicians; a more detailed discussion of the geometrical problem which is the object of this note would be out of place here.

291. Bertrand in the first paragraph of his note says that Lagrange is right in asserting that there is necessarily a minimum in the case considered; in the third paragraph of his note he says that Lagrange's statement is not necessarily exact except for an indefinitely small arc.

The remarks which Bertrand then makes on Jacobi's theorem coincide in substance with those of other writers on this subject ; see for example Mr Jellett's treatise, pages 90 and 98. These remarks depend on the following consideration ; Jacobi's method reduces the unintegrated part of the terms of the second order to the form

$$\frac{1}{2} \int \frac{d^2 f}{dy'^2} \left(\frac{1}{u} \frac{du}{dx} \delta y - \frac{d \delta y}{dx} \right)^2 dx,$$

and thus we cannot be sure of a minimum if u vanishes between the limits of integration. Bertrand however is alone in pointing out that this does not prove so much as Jacobi asserts in the

particular problem under consideration, for Jacobi asserts that there
will *not* be a minimum; and Bertrand conjectures that Jacobi here
overstated his results. But it has since been shewn by Ossian
Bonnet that Jacobi was quite correct; the proposition to which
Bertrand calls attention at the end of his note is also proved by
Bonnet.

Two notes have been written by Bonnet on the point we are
considering. The first note is entitled *On some properties of geodesic lines.* It was published in the *Comptes Rendus ...... de
l'Académie des Sciences*, Vol. 40, 1855, pages 1311—1313. We will
give it in the next article.

202. A line traced upon a surface is called a *geodesic line*,
when its osculating plane is always normal to the surface.

An arc of a geodesic line is the shortest line that can be
drawn on a curved surface between its two extremities, provided
the arc be comprised within certain limits which have been fixed
by Jacobi in the following manner. Consider a geodesic line AM
which starts from the point A, and let A' be the point where this
line is met by another geodesic line AM' which also starts from
the point A and is indefinitely close to AM. Between the points
A and A' the line AM will always be a minimum line; but beyond
the point A' the line AM will *generally* be neither a maximum nor
a minimum. Assuming this, let p denote the variable distance
MM' between two indefinitely close geodesic lines AM and AM'.
By a formula due to Gauss, p considered as a function of the
arc AM will satisfy the differential equation of the second order

$$\frac{d^2 p}{ds^2} + \frac{p}{RR'} = 0,$$

where $AM = s$, and R, R' are the principal radii of curvature of the
surface, and in addition, when $s = 0$ we have $p = 0$ and $\frac{dp}{ds} =$ the
angle $d\theta$ between the geodesic lines AM and AM', which will
completely determine p. Now suppose that the surface is of
opposite curvatures; $\frac{1}{RR'}$ will be negative, and we can assume

$$\frac{1}{RR'} < -\frac{1}{a^2},$$

where a is a real constant.

Let us take the equation

$$\frac{d^2 p_i}{ds^2} - \frac{p_i}{a^2} = 0,$$

and integrate it so that when $s = 0$ we may have $p_i = 0$ and $\frac{dp_i}{ds} = d\theta$; we shall obtain

$$p_i = \frac{a}{2} \left(e^{\frac{s}{a}} - e^{-\frac{s}{a}} \right) d\theta.$$

But from a theorem demonstrated by M. Sturm in his excellent Memoir on differential equations of the second order, it is known, that for any interval whatever starting from $s = 0$, the value of p_i must vanish at least as often as that of p; but p_i never does vanish, and so p cannot vanish. Thus in a surface of opposite curvatures a geodesic line is always a minimum throughout its length. This beautiful theorem was enunciated by Jacobi, but it had not been demonstrated up to the present time so far as I know.

Suppose in the next place that $\frac{1}{RR'}$ is positive and less than $\frac{1}{a^2}$. Consider the equation

$$\frac{d^2 p_i}{ds^2} + \frac{p_i}{a^2} = 0,$$

and integrate it so that when $s = 0$ we may have $p_i = 0$ and $\frac{dp_i}{ds} = d\theta$; we shall obtain

$$p_i = a d\theta \sin \frac{s}{a}.$$

But, from a second theorem demonstrated by M. Sturm, it is known that, starting from $s = 0$, p will vanish before p_i; but p_i vanishes when $s = \pi a$, therefore p vanishes before $s = \pi a$. Hence we infer that, in the case considered, a geodesic line cannot be *generally* a minimum line throughout a greater length than πa. Consequently the shortest distance between any two points on a convex surface is less than πa where a^2 is a number greater than the product RR' of the principal radii of curvature for all points of the surface.

293. The theorem due to Gauss which Bonnet quotes in the preceding article is contained in the *Disquisitiones generales circa superficies curvas*. This memoir was presented by Gauss to the Royal Society of Gottingen on October 8th, 1827, and was published in 1828 in the sixth volume of the *Commentationes Recentiores* of that Society. This memoir is reprinted in Liouville's edition of Monge's *Application de l'Analyse à la Géométrie*.

The theorem in question is also proved by Ossian Bonnet in his memoir on the general theory of surfaces in the *Journal de l'École Polytechnique*, Cahier XXXII, 1848.

The memoir by Sturm to which Bonnet refers will be found in the first volume of Liouville's Journal of Mathematics.

The second note by Bonnet is entitled *Second note on geodesic lines*. It was published in the *Comptes Rendus*... Vol. 41, 1855, pages 32—35. We give it in the next article.

294. In a note presented to the Academy on the 18th of June, I established some general properties of geodesic lines. My investigations depended on the following theorem due to Jacobi.

Let AM be any geodesic line which starts from the point A, and suppose A' to be the point where this geodesic line is met by a geodesic line which also starts from the point A and is indefinitely near to the first; then the line AM will be a minimum between the points A and A', and will cease to be a minimum beyond the point A'.

Jacobi did not demonstrate his theorem; he merely said that it might be easily deduced from the general rules which he gave for distinguishing maxima from minima in questions which depend upon the Calculus of Variations. M. Bertrand has given a proof of the first part of the theorem in the notes which he has added to his excellent edition of the *Mécanique Analytique;* that is, he has proved that between the points A and A' the line AM is a minimum. In the mode of proof M. Bertrand has followed the indications of Jacobi. With respect to the second part of the theorem M. Bertrand thinks that it may not be exact, and that at all events the method of Jacobi is not competent to decide the point. It is in fact certain that the general conditions found by Legendre and completed by Jacobi, for distinguishing between maxima and minima in problems which depend upon the calculus of variations are sufficient but not necessary. I have succeeded in proving by particular considerations both parts of Jacobi's theorem. I request permission from the Academy to communicate my demonstration, which thus removes the difficulties which relate to an important question, and at the same time gives more precision to the results of my previous investigations.

Let AMB be an arc of a geodesic line which starts from A and ends at B. (The reader is requested to make the figure for himself.) Draw any line AM_1B indefinitely close to AMB and having the same extremities. I proceed to estimate the difference of the lengths of AMB and AM_1B as far as small quantities of the second order; for this purpose I draw through the different points of AMB geodesic curves normal to AMB, and I denote in general by ω the portion of these curves comprised between AMB and AM_1B. Suppose the element MN of $AMB = ds$, and the corresponding element M_1N_1 of $AM_1B = ds_1$; then

$$M_1N_1 = ds_1 = \sqrt{[(M_1P)^2 + (PN_1)^2]},$$

P being the point in NN_1 such that $NP = MM_1$. But

$$PN_1 = \frac{d\omega}{ds}\,ds = \omega' ds,$$

and M_1P is, by a theorem due to Gauss, the integral of the equation

$$\frac{d^2u}{d\omega^2} + \frac{u}{RR} = 0,$$

which for $\omega = 0$ satisfies the conditions $u = ds$, $\dfrac{du}{d\omega} = 0$. Therefore

$$M_1P = ds\left(1 - \frac{\omega^2}{2RR}\right),$$

if we neglect powers of ω above the second. Therefore

$$ds_1 = ds\left\{\left(1 - \frac{\omega^2}{2RR}\right)^2 + \omega'^2\right\}^{\frac{1}{2}},$$

or more simply, to the order of approximation which we want,

$$ds_1 = ds\left(1 + \frac{1}{2}\omega'^2 - \frac{1}{2}\frac{\omega^2}{RR}\right).$$

Therefore the difference between AM_1B and AMB, that is the second variation of the integral $\int ds$, will be

$$\frac{1}{2}\int\left(\omega''-\frac{\omega^2}{RR'}\right)ds \dots\dots\dots\dots\dots\dots\dots\dots(1).$$

We see immediately that if RR' be negative this second variation is always positive; this proves the first theorem which I have established in another manner in my first note; *in any surface of opposite curvatures a geodesic line is a minimum throughout its length.*

Now let us call p the distance comprised between the line $AM\dot{B}$ and another geodesic line indefinitely close to it which also starts from A, so that we have

$$\frac{d^2p}{ds^2}+\frac{p}{RR'}=0,$$

and when $s=0$ we have $p=0$ and $\frac{dp}{ds}=$ the indefinitely small angle $d\theta$ between the two geodesic lines; the expression (1) can be put in the form

$$\frac{1}{2}\int\left(\omega''+\frac{d^2p}{ds^2}\frac{\omega^2}{p}\right)ds=\frac{1}{2}\int\left(\omega'-\frac{dp}{ds}\frac{\omega}{p}\right)^2 ds+\frac{1}{2}\int\left(\frac{\omega^2}{p}\frac{dp}{ds}\right)'ds.$$

But, if p does not vanish within the limits of integration,

$$\int\left(\frac{\omega^2}{p}\frac{dp}{ds}\right)'ds=0,$$

for ω is zero at the limits; thus the second variation is reduced to

$$\frac{1}{2}\int\left(\omega'-\frac{dp}{ds}\frac{\omega}{p}\right)^2 ds,$$

that is, to a positive result. I conclude therefore, that so long as the extremity B is not beyond the point A' where the line AMB is met by the geodesic line indefinitely close to it which also starts from the point A, the arc AMB of the geodesic line is a minimum between the point A and the point B; this is the first part of Jacobi's theorem.

If the point B is beyond A', then, since ω is only subject to the condition of vanishing at the points A and B, we can take for ω a value which satisfies an equation of the form

$$\frac{d^2\omega}{ds^2} + \omega\left(\frac{1}{RR'} - \frac{1}{k^2}\right) = 0,$$

where k is real, and which is such that $\omega = 0$ and $\frac{d\omega}{ds} = d\theta$ when $s = 0$. This follows from the fact that in an equation of the form

$$\frac{d^2p}{ds^2} + Gp = 0,$$

when G is diminished continuously the roots of the equation $p = 0$ increase continuously, (p and $\frac{dp}{ds}$ retaining the same values for $s = 0$). We have then for this particular value of ω

$$\omega'' + \frac{\omega}{RR'} = \frac{\omega}{k^2};$$

but, since ω is zero at the limits, we have also

$$\int\left(\omega''^2 - \frac{\omega^2}{RR'}\right) ds = -\int \omega\left(\omega'' + \frac{\omega}{RR'}\right) ds;$$

therefore

$$\int\left(\omega''^2 - \frac{\omega^2}{RR'}\right) ds = -\int \frac{\omega^2}{k^2} ds.$$

Thus the second variation of the integral $\int ds$ can become negative, and the arc AMB is neither a maximum nor a minimum between the point A and the point B. The second part of Jacobi's Theorem is thus established.

We have said above that when once Jacobi's Theorem is fully demonstrated we can give more precision to the enunciation of the results contained in the note of the 18th of June. In fact we can say that if in any convex surface the product RR' of the principal radii of curvature is less than the constant a^2, the shortest distance from one point to another upon the surface will always be less than πa. Hence it follows that every convex surface in which the principal radii of curvature do not become infinite is necessarily a closed surface.

295. Although so many proofs have been given of Jacobi's theorems that it may appear superfluous to present others, yet the following proofs are of interest as they depend on the principles of the Calculus of Variations itself. They were published in an article entitled *Observations on Jacobi's Memoir on the Calculus of Variations*, by E. Heine, in Crelle's Mathematical Journal, Vol. 54, 1857, pages 68—71. They will occupy our next two articles.

296. The proposition which Jacobi published in the 17th volume of Crelle's Journal and which was proved by Lebesgue and by Delaunay in the 6th volume of Liouville's Journal may be demonstrated also, without much trouble, in the following way, which depends on very different principles.

Let A be any given function of x, u any function of x, and let u', u'', ... denote the differential coefficients of u with respect to x. Put

$$2Z = (-1)^n \int A u^{(n)} u^{(n)} dx \dots\dots\dots\dots\dots (1),$$

where $u^{(n)}$ stands for $\dfrac{d^n u}{dx^n}$; then

$$\delta Z = (-1)^n \int A u^{(n)} \delta u^{(n)} dx.$$

Now by integrating by parts in the ordinary way δZ can be separated into two portions, namely, one which is free from the integral sign, and which we will call L, and another portion which remains under the integral sign, namely,

$$\int \frac{d^n (A u^{(n)})}{dx^n} \delta u\, dx.$$

Let y denote any given function of x, and put $u = yt$, so that $\delta u = y \delta t$; thus

$$\delta Z = L + \int y \frac{d^n (A u^{(n)})}{dx^n} \delta t\, dx \dots\dots\dots\dots\dots (2).$$

Now we must obtain an equivalent *value* for δZ if we first put yt for u in (1), and then effect the variation; the *form* however of the expression for δZ will differ from that in (2); and this difference in form accompanied with equivalence of value will give a proof of Jacobi's Theorem.

Put yt for u, then $u^{(n)}$ takes the form

$$at^{(n)} + a_1 t^{(n-1)} + \dots + a_{n-1}t' + a_n t,$$

where a, a_1, … are simple functions of y and therefore functions of x. Thus $Au^{(n)}u^{(n)}$ will consist of a series which we may denote by $\Sigma \beta t^{(m)} t^{(p)}$ where the indices m and p may take all values between 0 and n, and the functions denoted by β will be like a, a_1, …, given functions of x. Put this expression for $Au^{(n)}u^{(n)}$ in (1), then we shall shew that $2Z$ can be put in the form

$$2Z = M + \int (C_0 u - C_1 t't + C_2 t''t' - \dots \pm C_n t^{(n-1)}t^{(n)})\,dx \dots\dots (3),$$

where M contains no integral sign, and C_0, C_1, … are given functions of x.

For $\Sigma \int \beta t^{(m)} t^{(p)} dx$ consists partly of terms for which $m = p$, which thus have already the form in (3), and partly of terms in which m and p are different. Suppose then p greater than m, and first let $p = m + 1$; for such terms

$$\int \beta t^{(m)}t^{(p)} dx = \int \beta t^{(m)}t^{(m+1)} dx$$

$$= \frac{\beta t^{(m)}t^{(m)}}{2} - \int \frac{\beta}{2}\, t^{(m)}t^{(m)}\, dx,$$

and thus we obtain again terms of the form in (3). Next suppose $p - m$ greater than unity; then by using the following formula

$$\int \beta t^{(m)}t^{(p)} dx = \beta t^{(m)}t^{(p-1)} - \int \beta' t^{(m)}t^{(p-1)} dx - \int \beta t^{(m+1)}t^{(p-1)} dx,$$

as often as necessary, we shall obtain terms in which the indices of t are either equal or differ by unity; and thus finally we obtain terms of the form in (3).

Now take the variation of Z expressed as in (3); then by the ordinary formulæ of the Calculus of Variations the term in δZ which remains under the integral sign is

$$\int \left\{ C_0 t + \frac{d\,(C_1 t')}{dx} + \frac{d^2\,(C_2 t'')}{dx^2} + \dots + \frac{d^n\,(C_n t^{(n)})}{dx^n} \right\} \delta t\, dx \dots\dots (4).$$

The expression (4) must therefore be equal to the integral in (2); thus

$$y\frac{d^{n}(A_{n}u^{(n)})}{dx^{n}} = C_{0}t + \frac{d(C_{1}t')}{dx} + \frac{d^{2}(C_{2}t'')}{dx^{2}} + \ldots + \frac{d^{n}(C_{n}t^{(n)})}{dx^{n}} \ldots (5).$$

The quantity C_{0} is equal to $y\,\dfrac{d^{n}(Ay^{(n)})}{dx^{n}}$. For since $u = yt$, we have

$$u^{(n)} = y^{(n)}t + \frac{n}{1}y^{(n-1)}t' + \ldots;$$

thus the term

$$y\frac{d^{n}(Ay^{(n)})}{dx^{n}}$$

is the only term which can contribute any portion to $C_{0}t$, and thus obviously

$$C_{0}t = yt\,\frac{d^{n}(Ay^{(n)})}{dx^{n}}.$$

We can now prove Jacobi's Theorem.

Let
$$U = A_{0}u + \frac{d(A_{1}u')}{dx} + \ldots + \frac{d^{n}(A_{n}u^{(n)})}{dx^{n}},$$

where A_{0}, A_{1}, ... are given functions of x. Put $u = yt$ where y is a given function of x; then from what has been proved

$$yU = B_{0}t + \frac{d(B_{1}t')}{dx} + \ldots\ldots + \frac{d^{n}(B_{n}t^{(n)})}{dx^{n}},$$

where B_{0}, B_{1}, ... are known functions of x, like C_{0}, C_{1}, ... were.

Also
$$B_{0} = y\left\{A_{0}y + \frac{d(A_{1}y)}{dx} + \ldots + \frac{d^{n}(A_{n}y^{(n)})}{dx^{n}}\right\};$$

thus when y is so chosen that it is an integral of the differential equation $U = 0$, we have $B_{0} = 0$; and then

$$\int yUdx = B_{1}t' + \frac{d(B_{2}t'')}{dx} + \ldots + \frac{d^{n-1}(B_{n}t^{(n)})}{dx^{n-1}},$$

as Jacobi's Theorem asserts.

Remark. In order practically to determine the values of B_{1}, B_{2}, ... which do not come into consideration in Jacobi's memoir, the method may be modified by first integrating by parts and thus reducing $\int A v^{(m)} u^{(n)} dx$ to $\int u \dfrac{d^n (A u^{(m)})}{dx^n} dx$. Now put ty for u, and then we have to consider integrals of the form $\int \beta t\, t^{(n)} dx$, and not as before integrals of the form $\int \beta t^{(m)} t^{(n)} dx$.

297. Jacobi published another proposition in his Memoir, of which Delaunay has given a long demonstration in the place already named. This is the proposition;

$$\text{let} \quad J = \int f(x, y, y', \dots y^{(m)})\, dx,$$

then δJ consists of a part free from the integral sign together with the integral $\int V \delta y\, dx$, where

$$V = f(y) - \frac{df'(y)}{dx} + \dots \pm \frac{d^n f(y^{(n)})}{dx^n}.$$

This is well known; then Jacobi asserts that δV may be put in the form

$$A \delta y + \frac{d(A_1 \delta y)}{dx} + \dots + \frac{d^n (A_n \delta y^{(n)})}{dx^n} = W \dots\dots\dots\dots(6).$$

We proceed to prove this. Let δ and θ be symbols of variation which are independent of each other; then the double variation $\delta \theta J$ will be equal to

$$\Sigma \int f''(y^{(m)}, y^{(p)}) (\delta y^{(m)} \theta y^{(p)} + \theta y^{(m)} \delta y^{(p)})\, dx \dots\dots\dots (7),$$

where the sign of summation refers to all values of m and p which are comprised between 0 and n. But on the one hand this expression must be of the form

$$L + \int \delta V \theta y\, dx;$$

for if we vary J with the symbol θ we should obtain an integrated part and the unintegrated part $\int V \theta y\, dx$; and if we now vary the result with the symbol δ we obtain for the unintegrated part $\int \delta V \theta y\, dx$.

Moreover the expression given above for $\delta\theta J$ can be put in the form

$$M + \int (A\,\delta y\,\theta y - A_1\,\delta y'\,\theta y' + \ldots \pm A_m\,\delta y^{(m)}\,\theta y^{(m)})\,dx \ldots\ldots (\theta),$$

as we shall shew presently. Now by the ordinary method of integrating by parts the unintegrated part of the last expression is found to be $\int W\,\theta y\,dx$; and thus

$$\delta V = W,$$

which was to be proved.

We have then only to shew that $\delta\theta J$ really has the form (θ). The terms in (7) for which $m = p$ have already the required form; suppose then p greater than m, and first let $p = m + 1$. Then it is plain that by single integration

$$\int \beta\,(\delta y^{(m)}\,\theta y^{(m-1)} + \delta y^{(m-1)}\,\theta y^{(m)})\,dx$$

is referred to the form

$$\int \beta'\,\delta y^{(m)}\,\theta y^{(m)}\,dx.$$

If p be greater than $m + 1$, then by single integration we make

$$\int \beta\,(\delta y^{(m)}\,\theta y^{(p)} + \delta y^{(p)}\,\theta y^{(m)})\,dx$$

depend on

$$\int \beta\,(\delta y^{(m+1)}\,\theta y^{(p-1)} + \delta y^{(p-1)}\,\theta y^{(m+1)})\,dx$$

and

$$\int \beta'\,(\delta y^{(m)}\,\theta y^{(p-1)} + \delta y^{(p-1)}\,\theta y^{(m)})\,dx;$$

and by proceeding thus we shall ultimately arrive at the form in (θ).

298. There is an article by Minding entitled, *On the transformations which serve for distinguishing maxima from minima in the Calculus of Variations.* It was published in Crelle's Mathematical Journal, Vol. 55. 1858, pages 300—309. The object of

this article is to demonstrate two theorems used in Jacobi's memoir; namely, the theorem in Art. 222 in the form in which it is given in Arts. 229 and 231, and the theorem respecting the form of δV in Art. 223. The demonstrations are somewhat complex, but perfectly satisfactory; as they consist however almost entirely of ordinary algebraical transformations it will be unnecessary to enter upon them here.

209. We will close this chapter by giving two examples of the investigation of a maximum or minimum value.

For the first example we will apply Jacobi's method to the expression $\int V dx$ where $V = \left(p + \dfrac{y}{x}\right)^2 x + (2c + cy^2) x$. This is in fact the example given on page 108; the quantities which were there denoted by r, p, $\dfrac{dp}{dr}$ are now denoted respectively by x, y, p. The expression of the second order which determines whether there is a maximum or a minimum is here

$$\int \left\{ x\,(\delta p)^2 + 2\delta p \delta y + \left(cx + \frac{1}{x}\right)(\delta y)^2 \right\} dx.$$

Let
$$\beta = cxy - x\frac{d}{dx}\left(p + \frac{y}{x}\right),$$

therefore
$$\delta\beta = cx\delta y - x\frac{d}{dx}\left(\delta p + \frac{\delta y}{x}\right);$$

therefore
$$\int \delta\beta\,\delta y\,dx = \int cx\,(\delta y)^2\,dx - \int x\delta y\,\frac{d}{dx}\left(\delta p + \frac{\delta y}{x}\right) dx$$

$$= -x\delta y\left(\delta p + \frac{\delta y}{x}\right) + \int cx\,(\delta y)^2\,dx + \int \left(\delta p + \frac{\delta y}{x}\right)\frac{d}{dx}\,(x\delta y)\,dx$$

$$= -x\delta y\left(\delta p + \frac{\delta y}{x}\right) + \int \left\{ x\,(\delta p)^2 + 2\delta p\delta y + \left(cx + \frac{1}{x}\right)(\delta y)^2 \right\} dx.$$

Thus we see, since the limits are supposed fixed, that the terms which we have to examine can be put in the form $\int \delta\beta\,\delta y\,dx$; this is in accordance with Jacobi's theory.

Now $\int \delta\beta\, \delta y\, dx = \int u\,\delta\beta\, \dfrac{\delta y}{u}\, dx$, where u is at present undetermined; also if u be properly determined we shall have

$$\int u\,\delta\beta\, dx = - u^2 x \frac{d}{dx}\left(\frac{\delta y}{u}\right);$$

for this only requires that

$$u\left(x\omega + \frac{1}{x}\right)\delta y - u\frac{d}{dx}\left(x\frac{d\delta y}{dx}\right) = -\frac{d}{dx}\left\{u^2 x\frac{d}{dx}\left(\frac{\delta y}{u}\right)\right\},$$

$$= -\frac{d}{dx}\left\{ux\frac{d\delta y}{dx} - x\delta y\frac{du}{dx}\right\},$$

$$= -u\frac{d}{dx}\left(x\frac{d\delta y}{dx}\right) - x\frac{d\delta y}{dx}\frac{du}{dx} + \frac{d}{dx}\left(x\delta y\frac{du}{dx}\right);$$

that is, we must have

$$u\left(x\omega + \frac{1}{x}\right) = \frac{d}{dx}\left(x\frac{du}{dx}\right).$$

Suppose then that u is taken to satisfy this differential equation; then we get

$$\int \delta\beta\, \delta y\, dx = \int u^2 x\left\{\frac{d}{dx}\left(\frac{\delta y}{u}\right)\right\}^2 dx;$$

neglecting the terms free from the integral sign, which vanish at the limits if no infinite quantities occur.

Now u is such a quantity that if put for δy in $\delta\beta$ we get $\delta\beta = 0$; hence the value of u is known by Jacobi's theory; see Art. 220. The value of y which makes $\delta\int V dx = 0$ is in the present case to be obtained by finding $\dfrac{dz}{dr}$ from the value of z on page 108, and then changing r into x. Thus it is

$$A\frac{d}{dx}\int_0^\pi \epsilon^{-x\sqrt{-1}\cos\omega}\, d\omega + B\frac{d}{dx}\int_0^\pi \epsilon^{-x\sqrt{-1}\cos\omega}\log(x\sin^2\omega)\, d\omega;$$

and therefore the value of u is in the present case of the same form, with A and B replaced by new constants. The second constant must be supposed zero in order that u may not be infinite when $x = 0$; hence finally

$$u = a \int_0^x e^{-x\sqrt{(i-s)}} \cos s\, ds,$$

where a is an arbitrary constant.

This value of u however *vanishes* when $x = 0$, so that the expression under the integral sign in the value of $\int \delta\beta\, \delta y\, dx$ becomes *infinite* when $x = 0$. Hence we are not certain that in this case we really have obtained a minimum.

300. The next example is intended to draw attention to the case in which we have to discriminate between the maximum and minimum of a function when the limits are not fixed. Writers on the calculus of variations appear frequently to intimate that the fact of the limits being variable does not really render the problem more difficult; this however does not seem correct.

Let us consider the problem of the brachistochrone in which the moving particle is to pass from one given curve to another, starting with an assigned velocity. Take the axis of x vertically downwards; let h be the height due to the initial velocity, x_1 and x_2 the abscissæ of the starting-point and the final point respectively. Then we have to find the minimum value of $\int_{x_1}^{x_2} V dx$, where $V = \dfrac{\sqrt{(1 + p^2)}}{\sqrt{(h + x - x_1)}}$ and $p = \dfrac{dy}{dx}$. We shall treat the problem in what seems the best way; we shall attribute no *variation* to the independent variable x but shall obtain the requisite generality in our formulæ by changing the limits of the integration. Suppose then that p receives the variation δp, and that the limits x_1 and x_2 become respectively $x_1 + dx_1$ and $x_2 + dx_2$. In consequence of the change in p and x, a change takes place in V, and to the second order V becomes

$$V + \frac{dV}{dp}\, \delta p + \frac{dV}{dx_1}\, dx_1 + \frac{1}{2} \frac{d^2 V}{dp^2} (\delta p)^2 + \frac{d^2 V}{dp\, dx_1}\, \delta p\, dx_1 + \frac{1}{2} \frac{d^2 V}{dx_1^2} (dx_1)^2.$$

Hence the variation of the integral is

$$\int_{x_1 + dx_1}^{x_2 + dx_2} V dx - \int_{x_1}^{x_2} V dx$$

$$+ \int \left\{ \frac{dV}{dp} \delta p + \frac{dV}{dx_1} dx_1 + \frac{1}{2} \frac{d^2 V}{dp^2} (\delta p)^2 + \frac{d^2 V}{dp\, dx_1} \delta p\, dx_1 + \frac{1}{2} \frac{d^2 V}{dx_1^2} (dx_1)^2 \right\} dx,$$

the limits in the last line being $x_1 + dx_1$ and $x_2 + dx_2$.

Now we observe that if in an integral $\int_{x_1}^{x_2} \phi(x)\, dx$ the upper limit is increased by dx_2 the integral is increased by

$$dx_2\, \phi(x_2) + \frac{1}{2} (dx_2)^2 \phi'(x_2),$$

to the second order; and if the lower limit is increased by dx_1 the integral is *diminished* by

$$dx_1\, \phi(x_1) + \frac{1}{2} (dx_1)^2 \phi'(x_1),$$

to the second order. Thus the above variation becomes to the second order

$$V_2\, dx_2 - V_1\, dx_1 + \frac{1}{2} V_2' (dx_2)^2 - \frac{1}{2} V_1' (dx_1)^2$$

$$+ \int_{x_1 + dx_1}^{x_2 + dx_2} \left\{ \frac{dV}{dp} \delta p + \frac{dV}{dx_1} dx_1 \right\} dx$$

$$+ \frac{1}{2} \int_{x_1}^{x_2} \left\{ \frac{d^2 V}{dp^2} (\delta p)^2 + 2 \frac{d^2 V}{dp\, dx_1} \delta p\, dx_1 + \frac{d^2 V}{dx_1^2} (dx_1)^2 \right\} dx_1$$

where V' stands for the complete differential coefficient $\dfrac{dV}{dx}$, and the suffixes 1 and 2 indicate that x is made equal to x_1 and x_2 respectively.

By reducing the second of the above three lines the variation becomes to the second order

$$V_2\, dx_2 - V_1\, dx_1 + \frac{1}{2} V_2' (dx_2)^2 - \frac{1}{2} V_1' (dx_1)^2$$

$$+ \int_{x_1}^{x_2} \left\{ \frac{dV}{dp} \delta p + \frac{dV}{dx_1} dx_1 \right\} dx$$

$$+ \left(\frac{dV}{dp} \delta p + \frac{dV}{dx_1} dx_1 \right)_2 dx_2 - \left(\frac{dV}{dp} \delta p + \frac{dV}{dx_1} dx_1 \right)_1 dx_1$$

$$+ \frac{1}{2} \int_{x_1}^{x_2} \left\{ \frac{d^2 V}{dp^2} (\delta p)^2 + 2 \frac{d^2 V}{dp\, dx_1} \delta p\, dx_1 + \frac{d^2 V}{dx_1^2} (dx_1)^2 \right\} dx.$$

The term $\int \frac{dV}{dp} \, \delta p \, dx$ of the variation becomes by integration by parts

$$\left(\frac{dV}{dp}\right)_2 \delta y_2 - \left(\frac{dV}{dp}\right)_1 \delta y_1 - \int \frac{d}{dx}\left(\frac{dV}{dp}\right) \delta y \, dx.$$

Hence we infer that we must have $\frac{dV}{dp}$ equal to a constant, in order to obtain a minimum.

We have now to examine the remaining terms of the variation. We shall first transform δy_2 and δy_1.

Suppose $y = \chi(x)$ the equation to the upper limiting curve, and $y = \psi(x)$ the equation to the lower limiting curve. Then the co-ordinates x_2, y_2 satisfy the latter equation, and so also must the co-ordinates of the new extreme point which is obtained by changing the curve and the limits. The abscissa of the new extreme point is $x_2 + dx_2$; the ordinate of the new extreme point will be found by changing x_2 into $x_2 + dx_2$ in the function $y_2 + \delta y_2$, so that it will be

$$y + \delta y + dx_2 \frac{d(y + \delta y)}{dx} + \frac{1}{2}(dx_2)^2 \frac{d^2(y + \delta y)}{dx^2} + \ldots$$

in which we must suppose x put equal to x_2. Thus to the second order the ordinate in question is

$$\left\{ y + \delta y + dx_2 \frac{d(y + \delta y)}{dx} + \frac{1}{2}(dx_2)^2 \frac{d^2 y}{dx^2} \right\}_2 ;$$

and this must be equal to $\psi(x_2 + dx_2)$ estimated to the second order. Hence we get

$$\delta y_2 = \left\{ \psi'(x) - \frac{dy}{dx} \right\}_2 dx_2 + \frac{1}{2}\left\{ \psi''(x) - \frac{d^2 y}{dx^2} \right\}_2 (dx_2)^2 - \delta p_2 \, dx_2.$$

A similar expression holds for δy_1.

With these values of δy_1 and δy_2 we shall find that the variation reduces to the following terms of the first order,

$$\left(\frac{dV}{dp}\right)_2 \left\{ \psi'(x) - \frac{dy}{dx} \right\}_2 dx_2 - \left(\frac{dV}{dp}\right)_1 \left\{ \chi'(x) - \frac{dy}{dx} \right\}_1 dx_1$$

$$+ V_2 \, dx_2 - V_1 \, dx_1 + dx_1 \int_{x_1}^{x_2} \frac{dV}{dx_1} \, dx ;$$

together with the following terms of the second order,

$$\frac{1}{2}\left(\frac{dV}{dp}\right)_2\left(\psi''(x)-\frac{d^2y}{dx^2}\right)_2(dx_2)^2-\left(\frac{dV}{dp}\right)_2\delta p_2\,dx_2+\frac{1}{2}V_2''(dx_2)^2$$

$$-\frac{1}{2}\left(\frac{dV}{dp}\right)_1\left(\chi''(x)-\frac{d^2y}{dx^2}\right)_1(dx_1)^2+\left(\frac{dV}{dp}\right)_1\delta p_1\,dx_1-\frac{1}{2}V_1''(dx_1)^2$$

$$+\left(\frac{dV}{dp}\delta p+\frac{dV}{dx_1}dx_1\right)_2 dx_2-\left(\frac{dV}{dp}\delta p+\frac{dV}{dx_1}dx_1\right)_1 dx_1$$

$$+\frac{1}{2}\int_{x_1}^{x_2}\left\{\frac{d^2V}{dp^2}(\delta p)^2+2\frac{d^2V}{dp\,dx_1}\delta p\,dx_1+\frac{d^2V}{dx_1^2}(dx_1)^2\right\}dx.$$

The interpretation of the terms of the first order is well known, but we will give it here to render our investigation complete.

Equate to zero the coefficient of dx_2; thus

$$\left\{\frac{dV}{dp}\psi'(x)-\frac{dV}{dp}\frac{dy}{dx}+V\right\}_2=0;$$

substitute the values of V and $\dfrac{dV}{dp}$, and we obtain

$$\left\{\frac{p\psi'(x)+1}{\sqrt{(1+p^2)}\sqrt{(h+x-x_1)}}\right\}_2=0.$$

Thus $[p\psi'(x)+1]_2=0$, which shews that the curve described cuts the lower limiting curve at right angles.

Next equate to zero the coefficient of dx_1; thus

$$\left\{\frac{dV}{dp}\chi'(x)-\frac{dV}{dp}\frac{dy}{dx}+V\right\}_1-\int_{x_1}^{x_2}\frac{dV}{dx_1}dx=0.$$

Now $\dfrac{dV}{dx_1}=\dfrac{\sqrt{(1+p^2)}}{2\,(h+x-x_1)^{\frac{3}{2}}}$, and by supposition $\dfrac{dV}{dp}$ is equal to

a constant, that is $\dfrac{p}{\sqrt{(1+p^2)}\sqrt{(h+x-x_1)}}=\dfrac{1}{\sqrt{a}}$ say;

hence $\qquad p^2=\dfrac{h+x-x_1}{a-h-x+x_1}$, $\quad 1+p^2=\dfrac{a}{a-h-x+x_1}$.

Thus $\qquad \dfrac{dV}{dx_1}=\dfrac{\sqrt{a}}{2\,(a-h-x+x_1)^{\frac{1}{2}}(h+x-x_1)^{2}}$;

and
$$\int \frac{dV}{dx_i}\,dx = -\frac{\sqrt{(a-h-x+x_i)}}{\sqrt{a}\,\sqrt{(h+x-x_i)}} = -\frac{1}{p\sqrt{a}}.$$

Hence
$$\int_{x_i}^{x_2} \frac{dV}{dx_i}\,dx = -\frac{1}{\sqrt{a}}\left(\frac{1}{p_2}-\frac{1}{p_i}\right).$$

Thus our equation becomes

$$\left\{\frac{p\chi'(x)+1}{\sqrt{(1+p^2)}\,\sqrt{(h+x-x_i)}}\right\}_i + \frac{1}{\sqrt{a}}\left(\frac{1}{p_2}-\frac{1}{p_i}\right)=0,$$

that is
$$\frac{\chi'(x_i)}{\sqrt{a}}+\frac{1}{p_i\sqrt{a}}+\frac{1}{\sqrt{a}}\left(\frac{1}{p_2}-\frac{1}{p_i}\right)=0.$$

Therefore $\chi'(x_i)\,p_2 + 1 = 0$, and thus the tangents to the limiting curves at the points where the described curve meets them are parallel.

We have now remaining in the variation only terms of the second order; by reduction they become

$$\frac{1}{2}\left(\frac{dV}{dp}\right)_2\left\{\psi''(x)-\frac{d^2y}{dx^2}\right\}_2 (dx_2)^2 - \frac{1}{2}\left(\frac{dV}{dp}\right)_1\left\{\chi''(x)-\frac{d^2y}{dx^2}\right\}_1 (dx_1)^2$$

$$+\frac{1}{2}\,V_2'(dx_2)^2 - \frac{1}{2}\,V_1'(dx_1)^2 + \left(\frac{dV}{dx_i}\right)_2 dx_i\,dx_2 - \left(\frac{dV}{dx_i}\right)_1 (dx_1)^2$$

$$+\frac{1}{2}\int_{x_1}^{x_2}\left\{\frac{d^2V}{dp^2}(\delta p)^2 + 2\frac{d^2V}{dp\,dx_i}\,\delta p\,dx_i + \frac{d^2V}{dx_i^2}(dx_i)^2\right\}dx.$$

Now it is by no means evident that the above expression is necessarily positive, so that we are not sure of the existence of a minimum as asserted by Legendre; see Art. 203. Nor do Jacobi's investigations give us here any assistance. The above expression shews that *cæteris paribus* the suppositions that $\psi''(x_2)$ is positive and that $\chi''(x_1)$ is negative are favourable to the existence of a minimum. This makes the lower limiting curve convex to the axis of x and the upper limiting curve concave to the axis of x at the points where the described curve respectively meets them; and it is obvious from a figure that these circumstances are favourable to the existence of a minimum.

CHAPTER XII.

MISCELLANEOUS MEMOIRS.

301. THE present chapter contains an account in chronological order of various articles, memoirs, and treatises, connected with the Calculus of Variations.

302. Poisson, *Mémoires de l'Institut*, 1812, page 224.

Poisson here finds the differential equation to the surface of constant area which makes $\iint \sqrt{(1+p^2+q^2)} \left(\frac{1}{\rho}+\frac{1}{\rho'}\right)^2 dx\, dy$ a minimum, where ρ and ρ' are the principal radii of curvature at the point (x, y, z) of the surface. He adds that the equation obtained would also be obtained if we required that $\iint \sqrt{(1+p^2+q^2)} \left(\frac{1}{\rho}-\frac{1}{\rho'}\right)^2 dx\, dy$ should be a minimum, or that $\iint \sqrt{(1+p^2+q^2)} \left(\frac{1}{\rho}+\frac{1}{\rho'}\right) dx\, dy$ should be a minimum; for $\iint \delta \frac{\sqrt{(1+p^2+q^2)}}{\rho\rho'} dx\, dy$ vanishes, so far as the terms under the sign of double integration are concerned. There are two misprints in Poisson's remarks, but there can be no doubt that his meaning is what we have here given.

303. Rodrigue. *Bulletin des Sciences par la Société Philomatique de Paris*, 1815, pages 34—36.

This paper is on certain properties of double integrals and of the radii of curvature of surfaces. It is stated that the variation of the double integral $\iint \phi (p, q) (rt - s^2) dx\, dy$ contains only *terms relative to the limits.* This may be verified without much difficulty; that is, we can shew that the part of the variation under the double integral sign is identically zero. Hence we see that this statement is an extension of that quoted in the preceding article from Poisson.

304. Poisson. *Bulletin des Sciences par la Société Philomatique de Paris*, 1816, pages 82—86.

This paper is on the Calculus of Variations with respect to multiple integrals. Poisson refers to the difficulty which Lacroix had found in the variation of a double integral, which led him to infer that δx must be supposed a function of x only and δy a function of y only; see Art. 40. Lagrange adopted the same hypothesis as *sufficient* for his purpose without asserting its *necessity;* see *Mécanique Analytique*, 3rd edition, Vol. I. page 92. Poisson removes the difficulty by giving the correct expressions for $\delta x'$, $\delta x_{,}$, ... instead of those given by Lacroix. The substance of this paper was given by Lacroix in his third volume, pages 717—720; and it was afterwards incorporated by Poisson in his memoir on the Calculus of Variations. See Art. 102.

305. Choisy. *Essai Historique sur le problème des maximums et minimums et sur ses applications à la mécanique par J. D. Choisy,* Geneva, 1823.

This work consists of 66 quarto pages. It is divided into two parts. The first part is on the abstract problem of maxima and minima; this contains five chapters; (1) Preliminary considerations, (2) Elementary and synthetical methods, (3) Analytical methods up to those of the Bernouillis inclusive, (4) Methods of Euler, (5) Methods of Lagrange. The second part is on the applications of the theory of maxima and minima to Mechanics; this contains six chapters; (1) On the use of indeterminate coefficients in the applications of the Calculus of Variations to Mechanics, (2) On the principle of least action, (3) On the Cycloid, (4) On the Catenary, (5) On elastic curves, (6) On equilibrium.

At the end of the work is a list of authors on the subject; this list does not seem to contain anything of importance in addition to the usual references.

The present writer has never seen Choisy's work ; for the above notice of it he is indebted to a friend, who at his request examined the copy in the Bodleian Library at Oxford.

300.   C. H. Graeffe.   *Commentatio Historium Calculi Variationum inde ab origine Calculi Differentialis atque Integralis usque ad nostra tempora complectens.*

This essay obtained a prize from the University of Gottingen in 1825 ; the adjudicators however state that it is defective in giving so little information on the more recent investigations relating to the Calculus of Variations.   The author in his preface states his intention of going further into the subject in a future essay ; this intention however does not appear to have been ever carried out.

The essay occupies 60 quarto pages ; it traces the history of the subject from its origin until the time of Lagrange.   The essay thus goes over the same ground as the well-known work of Woodhouse. It is however not so full as the work of Woodhouse ; it sometimes merely states that certain results were obtained, without explaining the method by which they were obtained.

The essay does not bear upon the subject of the present volume, because it scarcely alludes to anything after the works of Lagrange. A few lines are given to Dirksen, a few to Ohm, and a few to Buquoy ; the latter two are not highly estimated by Graeffe. Thus he says : "Conatus quos Ohm ad hunc calculum stabiliendum publicavit parvi momenti sunt...," and "... ad calculi variationum principia fundanda Comitem de Buquoy etiam, quanquam frustra, vires tentasse ; non est tamen meum propositum hos conatus scientiam non augentes accurate explicare."   Graeffe refers to Lacroix in the following terms : "... inter eos qui libros quibus doctrinae mathescos exponuntur perscripserunt, Lacroix calculum variationum diligentissime tractasse."

These extracts are all taken from the last two pages of Graeffe's work.   The present writer has never seen the work of Buquoy to which Graeffe refers ; its title appears to be *Eine eigene Darstellung der Grundlehren der Variations-rechnung,* and the date 1812 is ascribed to it in a bookseller's catalogue.

307. Minding. *Crelle's Mathematical Journal*, Vol. 5, pages 297—304, 1830. This article is entitled *On curves of shortest perimeter on curved surfaces;* it contains a discussion of a problem proposed in the third volume of Crelle's Journal by Crelle himself. The problem is to find the shortest curve which can be drawn on a given surface so as to include a given area. Minding obtains the following results. If the given surface be a sphere the required curve is a plane curve, and therefore a circle. He obtains the required curve when the surface is a right cone. He remarks that if the surface be any developable surface, the required curve must be such as will become a circle when the surface is developed; this follows from the known fact that of all plane figures a circle is that of least perimeter which bounds a given plane area.

Minding also establishes the following result. Whatever be the surface the curve required has this property; the cosine of the angle between the osculating plane of the curve at any point and the tangent plane of the surface at that point is proportional to the radius of curvature of the curve at that point. This property has since been proved by other writers who have discussed the problem, namely, Delaunay, Bonnet, Jellett, and Schellbach.

The last five pages of the article are occupied with an investigation respecting another property of the curve; Minding appears to have here fallen into an error, and some detail will be required to illustrate the point.

A geodesic line is a curve drawn on a surface so that at every point its osculating plane contains the normal to the surface at that point. Now suppose a series of geodesic lines starting from a common point on a surface, and let a series of curves be drawn cutting these geodesic lines at right angles. The latter curves may be called *geodesic circles*, because it can be proved that the length of the geodesic line drawn from the common starting-point to any point of one of these curves is constant. This property of a *geodesic circle* from which its name is derived is proved by Minding, although he does not use this name. The name is used in Price's *Infinitesimal Calculus*, Vol. II. and the property is there proved; see also Bonnet's Memoir on the general theory of surfaces in the *Journal de l'Ecole Polytechnique*, Cahier 32, page 74.

The property then which Minding considers that he proves is that the curve of least perimeter which can be drawn on a given surface so as to include a given area is a *geodesic circle*. This is in fact true for any *developable surface* in virtue of the remark already made; but it does not appear to be generally true. It is however remarkable that Bonnet and Schellbach, who both seem to allude to Minding's solution, take no notice of this part of it.

We will indicate the grounds for considering this part of Minding's article to be erroneous. Let ρ be the radius of curvature at any point of the required curve, θ the angle which the osculating plane at any point of the curve makes with the tangent plane to the surface at that point. Then the characteristic property of the required curve is that $\dfrac{\cos\theta}{\rho} =$ a constant. If then Minding's result were correct it would follow that this property must necessarily belong to a geodesic circle. Suppose, for example, that we consider an ellipsoid; let the semiaxes be a, b, c in descending order of magnitude; and suppose we require the curve of least perimeter which can be drawn on the surface so as to enclose an area equal to half that of the ellipsoid. It would appear obvious that the required curve must in this case be the ellipse which has b and c for its semiaxes; for this curve satisfies the condition $\dfrac{\cos\theta}{\rho} =$ a constant, since $\cos\theta = 0$, and it encloses an area equal to half that of the ellipsoid. It is however also obvious that this curve cannot be a geodesic circle, for if it were, the pole of the circle must be the extremity of the longest axis of the ellipsoid, and the lengths of geodesic lines from this point to the ellipse in question are not all equal.

We will however examine Minding's solution. Let a series of geodesic lines be drawn on a given surface all starting from a fixed point. Let s denote the length of a portion of one of these measured from the fixed point, ψ the angle which the selected geodesic line makes at starting with some fixed line on the surface;

thus s and ψ serve as co-ordinates to determine a point on the surface.

Now let ϕ be such a function of s and ψ that $\phi d\psi$ represents the length of an element of the geodesic circle which passes through the point (s, ψ); then ϕ will be a known function because the surface is supposed a given surface. With this notation it will readily follow that the length of the perimeter of any curve is expressed by the integral $\int \sqrt{\phi^2(d\psi)^2 + (ds)^2}$ between suitable limits; and the area of the enclosed surface is expressed by $\iint \phi d\psi \, ds$ between suitable limits. Hence by the usual considerations we have to find the minimum of

$$h \int \sqrt{\phi^2(d\psi)^2 + (ds)^2} + \iint \phi d\psi \, ds,$$

where h is a constant.

Minding then proceeds thus. We have for determining the curve of shortest perimeter the equation

$$h\delta \int \sqrt{\phi^2(d\psi)^2 + (ds)^2} + \delta \iint \phi d\psi \, ds = 0.$$

For brevity put $dP^2 = \phi^2(d\psi)^2 + (ds)^2$, and suppose that only ψ varies since it is known that the two equations which are obtained by varying s and ψ must coincide; thus we obtain

$$\int \left\{ \frac{h\phi(d\psi)^2}{dP} \delta\phi + \frac{h\phi^2 d\psi}{dP} \delta d\psi + \phi \, ds \, \delta\psi \right\} = 0;$$

this gives the following as the differential equation of the curve of least perimeter,

$$h\phi \left(\frac{d\phi}{d\psi}\right) \frac{d\psi}{dP} d\psi - hd \left(\frac{\phi^2 d\psi}{dP}\right) + \phi \, ds = 0.$$

This equation will be satisfied by the supposition $ds = 0$, as it is easy to see. For it follows from this supposition that $dP = \phi d\psi$, so that the differential equation becomes $\left(\frac{d\phi}{d\psi}\right) d\psi - d\phi = 0$, and this is identically true, whether ϕ depends on ψ or, as in some cases may happen, is independent of ψ.

This is Minding's process. It appears from this process that when we take the variation of the proposed expression, the term remaining under the integral sign is

$$\int \left\{ h\phi\left(\frac{d\phi}{d\psi}\right) \frac{d\psi}{d\psi^2} \frac{d\psi}{ds} - h\frac{d}{ds}\left(\phi^2 \frac{d\psi}{d\psi^2}\right) + \phi \right\} \delta\psi \, ds.$$

Hence the equation for determining the required curve is

$$h\phi\left(\frac{d\phi}{d\psi}\right) \frac{d\psi}{d\psi^2} \frac{d\psi}{ds} - h\frac{d}{ds}\left(\phi^2 \frac{d\psi}{d\psi^2}\right) + \phi = 0.$$

Minding in effect multiplies the expression on the left-hand side of this equation by $\frac{ds}{d\psi}$, and then puts $\frac{ds}{d\psi} = 0$ as a solution. This is of course unsound.

We may put the solution in a slightly different form. Minding really takes s as the independent variable; it is however more natural to take ψ as the independent variable. The double integral $\iint \phi \, d\psi \, ds$ may be reduced to a single integral by supposing the integration $\int \phi \, ds$ effected; denote $\int \phi \, ds$ by v, where v will be a function of s and ψ. We have then to find the minimum of

$$\int \left\{ h\sqrt{\phi^2 + \left(\frac{ds}{d\psi}\right)^2} + v \right\} d\psi.$$

Hence in the usual way we obtain

$$\frac{dv}{ds} + \frac{h\phi\dfrac{d\phi}{ds}}{\sqrt{\phi^2 + \left(\dfrac{ds}{d\psi}\right)^2}} - \frac{d}{d\psi}\frac{h\dfrac{ds}{d\psi}}{\sqrt{\phi^2 + \left(\dfrac{ds}{d\psi}\right)^2}} = 0.$$

Now this equation cannot be generally satisfied by supposing $\frac{ds}{d\psi} = 0$; for this supposition leads to $\frac{dv}{ds} + h\frac{d\phi}{ds} = 0$, that is, $\phi + h\frac{d\phi}{ds} = 0$; and since ϕ is a function of s and ψ this equation connects s and ψ, and shews that s is a function of ψ, so that $\frac{ds}{d\psi}$ is not zero.

308. Goldschmidt. *Determinatio superficiei minimæ rotatione curvæ data duo puncta jungentis circa datum axem ortæ.* *Auctore Benjamin Goldschmidt.* Gottingen, 1831.

This essay obtained a prize from the university of Gottingen in 1831; it occupies 32 quarto pages. The problem discussed is to find the curve joining two given points which by revolving round a given axis will generate a minimum surface. The problem is solved in three different ways by using different formulæ for the area of a surface of revolution, and the result is, as is well known, that the surface is in general that obtained by the revolution of a catenary round its base. The author then investigates the possibility of drawing a catenary which shall have a given base and pass through two given points. The conclusion is that sometimes two such catenaries can be drawn, sometimes only one, and sometimes no catenary. When no catenary can be drawn it is inferred that the surface consists of two planes formed by the revolution round the axis of the perpendiculars from the given points on the axis; these planes may be supposed connected by means of the portion of the axis which they intercept between them. There is no investigation of the terms of the second order to shew that a minimum really is obtained.

In the course of the essay some interesting properties of the catenary are noticed; thus on page 17 is given a simple geometrical method of drawing a tangent to a catenary; on page 18 it is shewn that all the curves formed by varying the parameter c in the equation $2y = c \left(e^{\frac{x}{c}} + e^{-\frac{x}{c}} \right)$ touch two straight lines passing through the origin; on page 26 is given a simple geometrical method of determining the vertices of the two catenaries which have a given axis and pass through two points equally distant from that axis.

A short account of Goldschmidt will be found in the *Monthly Notices of the Royal Astronomical Society.* Vol. 12, page 64.

309. Poisson. *Crelle's Mathematical Journal*, Vol. 8, pages 361, 362. 1832.

This article is entitled *Note on the surface of which the area between given limits is a minimum.* We give a translation of it.

One of the first applications which Lagrange made of the Cal-

culus of Variations was to determine the surface of which the area
between given limits is a minimum. This was a very favourable
example for shewing the advantage of his new calculus over the in-
genious methods which had preceded it; for it would have been
difficult to extend these methods to the maxima and minima of
double integrals, and therefore to questions concerning surfaces.
The equation which Lagrange found is, as is well known, a partial
differential equation of the second order. Monge integrated it in
a finite form, but by considerations which appeared inadmissible,
and which gave rise to long discussions between him and Laplace.
Legendre afterwards obtained the same integral by a transformation applicable to a large class of equations of the second order,
so that no doubt remained as to the correctness of the result.
(Lacroix, *Differential and Integral Calculus*, Vol. 2, page 622.)
Unfortunately no advantage could be drawn from this integral,
which involved imaginary quantities and was expressed by a
system of three equations between two auxiliary variables and the
current co-ordinates of the surface. But besides the difficulty
which results from this form of the general integral, in which it
appears, to say the least, very difficult to determine the arbitrary
functions, there is another difficulty arising from the number of
these functions which the question can admit.

In fact the problem of a minimum area comprises two distinct questions; either two closed curves are given and we require
to connect them by a zone of surface of which the area shall be
the least possible, or else only one closed curve is given and we
have to find a surface such that the area of the portion bounded
by this curve shall be a minimum. When, for example, an aper-
ture is made in the surface of a vessel which contains a fluid, the
area of the surface by which we must multiply the velocity and the
time of the movement in order to calculate the volume of the fluid
discharged is precisely the minimum area corresponding to the
second case of the problem, which thus presents a useful application.

In the first case the question and the complete integral which
has been found have the same degree of generality, and the two
given curves determine implicitly the two arbitrary functions which
this integral includes. In the second case, on the contrary, the

given curve can only serve to determine one arbitrary function. One of these functions will then remain undetermined, and the integral will thus have more generality than the question which it serves to solve. If the given curve is plane the surface required is the plane of this curve. If it is a curve of double curvature this surface is not known *à priori*, but it ought to be some definite single surface, and the problem is not solved so long as there remains anything undetermined in the equation.

In order to resolve this difficulty I have considered specially the case in which the required surface does not deviate much from a given plane. By putting the integral of the partial differential equation under a form which differs from that hitherto used, I have found that the expression of one of the current co-ordinates as a function of the other two contains terms which become infinite at a point of the minimum area, in the second of the two cases of the problem; and these must be suppressed as foreign to the problem. In the first case these terms retain a finite value through the whole extent of the zone of surface which is to be determined, so that while they are to be suppressed in the other case they are to be retained in this. By this means the expression for the ordinate of any point of the surface has in each case the degree of generality which the question requires. Then, by the method which I have used in other memoirs, all the arbitrary quantities which enter into this expression are determined, by means of the two limiting curves of the minimum zone in the first case, and by means of the single curve which bounds the minimum area in the second case.

In this manner the solution of the problem is completely finished in the two parts which it presents, and which form two distinct questions with reference to the determination of the arbitrary functions, although they depend upon the same differential equation.

The Memoir from which this note is extracted will appear in another number of this Journal.

[The memoir in question seems never to have been published.]

310. Pagani. *Crelle's Mathematical Journal*, Vol. 15, pages 81—99, 1836.

This article is entitled *Solution of a problem relating to the Calculus of Variations*. The problem considered is that which was solved by Gauss; see Chapter III. Before considering the problem Pagani gives a brief investigation of the variation of a multiple integral. He arrives at the formulæ contained in Ostrogradsky's Memoir; see Art. 126. He then gives some remarks on the integration of the expressions when the number of the variables does not exceed three. The Memoir contains nothing that will not be found in Ostrogradsky, and from its brevity it would be difficult for a student who had not access to other works on the subject.

311. Björling. *Calculi Variationum Integralium Duplicium Exercitationes. Auctore Em. Gabr. Björling.* Upsal, 1842.

This treatise contains 57 quarto pages. The author refers to the memoirs by Poisson and Ostrogradsky, and expresses his surprise that neither of these mathematicians applied his general formulæ to the question of determining the surface of minimum area. He proposes to consider this problem. He gives by way of introduction an investigation of the variation of a double integral, with some remarks on the limiting equations which must be satisfied in order that the variation may vanish. This part of the treatise is taken from Ostrogradsky. This introductory part occupies the first 19 pages.

The author then proceeds to the problem of the surface of minimum area, and he arrives at the well-known result that such a surface must be determined from the equation

$$(1 + p^2)\, t - 2pq s + (1 + q^2)\, r = 0,$$

where the usual notation is adopted. Before considering this equation generally he gives two special examples in which it is satisfied; one example is a surface of revolution, and the other a ruled surface. The discussion of these examples occupies pages 20—28. Then pages 29—50 are devoted to the solution of the general partial differential equation given above. Björling quotes Monge's solution; but by means of transforming the variables he obtains the solution under another form, which he considers more suitable than that of Monge when we have to determine the arbitrary functions involved.

The author refers for Monge's solution to Monge's *Application de
l'Analyse à la Géométrie*, and to Lacroix, *Traité du Calc. Diff. et
Intég*. Vol. 2, page 630.   Monge's result is also established in
De Morgan's *Differential and Integral Calculus*, pages 473, 474.

The last seven pages of the treatise form an appendix in which
the author briefly discusses a particular case of the problem of
determining a solid which has a maximum volume while the area of
the surface is given.

It will be seen from this account of the treatise that it contains very little which strictly belongs to the Calculus of Variations;
in fact it should rather be considered as an essay on the integration
of the partial differential equation given above.   We may observe
that the part of the treatise which relates to the integration of the
equation is reproduced by the author in an article in Grunert's
Archiv der Mathematik und Physik, Vol. 4, pages 290—315, 1844.

The following four points of interest may be noticed in the
treatise.

(1) The author before considering the general problem takes
the case of a surface of revolution ; he then arrives at the known
result that the surface must be that which is formed by the
revolution of a catenary round its base. Supposing that the
surface is to connect two given circles which have their planes
perpendicular to the axis of revolution and their centres on this
axis, he obtains equations for determining the constants involved
in the equation to the catenary. He then asserts that the surface
thus obtained is that which has the minimum area out of *all*
possible surfaces that can be drawn so as to connect the two given
circles, and not merely the minimum area out of all surfaces of
revolution. He does not explain this remark. Perhaps he means
that we are first to conclude that in the case considered the surface
must be one of revolution ; suppose, for example, we divide it into
two parts by a plane containing the axis, then if the two parts are
not symmetrical one of them will generally be of greater area than
the other, we can then replace the part which has the greater area
by a part symmetrically equal to the other part, and thus obtain
a less total area than that which was assigned as the minimum.

Or perhaps the author argues that as the surface of revolution which he has obtained satisfies the general partial differential equation of the problem, and also satisfies the limiting conditions, it must be the surface required.

(2) Björling discusses another particular example before considering the general equation, namely, among all surfaces which can be formed by the motion of a straight line which always remains parallel to a fixed plane, to determine that of minimum area.

Take the plane of (x, y) as that to which the generating line is always to be parallel; then we have to find a relation between x, y, and z, so that the following partial differential equations may be satisfied,

$$q^2 r - 2pqs + p^2 t = 0,$$
$$(1 + p^2) t - 2pqs + (1 + q^2) r = 0.$$

The result is

$$x - a = (y - b) \tan \frac{z - c}{h}.$$

This result is however more general than appears from Björling's treatise. It has been shewn by Catalan that out of *all* ruled surfaces the surface determined by the equation just given is the only one which satisfies the condition for a minimum area; see Liouville's *Mathematical Journal*, Vol. 7, pages 203—211, 1842. This theorem is also proved by Bonnet in the *Journal de l'Ecole Polytechnique*, Cahier 32, page 134, 1848; it is there ascribed to Meunier.

(3) In the appendix which extends from page 51 to the end, Björling considers the following problem; among all surfaces of revolution to find that which has a given area and includes a maximum volume. He obtains the differential equation to the generating curve, and shews that this curve is that which is traced out by the focus of a conic section when the conic section is made to roll on a fixed line. This result he states is due to Delaunay; and he refers to the Journal called *L'Institut*, Number 394, 1841.

(4) On page 4 of his treatise Björling points out an important misprint in Poisson's Memoir; see Art. 107.

312. Bertrand.   Liouville's *Mathematical Journal*, Vol. 7, pages 55—58, 1842.

This article is entitled *Note on a point in the Calculus of Variations*.

Suppose we have to find the maximum or minimum of $\int U dx$, while $\int V dx$ is to remain constant; then the rule which was given by Euler is that we must find the maximum or minimum of $\int (V + cU)\, dx$ where c is a constant.   Bertrand's object is to prove this rule.   He says that his proof is not so simple as that which is commonly given, and which involves no calculation; but the common proof appears to him unsatisfactory, for it only shews that the solutions obtained do satisfy the conditions of the problem, but not that they are the only possible solutions.

Suppose then that $\int_a^b U dx$ is to be a maximum while $\int_a^b V dx$ remains constant; then we know that the variation $\delta \int_a^b U dx$ must be zero whenever the variation $\delta \int_a^b V dx$ is zero.   Suppose for simplicity that the terms outside the integral signs in the ordinary expressions for these variations vanish.   Then $\int_a^b \omega u\, dx$ must vanish whenever $\int_a^b \omega v\, dx$ vanishes, where u and v are certain functions derived in the well-known manner from U and V respectively, and ω admits of all values.

Now it is obvious that we can satisfy this condition by putting $u = cv$, where c is a constant; for then the two integrals have a constant ratio whatever ω may be, .and therefore they vanish simultaneously.   But we wish to prove that this relation $u = cv$ is not only sufficient but necessary.

Suppose then that $\frac{u}{v}$ is not a constant, and let $\frac{u}{v} = f(x)$; then we shall shew that there cannot be a maximum.   For we shall shew that it is possible to take ω such that $\int_a^b \omega v\, dx$ vanishes while

$\int_a^b \omega v f(x)\, dx$ does not vanish. For we may suppose that ω is zero for all values of x except when x lies between h_1 and h_2 or between h_3 and h_4; then we can take ω such that

$$\int_{h_1}^{h_2} \omega v\, dx + \int_{h_3}^{h_4} \omega v\, dx = 0.$$

For we can suppose that $h_2 - h_1$ is so small that the sign of v does not change while x lies between h_1 and h_2: and also that $h_4 - h_3$ is so small that the sign of v does not change while x lies between h_3 and h_4; then we can make ω have an unchangeable sign during each interval, and choose the same sign or contrary signs for the two intervals according as v has contrary signs or the same sign. By properly choosing h_1, h_2, h_3, and h_4 we can ensure that $f(x)$ does not change sign while x lies between h_1 and h_2 or between h_3 and h_4, and that the value of $f(x)$ throughout one of these intervals is always greater than throughout the other. Thus

$$\int_{h_1}^{h_2} \omega v f(x)\, dx + \int_{h_3}^{h_4} \omega v f(x)\, dx$$

will not be zero when the values of ω are adopted which we have supposed used to make

$$\int_{h_1}^{h_2} \omega v\, dx + \int_{h_3}^{h_4} \omega v\, dx$$

zero. Thus there is not a maximum.

Therefore there cannot be a relative maximum or minimum unless $\dfrac{u}{v}$ is constant.

Bertrand then considers the case in which the terms outside the integral sign in the two original variations do not vanish. It is however unnecessary to notice this part of his article; for what has been already given shews that there cannot be a solution at all of the problem proposed unless $\dfrac{u}{v}$ is constant, and the ordinary method shews, as Bertrand himself admits, that we can get a solution by supposing $\dfrac{u}{v}$ constant.

313. Bertrand.   Liouville's *Mathematical Journal*, Vol. 7, pages 212—214, 1842.

This article is entitled *Note on a Theorem in Mechanics*. The following theorem is proved; let there be two curves with their concavities downwards and terminated at the same extremities; then a particle moving under the action of gravity will take a longer time to describe the upper curve than the lower curve, the initial velocity being supposed the same in the two cases.

Take the axis of y vertically downwards, and the origin so that $\sqrt{2gy}$ may be the velocity when the ordinate of the particle is y. Then the time t of describing the arc is determined by the equation

$$t = \int_{x_0}^{x_1} \left(\frac{1+y'^2}{2gy}\right)^{\frac{1}{2}} dx.$$

Now from the usual expression for δt we shall obtain by reduction

$$\delta t = -\int_{x_0}^{x_1} \frac{1+y'^2+yy''}{y^{\frac{1}{2}}(1+y'^2)^{\frac{1}{2}}} \frac{\delta y}{2^{\frac{1}{2}}g^{\frac{1}{2}}} dx.$$

Now y'' is positive because the concavity of the curve is supposed downwards; and since we pass from the upper curve to the lower by assigning a *positive* value to δy, it follows that in passing from the upper curve to the lower δt is *negative*. Thus the time of motion is diminished in passing from one curve to another which is infinitesimally lower; and therefore *à fortiori* the time of motion is diminished in passing from one curve to another which is at a finite distance below the first, provided the passage can be effected through a series of curves indefinitely close to each other all having their concavities downwards, that is, provided the two extreme curves themselves both have their concavities downwards.

Bertrand uses the same method to shew that a convex arc is shorter than another which encloses it; and he intimates that the same method may be applied to shew that the area of a convex surface is smaller than the area of another which has the same boundary and which encloses the first.

314. Delaunay. *Liouville's Mathematical Journal*, Vol. 8, pages 241—244, 1843.

This article is entitled *Note on the line of given length which includes a maximum area on a surface.* The area is supposed to be bounded on three sides by curves which project on the plane of (x, y) into straight lines, two of them parallel to the axis of y and the other parallel to the axis of x; the fourth boundary of the area is supposed to be the curve required, which is to have a given length and to include with the other boundaries a maximum area.

The integral to be a maximum is therefore $\int_a^b dx \int_a^y dy \sqrt{(1+p^2+q^2)}$, where the superior limit in the integration relative to y is the ordinate for any point of the required curve. Moreover the length of the curve is supposed given.

Thus the problem coincides with that discussed by Minding and others; see Art. 307.'

315. Bonnet. *Journal de l'École Polytechnique.* Cahier 32, pages 1—146, 1848.

This Memoir is entitled *On the general theory of Surfaces.* It contains many interesting results with respect to geodesic lines, but it is not very closely connected with our subject; there are however three points which may be noticed here.

(1) On pages 37—39 the equation to the geodesic lines on any surface is obtained by means of the Calculus of Variations.

(2) On pages 44—46 the problem is solved by means of the Calculus of Variations which had been considered by Minding and Delaunay; see Arts. 307 and 314.

(3) On pages 134—136 is a note relative to the ruled surface which has at every point its principal radii of curvature equal and of opposite signs. It is stated that Meunier was the first person who proved that the *hélicoïde gauche* is the only ruled surface which has the property in question. Reference is made to solutions by Legendre and Olivier; and it is stated that other solutions have been given by writers in Liouville's Journal. Bonnet then gives a geometrical proof of the theorem originally established by Meunier.

Bonnet's treatment of the problems (1) and (2) by the Calculus of Variations is very interesting, but it is too closely connected with the notation and results of his Memoir to be extracted.

316. Hornstein. *Dissertatio de Maximis et Minimis integralium multiplicium quam pro gradu Doctoratus in celeberrima Universitate Bonnensi consequendo elaboravit auctor C. Hornstein.* Vienna, 1850.

This treatise consists of 26 quarto pages. No reference is given to preceding writers, but the treatise is obviously constructed under the guidance of the memoir by Cauchy which we have described in Chapter VIII. Hornstein adopts that modification of Cauchy's notation which we have given at the bottom of page 214.

The treatise consists essentially of two investigations. (1) An investigation of the variation of a double integral: this is such an investigation as we have given in Arts. 183 and 184. Hornstein gives completely the terms which arise from differential coefficients up to the second order inclusive, and indicates some of the terms which arise from differential coefficients of a higher order. (2) An investigation of the variation of a triple integral; Hornstein gives completely the terms which arise from differential coefficients up to the second order inclusive. This is similar to the investigation which we have given in Art. 195, so far as the terms arising from differential coefficients up to the first order inclusive.

The investigations are given very clearly, and the complicated expressions which necessarily occur have been very accurately printed.

317. Ostrogradsky. *Mémoire sur les équations différentielles relatives au problème des Isopérimètres.*

This Memoir was read to the Academy of Sciences at St Petersburg, on November 29th, 1848, and was published in 1850, in the Memoirs of the Academy. The volume which contains the memoir belongs to the sixth series; it is the *fourth* volume of the department of mathematical and physical sciences, and the *sixth* volume of the combined departments of mathematical, physical, and natural sciences. The memoir occupies pages 385—517 of the volume.

Suppose V to be a function of an independent variable t, and of the variables $x_1, x_2, \ldots x_m$, which are supposed to be functions of t, and of the differential coefficients of these functions with respect to t. Moreover suppose that V involves differential coefficients of each function $x_1, x_2, \ldots x_m$ up to that of the nth order inclusive. If $\int Vdt$ is to be a maximum or minimum $\delta \int Vdt$ must be zero. By the known principles of the Calculus of Variations this leads to m differential equations each of the order denoted by $2n$. Now it is shewn by Ostrogradsky that these differential equations are equivalent to a certain set of $2mn$ partial differential equations of the first order. The object of the first part of Ostrogradsky's Memoir is thus the same as that which was afterwards considered by Clebsch in the first part of his second Memoir; see Art. 286.

Ostrogradsky then enters at great length into the subject of the integration of the equations which are thus obtained, and the consideration of some remarkable properties connected with the equations.

The memoir is rather difficult and not very correctly printed. It is very slightly connected with the Calculus of Variations; its proper place is among the series of modern researches on the equations of Dynamics, and on the theory of the variation of the arbitrary constants; to these subjects Ostrogradsky often alludes.

The following points of interest may be noticed. In pages 419—430 Ostrogradsky makes some observations on that part of the *Mécanique Analytique* in which Lagrange deduces the equations of motion in Dynamics from the principle of Least Action combined with the principle of Vis Viva. Ostrogradsky says that Lagrange's analysis is inexact (page 424). The principle on which Ostrogradsky founds his objection is, that by virtue of the equation of Vis Viva there is a relation between certain variations which Lagrange assumes to be independent (page 423). The part of the *Mécanique Analytique* to which Ostrogradsky refers is that on page 296 and the following pages of the first volume; in one place Ostrogradsky refers to page 229, which must be a misprint for page 299.

In pages 472—480 Ostrogradsky applies his general theory to some examples; these are of great use as illustrations of his theory. In a note he says that he omits other illustrations because he has found during the printing of his memoir that it was possible to generalise and simplify these applications, and also that the general theory could be simplified and receive some development; this he promises to shew in a future memoir.

On page 512 Ostrogradsky indicates an important application of a formula originally obtained by Poisson, which application Poisson himself appears not to have observed.

318. Schellbach. *Crelle's Mathematical Journal*, Vol. 41, pages 293—363, 1851.

This Memoir is entitled *Problems of the Calculus of Variations*. The author states that students of mathematics often find the Calculus of Variations a difficult subject; he accordingly considers some problems which are usually treated by the Calculus of Variations and solves them without using the methods of that Calculus. His processes resemble those which were used by the early writers who solved such problems before the Calculus of Variations was reduced to a system. The memoir is interesting and instructive, especially for a student who is examining the foundations of the subject.

The memoir consists of 35 sections; we will indicate briefly the contents of these sections, and then give some specimens of the investigations.

(1) The ordinary formulæ for solving problems of maxima and minima are quoted from the Differential Calculus. (2) A curve of given length is to be drawn between two fixed points so as to. include with the axis of x and the bounding ordinate a minimum area. The problem is solved by first considering the case of a polygon, forming the necessary equations by (1), and then proceeding to the limit. (3), (4), (5) contain other solutions of the problem in (2). In (6) the problem is modified by supposing that the ends instead of being fixed are to lie on given curves. (7) The problem we have solved in Art. 99 after Poisson. (8) To

find the curve which joins two given points and by revolution round an axis in its plane generates a minimum surface. (9) To find the curve which by revolution round an axis in its plane generates a maximum or minimum volume, the ends of the curve lying on given curves. (10) A general discussion which amounts to finding the usual equation for a maximum or minimum in any integral expression with one dependent variable. (11) To find a curve such that the area between the curve and its evolute may be a minimum. (12) The solid of revolution of least resistance. (13), (14), (15), (16) and (19) The brachistochrone and allied problems. (17) The problem discussed by Minding and others; see Art. 307. Schellbach states that it has been discussed by another mathématician besides Minding and Delaunay, but he does not give a precise reference. (18) A curve of given length is drawn on a given surface; find the curve so that the volume determined by the curve and its orthogonal projection on one of the co-ordinate planes may be a maximum or minimum. (20) A problem which we shall consider presently; see Art. 320. (21) The curve which has its centre of gravity at a maximum depth. (22) The curve which bounds an area having its centre of gravity at a maximum depth. Sections (23)—(29) contain investigations which are not very closely connected with the Calculus of Variations; we shall recur to them again; see Art. 322. (30) To find a surface having a given boundary and a minimum area. (31) General investigation of the maxima and minima of double integrals. (32) General investigation of the maxima and minima of triple integrals. (33) and (34) The problem which Poisson quotes from Euler, and the problem which Poisson himself considers; see Arts. 116—120. (35) The transformation of the equations of motion in Dynamics given by Lagrange in the *Mécanique Analytique;* see De Morgan's *Differential and Integral Calculus,* page 520.

319. As an example of Schellbach's solutions we will take the problem of determining the brachistochrone when a particle moves in a resisting medium under the action of gravity; see section (14) of the memoir.

Instead of supposing the particle to describe a curve we will suppose it to describe a polygon of n sides, each side being ultimately made indefinitely small. Take the axis of x horizontal, and that of y vertically upwards. Let x_0, y_0 be the co-ordinates of the initial point; x_1, y_1 the co-ordinates of the beginning of the second side of the polygon; x_2, y_2 the co-ordinates of the beginning of the third side of the polygon; and so on. Let δs_0 be the length of the first side of the polygon, v_0 the velocity, supposed uniform, with which it is described; let δs_1 be the length of the second side of the polygon, v_1 the velocity, supposed uniform, with which it is described; and so on. Then the whole time of motion is

$$\frac{\delta s_0}{v_0} + \frac{\delta s_1}{v_1} + \frac{\delta s_2}{v_2} + \ldots\ldots + \frac{\delta s_{n-1}}{v_{n-1}}.$$

We have then to make this time of motion a minimum.

We must first however determine the connexion between the velocity at any point and the co-ordinates of that point, by mechanical principles. Suppose a particle to be moving on a curve; let p denote the reaction of the curve, gw the resistance where w is any function of the velocity; then the equations of motion are

$$\frac{d^2x}{dt^2} = p\,\frac{dy}{ds} - gw\,\frac{dx}{ds}, \quad \frac{d^2y}{dt^2} = -g - p\,\frac{dx}{ds} - gw\,\frac{dy}{ds}.$$

Eliminate p from these equations; thus

$$d\,v^2 = -2g\,dy - 2gw\,ds.$$

Assume $\qquad v^2 = 2gu$, so that

$$du + dy + w\,ds = 0 \ldots\ldots\ldots\ldots\ldots\ldots\ldots\ldots\ldots (1).$$

Now let us return to the supposition that the motion is to take place on a polygon and not on a curve; then from the equation last written we obtain the following n equations,

$$\left.\begin{array}{l} u_1 - u_0 + y_1 - y_0 + w_0\,\delta s_0 = 0 \\ u_2 - u_1 + y_2 - y_1 + w_1\,\delta s_1 = 0 \\ \ldots\ldots\ldots\ldots\ldots\ldots\ldots\ldots\ldots\ldots \\ u_n - u_{n-1} + y_n - y_{n-1} + w_{n-1}\,\delta s_{n-1} = 0 \end{array}\right\} \ldots\ldots\ldots (2).$$

The expression to be made a minimum is

$$\frac{\delta s_0}{\sqrt{u_0}} + \frac{\delta s_1}{\sqrt{u_1}} + \ldots\ldots + \frac{\delta s_{n-1}}{\sqrt{u_{n-1}}},$$

which we shall denote by T. Then we may consider T as a function of $2n$ unknown quantities, namely x_0, y_0, x_1, y_1, ..., x_{n-1}, y_{n-1}, and we must determine the values of these quantities so that T may be a minimum. Now by the ordinary principles of the Differential Calculus we may use the method of indeterminate multipliers in order to take account of the conditions expressed by the equations (2). So that we may consider we have to find the minimum value of $T + \Sigma \lambda_r M_r$, where

$$M_r = u_{r+1} - u_r + y_{r+1} - y_r + w_r \delta s_r,$$

λ_r is a constant, and the summation indicated by Σ extends from $r = 0$ to $r = n - 1$ both inclusive. We shall now differentiate $T + \Sigma \lambda_r M_r$ with respect to each variable, and equate each differential coefficient to zero. Let us take for example the variables x_r and y_r; each of these occurs in δs_r and in δs_{r-1}; for

$$(\delta s_{r-1})^2 = (x_r - x_{r-1})^2 + (y_r - y_{r-1})^2,$$

and

$$(\delta s_r)^2 = (x_{r+1} - x_r)^2 + (y_{r+1} - y_r)^2;$$

moreover y_r occurs explicitly in M_r and in M_{r-1}. Thus by differentiating with respect to x_r we get

$$-\frac{1}{\sqrt{u_{r-1}}} \frac{\delta x_{r-1}}{\delta s_{r-1}} - \frac{1}{\sqrt{u_r}} \frac{\delta x_r}{\delta s_r} + \lambda_{r-1} w_{r-1} \frac{\delta x_{r-1}}{\delta s_{r-1}} - \lambda_r w_r \frac{\delta x_r}{\delta s_r} = 0,$$

where δx_{r-1} is put for $x_r - x_{r-1}$ and δx_r for $x_{r+1} - x_r$.

The above equation may be written

$$\delta \frac{\delta x_{r-1}}{\sqrt{u_{r-1}} \cdot \delta s_{r-1}} + \delta \frac{\lambda_{r-1} w_{r-1} \delta x_{r-1}}{\delta s_{r-1}} = 0;$$

therefore by proceeding to the limit and integrating we obtain

$$\frac{1}{\sqrt{u}} \frac{dx}{ds} + \lambda w \frac{dx}{ds} = a \dots\dots\dots\dots\dots\dots (3),$$

where a is a constant. Here we have dropped the suffix $r-1$, that is, we use u, w, λ, $\dfrac{dx}{ds}$, as representing any one of the corresponding quantities with its appropriate suffix.

In the same manner by differentiating with respect to y, we obtain

$$\frac{1}{\sqrt{u_{r-1}}}\frac{\delta y_{r-1}}{\delta s_{r-1}} - \frac{1}{\sqrt{u_r}}\frac{\delta y_r}{\delta s_r} + \lambda_{r-1}w_{r-1}\frac{\delta y_{r-1}}{\delta s_{r-1}} - \lambda_r w_r\frac{\delta y_r}{\delta s_r} + \lambda_{r-1} - \lambda_r = 0;$$

this equation may be written

$$\delta\,\frac{\delta y_{r-1}}{\sqrt{u_{r-1}}\cdot\delta s_{r-1}} + \delta\,\frac{\lambda_{r-1}w_{r-1}\,\delta y_{r-1}}{\delta s_{r-1}} + \delta\lambda_{r-1} = 0;$$

therefore by proceeding to the limit and integrating we obtain

$$\frac{1}{\sqrt{u}}\frac{dy}{ds} + \lambda w\frac{dy}{ds} + \lambda = b \dots\dots\dots\dots\dots (4),$$

where b is a constant.

Equations (3) and (4) are the differential equations of the problem; they agree with the results obtained by the ordinary methods; see for example Mr Jellett's treatise, pages 298—300.

From (3) and (4) eliminate λ; then with the help of (1) we shall obtain

$$x = a\int \frac{du}{\left\{\left(bw + \frac{1}{\sqrt{u}}\right)^2 - a^2(1 - w^2)\right\}^{\frac{1}{2}}},$$

$$y = -\int \frac{w\left(bw + \frac{1}{\sqrt{u}}\right)du}{(1 - w^2)\left\{\left(bw + \frac{1}{\sqrt{u}}\right)^2 - a^2(1 - w^2)\right\}^{\frac{1}{2}}} - \int\frac{du}{1 - w^2}.$$

As w is supposed a given function of u we obtain from these two equations x and y as functions of an auxiliary variable u.

320.   In Schellbach's twentieth section the following problem is proposed.   The ends of a string of length l are fastened at the points A and B; the ends of a string of length λ are fastened at the points A' and B'.   The four points A, B, A', B' are not supposed to be all in the same plane.   A straight line passes from the position AB to the position $A'B'$ so that it moves over the threads l and λ in the same time with uniform velocity, and thus describes

a *developable* surface. Required to determine the forms of the strings so that this surface may be a maximum or a minimum.

This problem requires some observations.

It is no doubt meant that the straight line is to pass from the position AA' to the position BB', and not, as it is stated above, from the position AB to the position $A'B'$.

The meaning of the problem is best understood by examining the process of solution which the author adopts. Let P, Q denote adjacent points of one of the strings, and P', Q' corresponding adjacent points of the other string. Let a generating line be drawn from P to P'; let the end at P be supposed fixed, and let the line turn round this end remaining always in contact with PQ; thus an indefinitely small conical element is generated. Next let the end of the line at Q be supposed fixed, and let the line turn about this end remaining always in contact with PQ; thus another indefinitely small conical element is generated. Now it is the sum of all these pairs of elements which the author proposes to make a maximum or minimum. These elements do not form a continuous developable surface in the ordinary meaning of such a term; for that would require that the following three lines should be in one plane, the line PQ, the tangent to the guiding curve at P, and the tangent to the guiding curve at Q, and there is nothing in Schellbach's solution to secure this. Moreover there is nothing in the solution corresponding to the condition of moving with uniform velocity over the two curves, which occurs in the statement of the problem; the connexion between the lengths of the two curves described by the moving line in passing from its initial position to any other position is in fact one of the things sought in the solution.

Let x, y, z be the co-ordinates of one end of the moving line, s the length of the portion of the string which has been described; let ξ, η, ζ be the co-ordinates of the other end of the moving line, σ the length of the curve which has been described. Let r denote the distance of (x, y, z) from (ξ, η, ζ); if the first end of the line moves over an arc ds while the other end remains fixed, the area of the element of surface generated will be ultimately

$$\frac{1}{2}\,r\,ds\sqrt{1-\left(\frac{dr}{ds}\right)^2};$$

similarly if the second end of the line move over an arc $d\sigma$ while the first end remains fixed, the area of the element of surface generated will be ultimately

$$\frac{1}{2}\,r\,d\sigma\sqrt{1-\left(\frac{dr}{d\sigma}\right)^2}.$$

Thus since the lengths of the guiding curves are to be constant, we have, by the usual considerations, to find the maximum or minimum of

$$\int\left\{r\,ds\sqrt{1-\left(\frac{dr}{ds}\right)^2}+r\,d\sigma\sqrt{1-\left(\frac{dr}{d\sigma}\right)^2}+m\,ds+\mu\,d\sigma\right\},$$

where m and μ are constants. Schellbach then expresses r, $\frac{dr}{ds}$, $\frac{dr}{d\sigma}$, ds and $d\sigma$ in terms of x, y, z, ξ, η, ζ and their differentials; then by equating the coefficients of the variations to zero in the usual way he obtains equations for determining the required curves. The equations he obtains are susceptible of integration to a certain extent, but the problem cannot be completely solved.

Schellbach next considers a modification of the problem; he supposes that one of the curves is replaced by a straight line of given length and position, and that the other curve is to be determined so as to make the area a maximum or minimum. The solution of the problem in this form can be carried a little further than the solution of the original problem.

321. In his twenty-first section Schellbach suggests a problem which it will be instructive to examine.

ACB is a string of given length which is fastened at A and B; see figure 9; $A'C'B'$ is another string of given length fastened at A' and B'; CDC' is another string of given length, the ends of which are constrained to lie on the former strings. Each string is supposed uniform, but the weight of a unit of length is not necessarily the same for all the strings. Required the forms of the curves in order that the centre of gravity of the system may be at a maximum depth.

We know from Statics that the curves will all be portions of catenaries; and from Statics we can obtain certain equations for determining the constants involved in the equations to the catenaries. But the point of interest is to deduce these equations by means of the Calculus of Variations.

Take the axis of y vertically downwards, and put p for $\dfrac{dy}{dx}$. Let $w_1,\ w_2,\ w_3$ be the weights of a unit of length of the strings ACB, $A'C'B$, CDC' respectively. Then we require that the following expression should be a maximum,

$$w_1 \int y \sqrt{(1+p^2)}\, dx + w_2 \int y \sqrt{(1+p^2)}\, dx + w_3 \int y \sqrt{(1+p^2)}\, dx,$$

where the three integrals extend respectively over all the elements of the three curves. And the length of each curve is a constant. Hence the following expression is to be added to the former,

$$a_1 \int \sqrt{(1+p^2)}\, dx + a_2 \int \sqrt{(1+p^2)}\, dx + a_3 \int \sqrt{(1+p^2)}\, dx;$$

and the whole made a maximum, $a_1,\ a_2,\ a_3$ being constants, and the three integrals extending over all the elements of the three curves respectively.

We then make the variation of the whole vanish. This variation consists as usual of terms under the integral signs and terms outside the integral signs.

The terms under the integral signs vanish if we suppose equations to hold of which the type is

$$(wy + a)\sqrt{(1+p^2)} = \frac{(wy+a)\,p^2}{\sqrt{(1+p^2)}} + \text{constant},$$

that is,

$$\frac{(wy+a)}{\sqrt{(1+p^2)}} = \text{constant}.$$

In this equation w and a are to have the specific value belonging to the specific arc we are considering; the *constant* is not necessarily the same throughout, but will generally have five different values corresponding to the five arcs,

$$AC, \quad CB, \quad A'C', \quad C'B, \quad CDC'.$$

The general relation just obtained shews that each of these five arcs
is a portion of a catenary.

Now consider the terms outside the integral signs. We adopt
the usual supposition that both x and y vary, and we denote by
δx_0 and δy_0 the variations of the point C. Then δx_0 and δy_0 will
occur in three ways, arising from the three curves which meet at C.
The complete term involving δy_0 will be

$$\delta y_0 (L - M - N),$$

where L, M, N are respectively the values at the point C of the
expression of which the type is $\dfrac{(\kappa y + a) p}{\sqrt{(1 + p^2)}}$, obtained from the curves
AC, CB, CD respectively.

Thus the equation

$$L - M - N = 0$$

agrees with what we should obtain from the statical principle of
equating the sum of the vertical tensions at C of the two upper
curves to the vertical tension of the lower; for the value of p found
from the curve BC at C is negative.

Similarly by equating to zero the coefficient of δx_0 we shall
obtain an equation coincident with that which we should obtain
from the statical principle of equating the sum of the horizontal
tensions of the curves BC and CD at C to the horizontal tension
of the curve CA.

We have theoretically enough equations to determine the constants. For we have five constants from the general relation which
we have found above when it is applied to the five arcs, and five
more constants would be introduced by integrating that general
relation; we have also the three constants a_1, a_2, a_3; thus there are
thirteen constants on the whole. Now we have found two equations among the constants from the conditions which subsist at C,
and similarly we should obtain two more equations from the conditions which subsist at C'; the four fixed points A, B, A', B',
furnish four equations; the known lengths of the curves furnish
three equations; the fact that three arcs intersect at C furnishes
one equation, and the fact that three arcs intersect at C' furnishes
one equation. Thus on the whole we have thirteen equations.

322. From page 336 to page 347 of Schellbach's memoir is occupied with the investigation of some simple maxima and minima problems in mechanics and optics; this part of the memoir is interesting, though very slightly connected with the Calculus of Variations. The following example may be taken as a specimen of these investigations. Suppose we require the form of a solid of revolution of given mass which shall exert the greatest attraction in a given direction on a given particle, the attraction varying as any inverse power of the distance.

Take the given particle as the origin and the given direction as the line from which to measure angular distance; let r, θ be the polar co-ordinates of any point in a fixed plane passing through the given direction. Then if the attraction vary as the nth power of the distance the attraction of an element whose co-ordinates are r and θ may be denoted by μr^n; and the resolved part of this attraction in the given direction will be $\mu r^n \cos \theta$. Hence the equation

$$\mu r^n \cos \theta = \text{constant}$$

represents a curve such that a given element placed at any point of it will exert the same attraction on the given particle. Hence this equation represents the curve which by revolving round the fixed direction will generate the required solid of maximum attraction, the constant being determined so as to give to the solid the prescribed volume. It is obvious that such is the case because the surface we thus obtain separates space into two parts, and any particle outside the surface exercises a less attraction than it would if placed within the surface, n being supposed negative.

The result we thus obtain may of course also be obtained by the ordinary methods of the Calculus of Variations.

323. In pages 357—360 of the memoir we have an interesting application of the Calculus of Variations which Schellbach states that he has taken from a memoir by Jacobi in the 36th volume of Crelle's Mathematical Journal. We will explain this application rather more fully than Schellbach does.

Suppose in the triple integral $\iiint G\,dx\,dy\,dz$ that G is a function of $x, y, z, v, \dfrac{dv}{dx}, \dfrac{dv}{dy}, \dfrac{dv}{dz}$; where v is a function of x, y, z. Now suppose that x, y, z are expressed in terms of new variables λ, μ, ν by means of the equations

$$x = f_1(\lambda, \mu, \nu), \quad y = f_2(\lambda, \mu, \nu), \quad z = f_3(\lambda, \mu, \nu);$$

then v becomes a function of λ, μ, ν, which we shall denote by ϕ, and G becomes a function of λ, μ, ν, $\dfrac{d\phi}{d\lambda}$, $\dfrac{d\phi}{d\mu}$, $\dfrac{d\phi}{d\nu}$, which we shall denote by Γ. Then by the known theory of the transformation of multiple integrals we obtain

$$\iiint G\, dx\, dy\, dz = \iiint \Gamma\Pi\, d\lambda\, d\mu\, d\nu \quad \ldots\ldots\ldots\ldots (1),$$

where Π is a known expression which involves the differential coefficients of x, y, z with respect to λ, μ, ν, so that Π is in fact a known function of λ, μ, ν. Now take the variations of both members of this equation; these variations will be equal, and the unintegrated portions will be separately equal. Thus we obtain the result

$$\iiint Q\, \delta v\, dx\, dy\, dz = \iiint R\, \delta\phi\, d\lambda\, d\mu\, d\nu,$$

where Q is an expression derived in the well known way from G, and R is similarly derived from $\Gamma\Pi$. Now change the variables in the integral on the left-hand side of the equation; thus

$$\iiint Q\Pi\, \delta v\, d\lambda\, d\mu\, d\nu = \iiint R\, \delta\phi\, d\lambda\, d\mu\, d\nu.$$

Now δv is the same thing as $\delta\phi$, and is perfectly arbitrary, so that we obtain from the last equation

$$Q\Pi = R.$$

This equation written at full becomes

$$\Pi\left\{\frac{dG}{dv} - \frac{d}{dx}\left(\frac{dG}{d\frac{dv}{dx}}\right) - \frac{d}{dy}\left(\frac{dG}{d\frac{dv}{dy}}\right) - \frac{d}{dz}\left(\frac{dG}{d\frac{dv}{dz}}\right)\right\}$$

$$= \Pi\frac{d\Gamma}{d\phi} - \frac{d}{d\lambda}\left(\frac{\Pi d\Gamma}{d\frac{d\phi}{d\lambda}}\right) - \frac{d}{d\mu}\left(\frac{\Pi d\Gamma}{d\frac{d\phi}{d\mu}}\right) - \frac{d}{d\nu}\left(\frac{\Pi d\Gamma}{d\frac{d\phi}{d\nu}}\right) \ldots\ldots (2).$$

This transformation will sometimes be of use; and it is obvious that we might proceed in a similar way with a multiple integral of any order as we have proceeded with a triple integral; or we might suppose differential coefficients of a higher order than the first to occur in G.

For an example we will apply the formula to the transformation of the expression $\dfrac{d^2v}{dx^2} + \dfrac{d^2v}{dy^2} + \dfrac{d^2v}{dz^2}$.

Let
$$G = \left(\frac{dv}{dx}\right)^2 + \left(\frac{dv}{dy}\right)^2 + \left(\frac{dv}{dz}\right)^2, \text{ and}$$

$$x = \lambda \cos \mu, \quad y = \lambda \sin \mu \cos \nu, \quad z = \lambda \sin \mu \sin \nu.$$

Then, using v instead of its equivalent ϕ, we have

$$\frac{dv}{d\lambda} = \frac{dv}{dx}\frac{dx}{d\lambda} + \frac{dv}{dy}\frac{dy}{d\lambda} + \frac{dv}{dz}\frac{dz}{d\lambda}$$

$$= \frac{dv}{dx}\cos\mu + \frac{dv}{dy}\sin\mu\cos\nu + \frac{dv}{dz}\sin\mu\sin\nu,$$

$$\frac{dv}{d\mu} = \frac{dv}{dx}\frac{dx}{d\mu} + \frac{dv}{dy}\frac{dy}{d\mu} + \frac{dv}{dz}\frac{dz}{d\mu}$$

$$= -\frac{dv}{dx}\lambda\sin\mu + \frac{dv}{dy}\lambda\cos\mu\cos\nu + \frac{dv}{dz}\lambda\cos\mu\sin\nu,$$

$$\frac{dv}{d\nu} = \frac{dv}{dx}\frac{dx}{d\nu} + \frac{dv}{dy}\frac{dy}{d\nu} + \frac{dv}{dz}\frac{dz}{d\nu}$$

$$= -\frac{dv}{dy}\lambda\sin\mu\sin\nu + \frac{dv}{dz}\lambda\sin\mu\cos\nu.$$

Thus we obtain

$$\left(\frac{dv}{d\lambda}\right)^2 + \frac{1}{\lambda^2}\left(\frac{dv}{d\mu}\right)^2 + \frac{1}{\lambda^2\sin^2\mu}\left(\frac{dv}{d\nu}\right)^2 = \left(\frac{dv}{dx}\right)^2 + \left(\frac{dv}{dy}\right)^2 + \left(\frac{dv}{dz}\right)^2.$$

And in the present example $\Pi = \lambda^2 \sin\mu$; thus we obtain from (1)

$$\iiint \left\{ \left(\frac{dv}{dx}\right)^2 + \left(\frac{dv}{dy}\right)^2 + \left(\frac{dv}{dz}\right)^2 \right\} dx\, dy\, dz$$

$$= \iiint \left\{ \left(\frac{dv}{d\lambda}\right)^2 + \frac{1}{\lambda^2}\left(\frac{dv}{d\mu}\right)^2 + \frac{1}{\lambda^2\sin^2\mu}\left(\frac{dv}{d\nu}\right)^2 \right\} \lambda^2 \sin\mu\, d\lambda\, d\mu\, d\nu.$$

Then from the general formula (2) after division by $\lambda^2 \sin \mu$ we obtain

$$\frac{d^2 v}{dx^2} + \frac{d^2 v}{dy^2} + \frac{d^2 v}{dz^2}$$

$$= \frac{1}{\lambda^2 \sin \mu} \left\{ \frac{d}{d\lambda} \left(\lambda^2 \sin \mu \frac{dv}{d\lambda} \right) + \frac{d}{d\mu} \left(\sin \mu \frac{dv}{d\mu} \right) + \frac{d}{d\nu} \left(\frac{1}{\sin \mu} \frac{dv}{d\nu} \right) \right\}$$

$$= \frac{1}{\lambda^2} \frac{d}{d\lambda} \left(\lambda^2 \frac{dv}{d\lambda} \right) + \frac{1}{\lambda^2 \sin \mu} \frac{d}{d\mu} \left(\sin \mu \frac{dv}{d\mu} \right) + \frac{1}{\lambda^2 \sin^2 \mu} \frac{d^2 v}{d\nu^2}$$

$$= \frac{1}{\lambda} \frac{d^2 (\lambda v)}{d\lambda^2} + \frac{1}{\lambda^2 \sin \mu} \cdot \frac{d}{d\mu} \left(\sin \mu \frac{dv}{d\mu} \right) + \frac{1}{\lambda^2 \sin^2 \mu} \frac{d^2 v}{d\nu^2}.$$

Thus we obtain the well-known transformation first given by Laplace.

As another example let it be proposed to transform $\dfrac{d^2 z}{dx^2} + \dfrac{d^2 z}{dy^2}$ into an expression involving r and θ, where $x = r \cos \theta$ and $y = r \sin \theta$.

Here

$$\frac{dz}{dr} = \frac{dz}{dx} \frac{dx}{dr} + \frac{dz}{dy} \frac{dy}{dr} = \cos \theta \frac{dz}{dx} + \sin \theta \frac{dz}{dy},$$

$$\frac{dz}{d\theta} = \frac{dz}{dx} \frac{dx}{d\theta} + \frac{dz}{dy} \frac{dy}{d\theta} = - r \sin \theta \frac{dz}{dx} + r \cos \theta \frac{dz}{dy}.$$

Thus

$$\left(\frac{dz}{dx} \right)^2 + \left(\frac{dz}{dy} \right)^2 = \left(\frac{dz}{dr} \right)^2 + \frac{1}{r^2} \left(\frac{dz}{d\theta} \right)^2.$$

Therefore as in (1)

$$\iint \left\{ \left(\frac{dz}{dx} \right)^2 + \left(\frac{dz}{dy} \right)^2 \right\} dx\, dy = \iint \left\{ \left(\frac{dz}{dr} \right)^2 + \frac{1}{r^2} \left(\frac{dz}{d\theta} \right)^2 \right\} r\, dr\, d\theta.$$

Then as in (2) we obtain

$$\frac{d^2 z}{dx^2} + \frac{d^2 z}{dy^2} = \frac{1}{r} \left\{ \frac{d}{dr} \left(r \frac{dz}{dr} \right) + \frac{d}{d\theta} \left(\frac{1}{r} \frac{dz}{d\theta} \right) \right\} = \frac{d^2 z}{dr^2} + \frac{1}{r} \frac{dz}{dr} + \frac{1}{r^2} \frac{d^2 z}{d\theta^2}.$$

Thus, as Schellbach observes, the transformation used by Poisson can be readily effected. See Art. 119.

324. Spitzer. Grunert's *Archiv der Mathematik und Physik*, Vol. 28, pages 125, 126. 1854.

This article is entitled *Note on the shortest lines on curved surfaces*.

When a curved surface can be divided by a plane into two symmetrical portions the intersection of the plane and surface, when an intersection exists, is in general a line of minimum length on the surface.

The proof is very simple. Suppose in fact that the equation to such a surface, which is divided symmetrically by the plane of xz, is

$$z = F(x, y^2).$$

For a minimum line on the surface we must have the integral

$$s = \int \sqrt{(dx^2 + dy^2 + dz^2)}$$

a minimum. Put then $dz = pdx + qdy$, so that

$$s = \int \sqrt{[dx^2 + dy^2 + (pdx + qdy)^2]}$$

$$= \int \sqrt{[1 + y'^2 + (p + qy')^2]} \, dx;$$

then the condition for a maximum or minimum is

$$\frac{d\sqrt{[1 + y'^2 + (p + qy')^2]}}{dy} - \left[\frac{d\sqrt{[1 + y'^2 + (p + qy')^2]}}{dy'}\right]' = 0;$$

this gives

$$\frac{(p + qy')\left(\frac{dp}{dy} + y'\frac{dq}{dy}\right)}{\sqrt{[1 + y'^2 + (p + qy')^2]}} - \left[\frac{y' + (p + qy')q}{\sqrt{[1 + y'^2 + (p + qy')^2]}}\right]' = 0;$$

this may be reduced to

$$[y'' + q(p + qy')]\sqrt{[1 + y'^2 + (p + qy')^2]}$$

$$= [y' + (p + qy')q][\sqrt{[1 + y'^2 + (p + qy')^2]}]'.$$

This equation is satisfied when $y = 0$; for if $y = 0$, so are also $y' = 0$, $y'' = 0$, and $q = 0$.

As a sphere is divided symmetrically by any plane which passes through its centre, any great circle of a sphere is a line of maximum or minimum length.

325. Heine. Crelle's *Mathematical Journal*, Vol. 54, page 868. 1857.

This article is entitled *Lagrange's Theorem*. It consists of a proof of Lagrange's Theorem by the method previously used by the author for establishing Jacobi's Theorems; see Articles 296, 297.

Let
$$y - h f(y) = x \quad\dots\dots\dots\dots\dots\dots (1);$$

let $\psi(x) = z$ denote any function of x, and denote the differential coefficients of z with respect to x by z', z'', ...

Then
$$\psi\{x - h f(x)\} = z - \frac{h}{1} z' f(x) + \frac{h^2}{1 \cdot 2} z'' \left[f(x)\right]^2 - \dots\dots$$

If then $\phi(x)$ be any function of x whatever,

$$\int_a^b \phi(x)\, \psi\{x - h f(x)\}\, dx = \int_a^b \phi(x) \left[z - \frac{h}{1} z' f(x) + \frac{h^2}{1 \cdot 2} z'' \left[f(x)\right]^2 - \dots \right] dx$$
$$\dots\dots\dots (2).$$

Put y for x on the left-hand side of (2); then it becomes
$$\int_a^b \phi(y)\, \psi\{y - h f(y)\}\, dy,$$

and therefore by (1),
$$\int_a^b \phi(y)\, z\, dy,$$

and therefore
$$\int_\alpha^\beta \phi(y)\, z\, \frac{dy}{dx}\, dx,$$

where
$$\alpha = a - h f(a), \quad \beta = b - h f(b).$$

If h be small enough, at least a portion of the interval between a and b will coincide with a portion of the interval between α and β. Let z be so varied that within this common interval δz may have

any arbitrary value and be zero beyond it. The variation of the
right-hand member of (2) will consist of terms free from the integral
sign together with

$$\int_a^b B \,\delta z \, dx,$$

where

$$B = \phi(x) + \frac{h}{1} \frac{d\{\phi(x)f(x)\}}{dx} + \frac{h^2}{1 \cdot 2} \frac{d^2\{\phi(x)[f(x)]^2\}}{dx^2} + \ldots\ldots$$

And since we must have within the common interval

$$\int B \,\delta z \, dx = \int \delta z \, \frac{dy}{dx} \phi(y) \, dx,$$

therefore $$\frac{dy}{dx} \phi(y) = B.$$

This is in effect Lagrange's Theorem.

326. Giesel. *Geschichte der Variationsrechnung. Einladung-
schrift zu der Feier des Schröderschen Stifts-Actus im Gymnasium
zu Torgau aus 5 April*, 1857. Torgau, 1857.

This is the first part of a History of the Calculus of Variations.
It occupies 45 quarto pages, and details the history of the subject from its origin until the publication of Lagrange's memoir in
the *Miscellanea Taurinensia* in 1762. It is a valuable work, and
contains numerous quotations and exact references to the original
sources. It resembles in some degree the well-known work of
Woodhouse, but it is less didactic and more purely historical.

There is a brief notice of this treatise by Schlömilch in the
Zeitschrift für Mathematik und Physik, 1857, *Literaturzeitung*,
page 60. Schlömilch commends the treatise highly.

327. Löffler. *On the Method of finding the greatest and least
values of undetermined integral expressions.*

This article is printed in the 34th volume of the *Sitzungsberichte*
of the Academy of Sciences at Vienna, 1859. It occupies 30 octavo
pages. The article consists principally of remarks on the brachi-

stochrone problem; the remarks appear of no value, but seem to indicate that the writer has imperfectly grasped the subject.

328. Lindeloef. *New demonstration of a fundamental theorem of the Calculus of Variations.*

This article was published in the *Comptes Rendus...de l'Académie des Sciences.* Vol. 50, 1860, pages 85—88.

The fundamental theorem referred to is one given by Ostrogradsky, which was also proved by Cauchy; see Arts. 127 and 190. The object of Lindeloef's article is to establish this theorem by the method used by Poisson, in the case of two independent variables: see Arts. 102 and 103. We will give a translation of Lindeloef's article.

It is known that the variation of an integral can be presented under two forms, according as we do or do not vary the independent variables as well as the unknown functions. We propose to establish the first form, using only the principles of the differential calculus.

We adopt the method which Euler introduced into the calculus of variations, and thus regard every unknown function as involving an arbitrary parameter i, and the *variation* of the function means its differential coefficient with respect to this parameter. We regard the variables x, y, z, ... t, as unknown functions of other independent variables ξ, η, ζ, ... τ, and of the parameter i, and the *variations* of x, y, z, ... t, mean their differential coefficients with respect to the parameter i.

Thus any unknown function u of the variables x, y, z, ... t, is susceptible of two kinds of variations, since it depends upon the parameter i directly as well as by means of these variables, and it is advisable to distinguish them by a difference of notation. The partial differential coefficient of u with respect to i we shall call the *proper variation* of u, and we shall denote it by δu; the total differential coefficient of u with respect to i we shall call the *total variation* of u, and we shall denote it by Du. This distinction does not exist with respect to the variables x, y, z, ... t, and we might use either symbol D or δ for their variations; we shall adopt the latter symbol.

We now propose to investigate the variation of a multiple integral

$$S = \iiint \ldots v \, dx \, dy \, dz \ldots$$

when the limits are variable but continuous. For this purpose we first replace the variables $x, y, z, \ldots$, by others $\xi, \eta, \zeta \ldots$, which we suppose connected with the first by the differential equations

$$dx = a_1 d\xi + a_2 d\eta + a_3 d\zeta + \ldots + a_n d\tau,$$
$$dy = b_1 d\xi + b_2 d\eta + b_3 d\zeta + \ldots + b_n d\tau,$$
$$dz = c_1 d\xi + c_2 d\eta + c_3 d\zeta + \ldots + c_n d\tau,$$
$$\ldots \ldots \ldots \ldots \ldots \ldots \ldots \ldots$$
$$dt = h_1 d\xi + h_2 d\eta + h_3 d\zeta + \ldots + h_n d\tau.$$

Denote for shortness by the letter T the determinant

$$\Sigma \left(\pm a_1 b_2 c_3 \ldots h_n \right)$$

formed from the coefficients in these equations; then the integral may be transformed into

$$S' = \iiint \ldots VT \, d\xi \, d\eta \, d\zeta \ldots$$

With respect to the limits of the two integrals, if the first is to extend over all the values of $x, y, z, \ldots$, which render a certain function L negative, the second should extend over all the values of $\xi, \eta, \zeta, \ldots$, which render Λ negative, where Λ is what L becomes by the change of the variables.

As we suppose the limits of the proposed integral to be variable, L is a function of $x, y, z, \ldots$ the form of which changes with the parameter i, which gives rise to the proper variation δL. But we can dispose of the arbitrary functions $\delta x, \delta y, \delta z, \ldots$, so as to render the total variation of L zero, so that

$$\delta L + \frac{dL}{dx} \delta x + \frac{dL}{dy} \delta y + \frac{dL}{dz} \delta z + \ldots + \frac{dL}{dt} \delta t = 0.$$

Under this condition the limits of the new integral S' will not change with i; its total variation will therefore be

$$DS = \iiint \ldots (TDV + VDT)\, d\xi\, d\eta\, d\zeta \ldots,$$

and it only remains to develop DT. We observe then that the partial differential coefficients $a, b, c, \ldots$, with which the determinant T is made, must be of the nature of the preliminary functions $x, y, z, \ldots$, from which they spring, and they must consequently be regarded as functions of $\xi, \eta, \zeta, \ldots$, varying with the parameter i. We have therefore immediately

$$DT = \Sigma \frac{dT}{da}\, \delta a + \Sigma \frac{dT}{db}\, \delta b + \Sigma \frac{dT}{dc}\, \delta c + \ldots + \Sigma \frac{dT}{dh}\, \delta h.$$

In order to determine the sum $\Sigma \dfrac{dT}{da}\, \delta a$, we introduce n auxiliary quantities $a_1, a_2, a_3, \ldots a_n$, by the equations

$$a_1 a_1 + a_2 a_2 + a_3 a_3 + \ldots + a_n a_n = 1,$$

$$b_1 a_1 + b_2 a_2 + b_3 a_3 + \ldots + b_n a_n = 0,$$

$$c_1 a_1 + c_2 a_2 + c_3 a_3 + \ldots + c_n a_n = 0,$$

$$\ldots\ldots\ldots\ldots\ldots\ldots\ldots\ldots\ldots$$

$$h_1 a_1 + h_2 a_2 + h_3 a_3 + \ldots + h_n a_n = 0.$$

Solve these with respect to a_1; thus we obtain

$$a_1 T = \Sigma\, (\pm\, b_2 c_3 \ldots h_n),$$

which shews that the product $a_1 T$ does not involve any of the quantities a. We can prove the same thing with respect to the products $a_2 T, a_3 T, \ldots, a_n T$.

From the identical equation

$$T = a_1 a_1 T + a_2 a_2 T + a_3 a_3 T + \ldots + a_n a_n T$$

we obtain immediately

$$\frac{dT}{da_1} = a_1 T, \quad \frac{dT}{da_2} = a_2 T, \quad \frac{dT}{da_3} = a_3 T, \quad ...., \quad \frac{dT}{da_n} = a_n T.$$

On the other hand, if we regard δx, δy, δz, ..., as immediate functions of x, y, z, ..., we shall evidently have

$$\delta a_1 = a_1 \frac{d\delta x}{dx} + b_1 \frac{d\delta x}{dy} + c_1 \frac{d\delta x}{dz} + ... + h_1 \frac{d\delta x}{dt},$$

$$\delta a_2 = a_2 \frac{d\delta x}{dx} + b_2 \frac{d\delta x}{dy} + c_2 \frac{d\delta x}{dz} + ... + h_2 \frac{d\delta x}{dt},$$

$$\delta a_3 = a_3 \frac{d\delta x}{dx} + b_3 \frac{d\delta x}{dy} + c_3 \frac{d\delta x}{dz} + ... + h_3 \frac{d\delta x}{dt},$$

$$..$$

$$\delta a_n = a_n \frac{d\delta x}{dx} + b_n \frac{d\delta x}{dy} + c_n \frac{d\delta x}{dz} + ... + h_n \frac{d\delta x}{dt}.$$

By means of these developments the sum

$$\frac{dT}{da_1} \delta a_1 + \frac{dT}{da_2} \delta a_2 + \frac{dT}{da_3} \delta a_3 + ... + \frac{dT}{da_n} \delta a_n$$

reduces to

$$\Sigma \frac{dT}{da} \delta a = \frac{d\delta x}{dx} T.$$

A similar process would give

$$\Sigma \frac{dT}{db} \delta b = \frac{d\delta y}{dy} T,$$

and so on.   Hence finally

$$DT = \left(\frac{d\delta x}{dx} + \frac{d\delta y}{dy} + \frac{d\delta z}{dz} + ... + \frac{d\delta t}{dt} \right) T.$$

If we put this value in the expression DS and restore the original variables we have definitely for the variation of the proposed integral

$$DS = \iiint \ldots \left\{ \delta V + \frac{d\,(V\delta x)}{dx} + \frac{d\,(V\delta y)}{dy} + \frac{d\,(V\delta z)}{dz} + \ldots \right\} dx\,dy\,dz \ldots$$

This formula is due to M. Ostrogradsky, who established it by the infinitesimal method; afterwards M. Cauchy arrived at it by other considerations. As to the demonstration just proposed, which depends essentially on a change of variables, it is right to remark that the same expedient had been already employed by Poisson, when he investigated the variation of a double integral.

[The part of the preceding article in which it is inferred that the limits of S' do not change with i seems difficult; and it might with advantage be replaced by the method of Poisson given in Art. 86.]

CHAPTER XIII.

SYSTEMATIC TREATISES.

329. We shall now give an account of the works which have been published as systematic treatises on the whole subject. There are three which from their extent and importance demand particular notice; these we shall describe in the present chapter. In the next chapter we shall take the remaining works. In each chapter we shall follow the chronological order.

330. The first of the three treatises is that by Dr G. W. Strauch. Its title is *Theorie und Anwendung des sogenannten Variationscalcul's*. Zurich, 1849.

This work consists of two closely printed volumes of large octavo size. The first volume contains 499 pages, and the second 788; the first volume also contains a preface of 32 pages.

The Preface begins with a sketch of the history of the subject from the earliest period until the publication of Lagrange's *Théorie des fonctions analytiques* in 1797; this sketch is furnished with references to the original memoirs. The remainder of the preface is devoted to an account of the contents of the work and an indication of the points in which the author believes that he has improved or corrected the methods of his predecessors. Of the writers in the present century, Strauch mentions Lacroix, Gergonne, Dirksen, Poisson, Ohm, and Ostrogradsky. It is remarkable however that he takes no notice of Jacobi's theorems, nor does he refer to the memoirs of Gauss, Delaunay, Sarrus, and Cauchy, which we have described in preceding chapters.

331. The work may be divided into four parts. The first part occupies pages 1—356 of the first volume; these pages contain all the ordinary theoretical investigations of the subject, exclusive of those which refer to double or multiple integrals. The second part occupies the remainder of the first volume, and consists of the solution of 60 problems of maxima and minima, in which neither integrals nor differential coefficients appear; these problems are in fact almost entirely examples of the ordinary theory of maxima and minima values which is given in the Differential Calculus. The third part occupies pages 1—211 of the second volume, and consists of the solution of 93 problems of the maxima and minima values of expressions which involve differential coefficients but not integrals; these problems thus resemble that which we have given in Art. 3, from Lagrange. The fourth part occupies pages 212—739 of the second volume, and consists of the solution of 135 problems respecting the maxima and minima values of expressions which involve single or double integrals. The remainder of the second volume forms a supplement which is chiefly devoted to the theory of relative maxima and minima values.

332. Strauch may be considered as the successor of Ohm, whose methods he chiefly follows. The most valuable part of his work is that which we have called the fourth part. The problems there given are discussed with great fulness and clearness, and the terms of the second order are almost always completely exhibited in order to discriminate between maxima and minima values. Strauch is however content with Legendre's treatment of the terms of the second order, that is, he generally assumes that certain differential equations can be solved, and that the solutions of such differential equations will not introduce quantities that can become infinite; see Art. 5. In a few simple cases however Strauch actually solves the equations which are analogous to equation (2) of Art. 5. With the single exception of the general problem of the shortest line on any surface, all the great problems of the Calculus of Variations occur in Strauch's collection; and although he has not given the shortest line on any surface, he has given cases of the shortest line on specific surfaces. The problems are always accompanied by excellent historical

accounts of their origin and progress. On the whole, although the work contains much that is superfluous, and much that is of very inferior interest, and very little so far as the theory is concerned which had not appeared before, yet the large collection of carefully solved examples which it contains, recommends it to the notice of every student of the Calculus of Variations. The work is distinguished for remarkable accuracy, both in the investigations and in the printing.

333. We proceed to give a more detailed account of the contents of these volumes. We begin with the first volume.

The first section occupies pages 1—8; it is entitled *Propositions which belong to the Differential Calculus.* These pages contain nothing of importance; they are principally explanatory of the notation which the author adopts for distinguishing differential coefficients formed on different suppositions, such as partial and complete differential coefficients. The second section occupies pages 8—13; it is entitled *Propositions which belong to the Integral Calculus.* These pages contain nothing new; they principally refer to the differentiation of an integral with respect to any parameter which may occur in the expression to be integrated. The third section occupies pages 13—20; it consists of an investigation of the conditions under which certain homogeneous functions will retain an invariable sign. For example, consider the expression

$$Ap^2 + 2Bpq + Cq^2 + 2Dpr + 2Eqr + Fr^2,$$

and suppose that A, B, C, D, E, F are fixed quantities, and that p, q, r are variables which may have any value; then Strauch investigates the conditions that must hold among A, B, C, D, E, F in order that the expression may be of invariable sign. The fourth section occupies pages 20—69; it treats of the development of a function in powers of a variable, the function being connected with the variable by means of an unsolved equation. Thus, for example, on page 44, Strauch proposes to express u in a series of ascending powers of v, the equation which connects u and v being

$$u^3 - 3auv + v^3 = 0.$$

From this equation three series are deduced for u. For it is shewn that we may have

$$u = A_1 v^3 + A_2 v^5 + A_3 v^9 + A_4 v^{11} + \ldots$$

where A_1, A_2, A_3, A_4,... are successively determined, and each has only one value. Or we may have

$$u = B_1 v^{\frac{1}{2}} + B_2 v^3 + B_3 v^{\frac{5}{2}} + B_4 v^4 + \ldots$$

where B_1, B_2, B_3, B_4,... are successively determined. In this case it is found that B_1 may have two different values, and as the subsequent coefficients B_2, B_3, B_4,... are found in terms of B_1, each value of B_1 gives rise to a series for u, so that we have two different series for u. Thus, on the whole we have three forms for the expansion of u in terms of v; this might of course have been anticipated from the fact that the original equation is of the third degree in u, and therefore furnishes three values of u.

The method used by the author throughout this section is that of indeterminate coefficients. He is very careful in his examples to obtain all the different expansions which his expressions will furnish; and he has thus given a more complete exemplification of the method of indeterminate coefficients than is usual in works on algebra. The subject however is not very closely connected with the Calculus of Variations; and the chief use of this section is in relation to the first series of examples in the book, which as we have said belong to the ordinary theory of maxima and minima.

Thus the first four sections of the work are only introductory to the Calculus of Variations.

334. The fifth section occupies pages 69—131; it is entitled *Theory of the so-called Calculus of Variations*. In this section Strauch explains what is meant by a variation, and shews how to find the variations of different expressions. He objects to the word *variation* as not sufficiently distinctive, since the notion of variables runs through the whole of the Differential Calculus;

moreover the word *variation* is used in a peculiar sense in algebra.
Accordingly he adopts the word *mutation* instead of *variation*.
We shall however generally retain the usual word. His definition
of a variation coincides in fact with that which has been adopted
by Euler, Lagrange and Ohm; see Arts. 22, 15, 55. Let y stand
for $\phi(x)$; then he supposes $\phi(x)$ changed into $\phi(x, \kappa)$, and $\phi(x, \kappa)$
expanded in powers of κ by Maclaurin's Theorem; this expansion
he denotes by

$$y + \kappa \delta y + \frac{\kappa^2}{1 \cdot 2} \delta^2 y + \frac{\kappa^3}{\lfloor 3} \delta^3 y + \dots$$

Then supposing κ indefinitely small the series

$$\kappa \delta y + \frac{\kappa^2}{1 \cdot 2} \delta^2 y + \frac{\kappa^3}{\lfloor 3} \delta^3 y + \dots$$

is called the *variation* of y. The quantity κ is considered independent of x; thus the variation of $\dfrac{dy}{dx}$ is

$$\kappa \frac{d\delta y}{dx} + \frac{\kappa^2}{1 \cdot 2} \frac{d\delta^2 y}{dx} + \frac{\kappa^3}{\lfloor 3} \frac{d\delta^3 y}{dx} + \dots \, ;$$

and by differentiating this series with respect to x we obtain the
variation of $\dfrac{d^2 y}{dx^2}$, and so on.

Strauch lays great stress on the view he takes of a variation, and
asserts that the common method of denoting the variation of y by
a single term as δy or $\kappa \delta y$ leads to a number of absurdities and con-
tradictions. This assertion seems however quite arbitrary, and a very
careful examination of his theory and problems has not afforded
any confirmation of it. On the contrary, his method leads to a
great and needless complexity in the exhibition of the terms of
the second order in the variations of expressions, with the view
of discriminating between maxima and minima. The student of
Strauch's work will effect a great simplification, without any loss,
by supposing that such expressions as $\delta^2 y$, $\delta^3 y$, ..., are all zero, so
as to reduce each variation to its first term.

In the latter part of his fifth section Strauch explains a distinction on which he also lays great stress. A function is said to experience a *mixed mutation* when some of the variables undergo that kind of change which the Calculus of Variations contemplates, and others that kind of change which the Differential Calculus contemplates. We can illustrate this by considering an Integral, although Strauch himself does not introduce Integrals until the next section of his work. In varying an integral then he does not ascribe any *variation* to the independent variable, but makes changes in the *limits* of the integration. Thus he calls the whole change in the integral a *mixed mutation*, since it partly consists of an ordinary change of *value* of the limits of the independent variable, and partly of a change of *form* of the dependent variable which is strictly a variation or mutation. This restriction of variations to the dependent variables seems to possess all the advantages which Strauch claims for it.

The sixth section occupies pages 132—165; it treats of some special points in the theory of variations. This section presents nothing remarkable or important; it is chiefly occupied with inferences which follow from the view the author takes of a variation as consisting of an infinite series of terms.

335. The seventh section occupies pages 165—356; this contains the general theory of maxima and minima values. This section is divided into three parts; in the first Strauch considers expressions which involve neither integrals nor differential coefficients, in the second expressions which involve differential coefficients, in the third expressions which involve also single integrals.

Some general remarks and definitions are given on pages 165—171, and then the theory of the maxima and minima values of functions involving neither integrals nor differential coefficients occupies pages 171—231. This part of the book contains the ordinary theory of maxima and minima values which is explained in treatises on the Differential Calculus; the language is rather different from that which is usually employed and the various cases which occur are treated separately with great care; nothing however is given which might not be obtained from the ordinary treatises on the Differential Calculus. This part of the work is illustrated by a series of sixty problems occupying pages 357—480 of the first volume. These sixty problems are all, with the exception of the last six, ordinary problems of maxima and minima; the last six are of a slightly different character. Take for example problem 55. Let a be a given quantity, and let it be required to determine the function ϕ so that the following expression shall be a maximum or a minimum, without assigning a specific value to x,

$$a^2 - [\phi(x)]^2 + 2\phi(x)\,\phi(a) - [\phi(a)]^2 - 2x\,\phi(x) - 2a\,\phi(a).$$

Let y stand for $\phi(x)$ and y_a for $\phi(a)$, and denote the expression by U; then

$$\delta U = -2\,(y - y_a + x)\,\delta y - 2\,(y_a - y + a)\,\delta y_a.$$

Thus δU will vanish if

$$y - y_a + x = 0 \text{ and } y_a - y + a = 0.$$

These lead to $x = a$; this however is inconsistent with the supposition that x is not to have any specific value. Suppose the problem then limited by the condition that y_a is always to be invariable. Then to make δU vanish we only require $y - y_a + x = 0$. Suppose $x = a$ in this equation; thus $y_a - y_a + a = 0$; therefore $a = 0$. So the problem does not admit of a solution in the limited sense unless a be zero. In this case the only term of the second order is $-(\delta y)^2$, indicating that there is a maximum.

It is known that a function of any variable may be a maximum or minimum when its differential coefficient with respect to that variable is infinite as well as when it is zero; Strauch accordingly in his examples takes account of such infinite values very carefully.

The second part of the seventh section occupies pages 231—274; it investigates the conditions for the maxima and minima values of expressions which involve differential coefficients. We take his first case for an example. Suppose U a given function of x, y, and p, where p stands for $\frac{dy}{dx}$; and let it be required to find y in terms of x so that U may be a maximum or minimum. If we regard y and p both as variable, then, since the variations of y and p are independent, we must have in order that the variation of U should vanish

$$\frac{dU}{dy} = 0, \quad \text{and} \quad \frac{dU}{dp} = 0.$$

If we can find y in terms of x so as to satisfy simultaneously these two equations, we obtain a maximum or a minimum value of U provided that

$$\frac{d^2U}{dy^2}(\delta y)^2 + 2\frac{d^2U}{dy\,dp}\delta y\,\delta p + \frac{d^2U}{dp^2}(\delta p)^2$$

is of invariable sign for all indefinitely small values of δy and δp.

Also solutions may sometimes be found by taking y so that simultaneously

$$\frac{dU}{dy} = 0, \quad \text{and} \quad \frac{dU}{dp} = \infty,$$

$$\text{or so that } \frac{dU}{dy} = \infty, \quad \text{and} \quad \frac{dU}{dp} = 0,$$

$$\text{or so that } \frac{dU}{dy} = \infty, \quad \text{and} \quad \frac{dU}{dp} = \infty.$$

But we may if we please modify our original problem thus; required the relation that must hold between x and y in order that for a given value of y we may have U a maximum or minimum. That, is, we may suppose p susceptible of variation but not y. In this case we have to find y from the equation $\frac{dU}{dp} = 0$, and then we have a maximum or minimum according as $\frac{d^2U}{dp^2}$ is negative or positive. And a solution may sometimes be found by supposing

$$\frac{dU}{dp} = \infty .$$

Or we may suppose y susceptible of variation but not p; and then we have to seek for solutions from the equations

$$\frac{dU}{dy} = 0, \quad \text{and} \quad \frac{dU}{dy} = \infty .$$

Strauch then proceeds to the case in which U is a given function of x, y, p, q, ..., and is to be made a maximum or a minimum; then to cases in which such an expression is to be made a maximum or a minimum, while at the same time one or more relations are to hold between x, y, p, q, ... Then follow similar cases in which U is a given function of x, y, z, $\frac{dy}{dx}$, $\frac{dz}{dx}$, ...

Lagrange first considered a problem of the kind to which Strauch devotes this part of his seventh section, and Ohm first treated the subject in detail; see Arts. 3 and 56. The subject is neither difficult nor important. In his second volume Strauch illustrates this part of his work by a series of 93 examples, which occupy pages 1—211. One of these examples is that given by Lagrange, and three are taken from Ohm; the remainder are supplied by Strauch himself. See his preface, page xxix. Most of these examples are fully worked out, but a few are left with only indications of the steps.

The third part of the seventh section occupies pages 275—356; this contains such investigations as are usually comprised in the Calculus of Variations, so far as single integrals are concerned. Strauch proceeds in the same way as Ohm, beginning with simple cases and gradually rising to the more complex cases; see Art. 57. In order to distinguish between maxima and minima values he adopts Legendre's method, without any attention to the imperfections of the method indicated by Lagrange and others; see

Arts. 5, 6, 219.   He considers the case in which the integral involves more than one dependent variable, and he adapts Legendre's method to the discrimination of the maxima and minima values. This extension of Legendre's method he attributes to Ohm; see Strauch, Vol. I. page 311.

330.   We now come to the most valuable part of Strauch's work, namely, the collection of problems relating to the maxima and minima of integrals; this occupies pages 212—739 of the second volume.

The problems which relate to single integrals occupy pages 212—562; these are all examples of the theory which is developed in the third part of the seventh section. There are 95 problems according to the author's enumeration, but this number is obtained by counting as different problems many which are only varieties of one problem. Strauch says that he has taken 32 of these problems from Euler's *Methodus Inveniendi...*, and 14 of them from the writings of Lagrange; see Strauch's preface, page xxix. The problems are very carefully solved by Strauch; the various limiting cases that can occur are fully distinguished, and the terms of the second order are almost always investigated. Valuable historical notes are added to the discussion of the problems which have been proposed by the great writers on the subject.

The problems which relate to double integrals occupy pages 562—739. There are 40 problems according to the author's enumeration. These are principally strictly *examples;* but a few of them are theoretical investigations of the variations of double integrals, which Strauch had not previously considered. The theoretical investigations are given in his usual way by Strauch; he begins with the more simple cases and proceeds to the more complex. Thus on pages 674—676 he gives an investigation like that we have given in Art. 59 from Ohm; Strauch however supplies an investigation of the terms of the second order. Then on pages 713—717 he gives a similar investigation for the case in which the function under the integral sign involves x, y, z, $\dfrac{dz}{dx}$, $\dfrac{dz}{dy}$, $\dfrac{d^2z}{dx^2}$,

$\dfrac{d^2s}{dx\,dy}$ and $\dfrac{d^2z}{dy^2}$; here he does not supply an investigation of the
terms of the second order. This investigation on pages 713—717
does in fact sum up all that Strauch accomplishes with the variation of multiple integrals; his result coincides with that which we
have already given after Sarrus; see Arts. 183, 184.

Strauch, as we have already stated, does not refer to some of the
writers whose works had preceded his own; see Art. 330. He is
consequently disposed to claim as new investigations which had
already been made. Thus on his page 574 he supposes that he
is the first to investigate the terms of the second order in a certain double integral; Brunacci however had preceded him; see
Art. 213. Again, on his pages 737, 738 he institutes a comparison
between his own results and those of Poisson and Ostrogradsky;
and he justly states that his own are in some points more general. But, as we have stated above, Sarrus had preceded him in
the investigation which really involves all that he accomplishes.
See Art. 138.

We will now consider some special points suggested by the
work of Strauch.

337. We have spoken above of the extreme accuracy of the
work in general; we will here indicate a few points which appear
to be incorrect.

On page 438 of Vol. II. a case of the brachistochrone is discussed;
a heavy particle is supposed to be constrained to move on a fixed
plane, and there is a resistance which varies as the square of the
velocity. Here Strauch obtains the result that the curve becomes a
straight line. But he has interchanged the values of the quantities
which he obtains from his equations XXIV. and XXXI.; and he does
not observe that the true values render his $F(y)$ infinite and vitiate
his solution. He does not observe also that we can resolve the
force of gravity into two components, one in the fixed plane and the
other perpendicular to it, and then neglecting the latter component
the problem is the same as if the particle moved in a vertical
plane. The latter remark applies again on page 454.

On page 445 of Vol. 11. Strauch is discussing a problem given by Euler; the curve is required down which a heavy particle must move so as to acquire the greatest velocity, supposing a resistance varying as the square of the velocity. Strauch exhibits some investigations for discriminating between a maximum and a minimum. His equation XXV. cannot however be allowed, because his equation XXIV. from which he deduces it, is true for the curve which the particle is supposed actually to describe, but not true necessarily for any other curve.

On pages 461 and 462 of Vol. 11. he attempts to shew that it is possible that $\dfrac{Lp}{\sqrt{(1+p^2)}}$ can always be equal to a constant B, and yet L vanish when $x = a$. This is impossible, for $\dfrac{p}{\sqrt{(1+p^2)}}$ is always finite, and $\dfrac{Lp}{\sqrt{(1+p^2)}}$ is less than L. In fact his equation XXVIII. shews that y is impossible when $x = a$ if B is not zero. The only conclusion is that $B = 0$; then $p = 0$, and the curve becomes a straight line, as might have been anticipated. Similar remarks apply to page 466; it is impossible that $L_a = 0$ and $\dfrac{Lp}{\sqrt{(1+p^2)}} = a$ constant, unless that constant is zero.

838. Suppose we require the maximum or minimum value of an expression $\int \phi\, dx$, where ϕ involves x, y, and the differential coefficients of y with respect to x. Now the well-known process is to obtain $\int \delta\phi\, dx$, and to reduce this expression as much as possible by integration by parts until it takes the form $L + \int M \delta y\, dx$, where M contains no variation; then we put $M = 0$. Strauch has a very singular notion on this subject. He says it cannot be proved that we *must* have $M = 0$; although he allows that we do get solutions of our problem thus. Accordingly he proposes to try if solutions cannot be obtained by putting $\delta\phi = 0$. See his Preface, pages xxv. and xxvi. Thus he frequently tries two

processes of solution of his problems. It may be safely asserted that the ordinary view of the *necessity* of the equation $M = 0$ is sound; supposing that whatever series of values δy can assume it can also assume the corresponding series of values numerically equal but of opposite sign, without changing the limiting values of the variations. And on examination it will be found that nothing is gained in any part of Strauch's work by paying attention to what he considers a second solution of some of his problems. Let us take for example the case which he himself brings forward in the preface. Required the maximum or minimum value of the expression

$$\int_{a}^{b} (y^2 - 2xy + 2p - p^2)\, dx.$$

The ordinary method furnishes the equation

$$y - x - \frac{d}{dx}(1 - p) = 0,$$

that is,

$$y - x + \frac{d^2 y}{dx^2} = 0 \dots\dots\dots\dots\dots\dots\dots\dots (1).$$

And we have also the limiting equation

$$(1 - p)_b\, \delta y_b - (1 - p)_a\, \delta y_a = 0 \dots\dots\dots\dots\dots\dots (2).$$

Strauch then proposes the following as another solution. The variation of the proposed expression is

$$\int_{a}^{b} 2\left[(y - x)\, \delta y + 2(1 - p)\, \delta p\right] dx.$$

Without effecting any reduction by integration by parts, make this expression vanish; this we can do by supposing

$$y - x = 0 \quad \text{and} \quad 1 - p = 0 \dots\dots\dots\dots\dots\dots (3).$$

The second of equations (3) is in this case consistent with the first, so that we do get a solution. This however is not a *new* solution; it is comprised in (1); for $y = x$ is a particular solution of the differential equation (1); and $y = x$ also satisfies (2). Thus Strauch's supposed second solution is really included, as it should be, in the ordinary solution.

Before leaving this part of our subject we will offer some remarks with the view of guarding against a possible misconception of the principle of equating separately to zero the two parts of the variation of an integral, in order to obtain a maximum or minimum value of the integral. Consider the problem of finding the curve which with its evolute includes a minimum area. Let ρ denote the radius of curvature at any point of the curve, s the length of the arc of the curve measured from any fixed origin up to this point; then we require that $\int_{s_0}^{s_1} \rho \, ds$ should be a minimum. Let ρ receive the variation $\delta\rho$, and let s_0 and s_1 receive the increments ds_0 and ds_1 respectively; then the change in the integral is

$$\int_{s_0}^{s_1} \delta\rho \, ds + \rho_1 \, ds_1 - \rho_0 \, ds_0.$$

Here the coefficient of $\delta\rho$ under the integral sign is unity, which cannot be made to vanish; so that it might perhaps be supposed at once that the solution of the problem is impossible.

But the fact is that we cannot prove in such a case that in order to obtain a solution we *must* make the integrated part and the unintegrated part separately vanish. For when we take the arc s as the independent variable, and pass from one curve to an adjacent curve the length of the arc will in general be changed; and if we make any change in that part of the variation of an integral which remains under the integral sign, the part outside the integral sign also undergoes a change. In other words, the two parts which constitute the whole variation of a proposed integral are *not independent*, so that we are not *compelled* to make them separately vanish in order that the whole variation may vanish. If we *can* make them separately vanish we obtain a solution of the problem, subject of course to an examination of the terms of the second order; but we are not certain that this is the *only* solution. And if we cannot make them separately vanish we must not therefore conclude that the problem is impossible.

The point we are now considering is perhaps sufficiently obvious; but as it is sometimes a source of difficulty to students it may be useful to refer to two other examples.

Suppose we require a curve which has the property of making $\int \sqrt{\left(c + \dfrac{2}{r}\right)}\, ds$ a minimum, the ends of the curve being supposed fixed; c is a constant and r is the radius vector drawn from a fixed pole. The problem is thus equivalent to the following; assuming the principle of least action in Dynamics, and the ordinary law of attraction, determine the curve which a particle will describe. The result ought to be a conic section, and we shall obtain this result if we adopt the usual independent variable θ, and put

$$\sqrt{r^2 + \left(\frac{dr}{d\theta}\right)^2}\, d\theta \text{ for } ds.$$

But no result will be obtained by attempting to determine r as a function of s and operating in the usual way immediately on

$$\int \sqrt{\left(c + \frac{2}{r}\right)}\, ds.$$

Again, suppose we require to describe on a given chord a curve of given length, such that the area included by the curve and the chord may be a maximum. This can be easily solved in the usual way by taking x as the independent variable; the result is that the curve must be a circular arc. But suppose we take s as the independent variable, and take a fixed point as pole. Then the polar area between the curve and the extreme radii will be

$$\frac{1}{2} \int r \sqrt{1 - \left(\frac{dr}{ds}\right)^2}\, ds,$$

and as the triangle included by the given chord and the extreme radii is itself constant, we have to make the above area a maximum; also the length of the given curve is to be constant. Thus in the usual way we have to make the following expression a maximum,

$$\int \left\{ r \sqrt{1 - \left(\frac{dr}{ds}\right)^2} + c \right\} ds,$$

where c is a constant. Proceeding in the usual way we shall have the equation

$$r\sqrt{1 - \left(\frac{dr}{ds}\right)^2} + c = \frac{-r\left(\frac{dr}{ds}\right)^2}{\sqrt{1 - \left(\frac{dr}{ds}\right)^2}} + \text{constant,}$$

therefore $\dfrac{r}{\sqrt{1 - \left(\frac{dr}{ds}\right)^2}} = a$, where a is some constant.

Therefore $\left(\dfrac{ds}{dr}\right)^2 = \dfrac{a^2}{a^2 - r^2}$, that is, $1 + r^2\left(\dfrac{d\theta}{dr}\right)^2 = \dfrac{a^2}{a^2 - r^2}$;

therefore $\left(\dfrac{d\theta}{dr}\right)^2 = \dfrac{1}{a^2 - r^2}$.

From this we should obtain for the required curve a circle passing through the arbitrary pole; and this is inadmissible, because the circle is determined by the fact that it is to pass through the ends of the given chord and that its arc cut off by the chord is to have a constant length, so that it cannot in addition be made to pass through an arbitrary point.

If p denote the perpendicular from the pole on the tangent to the curve, the problem amounts to requiring that $\int (p + c)\, ds$ shall be a maximum; and in this form we see at once that no solution can be obtained by the ordinary method if we keep s as the independent variable and endeavour to determine p as a function of s.

We have hitherto spoken only for simplicity of the use of the arc s as an *independent* variable; but our remarks apply also to the use of the arc s as a *dependent* variable. Thus, taking the example already used, we have

$$\int\left\{r\sqrt{1 - \left(\frac{dr}{ds}\right)^2} + c\right\} ds = \int\left\{r\sqrt{\left(\frac{ds}{dr}\right)^2 - 1} + c\,\frac{ds}{dr}\right\} dr;$$

but if we adopt the right-hand form and thus treat r as the independent variable we shall arrive at the same untenable solution as before. The objection to the process is easily seen. Suppose we draw one curve through two fixed points, and then draw an adjacent curve by changing every s into $s + \delta s$, and also pass from the first curve to a third curve by changing every s into $s - \delta s$; then if we make the second curve to have the fixed initial and final points, the first and the third curves will not in general have the same final points. That is, we cannot change the sign of δs arbitrarily, and therefore we have no right to conclude that the coefficient of δs in the part remaining under the integral sign in the variation of the integral must be zero.

We may add that the fact that when we use the ordinary variables x and y we must equate to zero the coefficient of the variation under the integral sign, seems more obvious when we ascribe a variation to the dependent variable only than when we also vary the independent variable; this is an additional argument in favour of an opinion already expressed. See Art. 204.

339. Problems of maxima and minima which involve the product or quotient of integrals are sometimes incompletely solved. Strauch has given some examples for the purpose of drawing attention to the point which is liable to be overlooked; see his Preface, pages xxx. and xxxi. This deserves to be illustrated fully, and we will accordingly give two problems in addition to his.

I. Determine the form of a curve symmetrical with respect to its axis such that when suspended by its vertex the time of a small oscillation of the segment cut off by the ordinate which corresponds to a given abscissa may be a minimum.

Take the vertex as the origin, the tangent at the vertex as the axis of y and the axis of x vertically downwards; let c denote the given abscissa. The area cut off by the ordinate which corresponds to c is supposed to oscillate about an axis through the origin perpendicular to the plane of the curve. Then by the principles of mechanics the length of the equivalent simple pendulum is

$$\frac{\int_a^c \left(\frac{y^2}{3} + x^2\right) y\,dx}{\int_0^c yx\,dx},$$

and this expression must therefore be a minimum.

Denote the numerator and denominator of this fraction by u and v respectively. Then that $\dfrac{u}{v}$ may be a minimum we must have

$$\frac{\delta u}{v} - \frac{u\,\delta v}{v^2} = 0,$$

therefore

$$\delta u - \frac{u}{v}\,\delta v = 0;$$

that is,

$$\int_0^c (y^2 + x^2)\,\delta y\,dx - \frac{u}{v}\int_0^c x\,\delta y\,dx = 0.$$

Now let $\dfrac{u}{v}$ be denoted by l; then l is a constant for our purpose, so that the last equation may be written

$$\int_0^a (y^2 + x^2 - lx)\,\delta y\,dx = 0.$$

Hence in the usual way we infer that

$$y^2 + x^2 - lx = 0,$$

and so we apparently obtain a circle as a solution of the proposed problem.

The solution however *is not yet completed;* for we require that $\dfrac{u}{v}$ should be equal to l. Substitute for y its value in terms of x which has just been obtained; then we require that

$$\frac{\dfrac{1}{3}\displaystyle\int_0^a (lx + 2x^2)\,\sqrt{(lx - x^2)}\,dx}{\displaystyle\int_0^a x\,\sqrt{(lx - x^2)}\,dx} = l,$$

therefore

$$\frac{\dfrac{2}{3}\displaystyle\int_0^a x^2\,\sqrt{(lx - x^2)}\,dx}{\displaystyle\int_0^a x\,\sqrt{(lx - x^2)}\,dx} = \frac{2l}{3},$$

therefore

$$\int_0^c (x^2 - lx) \sqrt{(lx - x^2)}\, dx = 0,$$

that is,

$$-\int_0^c (lx - x^2)^{\frac{3}{2}}\, dx = 0.$$

This is impossible; so that the proposed problem does not admit of a solution.

In fact in this problem as there is no limitation about the area we can suppose it to diminish down to an indefinitely small area in the neighbourhood of the origin, and so make the time of a small oscillation indefinitely small.

In such a problem as the above, the investigation as to whether such a condition as that denoted by $\dfrac{u}{v} = l$ can be satisfied, is sometimes omitted; in the present case it appears that this condition cannot be satisfied. We will now give a problem of the same kind which does admit of a solution.

II. A given volume of a given substance is to be formed into a solid of revolution, such that the time of a small oscillation about a horizontal axis perpendicular to the axis of the figure may be a minimum; determine the form of the solid.

Take the axis of x coincident with the axis of figure, and the axis of y coincident with the line about which the body is to revolve; let x_1 be the abscissa of the lowest point of the body. We have to find the equation to the curve, which by revolution round the axis of x will generate the required solid; we suppose the curve to lie in the plane of (x, y). By the principles of mechanics the length of the equivalent simple pendulum is

$$\frac{\int_0^{x_1} \left(\frac{y^2}{4} + x^2\right) y^2\, dx}{\int_0^{x_1} y^2 x\, dx};$$

this expression must therefore be a minimum, while $\pi \int_0^{x_1} y^2\, dx$ is to be equal to a constant, namely to the given volume. Hence, by the usual principle we must have

$$\frac{\displaystyle\int_{_0}^{^{x_1}}\left(\frac{y^2}{4}+x^2\right)y^2\,dx}{\displaystyle\int_{_0}^{^{x_1}}y^2x\,dx}+\beta\int_{_0}^{^{x_1}}y^2\,dx.$$

a minimum, where β is some constant.

We will at first vary y, and afterwards examine the terms which arise from a change in the limit x_1 of the integrations. Let u and v denote the numerator and denominator respectively of the fraction which occurs in the above expression; then in order that the expression may be a minimum, we must have

$$\frac{\delta u}{v}-\frac{u\,\delta v}{v^2}+\beta\delta\int_{_0}^{^{x_1}}y^2\,dx=0,$$

therefore

$$\delta u-\frac{u}{v}\,\delta v+\beta v\delta\int_{_0}^{^{x_1}}y^2\,dx=0,$$

that is,

$$\int_{_0}^{^{x_1}}(y^2+2yx^2)\,\delta y\,dx-\frac{u}{v}\int_{_0}^{^{x_1}}2yx\,\delta y\,dx+\beta v\int_{_0}^{^{x_1}}2y\,\delta y\,dx=0.$$

Now let $\dfrac{u}{v}$ be denoted by l, and βv by β'; then l and β' are constants for our purpose, so that the last equation may be written

$$\int_{_0}^{^{x_1}}(y^2+2yx^2-2lyx+2\beta'y)\,\delta y\,dx=0.$$

Hence, we infer that

$$y^2+2yx^2-2lyx+2\beta'y=0,$$

so that

$$y^2+2x^2-2lx+2\beta'=0\ \dots\dots\dots\dots\dots\dots(1).$$

This indicates that the generating curve is an ellipse with the axes in the ratio of 1 to $\sqrt{2}$. The solution however is not yet completed; for we must shew that the relation just found will

make $\dfrac{u}{v} = l$. This we will shew presently; but we will previously
advert to the terms which arise from a change in the limit x_i of
the integrations. Suppose then that x_i becomes $x_i + dx_i$, then
to the first order the following is the increment of the expression
which we have to make a minimum,

$$\frac{\left(\frac{y^4}{4} + y^2 x^2\right)_i}{v}\, dx_i - \frac{u}{v}\, (y^2 x)_i\, dx_i + \beta y_i^2\, dx_i,$$

where the subscript denotes that x is to be made equal to x_i. In
order that this increment may vanish, we must have either
$y_i = 0$, or

$$\left(\frac{y^2}{4} + x^2 - Lx + \beta\right)_i = 0,$$

and the latter combined with the general relation (1) leads also
to $y_i = 0$. Thus at the lower limit the generating curve meets
the axis of figure.

We have now to shew that it is possible to have

$$\frac{\displaystyle\int_a^{x_i} \left(\frac{y^4}{4} + y^2 x^2\right) dx}{\displaystyle\int_a^{x_i} y^2 x\, dx} = l,$$

when y is determined by equation (1), and x_i is such that y
vanishes when $x = x_i$.

We have from (1)

$$y^2 + 2\left(x - \frac{l}{2}\right)^2 = \frac{l^2}{2} - 2\beta;$$

let a and $a\sqrt{2}$ be the semiaxes of the ellipse, determined by this
equation; then $\dfrac{l^2}{2} - 2\beta = 2a^2$, and (1) becomes

$$y^2 + 2\left(x - \frac{l}{2}\right)^2 = 2a^2.$$

This equation indicates that the centre of the ellipse is at the distance $\frac{l}{2}$ from the origin. Assume $x_1 = 2a - c$, then

$$\frac{l}{2} = x_1 - a = a - c.$$

Hence we have to shew that

$$\frac{\int_0^{2a-c} \left(\frac{y^4}{4} + y^2 x^2\right) dx}{\int_0^{2a-c} y^2 x\, dx} = 2(a-c) \quad\dots\dots\dots\dots (2);$$

when

$$y^2 + 2(x - a + c)^2 = 2a^2.$$

We have

$$y^2 = 4ac - 2c^2 + 4x(a-c) - 2x^2;$$

therefore

$$\frac{y^4}{4} + y^2 x^2 = \frac{1}{4} y^2 (y^2 + 4x^2) = \left\{2ac - c^2 + 2x(a-c)\right\}^2 - x^4$$

$$= (2ac - c^2)^2 + 4x(2ac - c^2)(a-c) + 4x^2(a-c)^2 - x^4.$$

Integrate from $x = 0$, to $x = 2a - c$; thus we obtain

$$\int_0^{2a-c} \left(\frac{y^4}{4} + y^2 x^2\right) dx =$$

$$c^2 (2a - c)^2 + 2c(a-c)(2a-c)^2 + \frac{4}{3}(a-c)^2(2a-c)^3 - \frac{1}{5}(2a-c)^5.$$

And

$$\int_0^{2a-c} y^2 x\, dx = c(2a - c)^2 + \frac{4}{3}(a-c)(2a-c)^3 - \frac{1}{2}(2a-c)^4.$$

Thus the left-hand member of (2) becomes

$$\frac{c^2 + 2c(a-c) + \frac{4}{3}(a-c)^2 - \frac{1}{5}(2a-c)^2}{c + \frac{4}{3}(a-c) - \frac{1}{2}(2a-c)},$$

that is

$$\frac{4\left(c^{2}+ac+4a^{2}\right)}{5\left(c+2a\right)};$$

and (2) becomes

$$\frac{2\left(c^{2}+ac+4a^{2}\right)}{5\left(c+2a\right)}=a-c,$$

therefore $\qquad 7c^{2}+7ac-2a^{2}=0.$

This equation furnishes one positive value of $\frac{c}{a}$; it is approximately equal to $\frac{8}{14}$.

Then β' is to be found in terms of a from the equation

$$\frac{\Gamma}{2}-2\beta'=2a^{2};$$

this gives a negative value for β', as should be the case, because from (1) we obtain $y^{2}=-2\beta'$ when $x=0$. The constant a is to be determined from the given volume, that is by means of the equation

$$\pi\int_{0}^{a-c}2\left[a^{2}-(x-a+c)^{2}\right]dx=\text{the given volume.}$$

To shew that we have really obtained a minimum we should investigate the terms of the second order in the variation of $\frac{u}{v}$; to this we shall now proceed. The variation of $\frac{u}{v}$ arises partly from the change of y into $y+\delta y$, and partly from the change of x_{1} into $x_{1}+dx_{1}$. We shall first shew that by reason of the supposition that y vanishes when $x=x_{1}$, the change in u or v arising from the change of x_{1} into $x_{1}+dx_{1}$ may be disregarded. For example, consider v; the change in v produced by the change is $\int_{x_{1}}^{x_{1}+dx_{1}}y^{2}x\,dx$; and as y itself is indefinitely small for values of x lying between x_{1} and $x_{1}+dx_{1}$, the above integral may be considered of the *third* order of small quantities. Similar remarks hold with respect to the change of u. Thus to the second order we may say that the complete variation of $\dfrac{u}{v}$ is

$$\frac{\int_0^{x_1}\left\{\dfrac{(y+\delta y)^4}{4} + (y+\delta y)^2 x^2\right\}dx}{\int_0^{x_1}(y+\delta y)^2 x\,dx} - \frac{\int_0^{x_1}\left(\dfrac{y^4}{4}+y^2x^2\right)dx}{\int_0^{x_1}y^2 x\,dx} . \quad .$$

Thus to the second order we obtain $\dfrac{P}{Q}-\dfrac{u}{v}$, where

$$P = \frac{u}{v} + \frac{1}{v}\int_0^{x_1}(y^3 + 2yzx^2)\,\delta y\,dx + \frac{1}{v}\int_0^{x_1}\left(\frac{3y^2}{2} + x^2\right)(\delta y)^2\,dx,$$

and

$$Q = 1 + \frac{2}{v}\int_0^{x_1}yx\,\delta y\,dx + \frac{1}{v}\int_0^{x_1}(\delta y)^2 x\,dx.$$

This gives for the variation the following terms of the first order,

$$\frac{1}{v}\int_0^{x_1}(y^3 + 2yzx^2)\,\delta y\,dx - \frac{2u}{v^2}\int_0^{x_1}yx\,\delta y\,dx,$$

together with the following terms of the second order,

$$\frac{1}{v}\int_0^{x_1}\left(\frac{3y^2}{2} + x^2\right)(\delta y)^2\,dx - \frac{2}{v^2}\left(\int_0^{x_1}yx\,\delta y\,dx\right)\left(\int_0^{x_1}(y^3 + 2yzx^2)\,\delta y\,dx\right)$$

$$-\frac{u}{v^2}\int_0^{x_1}(\delta y)^2 x\,dx + \frac{4u}{v^3}\left(\int_0^{x_1}yx\,\delta y\,dx\right)^2.$$

We shall denote the terms of the first order by M_1 and those of the second order by M_2; so that if the complete variation of $\dfrac{u}{v}$ to the second order be denoted by $\delta\dfrac{u}{v}$, we have

$$\delta\frac{u}{v} = M_1 + M_2 \quad\dotfill\quad (8).$$

Now since the volume is to be constant we have

$$\int_0^{x_1}(y+\delta y)^2\,dx - \int_0^{x_1}y^2\,dx = 0,$$

that is
$$2 \int_0^{x_1} y \delta y \, dx + \int_0^{x_1} (\delta y)^2 \, dx = 0 \quad \ldots\ldots\ldots\ldots\ldots (4).$$

Multiply (4) by β and add to (3); thus

$$\delta \frac{u}{v} = M_1 + 2\beta \int_0^{x_1} y \delta y \, dx + M_2 + \beta \int_0^{x_1} (\delta y)^2 \, dx.$$

And $M_1 + 2\beta \int_0^{x_1} y \delta y \, dx$ vanishes by (1); thus

$$\delta \frac{u}{v} = M_2 + \beta \int_0^{x_1} (\delta y)^2 \, dx,$$

that is
$$\delta \frac{u}{v} = \frac{1}{v} \int_0^{x_1} \left(\frac{3y^2}{2} + x^2 - lx + \beta \right) (\delta y)^2 \, dx$$

$$- \frac{2}{v^2} \left(\int_0^{x_1} yx \, \delta y \, dx \right) \left(\int_0^{x_1} 2(lx - \beta) \, y \delta y \, dx \right) + \frac{4l}{v^2} \left(\int_0^{x_1} yx \, \delta y \, dx \right)^2,$$

that is

$$\delta \frac{u}{v} = \frac{1}{v} \int_0^{x_1} y^2 (\delta y)^2 \, dx + \frac{4\beta}{v^2} \left(\int_0^{x_1} yx \, \delta y \, dx \right) \left(\int_0^{x_1} y \delta y \, dx \right).$$

This value of $\delta \frac{u}{v}$ is true to the second order, that is, no term of the second order has been omitted.

But from (4) we see that $\int_0^{x_1} y \delta y \, dx$ is itself of the second order, so that the latter of the above two terms is really of the *third* order. Hence finally to the second order

$$\delta \frac{u}{v} = \frac{1}{v} \int_0^{x_1} y^2 (\delta y)^2 \, dx;$$

and as the right-hand member of this equation is *positive* we have obtained a minimum value of $\frac{u}{v}$.

340. The criticisms which Strauch offers on preceding writers are sometimes of a very trifling character; we have already seen an instance in Art. 39, and we will now notice two others.

In the problem solved by Poisson which we have reproduced in Art. 99, Poisson's own result has θ instead of $\theta + \Delta$; that is, Poisson has not explicitly introduced the constant Δ in his last integration. Strauch refers to this slight omission in such a manner as almost to lead a reader to suppose that Poisson's investigation must be altogether unsatisfactory. See Vol. II. page 504.

On pages 747, 748 of his second volume Strauch solves a problem of a relative minimum as an example of Euler's method. It required a curve such that the area bounded by the curve the axis of x and ordinates at fixed points of this axis shall be constant, and at the same time the centre of gravity of this area at a minimum distance from the axis of x.

Let the abscissae of the fixed points be a and z; then $\dfrac{\int_a^z y^2\, dx}{2\int_a^z y\, dx}$ is to be a minimum while $\int_a^z y\, dx$ is constant.

Let
$$U = \frac{\int_a^z y^2\, dx}{2\int_a^z y\, dx} + L \int_a^z y\, dx \quad\dots\dots\dots\dots\dots (1),$$

where L is a constant; and let $\int_a^z y\, dx$ be denoted by Δ.

Then
$$\delta U = \frac{\int_a^z y\,\delta y\, dx}{\Delta} - \frac{\int_a^z y^2\, dx}{2\Delta^2} \int_a^z \delta y\, dx + L \int_a^z \delta y\, dx \dots\dots (2).$$

Now put
$$\int_a^z y^2\, dx = C \int_a^z y\, dx \quad\dots\dots\dots\dots\dots\dots (3),$$

then (2) may be expressed thus,
$$\delta U = \frac{1}{2\Delta} \int_a^z (2y - C + 2\Delta L)\,\delta y\, dx.$$

Thus
$$2y - C + 2\Delta L = 0 \quad\dots\dots\dots\dots\dots (4),$$

so that we obtain a straight line parallel to the axis of x for the required curve. Then from (3) we obtain

$$\left(\frac{C-2AL}{2}\right)^2 (a-a) = C\,\frac{C-2AL}{2}\,(a-a),$$

therefore $C = 2AL$ or $= -2AL$; the former by (4) gives the inadmissible result $y = 0$, the latter gives $y = C$.

Now let the constant area be denoted by g^2; then since

$$\int_a^a y\,dx = g^2,$$

we obtain $\qquad\qquad C(a-a) = g^2.$

Strauch now proceeds to investigate the terms of the second order; he arrives at the result that the sign of these terms is the same as that of

$$\int_a^a (\delta y)^2\,dx - \frac{1}{a-a}\left(\int_a^a \delta y\,dx\right)^2,$$

and he says that as we cannot assert that the sign of this expression is positive we are not justified in concluding by this method that there is a minimum, although it is obvious from statical considerations that our result does give a minimum. He therefore concludes that Euler's process is defective. The answer is obvious. Since the area is to be constant $\int_a^a \delta y\,dx$ is absolutely zero, so that we are sure of a minimum from Strauch's own process. It will be found on examining Strauch's investigation of the terms of the second order that he has in effect in one place himself recognized that $\int_a^a \delta y\,dx$ is zero. The whole solution is more laborious than was necessary; for since $\int_a^a y\,dx$ is constant we might instead of Strauch's value of U have used the more simple value given by

$$U = \int_a^a y^2\,dx + L\int_a^a y\,dx.$$

Strauch's objections to the methods of Euler and Lagrange for solving problems of relative maxima and minima seem unimportant; and his own method is unnecessarily complex. See Vol. I. pages 339—355, and Vol. II. pages 740—763.

341. It will be convenient to notice in connexion with the work of Strauch an elaborate memoir which he presented to the Academy of Sciences at Vienna in 1856, and which may be regarded as a continuation of his work. The title of the memoir is *Anwendung des sogenannten Variationscalcul's auf zweifache und dreifache Integrale;* it was published in 1859 in the 16th volume of the *Denkschriften* of the Academy. The memoir occupies 156 large quarto pages, and is remarkable for the accuracy and beauty of the printing.

The introduction refers to the memoirs of Delaunay, Sarrus and Cauchy, which we have described in Chapters VI, VII, VIII. Strauch considers that these memoirs do not really effect what was required by the Academy of Sciences at Paris when they proposed their prize subject; see Art. 133. Accordingly he undertakes in the present memoir to investigate the variations of double and triple integrals.

After some explanatory remarks respecting his notation he proceeds to the variation of double integrals; this subject occupies pages 8—78 of the memoir. This part of the memoir contains little more than the author had already given in his work, for the most general investigation which occurs is that which we have already stated to be the most general investigation in his work; see Art. 336. The methods are the same as in his work; he begins with simple cases and proceeds to those which are more complex; he gives a full account of the various suppositions which can be made respecting the limits of the integrations, although his statement of the manner in which the arbitrary functions or constants must be determined is too vague and general to be of much value. He usually investigates the terms of the second order, but in transforming these terms he is content with imitating the method of Legendre. The variation of triple integrals occupies pages 79—132 of the memoir, and is treated in his usual manner by the author. The most general investigation which is completely worked out is the variation of a triple integral in which no differential coefficient occurs of an order higher than the first; some more general investigations are partially worked out. Four problems occur as examples in this part of the memoir. The first is to find w so that the following triple integral may have a maximum or minimum value,

$$\iiint \left\{ \varDelta^2 - \left(\frac{d^3 w}{dx\, dy\, dz} \right)^2 \right\} dx\, dy\, dz,$$

where $\varDelta$ is a constant, and the limits of the integrations are all constants. The other three problems are modifications of that which we have given from Sarrus in Art. 180.

The pages 133—154 of the memoir contain some remarks on the memoirs of Sarrus, Cauchy and Delaunay. Strauch quotes at full the result which Sarrus obtains for the problem which we have explained in Art. 194, and compares this result with that which he obtains by his own processes and in his own notation. Strauch gives that result from Cauchy's memoir which we have investigated in Art. 192, and compares it with that which he obtains by his own processes and in his own notation. In his remarks on Delaunay he intimates that some terms are omitted by Delaunay in his formulæ; see pages 147 and 148 of the memoir. There is however no error in Delaunay's formulæ; the terms in question do not appear because the problem which Delaunay considers is not the most general that could be proposed, as we have already stated in Art. 138.

Again on page 149 Strauch intimates that Delaunay has only *two* equations for determining certain arbitrary functions, while *four* are required, which he has himself supplied; Strauch's four equations would however reduce to two in the particular case which Delaunay considers.

342. The next of the three comprehensive treatises is Mr Jellett's, entitled *An elementary treatise on the Calculus of Variations by the Rev. J. H. Jellett*. Dublin 1850. It is an octavo volume of 377 pages, with a preface and introduction of 20 pages.

This valuable work constitutes the only complete treatise on the Calculus of Variations in the English language, and will necessarily be studied by all who wish to pass beyond the rudiments of the subject. A brief outline of the work with some remarks on a few incidental points is consequently all that will be required here.

343. The introduction contains a sketch of the history of the subject; it appears that the author had studied the memoirs of Poisson, Ostrogradsky, Jacobi and Delaunay, but had not seen that of Sarrus. The first chapter is entitled *Definitions and Principles;* it occupies pages 1—10, and explains what is meant by a variation. A very important remark occurs on page 5, " .... many writers on the Calculus of Variations have been led into considerable difficulties by an unsteady use of the symbol δ, a symbol which they employ sometimes to express the increment which a function receives in consequence of a change of form *only*, and sometimes to express the increment which it receives from the variation, not only of its form, but also of its independent variables. We shall then use the symbol δ to denote that species of increment which is peculiar to the Calculus of Variations, that, namely, which a function receives in consequence of a change in its form *only*. We shall, as in the Differential Calculus, denote by the symbol d that increment which a function receives in consequence of a change in the magnitude of its independent variables."

Accordingly in Mr Jellett's work the independent variable is not supposed to undergo *variation*. It has already been stated in the course of the present work that this appears the best method of treating the subject.

344. The second chapter is entitled *Functions of one independent variable;* it occupies pages 11—30. It contains the ordinary investigations and transformations of the variation of a single integral so far as terms of the first order, and also an investigation of the terms of the second order; the usual expression *second variation* is adopted for these terms, but a good note is given on page 355 respecting the ambiguity of this expression. The third chapter is entitled, *Maxima and minima of indeterminate functions of one independent variable;* it occupies pages 31—136. This chapter contains the ordinary investigation of the equation or equations which must hold in order that an integral may have a

maximum or a minimum value. Jacobi's theory for distinguishing between a maximum and a minimum is fully developed; the author here follows the guidance of Delaunay, see Arts. 230—236. This chapter contains a very important discussion as to the number of constants which can occur in the solution of a certain problem, and as to the number of them which are indeterminate. Let it be required to make the integral $\int_{x_0}^{x_1} V dx$ a maximum or a minimum, where V contains x, y, z, and the differential coefficients of y and z with respect to x; while at the same time a relation $L = 0$ is always to hold among these quantities. The following is the conclusion. Suppose that V contains y and its differential coefficients as far as that of the order n inclusive, and z and its differential coefficients as far as that of the order m; suppose that the equation $L = 0$ is of the order n' in differential coefficients of y and of the order m' in differential coefficients of z.   Then

(1) If m be greater then m' and n greater than n' the order of the final differential equation will be the greater of the two quantities

$$2 (m + n') \text{ and } 2 (m' + n),$$

and there will be a sufficient number of ancillary equations to determine the arbitrary constants which enter into its solution.

(2) The same conclusion holds for the case in which m is greater than m' and n less than n'.

(3) If m' is greater than m and n' greater than n, the order of the final equation will be in general

$$2 (m' + n');$$

and its solution may contain any number of indeterminate constants not exceeding the lesser of the two quantities

$$2 (m' - m) \text{ and } 2 (n' - n).$$

Mr Jellett points out that a remark made by Poisson in the ninth section of his memoir is inconsistent with these results.

The whole of this chapter is illustrated by examples which are fully solved.

345. The fourth chapter is entitled *Application of the Calculus of Variations to Geometry.* I. *Theory of Curves;* it occupies pages 137—202. This chapter consists of a collection of problems, including those of historical celebrity; they are all fully solved. The fifth chapter is entitled *On multiple Integrals in general;* it occupies pages 203—218. The sixth chapter is entitled *Functions of two or more independent variables;* it occupies pages 219—238. The fifth and sixth chapters contain the variation of multiple integrals; the methods are those of Ostrogradsky and Delaunay. The most general result obtained is equivalent to that which we have given in Art. 144 after Delaunay. The seventh chapter is entitled *On maxima and minima of functions of two or more independent variables;* it occupies pages 239—275. This chapter illustrates and applies the results of the preceding chapter; several examples are discussed in order to shew the treatment of the limiting equations.

346. The eighth chapter is entitled *Application of the Calculus of Variations to Geometry.* II. *Theory of Surfaces;* it occupies pages 276—286. The ninth chapter is entitled *Application of the Calculus of Variations to Mechanics;* it occupies pages 287—334. This chapter besides the usual examples contains a section on the application of the Calculus of Variations to the deduction of equations of equilibrium and motion. The tenth chapter is entitled *Application of the Calculus of Variations to the integration of functions of one or more independent variables;* it occupies pages 335—354. This chapter investigates the *conditions of integrability* of various expressions. The remainder of the work consists of notes.

347. It may be of service to students into whose hands the work under consideration may come, to advert to some points which may occasion a little difficulty; and on this ground we shall now venture to offer some remarks.

348. In the fourth chapter of Mr Jellett's treatise many of the problems are solved by using the arc *s* of a curve as the inde-

pendent variable; the method however is free from the objection stated in Art. 338. There is an example on page 138 and the following pages. In the course of the solution a constant a occurs, and it is stated that the "existence of the arbitrary constant a is an ambiguity necessarily introduced by the selection of s for the independent variable." A reason is then assigned for making $a = 0$; but the reason does not seem satisfactory. It appears that the term $\mu_1 ds_1 - \mu_0 ds_0$ is omitted in the discussion of the limiting terms on page 141. The whole expression relative to the upper limit should be

$$\mu_1 ds_1 + \lambda_1 \left\{ \left(\frac{dx}{ds}\right)_1 \delta x_1 + \left(\frac{dy}{ds}\right)_1 \delta y_1 \right\};$$

then giving to m_1 the same meaning as Mr Jellett does, we have

$$\delta y_1 + \left(\frac{dy}{ds}\right)_1 ds_1 = m_1 \left\{ \delta x_1 + \left(\frac{dx}{ds}\right)_1 ds_1 \right\} \ \dots\dots\dots\dots (1).$$

By means of (1) the expression relative to the upper limit becomes

$$\mu_1 ds_1 + \lambda_1 \left(\frac{dx}{ds}\right)_1 \delta x_1 + \lambda_1 \left(\frac{dy}{ds}\right)_1 \left\{ m_1 \delta x_1 + m_1 \left(\frac{dx}{ds}\right)_1 ds_1 - \left(\frac{dy}{ds}\right)_1 ds_1 \right\}.$$

Hence

$$\mu_1 + \lambda_1 \left(\frac{dy}{ds}\right)_1 \left\{ m_1 \left(\frac{dx}{ds}\right)_1 - \left(\frac{dy}{ds}\right)_1 \right\} = 0 \ \dots\dots\dots\dots (2),$$

and

$$\left(\frac{dx}{ds}\right)_1 + m_1 \left(\frac{dy}{ds}\right)_1 = 0 \ \dots\dots\dots\dots\dots\dots (3).$$

Substitute from (3) in (2); thus

$$\mu_1 - \lambda_1 \left\{ \left(\frac{dx}{ds}\right)_1^2 + \left(\frac{dy}{ds}\right)_1^2 \right\} = 0;$$

therefore $\mu_1 = \lambda_1$.

This proves that $a = 0$; since the book proves that $\lambda = \mu + a$.

349. We have stated in the preceding Article that it appears that $\mu_1 ds_1 - \mu_0 ds_0$ is omitted in the discussion of the limiting terms.

In support of this remark we may advert to Art. 152 of the present work. There by taking account of certain limiting terms we obtain the equation

$$\frac{\lambda'}{\rho^2} = 1 + a\frac{dx}{ds} + b\frac{dy}{ds} + c\frac{dz}{ds};$$

this equation does not occur in Mr Jellett's investigation. The truth of this equation is confirmed in Art. 157 by its agreement with a result obtained by Delaunay.

There is a difference in the methods we have used in Arts. 152 and 348. In Art. 152 we followed the ordinary method and ascribed a variation to the independent variable s; in Art. 348 we do not ascribe a variation to s. The final results will agree in the two methods, but the processes will differ. Thus in Art. 348, if we follow the ordinary method the whole expression relative to the upper limit will be

$$\mu_1\delta s_1 + \lambda_1\left[\left(\frac{dx}{ds}\right)_1\left\{\delta x_1 - \left(\frac{dx}{ds}\right)_1\delta s_1\right\} + \left(\frac{dy}{ds}\right)_1\left\{\delta y_1 - \left(\frac{dy}{ds}\right)_1\delta s_1\right\}\right],$$

instead of what we have given; and instead of (1) we shall have

$$\delta y_1 = m_1\,\delta x_1.$$

Thus the expression above becomes

$$(\mu_1 - \lambda_1)\,\delta s_1 + \lambda_1\left\{\left(\frac{dx}{ds}\right)_1 + m_1\left(\frac{dy}{ds}\right)_1\right\}\delta y_1,$$

and from this we obtain as before

$$\mu_1 - \lambda_1 = 0, \quad \text{and} \left(\frac{dx}{ds}\right)_1 + m_1\left(\frac{dy}{ds}\right)_1 = 0.$$

On the other hand, suppose that in Art. 152 we follow the second method. Then instead of the term

$$\left(V + a\frac{dx}{ds} + b\frac{dy}{ds} + c\frac{ds}{ds} - \frac{\lambda'}{\rho^2}\right)\delta s$$

which is there given, we should have simply $V ds$. But now the variations of the limiting co-ordinates will not be simply δx, δy, δz, as in Art. 152, but

$$\delta x + \frac{dx}{ds}\, ds, \quad \delta y + \frac{dy}{ds}\, ds, \quad \delta z + \frac{dz}{ds}\, ds$$

respectively; and these must vanish at the limits, since the limits are supposed fixed. Thus we shall obtain finally the same result as before.

Of the two methods which can be used, Mr Jellett has decided in favour of that which does not ascribe a variation to the independent variable, see Art. 343. But it would seem that in the fourth chapter of his work he has not adopted uniformly the consequences which follow from this decision.

350. Remarks similar to those already made apply with respect to pages 153, 155, 178, 181, 183 and 299 of the book.

Again, on page 170 it is remarked, "and the remaining constant, a, depending upon the given length of the curve...." Nothing however has been previously said respecting the given length; and it appears here as before that $\mu_1\, ds_1 - \mu_0\, ds_0$ should be added to the limiting terms if we adopt the method of Art. 349. Or if we adopt the method of Art. 152 we must add

$$(\mu - \lambda + \mu' \rho)_1\, \delta s_1 - (\mu - \lambda + \mu' \rho)_0\, \delta s_0.$$

Again, on page 175 it is stated, "the superfluous constant a will be determined by expressing the area as a function of that constant and equating its differential to zero." This reference to the ordinary Differential Calculus is unnecessary; for the Calculus of Variations supplies sufficient conditions for determining the constants. The problem under discussion is, to find a curve of given length such that the area bounded by the curve itself, its two extreme radii of curvature, and the arc of the evolute between them may be a minimum. This problem is solved in most elementary treatises, and the result obtained is that the curve must be a cycloid; this result is obtained by the ordinary processes of the Calculus of Variations. In fact if we adopt the method of Art. 152

we shall find that the following limiting terms have been omitted
in the book,

$$(\mu - \lambda + \mu'\rho)_1 \, \delta s_1 - (\mu - \lambda + \mu'\rho)_0 \, \delta s_0,$$

where $\mu' = 1$ and $\mu = \rho + $ a constant.

From considering these we find that we must have

$$\lambda_1 = 0, \quad \text{and} \quad \lambda_0 = 0,$$

since ρ_1 and ρ_0 vanish. Then by page 168 of the work, we have

$$\lambda = a \frac{dx}{ds} + \mu'\rho,$$

for it is shewn on page 169 that $b = 0$. Thus $\left(\dfrac{dx}{ds}\right)_1$ and $\left(\dfrac{dx}{ds}\right)_0$ must

vanish. Then by page 174 since $y_1 = 0$ and $\left(\dfrac{dx}{ds}\right)_1 = 0$ we have $c = 0$;

and this is the result which is established in the book by appealing
to the Differential Calculus.

351. On page 165 some results are given without demonstration. The results refer to a segment of a sphere which is
required to have a maximum or minimum volume, while the surface
is given. Let a denote the radius of the sphere, h the height of the

segment, then the volume of the segment is $\pi\left(ah^2 - \dfrac{h^3}{3}\right)$. Since

the surface is given, ah is equal to a constant, which we will denote
by k^2. Let y denote the radius of the plane base of the segment;
then

$$y^2 = 2ah - h^2 = 2k^2 - h^2,$$

therefore $h^2 = 2k^2 - y^2.$

Thus the volume $= \pi\left\{k^2\sqrt{(2k^2 - y^2)} - \dfrac{(2k^2 - y^2)^{\frac{3}{2}}}{3}\right\} = V$ suppose.

Now y is supposed to be an ordinate of a given curve, and V is
to be made a maximum or a minimum by properly choosing this
ordinate. Let x denote the abscissa corresponding to the ordinate y.
Then we have

$$\frac{dV}{dy} = \pi \left\{ \frac{-k^2 y}{\sqrt{(2k^2 - y^2)}} + y \sqrt{(2k^2 - y^2)} \right\} = \frac{\pi y (k^2 - y^2)}{\sqrt{(2k^2 - y^2)}},$$

therefore $\dfrac{dV}{dx} = \dfrac{\pi y (k^2 - y^2)}{\sqrt{(2k^2 - y^2)}} \dfrac{dy}{dx}.$

We have now three cases to examine, namely

$$\frac{dy}{dx} = 0, \quad y = k, \quad y = 0.$$

(1) If y itself be a maximum or minimum V will be a maximum or minimum respectively provided $k^2 - y^2$ be positive, and a minimum or maximum respectively provided $k^2 - y^2$ be negative.

(2) The value $y = k$ makes $\dfrac{dV}{dx}$ zero, and makes $\dfrac{d^2V}{dx^2}$ negative provided $\dfrac{dy}{dx}$ be not zero; thus in this case V is a maximum. If y is itself a maximum or minimum when $y = k$, then $\dfrac{dV}{dx}$ changes sign when $y = k$, and so V is itself a maximum or minimum respectively.

(3) With respect to the case of $y = 0$ we must remark that the question does not suppose that y is capable of becoming negative. If the given curve touches the axis of x then the value $y = 0$ occurs simultaneously with $\dfrac{dy}{dx} = 0$, so that y is then a minimum and so is V.

These results do not agree with those in the book. The case in which $y = k$ seems there overlooked.

If $y = k$ we have $h = k = a$. And it may be seen that the relation on the 14th line of page 165 of the book may be satisfied by supposing $a = y$ and the angle CPY zero.

352. On page 365 the following problem is suggested; to construct upon a given base a curve such that the superficial area of the surface generated by its revolution round AB may be given, and that its solid content may be a maximum.

Take the axis of x as that of revolution; then adopting the usual notation we require that $\pi \int y^2 dx$ should be a maximum while $2\pi \int y \sqrt{(1 + p^2)}\, dx$ is given, the limits of x being supposed fixed. Thus if a be a constant we have to find the maximum value of

$$\int \left\{ y^2 + 2ay \sqrt{(1 + p^2)} \right\} dx.$$

Hence we must have $y + a \sqrt{(1 + p^2)} = \dfrac{d}{dx} \dfrac{ayp}{\sqrt{(1 + p^2)}} \ \ldots\ldots (1);$ this we know leads to

$$y^2 + 2ay \sqrt{(1 + p^2)} = \frac{2ayp^2}{\sqrt{(1 + p^2)}} + b,$$

therefore $\qquad \dfrac{2ay}{\sqrt{(1 + p^2)}} = b - y^2 \ \ldots\ldots\ldots\ldots\ldots\ldots (2),$

where b is a constant.

Then since y is to vanish at the two fixed points we have $b = 0$, and then by completing the solution we obtain a semicircle for the required curve, and therefore a sphere for the solid generated.

Mr Jellett points out that this solution is unsatisfactory, because the superficial area of a sphere described upon a given diameter is a determinate function of that diameter, and cannot therefore be made equal to any given quantity. Mr Jellett proceeds to remark that the process of the Calculus of Variations fails in this case.

We suggest the following as a solution of the problem.

Let the figure $ACEDB$ consist of two straight lines AC, BD perpendicular to the axis of x, and of the arc CED which satisfies the differential equation (2); see figure 10. Take A as the origin; let $AC = y_0$, $BD = y_1$, $AB = x_1$.

Then the volume of the figure formed by the revolution of $ACEDB$ round AB is $\pi \int_0^{x_1} y^2 dx$; and the surface, including the circular ends, is

$$\pi y_1^2 + \pi y_0^2 + 2\pi \int_0^{x_1} y \sqrt{(1 + p^2)}\, dx.$$

Now suppose that y is changed into $y + \delta y$, then the variation of the volume is $2\pi \int_0^{x_1} y\,\delta y\,dx$, and we have to make this zero for such variations as leave the surface unchanged; that is, for such variations as make

$$2\pi y_1\,\delta y_1 + 2\pi y_0\,\delta y_0 + 2\pi\,\delta \int_0^{x_1} y\,\sqrt{(1 + p^2)}\,dx = 0 \dots\dots\dots (3).$$

Thus if a represent a constant we must make

$$\int_0^{x_1} \left\{ y + a\sqrt{1 + p^2} - \frac{d}{dx}\,\frac{apy}{\sqrt{(1 + p^2)}} \right\} \delta y\,dx$$

$$+ \left\{ \frac{apy\,\delta y}{\sqrt{(1 + p^2)}} \right\}_1 - \left\{ \frac{apy\,\delta y}{\sqrt{(1 + p^2)}} \right\}_0 + ay_1\,\delta y_1 + ay_0\,\delta y_0 = 0 \dots (4).$$

The part under the integral sign vanishes because we suppose equation (1) satisfied. So that we only require in addition

$$\left\{ \frac{p}{\sqrt{(1 + p^2)}} - 1 \right\}_0 = 0, \quad \text{and} \quad \left\{ \frac{p}{\sqrt{(1 + p^2)}} + 1 \right\}_1 = 0.$$

This leads to $p_0 = +\infty$ and $p_1 = -\infty$; that is, the curve must join on continuously to the straight lines at C and D. Then it appears from (2) that $y^2 = b$ when p is infinite, so that $AC = BD$.

The constants a and b, and that which would arise from integrating (2), must then be determined so that $y^2 = b$ when $x = 0$ and when $x = x_1$, and that the surface may have the given value.

Suppose however the circular ends are not to be included in the given surface. In this case $y = -a$ furnishes a solution. For the terms $ay_1\,\delta y_1 + ay_0\,\delta y_0$ do not now occur in (4); and the value $y = -a$ makes

$$y + a\sqrt{(1 + p^2)} - \frac{d}{dx}\,\frac{apy}{\sqrt{(1 + p^2)}}$$

vanish, and it gives $p = 0$ so that $\dfrac{apy\,\delta y}{\sqrt{(1 + p^2)}}$ also vanishes. Thus we obtain a cylindrical surface; a will of course be negative, and will be determined by the condition that $-2\pi ax_1$ must be equal to the given surface.

353.   A mistake occurs on page 876 of the book which may be noticed.   The integral $\int_{0}^{\pi} \tan^{3}\theta \sin\theta\, d\theta$ is made equal to a finite negative value, the fact being overlooked that $\tan^{3}\theta$ becomes infinite between the limits of integration.   And the same mistake occurs on page 377 where the integral $\int \dfrac{y'dp}{p'\sqrt{(1+p'^{2})}}$ is taken between limits which include $p = 0$ and make the integral really infinite.

In concluding we may strongly recommend the student of the Calculus of Variations to master this important volume.   A translation of it into German has been advertised, but the present writer has not had the opportunity of consulting it.

354.   The last of the three comprehensive treatises is by Dr Stegmann, entitled *Lehrbuch der Variationsrechnung und ihrer Anwendung bei Untersuchungen über das Maximum und Minimum.* Kassel, 1854.   It is an octavo volume of 417 pages with a preface of 16 pages.

In the preface the author states that he had long been of opinion that the Calculus of Variations was treated in a meagre and unsatisfactory manner in elementary treatises, and had resolved to undertake the task of producing a more complete work on the subject.   The work of Strauch had not appeared when first this resolution was formed; after it was published the question arose with Stegmann whether he should continue his design, since he had no intention of offering to his readers such a rich collection of problems as Strauch had supplied.   Ultimately he resolved to complete his original design.

In addition to the works of Dirksen, Ohm and Strauch, Stegmann refers to the memoirs of Poisson and Ostrogradsky.   He has discussed numerous problems as illustrations of his theory, but he does not present his work as a collection of problems, for the development of the general theory has been his main object.   In solving his problems he has imitated Ohm and Strauch in investigating the terms of the second order so as to discriminate between maxima and minima values.

355. The work consists of six chapters and two supplements.

The first chapter is entitled *On variations generally;* it occupies pages 1—11. The following is Stegmann's view of a variation; let y denote any function of x as $f(x)$, and let $\phi(x, t)$ be any function of x and t which reduces to $f(x)$ when $t = 0$; then the variation of y is denoted by δy, where

$$\delta y = \left\{\frac{d\phi(x, t)}{dt}\right\}_0 dt,$$

the suffix 0 indicating that t is to be made zero after the differentiation.

On page 7 we have the usual geometrical illustration of the relation $d\delta y = \delta dy$.

In the first four chapters of the work no variation is supposed ascribed to the independent variable, and no change of value is made in the limits of the integrals which occur.

356. The second chapter is entitled *Variations of expressions in which Functions of one independent variable occur, but no Integrals;* it occupies pages 11—64.

This chapter gives that portion of the subject which has been developed by Ohm and Strauch; see Arts. 56 and 385. The theory is illustrated by the discussion of the problem originally given by Lagrange; see Art. 3. Stegmann also gives four problems which are to be found in the volumes of Strauch, namely those numbered 1, 76, 65 and 66 by Strauch. Stegmann indicates on page 60 another problem of the same kind as Lagrange's, namely, to find a curve such that the product of the perpendiculars let fall on any tangent from two fixed points shall be a maximum. It is supposed as in Art. 3 that at any point $\frac{dy}{dx}$ alone is susceptible of variation. The result is that the curve must be an ellipse or hyperbola of which the two fixed points are the foci.

On page 68 Stegmann discusses another problem of this kind, namely, to find the curve for which yp shall be a maximum or minimum, the variations of y and p being so taken that at any point considered $y\left(x - \dfrac{y}{p}\right)$ shall undergo no change by variation. Thus with the usual notation we must have

$$p\,\delta y + y\,\delta p = 0 \dots\dots\dots\dots\dots\dots (1),$$

and

$$\left(x - \frac{2y}{p}\right)\delta y + \frac{y^2}{p^2}\,\delta p = 0 \dots\dots\dots\dots (2);$$

from these equations we obtain

$$\frac{p}{y} = \frac{p^2}{y^2}\left(x - \frac{2y}{p}\right) \dots\dots\dots\dots\dots (3);$$

therefore $\dfrac{3}{x} = \dfrac{p}{y}$, therefore $y = \dfrac{x^3}{A}$, where A is a constant.

Now let us retain the terms of the second order in order to ascertain whether the result gives a maximum or a minimum. Let $U = yp$, then accurately

$$\delta U = (y + \delta y)(p + \delta p) - yp = p\,\delta y + y\,\delta p + \delta y\,\delta p,$$

and $(y + \delta y)\,x - \dfrac{(y + \delta y)^2}{p + \delta p} - yx + \dfrac{y^2}{p} = 0$ accurately.

Multiply the last expression by λ and add it to δU; thus

$$\delta U = p\,\delta y + y\,\delta p + \delta y\,\delta p$$
$$+ \lambda\left\{\left(x - \frac{2y}{p}\right)\delta y + \frac{y^2}{p^2}\,\delta p - \frac{(\delta y)^2}{p} + \frac{2y\,\delta y\,\delta p}{p^2} - \frac{y^2\,(\delta p)^2}{p^3} + \dots\right\},$$

where the omitted terms are of the third and higher orders. Assume λ such that

$$p + \lambda\left(x - \frac{2y}{p}\right) = 0 \dots\dots\dots\dots\dots (4);$$

then by means of (3) and (4) the terms of the first order disappear from δU; also we get $\lambda = -\dfrac{p^2}{y}$, and thus to the second order

$$\delta U = \delta y \, \delta p + \frac{p^2}{y} \left\{ \frac{(\delta y)^2}{p} - \frac{2y \, \delta y \, \delta p}{p^2} + \frac{y^2 (\delta p)^2}{p^4} \right\}$$

$$= (\delta y)^2 \left\{ -\frac{p}{y} + \frac{p}{y} + \frac{2p}{y} + \frac{p}{y} \right\} , \text{ by (2)},$$

$$= \frac{3p}{y} (\delta y)^2 = \frac{9 \, (\delta y)^2}{x} .$$

Thus supposing x positive we have obtained a minimum.

357. The third chapter is entitled *Variations of single Integral expressions with one independent variable*; it occupies pages 84—165.

This chapter contains the ordinary theory of the maxima and minima values of Integrals, illustrated by four examples; it also contains an investigation of the *criterion of integrability* of an expression, and an investigation of Jacobi's method of distinguishing between maxima and minima values.

The examples discussed are the following: (1) The shortest line between two given points. (2) The brachistochrone between a fixed point and a fixed horizontal line; the cycloid is obtained as the general solution, but it is shewn that in the particular case when the position of the lower limiting point is not fixed on the fixed horizontal line the result becomes a vertical straight line. (3) The maximum or minimum value of

$$\int \left\{ \frac{2ay}{x} - \left(\frac{dy}{dx} \right)^2 \right\} dx.$$

(4) The curve which with its evolute includes a minimum area. In all these examples the terms of the second order are examined.

In investigating Jacobi's method Stegmann proves the first part of the theorem of Art. 222 universally, that is, he proves that a certain expression is integrable; his proof depends on his previous investigation of the *condition of integrability*. With respect to the second part of the theorem he confines himself to proving that $\int y U dx$ has the required form when B_n is the last of the series of terms $B, B_1, B_2, \ldots$; and he exhibits completely the values of B, B_1 and B_2. He gives an investigation similar to that in Art. 224, and as in that Article he preserves the terms which are outside the

integral signs. At the bottom of his page 163 he makes a certain
expression to be zero which should be equal to a constant; there
seem indications however on the last page of the chapter that he
had perceived some inconsistency in this proceeding with respect
to the number of constants involved; see Art. 232.

858. The fourth chapter is entitled, *On the determination of
the maximum or minimum in combinations of simple integrals, or
when certain conditions are prescribed;* it occupies pages 165—265.

This chapter contains the following subjects: (1) Relative
maxima and minima problems or isoperimetrical problems. (2) Problems in which the limiting values are subject to certain conditions; here Stegmann draws attention to the terms of the second
order, and he keeps them all in, so that he has terms outside the
integral sign besides the terms under the integral sign which may
be supposed treated by Jacobi's method; see pages 187—196 of the
work. (3) Maximum or minimum of an integral which involves
more than one dependent variable, with or without a given equa-.
tion connecting the variables. (4) Maximum or minimum of an
integral which involves x, y, differential coefficients of y, and also Z
where Z is an integral expression involving x, y, and the differential
coefficients of y. (5) Maximum or minimum of $\int V dx$, where V is
supposed determined by a differential equation. (6) Maximum or
minimum of an integral involving x, y, s and the differential
coefficients of y and s, where the limiting values of y and s and
their differential coefficients occur in the integral.

This chapter contains the following examples. (1) To find the
curve of given length joining two fixed points which with the ordinates of the two fixed points and the axis of x includes the greatest
or least area. (2) The curve of given length fastened at its ends to
two fixed points, which has its centre of gravity lowest. (3) To
find the shortest line that can be drawn between two fixed lines
perpendicular to the axis of x, under the condition that the
product of the extreme ordinates shall have a prescribed value.
In these three problems the terms of the second order are examined. (4) The shortest line on a curved surface; the general

differential equation is obtained and then particular applications
are given; for example, the case of the ellipsoid is examined.
(5) Of all curves which have the property that the normal plane
passes through a fixed point, to find that which has the least
length between two fixed parallel planes; this is in Strauch, Vol. II.
pages 379—381. (6) The brachistochrone in a resisting medium.
(7) The minimum value of $\int_a^b Z^n dx$, where $Z = \int_a^x \sqrt{(1 + p^2)}\, dx$.
(8) The curve down which a body must fall in a resisting medium
so as to acquire the greatest velocity. (9) To find the minimum
value of $\int_a^1 \left(\frac{dy}{dx}\right)^2 dx$, under the conditions that $y_0 = 1$ and that
$\int_a^1 y\, dx = - y_1$. (10) The problem we have enunciated in para-
graph (3) of Art. 311; Stegmann does not however allude to
the difficulty which occurs in the particular case which we have
examined in Art. 352.

359. The fifth chapter is entitled *On Mixed Variations with
simultaneous changes of the independent variable;* it occupies pages
265—327.

In all the investigations hitherto given in the book the limits of
the integrations have been supposed fixed and the independent
variable unsusceptible of variation; Stegmann proceeds in the present chapter to give that extension to his formulæ which they
require in order to apply to problems in which the initial and final
values of all the quantities which occur are changed. He now
adopts the common method of ascribing a variation to the independent variable. Suppose x the independent variable and y the
dependent variable, let these become by variation $x + \delta x$ and
$y + \delta y$ respectively; then Stegmann obtains a relation denoted thus

$$\delta y = (\delta) y + p \delta x.$$

This result might be presented as a definition, namely, let
$\delta y - p \delta x$ be denoted by $(\delta) y$, and then it might of course be
considered absolutely true. Stegmann however adopts a different

method; he *defines* $(\delta) y$ and by means of geometrical considerations establishes the truth of the relation as far as the first order of small quantities.

It is then necessary for him to shew that

$$\delta p = \frac{d\,(\delta)\,y}{dx} + q\delta x,$$

where $\qquad q = \frac{dp}{dx} = \frac{d^2 y}{dx^2}$; and generally that

$$\delta \frac{d^n y}{dx^n} = \frac{d^n\,(\delta)\,y}{dx^n} + \frac{d^{n+1} y}{dx^{n+1}}\,\delta x.$$

His method is the following,

$$\delta p = \delta \frac{dy}{dx} = \frac{dx\,d\delta y - dy\,d\delta x}{dx^2} = \frac{d\delta y}{dx} - p\,\frac{d\delta x}{dx};$$

put $(\delta) y + p\delta x$ for δy and $q dx$ for dp, thus

$$\delta p = \frac{d\,(\delta)\,y}{dx} + q\delta x;$$

this may be written $\delta p = (\delta)\,p + q\delta x$.

Stegmann subsequently gives the common geometrical illustration of the relation $\delta dx = d\delta x$.

The above investigation of the value of δp cannot be regarded as absolutely true, but only as true to the first order.

Suppose now that $U = \int_a^t V dx$, and that the variation of U is required; Stegmann proves that the result obtained when x was supposed unsusceptible of variation, so far as terms of the first order are involved, requires only the following modifications; δy, δp, ... have to be changed into $(\delta) y$, $(\delta) p$, ... respectively, and the following limiting terms added, $V_t \delta \xi - V_a \delta a$. Two proofs are given of this statement.

The formulæ are illustrated by discussing the problem of the brachistochrone in the case where there is no resistance, and also in the case where there is, and the problem of the shortest line.   In

both these problems various suppositions are made with respect to
the limiting conditions and carefully examined. For example,
take the problem we have considered in Art. 300; Stegmann adopts
the suppositions there made and arrives at the results there obtained by interpreting the terms of the first order. Then he makes
another supposition; let the limiting values x_1 and x_2 be connected
by the relation

$$x_2 - x_1 = \text{a constant},$$

then $dx_1 = dx_2$, and instead of the two equations obtained by
equating to zero the coefficients of dx_1 and dx_2 we have now the
single equation

$$\left\{ \frac{p\psi'(x) + 1}{\sqrt{(1+p^2)}\,\sqrt{(h+x-x_1)}} \right\}_2 - \left\{ \frac{p\chi'(x) + 1}{\sqrt{(1+p^2)}\,\sqrt{(h+x-x_1)}} \right\}_1 + \int_{x_1}^{x_2} \frac{dV}{dx_1}\, dx = 0;$$

this reduces to

$$\left\{ \frac{p\psi'(x) + 1}{p\sqrt{a}} \right\}_2 - \left\{ \frac{p\chi'(x) + 1}{p\sqrt{a}} \right\}_1 - \frac{1}{\sqrt{a}} \left(\frac{1}{P_2} - \frac{1}{P_1} \right) = 0,$$

therefore $$\psi'(x_2) = \chi'(x_1);$$

thus the tangents to the limiting curves at the points where the
described curve meets them are parallel.

Stegmann also considers briefly the subject of the discrimination between maxima and minima values when the independent
variable is supposed to undergo a variation. Here of course allow-
ance has to be made for the circumstance that some of the formulæ
employed were only true to the first order. He illustrates his
remarks by considering the problem of the shortest line between
a given point and a given curve.

On the whole the chapter appears to be a good exhibition of
the method which the author selects, but the method seems far
less simple and satisfactory than that of not allowing the independent variable to undergo variation, but obtaining the requisite
generality by changing the limits of the integrations.

Two other subjects may be mentioned which are introduced
into this chapter. On pages 278, 279 Stegmann proves the theorem

which we have expressed in Art. 93 thus, $\Pi y' + K z' = 0$; the proof does not depend on the Calculus of Variations. On page 292 Stegmann considers the case in which the function under the integral sign may itself involve the limiting values of the variables or differential coefficients; he points out however that the limiting values of the highest differential coefficient when there is only one dependent variable must not occur; because if in such a case we wish to make the integral a maximum or a minimum we have in general more conditions than disposable quantities. A similar remark holds when there is more than one dependent variable.

360. A supplement to the third, fourth, and fifth chapters occupies pages 327—338; it draws attention to the method of solving problems in this subject which was adopted by the early writers, and refers to the memoir of Schellbach. Stegmann solves two problems by this method. (1) To find among all curves of given length that for which $\int_a^b F(y)\, dx$ is a maximum or a minimum. (2) The shortest line on a surface of revolution.

361. The sixth chapter is entitled, *On the variations of functions of two independent variables*; it occupies pages 338—395.

On page 11 of his work Stegmann seems to indicate that *mixed* variations occur only in the fifth chapter, but we find them again in the first section of the sixth chapter.

Suppose z any function of x and y, say $z = f(x, y)$; let $\phi(x, y, t)$ denote any function of x, y, and t, which reduces to $f(x, y)$ when t vanishes. In $\phi(x, y, t)$ change x into $x + \delta x$, y into $y + \delta y$, and t into $t + \delta t$; then a result is obtained which is denoted thus,

$$\delta z = \frac{d\phi}{dt}\,\delta t + \frac{d\phi}{dx}\,\delta x + \frac{d\phi}{dy}\,\delta y,$$

or by supposing $t = 0$,

$$\delta z = (\delta)\,z + \frac{dz}{dx}\,\delta x + \frac{dz}{dy}\,\delta y.$$

Then since this is true whatever function of x and y is denoted by z, Stegmann says we have

$$\delta p = \frac{d(\delta)z}{dx} + \frac{d^2z}{dx^2}\,\delta x + \frac{d^2z}{dx\,dy}\,\delta y,$$

$$\delta q = \frac{d(\delta)z}{dy} + \frac{d^2z}{dx\,dy}\,\delta x + \frac{d^2z}{dy^2}\,\delta y,$$

and so on.

This method seems however an unsatisfactory proof of these formulæ; see Arts. 102 and 124.

Stegmann next refers to questions similar to that in Art. 8, but involving more than one independent variable. He solves the following problem; to determine a surface having the property that the sum of the squares of the intercepts cut off from the co-ordinate axes by the tangent plane at any point shall be a minimum. Thus in the usual notation

$$\frac{(p^2q^2 + p^2 + q^2)(z - px - qy)^2}{p^2q^2}$$

is to be a minimum. Here p and q are supposed susceptible of variation; the result is that the required surface is determined by the equation

$$x^{\frac{2}{3}} + y^{\frac{2}{3}} + z^{\frac{2}{3}} = a^{\frac{2}{3}}.$$

Stegmann now proceeds to the variation of a double integral; here he restricts himself to supposing δx and δy to be zero, and he gives the complete development of the variation as far as terms of the first order, supposing that no differential coefficient occurs of a higher order than the second. As δx and δy are supposed zero, and no change is made in the limits of the integrations, the investigation is less general than that which we have given in Arts. 143 and 183. Stegmann illustrates this investigation by the following examples.   (1) To find the minimum of

$$\int_a^\xi \int_\beta^\eta (z + xp + yp^2)\,dy\,dx;$$

this example is taken from Strauch, Vol. II. page 579.   (2) The

curved surface of minimum area between given limits. In this
case Stegmann obtains the ordinary differential equation and then
gives a long investigation by which he arrives at Monge's integral;
see Art. 311. Then as an example, he shews that the particular
surface considered by Björling and others is included among the
general class of surfaces which is required; see Arts. 311 and 315.
With respect to this example however, he states more than he has
proved; see his page 377. He states that if the surface is to
be bounded by two fixed straight lines AC, BD and two fixed
curves AB, CD which constitute a closed four-cornered figure,
then the particular surface referred to does possess the least area.
Now he has not examined the terms of the second order so as
to ascertain that there really is a minimum, and moreover his
solution does not shew that the particular surface referred to is
the *only* surface that will satisfy the conditions of the problem
so far as making the terms of the first order vanish, but the only
surface out of all those which can be generated by a straight
line which moves so as always to be parallel to a fixed plane. We
shall hereafter see that Stegmann has stated more than is true.

The last three sections of the sixth chapter are devoted to the
consideration of the modification of the formulæ for the variation
of a double integral which is produced by supposing that δx and
δy are not zero. Stegmann refers to Poisson and Ostrogradsky;
but it appears probable from coincidence in notation that he has
chiefly followed Björling; the latter however, as we have stated,
may be considered to have only reproduced Ostrogradsky's method.
In illustration of the formulæ Stegmann considers three particular
cases; these are all included in those results of Poisson which we
have given in Arts. 113 and 114.

862. A supplement on the use of variations in Mechanics
occupies pages 396—417.

Stegmann shews here how certain mechanical problems may
coincide with problems of the Calculus of Variations. For example, the principle of Virtual Velocities supplies for the condition
of equilibrium of any system an equation of the form

$$\Sigma (X \delta x + Y \delta y + Z \delta z) = 0;$$

then if we suppose U a function determined by the relation

$$dU = \Sigma\, (Xdx + Ydy + Zdz),$$

the condition for equilibrium amounts to the statement that in general U must be a maximum or a minimum.

Lagrange's transformation of the equations of motion in Dynamics is also investigated; see Art. 818.

The principle of least action is also investigated. Stegmann considers this principle under the following form; required the curve for which $\int v ds$ is a maximum or minimum, where v is supposed a given function of the co-ordinates x, y, z. He shews that the differential equations which determine the curve, are the same as those which are furnished by Dynamics for the curve which would be described by a particle under forces which would generate a velocity denoted by the given function v. He draws attention to the fact that $\int v ds$ is not necessarily a minimum. For example, when v is constant and the particle moves on a smooth surface, the curve obtained may be in general the shortest line that can be drawn on that surface between fixed points, but will not be so necessarily. A particle may move on a smooth sphere acted on by no forces except the normal action of the sphere, and describe the shortest line between two points, namely the *shorter* arc of the great circle joining those points; but it may also describe the *longer* arc of the great circle joining those points.

We shall now consider in detail a few points connected with Stegmann's work.

363. Suppose we require the maximum or minimum of $\int \phi\, dx$, where ϕ involves $x, y,$ and the differential coefficients of y; before reducing $\int \delta\phi\, dx$ in the ordinary way by integration by parts, Stegmann makes some remarks on the attempt to solve the problem

which is made by supposing $\delta\phi = 0$; see his page 85. The relation $\delta\phi = 0$ can only indicate one of these two things, either ϕ does not change by ascribing a variation to y and its differential coefficients, or else ϕ is itself a maximum or minimum. The former supposition is impossible, since

$$\delta\phi = \frac{d\phi}{dy}\,\delta y + \frac{d\phi}{dp}\,\delta p + \ldots.$$

With respect to the latter supposition it is to be observed that if ϕ be itself a maximum or minimum for all values of x between given limits, then $\int \phi\, dx$ will also be a maximum or minimum respectively, the integral being taken between those limits. This Stegmann proves by means of a figure which is constructed by taking the ordinate of a curve always equal to ϕ. The proof amounts to the consideration that the integral must be a maximum or a minimum, because each of the elements of which it may be ultimately regarded as the sum is a maximum or minimum respectively. It is however not true conversely that any relation which renders $\int_a^{\xi} \phi\, dx$ a maximum or minimum will make ϕ also such for all values of x between a and ξ. This is illustrated by a figure which amounts to the consideration that $\int_a^{\xi} \phi_1\, dx$ may be greater than $\int_a^{\xi} \phi_2\, dx$, even although some of the values of ϕ_1 are less than the corresponding values of ϕ_2; for other values of ϕ_1 may be greater than the corresponding values of ϕ_2.

Thus the conclusion is that the relation $\delta\phi = 0$ will not necessarily supply all possible solutions of the problem of finding the maximum or minimum value of $\int \phi\, dx$.

364. On page 109 of his work Stegmann makes a remark which relates to the use of a series to represent a variation instead of a single term; see Art. 334. Stegmann is investigating the maximum or minimum of $\int_a^{\xi} \frac{\sqrt{(1+p^2)}}{\sqrt{x}}\, dx$. The ordinary mode would be to change p into $p + \delta p$, and then to examine the terms

involving δp and $(\delta p)^2$. But suppose we change p not into $p + \delta p$ but into a series, after the manner of Strauch; let this series be

$$p + x\Omega'(x) + \frac{x^2}{1 \cdot 2}\Psi'(x) + \ldots$$

Arrange the variation of the proposed integral according to powers of x; thus we obtain for the variation

$$x\int_a^b \frac{p\,\Omega'(x)\,dx}{\sqrt{x}\sqrt{(1+p^2)}} + \frac{x^2}{2}\int_a^b \left[\frac{[\Omega'(x)]^2}{1+p^2} + p\Psi'(x)\right]\frac{dx}{\sqrt{x}\sqrt{(1+p^2)}} + \ldots$$

In order that there may be a maximum or minimum we must have in the usual way

$$\frac{p}{\sqrt{x}\sqrt{(1+p^2)}} = \text{a constant.}$$

Stegmann then remarks that we are prevented from ascertaining what the sign of the term involving x^2 is, by reason of the presence of $\Psi'(x)$ which is altogether independent of $\Omega'(x)$. He does not notice that the relation which has been already assumed in order to make the coefficient of x vanish, also makes the coefficient of $\Psi'(x)$ constant in the term involving x^2; hence it will be found that since the limiting terms of the first order are made to vanish, the terms of the second order which depend on $\Psi'x$ will also vanish. It is in fact this circumstance that renders it useless to adopt the form of a series instead of a single term in order to denote a variation.

365. On page 140 of his work Stegmann is discussing the problem of finding the curve which with its evolute includes a minimum area.

Let
$$U = \int_a^b \frac{(1+p^2)^{\frac{3}{2}}}{q}\,dx;$$

by making the terms of the first order vanish in the variation of U we obtain a cycloid for the curve. The terms of the second order may be put in the form

$$\int_a^b \left\{3(1+p^2)(\delta p)^2 + \left(2p\,\delta p - \frac{1+p^2}{q}\,\delta q\right)^2\right\}\frac{dx}{q},$$

and Stegmann says that neither $\dfrac{1}{q}$ nor p can become infinite between the limits of integration; so that the solution he has obtained gives a minimum. But p *is infinite* at the cusps of the cycloid, and thus Stegmann is wrong. But although p is infinite yet $\dfrac{(1+p'^2)^{\frac{3}{2}}}{q}$ does not become infinite, this being the radius of curvature of the curve; hence *à fortiori* $\dfrac{1+p'^2}{q}$, $\dfrac{p^2}{q}$, $\dfrac{p(1+p'^2)}{q^2}$ and $\dfrac{(1+p'^2)^2}{q^3}$ do not become infinite. Thus if δp and δq are indefinitely small throughout the limits of the integration the quantity under the integral sign in the above expression will not become infinite; so that the result obtained is really a minimum in comparison with all adjacent curves which can be obtained under the limitation that δp and δq shall be indefinitely small.

With respect to the problem in question it will be useful to notice the conclusions of other writers. Thus in De Morgan's Differential Calculus, page 463, the following statement is made, ".... the radii of curvature at the extreme points are both $= 0$; which in the cycloid only happens at the cusps. Hence if A and B be the given points, every such figure as that in the diagram gives an algebraical minimum: that is to say, any slight variation of the upper curves with a corresponding variation of the lower evolutes would increase the area contained. There is no absolute arithmetical minimum; for by sufficiently increasing the number of revolutions of the generating circle we might diminish the whole area without limit." The diagram referred to supposes the generating circle to have turned round three times completely, so that there are three complete arcs of a cycloid between the two fixed points. There is no investigation of the terms of the second order to shew that any slight variation would increase the area.

The problem is solved by Strauch, and he exhibits the terms of the second order, but makes no remarks of importance. See his Vol. II. pages 289—291.

Mr Jellett discusses the problem, and makes some remarks on the result; see pages 172 and 177 of his work. He gives a

figure consisting of a single complete arc of a cycloid with its
extremities at the two fixed points; the two fixed points are also
connected by a curve which is composed of two complete arcs of a
cycloid, one of which may if we please be supposed indefinitely
small, and the other finite and differing infinitesimally from the
single complete arc first considered. It is easy to shew that the
area in the second case is less than the area in the first case;
nevertheless the first is to be considered a real minimum in
the proper sense of that term, because the second curve cannot
be deduced from the first by a legitimate variation.

366. In Art. 202 we have referred to a result obtained by
Legendre in discussing the following problem; required to connect
two fixed points by a curve of given length so that the area
bounded by the curve, the ordinates of the fixed points, and the
axis of abscissæ shall be a maximum. Stegmann discusses this
problem and arrives at the same results as Legendre, though he
does not refer to him; see Stegmann's work, pages 175—180.

Let h_1, k_1 be the co-ordinates of one of the fixed points, which
we will denote by A; let h_2, k_2 be the co-ordinates of the other fixed
point, which we will denote by B; and we will suppose h_1 less than
h_2, and k_1 less than k_2. Then with the usual notation $\int_{h_1}^{h_2} y\,dx$ is
to be a maximum while $\int_{h_1}^{h_2} \sqrt{(1+p^2)}\,dx$ is to have a given value.

Then we proceed to make $\int_{h_1}^{h_2} [y + \lambda \sqrt{(1+p^2)}]\,dx$ a maximum where
λ is a constant.

Therefore
$$1 - \lambda \frac{d}{dx}\frac{p}{\sqrt{(1+p^2)}} = 0 \quad\ldots\ldots\ldots\ldots\ldots\ldots(1),$$

therefore
$$x - C_1 = \frac{\lambda p}{\sqrt{(1+p^2)}},$$

therefore
$$\frac{dy}{dx} = \frac{x - C_1}{\pm \sqrt{[\lambda^2 - (x - C_1)^2]}},$$

therefore
$$y - C_2 = \mp \sqrt{[\lambda^2 - (x - C_1)^2]} \quad\ldots\ldots\ldots\ldots\ldots(2).$$

It is easy to see that the sign of the terms of the second order is the same as that of

$$\lambda \int_{h_1}^{h_2} \frac{(\delta p)^2}{(1+p^2)^{\frac{3}{2}}}\, dx,$$

and is therefore the same as the sign of λ. Then (2) gives for the required curve an arc of a circle of which λ^2 is the square of the radius, and from (1) it may be shewn that this arc will be concave to the axis of x if λ be negative; so that an arc of a circle concave to the axis of x gives a maximum area. The constants λ, C_1, and C_2 are to be determined by making the arc go through the points A and B and have the given length. This given length must of course be greater than the straight line which joins A and B.

The solution thus obtained is satisfactory as long as the concave circular arc joining A and B falls entirely between the lines drawn through A and B perpendicular to the axis of x; the extreme admissible case is that in which the ordinate at A is the tangent to the circular arc at A.

Supposing then that the given length exceeds that which corresponds to the extreme admissible case just referred to, we must modify the problem. Let the ordinate at A be produced through A to a point distant y_1 from the axis of x; and let the straight line of length $y_1 - k_1$ be considered part of the curve connecting A and B. Thus we now propose to make $\int_{h_1}^{h_2} y\, dx$ a maximum while $y_1 - k_1 + \int_{h_1}^{h_2} \sqrt{(1+p^2)}\, dx$ has a given value. No change is thus required in the solution of the problem except so far as relates to the terms at the limits; these formerly vanished because the extreme points were both fixed. Now we have corresponding to the lower limit the expression

$$\lambda \left\{ 1 - \frac{p}{\sqrt{(1+p^2)}} \right\}_1 \delta y_1\,;$$

and to make this vanish we must have

$$\left\{ 1 - \frac{p}{\sqrt{(1+p^2)}} \right\}_1 = 0,$$

therefore
$$p_1 = \infty\,.$$

This requires the circular arc to have its tangent at the point (k_1, y_1) where it joins the ordinate produced through A, coincident with that ordinate produced. Thus $y_1 = C_2$, and $C_1 - k_1 =$ the radius of the circle; and the constants will be found from these relations combined with the conditions that the circle shall pass through B, and that the length of the circular arc together with $y_1 - k_1$ shall be equal to the given length.

In this case then the required curve is made up of a straight line of the length $y_1 - k_1$ and of an arc of a circle.

The solution thus obtained is satisfactory so long as the concave circular arc is not cut by the ordinate at B produced through B; the extreme admissible case is that in which the ordinate at B is the tangent to the circular arc at B.

Supposing then that the given length exceeds that which corresponds to the extreme admissible case just referred to, we must again modify the problem. Let the ordinate at B be produced to a point distant y_2 from the axis of x, and let the straight line of length $y_2 - k_2$ as well as the straight line of length $y_1 - k_1$ be considered part of the curve connecting A and B. Thus we now propose to make $\int_{k_1}^{k_2} y\, dx$ a maximum, while

$$y_1 - k_1 + y_2 - k_2 + \int_{k_1}^{k_2} \sqrt{(1 + p^2)}\, dx$$

has a given value. No change is thus required in the solution of the problem except so far as relates to the terms at the limits. We now have the expression

$$\lambda \left\{ 1 + \frac{p}{\sqrt{(1 + p^2)}} \right\}_2 \delta y_2 + \lambda \left\{ 1 - \frac{p}{\sqrt{(1 + p^2)}} \right\}_1 \delta y_1;$$

and to make this vanish we must have

$$\left\{ 1 + \frac{p}{\sqrt{(1 + p^2)}} \right\}_2 = 0, \text{ and } \left\{ 1 - \frac{p}{\sqrt{(1 + p^2)}} \right\}_1 = 0,$$

therefore $\qquad\qquad p_1 = \infty, \text{ and } p_2 = -\infty.$

This requires the circular arc to have its tangent at the point (h_1, y_1) where it joins the ordinate produced through A, coincident with that ordinate produced; and also its tangent at the point (h_2, y_2) where it joins the ordinate produced through B, coincident with that ordinate produced. This requires the circular arc to be a semicircle, so that $y_1 = y_2 = C_2$; and $C_1 = \frac{1}{2}(h_1 + h_2)$, and the radius of the circle $= \frac{1}{2}(h_2 - h_1)$. The constant C_2 is to be found from the condition that the sum of the length of the circular arc and $y_1 - k_1$ and $y_2 - k_2$ is to be equal to the given length.

In this case then the required curve consists of a semicircular arc and two straight lines.

367. In his fourth Chapter, pages 222—227, Stegmann gives an investigation of the number of the constants which can occur in the solution of a certain problem, and of the number of the equations which serve to determine these constants; see Art. 344. Stegmann's conclusion is that in general these constants can all be determined; he does not shew that the auxiliary equations may diminish in number in certain cases, and thus some of the constants remain indeterminate. He draws attention however to some exceptional cases, in which the number of the constants may be less than the general theory indicates. Take for example the first case considered in Art. 273; here no arbitrary constants occur in the solution, so that the terms which relate to the limits must be supposed to vanish of themselves, or they will not vanish at all. In other words, if we use geometrical language, the limiting points must be supposed *fixed* through which the curve is to be drawn.

368. On his pages 245—247, Stegmann solves a problem which we will here notice. Let $U = \int_a^\xi Z^n dx$, where

$$Z = \int_a^x \sqrt{(1 + p^2)}\, dx\,;$$

required to find the value of y which makes U a maximum or minimum. Here we have as far as terms of the second order

$$\delta Z = \int_a^x \left\{ \frac{p\,\delta p}{\sqrt{(1+p^2)}} + \frac{(\delta p)^2}{2(1+p^2)^{\frac{3}{2}}} + \dots \right\} dx,$$

and $\quad \delta U = \int_a^\xi \left\{ nZ^{n-1}\,\delta Z + \frac{n(n-1)}{2}\, Z^{n-2}\,(\delta Z)^2 + \dots \right\} dx.$

The investigation of Art. 38 may be applied to this problem. The quantity there denoted by v is here denoted by Z, and $L = nZ^{n-1}$. Also $P' = \dfrac{p}{\sqrt{(1+p^2)}}$, while $N,\ N',\ P,\ Q,\ Q',\ \dots$ are zero. Thus we obtain

$$(A - I)\,P' = \text{a constant};$$

and as $A - I$ vanishes when x has its superior limiting value, the constant must vanish; this leads to $P' = 0$, so that $p = 0$. The integrated part of the variation also vanishes since the above constant vanishes.

Since $p = 0$ the only term of the second order which remains in δU is

$$\frac{n}{2} \int_a^\xi Z^{n-1} \left\{ \int_a^x (\delta p)^2\, dx \right\} dx,$$

which is positive, and so we obtain a minimum.

Stegmann's solution is effected by the use of an arbitrary multiplier, and leads to the same result. In discriminating however between a maximum and a minimum, he retains the term

$$\frac{n(n-1)}{2} \int_a^\xi Z^{n-2}\,(\delta Z)^2\, dx,$$

and this leads him to make the supposition that n is positive and not less than unity, in order to ensure a minimum. But as p is zero, δZ is itself of the *second* order of small quantities, and thus the term just expressed is of the *fourth* order, and therefore does not require to be retained.

It will be observed that the solution $p = 0$ can only apply when the limiting values of y are either not given or are given equal.

When the limiting values of y are given and unequal suppose these values to be β and η corresponding to the values a and ξ of x. Then putting the problem into a geometrical form, the curve required appears to be made up of the straight line which joins the point (a, β) with the point (ξ, β), and the straight line which joins the point (ξ, β) with the point (ξ, η); or at least the nearer we approach to this limit the smaller does U become.

This problem is taken from Euler's *Methodus Inveniendi* ... page 94. Euler considers any function of Z instead of Z^2, and he arrives at the result $p = 0$ as necessary for a maximum or a minimum.

369. An example of a relative minimum is solved by Stegmann on his pages 255—258, which we will give here. Required the minimum value of $\dfrac{1}{2}\displaystyle\int_0^1 p^2\, dx$ under the following conditions;

$$y_0 = 1 \dotfill (1),$$

$$\int_0^1 \frac{y}{y_1}\, dx = -1 \dotfill (2).$$

Let λ be a constant, and let

$$U = \int_0^1 \left(\frac{1}{2} p^2 + \frac{\lambda y}{y_1} \right) dx;$$

then to the first order

$$\delta U = \left\{ p_1 - \frac{\lambda}{y_1} \int_0^1 y\, dx \right\} \delta y_1 + \int_0^1 \left(\frac{\lambda}{y_1} - \frac{dp}{dx} \right) \delta y\, dx.$$

Hence
$$\frac{\lambda}{y_1} - \frac{dp}{dx} = 0 \dotfill (3)$$

and
$$p_1 - \frac{\lambda}{y_1} \int_0^1 y\, dx = 0 \dotfill (4).$$

From (3) we have

$$\frac{\lambda}{y_1}(x - A) = p,$$

therefore
$$\frac{\lambda}{2y_1}(x - A)^2 = y + B,$$

where A and B are constants.

The condition (1) gives

$$\frac{\lambda A^2}{2y_1} = 1 + B,$$

therefore

$$y = 1 + \frac{\lambda}{2y_1}(x^2 - 2Ax) \dots\dots\dots\dots(5).$$

The condition (2) gives

$$1 + \frac{\lambda}{6y_1} - \frac{\lambda A}{2y_1} = -y_1 \dots\dots\dots\dots (6).$$

From (2) and (4) we obtain

$$p_1 + \frac{\lambda y_1}{y_1} = 0, \quad \text{that is } \frac{\lambda}{y_1}(1 - A) + \frac{\lambda}{y_1} = 0,$$

that is

$$\frac{\lambda}{y_1}(2 - A) = 0 \dots\dots\dots\dots (7).$$

By putting $x = 1$ in (5), we obtain

$$y_1 = 1 + \frac{\lambda}{2y_1}(1 - 2A) \dots\dots\dots\dots (8).$$

The solution $\lambda = 0$ of (7) is inadmissible, for that would make $y = 1$ by (5), and then (2) would not be satisfied. Hence we deduce $A = 2$ from (7), and then from (6) and (8) we deduce

$$\lambda = -\frac{12}{49}, \quad y_1 = -\frac{2}{7}.$$

Now to determine whether a minimum is thus obtained, we must form the expression for δU correct to the second order; now we have exactly

$$\delta U = \int_0^1 \left\{ \frac{1}{2}(p + \delta p)^2 - \frac{1}{2}p^2 + \frac{\lambda(y + \delta y)}{y_1 + \delta y_1} - \frac{\lambda y}{y_1} \right\} dx,$$

and therefore to the second order.

$$\delta U = \int_0^1 \left(p\delta p + \frac{\lambda \delta y}{y_1} - \frac{\lambda y\, \delta y_1}{y_1^2} \right) dx$$

$$+ \int_0^1 \left\{ \frac{1}{2}(\delta p)^2 - \frac{\lambda \delta y\, \delta y_1}{y_1^2} + \frac{\lambda y\,(\delta y_1)^2}{y_1^3} \right\} dx$$

$$= \int_0^1 \left\{ \frac{1}{2}(\delta p)^2 - \frac{\lambda \delta y\, \delta y_1}{y_1^2} + \frac{\lambda y\,(\delta y_1)^2}{y_1^3} \right\} dx, \text{ by (3) and (4)}.$$

By integrating by parts we have

$$\int \frac{\lambda \delta y \, \delta y_1}{y_1^3} \, dx = \frac{\lambda \delta y_1}{y_1^3} \left(x \delta y - \int x \delta p \, dx \right);$$

thus
$$\delta U = \int_0^1 \left\{ \frac{1}{2} (\delta p)^2 + \frac{\lambda \delta y_1}{y_1^3} x \delta p \right\} dx$$
$$+ \frac{\lambda (\delta y_1)^2}{y_1^3} \int_0^1 y \, dx - \frac{\lambda (\delta y_1)^2}{y_1^3}$$
$$= \frac{1}{2} \int_0^1 \left(\delta p + \frac{\lambda x \, \delta y_1}{y_1^3} \right)^2 dx + \frac{\lambda (\delta y_1)^2}{y_1^3} \left(\frac{1}{y_1} \int_0^1 y \, dx - 1 - \frac{\lambda}{6 y_1^3} \right).$$

Now $\dfrac{\lambda}{y_1^3} = -3$, and $\dfrac{1}{y_1} \displaystyle\int_0^1 y \, dx = -1$; thus finally

$$\delta U = \frac{1}{2} \int_0^1 \left(\delta p + \frac{\lambda x \, \delta y_1}{y_1^3} \right)^2 dx + \frac{9}{2} (\delta y_1)^2,$$

so that we have obtained a minimum.

370.   Stegmann gives on his page 395 one application of the formulæ relating to double integrals which we will reproduce.

Suppose we have to find a surface of minimum area under the condition that the length of the boundary is given.

The equations which must hold at the boundary are the first two of equations (13) of Art. 114.

Here
$$V = \sqrt{(1 + z^2 + z_i^2)}, \quad X = \frac{z'}{V}, \quad Y = \frac{z_i}{V},$$

$$h = - \frac{d}{ds} \left(\frac{dx}{ds} \right) = - \frac{d^2 x}{ds^2} \frac{ds}{ds}, \qquad k = - \frac{d}{ds} \left(\frac{dy}{ds} \right) = - \frac{d^2 y}{ds^2} \frac{ds}{ds}.$$

Thus the equations are

$$\sqrt{(1 + z^2 + z_i^2)} + c \frac{ds}{ds} \left(\frac{d^2 x}{ds^2} z_i - \frac{d^2 y}{ds^2} z' \right) = 0,$$

$$\frac{z_i \, dx - z' \, dy}{\sqrt{(1 + z^2 + z_i^2)}} + c \left(\frac{d^2 x}{ds^2} dx + \frac{d^2 y}{ds^2} dy \right) \frac{ds}{ds} = 0.$$

By ordinary transformations these equations become respectively

$$\sqrt{(1 + z'^2 + z_,^2)} - c\,\frac{dx}{ds}\left(\frac{d^2y}{ds^2} + z_,\,\frac{d^2z}{ds^2}\right) = 0 \quad\dots\dots\dots\dots (1),$$

and

$$\frac{z_,\,dx - z'\,dy}{\sqrt{(1 + z'^2 + z_,^2)}} - c\,\frac{d^2z}{ds^2}\,ds = 0 \quad\dots\dots\dots\dots\dots (2);$$

and this is the form in which Stegmann gives them.

He now takes another condition, namely that z shall be constant round the boundary, so that round the boundary

$$dz = z'\,dx + z_,\,dy = 0 \quad\dots\dots\dots\dots\dots (3),$$

and since z is constant round the boundary (2) gives

$$z_,\,dx - z'\,dy = 0 \quad\dots\dots\dots\dots\dots\dots (4).$$

From (3) and (4) we have round the boundary

$$z' = 0 \quad\text{and}\quad z_, = 0.$$

Also (1) becomes round the boundary

$$1 - c\,\frac{d^2y}{ds^2}\,\frac{ds}{dx} = 0 \quad\dots\dots\dots\dots\dots\dots (5).$$

From (5) by integration we obtain the equation to a circle of which the radius is numerically equal to c; that is, the projection of the boundary on the plane of (x, y) is a circle.

Then Stegmann observes that this cannot give a minimum area but a maximum area, since the boundary is supposed to be a closed curve. But the result may be made useful by modifying the problem. The modification appears to be that the projection of the boundary shall be a four-sided figure having for two of its sides fixed straight lines perpendicular to the axis of x, and the other two sides remaining to be determined and each being of given length. Then Stegmann says these other two sides should be arcs of circles with their convexities turned towards each other.

CHAPTER XIV.

MINOR TREATISES.

371. This chapter is intended to give an account of the minor treatises on the Calculus of Variations. It includes all the separate works which have come to the writer's knowledge, but does not attempt to notice every case in which a chapter has been devoted to this subject in the course of a general work on analysis. A few such cases have been however included in the present list.

372. Brunacci. A treatise on the Calculus of Variations occupies pages 166—255 of the fourth volume of Brunacci's *Corso di Matematica Sublime.* Florence, 1808.

Brunacci begins with some general remarks similar to those which we have given in Art. 363 after Stegmann. He considers the case in which $F(x, y)$ is to be a maximum or minimum by the variation of y, and then the case in which $F(x, y, p)$ is to be a maximum or minimum by the variation of y and p or of one of them; and he gives Lagrange's example; see Art. 3. He makes some brief remarks on the history of the subject, and states that Lagrange had finally relieved it from any consideration of infinitesimal quantities; he proposes to follow Lagrange's method in discussing the subject. He does not use the symbol δy, but $i\omega$ instead, where i is supposed indefinitely small and ω an arbitrary function.

In finding the maximum or minimum value of an integral $\int \phi\, dx$ he first supposes that ϕ contains only x and y; he illustrates this by two examples taken from Euler's *Methodus Inveniendi ...*, pages 39 and 40, and in the second example he agrees with Dirksen in distinguishing between a maximum and a minimum more carefully than Euler did; see Art. 52, and Dirksen, page 202. He next supposes that ϕ is a function of x, y, and p, and that $\int \phi \, dx$ is to be made a maximum or minimum; this case he illustrates by discussing the problems of the shortest line and the brachistochrone. He insists on the propriety of separating the problems which occur into two parts, one depending strictly on the Calculus of Variations and the other on the Differential Calculus; see Arts. 90 and 91. He says that this idea was communicated to him by a distinguished scholar and mathematician Paradisi, and that Euler himself would have judged it worthy of his own immortal work, the *Methodus Inveniendi ......* Accordingly Brunacci in treating the problem of the brachistochrone between two given curves first supposes the extreme points fixed and obtains a cycloid by the Calculus of Variations as the required curve; then he determines by the Differential Calculus the position which the cycloid must have when its ends are supposed moveable on two curves; in spite of Brunacci's opinion his process seems longer and not clearer than that usually given which depends on the Calculus of Variations solely. Brunacci next supposes that ϕ is a function of x, y, p, and q, and that the maximum or minimum of $\int \phi \, dx$ is required; this he illustrates by examples drawn from pages 61 and 247 of the *Methodus Inveniendi ......*

Brunacci supplies investigations of the terms of the second order for distinguishing between maxima and minima values; he repeats the investigation to which we have alluded in Art. 216; he says however that it is now presented in a better form.

Brunacci gives some account of problems of relative maxima and minima, and considers a few simple examples.

With respect to the variation of double integrals he gives an investigation which is correct so far as it goes; see Art. 29. He applies the result to obtain the differential equation to the surface which is a minimum among those which include the same volume. He says however that owing to the difficulty of integrating partial differential equations, to the difficulty of determining the arbitrary functions which occur in the solutions, and to other difficulties which arise from the nature of the problems, very little can be effected in this part of the subject; in his own words "... siamo sopra una spiaggia da cui si scopre un mar senza fine, e non ci è dato per anche d'inoltrarvisi, onde fare delle scoperte."

It would appear from his page 248 that Brunacci considered that his treatise on the Calculus of Variations might be contrasted favourably with those which had been previously published. It is not however very accurate in language or investigation; we have already in Art. 208 pointed out an objectionable statement, and we will now indicate some others. Brunacci says on his page 168 that $\int_a^h f(x)\,dx$ is the sum of all possible values of $f(x)$ between those which correspond to $x = a$ and $x = h$; this amounts to overlooking the dx which occurs in the symbol $\int_a^h f(x)\,dx$. On his page 245 he interprets the equation $xy = 3z^2$ to mean that the vertical ordinate is a third of the rectangle of the horizontal co-ordinates, instead of saying that the *square* of the vertical ordinate is so; here he had previously given the statement correctly. On his page 229 he discusses the maximum or minimum of $\int \psi\,dx$, where ψ is a function of Z, and $Z = \int \sqrt{(1 + p^2)}\,dx$. We have already considered a case of this problem in Art. 368. Brunacci by an obscure method arrives at a differential equation, and he shews that when a certain constant c' vanishes the solution is $p = 0$; but this he says is only a particular solution. It will be seen, however, on his page 230 that he requires a to vanish at the limits, and

$$a = -\frac{c'\sqrt{(1 + p^2)}}{p},$$

so that his solution leads necessarily to $c' = 0$.

373. Lacroix. *An elementary treatise on the Differential and Integral Calculus, by S. F. Lacroix.* Translated from the French. Cambridge, 1816.

This work contains a brief treatise on the Calculus of Variations on pages 436—463, and 706—711. The treatise has been described with great justice as "singularly confused and unintelligible."

374. Gergonne. Gergonne's *Annales de Mathématiques* ......
Vol. 18, 1822, pages 1—93.

This memoir is on the investigation of the maxima and minima of undetermined integral formulæ. Gergonne considers that with many persons the Calculus of Variations is merely a mechanical process of which they do not comprehend the spirit. He proposes to shew that the questions of maxima and minima for which this Calculus was principally invented can be treated in the clearest and briefest manner by the principles of the ordinary Differential Calculus. He does not use the distinctive notation of the Calculus of Variations; thus for what is usually denoted by δy he puts iY, where i is an indefinitely small quantity and Y is an arbitrary function.

This memoir seems of no great use; any student who could understand it could understand the ordinary exhibitions of the Calculus of Variations. The distinctive notation of the Calculus of Variations has always been considered one of its great advantages, and nothing is gained by discarding this notation. There are also passages in this memoir which would probably appear more difficult to a beginner than the corresponding passages in the ordinary treatises. Thus, for example, we may refer to the way in which Gergonne shews that the integrated and the unintegrated part of the variation of an integral must separately vanish in order that the integral may be a maximum or a minimum.

The memoir is written with remarkable diffuseness. As an instance the following may be noticed. When Gergonne is dis-

cussing the question of the shortest line he obtains these two
equations,

$$\frac{d}{ds}\frac{x'}{\sqrt{(1 + x'^2 + y'^2)}} = 0, \quad \frac{d}{ds}\frac{y'}{\sqrt{(1 + x'^2 + y'^2)}} = 0,$$

and instead of inferring at once that

$$\frac{x'}{\sqrt{(1 + x'^2 + y'^2)}} = \text{a constant, and } \frac{y'}{\sqrt{(1 + x'^2 + y'^2)}} = \text{a constant,}$$

he devotes a page to performing the differentiations first and then
retracing his steps by integration; and he makes a temporary mistake in the course of his process by omitting $\frac{1}{4}$ in the fifth line of
his page 86.   Page 89 is quite wrong; the equations in the fourth
line are false, since they ought to involve the partial differential coefficients of S; the equations given by Gergonne would
make the osculating plane of the curve perpendicular to its tangent.

The following paragraph forms the last of Gergonne's memoir.

In conclusion we must ask the indulgence of the reader for the
numerous imperfections and even errors which may be found in
this memoir.   If we may believe what is stated by Dr Prompt in a
small treatise published in 1820, the work even of the illustrious
Lagrange on this subject is not free from objections.   The em-
barrassing notation of that great mathematician on the one hand,
and the brevity of Dr Prompt on the other hand, have prevented
us from ascertaining to what extent these objections are well
founded; but this is a point to which we will return on another
occasion.

[It does not appear that Gergonne ever returned to the subject.
The present writer has not seen any other notice of Dr Prompt's
work.]

375.   Ampère.   Gergonne's *Annales de Mathématiques* ......
Vol. 16, 1825, pages 133—167.

This memoir is an exposition of the principles of the Calculus
of Variations, and is said to have been drawn up by Ampère for his

course of lectures at the Polytechnique School. It constitutes such an elementary treatise on the Calculus of Variations as is frequently given in works on the Differential and Integral Calculus, and presents no peculiarity. After establishing the formula for the variation of an integral Ampère shews that in order that the integral may be a maximum or a minimum the two parts of the variation must separately vanish. This he shews by supposing in the first place that the limiting values of the variables and of the differential coefficients are given; then the part of the variation which remains under the integral sign must vanish because the other part vanishes of itself. Next he supposes that the limiting values are not given; still it is in our power to suppose such a variation as leaves the limiting values unchanged, and this variation must be zero, so that, as before, the part under the integral sign must vanish. Gergonne himself says in a note that Ampère is the first who has shewn distinctly that the part of the variation which is under the integral sign must separately vanish, and he admits that his own memoir was unsatisfactory on this point.

370. Verdam and Verhulst. The subject of maxima and minima appears to have been proposed for a prize exercise in the University of Leyden in 1823. Essays by Verdam and Verhulst obtained prizes; they were published in 1824. The title of the two essays is the same ... *Commentatio ad Quæstionem Mathematicam ... in Academia Lugduno-Batava ... propositam ...*

Verdam's essay occupies 100 quarto pages; from page 76 to the end is devoted to the Calculus of Variations. The writer confesses that he has a very imperfect knowledge of this branch of the subject. Some of the ordinary formulæ are given, but the demonstrations are only sketched, and reference is made to Lacroix for the details; a few of the usual problems are given in illustration. The essay is not free from error; we may refer for example to the treatment of the limiting equations. Verdam says in effect, that in a term of the form $A\delta y$, if the limits of y are fixed we still have $A = 0$, whereas the term vanishes because $\delta y = 0$ and the relation $A = 0$ does not in general hold. And on his page 94 he gives an example from Euler's *Methodus Inveniendi* ... page 88, which he treats by means of that formula given by Lacroix which we have discussed in Art. 38. Verdam's result is correct for the case which Euler considers in which L is a function of Π, but is not true if, as Verdam says, L is a function of x and y.

Verhulst's essay occupies 30 quarto pages; about three pages are devoted to the formulæ of the Calculus of Variations, and three more to some of the common problems.

377. Verhulst.   There is another essay by Verhulst, which is on the Calculus of Variations exclusively.   This obtained a prize which was offered in 1823 by the University of Ghent, and was published in 1824 under the title ... *Commentatio ad Quæstionem Mathematicam ... Academiæ Gandavensis propositam*....

The essay contains a brief sketch of the subject, and discusses seven problems; it gives some account of the application of the subject to Mechanics, and demonstrates the principle of least action.   It is chiefly remarkable for grave errors.

378. Airy.   In Airy's *Mathematical Tracts*, published at Cambridge in 1826, twenty-three pages are devoted to the Calculus of Variations.   These pages form an excellent elementary treatise on the subject.   The author in his preface speaks of the subject as the "most beautiful of all the branches of the Differential Calculus."   He says of his treatise, "by adhering rigorously to principles, by exemplifying every formula, and by avoiding the investigation of useless theorems, the author hopes that he has removed many of the difficulties which have been thought to beset this theory."

The fourth edition of the *Mathematical Tracts* was published in 1858; the treatise on the Calculus of Variations is here increased by two pages, namely pages 240 and 241 of the work.

379. Bordoni. *Lezioni di Calcolo Sublime*. Milan, 1831. This work is in two octavo volumes; the Calculus of Variations

occupies pages 192—298 of the second volume. Bordoni adopts the method and notation of Lagrange which we have described in Art. 15; and the work is rendered extremely perplexing by the profusion of dots and dashes and affixes with which the symbols are loaded. Scarcely any examples are given in illustration of the theory. This appears to be the first elementary work which introduced Poisson's formulæ for the variations of the differential coefficients of a function of two independent variables; see Art. 262.

We will notice a few points in the treatise in detail.

380. Two examples of the use of Variations are given by Bordoni on his pages 261—265, which we will briefly explain.

I. Suppose a fixed surface and two fixed points outside it; let a string have its extremities fixed to these points, and let it be stretched and kept in contact with the surface by means of a point moving on the surface and against the string; thus the whole string consists of four portions, namely two straight lines outside the surface and two curved portions on the surface. The moving point will trace out a locus on the surface after the manner in which an ellipse is traced out on a plane by a moving point which stretches a string having its ends fixed. Then the locus traced on the surface has this property analogous to a property of the ellipse; the tangent at any point of the locus makes equal angles with the two curved portions of the string meeting in that point. This we shall now prove. The string is inextensible, and therefore the sum of the variations of the four parts is zero. Let x, y, z denote the co-ordinates of a point in one of the curved portions, so that the length of this portion is

$\int \sqrt{(1 + y'^2 + z'^2)}\, dx$ between proper limits, where y' stands for $\dfrac{dy}{dx}$

and z' stands for $\dfrac{dz}{dx}$. The variation of this integral according to the usual notation consists of an integrated part

$$\sqrt{(1 + y'^2 + z'^2)}\, \delta x + \frac{y'\, (\delta y - y'\delta x) + z'\, (\delta z - z'\delta x)}{\sqrt{(1 + y'^2 + z'^2)}},$$

and an unintegrated part

$$-\int\left\{(\delta y - y'\delta x)\frac{d}{dx}\frac{y'}{\sqrt{(1 + y'^2 + z'^2)}} + (\delta z - z'\delta x)\frac{d}{dx}\frac{z'}{\sqrt{(1 + y'^2 + z'^2)}}\right\}dx.$$

Now this unintegrated part vanishes, because we know from statical considerations, that the curved portions of the string assume the forms of the lines of maximum or minimum length on the surface, and for such lines the unintegrated part of the variation of the length of an arc vanishes. We have therefore only the integrated part remaining, and this may be put in the form

$$\frac{\delta x + y'\delta y + z'\delta z}{\sqrt{(1 + y'^2 + z'^2)}},$$

that is, $\delta s \cos \phi$, where $\delta s^2 = \delta x^2 + \delta y^2 + \delta z^2$, and ϕ is the angle between two lines, one having its direction-cosines proportional to δx, δy, δz respectively, and the other having its direction-cosines proportional to 1, y', z' respectively.

Now at the point which is common to one of the straight portions of the string and one of the curved portions, δs and ϕ have the same values for each portion; so that the two terms which are thus contributed to the variation of the whole length cancel. Then at the point common to the curved portions δs is the same for the two portions, and therefore ϕ must have the same value in order that the whole variation may vanish.

II. Suppose one end of a string fixed to a point in a curve on a fixed surface; and let the string be stretched so that a part is kept in contact with this curve, a part kept in contact with the surface, and a part is free from the surface. Then whatever may be the position of the string, provided that the three parts are kept stretched, the third part is always a normal to the surface traced out by its free end.

This is proved in the same manner as before. Let ξ, η, ζ be the co-ordinates of the free end; x, y, z the co-ordinates of the point where the string leaves the surface. Let s_1 be the length of the straight portion, s_2 the length of the part which is only kept

on the surface, s_3 the length of the part which is kept against
the curve. The whole variation of $s_1 + s_2 + s_3$ must be zero. The
unintegrated part of the variation of s_2 vanishes as before; the
only variation in s_3 is that which is produced by lengthening or
shortening the portion in contact with the curve; and this variation
is cancelled by the corresponding term in the integrated part of
the variation of s_2. The variation of s_1 so far as it depends on
the variation of the point (x, y, z) is cancelled by the corresponding term in the integrated part of the variation of s_2. Thus
that part of the variation of s_1 which arises from the variation
of the point (ξ, η, ζ) must separately vanish.

But
$$s_1{}^2 = (x - \xi)^2 + (y - \eta)^2 + (z - \zeta)^2,$$

therefore
$$\frac{(x - \xi)\,\delta\xi + (y - \eta)\,\delta\eta + (z - \zeta)\,\delta\zeta}{s_1} = 0;$$

this equation shews that two lines are at right angles, namely
the line which has its direction-cosines proportional to $\delta\xi$, $\delta\eta$, $\delta\zeta$
respectively, and the line which has its direction-cosines pro-
portional to $x - \xi$, $y - \eta$, $z - \zeta$ respectively. This proves the
theorem.

381. On pages 281—298 of his work, Bordoni discusses the
criteria for distinguishing between maxima and minima values;
here he follows the method of Legendre. Suppose we have to
investigate the maximum or minimum of $\int \phi\,(x, y, y')\,dx$. The
terms of the first order are supposed treated in the usual way
We have then to examine the sign of

$$\int \left\{ A(\delta y)^2 + 2B\,\delta y\,\delta y' + C\,(\delta y')^2 \right\} dx,$$

where
$$A = \frac{d^2\phi}{dy^2}, \quad B = \frac{d^2\phi}{dy\,dy'}, \quad C = \frac{d^2\phi}{dy'^2}.$$

Now we have identically, whatever a may be,

$$A\,(\delta y)^2 + 2B\,\delta y\,\delta y' + C\,(\delta y')^2$$
$$= (A - a')\,(\delta y)^2 + 2\,(B - a)\,\delta y\,\delta y' + C\,(\delta y')^2 + \{a\,(\delta y)^2\}'.$$

Thus the above integral becomes

$$a\,(\delta y)^2 + \int \left\{ (A - a')\,(\delta y)^2 + 2\,(B - a)\,\delta y\,\delta y' + C\,(\delta y')^2 \right\}\,dx.$$

Then if a can be found so as to make

$$(A - a')\,C \text{ greater than } (B - a)^2,$$

the sign of the expression remaining under the integral sign will be the same as the sign of C; and thus we shall be able to determine whether there is a maximum or a minimum.

A suitable value of a may be found thus. Let c be the least value of C between the limits of integration, b the least value of $A - B'$; find μ from the equation

$$(b + \mu') \, c = \mu^2,$$

so that
$$\mu = \sqrt{(bc)}\;\frac{1 + ke^{\frac{2x\sqrt{b}}{\sqrt{c}}}}{1 - ke^{\frac{2x\sqrt{b}}{\sqrt{c}}}},$$

where k is a constant.

Then $a = B - \mu$ is a suitable value. For

$$b + \mu' \text{ is less than } A - B' + \mu', \text{ and } c \text{ less than } C;$$

therefore $(b + \mu')\,c$ is less than $C\,(A - B' + \mu')$,

that is $C\,(A - B' + \mu')$ is greater than μ^2,

that is $C\,(A - a')$ greater than $(B - a)^2$.

Bordoni does not however allow for the exceptions which may arise; thus in applying the test to a geodesic line, he says that such a line is a line of minimum length, which we know is not necessarily the case.

382. One of the investigations which Bordoni gives is intended to discriminate between the maximum and minimum of $\int \phi\,(x, y, z, y', z')\,dx$ when a relation $F\,(x, y, z, y', z') = 0$ is supposed to hold. In this case by the use of a multiplier λ we find that we have to investigate the sign of the terms of the second

order in the variation of $\int (\phi + \lambda F)\, dx$. These terms form a polynomial of the second degree in $\delta z'$, $\delta y'$, δz, δy; then $\delta z'$ is eliminated by means of the relation

$$\frac{dF}{dz'}\,\delta z' + \frac{dF}{dy'}\,\delta y' + \frac{dF}{dz}\,\delta z + \frac{dF}{dy}\,\delta y = 0.$$

We thus obtain under the integral sign a polynomial of the second degree in $\delta y'$, δz, δy, say

$$A\,(\delta y)^2 + 2B\,\delta y\,\delta y' + \ldots\ldots + G\,(\delta y')^2;$$

and

$$G = \frac{d^2(\phi + \lambda F)}{dy'^2} + 2r\,\frac{d^2(\phi + \lambda F)}{dy'\,dz'} + r^2\,\frac{d^2(\phi + \lambda F)}{dz'^2},$$

where

$$r = -\frac{\dfrac{dF}{dy'}}{\dfrac{dF}{dz'}}.$$

This polynomial is then modified by adding to it the term $[a\,(\delta y)^2 + 2\beta\,\delta y\,\delta z + \gamma\,(\delta z)^2]'$ and taking away the same term, in the manner of the preceding article. Then $a\,(\delta y)^2 + 2\beta\,\delta y\,\delta z + \gamma\,(\delta z)^2$ is brought outside the integral sign, and the polynomial under the integral sign involves a, β, γ and their differential coefficients. The polynomial under the integral sign may then be arranged by the theorem given in Art. 260; and finally by properly choosing the values of a, β, γ we may make the polynomial have the same sign as G. Thus we have a minimum if G be positive throughout the limits of the integration, and a maximum if G be negative throughout the limits of the integration.

This general result Bordoni applies to two special cases. First, suppose that ϕ involves only x, y, z and y', and that F is of the form $z' - \psi\,(x, y, z, y')$; then the case coincides with that considered by Brunacci, and the result is the same as he obtained; see Art. 206.

Next, suppose $\phi\,(x, y, z, y', z')$ reduces to z'; then G becomes

$$\lambda\left(\frac{d^2F}{dy'^2} + 2r\,\frac{d^2F}{dy'\,dz} + r^2\,\frac{d^2F}{dz'^2}\right).$$

Bordoni says that this is equal to $-\lambda \dfrac{dF}{dz}\dfrac{d^n z'}{dy^n}$, because

$$\frac{d^n F}{dy^n} + 2r\,\frac{d^n F}{dy'\,dz} + r^2\,\frac{d^n F}{dz^n} + \frac{dF}{dz}\,\frac{d^n z'}{dy^n} = 0,$$

which is altogether inadmissible.

383. In Klügel's *Mathematisches Wörterbuch*, Vol. 5, 1831, an article occurs on *Variationsrechnung* which occupies pages 600—715. This article presents nothing remarkable. The early part of it is encumbered with useless generalities. It concludes with a brief sketch of the early history of the subject, accompanied with some references to writers, chiefly of the 18th century.

384. Momsen. *Elementa Calculi Variationum ratione ad analysin infinitorum quam proxime accedente tractata.* Altona, 1833.

This treatise was written as an exercise for a degree in the University of Kiel; it occupies 73 quarto pages. In the introduction the author treats of the different ways in which the notion of a variation has been presented by mathematicians, and gives the preference to that which has been adopted by Euler, Lagrange, Ohm and Strauch; see Art. 334. The work consists of four sections besides the introduction. The first section considers the maxima and minima values of single integrals. The second section considers the maxima and minima values of compound expressions, such as an integral which involves another integral, or the product of two integrals, or the quotient of one integral by another integral. The third section considers problems of relative maxima and minima values. The fourth section considers the maxima and minima values of double integrals. The treatise possesses no merit as regards the theory of the subject; it may be considered as a collection of examples taken almost entirely from Euler's *Methodus Inveniendi...* Momsen however adds to the solutions given by Euler some investigations of the terms of the second order in order to distinguish between maxima and minima values. Momsen ascribes no variation to the independent variable in his solutions, nor does he make any changes in the limits of his integrations; all investigations respecting the limiting values of the quantities which occur he considers to belong to the ordinary Differential and Integral Calculus; see his pages 27—29.

We will make some remarks on certain parts of the treatise.

885. On his page 14 Momsen shews that $\int (2xy - y^2)\, dx$ is a *maximum* when $y = x$; Euler, in the memoir to which we have referred in Art. 22, erroneously stated that the result is a *minimum*. On his page 15 Momsen discusses an example given by Euler in his *Methodus Inveniendi*... page 41; see Art. 52. Momsen agrees with Dirksen in correcting Euler's statement as to the nature of the result. See Dirksen, page 204, and also page 7 of the preface to Ohm's work, entitled *Die Lehre vom Grössten und Kleinsten.*

On his pages 18 and 19 Momsen considers the problem of the solid of least resistance. In examining whether the result obtained is really a maximum or a minimum Momsen makes a mistake in his work; the mistake occurs in the last two lines of page 18, where he has $\dfrac{-6yp}{(1 + p^2)^3}$ instead of $\dfrac{(6p - 2p^3)\, y}{(1 + p^2)^3}$. Hence, he erroneously concludes that the solid is really a solid of maximum resistance, and he says, " hinc igitur satis perspicitur, ex hac quæstione, quæ in omnibus fere libris de hoc argumento conscriptis occurrere solet, soluta parum sane emolumenti ad societatem humanam redundare." The true results respecting this problem have been given by Legendre in the memoir which we have cited in Art. 197.

On his pages 32—34 Momsen examines the problem of finding the maximum or minimum of the product of $\int y\, dx$ and $\int \sqrt{(1 + p^2)}\, dx$. The result apparently obtained is a circle, but Momsen shews that there is really neither a maximum nor a minimum; Strauch arrives at the same result on page 541 of his second volume. Euler erroneously concluded that a circle convex to the axis of abscissæ would give a maximum; see the *Methodus Inveniendi* ... page 149.

386. On his pages 35—37 Momsen discusses a problem given by Euler in his *Methodus Inveniendi* ... pages 122—126. It is required to find the curve in which Π is a maximum or minimum, where Π is to be found by the differential equation

$$d\Pi - g\,dx + a\Pi^{a}\,\surd(1+p^{2})\,dx = 0 \;\ldots\ldots\ldots\ldots\ldots\; (1).$$

This is easily seen to be a problem in Dynamics; the curve is required down which a particle must move so as to acquire a maximum velocity, supposing a resistance varying as the $2n^{th}$ power of the velocity. Strauch has considered the case in which $n = 1$, but in examining the terms of the second order he has made a mistake; see Art. 337. Momsen also is wrong in his investigation of the terms of the second order. We will here examine the problem briefly. We shall denote initial and final values by the suffixes 0 and 1 respectively, and we shall suppose Π_{0} given. Suppose Π receives an increment $\delta\Pi$; then from (1) retaining terms of the second order, we have

$$d\,\delta\Pi + an\Pi^{a-1}\delta\Pi\,\surd(1+p^{2})\,dx + \frac{a\Pi^{a}p\,\delta p\,dx}{\surd(1+p^{2})} + M\,dx = 0 \;\ldots\; (2),$$

where

$$2M = an\,(n-1)\,\Pi^{a-2}\,(\delta\Pi)^{2}\,\surd(1+p^{2}) + \frac{2an\,\Pi^{a-1}\delta\Pi\,p\,\delta p}{\surd(1+p^{2})} + \frac{a\Pi^{a}\,(\delta p)^{2}}{(1+p^{2})^{\frac{3}{2}}}.$$

Multiply (2) by λ, where λ is a function of x at present undetermined, and integrate; thus

$$(\lambda\delta\Pi)_{1} + \left\{\frac{\lambda a\,\Pi^{a}p\,\delta y}{\surd(1+p^{2})}\right\}_{1} - \left\{\frac{\lambda a\,\Pi^{a}p\,\delta y}{\surd(1+p^{2})}\right\}_{0}$$

$$+ \int_{x_{0}}^{x_{1}} \left[\left\{an\,\lambda\Pi^{a-1}\,\surd(1+p^{2}) - \frac{d\lambda}{dx}\right\}\delta\Pi - a\,\delta y\,\frac{d}{dx}\frac{\lambda\Pi^{a}p}{\surd(1+p^{2})} + \lambda M\right]dx = 0.$$

Now as λ is in our power, we may assume

$$an\,\lambda\Pi^{a-1}\,\surd(1+p^{2}) - \frac{d\lambda}{dx} = 0 \;\ldots\ldots\ldots\ldots\ldots\; (3);$$

then the coefficient of δy must vanish in the expression under the integral sign in order that $(\delta\Pi)_1$ may be of the second order; thus

$$\frac{a\lambda\,\Pi^n p}{\sqrt{(1+p^2)}} = \text{a constant} = C \text{ say} \dots\dots\dots\dots (4).$$

Moreover it will be necessary that the terms outside the integral sign in the value of $(\delta\Pi)_1$ should vanish. If the initial and final points are fixed, these terms vanish because δy_0 and δy_1 are then zero; if these points are not fixed, we should require $C = 0$, and this would lead to $p = 0$, and so the required curve would become a vertical straight line. We take the former supposition, namely that y_0 and y_1 are constants.

From (4) by taking logarithms we can get an expression for $\frac{1}{\lambda}\frac{d\lambda}{dx}$; equate this to the value given by (3), and substitute for $\frac{d\Pi}{dx}$ from (1); thus we shall finally obtain

$$\Pi\frac{dp}{dx} = -ng\,p\,(1+p^2)\dots\dots\dots\dots\dots (5).$$

Thus we now have

$$(\lambda\delta\Pi)_1 = -\int_{s_0}^{s_1}\lambda M\,dx,$$

so that $(\delta\Pi)_1$ is of the second order.

Now it is shewn by Euler that we can proceed one step further in the integration and obtain Π as a function of p. Strauch having obtained Π as a function of p, differentiates with the symbol δ, and thus he obtains a relation between $\delta\Pi$ and δp, and by using this relation he simplifies the expression for M; see his Vol. II. page 445. He thus in fact assumes that the velocity is the same *particular* function of p both for the curve which we suppose to be under examination and for an adjacent curve; this is altogether inadmissible. Thus Strauch's equation XXVI is not true; moreover in the equation immediately preceding instead of $2Lmw$ under the integral sign he ought to have $4Lmw$.

Although the way in which Strauch tries to connect $\delta\Pi$ and δp is inadmissible, yet by another method we may find an expression

for $\delta\Pi$ which may be used in transforming M. If (1) could be
integrated so as to give Π in terms of p for any curve, we could .
connect $\delta\Pi$ and δp; but this integration cannot be effected. But
from (1) we have universally to the first order

$$\frac{d\,\delta\Pi}{dx} + an\Pi^{n-1}\delta\Pi\,\sqrt{(1+p^2)} + \frac{a\Pi^n p\,\delta p}{\sqrt{(1+p^2)}} = 0.$$

Let $an\Pi^{n-1}\sqrt{(1+p^2)}$ be denoted by Q and $\dfrac{a\Pi^n p}{\sqrt{(1+p^2)}}$ by R, so
that

$$\frac{d\,\delta\Pi}{dx} + Q\,\delta\Pi + R\,\delta p = 0,$$

therefore

$$\frac{d}{dx}\left(e^{\int Q dx}\delta\Pi\right) + e^{\int Q dx} R\,\delta p = 0,$$

and by integrating from x_0 to x

$$e^{\int Q dx}\delta\Pi = -\int_{x_0}^{x} e^{\int Q dx} R\,\delta p\,dx.$$

The last result is universally true; and when we apply it to
the curve under consideration we may put λ for $e^{\int Q dx}$ and C for λR;
thus

$$\lambda\,\delta\Pi = -\int_{x_0}^{x} C\delta p\,dx = -C\delta y, \text{ supposing } \delta y_0 = 0.$$

If we use this relation we can remove $\delta\Pi$ from M, and thus
express M as a function of the variations δy and δp.

Momsen's investigation of the terms of the second order is
wrong. If his process be followed out correctly, the result obtained
expressed in our notation will be

$$2(\lambda\delta\Pi)_1 = -\int_{x_0}^{x_1}\delta p\left\{\frac{an\,\lambda\Pi^{n-1}p\,\delta\Pi}{\sqrt{(1+p^2)}} + \frac{a\lambda\,\Pi^n\delta p}{(1+p^2)^{\frac{3}{2}}}\right\}dx$$

$$+ C\int_{x_0}^{x_1}\delta y\left\{n(n-1)a\Pi^{n-2}\sqrt{(1+p^2)}\delta\Pi + \frac{an\,\Pi^{n-1}p}{\sqrt{(1+p^2)}}\delta p\right\}dx;$$

and if we put $-\lambda\,\delta\Pi$ for $C\delta y$, this result agrees with that which we have obtained. But Momsen assumes that because $(\delta\Pi)_1$ is zero to the first order, therefore $\delta\Pi$ is so also; by this error he obtains

$$2\left(\lambda\,\delta\Pi\right)_1 = -\int_{x_0}^{x_1}\frac{a\lambda\,\Pi^a(\delta p)^2}{(1+p^2)^{\frac{3}{2}}}\,dx + C\int_{x_0}^{x_1}\frac{an\,\Pi^{a-1}p\,\delta y\,\delta p}{\sqrt{(1+p^2)}}\,dx.$$

By integration by parts the second term gives

$$-\frac{C}{2}\int_{x_0}^{x_1}(\delta y)^2\frac{d}{dx}\frac{an\,\Pi^{a-1}p}{\sqrt{(1+p^2)}}\,dx;$$

in this form Momsen leaves it, and asserts that there is a maximum; so that he appears to assume that $\dfrac{d}{dx}\dfrac{an\,\Pi^{a-1}p}{\sqrt{(1+p^2)}}$ is necessarily positive.

We may remark that although Momsen does not explicitly say so, yet from the beginning of his page 36 it appears that he takes Π_0 to be given and also y_0 and y_1.

387. Some remarks may be made on a problem which Momsen discusses on his pages 45 and 46. The problem is a particular case of the second of the two famous isoperimetrical problems proposed by James Bernouilli. Bernouilli's problem is the following; let s denote $\int_0^x \sqrt{(1+p^2)}\,dx$, and $\phi(s)$ any function of s; then the relation between x and y is required which makes $\int_0^a \phi(s)\,dx$ a maximum or minimum while $\int_0^a \sqrt{(1+p^2)}\,dx$ has a given value, a being a constant. In the figure which is usually given to illustrate this problem it is in fact assumed that $\phi(s)$ vanishes when $x=0$ and when $x=a$; this limitation is altogether unnecessary, and is never regarded in the solution. The enunciation implies that the limiting values of x are constants. The usual figure makes the limiting values of y both *zero*; this limitation is also unnecessary, it is sufficient that the limiting values of y should be constants. Thus the figure may be drawn as in figure 11, and the enunciation be given thus; A and B are fixed points, it is required to find a curve ASB of given length such that the area $OEDF$ may be a maximum or a minimum where PN is always a given function of AS.

Since $\int_0^a \phi(s)\,dx$ is to be a maximum or minimum while $\int_0^a \sqrt{(1+p^2)}\,dx$ is constant, we proceed to find the maximum or minimum of $\int_0^a \left\{ \phi(s) + \lambda \sqrt{(1+p^2)} \right\} dx$. We can then apply the formula of Art. 38, supposing that

$$v = s, \quad L = \phi'(s), \quad P = \frac{\lambda p}{\sqrt{(1+p^2)}} \text{ and } P' = \frac{p}{\sqrt{(1+p^2)}}.$$

The integrated part of $\delta \int V dx$ in that formula vanishes because the limiting values of x and y are constant; hence for a maximum or minimum we have

$$P + (A - I) P' = \text{a constant} = C \text{ say,}$$

therefore $\qquad \lambda p + (A - I) p = C \sqrt{(1+p^2)},$

therefore $\qquad \lambda + A - I = \frac{C}{p} \sqrt{(1+p^2)} \quad\ldots\ldots\ldots\ldots (1);$

by differentiating we obtain

$$-\frac{dI}{dx} = \frac{-C}{p^2 \sqrt{(1+p^2)}} \frac{dp}{dx},$$

that is $\qquad L \text{ or } \phi'(s) = \frac{C}{p^2 \sqrt{(1+p^2)}} \frac{dp}{dx},$

therefore $\qquad \phi'(s) \frac{ds}{dx} = \frac{C}{p^2} \frac{dp}{dx} \quad\ldots\ldots\ldots\ldots\ldots (2),$

therefore $\qquad \phi(s) = -\frac{C}{p} + C_1,$

therefore $\qquad \dfrac{dy}{dx} = \dfrac{C}{C_1 - \phi(s)},$

therefore $\qquad \dfrac{dy}{ds} = \dfrac{C}{\sqrt{[C^2 + \{C_1 - \phi(s)\}^2]}},$

and $\qquad \dfrac{dx}{ds} = \dfrac{C_1 - \phi(s)}{\sqrt{[C^2 + \{C_1 - \phi(s)\}^2]}}.$

From the last two equations x and y must be found in terms of s; two constants already appear, and two more will occur in the integrations for finding x and y. These constants must be determined from the consideration that when $s=0$ the values of x and y must be the co-ordinates of the given point A, and when s is equal to the given length the values of x and y must be the co-ordinates of the given point B. A different view of this part of the solution is given in De Morgan's *Differential Calculus*, page 468.

In the particular case considered by Momsen $\phi(s)=s$; thus $\frac{dy}{dx}=\frac{C}{C_1-s}$; and this shews that the curve must be a catenary having its directrix parallel to the axis of y. And thus we see that the ordinary figure with A and B on the axis of x is impossible in the present case, because a catenary cannot be cut in two points by a straight line perpendicular to its directrix.

We proceed to investigate the terms of the second order in the variation of $\int_0^a \left\{\phi(s)+\lambda\sqrt{(1+p^2)}\right\} dx$ in the particular case in which $\phi(s)=s$.

We have to the second order

$$\delta s=\int_0^x \left\{\frac{p\delta p}{\sqrt{(1+p^2)}}+\frac{(\delta p)^2}{2(1+p^2)^{\frac{3}{2}}}\right\} dx.$$

Thus the required terms consist of

$$\frac{1}{2}\int_0^a \left[\int_0^x \frac{(\delta p)^2\,dx}{(1+p^2)^{\frac{3}{2}}}+\frac{\lambda(\delta p)^2}{(1+p^2)^{\frac{3}{2}}}\right] dx.$$

And $$\int dx \left[\int_0^x \frac{(\delta p)^2\,dx}{(1+p^2)^{\frac{3}{2}}}\right]=x\int_0^x \frac{(\delta p)^2\,dx}{(1+p^2)^{\frac{3}{2}}}-\int \frac{x(\delta p)^2\,dx}{(1+p^2)^{\frac{3}{2}}};$$

therefore $$\int_0^a dx \left[\int_0^x \frac{(\delta p)^2\,dx}{(1+p^2)^{\frac{3}{2}}}\right]=\int_0^a \frac{(a-x)(\delta p)^2\,dx}{(1+p^2)^{\frac{3}{2}}}.$$

Thus the expression to be examined becomes

$$\frac{1}{2}\int_0^a \frac{(\lambda+a-x)(\delta p)^2\,dx}{(1+p^2)^{\frac{3}{2}}}.$$

We must now consider the sign and value of λ. From equation (1), by supposing $x = a$, we obtain

$$\lambda = \left\{ \frac{C \sqrt{(1 + p^2)}}{p} \right\}_{x=a} \quad \dots\dots\dots\dots\dots\dots (3).$$

From equation (2)

$$\frac{ds}{dx} = \frac{C}{p^2} \frac{dp}{dx};$$

therefore

$$\lambda = \left\{ \frac{p \left(\frac{ds}{dx} \right)^2}{\frac{dp}{dx}} \right\}_{x=a} \quad \dots\dots\dots\dots\dots (4).$$

Hence by the nature of the catenary it may be shewn that λ is numerically equal to the distance of the point B from the directrix of the catenary.

Suppose in the first place that the ordinate of A is less than that of B; if the catenary is concave to the axis of x, then λ is negative and is numerically greater than a, so that $\lambda + a - x$ is negative and we have a maximum; if the catenary is convex to the axis of x, then λ is positive and we have a minimum. Next suppose that the ordinate of A is greater than that of B; if the catenary is concave to the axis of x, then λ is positive and we have a minimum; if the catenary is convex to the axis of x, then λ is negative and is numerically greater than a, so that $\lambda + a - x$ is negative and we have a maximum.

The last eight lines of Momsen's investigation are unsatisfactory; he comes to the conclusion that there is always a minimum. He argues thus; let

$$W = \int_0^a [s + \lambda \sqrt{(1 + p^2)}] \, dx;$$

by integration by parts we have

$$\int_0^a s \, dx = sx - \int_0^a x \frac{ds}{dx} \, dx,$$

therefore

$$\int_0^a s \, dx = \int_0^a (a - x) \frac{ds}{dx} \, dx;$$

thus
$$W = \int_a^b (\lambda + a - x)\, \sqrt{(1 + p^2)}\, dx.$$

Hence Momsen says that W is of the same sign as the expression of the second order

$$\frac{1}{2} \int_a^b \frac{(\lambda + a - x)\,(\delta p)^2\, dx}{(1 + p^2)^{\frac{3}{2}}};$$

and this is true from what we have given although Momsen does not prove it. Then Momsen concludes that the result necessarily makes W a minimum. This is inadmissible; the sign of W has nothing to do with the question of the maximum or minimum of $\int_a^b s\, dx$.

It should be observed that the solution here given is liable to fail, for the given length of curve may be too great to constitute an arc of a catenary joining the two given points. We will consider one case, and treat it after the manner of Art. 852. Let k_0 and k_1 be the ordinates of A and B, and suppose k_0 less than k_1. Suppose a maximum is required, and let us try if the problem can be solved by supposing the curve joining A and B to be made up of a straight line of length $y_0 - k_0$ formed by producing OA through A, and an arc joining the point $(0, y_0)$ to B. The expression which is now to be a maximum is

$$\int_0^a [y_0 - k_0 + s]\, dx, \quad \text{where } s = \int_0^x \sqrt{(1 + p^2)}\, dx;$$

and the whole length is $y_0 - k_0 + \int_0^a \sqrt{(1 + p^2)}\, dx$.

Thus we may consider that we have now to find the maximum of

$$\int_0^a [y_0 - k_0 + s + \lambda \sqrt{(1 + p^2)}]\, dx + \lambda\, (y_0 - k_0),$$

that is of $\int_0^a [s + \lambda \sqrt{(1 + p^2)}]\, dx + (a + \lambda)\, (y_0 - k_0)$.

The only point in which the solution will differ from that formerly given is in the terms outside the integral sign. We have $(a + \lambda)\, \delta y_0$ from the term $(a + \lambda)\, y_0$; and there is the term

$(P + \Delta P' - IP')\,\omega$ in the notation of Art. 38, which gives us $- C\delta y_o$. Thus we require that

$$a + \lambda - C = 0 \dots\dots\dots\dots\dots\dots\dots\dots\dots(5).$$

We have already stated that from (4) it follows that λ is numerically equal to the distance of B from the directrix of the catenary; then from (3) it follows that C is numerically equal to the parameter of the catenary, that is, to the distance of the directrix from the nearest point of the curve. And if the catenary is concave to the axis of x both λ and C are negative. Thus we shall deduce from (5) that the catenary must *touch* the axis of y at the point $(0, y_o)$.

This holds so long as y_o is not greater than k_1. If we cannot consistently with the given length have y_o not greater than k_1, we must make the catenary convex to the axis of x and make it touch the axis of y at the point $(0, y_o)$.

If a minimum be required, the curve consists of a catenary beginning at A and ending at the point (a, y_o), and having its tangent parallel to the axis of y at this point; and the length consists of that of the arc of the catenary together with that of the line joining the points (a, y_1) and (a, k_1).

388. The following problems relating to the maxima and minima values of double integrals are solved in Momsen's fourth section, the limits of x and y being supposed given in all cases.

(1)　The maximum of $\iint z\,(x^2 + y^2 - az)\,dx\,dy$; this is in Strauch, Vol. II. page 562.

(2)　The maximum of $\iint \left\{ 2\sqrt{(x^2 + y^2 + z^2)} - \dfrac{z^2}{r} \right\} dx\,dy$.

(3)　The minimum of $\iint \left\{ z\sqrt{(x^2 + y^2)} + \dfrac{m}{2}(z - c)^2 \right\} dx\,dy$.

(4)　The surface of maximum or minimum area having a given boundary.

(5)　The surface of maximum or minimum area among all those which correspond to a constant volume.

(6)   The volume of a solid being given, it is required to find its bounding surface so that its centre of gravity may be at a maximum distance from the plane of (x, y).   This problem is in Strauch, Vol. II. page 610.   The problem is analogous to that considered in Art. 340; the result is that the required surface is a plane.   Both Momsen and Strauch encumber their solution by not paying attention to the remark at the end of Art. 340.

(7)   Among surfaces of given area to find that which has its centre of gravity at a maximum distance from the plane of (x, y); the differential equation of the required surface is here obtained, and as in the preceding problem the investigation is needlessly encumbered.

A general formula for the variation of double integrals is given by Momsen from Lacroix, which involves the errors already indicated; see Art. 27.

389.   Besides the errors we have already noted in Momsen's treatise, a few more may be given.

On his page 32 Momsen is speaking of the determination of the constants in the problem we have given in Art. 65.   He has a condition equivalent to $\lambda_4 = 0$, so that $\dfrac{d}{dx}\left(\dfrac{z}{p}\right)$ must $= 0$ when $x = b$. This equation which holds for a particular value of x he integrates, and deduces $z = Cp'$, which is inadmissible.

On his page 39 Momsen is speaking of the determination of the four constants which occur in the solution of the problem of the brachistochrone in a resisting medium.   He says that two are to be determined by making the curve pass through given initial and final points; he proposes what he considers two conditions for determining the other two, but these two conditions amount really to only one condition.   The condition which he omits is that the initial velocity must be supposed given, as he has really assumed at the top of his page 38.   Remarks similar to that which we have noticed in Art. 387 as occurring in the last eight lines of Momsen's investigation occur in other places of Momsen's treatise; see his sections 36, 37, and 40.   At the end of his section 48 he assumes without any proof that the sign of C can be easily ascertained to be positive when the curve is convex to the axis of x; the quantity C is the same as that denoted by M in Strauch, Vol. II. page 516, and its sign is not determined by Strauch. In his sections 38 and 58 Momsen retains terms which are absolutely zero, in the same way as $\int_a^a \delta y\, dx$ is zero in Art. 340.

390. Abbatt. *A Treatise on the Calculus of Variations*, by Richard Abbatt. London, 1837.

This is a volume in foolscap octavo, of 207 pages, with a preface of 11 pages. The writer in his preface refers to Lacroix, Lagrange, Euler, Woodhouse and Airy; and on page 203 he refers to Poisson's memoir. He appears to have used Poisson's memoir also on his pages 16, 62, 115—121 and 194—203. Nevertheless he gives on his pages 192 and 193 the erroneous formulæ which we have noticed in Arts. 39 and 40. He gives the correct formulæ on his pages 197 and 198, but his mode of obtaining them is not satisfactory.

The treatise contains numerous examples selected from preceding writers on the subject.

391. De Morgan. In Professor De Morgan's *Differential and Integral Calculus*, pages 446—475 are devoted to the Calculus of Variations; this part of the work was published in 1840. By adopting a condensed yet expressive notation a large quantity of information on the subject is compressed into a brief space. There is no investigation of the terms of the second order, but with this exception the student is introduced to all the important parts of the subject. In the formulæ respecting the variation of double integrals the limits with respect to both variables must be understood to be all *constants*, for the reason which we have given in Art. 28.

On pages 470 and 471 the problem of the brachistochrone in a resisting medium is discussed, and the way of determining the four constants which occur is carefully explained. Mr De Morgan observes that this part of the problem is omitted in silence by Woodhouse and Lacroix, and that " Lagrange merely says that δx_1 is indeterminate, but does not give any reason..." Lagrange's meaning is to be found however from what he had previously given on page 465 of the *Leçons* ..., edition of 1806; and it appears from this that Lagrange's view was correct.

We may observe that in Stegmann's discussion of the problem the constants are determined in the same way as by Mr De Morgan; see Stegmann's work, pages 818—321. Strauch is not satisfactory on this point; see his Vol. II. page 418.

392. Cournot. Two chapters are devoted to the Calculus of Variations in Cournot's *Traité élémentaire de la Théorie des Fonctions...* Paris, 1841. These chapters occupy pages 113—155 of the second volume of the work; they form a good elementary treatise on the subject. It should be observed however that in the variation of double integrals Cournot reproduces the error which we have explained in Art. 27.

393. Hall. The *Encyclopædia Metropolitana* contains a brief treatise on the Calculus of Variations by Professor Hall. It occupies pages 209—226 of the second volume of the first division of the Encyclopædia; the date of this volume is 1843. The treatise gives the usual theory so far as terms of the first order in the variation of single integrals, and applies the theory to a few examples.

394. Bruun. *A Manual of the Calculus of Variations*. Odessa, 1848.

This is an octavo volume of 195 pages in the Russian language. The difficulty of the language will prevent any detailed account of the work. It is divided into four parts. The first part occupies pages 1—36, and gives the variations of expressions. The second part occupies pages 37—56, and discusses the criteria of integrability of expressions. The third part occupies pages 57—181, and contains the investigation of maxima and minima values. The fourth part occupies pages 182—195, and consists of a sketch of the history of the subject.

In the third part of the work the terms of the second order in the variations of integrals are investigated with the view of distinguishing between maxima and minima values. Bruun takes in succession the case in which the function under the integral sign involves only x, y and y', and the case in which the function under the integral sign involves x, y, y' and y''. He gives both Legendre's method and Jacobi's method, and of course by comparing the results of the two methods the auxiliary quantities introduced by Legendre's method become determined; see Art. 235.

The only passage in the third part which presents any appearance of novelty is that on pages 103—108. After having finished the discussion of the method of Jacobi applied to $\int \phi(x, y, y', y'')\, dx$, Bruun intimates that this method is very complex, and that he will explain another method of discriminating between maxima and minima values, given by Sokoloff. He does not however do more than introduce the method to the reader and refer for detail and exemplification to the memoir of Sokoloff. The title of this memoir appears to be *Researches on a certain point of the Calculus of Variations*. Charkoff, 1842. The following process will give an idea of the method so far as it is explained by Bruun.

Suppose we are investigating the sign of the terms of the second order in the variation of $\int_{x_0}^{x_1} \phi(x, y, y')\, dx$. The expression we have to examine may be written thus,

$$\int_{x_0}^{x_1} \left[A\,(\delta y)^2 + 2B\delta y\,\delta y' + C\,(\delta y')^2 \right]\, dx,$$

where A, B, C are functions of x. We wish to know if this expression retains the same sign for all values of δy and $\delta y'$; we will test this by ascribing a certain convenient value to δy.

We have
$$\int \left[A\,(\delta y)^2 + 2B\,\delta y\,\delta y' + C\,(\delta y')^2 \right]\, dx$$

$$= \int \left[(A\,\delta y + B\,\delta y')\,\delta y + (B\,\delta y + C\,\delta y')\,\delta y' \right]\, dx$$

$$= (B\delta y + C\delta y')\,\delta y + \int \left[A\,\delta y + B\,\delta y' - \frac{d}{dx}(B\delta y + C\delta y') \right] \delta y\, dx.$$

Thus if we choose for δy a value which makes

$$A\delta y + B\delta y' - \frac{d}{dx}(B\delta y + C\delta y') = 0,$$

the term we wish to examine can be actually integrated, and so its sign can be easily ascertained. Now a value of δy which will satisfy the above equation can be found, supposing that we can solve the differential equation which arises from making the terms of the first order vanish in the variation of $\int \phi\,(x,\,y,\,y')\,dx$; see Art. 251. Such a value will be of the form $\beta_1 u_1 + \beta_2 u_2$, where β_1 and β_2 are arbitrary constants, and u_1 and u_2 are known functions of x. Thus $(B\delta y + C\delta y')\,\delta y$ will be a homogeneous function of the second order of the arbitrary constants β_1 and β_2, and so we may by ordinary methods investigate whether

$$\{(B\delta y + C\delta y')\,\delta y\}_1 - \{(B\delta y + C\delta y')\,\delta y\}_0$$

is positive or negative for all values of these arbitrary constants.

Such appears to be essentially all that Bruun gives. It is obvious that by this method we may in some cases succeed in shewing that a proposed expression has neither a maximum nor a minimum value; but it does not appear obvious how we can deduce a positive test which shall shew when a proposed expression *is* a maximum or a minimum.

The pages 193—195 of the work contain a list of references to writers on the subject. In this list, besides the memoir of Sokoloff, two works are named which the present writer has not had an opportunity of consulting. These works are the following.

Textor. *Kurze Darstellung der höhern Analysis, nebst einem Anhange von dem Variationencalcul.* Berlin, 1809.

Senff. *Elementa Calculi Variationum.* Dorpat, 1838.

The present writer is indebted to the kindness of Professor Bruun for a copy of his *Manual of the Calculus of Variations.*

395. Price. A treatise on the Calculus of Variations forms part of the second volume of Professor Price's *Treatise on Infinitesimal Calculus.* Oxford, 1854. The Calculus of Variations occupies pages 234—334; and there is an application of the subject to the conditions of integrability on pages 440—446. The author refers to the works of Euler, Lagrange, Poisson, Jacobi, Ostrogradsky,

Delaunay, Strauch, Jellett, and Schellbach. The treatise gives the usual theory of the variation of single integrals; it explains Jacobi's method of distinguishing between maxima and minima values; it treats copiously of geodesic lines; and it touches briefly on the variation of double integrals.

398. It may be of service to a student of Professor Price's work to refer to a few points in which he may find some difficulty.

In Art. 93 we have given Poisson's proof of a certain relation, namely, $Hy' + Kz' = 0$, and we have stated in Art. 94, that Lagrange had proved this relation repeatedly. Mr Price on his pages 269 and 272 makes a remark which amounts to assuming that this result is obvious without demonstration.

On page 270 some remarks are made on the method of determining the arbitrary constants which occur in solving problems in the Calculus of Variations. If the limiting values of the quantities are not restricted, the coefficients of the terms $\delta x_0, \delta x_1, \delta y_0, \delta y_1, \ldots$ must be equated to zero. The book proceeds, "Suppose, however, that equations are given connecting the variables at the limits, that is, that equations are given between x_0 and y_0 and between x_1 and y_1: then if $T = 0$ is the integral of $II = 0$, there will be given

$$T_0, \left(\frac{dT}{dy}\right)_0, \left(\frac{dT}{dy^2}\right)_0, \ldots \left(\frac{d^{n-1}T}{dy^{n-1}}\right)_0, \quad T_1, \left(\frac{dT}{dy}\right)_1, \ldots \left(\frac{d^{n-1}T}{dy^{n-1}}\right)_1, \ldots "$$

This seems unsatisfactory. If, for example, $T = 0$ then $T_0 = 0$ and $T_1 = 0$ necessarily, and no new information is supplied by these equations. The true method when relations are given between the limiting values of quantities is to deduce relations between the variations of these limiting values; thus some of the variations are expressible in terms of the others, and the number left arbitrary is diminished; we then equate to zero the coefficients of these remaining variations, and the equations so obtained together with the given relations can be used to determine the arbitrary constants.

In some cases, as we have seen in Arts. 276 and 367 the number of arbitrary constants occurring in a solution may be too small. Mr Price speaks of such a problem as *indeterminate* on page 270; it should rather be called *impossible*, for the problem cannot be solved at all, unless certain restrictions are imposed. See Mr Jellett's Treatise, page 44.

On page 274 instead of "... $F_0(a, b) = 0$, $F_1(a, b) = 0$. By means of which four equations we can determine $\frac{a}{\beta}$, a and b, and thereby definitely fix the line whose equation is (32)," read

$$\text{"... } F_0(x_0, y_0) = 0, \ F_1(x_1, y_1) = 0; \text{ also } \frac{x_1 - x_0}{\alpha} = \frac{y_1 - y_0}{\beta}.$$

We have now five equations for finding x_0, y_0, x_1, y_1, $\frac{a}{\beta}$."

An important mistake occurs on page 296. The equations (131) cannot be deduced in the way given in the book. Equations (131) involve important properties of *geodesic* lines, but the equations (127), (128), (129), (130), from which the book deduces (131), are *not at all restricted* to geodesic lines. Equations (131) may be proved thus; we may shew by direct investigation that

$$\frac{d\lambda}{ds\,d''x - dx\,d''s} = \frac{d\mu}{ds\,d''y - dy\,d''s} = \frac{d\nu}{ds\,d''z - dz\,d''s},$$

and then by means of equations (115) of the book, we have

$$\frac{d\lambda}{U} = \frac{d\mu}{V} = \frac{d\nu}{W}.$$

On page 307 we read "suppose a series of geodesic lines to originate at a point (μ_1, ν_1) and to touch the line of curvature (μ_0); then at that point ...." It is not possible to have a series of geodesic lines passing through a point and touching a given line of curvature. In fact the words "originating at a point" should be omitted, as they are not required or used.

On page 308 we read "it may be proved in the same way as the analogous theorem in plane geometry, that the geodesic radii vectores make equal angles with the curve of curvature." The proposition in question has been assumed to be true in writing the equations

$$dr_1 = d_0 s \cos i, \quad dr_2 = -d_0 s \cos i,$$

which occur immediately before, so that of course we cannot use
any consequence drawn from these equations in order to establish
the proposition.

On page 329 the same mistake occurs which we have noticed
in Art. 232.   We have an equation

$$\int_0^1 u \delta H \, dx = B_1 \left(\frac{u}{z}\right)' + \frac{d}{dx} B_1 \left(\frac{u}{z}\right)'',$$

and it is stated that any value of u which makes $\delta H = 0$ will also
satisfy the right-hand member of the equation.   Either the limits
0 and 1 should be omitted from the left-hand side and then the
conclusion is that any value of u which makes $\delta H = 0$ will make
the right-hand member equal to a constant; or if the limits 0 and 1
are retained on the left-hand side the right-hand side must be
written

$$\left\{ B_1 \left(\frac{u}{z}\right)' + \frac{d}{dx} B_1 \left(\frac{u}{z}\right)'' \right\}_1 - \left\{ B_1 \left(\frac{u}{z}\right)' + \frac{d}{dx} B_1 \left(\frac{u}{z}\right)'' \right\}_0,$$

and then any value of u which makes $\delta H = 0$ makes this expression
vanish.

897.   There are some passages in the treatise which do not
appear treated with sufficient detail for those who are studying the
subject for the first time.   For example, the process of page 258 of
the treatise may be compared with Ostrogradsky's corresponding
process, which we have reproduced in Art. 128.   The statement on
page 283 respecting the equating certain ratios to a *constant* quantity
seems to need explanation.   On page 310 it is stated that the
directions of the principal lines of curvature at any point of an
ellipsoid are *evidently* parallel to the principal axes of a section of
the ellipsoid made by a plane parallel to the tangent plane at the
point in question; they are parallel but not evidently so without
demonstration.

398.   Meyer.   *Nouveaux Éléments du Calcul des Variations.*
Liége et Leipzig, 1856.

This treatise consists of 132 octavo pages.   In the preface the
author says he has preserved the classification of variations into
simple and compound, pure and mixed, given by Strauch, and that

he has borrowed from the profound work of that writer the formula for the variation of a double integral when the limits of the first integration are themselves susceptible of variation. He says that he has given a new method of explaining the principles of the subject, and he considers this method to have the threefold advantage of deducing the subject from Taylor's Theorem, of freeing it from the consideration of infinitesimals, and of freeing it from any question about the convergence of series. As he only proposed to write an elementary treatise he has not entered upon the calculation of the variations of the second order. He says that for isoperimetrical problems he has given a method which is substantially Euler's, but that he has introduced a modification which removes some objections that are brought against the methods of Euler and Lagrange. For the composition of the treatise he has consulted the most eminent writers, especially Euler, Lagrange, Poisson, Dirksen, Ohm and Strauch; but as his method of explaining the principles of the subject differs from those of all the authors whom he consulted, he calls his treatise, *New* Elements of the Calculus of Variations.

The treatise however does not seem to possess any claims to attention; the method which the author adopts for explaining the principles of the subject would probably present serious difficulties to a beginner. In many of his earlier formulæ Meyer retains terms of a higher order than the first; this is a useless encumbrance, because he makes no use of those terms afterwards. It should be added that the book has been obviously printed at a press which is rarely used for mathematical works, and thus it presents an awkward and almost repulsive appearance. Meyer's method will be seen from the following example which he gives. Let $f(x)$ and $F(x)$ be two functions of x; form the equation

$$f(x + \eta) = F(x);$$

from this we may find for η a value, say $\eta = \zeta(x)$, so that identically

$$f[x + \zeta(x)] = F(x).$$

Thus the original function $f(x)$ changes its properties and is transformed into $F(x)$. For example,

put $\qquad\qquad\qquad a(x + \eta) = \sin x,$

then
$$\eta = \frac{\sin x - ax}{a},$$

and
$$a\left(x + \frac{\sin x - ax}{a}\right) = \sin x.$$

Thus if $y = f(x)$, Meyer puts

$$Dy = F(x) - f(x) = f(x + \eta) - f(x)$$

$$= \frac{dy}{dx}\eta + \frac{d^2y}{dx^2}\frac{\eta^2}{1.2} + \dots$$

$$= \delta y + \frac{1}{1.2}\delta^2 y + \dots$$

Thus with him $\delta y = \dfrac{dy}{dx}\eta,\ \delta^2 y = \dfrac{d^2 y}{dx^2}\eta^2,\ \dots,$ where η is an arbitrary function of x.

This method appears unsatisfactory. In the first place it is deficient *in generality*. The usual method is to suppose $f(x)$ changed into $\phi(x, t)$ and not necessarily into the restricted form $f(x + t)$.

Meyer seems to want to consider δy and $\delta^2 y$ as arbitrary and unconnected; this however is not the case in his system, for

$$\delta^2 y = \frac{\dfrac{d^2 y}{dx^2}}{\left(\dfrac{dy}{dx}\right)^2}(\delta y)^2.$$

In the next place, a beginner would be perplexed by the author's speaking of η as a *constant*, after the explanation and example which have been given of it. This language occurs however on page 6. Again, on page 22 we have this process. Having given the function $p = \dfrac{d^m y}{dx^m}$, in which x is the constant element, required δp, $\delta^2 p$, ..., y being a function of x.

We have by definition

$$p + Dp = \frac{d^m (y + Dy)}{dx^m} = \frac{d^m \left(y + \delta y + \frac{1}{2}\,\delta^2 y + \ldots\right)}{dx^m}$$

$$= \frac{d^m y}{dx^m} + \frac{d^m \delta y}{dx^m} + \frac{1}{2}\frac{d^m \delta^2 y}{dx^m} + \ldots;$$

but
$$\delta y = \frac{dy}{dx}\,\eta, \quad \delta^2 y = \frac{d^2 y}{dx^2}\,\eta^2, \ldots;$$

moreover η being an arbitrary function of the constant element x, we must regard η, η', ... as constants.... Here the last statement would appear obscure to a beginner.

On page 81 there is some novelty, but it cannot be commended. The subject of isoperimetrical problems is considered on pages 89 and 90; but it is not obvious what modification or improvement the author has made of the common method.

CHAPTER XV.

MISCELLANEOUS ARTICLES.

399. The present chapter contains a brief account of some miscellaneous articles connected with the Calculus of Variations; the connection is in some cases very slight, but it is useful for purposes of reference to notice all the articles which bear on the subject. The notices will take the articles in chronological order.

400. Ampère. Remarks on the application of the general formulæ of the Calculus of Variations to mechanical problems.

This memoir was published in 1805, in the first volume of the *Mémoires présentés à l'Institut ... par Divers Savans*. It occupies pages 493—523 of the volume. This memoir contributes nothing to the theory of the Calculus of Variations; its only interest arises from its relation to mechanics. Lagrange had remarked in the *Mécanique Analytique*, that there is an analogy between the equations of equilibrium in mechanical problems and the equations furnished by the Calculus of Variations for determining the maxima and minima values of integral expressions. Ampère makes some general remarks on this analogy; he illustrates his remarks by the example of a uniform inextensible string suspended by its extremities and acted on by gravity. In connection with this example he indicates several properties of the common catenary.

On his page 503 Ampère makes some remarks to the following effect. The Calculus of Variations consists of two parts, one in which it is sufficient to attribute variations to the dependent variables only, the other in which variations must be attributed to all the variables dependent and independent; writers on the subject

have however confined themselves as much as possible to the
former part. The theory of the Calculus of Variations is therefore,
according to Ampère, not yet established upon absolutely rigorous
principles. There remains in this respect a deficiency in Mathematics which Ampère proposes to consider elsewhere.

It does not however appear that this purpose was accomplished;
for the memoir in Gergonne's *Annales* ... which we have noticed
in Art. 375, can hardly be considered of sufficient importance to
correspond to the purpose here expressed. On his page 516
Ampère refers to some other memoir, without however indicating
where it is to be found.

401. Lagrange. The first volume of the second edition of
Lagrange's *Mécanique Analytique* was published in 1811; the
second volume was published in 1815, after Lagrange's death.
Lagrange uses the notation and the processes of the Calculus of
Variations freely throughout the work, but the great interest which
belongs to his investigations is derived from their connection with
Mechanics. The theory of the Calculus of Variations receives no
accession from the work.

402. Crelle. In the article *Variationsrechnung* of Klügel's
Mathematisches Wörterbuch, page 713, reference is made to a work
by Crelle. The article says, "Crelle's views on the principles of
the Calculus of Variations seem not sufficiently known; they are
contained in his *Versuch einer rein algebraischen Darstellung der
Rechnung mit verandlichen Grössen*, I. Gottingen, 1813, pages
527—776. The numerous new symbols render the work difficult
for study. The application to maxima and minima is not included
in the work." The present writer has not seen this work by
Crelle.

403. On the surface of minimum area between given limits.
Gergonne's *Annales de Mathématiques*, Vol. 7, pages 68, 99,
143—155, 283—287. 1816.

These pages contain some problems proposed for solution; the
problems are particular cases of the question of the surface of

minimum area, various conditions being given with respect to the limits of the required surface. There is an attempt at the solution of one of the problems by M. Tédénat, and criticisms on this attempt by Gergonne; Gergonne also makes some observations on the general question.

The particular case considered by Tédénat is the following; it is required to determine a surface which shall pass through the inverse diagonals of two opposite faces of a cube, and so that the area of the portion of the surface intercepted by the cube may be a minimum. By mechanical considerations relating to a flexible elastic membrane, Tédénat considers that he proves that the surface must be that which is determined by the equation $y = x \tan \dfrac{\pi z}{4a}$. Gergonne admits that this surface satisfies the general partial differential equation for a surface of minimum area, but objects that it is not proved that this surface gives *the* solution of the problem with the prescribed limiting conditions. Gergonne's criticisms indicate that he had considered the problem more closely than Tédénat had.

Gergonne gives an interesting account of the circumstances which drew his attention to these problems. A distinguished mathematician informed Gergonne that he had serious doubts as to the legitimacy of the methods given in the Calculus of Variations. Gergonne invited him to write an article upon the subject which might appear in the *Annales* ...; but the article was never sent for publication. One of the objections of the distinguished mathematician is expressed thus; suppose the so-called minimum surface to be determined by conditions which preclude it from being a plane surface; draw any plane curve upon it; then remove the piece of the so-called minimum surface which is bounded by this plane curve, and replace it by a plane having the same boundary; thus a surface is obtained which is less than the so-called minimum surface. Gergonne replies that this objection only amounts to a proof that it would be impossible to draw on the minimum surface a plane closed curve; and this impossibility is consistent with the fact that the minimum surface has at every point its principal curvatures in opposite directions.

Gergonne states that it appeared to him that it would be useful to propose certain problems relative to the minimum surface in which there should be definite limiting conditions. Besides the problem already given, the following are proposed.

To find the surface of minimum area among all those which are bounded by the curve of intersection of two cylinders of the same radius, the cylinders having their axes at right angles to each other, and the axis of each cylinder being a tangent to the other cylinder.

A quadrilateral is given having its sides not all in the same plane; find the surface of minimum area among all those which are bounded by the sides of this quadrilateral.

Find the surface of minimum area among all those which are bounded by two circles given in magnitude and position.

Find the surface of minimum area among all those which are bounded by the sides of a given square, and which include between themselves and the square a given volume.

Among all surfaces which are bounded by the sides of a given square, and which have within this boundary a given area, find that which includes between itself and the square a maximum volume.

No attempts seem to have been made to solve these problems, except that Tédénat intimates that he believes that no continuous surface can be found as a solution of a certain special case of the problem in which the given boundary is a quadrilateral having its sides not all in the same plane; see page 286 of the seventh volume of the *Annales. ...*

404. Crelle. Remarks on the Calculus of Variations.

These remarks form part of a collection of mathematical treatises published by Crelle under the title of *Sammlung Mathematischer Aufsätze und Bemerkungen.* The work consists of two octavo volumes; the first was published in 1821, and the second in 1822, both at Berlin. The remarks on the Calculus of Variations occur in the second volume; they occupy pages 44—174. These remarks constitute an elementary treatise on the subject; the treatise however does not seem to possess any special merit, and the

notation is repulsive. On his page 47 Crelle refers to his former
work on the subject, but not in terms of commendation; see
Art. 383.

405. Crelle. Remarks on the principles of the Calculus of
Variations.

This memoir forms part of the Transactions of the Academy of
Sciences of Berlin for 1833; the date of publication of the volume
is 1835. The memoir occupies 40 pages; it proves the ordinary
formulæ for the variation of a single integral, both for constant
and variable limits of integration. The method and notation differ
from those in common use, but present no obvious advantages.

406. Muller. On establishing and extending the Calculus of
Variations. Crelle's *Mathematical Journal*, Vol. 13, pages 240—249.
1835.

This article contains some general remarks on functions without
any obvious reference to the Calculus of Variations. At the end of
the article the author says that he will on another occasion explain
the method of applying these remarks; it does not however appear
that this design was accomplished.

407. Boole. On certain theorems in the Calculus of Variations, *Cambridge Mathematical Journal*, Vol. 2, pages 97—102.
1840.

The author says at the beginning of this article, "It would
perhaps have been more just to entitle this communication 'Notes
on Lagrange.' The papers from which it is selected were written
towards the close of the year 1838, during the perusal of the
Mécanique Analytique." The article contains a simple demonstration of a theorem which forms the basis of Lagrange's investigations
on the great problem of the variation of the arbitrary constants.
The theorem is that which Mr De Morgan speaks of as "perhaps
the most characteristic specimen of the genius of Lagrange which
could be given;" see his *Differential and Integral Calculus*,
page 532.

The author thus indicates the object of the latter part of his
article. "I shall now proceed to demonstrate from the general

transformed equation of motion the principles of the conservation of living forces, and of least action. The former of these has been thence deduced by Lagrange. I am not however aware that the latter has been obtained from the same equation, either by the discoverer of the Calculus of Variations, or by any subsequent author."

408. Delaunay. On the surface of revolution which has its mean curvature constant. Liouville's *Journal of Mathematics*, Vol. 6, pages 309—315. 1841.

When we investigate the problem of finding the surface which with a given area includes a maximum volume, we arrive at a certain partial differential equation which expresses that the sum of the principal curvatures at any point of the surface is constant. Delaunay proposes to determine what surface of revolution has this property. He finds that the generating curve must be such as would be traced out by the focus of a conic section, if the conic section itself were to roll without sliding on a fixed straight line. There is a note by Sturm immediately after Delaunay's article, in which the same result is obtained in a different manner. The result is also given in Mr Jellett's treatise; see his page 364.

409. Strauch. Problems in the Calculus of Variations. Grunert's *Archiv der Mathematik und Physik*, Vol. 3, pages 119—195. 1843.

This article contains some problems which Strauch published as a specimen of his work on the Calculus of Variations. The first seven pages of the article contain some introductory remarks and definitions, and then follow the problems. A few of the problems relate to expressions involving neither symbols of differentiation nor symbols of integration; the remainder relate to expressions which involve differential coefficients but not integrals. All these problems are reproduced by Strauch in his work.

In the same volume of Grunert's *Archiv* ... a few remarks are made on Strauch's article by Göpel; these remarks occupy pages 405—407 of the volume. Göpel says that the problems of the first

kind which Strauch considers are only ordinary problems of maxima
and minima values; and he makes a few other observations.
Göpel's remarks did not convince Strauch of the necessity of
making any change, as the parts which are criticised appear again
in substantially the same form in Strauch's work.

410. Laurent. A memoir on the Calculus of Variations was
written by Laurent in competition for the prize offered by the
Academy of Sciences at Paris; see Art. 133. Laurent's memoir
was sent to the Academy after the time fixed for the reception of
the memoirs, but before the judges had published their award.
A report on Laurent's memoir is given by Cauchy in the *Comptes
Rendus* ... Vol. 18, pages 920, 921. 1844. We will give a translation of the essential part of this report.

The application of the Calculus of Variations to the investigation of the maxima and minima values of multiple integrals
required especially new formulæ of integration by parts and a new
notation which should afford an easy expression of these new
formulæ. The judges of the prize had particularly noticed the
paragraphs relating to these two objects in the memoir of Sarrus.
The corresponding paragraphs in the memoir of Laurent are also
worthy of notice. The two authors have employed different methods
of establishing the formulæ of integration by parts. But the
formulæ are in reality the same in the two memoirs, although they
are expressed by two distinct notations. We may add that when
once these formulæ are established Laurent uses methods analogous
to those of Sarrus in order to obtain the limiting equations.

The memoir of Laurent contains besides some observations,
which are not without interest, respecting the different ways of
verifying the limiting equations.

We will not conceal the fact that among the methods employed
by Laurent some may be considered rather as methods of induction
than as perfectly rigorous methods. But it is generally very easy
to verify the exactness of the results obtained by these methods, as
the calculations commonly can be easily effected.

To sum up we think the memoir of Laurent deserves to be

approved by the Academy, and to be inserted in the *Recueil des Savants étrangers*.

We may add that the memoir does not seem to have been printed as yet. There is a report on two memoirs by Laurent in the *Comptes Rendus* ... Vol. 40, pages 632—634. 1855. The report is by Cauchy, and it gives a short account of the scientific labours of Laurent then recently deceased.

411. Strauch. On the sign of the second variation and on relative maxima and minima. Grunert's *Archiv der Mathematik und Physik*, Vol. 4, pages 39—68. 1844.

This article contains some problems in which the second variation of an expression is examined in order to determine whether the expression is really a maximum or a minimum; and some problems of relative maxima and minima values are discussed. All these problems are reproduced by Strauch in his work.

412. Strauch. Remarks on the words *variation, variable*,.... Grunert's *Archiv der Mathematik und Physik*, Vol. 7, pages 221—224. 1846.

This article contains some remarks by Strauch on some of the terms used in the Calculus of Variations; the remarks are reproduced by Strauch in his work, Vol. I., pages 69—71.

413. Roger. Essay on Brachistochrones. Liouville's *Journal of Mathematics*, Vol. 13, pages 41—71. 1848.

In this essay the author demonstrates several properties relative to brachistochrones. He considers the case when the moving particle is constrained to remain on a surface as well as the case of a free particle. The differential equations of the problem are obtained by the ordinary principles of the Calculus of Variations, and many interesting results are deduced from these equations.

414. Goodwin. *Cambridge and Dublin Mathematical Journal*, Vol. 3, pages 225—236. 1848.

This article is entitled, On certain points in the theory of the Calculus of Variations. The article is chiefly devoted to the expla-

notion of a certain geometrical conception relative to variations.
Suppose x and y the co-ordinates of a point in a curve.   Then it
is manifest that we may give the most general infinitesimal variation possible to the position of the point (x, y) by giving it a
small tangential displacement and also a small normal displacement.   Let the tangential and normal displacements be denoted
by τ and ν respectively; then if δx and δy be the corresponding
displacements parallel to the axes of co-ordinates, and ds an element
of the arc of the curve, we have

$$\tau = \delta x \frac{dx}{ds} + \delta y \frac{dy}{ds}, \quad \nu = \delta x \frac{dy}{ds} - \delta y \frac{dx}{ds};$$

and these are equivalent to

$$\delta x = \tau \frac{dx}{ds} + \nu \frac{dy}{ds}, \quad \delta y = \tau \frac{dy}{ds} - \nu \frac{dx}{ds}.$$

The variation of an integral is then expressed so as to involve τ
and ν, and it appears that τ does not occur at all in the unintegrated part, and only once in the integrated part.

It is not difficult to illustrate geometrically the fact that τ does
not occur in the unintegrated part.   The unintegrated part may
be denoted by $\int U\nu\, ds$, and then the equation $U = 0$ gives the *form*
of the curve which is required, and it is manifest that a curve may
be made to pass into another which differs infinitesimally from
itself by a normal variation only, and that in fact a tangential
variation can have no effect upon the form of the curve, because if
a point receive an indefinitely small displacement along the tangent,
or which is the same thing along the curve, it still remains in the
same curve.

The fact that τ does not occur in the unintegrated part of the
variation of an integral is the principal topic discussed in this
article, and it is illustrated and developed in various ways.   Three
examples are given of the application of the formulæ which are
investigated.

The article concludes with some remarks on the *condition of
integrability* of a function $V dx$.   In reference to the well-known

equation which is obtained as the condition the author says,
" I think it would be more proper to say that the equation expresses *a* condition of $V dx$ being a perfect differential rather than
the condition, for it is nowhere proved that there may not be an
indefinite number of other conditions." It must however be remarked here, that it has been distinctly proved that the equation
referred to is *sufficient* to ensure that $V dx$ should be integrable as
well as *necessary;* see the last Chapter of the present work.

415. Vieille. *Cours complémentaire d'analyse et de Mécanique
rationelle.* Paris, 1851.

This valuable work contains some investigations relating to our
subject.

An excellent demonstration of Lagrange's transformation of the
equations of motion in Dynamics is given in pages 1—9.

A chapter entitled *Développements sur le calcul des variations,*
occupies pages 38—50. This chapter contains four articles. (1) The
investigation of the maximum or minimum of $\int_{x_0}^{x_1} V dx$, where V
contains x, y, z and the differential coefficients of y and z with
respect to x; and an equation is given which connects the variables
and differential coefficients. (2) To determine the conditions which
must subsist among p, q, r which are all functions of x, y, and z,
in order that $\int_{x_0}^{x_1} (p dx + q dy + r dz)$ may retain a constant value
whatever functions of t may be denoted by x, y, z; the conditions
are found to be those which ensure that $p dx + q dy + r dz$ is an
exact differential with respect to x, y, and z, considered as independen-
dent. (3) Having given $dT = p dx + q dy + r dz$, where x, y, z are
any functions of t, and p, q, r are any functions of x, y, z which
may also contain t, it is required to determine under what con-
ditions we shall also have $\delta T = p \delta x + q \delta y + r \delta z$; the conditions
are found to be the same as in the preceding example. (4) The
example just given is now modified by the supposition that x, y,
and z are connected by a relation $z = F(x, y)$; the condition now is
found to amount to this, that $p dx + q dy + r dz$ must be an exact

differential after one of the variables has been eliminated by means of the given relation $z = F(x, y)$.

A chapter of exercises on the Calculus of Variations occupies pages 113—127. Four examples are discussed. (1) Among all curves of given length which are terminated in two fixed points A and B, to find that for which the sum of the products of each element by the square of its distance from the line AB is a maximum. (2) To find the maximum value of $\int_{x_0}^{x_1} \sqrt{(dx^2 + dy^2)}$, subject to the relation that $\int_{x_0}^{x_1} \sqrt{(dx^2 + dy^2 + dz^2)}$ shall be equal to a given constant. This question admits of easy geometrical treatment, but the process of the Calculus of Variations does not completely succeed, so that Euler's method for solving problems of relative maxima and minima appears to fail. The reason appears to be, as Vieille conjectures, that the second integral involves a new variable z which is quite independent of the other variables x and y which alone occurred in the first integral. (3) Assuming that $dT = X\,dx + Y\,dy + Z\,dz$, it is required to find the curve for which $\int_{x_0}^{x_1} T\,ds$ is a minimum; the result is that the curve must be that which a flexible string would form when in equilibrium under forces on each element which referred to a unit of length of string would be X, Y, Z, respectively parallel to the axes of x, y, z. (4) To find a curve of given length terminated at two fixed points for which $\int_{x_0}^{x_1} y^2\,dx$ is a maximum; this is an example of the first of James Bernouilli's celebrated isoperimetrical problems; see Art. 387. Vieille gives a figure similar to that which we have recommended in Art. 387.

Some results relative to brachistochrones are given on pages 299—308 of the work.

410. Cauchy. *Variations employées comme clefs algébriques.* This article occurs in the *Comptes Rendus* ... Vol. 37, pages 57—64. 1853. The article presents nothing of interest so far as the Calculus of Variations is concerned; it merely uses the symbol δ to

express certain infinitesimal changes in the values of arbitrary constants. At the end of the article Cauchy promises another article on the subject. The student who wishes for information on what Cauchy calls *clefs algébriques* may consult the *Comptes Rendus* ... Vol. 36, page 70, and a memoir on the subject in Vol. 4 of Cauchy's *Exercices d'Analyse et de Physique Mathématique*.

417. Cauchy. On the advantages which arise from the introduction of a variable parameter and of the notation of the Calculus of Variations into some of the principal formulæ of infinitesimal analysis. *Comptes Rendus*, Vol. 40, pages 261—267. 1855.

The following sentences will give an idea of this article by Cauchy.

Let u be any function of the variables x, y, z; suppose

$$u = f(x, y, z);$$

and let u_i be the value which is obtained from u by changing x, y, z into $x + h$, $y + k$, $z + l$ respectively, so that

$$u_i = f(x + h, y + k, z + l).$$

Then put $h = ah'$, $k = ak'$, $l = al'$; thus u_i may be considered a function of the parameter a, and may be developed by Maclaurin's theorem in a series, which we may express thus;

$$u_i = u + a\,\delta u + \frac{a^2}{1 \cdot 2}\,\delta^2 u + \frac{a^3}{\underline{|3}}\,\delta^3 u + \dots$$

This notation is also applied by Cauchy to the case of a system of differential equations. Cauchy says at the end that he will give another article on the subject.

418. Carmichael. The treatise on the *Calculus of Operations*, published by Mr Carmichael in 1855, contains some investigations bearing upon the Calculus of Variations; they occupy pages 153—160 of the work. These investigations include generalisations of the results which occur on pages 253, 262, and 840 of Mr Jellett's treatise, and also some interesting theorems respecting attractions.

31

419. **Braschmann.** On the Principle of Least Action. *Bulletin...Physico-Mathématique de l'Académie...de St Pétersbourg.* Vol. 17, pages 487—489. 1859.

We have remarked in Art. 817 that Ostrogradsky criticises some parts of Lagrange's *Mécanique Analytique.* On page 139 of the 16th volume of the *Bulletin...de St Pétersbourg* we read that M. Ostrogradsky announced a memoir on the principle of least action; and it is stated that he considers the ordinary enunciation of the principle to require modification. Braschmann's article bears on this point. It does not appear obvious what error Ostrogradsky thinks he detects in the common account of the principle. We will however translate part of Braschmann's article.

Let there be a system of masses $m, m', m'', m''', ...$ considered as points and acted upon by given forces. Let X, Y, Z denote the projections of the accelerating force which acts upon the mass m, let v denote the velocity of this particle at the end of the time t. Put

$$\Sigma m \left(X dx + Y dy + Z dz \right) = d\Pi, \quad \tfrac{1}{2} \Sigma m v^2 = T;$$

then the equation of motion of the system may be written under the following form;

$$\delta\Pi = \frac{d}{dt} \Sigma m \left(\frac{dx}{dt} \delta x + \frac{dy}{dt} \delta y + \frac{dz}{dt} \delta z \right) - \delta T,$$

the characteristic δ relating to all possible displacements of the masses $m, m', m'', m''' ....$ We see by this equation, as M. Ostrogradsky has shewn in his memoir on isoperimetrical problems, that in the passage of a system from one position to another

$$\delta \int (\Pi + T) \, dt = 0;$$

that is, between given limits the integral $\int (\Pi + T) \, dt$ is a maximum or a minimum. Nevertheless in the treatises on Mechanics which have appeared since the publication of this memoir, we find the principle of least action still treated after the manner of Lagrange. This great mathematician replaces in the equation $d\Pi = dT$ the differential d by the letter δ, which relates to possible displacements, and concludes that

$$2 \int T dt \text{ or } \int \Sigma m v ds$$

must be a maximum or a minimum. Although it seems evident that we cannot substitute δ for d in the equation of Vis Viva, yet it will perhaps be useful for those who are studying rational mechanics, still to prove by a simple example, that the true principle of least action is that given by M. Ostrogradsky, and that we are not at liberty to replace d by δ in the equation of Vis Viva.

Braschmann then proceeds to his example. It merely shews what no one will dispute, that d and δ are not to be interchanged arbitrarily; but it does not shew that there is any error in the ordinary conception or proof of the principle of least action.

420. In the second edition of the Catalogue of the Library of the Observatory of Pulkova, St Petersburg, 1860, the titles of some treatises occur bearing on the Calculus of Variations which the present writer has not had the opportunity of consulting. These titles are the following.

Wiedebeck, J. S. *In methodum Variationum*, Upsal, 1823.

Svanberg, J. *In Theoriam Maximorum et Minimorum*, Upsal, 1830.

Almquist, E. *De Principiis Calculi Variationis*, I. II., Upsal, 1837.

Senff, C. E. *Elementa Calculi Variationum* ... Dorpat, 1838.

Lindelöf, L. L. *Variations-kalkylens theori och dess användning* ... Hfs, 1856.

Popoff, A. *Elements of the Calculus of Variations*, Kazan, 1856 (in Russian).

Simon, O. *Die Theorie der Variationsrechnung*, Berlin, 1857.

CHAPTER XVI.

421. THE following chapter contains brief accounts of some articles and memoirs on geometry and mechanics which have some connection with the Calculus of Variations; and a few works are noticed which really belong to the ordinary theory of maxima and minima values given in the Differential Calculus, but the titles of which might suggest that they were treatises on the Calculus of Variations. We adopt the chronological order.

422. Busse. *Neue Methode des Grössten und Kleinsten nebst Beurtheilung und einiger Verbesserung des bisherigen Systemes.* Freyberg, 1808.

This is an octavo volume of 108 pages with a preface of 12 pages. It is devoted to the ordinary theory of maxima and minima values, and does not touch on the Calculus of Variations. The chief point in it seems to be that it draws attention to the fact that a function of a variable may have a maximum or minimum value when its differential coefficient with respect to that variable is *infinite* as well as when it is *zero*. It is stated in the preface that a second part will soon appear; this has not come to the knowledge of the present writer, and perhaps never appeared.

Ohm speaks unfavourably of the views of Busse; see Ohm's *System of Mathematics*, Vol. 4, Berlin, 1830, page 127.

423. Playfair. *Of the solids of Greatest Attraction, or those which among all the Solids that have certain properties attract with the greatest Force in a given direction.* Read 5th January, 1807. Published in the Transactions of the Royal Society of Edinburgh, Vol. 6, 1812.

This memoir occupies pages 187—243 of the volume. The problems on Solids of Greatest Attraction are not treated by the Calculus of Variations, but by the method which we have illustrated in Art. 322.

It is stated on page 204, "In general, if x, y, and z, are three rectangular co-ordinates that determine the position of any point of a solid given in magnitude, and if the value of a certain function Q, of x, y, and z, be computed for each point of the solid, and if the sum of all these values of Q added together be a maximum or a minimum, the solid is bounded by a superficies in which the function Q is everywhere of the same magnitude."

And on page 205, "All the questions, therefore, which come under this description, though they belong to an order of problems, which requires in general the application of one of the most refined inventions of the New Geometry, the *Calculus Variationum*, form a particular division admitting of resolution by much simpler means, and directly reducible to the construction of loci."

The problems respecting solids that have certain properties and attract with the greatest force in given directions are examples of the ordinary methods of maxima and minima explained in the Differential Calculus.

424. Knight. *Of the attractions of such Solids as are terminated by Planes; and of Solids of greatest attraction.* Read March 19, 1812. Published in the *Philosophical Transactions*, 1812.

This memoir occupies pages 247—309 of the volume. It contains investigations of the attractions of solids of various forms. Knight refers frequently to Playfair's memoir which we noticed in the preceding Article. One section of Knight's memoir occupying pages 283—301 is devoted to *Solids of greatest attraction*. Knight states that besides Playfair this subject had been considered by Silvabelle and Frisi, but that these mathematicians had confined themselves to the case of a homogeneous solid of revolution. Knight obtains his solutions by a simple application of the Calculus of Variations. He proves the well-known result for the figure of a homogeneous solid of revolution of given mass which exerts the greatest attraction on a particle in its axis; and he notices that the generating curve is the same as would be obtained if the problem proposed were to find the form of a curve such that the area included may be a given quantity, and the attraction on a given point a maximum. Playfair had established these results. Knight then shews that the same form is obtained for the solid of revolution of given mass and greatest attraction on a point in its axis if the solid be not homogeneous, provided the density at any point is a function of the distance of that point from the axis and of the distance between the foot of the perpendicular from that point on the axis and the attracted particle.

425. Lehmus. *Uebungs-Aufgaben zur Lehre vom Grössten und Kleinsten*. Berlin, 1823.

This is an octavo volume of 209 pages, containing examples of ordinary maxima and minima problems; it does not touch upon the Calculus of Variations. The problems are principally of a geometrical character. Ohm refers to the work in favourable terms; see *Die Lehre vom Grössten und Kleinsten*, page 209.

426. Crelle's *Mathematical Journal*, Vol. 6, pages 81—83. 1830.

This is an anonymous article respecting Minding's solution which we have examined in Article 307, which was not known to the present writer when that Article 307 was printed. The anonymous article agrees with what we have stated respecting the inaccuracy of Minding's result. The equation given by Minding

$$h\phi\left(\frac{d\phi}{d\psi}\right)\frac{d\psi}{dP}\,d\psi - hd\left(\frac{\phi'd\psi}{dP}\right) + \phi\,ds = 0$$

is here developed into the form

$$h\left\{\phi\frac{d^2s}{d\psi^2} - 2\left(\frac{d\phi}{ds}\right)\frac{ds^2}{d\psi^3} - \left(\frac{d\phi}{d\psi}\right)\frac{ds}{d\psi} - \phi'\left(\frac{d\phi}{ds}\right)\right\}\phi\frac{ds}{d\psi}$$
$$+ \left(\phi' + \frac{ds^2}{d\psi^2}\right)^2 \phi\frac{ds}{d\psi} = 0.$$

The writer says that neither $\phi = 0$ nor $\dfrac{ds}{d\psi} = 0$ can give the general solution; that must be found from the equation in the form which it takes after removing the factor $\phi \dfrac{ds}{d\psi}$ by division.

The writer gives a geometrical interpretation of the result $\dfrac{\cos\theta}{\rho} = $ a constant, which belongs to the required curve. Suppose tangent planes drawn to the given surface at all the points of the required curve; we may suppose a developable surface generated by the lines which form the perpetual intersections of these tangent planes. The required curve is then common to the given surface and the generated developable surface. Then if the developable surface be developed into a plane the required curve becomes a circle on that plane.

It appears from page 161 of the same volume of Crelle's *Mathematical Journal* that Minding admitted his error.

427. Arndt. *Disquisitiones historicæ de maximis et minimis.* Berlin, 1833.

This essay was written for a degree in the University of Berlin. It contains a history of the ordinary theory of maxima and minima values without any reference to the Calculus of Variations. Giesel refers to it on page 38 of his work.

428. Scherk. Remarks on the least surface between given limits. Crelle's *Mathematical Journal*, Vol. 13, pages 185—208. 1835.

This memoir was presented to the Royal Academy of Sciences at Copenhagen in September, 1833. Some historical information is supplied as to the problem of the least surface. Lagrange found the partial differential equation. Meunier shewed the geometrical interpretation of the equation, namely, that the required surface must have at every point its two principal radii of curvature equal in magnitude and opposite in sign. Meunier also indicated two surfaces which satisfy this equation, namely, the surface called the *hélicoïde gauche* by the French writers, and the surface formed by revolving a catenary round its directrix. Reference is then made to the general integral of the partial differential equation found by Monge, and to the note on the problem by Poisson in the eighth volume of Crelle's *Mathematical Journal*.

The surface in question was proposed as the subject of a prize essay by a scientific society in Leipsic, and the prize was awarded to Professor Scherk in Nov. 1830.

The essay which gained the prize is printed in the *Acta Societatis Jablonovianæ*, Vol. IV. Fasc. II. pages 204—280, under the title *De proprietatibus superficiei quæ hac continetur æquatione*

$$(1 + q^2)\, r - 2pqs + (1 + p^2)\, t = 0$$

disquisitiones analyticæ.

The two memoirs by Professor Scherk belong to the subject of differential equations rather than to the *Calculus of Variations*. The result of them appears to be that some additional surfaces are indicated which satisfy the differential equation in question. An investigation is given with the view of shewing that the *hélicoïde gauche* is the only ruled surface which satisfies the differential equation, but the author admits that he has not fully established this proposition.

The following are the equations to three surfaces which are shewn by the author to satisfy the differential equation,

(1) $\quad e^{az} = \dfrac{\cos ay}{\cos ax}.$

(2) $\quad (e^{az} - e^{-az})(e^{ax} - e^{-ax}) = \pm\, 4 \sin ay.$

(3) $\quad z = b \log\left\{ \sqrt{(r^2 + a^2)} + \sqrt{(r^2 - b^2)} \right\} - a \tan^{-1} \dfrac{b \sqrt{(r^2 + a^2)}}{a \sqrt{(r^2 - b^2)}} + a\theta + c,$

where, as usual, $r \cos \theta = x$ and $r \sin \theta = y$.

The last result includes two well-known results; for by putting $a = 0$ we obtain the solid formed by revolving a catenary round its directrix, and by putting $b = 0$ we obtain the *hélicoïde gauche*. Two other equations are given by the author, but they are very complicated.

We take this opportunity of adverting to a point in the history of the problem here considered.

The statements which we have noticed in Art. 315 as made by Bonnet are not correct. Bonnet's words are, On sait que l'hélicoïde gauche à plan directeur est la seule surface réglée qui ait en chacun de ses points ses rayons de courbure principaux égaux et de signes contraires. Meunier a le premier démontré cette proposition remarquable dans son Mémoire sur les surfaces, qui a été inséré au *Recueil des Savants étrangers*. Plus tard Legendre y a été aussi conduit (*voir* les *Mémoires de l'Académie des Sciences*, année 1787).

The memoir of Meunier is in the *Mémoires présentés … par Divers Savans* … Vol. 10, 1785; see page 504 of the volume. Meunier proves that the *hélicoïde gauche* is the surface of minimum area among all surfaces that can be generated by the motion of a line which always remains parallel to a fixed plane, not among all ruled surfaces; thus he does not prove so much as Bonnet says. Legendre does not *prove* any thing, but he *asserts* more than Bonnet intimates. His words are, Si on cherche la surface la moindre entre deux lignes droites données, non situées dans le même plan, soit *m* la plus courte distance de ces lignes, λ l'angle qu'elles font entr'elles … il en résultera pour l'équation de la surface cherchée, réduite à la forme la plus simple,

$$ z = x \tan \frac{\lambda y}{m}. $$

These words occur on page 314 of the volume cited by Bonnet. Thus Legendre asserts that the *hélicoïde gauche* is the surface of minimum area among all surfaces which have two rectilinear boundaries not in one plane; this is not true; see Art. 442.

429. Michaelis. *De lineis brevissimis in datis superficiebus, imprimis de Linea Geodetica*. Berlin, 1837.

This is an exercise for a degree in the University of Berlin; it consists of 27 quarto pages. The differential equations are investigated by the Calculus of Variations for two problems. (1) The shortest line on a given surface. (2) The problem considered by

Minding and others; see Art. 307. The investigations are given in two forms, first by using the ordinary variables x, y, z, and secondly by using two variables p and q in the manner explained by Gauss in his *Disquisitiones generales circa superficies curvas*. In the second problem Michaelis gives the result which had been published in the sixth volume of Crelle's *Mathematical Journal*; see Art. 427.

A large part of the memoir is devoted to the geodetic line, by which the author means the shortest line on the surface of an oblate spheroid. The investigations in this part chiefly involve the theory of elliptic integrals.

430. Minding. On the shortest lines on curved surfaces. Crelle's *Mathematical Journal*, Vol. 20, pages 323—327, 1840.

In this article the differential equations furnished by the Calculus of Variations are assumed, and some inferences are deduced from them with respect to the shortest lines on developable surfaces.

431. Catalan. On ruled surfaces with a minimum area. Liouville's *Journal of Mathematics*, Vol. 7, pages 203—211. 1842.

The problem discussed is the following; among all ruled surfaces to find that of which the area is a minimum, or which amounts to the same thing, to find that which has its two principal radii of curvature at every point equal in magnitude and of opposite sign. The memoir does not make any use of the Calculus of Variations. The result has been already stated; see Art. 311.

432. Catalan. On the line of given length, which includes a maximum area upon a surface. *Journal de l'Ecole Polytechnique*, Cahier 29, pages 151—156. 1843.

Reference is made to an investigation by Delaunay in the eighth volume of Liouville's Journal of Mathematics; see Art. 314. (Catalan by mistake names the *seventh* volume).

The following theorems are demonstrated by Catalan in his interesting article.

(1) Suppose any surface S, and let there be a curve L of given length described on it so as to include a maximum area; construct a developable surface Σ which touches the surface S along the curve L; then if the surface Σ be developed the curve L is transformed into a circle. This theorem had been obtained however by previous writers; see Arts. 427 and 429.

(2) Suppose any surface S and on it a curve L of minimum length; construct a developable surface Σ which touches the surface S along the line L; then if the surface Σ be developed the curve L is transformed into a straight line.

433. Björling. *In integrationem æquationis Derivatarum partialium superficiei, cujus in puncto unoquoque principales ambo radii curvedinis æquales sunt signoque contrario.* Grunert's *Archiv der Mathematik und Physik*, Vol. 4, pages 290—315. 1844.

In the beginning of 1842 Björling published a treatise entitled *Calculi Variationum Integralium Duplicium Exercitationes*, of which an account has already been given in Art. 811. A large part of that treatise was devoted to the integration of the differential equation which belongs to surfaces of minimum area. In a French scientific journal called *L'Institut*, Björling saw it stated that Wantzel and Catalan had proved that the only ruled surface of minimum area was the *hélicoïde gauche*. Björling then resolved to reprint his investigations on the integration of the partial differential equation, with some modifications and additions.

Thus the present memoir is devoted to the solution of the partial differential equation, and the results obtained coincide essentially with those of the treatise already referred to, namely, that of all surfaces of revolution, the only one which satisfies the proposed differential equation is that formed by the revolution of a catenary round its directrix, and that of all surfaces which can be formed by the motion of a straight line which always remains parallel to a fixed plane, the only one which satisfies the proposed differential equation is the *hélicoïde gauche*. Björling expresses a hope that the demonstrations of Wantzel and Catalan of the statement that this is the only surface out of *all ruled surfaces* which satisfies the proposed differential equation, will soon be published; Catalan's has since been published, as we have seen in Art. 431.

There are two points in the memoir to which we will advert.

In a note on page 303 Björling makes a statement to which he refers more than once afterwards; it is to the effect that if we are seeking the surface for which $\iint dx\, dy\, \sqrt{(1 + p^2 + q^2)}$ is a minimum, and suppose the surface to be bounded by two given curves, the curves must be such that when they are projected on the plane of (x, y) one projection must be entirely within the other. It is not obvious what he means to be inferred when this condition does not hold, whether he regards the problem as then impossible, or whether he thinks that the ordinary formulæ of the Calculus of Variations cannot be applied to it.

On page 312 Björling considers a certain special example. Suppose we have two circles in parallel planes at a distance 2, and suppose that the line joining their centres is perpendicular to the planes of the circles, and that the radius of each circle is $\frac{1}{2}\left(e + \frac{1}{e}\right)$. Take the line joining the centres as the axis of x and the origin midway between the centres. Then it might be supposed that the minimum surface would be that formed by revolving round the axis of x, the catenary determined by

$$y = \frac{1}{2}\left(e^x + e^{-x}\right),$$

and taking that portion of it comprised between $x = -1$ and $x = 1$. But it will be found on trial that the surface thus obtained is not necessarily less than that which would be obtained by taking a cylindrical surface round the axis of x as axis with any radius r which is less than $\frac{1}{2}\left(e + \frac{1}{e}\right)$, and forming the surface of the part of this cylindrical surface which is contained between $x = -1$ and $x = 1$, together with the plane circular strips at each end which are necessary to connect the cylindrical surface with the given limiting circles. In fact the area of the surface formed by the revolution of the catenary will be found to be

$$2\pi \left\{ 1 + \frac{1}{4}\left(c^2 - \frac{1}{c^2} \right) \right\},$$

and the area of the surface made up of the cylindrical surface and the plane circular strips is

$$2\pi \left\{ 2r - r^2 + \frac{1}{4}\left(c + \frac{1}{c} \right)^2 \right\}.$$

Now it is quite possible for the former expression to exceed the latter; for example, the former will exceed the latter by $\pi\left(\frac{1}{4} - \frac{1}{c^2}\right)$, if r be taken so that $r^2 - 2r + \frac{3}{8} = 0$, that is if r be taken about $= \cdot 2$. Björling brings this forward as an example of the necessity of the restriction he proposed in his note on page 303. It seems to shew no more than this; a result furnished by the Calculus of Variations must not be assumed to be a maximum or a minimum without investigating the terms of the second order.

434. Grunert. On the Cycloid as the Brachistochrone. Grunert's *Archiv der Mathematik und Physik*, Vol. 7, pages 308—315. 1846.

This article contains an elementary proof of the fact that the cycloid is the brachistochrone, without the use of the Calculus of Variations.

435. Jacobi. On a particular solution of the partial differential equation

$$\frac{d^2 V}{dx^2} + \frac{d^2 V}{dy^2} + \frac{d^2 V}{dz^2} = 0.$$

Crelle's *Mathematical Journal*, Vol. 36, pages 113—134. 1848. In the course of this memoir, Jacobi makes that application of the Calculus of Variations which we have given in Art. 323.

436. Schlaeffli. On the minimum of a certain Integral. Crelle's *Mathematical Journal*, Vol. 43, pages 23—36. 1852.

The problem of finding the shortest line on a surface of the second order amounts to making the integral $\int \sqrt{(dx_1^2 + dx_2^2 + dx_3^2)}$ a minimum, where x_1, x_2, x_3 are connected by an equation of the second degree. In the present memoir the problem considered is to make the integral $\int \sqrt{(dx_1^2 + dx_2^2 + \ldots + dx_n^2)}$ a minimum, where the variables x_1, x_2, ... x_n are connected by an equation of the second degree. The memoir however does not belong to the Calculus of Variations, as there is only one line connected with that subject; in this line the equations for a minimum value furnished by the Calculus of Variations are written down, merely for the purpose of indicating the number of arbitrary constants which should occur in the solution. The solution of the problem considered in the memoir is effected by some complex algebraical investigations which do not involve the Calculus of Variations.

437. Hohl. *Aufgaben zur Lehre vom Grössten und Kleinsten der Differenzial-Functionen* ... Stuttgart, 1852.

This is an octavo volume of 162 pages; the author is a professor of Mathematics in the University of Tübingen. The problems are of the same kind as that which we have considered in Art. 8, after Lagrange. Three cases are considered by the author. (1) The maximum or minimum of $F\left(x, y, \dfrac{dy}{dx}\right)$. (2) The maximum or minimum of $F\left(x, y, \dfrac{dy}{dx}, \dfrac{d^2y}{dx^2}\right)$. (3) The maximum or minimum of $F\left(x, y, z, \dfrac{dz}{dx}, \dfrac{dz}{dy}\right)$. Each case is illustrated by the solution of numerous simple examples. The author says that the examples are intended for the exercise of beginners, in Differentiation, in Integration, and in the higher Geometry.

The author says in his preface that he did not become acquainted with the work of Strauch before the printing of his own had advanced to the last sheet. He promises if his work is favourably received, to follow it up by a similar collection of examples on the maxima and minima values of integral expressions; the present writer is not aware that this continuation has appeared.

438. **Wituski.** *De Maximis atque Minimis valoribus Functionum Algebraicarum* ... Berlin, 1853.

This is an essay written for a degree in the University of Berlin; it contains 25 quarto pages. The essay has no relation to the Calculus of Variations; it consists of investigations partly respecting the equations furnished by the Differential Calculus for determining the maxima and minima values of expressions, but chiefly respecting the tests for ascertaining whether a maximum or minimum value really exists.

439. **Jellett.** On the surface which has its mean curvature constant. Liouville's *Journal of Mathematics*, Vol. 18, pages 163—167. 1853.

The Calculus of Variations shews that for a surface which includes a maximum volume under a given surface, the mean curvature must be constant. The object of the article is to prove that among all the surfaces whose volume can be expressed by the integral

$$\int_0^R \int_0^\pi \int_0^{2\pi} r^2 dr \sin\theta\, d\theta\, d\phi,$$

the sphere is the only surface which has its mean curvature constant. The proof depends upon two theorems.

(1) For any closed surface

$$\iint \left(\frac{1}{R} + \frac{1}{R'}\right) dS = 2 \iint P d\omega;$$

see Mr Jellett's *Calculus of Variations*, page 353.

(2) For any closed surface the whole area of the surface

$$= \frac{1}{2} \iint P \left(\frac{1}{R} + \frac{1}{R'}\right) dS.$$

the integral being taken over the whole surface.   This remarkable
theorem is proved in the article.   .

440.   Bonnet.   Note on the general theory of Surfaces.
Comptes Rendus ... Vol. 37, pages 529—532.   1853.

This note contains some results relative to the surface of minimum area.   A new form is proposed for the integral of the differential equation which belongs to such a surface, the new form being
in Bonnet's opinion preferable to that given by Monge.   Some new
properties of such surfaces are enunciated without demonstration.
The investigations relative to the integral depend upon a method
of considering surfaces which is due to Gauss.   Bonnet does not
demonstrate the fundamental formulæ which he uses.

441.   Grunert.   On the shortest line between two points on
any surface and on the fundamental formulæ of spheroidal Trigono-
metry.   Grunert's *Archiv der Mathematik und Physik*, Vol. 22,
pages 64—106.   1854.

The design of this memoir is to discuss in an elementary
manner the subjects mentioned in its title, and there is no reference
in it to the Calculus of Variations.

442.   Serret.   On the least surface comprised between given
right lines not situated in the same plane. *Comptes Rendus* ...
Vol. 40, pages 1078—1082.   1855.

Legendre asserted that the least surface comprised between two
given right lines which are not situated in the same plane is the
hélicoïde gauche; see Art. 428.   Serret shews that this assertion
is incorrect, for there is an infinite number of such surfaces, and
the *hélicoïde gauche* is only a particular case of them.   Serret's
investigation is based on Monge's form of the integral of the
differential equation belonging to surfaces of minimum area.

443.   Bonnet.   On the determination of the arbitrary functions
which occur in the integral of the equation for surfaces of minimum
area. *Comptes Rendus* ... Vol. 40, pages 1107—1110.   1855.

Bonnet's design is to shew that the question discussed by Serret on pages 1078—1082 of this volume of the *Comptes Rendus* ..., and similar questions of greater difficulty, may be investigated by means of the formula which he himself gave in the 37th volume of the *Comptes Rendus* ...; see Art. 440.

444. Roger. Memoir on a certain class of curves. *Comptes Rendus* ... Vol. 40, pages 1176, 1177. 1855.

This is a brief account by the author of the results of his investigations. It is as follows.

We may imagine in space or on a given surface an infinite number of different trajectories which a particle can describe under the action of a given system of forces. Among these trajectories I have considered those which make an integral of the form $\int_0^s \phi(v)\,ds$ a minimum, where $\phi(v)$ is a certain function of the velocity, supposed known in terms of the co-ordinates of the moving particle, and s is the arc described from the starting-point.

Some curves which have been already studied under various points of view fall under the class which I have defined, and form particular cases of it. The principal are the following. 1. Geodesic lines which correspond to the case for which $\phi(v) =$ a constant. 2. Brachistochrones for which $\phi(v) = \frac{1}{v}$. 3. The trajectories of least action which are obtained by taking $\phi(v) = v$; these trajectories by a well-known principle due to Euler are those which the moving particle is naturally led to describe under the action of the given forces. 4. The lines of greatest slope (*lignes de plus grande pente*); these form a peculiar species, which I find corresponds to the case of $\dfrac{\phi(v)}{\phi'(v)} = 0$, whatever v may be.

The lines belonging to these different species and to other species of the same class which have not as yet obtained a definition, or rather a distinctive appellation, possess on the one hand a set of common properties, and on the other hand properties peculiar to the different species; the study of these properties appears to me to have some interest. The most striking results which I have obtained are the following.

I. If we suppose on a given surface a series of trajectories of the same species which start normally from the same curve, and take on each of them arcs described in the same time, the curve formed by the extremities of these arcs will be itself normal to every one of the trajectories, if these trajectories are geodesic lines or brachistochrones, and only in these two cases. (This theorem has already been demonstrated for geodesic lines by Gauss and for brachistochrones by Bertrand.)

II. The trajectories of least action, the brachistochrones, and generally the species for which the ratio $\dfrac{\phi\,(v)}{\phi'\,(v)}$ vanishes when $v = 0$, are tangents to the lines of greatest slope, or, which is the same thing, are normals to the curves of level (*courbes de niveau*), in all the points where the velocity is zero.

III. If we suppose the moving particle to be free or to be constrained to move on a plane, and consider the ratio of the centrifugal force $\dfrac{v^2}{r}$ to the component N of the force estimated along the radius of curvature of the path described by the particle, then

1. For all the curves which make the integral $\int \phi\,(v)\,ds$ a minimum the ratio of the component N to the centrifugal force is constant throughout the extent of any curve of level.

2. This ratio is absolutely invariable for all the particular species determined by a function of the form $\phi\,(v) = v^k$, where k is an arbitrary constant, which is in fact the value of the ratio of N to $\dfrac{v^2}{r}$.

3. In a more special manner this ratio reduces to ± 1 for brachistochrones and for curves of least action; so that in these two species the component N is equal, in actual magnitude, to the centrifugal force $\dfrac{v^2}{r}$, and this property belongs exclusively to these

two curves, including the right line, which may be considered as
a variety of either of them.

IV. If a curve belongs to two different species it will possess
the properties of all the species; that is, it will be at every point
geodesic, curve of least action, brachistochrone, line of greatest
slope, &c. For example, in the case of gravity, any meridian of
a surface of revolution with its axis vertical.

This is the end of the author's account of the results of his
investigations. It would appear that these investigations constitute
a development of the memoir published in Vol. 13 of Liouville's
Journal of Mathematics; see Art. 413. In that memoir Roger
explains what he means by a *line of greatest slope* and by *surfaces
of level.* It is there stated that the theorem attributed to Gauss
was published by him in the memoir in the 6th volume of the
Gottingen Transactions. The theorem attributed to Bertrand is
there proved by Roger. Roger first supposes the curves to start
all *from the same point;* he says that this theorem was communicated to him by Bertrand, and he also gives Bertrand's proof, which
is as follows.

Suppose a point on a surface; see figure 12. Let AM, AM', ...
be brachistochrones, commencing at the same point A, such that
they would be described in equal times by particles starting from
A with the same velocity; then the locus of the points M, M', ...
will be normal to every brachistochrone. For if the angle at M'
be acute we can make at M an angle NMM' greater than $NM'M$;
then we shall have MN less than $M'N$; thus the moving particle
having arrived at N with a certain velocity would describe the
element NM in less time than it would describe the element NM', its
velocity not being sensibly altered while describing the element;
thus the curve ANM would be described in less time than ANM',
that is in less time than AM, which is absurd.

445. Catalan. Note on a surface at every point of which the
radii of curvature are equal and of opposite sign. *Comptes Rendus...*
Vol. 41, pages 85—88. 1855.

Catalan proposes to consider whether the well-known differential
equation admits of a solution of the form $s = \phi(x) + \psi(y)$. He

shews that the only solution of such a form is one which in its simplest form may be written $z = \log \cos y - \log \cos x$. He also points out many properties of the surface denoted by this equation.

This equation had been noticed before; see Art. 428.

446. Catalan. Note on two surfaces which have at every point their radii of curvature equal and of opposite sign. *Comptes Rendus* ... Vol. 41, pages 274—276. 1855.

Two surfaces are here given which satisfy the well-known differential equation. One of them is that determined by equation (3) of Art. 428. Catalan points out some properties of this surface.

447. Catalan. On the surfaces which have at every point their radii of curvature equal and of opposite sign. *Comptes Rendus* ... Vol. 41, pages 1019—1023. 1855.

This is an extract from a memoir on the subject named. Some results are given without demonstration. Catalan appears to have transformed the differential equation into forms more convenient for integration than the common form. He is thus enabled to obtain the integral in a more convenient form than Monge's. Some new examples are given of surfaces which have the property considered.

448. Bonnet. Observations on Minima Surfaces. *Comptes Rendus* ... Vol. 41, pages 1057, 1058. 1855.

Bonnet adverts to three notes on the subject of Surfaces of minimum area which Serret had communicated to this volume of the *Comptes Rendus* ... Bonnet intimates that his own formulæ in the 37th volume of the *Comptes Rendus* ... had rendered such investigations superfluous. Bonnet claims for himself the example given by Catalan in his second note, which as we have seen had been given before either of them by Scherk; see Arts. 446 and 428. Bonnet then adds two more examples of the use of his formulæ.

On page 1155 of the 41st volume of the *Comptes Rendus* ... Catalan offers a brief reply to the remarks of Bonnet. This reply was referred by the Academy to the members who had already been appointed to examine Catalan's memoir, namely Liouville, Binet and Chasles.

449. Bonnet. Note on the surfaces for which the sum of the two principal radii of curvature is equal to twice the normal. *Comptes Rendus* ... Vol. 42, pages 110—112. 1856.

This is an application of the formulæ which Bonnet gave, as he says, in the *Comptes Rendus* ... Vol. 37, page 349, to the determination of a class of surfaces which have a remarkable analogy to the surfaces of minimum area. Page 349 seems to be put by mistake for page 529.

450. Bonnet. New remarks on surfaces of minimum area. *Comptes Rendus* ... Vol. 42, pages 532—535. 1856.

Bonnet says that this article contains a simpler solution than that which he had given in Vol. 40 of the *Comptes Rendus* ... of the problem to determine the surface of minimum area which touches a given surface along a given curve.

451. Liouville. Remarkable expression of the quantity which by the principle of least action is a minimum in the movement of a system of material particles subject to any connexions. *Comptes Rendus* ... Vol. 42, pages 1146—1154. 1856.

This article is not connected with the Calculus of Variations; it is interesting in its relation to Dynamics.

452. Richelot. Remarks on the theory of Maxima and Minima. Schumacher's *Astronomische Nachrichten*. No. 1146. 1858.

This article relates to the ordinary theory of maxima and minima values of the Differential Calculus.

453. Richelot. On the theory of elliptic functions, and on the differential equations of the Calculus of Variations. *Comptes Rendus* ... Vol. 49, pages 611—645. 1859.

This article states that the differential equations furnished by the Calculus of Variations for the maximum or minimum of an integral may be transformed into other differential equations of the first order and first degree, which take what the author calls the *canonical form*; this term is used because the form agrees with the analogous form in Dynamics. Richelot's object is thus the same as that of Ostrogradsky and Clebsch; see Art. 317.

454. Bode and Fischer. *Mathematische Lehrstunden von K. H. Schellbach. Aufgaben aus der Lehre vom Grössten und Kleinsten, bearbeitet und herausgegeben von A. Bode und E. Fischer.* 1860.

This is an octavo volume of 154 pages containing elementary problems not involving the Differential Calculus.

455. We have in Art. 327 referred to some remarks by Löffler as destitute of value; since that article was printed the present writer has seen a later paper by Löffler. This paper is entitled *Beitrag zum Probleme der Brachystochrone;* it is published in the 41st volume of the *Sitzungsberichte* of the Academy of Sciences of Vienna, pages 53—59, 1860. It is remarkable that a scientific society should print a communication with so little to recommend it.

Löffler's notion is that the *limiting equations* in problems of maxima and minima are often inadmissible or contradictory, and that in the brachistochrone problem they do not supply sufficient conditions.

He takes for example the case in which we require the maximum or minimum value of

$$\int_a^b \left(y'^2 + \frac{y}{a-x} \right) dx,$$

and supposes that the limiting values of y are not fixed. The term outside the integral sign in the variation of $\int \left(y'^2 + \frac{y}{a-x} \right) dx$ is $2y'\delta y$; and Löffler says that it is equal to $\left(a_1 + \frac{1}{a-x} \right) \delta y$, where a_1 is a constant. Thus the coefficient of δy is infinite when $x = a$, and so we cannot make the integrated part vanish at the lower limit. Löffler has not given the coefficient of δy correctly; for to make the proposed expression a maximum or minimum, we have the equation

$$\frac{1}{a-x} = 2y'',$$

and this leads to

$$2y = a_1 x + a_2 - (x-a) \log (x-a),$$

where a_1 and a_2 are arbitrary constants.

Thus $$2y' = a_1 - 1 - \log (x-a),$$

and this should be the coefficient of δy instead of what Löffler gives. Nevertheless it is true, as he says, that this coefficient is infinite when $x = a$; this indicates that if the limiting values of y are not fixed the proposed integral cannot be made a maximum or a minimum, and this involves no contradiction and no difficulty.

Löffler next considers the brachistochrone problem on the supposition that the initial point is constrained to lie on one fixed vertical line and the final point on another fixed vertical line. Take the axis of y vertically downwards, and let

$$U = \int_a^b \frac{\sqrt{(1+y'^2)}}{\sqrt{(A-y)}} \, dx.$$

If we proceed to make U a minimum, we obtain in the usual way

$$\sqrt{(a_1)} = \sqrt{(A-y)} \sqrt{(1+y'^2)},$$

where a_1 is a constant. The integrated part of the variation reduces to

$$\left\{ \frac{y'\delta y}{\sqrt{(a_1)}} \right\}_{x=b} - \left\{ \frac{y'\delta y}{\sqrt{(a_1)}} \right\}_{x=a},$$

and this will not vanish if δy is arbitrary at both the limits unless y' vanishes at both limits. Löffler says that this is inadmissible, because the first element of the cycloid must be vertical and not horizontal. There is no reason for saying that the first element of the cycloid must be vertical; the fact is that our result indicates that there is no minimum in the present case; see Art. 23. There is therefore here no contradiction and no difficulty.

Löffler now takes the general brachistochrone problem when the initial and final points are constrained to lie on given curves, and the velocity is supposed given at the initial point. He puts down a few of the steps and arrives at the results which we have denoted thus in Art. 300,

$$[p\,\psi'(x)+1]_1 = 0, \quad \chi'(x_1)\,p_2 + 1 = 0;$$

therefore $$\psi'(x_0) = \chi'(x_1).$$

He then asserts, quite untruly, that from the nature of the cycloid, we must have

$$\psi(x_0) = \chi(x_1),$$

and on this error he constructs a large figure and a corresponding page of text.

Lastly, he considers that there are not enough conditions for determining the constants of the problem; he seems to be in difficulty with respect to the quantity A. But in the case which he has himself considered, A is equal to the value of y at the initial point; and if A were any given function of the value of y at the initial point the problem could be discussed in a similar manner. Löffler's difficulties arise solely from his own misconceptions.

CHAPTER XVII.

CONDITIONS OF INTEGRABILITY.

456. The present chapter will be devoted to the subject of the criteria which determine whether proposed expressions are immediately integrable. The history of the subject has not hitherto been fully treated; and it will be seen that the statements which have been made are deficient in precision.

457. In Gregory's *Examples of the processes of the Differential and Integral Calculus*, first edition, page 285, the relations are given which must hold in order that a function involving two variables and their differentials may be integrable once, twice, thrice, ... Gregory says, "these remarkable formulæ were first discovered by Euler (*Comm. Petrop.* Vol. VIII.) in his investigations concerning maxima and minima." This does not appear correct; Euler first gave the relation which must hold in order that a function of one variable and its differential coefficients may be integrable once, but not in the place which Gregory cites.

The eighth volume of the *Comm. Petrop.* is represented to be for the year 1736, and was published in 1741. It contains a memoir by Euler, entitled *Curoarum maximi minimive proprietate gaudentium inrentio;* there is nothing in this memoir relating to the conditions of integrability.

The eighth volume of the *Novi Comm. ... Petrop.* is represented to be for 1760 and 1761, and was published in 1763; it has nothing bearing on the conditions of integrability.

458. The tenth volume of the *Novi Comm. ... Petrop.* is represented to be for 1764, and was published in 1766; this volume

contains two memoirs by Euler, connected with the Calculus of Variations. The first memoir is entitled *Elementa Calculi Variationum;* the second memoir is entitled *Analytica explicatio methodi maximorum et minimorum.* At the end of the second memoir Euler says: Antequam autem finiam examini Analystarum egregium Theorema subjiciam cujus Veritas ex principiis hactenus positis haud difficulter perspicitur, et quod in Calculo integrali eximium usum præstare videtur. The theorem is that Zdx is integrable if

$$N - \frac{dP}{dx} + \frac{d^2Q}{dx^2} - \frac{d^3R}{dx^3} + \frac{d^4S}{dx^4} - \ldots = 0,$$

and that Zdx is not integrable unless this relation holds; $N, P, Q, \ldots$ being derived from Z in the well-known manner.

This appears to be the earliest reference to the Theorem.

459. The third volume of the first edition of Euler's treatise on the Integral Calculus was published in 1770; the present writer has not seen it, but this date is assigned to it by Strauch in his preface, page x, and the date is confirmed by the testimony given in Vol. 15 of the *Novi Comm. ... Petrop.* which will presently be quoted.

It appears that the third chapter of the part which treats of the Calculus of Variations contains the theorem, that the necessary and sufficient condition for the integrability of Vdx is that

$$N - \frac{dP}{dx} + \frac{d^2Q}{dx^2} - \frac{d^3R}{dx^3} + \frac{d^4S}{dx^4} - \ldots = 0;$$

the proof given is in substance the same that has usually been adopted in Treatises on the Calculus of Variations. The present writer has not had the opportunity of consulting the first edition of Euler's Integral Calculus, so that he cannot assert positively that the proof is there given. Bertrand, in his Memoir in Cahier 28 of the *Journal de l'Ecole Polytechnique,* quotes Euler's proof but without giving any precise reference. The passage Bertrand quotes occurs in Art. 92, page 425 of the *second* edition of Euler's Integral Calculus; the date of the volume is 1793. In the same volume,

Art. 129, page 454, Euler gives the form of the variation of $\int V' dx$, where V' contains *two* dependent variables y and z, and their differential coefficients with respect to x. From his result he infers in Art. 131 that two relations must be satisfied in order that $V' dx$ may be integrable, namely,

$$N - \frac{dP}{dx} + \frac{d^2Q}{dx^2} - \frac{d^3R}{dx^3} + \frac{d^4S}{dx^4} - \ldots = 0,$$

and a similar relation in connexion with z and its differential coefficients.

460. The fifteenth volume of the *Novi Comm. ... Petrop.* is represented to be for the year 1770, and was published in 1771. It contains a memoir of 68 pages by Lexell, entitled *De criteriis Integrabilitatis Formularum Differentialium.* There is a short account of this memoir given in pages 18—22 of the volume. In this account Euler's theorem is referred to as, insigne Theorema ab Ill. Eulero in Tomo III. Calculi Integralis allatum, and the following statement is made. Hoc autem Theorema, licet jam demum anno praeterito in nunquam satis laudato opere *Calculi Integralis* evulgatum fuit, tamen ad minimum ante 16 annos ab Illustris. ejus Auctore inventum fuisse certissime nobis habemus perspectum. Quam vero interea Illustr. Eulerus hoc Theorema cum insigni quodam Galliæ Mathematico communicasset, probabile omnino est, Illustr. Marchionem de *Condorcet* per eum in cognitionem hujus Theorematis pervenisse. Ex Historia enim Illustrissimæ Academ. Scient. Parisinæ pro annis 1764 et 1765 accepimus, modo laudatum Marchionem primum demonstrationem hujus Theorematis cum Illustr. Acad. Parisina communicasse, tum vero conscripto Tractatu de *Calculo Integrali* doctrinam de criteriis integrabilitatis omnino fusius explicasse.

It seems singular that in this passage, which claims priority for Euler, it is implied that the theorem was first given by Euler in his Integral Calculus in 1770, when we have seen that it was really given by him in the volume of the *Novi Comm. ...* published in 1766. Lexell, in his memoir, gives the criteria which determine when an expression admits of integration several times in succession.

461. The volume of the *Histoire de l'Académie ...de Paris...* for the year 1765 was published in 1768. Here on pages 54 and 55 we find the following statements. M. Le Marquis de Condorcet presented to the Academy a treatise on the Integral Calculus. He solves this problem; given a differential equation of any order with any number of variables, required to determine if this equation in the state in which it is proposed admits or does not admit of an integral of an inferior degree. This important solution is given with all the elegance and all the generality possible.

Lacroix, *Traité du Calc. Diff. ...* Vol. 2, page 238, says "... je passerai aux équations de condition qu'Euler a rencontrées par une sorte de hasard, et qui ont été démontrées pour la première fois directement par Condorcet, dont je suivrai d'abord la marche." Accordingly we may presume that Lacroix gives Condorcet's method. The necessity of the condition is shewn very distinctly, and the conditions are given which must hold for a function to admit of integration twice, thrice, &c.

462. The sixteenth volume of the *Novi Comm. ... Petrop.* is represented to be for the year 1771, and was published in 1772. It contains a memoir by Lexell which occupies 59 pages. Lexell says that he wished to give some examples of the application of the criteria of integrability, and also to give a new demonstration of Euler's theorem, since that which he formerly gave was liable to objection.

Lacroix, in his *Traité du Calc. Diff. ...* Vol. 2, page 249, says, On trouve dans les *Novi Commentarii Acad. Petrop.* T. xv. et xvi. deux Mémoires dans lesquels M. Lexell s'est proposé de prouver la proposition ci-dessus; mais ses procédés sont extrêmement compliqués, et ont paru tels à M. Lagrange. (*Leçons sur le Calcul des Fonctions*, p. 409, de l'édition *in-8'* imprimée par M. Courcier, en 1806.) Lagrange's words are quoted in the next article, and they do not bear out the remark of Lacroix; Lagrange says that the demonstration in the fifteenth volume is complicated, and says nothing of the other demonstration, while Lacroix speaks of Lagrange's opinion of *both* demonstrations.

403. Lagrange has proved both the necessity and sufficiency of the condition of integrability for the case of a single dependent variable; and he adds that in the same way the two conditions can be obtained which must hold when there are two dependent variables. See the *Théorie des Fonctions*, first edition, page 217; and the *Leçons sur le Calcul des Fonctions*, edition of 1806, page 402. It is usual on this point to refer to the latter work, but the proof is substantially the same in the two works, though the nature of it is perhaps seen more readily in the former work.

On page 409 of the latter work, after Lagrange has given his proof, he remarks, Nous venons de prouver non seulement que la fonction proposée ne peut être une fonction dérivée exacte, à moins que l'équation de condition n'ait lieu, comme Euler et Condorcet l'avaient trouvée, mais encore que si cette équation a lieu, la fonction sera nécessairement une dérivée exacte, ce qui restait, ce me semble, à démontrer; car la démonstration qu'on en trouve dans le tome xv. des *Novi Commentarii* de Pétersbourg, est si compliquée, qu'il est difficile de juger de sa justesse et de sa généralité.

464. In the *Leçons*... Lagrange, after investigating the conditions of integrability, gives some examples of their use; see pages 417—421 of the work. Suppose in the first place that we have a function of the first order $f(x, y, y')$; the condition that it may be an exact differential is

$$f'(y) - [f'(y')]' = 0.$$

In order that this may be identical $f'(y)$ must not contain y', for if it did $[f'(y')]'$ would contain y'', and as y'' would not occur in $f'(y)$, the whole expression $f'(y) - [f'(y')]'$ would not vanish identically.

Thus $f(x, y, y')$ must be of the form

$$\psi(x, y) + y'\,\phi(x, y);$$

then it will be found that the condition reduces to

$$\psi'(y) = \phi'(x).$$

Next, consider a function of the second order $f(x, y, y', y'')$; the condition that it may be an exact differential is

$$f'(y) - [f'(y')]' + [f'(y'')]'' = 0.$$

As before, it is necessary that $f'(y'')$ should not contain y''; so that $f(x, y, y', y'')$ must be of the form

$$\psi(x, y, y') + y'' \phi(x, y, y').$$

Then it will be found that the equation of condition will become

$$\psi'(y) + y'' \phi'(y) - [\psi'(y')]' + [\phi'(x)]' + [y'\phi'(y)]' = 0.$$

Let $\phi'(x) + y'\phi'(y) - \psi'(y')$ be denoted by $\chi(x, y, y')$, so that the condition becomes

$$\psi'(y) + y'' \phi'(y) + [\chi(x, y, y')]' = 0;$$

that is

$$\psi'(y) + \chi'(x) + y'\chi'(y) + y'' [\phi'(y) + \chi'(y')] = 0.$$

And y'' does not occur in any of the functions $\psi'(y)$, $\chi'(x)$, $\chi'(y)$, so that the last equation cannot be identically true unless

$$\phi'(y) + \chi'(y') = 0,$$

and
$$\psi'(y) + \chi'(x) + y'\chi'(y) = 0.$$

Lagrange adds on page 421—In like manner as in the case of a function of the second order, the equation of condition decomposes into two which must hold simultaneously, so it may be proved that for a function of the third order it will decompose into three, for a function of the fourth order it will decompose into four; and so on. This statement has been developed in two elaborate memoirs by Raabe and Joachimsthal. Raabe's memoir is in Crelle's *Mathematical Journal*, Vol. 31, pages 181—212. 1846. Joachimsthal's memoir is in Crelle's *Mathematical Journal*, Vol. 33, pages 95—116. 1846.

405. As we have already stated, Lacroix gives a proof of the *necessity* of the conditions of integrability. His method is independent of the Calculus of Variations. But he does not prove the *sufficiency* of the conditions by this method, but refers to the Calculus of Variations on this point. Accordingly he returns to the subject in the chapter on the Calculus of Variations, and there he improves, as he considers, Euler's proof; see the *Traité du Calc. Diff.* ... Vol. 2, pages 249 and 764.

406. The fourteenth volume of Gergonne's *Annales de Mathématiques* contains a memoir on the integrability of differential expressions by M. F. Sarrus; the date of publication is January, 1824. The memoir occupies pages 197—205 of the volume.

Sarrus begins by referring to the remarks of Lagrange which we have quoted in Art. 463. He then proves that the conditions of integrability are *necessary;* he takes the case in which two variables x and y are functions of a third variable t, and an expression involves x and y and their differential coefficients. In proving that the conditions are necessary, Sarrus adopts precisely the same method as Lacroix, but he does not give any reference to him or to Condorcet. Sarrus then proves that the conditions are *sufficient.*

The demonstration given by Sarrus is perhaps the best for elementary purposes that has yet appeared, unless it be considered preferable to prove the *necessity* of the conditions in the manner given by Sarrus, and the *sufficiency* of the conditions in the manner given in Moigno's *Leçons de Calc. Diff. et de Calc. Int.*

407. Another memoir on the conditions of integrability appeared in the fourteenth volume of Gergonne's *Annales* ..., pages 319—323.

The question considered is the following. Suppose V a function of x and y and their differential coefficients with respect to a third variable t. Then the two conditions which must hold in order that Vdt may be integrable are known from the memoir of Sarrus. Now suppose that y is made a function of x, it is obvious that a

single condition would ensure the integrability of Vdt; it is required
to find that condition.   The result is

$$X\frac{dx}{dt} + Y\frac{dy}{dt} = 0,$$

where X and Y are the functions which we should have to equate
to zero to ensure the integrability of Vdt if y had not been made
a function of x.   This result is obtained by simple transformations.
The result may be easily obtained by the Calculus of Variations;
for if y be not supposed a function of x, we obtain in the ordinary
way for the unintegrated part of $\delta \int Vdt$ the expression

$$\int \left\{ X\left(\delta x - \frac{dx}{dt}\delta t\right) + Y\left(\delta y - \frac{dy}{dt}\delta t\right)\right\} dt;$$

suppose y is made a function of x, then this term becomes

$$\int \left\{ X + Y\frac{\frac{dy}{dt}}{\frac{dx}{dt}} \right\} \left\{ \delta x - \frac{dx}{dt}\delta t \right\} dt.$$

Thus in order that Vdt may be integrable, we must have

$$X + Y\frac{\frac{dy}{dt}}{\frac{dx}{dt}} = 0.$$

At the end of the memoir the writer says that the condition is
exactly that of Lagrange, *Leçons* ... page 412 of the edition of 1806.
But Lagrange has there a different question before him; Lagrange's
result is in fact that which we have noticed in Art. 93, and have
expressed thus,

$$Hy' + Kz' = 0.$$

468.   Graeffe briefly refers to the condition of integrability on
page 46 of his essay; see Art. 305.   He quotes the theorem of

Euler as we have given it in Art. 458, and says, Manifesto Eulerus ad illam æquationem in quæstionibus quæ ad calculum variationum spectant, instituendis venit, unde accidit, ut his principiis theorema superstrueret. Sed ejusdem evidentia adhuc desiderabatur et quanquam Condorcet et Lexell demonstrationem in solius calculi integralis notionibus fundatam tentabant, Lagrange tamen primus rite confirmavit, si formula V evanescat, semper quantitatem Zdx integrari posse. Graeffe refers to Condorcet, *du Calcul Integral*, p. 16 *seq.* Novi. Comm. ... Petrop. T. xv. p. 127. Lagrange *Leçons* ... p. 401 *seq.*

469. In Poisson's Memoir on the Calculus of Variations, pages 260—270 are devoted to our present subject; see Art. 96. Poisson first shews very briefly the necessity of the condition. He says that if Vdx is an exact differential the integral U will be a function of $x_{o}, y_{o}, y_{o}', y_{o}'', ... y_{i}', y_{i}'', ...$; thus the value of δU must reduce to the part Γ, and therefore the factor Π under the integral sign must vanish; see equation (3) of Art. 86. Poisson adds the following words: "Thus the same equation $H=0$ which determines the value of y corresponding to the maximum or minimum of U, when Vdx is not an exact differential, must become identical when Vdx is an exact differential. This remark is due to Euler, who has thus been the first to express by an equation the necessary condition for the integrability of a differential formula of any order. Lagrange has proved by means of very complicated series not only that the equation $H=0$ is necessary, but that it is sufficient for the integrability of Vdx; *Leçons* ... page 409 of the edition of 1806."

Poisson then says that he will give a demonstration of the second part of the proposition which appears more simple to him, and which has the advantage of presenting the integral of Vdx under a finite form, when the condition $H=0$ holds.

470. A note by Sarrus is given in the *Comptes Rendus...* Vol. i. pages 115—117, 1835. This note enunciates some results, which the author had obtained as generalisations of his memoir in Gergonne's *Annales....*

471. A memoir by Dirksen on the conditions of integrability of functions of several variables occurs in the volume for 1836 of

the Transactions of the Academy of Sciences of Berlin ; the date of
the volume is 1838.   This memoir names Euler, Condorcet, Lexell,
Lagrange and Poisson.   Dirksen agrees with Lagrange in speaking unfavourably of Lexell's first memoir ; and Dirksen adds that
Lexell's second memoir, which Lagrange does not mention, is unsatisfactory.   Dirksen objects to Poisson's proof, because it depends
on the Calculus of Variations, and intimates that a proof depending
upon considerations which are not foreign to the subject, is still
required.   Accordingly, he supplies some tedious investigations on
the subject ; he proves both the necessity and sufficiency of the condition, considering the case of one variable.

472.   A memoir by Bertrand on the conditions of integrability
of differential functions was published in the *Journal de l'École
Polytechnique*, Cahier 28, 1841, pages 249—275.   Bertrand infers
from the words of Lagrange and Poisson that they did not know
that Euler had professed to prove the sufficiency as well as the
necessity of the condition.   Bertrand quotes Euler's words as we
have already stated in Art. 459.   After some remarks on the history
of the subject, Bertrand's memoir is divided into three sections.

In his first section, Bertrand proves the necessity and sufficiency
of the condition.   He says himself that his proof agrees with
Euler's when the latter is so modified as to be placed beyond the
reach of objection.   He then shews how to effect the integration
when the condition is satisfied.   Bertrand then investigates the
conditions when a function is to admit of successive integration ;
next he considers the case when there are two dependent variables ;
and lastly, he considers the condition which must hold in order that

$$\iint V\,dx\,dy$$ may be capable of expression without assigning any par-

ticular relation between z, x and y, where V is a function of x, y, z,
and the differential coefficients of z with respect to x and y.   All
these investigations are simple and conclusive.

Bertrand begins his second section by saying that his demonstration in the first section depended entirely on the Calculus of Variations, and so he says, diffère en cela de celles qui avaient été pro-
posées jusqu'ici par Lexell, Lagrange, Poisson, et dernièrement

encore par M. Sarrus. These words would suggest to a reader that
the memoir of Sarrus was subsequent to that of Poisson, which we
know, however, is not the case. Bertrand adds that those mathematicians establish the sufficiency of the condition by effecting the
integration, the possibility of which they wish to prove, and he says
that they seem to regard this as the only difficulty in the question.
He considers all the demonstrations which have been given very
complicated, and thinks he has found a simple demonstration. Accordingly, he establishes the sufficiency of the condition. His proof
is, as he says, founded on the same principle as Poisson's, but it
avoids the use of the Calculus of Variations. Bertrand's proof is a
simplification of Poisson's. Bertrand next proves the necessity of
the condition; this proof seems rather difficult but decisive.

In his third section Bertrand gives some interesting applications
to Mechanics.

473. The second volume of Moigno's *Leçons de Calc. Diff. et
de Calc. Integ.* is dated 1844. Moigno refers to our present subject
on page xxxvii. of his preface, and considers it on pages 550—563
of the work. Moigno states that Lexell, Lagrange, and Poisson
seem not to have been aware that Euler had proved not only that
the condition is necessary, but that it is sufficient. This seems incorrect so far as Lexell is concerned; for Lexell says that his object
was to give a proof without *using the Calculus of Variations*, so that
he appears to imply that the proposition had been established by the
use of that calculus.

Moigno's proof was communicated to him by M. Jacques Binet.
The method of proving the sufficiency of the condition may be described as an improvement on Bertrand's simplification of Poisson's
proof. The proofs of Poisson and Bertrand are liable to failure, because a certain quantity which occurs may become infinite or indeterminate; the proof given by Moigno is free from this difficulty.

The proof of the necessity of the condition given by Moigno
seems open to an objection urged by Professor De Morgan in a
memoir which we shall presently notice. Mr De Morgan says :—
" Again, it is to be shewn, not only that the criterion is *sufficient*,
but that it is *necessary*. Some of the proofs of the latter point

appear to me to fail entirely. They depend upon the reduction of $\int V dx$ to an integrated portion together with an integral of the *form*

$\int (V_y - V_{y'}' + \dots) Q\, dx.$ This, it is assumed, must vanish; which though clear enough in the common case in which $Q = y$, and $V_y - \dots$ is a function of x only, is not sufficiently supported in any other. Why may not $(V_y - \dots) Q$ be a new integrable function?" It does not seem that this objection holds against any other proof besides that given by Moigno.

Both Bertrand's proof and that given by Moigno of the sufficiency of the conditions allow us to draw the two inferences drawn by Poisson; see Art. 96.

474. An article on the integrability of functions by Professor Bruun, of Odessa, was published in 1848, in the eighth number of the seventh volume of the *Bulletin... Physico-Mathematique* of the Academy of St Petersburg; the article is in German. This article proves both the necessity and sufficiency of the condition; the proof depends on the Calculus of Variations. The method resembles Poisson's, but is much simpler. This article is included in Professor Bruun's *Manual of the Calculus of Variations*.

475. We may now refer to some investigations by Bertrand and Sarrus which are connected with the present subject. Bertrand's investigations were mentioned in the *Comptes Rendus ...* Vol. 28, pages 350, 351. 1849. Sarrus gave on pages 439—442 of the same volume a brief account of the method which he had for many years explained in his lectures, and which he presumed would be found to agree with Bertrand's. A memoir by Bertrand explaining his method was published in Liouville's *Journal of Mathematics*, Vol. 14, pages 123—131. 1849. This memoir is followed by a note by Sarrus, which occupies pages 131—134 of the volume.

. The method of Bertrand and Sarrus is different from that of previous writers on the subject. Bertrand's own words will give an idea of it. After referring to Euler's well-known condition of integrability, which had been so often demonstrated, Bertrand makes the following remarks. Notwithstanding the elegant form of this condition the application of it is very laborious. In order to make use of the condition, we have to perform a large number of differentiations, and when the condition is satisfied we have to perform a new set of operations in order to obtain the integral which is thus known to exist. The method which I propose in this memoir differs widely from that of Euler, and it would require some complicated investigations to establish their agreement in a direct manner; the method does not certainly lead to such an elegant condition as Euler's, but the operations which it requires have the great advantage of simplicity. It is by integrating a proposed function that we ascertain that it is integrable; each operation is followed by a verification, and we are relieved from the necessity of continuing the process if the verification does not succeed. We have thus an advantage analogous to that of the method of commensurable roots in the Theory of Equations; for this method, although it does not give us a formula for the roots, indicates a series of operations by which we may find these roots, and a single operation will often shew that such a root does not exist.

We may add that the method is explained in Professor Boole's *Differential Equations*, pages 219—222.

476. Minich. An article on the present subject occurs in Tortolini's *Annali di Scienze Matematiche e Fisiche*, Vol. 1, pages 321—336. 1850. The article is said to be an extract from an unpublished memoir. The article is divided into three sections.

In the first section Minich proposes to exhibit the conditions which ensure that a function shall be susceptible of repeated integration, under a simpler form than the well-known form. An example will give a clear idea of Minich's object. Suppose we have an expression V which involves x and y and the differential coefficients of y with respect to x up to $\dfrac{d^4y}{dx^4}$; and let the partial differential coefficients of V with respect to y, $\dfrac{dy}{dx}$, $\dfrac{d^2y}{dx^2}$, $\dfrac{d^3y}{dx^3}$ and $\dfrac{d^4y}{dx^4}$, be denoted by N, P, Q, R, S respectively. Then the conditions which are necessary and sufficient in order that V may be immediately integrable *four* times in succession are known to be

$$N - \frac{dP}{dx} + \frac{d^2Q}{dx^2} - \frac{d^3R}{dx^3} + \frac{d^4S}{dx^4} = 0,$$

$$P - 2\frac{dQ}{dx} + 3\frac{d^2R}{dx^2} - 4\frac{d^3S}{dx^3} = 0,$$

$$Q - 3\frac{dR}{dx} + 6\frac{d^2S}{dx^2} = 0,$$

$$R - 4\frac{dS}{dx} = 0.$$

Minich substitutes for this system the following more simple system,

$$4N - \frac{dP}{dx} = 0, \quad 3P - 2\frac{dQ}{dx} = 0, \quad 2Q - 3\frac{dR}{dx} = 0, \quad R - 4\frac{dS}{dx} = 0.$$

If we only require that V shall be immediately integrable *three* times in succession, the conditions will consist of the first three of the first system given above; and Minich substitutes for them the following,

$$6N - 3\frac{dP}{dx} + \frac{d^2Q}{dx^2} = 0,$$

$$3P - 4\frac{dQ}{dx} + 3\frac{d^2R}{dx^2} = 0,$$

$$Q - 3\frac{dR}{dx} + 6\frac{d^2S}{dx^2} = 0.$$

And similarly if V is to be immediately integrable *twice* in succession, Minich gives the two conditions,

$$4N - 3\frac{dP}{dx} + 2\frac{d^2Q}{dx^2} - \frac{d^3R}{dx^3} = 0,$$

$$P - 2\frac{dQ}{dx} + 3\frac{d^2R}{dx^2} - 4\frac{d^3S}{dx^3} = 0.$$

Thus in every case the last condition of Minich's system is the same as the last condition of the ordinary system, and the other conditions of Minich's system are simpler than the conditions of the ordinary system. Minich gives a general investigation, and shews that the ordinary system can be deduced from his system. He does not shew conversely that his system can be deduced from the ordinary system; this however is the case, and it can be easily verified in the example which we have given.

The object of the second section of Minich's article may be seen from an example which occurs in it. Suppose we require the condition which must hold in order that a given expression

$$R\,dx^2 + S\,dx\,dy + T\,dy^2$$

may result by differentiating an expression of the form $P\,dx + Q\,dy$, on the supposition that dx and dy are both constant. The required condition is found to be

$$\frac{d^2R}{dy^2} - \frac{d^2S}{dx\,dy} + \frac{d^2T}{dx^2} = 0.$$

The third section of Minich's article relates to the integration of expressions in Finite Differences. Lacroix intimates that Condorcet was the first to consider this subject, and Lacroix considers the subject more curious than useful; see the *Traité du Calc. Diff. et du Calc. Int.* Vol. 3, page 311. Minich investigates the condition which is necessary in order that one immediate Finite Integration may be possible. Suppose V any function of x, y, Δy, $\Delta^2 y$, ... $\Delta^n y$; let Δy be denoted by p_1, and $\Delta^2 y$ by p_2, and so on. Let the symbol E be equivalent to $1 + \Delta$. Then the necessary condition is

$$E\,\frac{dV}{dy} - \Delta E^{-1}\frac{dV}{dp_1} + \Delta^2 E^{-1}\frac{dV}{dp_2} - \ldots\ldots + (-1)^n \Delta^n\frac{dV}{dp_n} = 0.$$

This condition may also be put in another form.

Suppose that in V we put for Δy, $\Delta^2 y$, ... their values in terms of y, y_1, y_2, ... ; namely

$$\Delta y = y_1 - y, \quad \Delta^2 y = y_2 - 2y_1 + y, \ldots$$

then V becomes a function of $x, y, y_1, y_2, \ldots y_n$. The condition may now be expressed thus,

$$E^n \frac{dV}{dy} + E^{n-1} \frac{dV}{dy_1} + E^{n-2} \frac{dV}{dy_2} + \ldots + \frac{dV}{dy_n} = 0.$$

In this form of the condition $\dfrac{dV}{dy}$ is not the same thing as was

denoted by $\dfrac{dV}{dy}$ in the first form of the condition.

Minich then briefly indicates the conditions necessary in order that it may be possible to effect immediate Finite Integration any number of times in succession; and he shews that the system of conditions which he first obtains is deducible from a second system which is more simple, so that this part of the third section is analogous to the first section.

477. In Mr Jellett's treatise on the Calculus of Variations a chapter is devoted to the present subject. The ordinary proof by the Calculus of Variations of the necessity and sufficiency of the condition of integrability is given, and then five propositions are discussed. (1) To investigate the conditions under which a function will admit of immediate integration m times successively. (2) To find the form of the function V in order that $\iint V dx\, dy$ may be reduced to a single integral, when V is a function of $x, y, z, p,$ and q. (3) To find the form of the function V in order that $\iint V dx\, dy$ may be reducible to a single integral, when V is a function of $x, y, z, p, q, r, s,$ and t. (4) To find whether it is possible to represent the superficial area of a surface by any such formula as

$$\Gamma + \iint F(P, \theta, \phi)\, d\theta\, d\phi,$$

where Γ is a quantity referring solely to the limits of integration, P is the perpendicular from the origin upon the tangent plane, and θ and ϕ are the polar angles which determine the position of this perpendicular. (5) Let R and R' be the principal radii of curvature of a closed surface, P the perpendicular on the tangent plane, and $d\omega$ the element of the spherical surface described by a portion of this perpendicular whose length is equal to unity. Then

$$\iint (R + R') \, d\omega = 2 \iint P \, d\omega,$$

the integrals being extended throughout the entire of the closed surface.

478. A memoir On some points of the Integral Calculus by Professor De Morgan was published in 1851 in the second part of the ninth volume of the *Transactions of the Cambridge Philosophical Society*. The fourth section of the Memoir is devoted to the condition of integrability of a differential expression. After the memoir had been read before the Society Mr De Morgan became acquainted with the memoir of Sarrus, which we have noticed in Art. 466; but as Mr De Morgan's copy of this memoir was detached from the volume to which it belonged, he did not know in what journal it had been published, and made a wrong conjecture. Mr De Morgan says with respect to Sarrus's memoir, "This memoir contains the proof here given, in substance, though the equations on which the condition is founded are not demonstrated. It is singular that M. Bertrand takes no notice of it, except to observe that M. Sarrus does not use the calculus of variations. MM. Cauchy and Moigno pass it over altogether. But it must be observed that M. Sarrus establishes only the *necessity* of the condition, and does not establish its *sufficiency*, except when the equations that give it are presented with it." The statement that Sarrus does not prove the *sufficiency* of the condition is incorrect. By "MM. Cauchy and Moigno" is meant the work published under the name of Moigno which we have noticed in Art. 473. It is not obvious what is meant by the remark that "the equations on which the condition is founded are not demonstrated."

479. There is a very good elementary discussion of the subject in Stegmann's treatise on the Calculus of Variations, pages 118—132. Stegmann begins by remarking that the equation furnished by the Calculus of Variations for the maximum or minimum

of an integral may in some cases be impossible and in some cases
identical. An instance of the first kind is supplied by endeavour-
ing to find the maximum or minimum of $\int (xp - y)\, dx$. Here we
should obtain as the condition for a maximum or a minimum
$-1 - \dfrac{d}{dx} x = 0$, that is $-2 = 0$, which is impossible. In fact if we
transform the proposed expression to polar co-ordinates we find
that we are requiring the maximum or minimum of $\int r^2 d\theta$, and it
is obvious that this function may be made either as great as we
please or as small as we please. Stegmann then passes on to the
case in which the equation becomes an identity, and this leads him
to discuss the condition of integrability. He proves the necessity
of the condition in the same way as Sarrus, and the sufficiency
of the condition in the same way as Binet in Moigno's work.

Stegmann makes a remark on his page 123 which we will give
here. Suppose $V\,dx$ a perfect differential of u, where u involves x
and y and the differential coefficients of y with respect to x up to
$\dfrac{d^n y}{dx^n}$. Let y_r stand for $\dfrac{d^r y}{dx^r}$. Then

$$V = \frac{du}{dx} + \frac{du}{dy}\, y_1 + \frac{du}{dy_1}\, y_2 + \ldots + \frac{du}{dy_n}\, y_{n+1};$$

therefore $\dfrac{dV}{dy} = \dfrac{d^2 u}{dy\,dx} + \dfrac{d^2 u}{dy^2}\, y_1 + \dfrac{d^2 u}{dy\,dy_1}\, y_2 + \ldots + \dfrac{d^2 u}{dy\,dy_n}\, y_{n+1}.$

Thus $\dfrac{dV}{dy} = \dfrac{d}{dx}\dfrac{du}{dy}$,

where the right-hand member means the complete differential coefficient of $\dfrac{du}{dy}$ with respect to x.

Therefore $\qquad\qquad\qquad \dfrac{du}{dy} = \displaystyle\int \dfrac{dV}{dy}\, dx,$

that is $\qquad\qquad\qquad \dfrac{d}{dy}\displaystyle\int V\,dx = \int \dfrac{dV}{dy}\, dx,$

so that if $V dx$ is a perfect differential, the two operations of complete integration with respect to x and partial differentiation with respect to y, may be performed on V in either order.

480. We will close this chapter by giving a translation of the memoir of Sarrus which we have noticed in Art. 466, and also an account of the method adopted by Bruun which we have noticed in Art. 474.

481. The present article is a translation of the memoir of Sarrus.

The investigation of the conditions of integrability of differential functions which has chiefly engaged Euler and Condorcet constitutes one of the most important branches of the higher analysis. The method of variations leads very simply to these conditions, but the use of this method in investigations which strictly belong to the Integral Calculus seems indirect, and moreover it does not assist us in arriving at the integral when these conditions are fulfilled.

Euler and Condorcet proved satisfactorily by their analysis that the conditions which they obtained are *necessary;* but Lexell appears to be the first who without using any considerations foreign to the integral calculus, tried to demonstrate that these conditions are *sufficient*, that is, that they assure us of the possibility of effecting the integration, which is the important point in the theory (*Novi Comm. ... Pet.* Vol. xv). Unfortunately, as Lagrange remarks, the demonstration of Lexell is so complicated that it is difficult to judge of its accuracy and its generality.

In reflecting on this subject it appears to us that the processes of the differential calculus, strictly so called, are sufficient by themselves to lead in a simple manner to the conditions of integrability and to the demonstration of the important proposition of Lexell; and this we propose to shew in this brief memoir.

In all that follows x and y will be any functions of a third variable, the differential of which we shall take for unity, and of any number of constants. For abridgement, we shall represent $dx, d^2x, d^3x, \ldots$ by $x_1, x_2, x_3, \ldots$, and $dy, d^2y, d^3y, \ldots$ by $y_1, y_2, y_3, \ldots$:

P, P_1, P_2, P_3, ... will be any functions of x, x_1, x_2, x_3, ... x_{m-1}, y, y_1, y_2, y_3, ... y_{m-1}, and their differentials will be respectively p, p_1, p_2, p_3, ...

Thus we have identically,

$$p = \frac{dP}{dx}x_1 + \frac{dP}{dx_1}x_2 + \frac{dP}{dx_2}x_3 + \ldots$$

$$\ldots + \frac{dP}{dx_{m-1}}x_m + \frac{dP}{dy}y_1 + \frac{dP}{dy_1}y_2 + \frac{dP}{dy_2}y_3 + \ldots + \frac{dP}{dy_{m-1}}y_m,$$

and therefore

$$\left.\begin{aligned}
&\frac{dp}{dx} = d\frac{dP}{dx}, \quad \frac{dp}{dx_1} = d\frac{dP}{dx_1} + \frac{dP}{dx}, \quad \frac{dp}{dx_2} = d\frac{dP}{dx_2} + \frac{dP}{dx_1}, \ldots \\
&\ldots\ldots\ldots, \quad \frac{dp}{dx_{m-1}} = d\frac{dP}{dx_{m-1}} + \frac{dP}{dx_{m-2}}, \quad \frac{dp}{dx_m} = \frac{dP}{dx_{m-1}}
\end{aligned}\right\} \quad \ldots\ldots (1),$$

$$\left.\begin{aligned}
&\frac{dp}{dy} = d\frac{dP}{dy}, \quad \frac{dp}{dy_1} = d\frac{dP}{dy_1} + \frac{dP}{dy}, \quad \frac{dp}{dy_2} = d\frac{dP}{dy_2} + \frac{dP}{dy_1}, \ldots \\
&\ldots\ldots\ldots, \quad \frac{dp}{dy_{m-1}} = d\frac{dP}{dy_{m-1}} + \frac{dP}{dy_{m-2}}, \quad \frac{dp}{dy_m} = \frac{dP}{dy_{m-1}}
\end{aligned}\right\} \quad \ldots\ldots (2).$$

From the first of these systems of equations we obtain by successively eliminating the differentials of $\dfrac{dP}{dx_{m-1}}$, $\dfrac{dP}{dx_{m-2}}$, ..., $\dfrac{dP}{dx_1}$, $\dfrac{dP}{dx}$,

$$\left.\begin{aligned}
&\frac{dP}{dx_{m-1}} = \frac{dp}{dx_m} \\
&\frac{dP}{dx_{m-2}} = \frac{dp}{dx_{m-1}} - d\frac{dp}{dx_m} \\
&\frac{dP}{dx_{m-3}} = \frac{dp}{dx_{m-2}} - d\frac{dp}{dx_{m-1}} + d^2\frac{dp}{dx_m} \\
&\qquad\ldots\ldots\ldots\ldots\ldots\ldots\ldots \\
&\frac{dP}{dx} = \frac{dp}{dx_1} - d\frac{dp}{dx_2} + d^2\frac{dp}{dx_3} - \ldots \mp d^{m-1}\frac{dp}{dx_m}, \\
&0 = \frac{dp}{dx} - d\frac{dp}{dx_1} + d^2\frac{dp}{dx_2} - \ldots \mp d^{m-1}\frac{dp}{dx_{m-1}} \pm d^m\frac{dp}{dx_m}
\end{aligned}\right\} \quad \ldots\ldots (3).$$

The last of these equations is an equation of condition which must be satisfied by the differential p of the function P.

The equations (2) treated in the same manner give a similar system to (3), namely

$$
\left.
\begin{aligned}
\frac{dP}{dy_{n-1}} &= \frac{dp}{dy_n} \\[4pt]
\frac{dP}{dy_{n-1}} &= \frac{dp}{dy_{n-1}} - d\,\frac{dp}{dy_n} \\[4pt]
&\dotfill \\[4pt]
\frac{dP}{dy} &= \frac{dp}{dy_1} - d\,\frac{dp}{dy_2} + d^2\,\frac{dp}{dy_3} - \ldots\ldots \mp d^{n-1}\,\frac{dp}{dy_n} \\[4pt]
0 &= \frac{dp}{dy} - d\,\frac{dp}{dy_1} + d^2\,\frac{dp}{dy_2} - \ldots \mp d^{n-1}\,\frac{dp}{dy_{n-1}} \pm d^n\,\frac{dp}{dy_n}
\end{aligned}
\right\} \quad \ldots\ldots (4).
$$

The last of these is a new equation of condition which must be satisfied by the differential p of the function P.

Before we proceed further we may remark that if P is a function of x_i, x_{i+1}, x_{i+2}, $\ldots x_{n-1}$, y, y_1, y_2, $\ldots y_{n-1}$, only, that is, if this function does not contain any of the quantities x, x_1, x_2, $\ldots x_{i-1}$, we shall have

$$
\frac{dP}{dx} = 0, \quad \frac{dP}{dx_1} = 0, \quad \frac{dP}{dx_2} = 0, \ldots\ldots \frac{dP}{dx_{i-1}} = 0,
$$

$$
\frac{dp}{dx} = 0, \quad \frac{dp}{dx_1} = 0, \quad \frac{dp}{dx_2} = 0, \ldots\ldots \frac{dp}{dx_{i-1}} = 0;
$$

the application of the same method will then lead to the results

$$
d\,\frac{dP}{dx_i} = \frac{dp}{dx_i} \dotfill (5),
$$

$$
0 = \frac{dp}{dx_i} - d\,\frac{dp}{dx_{i+1}} + d^2\,\frac{dp}{dx_{i+2}} - \ldots\ldots \pm d^{n-i}\,\frac{dp}{dx_n} \dotfill (6).
$$

This remark will be useful to us in the sequel.

When we are sure that p is an exact differential the equations (3) and (4) will supply the simplest means for obtaining the integral P by quadratures only. But we have now to prove that any differential function which satisfies identically equations (3) and (4) is necessarily an exact differential.

In the first place let u_i be any function whatever of

$$x_i,\ x_{i+1},\ x_{i+2},\ \dots x_m,\ y,\ y_1,\ y_2,\ \dots, y_n,$$

subject only to the condition of satisfying the equation

$$A_i = \frac{du_i}{dx_i} - d\,\frac{du_i}{dx_{i+1}} + d^2\,\frac{du_i}{dx_{i+2}} - \dots \pm d^{m-i}\frac{du_i}{dx_m} \dots\dots (7),$$

in which A_i is any constant quantity whatever. This equation may be put in the form

$$\frac{du_i}{dx_i} = A_i + d\left\{\frac{du_i}{dx_{i+1}} - d\,\frac{du_i}{dx_{i+2}} + d^2\,\frac{du_i}{dx_{i+3}} - \dots \mp d^{m-i+1}\frac{du_i}{dx_m}\right\};$$

and hence we infer that since the first member does not involve differentials of x and y of a higher order than x_m, y_n, the part of the second member comprised between the brackets cannot involve differentials of the same variables of a higher order than x_{m-1} and y_{n-1}; and therefore it will be possible to find a function P_i of x_i, $x_{i+1}, \dots, x_{m-1}, y, y_1, y_2, \dots, y_{n-1}$, which satisfies the equation

$$\frac{dP_i}{dx_i} = \frac{du_i}{dx_{i+1}} - d\,\frac{du_i}{dx_{i+2}} + d^2\,\frac{du_i}{dx_{i+3}} - \dots \mp d^{m-i+1}\frac{du_i}{dx_m},$$

and from this by means of (5) we shall have

$$\frac{du_i}{dx_i} = A_i + d\,\frac{dP_i}{dx_i} = A_i + \frac{dp_i}{dx_i},$$

and therefore $\qquad u_i = A_i x_i + p_i + u_{i+1} \dots\dots\dots\dots (8),$

where u_{i+1} denotes a function of $x_{i+1},\ x_{i+2}, \dots, x_m,\ y,\ y_1,\ y_2, \dots, y_n,$ which must be determined in a suitable manner. Substitute this value of u_i in (7), and observing that since p_i is an exact differential we have by (6)

$$0 = \frac{dp_i}{dx_i} - d\,\frac{dp_i}{dx_{i+1}} + d^2\,\frac{dp_i}{dx_{i+2}} - \dots \mp d^{m-i}\frac{dp_i}{dx_m},$$

we shall find after reduction

$$0 = d\,\frac{du_{i+1}}{dx_{i+1}} - d^2\,\frac{du_{i+1}}{dx_{i+2}} + d^3\,\frac{du_{i+1}}{dx_{i+3}} - \dots \mp d^{m-i}\frac{du_{i+1}}{dx_m},$$

and therefore by integrating

$$A_{i+1} = \frac{du_{i+1}}{dx_{i+1}} - d\,\frac{du_{i+2}}{dx_{i+2}} + d^2\,\frac{du_{i+1}}{dx_{i+2}} - \dots \mp d^{m-i-1}\,\frac{du_{i+1}}{dx_m},$$

which shews that u_{i+1} is entirely of the same nature as u_i.

Let us now suppose that u is a function of x, x_1, x_2, ... , x_m, y, y_1, y_2, ... , y_n, which satisfies the condition

$$0 = \frac{du}{dx} - d\,\frac{du}{dx_1} + d^2\,\frac{du}{dx_2} - \dots \pm d^m\,\frac{du}{dx_m};$$

by operations analogous to those which gave us equation (8) we shall obtain

$$u = p + u_1,$$
$$u_1 = A_1 x_1 + p_1 + u_2,$$
$$u_2 = A_2 x_2 + p_2 + u_3,$$
$$u_3 = A_3 x_3 + p_3 + u_4,$$
$$\dots\dots\dots\dots\dots\dots$$
$$u_{m-1} = A_{m-1} x_{m-1} + p_{m-1} + u_m,$$
$$u_m = A_m x_m \quad + p_m \quad + Y,$$

Y being a function of y, y_1, y_2, ... , y_n only.

Add these equations and put for abridgement

$$q = A_1 x_1 + A_2 x_2 + A_3 x_3 + \dots + A_m x_m$$
$$+ p_1 + \quad p_2 + \dots \qquad + p_m;$$

thus $\qquad\qquad u = q + Y,$

in which q is evidently an exact differential because each of the terms of which it is composed is an exact differential.

If u did not involve y and its differential coefficients y_1, y_2, y_3, ... , y_n, the function which we have represented by Y would be a constant and therefore zero, otherwise u would be composed of heterogeneous terms, which can never be the case; thus u would then be an exact differential.

If on the contrary u involves y and its differential coefficients $y_1, y_2, y_3, \ldots, y_n$, but so that the following equation is identically satisfied,

$$0 = \frac{du}{dy} - d\,\frac{du}{dy_1} + d^2\,\frac{du}{dy_2} - \ldots \pm d^n\,\frac{du}{dy_n},$$

the function Y may be different from zero; but by substituting in this equation the value of u just given, and observing that since q is an exact differential we have

$$0 = \frac{dq}{dy} - d\,\frac{dq}{dy_1} + d^2\,\frac{dq}{dy_2} - \ldots\ldots \pm d^n\,\frac{dq}{dy_n},$$

we obtain, by reduction,

$$0 = \frac{dY}{dy} - d\,\frac{dY}{dy_1} + d^2\,\frac{dY}{dy_2} - \ldots \pm d^n\,\frac{dY}{dy_n};$$

from this we conclude as before, that since Y only involves y and its differential coefficients $y_1, y_2, y_3, \ldots, y_n$, this function Y is necessarily an exact differential, so that in this case, as in the preceding, u is still an exact differential.

In order to simplify the question we have supposed that all the functions involved only two variables x and y and their differential coefficients; but it is easy to see that the question would not become very much complicated if we wished to consider more than two variables, and that moreover the conclusions would be absolutely the same.

[It would perhaps have been clearer if Sarrus had explicitly introduced the third variable, say t, of which x and y may be supposed functions; thus in his value of p we should add a term on the right $\frac{dP}{dt}$; his equations (1) and (2) would still hold. His method really amounts to the following; let V be any function of x, y, t, and the differential coefficients of x and y with respect to t; then suppose $\int V\,dt$ separated into two parts, first, that part which would arise from supposing t variable, but not x, y, and their differential coefficients, secondly, that part which would arise from regarding x, y and their differential coefficients as variables. Then the first part may be supposed obtained by ordinary explicit integration, and Sarrus disregards it.

Dirksen's process, which we have referred to in Art. 471, resembles that of Sarrus in this respect; both in fact follow Condorcet's method as given by Lacroix.]

482. We will now give an account of the method adopted by Bruun which we have noticed in Art. 474.

Bruun proves the *necessity* of the condition in the same way as it is usually proved in works on the Calculus of Variations. His proof of the *sufficiency* of the condition is substantially the following. Let V be a function of x and y and the differential coefficients of y with respect to x, which satisfies the condition of integrability, say $V = f(x, y, y', y'', ...)$. Change y into $y + t\delta y$, and let V_i denote what V now becomes, so that

$$V_i = f(x, y + t\delta y, \ y' + t\delta y', \ y'' + t\delta y'', \ ...).$$

Then let
$$U = \int V_i \, dx, \text{ so that}$$

$$\frac{dU}{dt} = \int \frac{dV_i}{dt} \, dx.$$

Now $\dfrac{dV_i}{dt}$ will consist of a series of terms which we may denote by

$$L\delta y + M\delta y' + N\delta y'' + P\delta y''' + ...$$

Apply the process of integration by parts in the usual manner of the Calculus of Variations, and we shall obtain

$$\frac{dU}{dt} = \delta y \left(M - \frac{dN}{dx} + \frac{d^2 P}{dx^2} - ... \right)$$
$$+ \delta y' \left(N - \frac{dP}{dx} + ... \right)$$
$$+ \delta y'' \left(P - ...... \right)$$
$$+ ......$$
$$+ \int \delta y \left(L - \frac{dM}{dx} + \frac{d^2 N}{dx^2} - \frac{d^3 P}{dx^3} + ... \right) dx.$$

The part under the integral sign vanishes, because the condition of integrability is supposed to be satisfied with respect to $f(x, y, y', y'', ...)$, and it will therefore be satisfied when y is changed into $y + t\delta y$. Thus we may express our result as follows,

$$\frac{dU}{dt} = \delta y\, \psi\, (x,\, y + t\delta y,\ y' + t\delta y',\ y'' + t\delta y'',\ ...)$$
$$+ \delta y'\, \psi_1\, (x,\, y + t\delta y,\ y' + t\delta y',\ y'' + t\delta y'',\ ...)$$
$$+ \delta y''\, \psi_2\, (x,\, y + t\delta y,\ y' + t\delta y',\ y'' + t\delta y'',\ ...)$$
$$+ ......$$

Integrate with respect to t from $t = 0$ to $t = 1$; then the left-hand member gives us $U_1 - U_0$, so that

$$\int f(x,\, y + \delta y,\ y' + \delta y',\ y'' + \delta y'',\ ...)\, dx - \int f(x,\, y,\ y',\ y'',\ ...)\, dx$$
$$= \int_0^1 \Big\{ \delta y\, \psi\, (x,\, y + t\delta y,\ y' + t\delta y',\ y'' + t\delta y'',\ ...)$$
$$+ \delta y'\, \psi_1\, (x,\, y + t\delta y,\ y' + t\delta y',\ y'' + t\delta y'',\ ...)$$
$$+ \delta y''\, \psi_2\, (x,\, y + t\delta y,\ y' + t\delta y',\ y'' + t\delta y'',\ ...)$$
$$+ ...... \Big\}\, dt.$$

In this result put 0 for y and y for δy; thus

$$\int f(x,\, y,\ y',\ y'',\ ...)\, dx - \int f(x,\, 0,\ 0,\ 0,\ ...)\, dx$$
$$= \int_0^1 \Big\{ \delta y\, \psi\, (x,\, ty,\ ty',\ ty'',\ ...) + \delta y'\, \psi_1\, (x,\, ty,\ ty',\ ty'',\ ...)$$
$$+ \delta y''\, \psi_2\, (x,\, ty,\ ty',\ ty'',\ ...) + ... \Big\}\, dt.$$

This is in fact the result originally obtained by Poisson; see Art. 96.

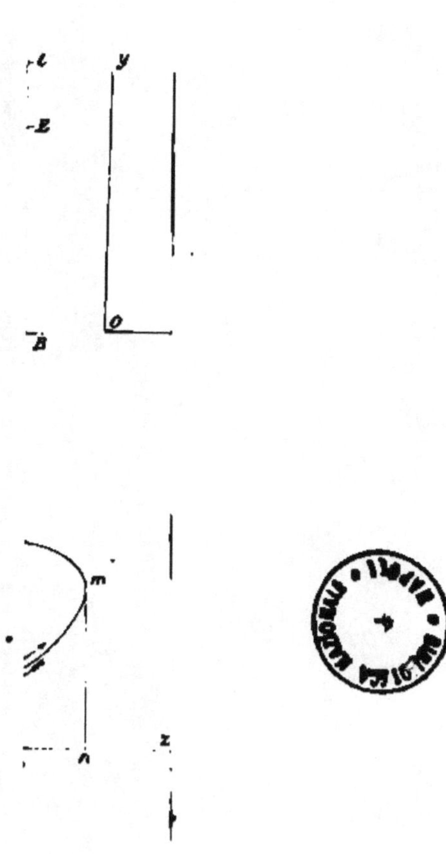